FEB 17

D0046762

this book
belongs to:

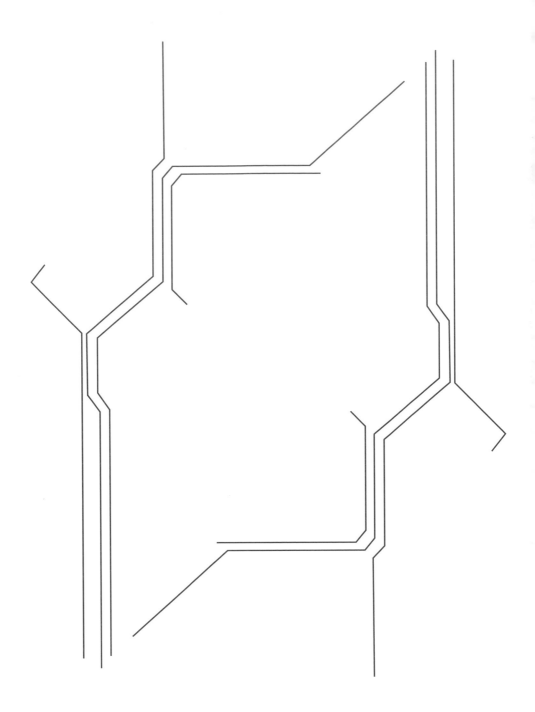

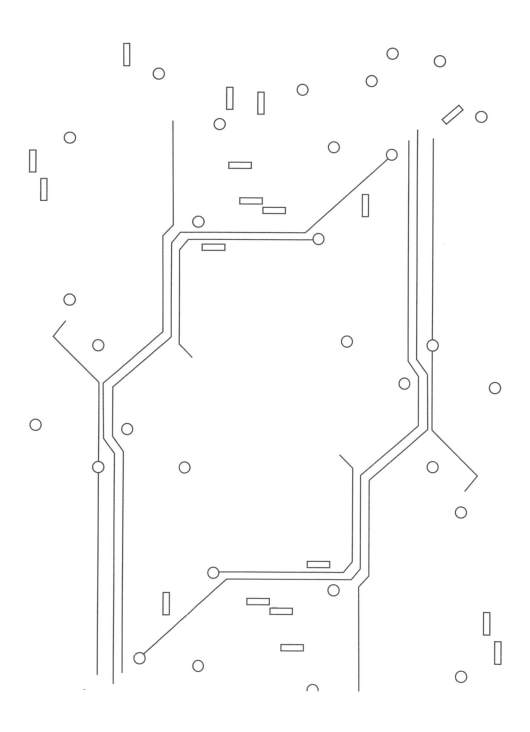

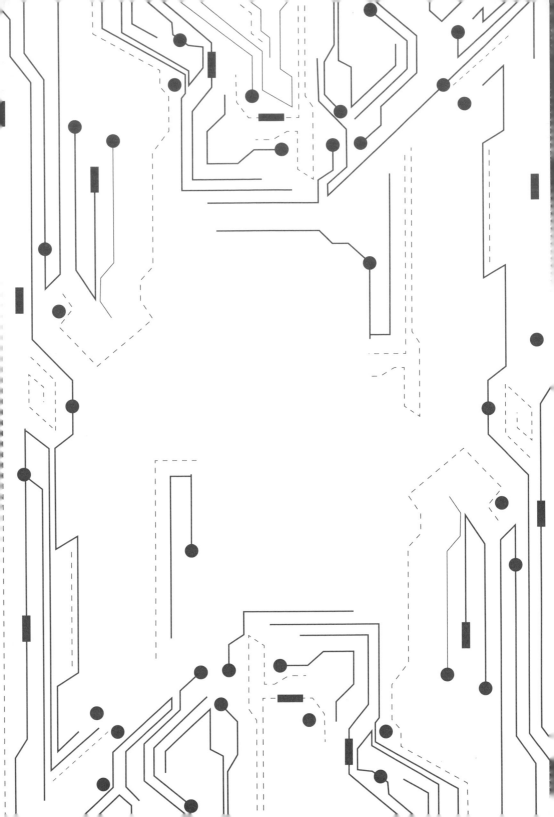

WIRES

AND

NERVE

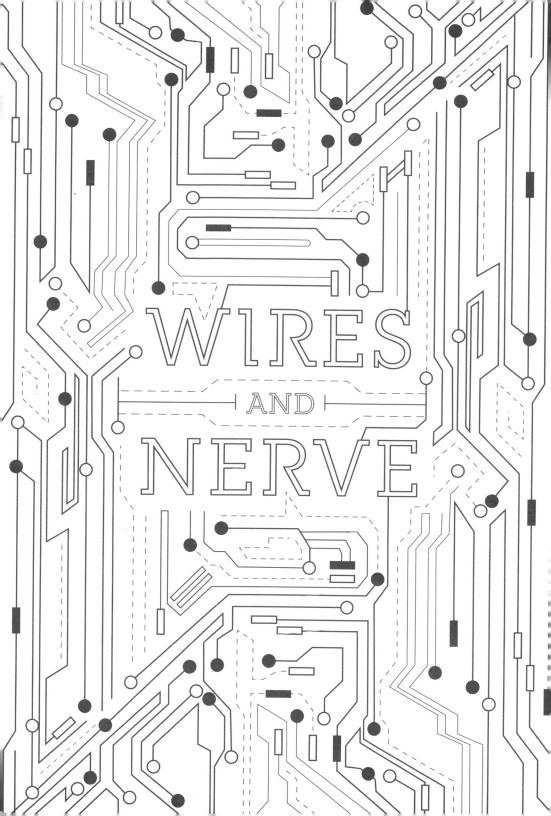

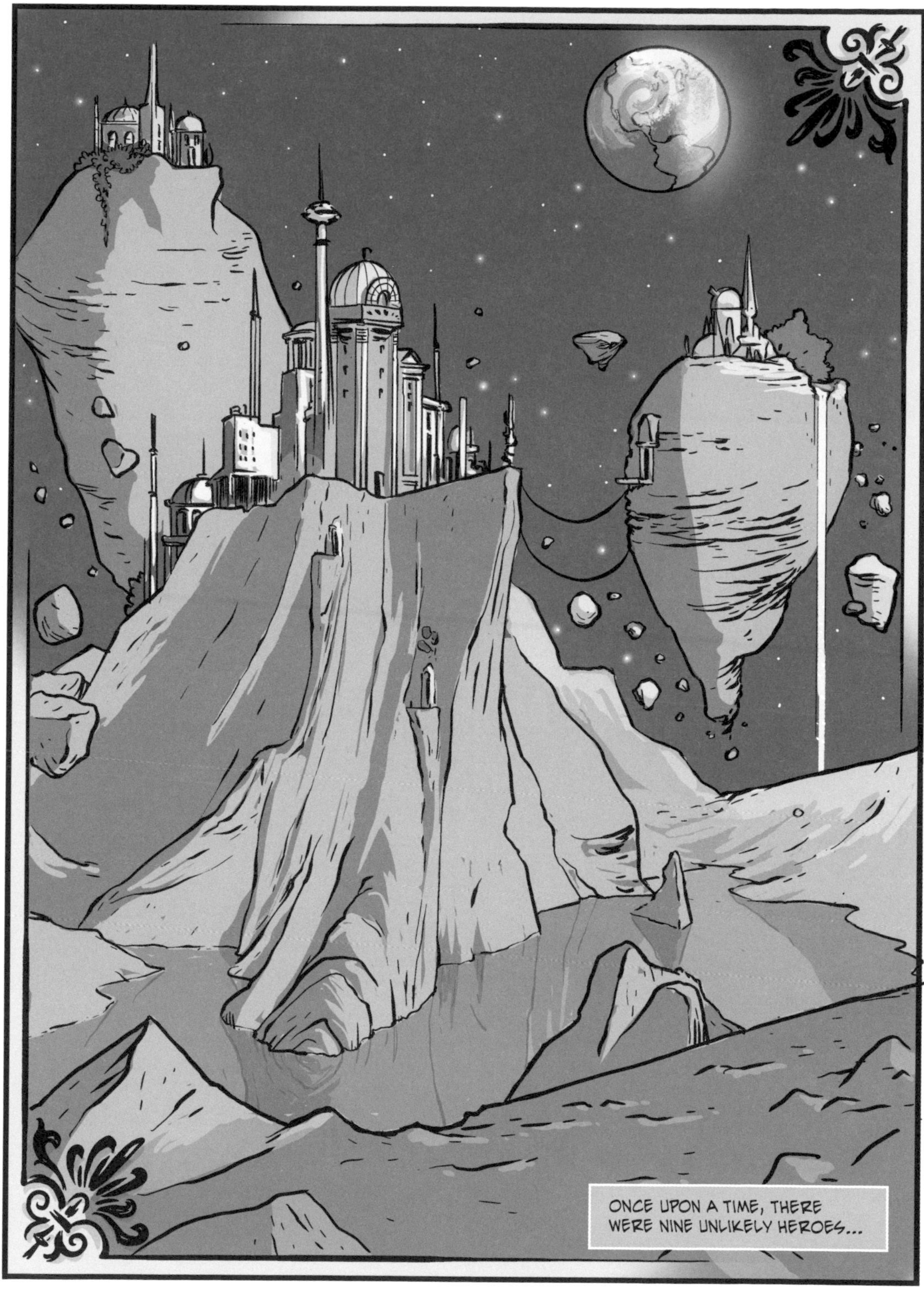
ONCE UPON A TIME, THERE WERE NINE UNLIKELY HEROES...

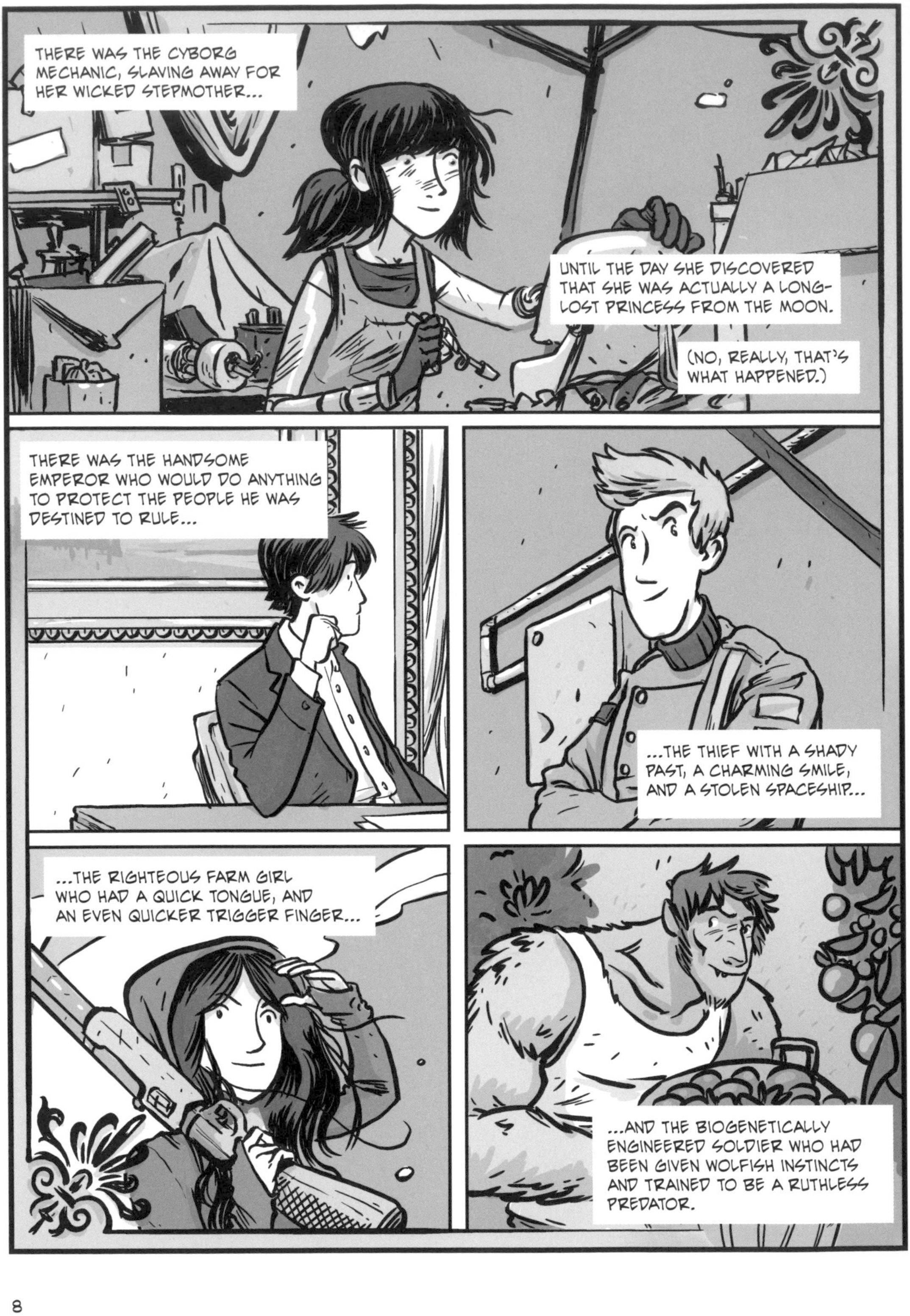

THERE WAS THE CYBORG MECHANIC, SLAVING AWAY FOR HER WICKED STEPMOTHER...
UNTIL THE DAY SHE DISCOVERED THAT SHE WAS ACTUALLY A LONG-LOST PRINCESS FROM THE MOON.
(NO, REALLY, THAT'S WHAT HAPPENED.)
THERE WAS THE HANDSOME EMPEROR WHO WOULD DO ANYTHING TO PROTECT THE PEOPLE HE WAS DESTINED TO RULE...
...THE THIEF WITH A SHADY PAST, A CHARMING SMILE, AND A STOLEN SPACESHIP...
...THE RIGHTEOUS FARM GIRL WHO HAD A QUICK TONGUE, AND AN EVEN QUICKER TRIGGER FINGER...
...AND THE BIOGENETICALLY ENGINEERED SOLDIER WHO HAD BEEN GIVEN WOLFISH INSTINCTS AND TRAINED TO BE A RUTHLESS PREDATOR.

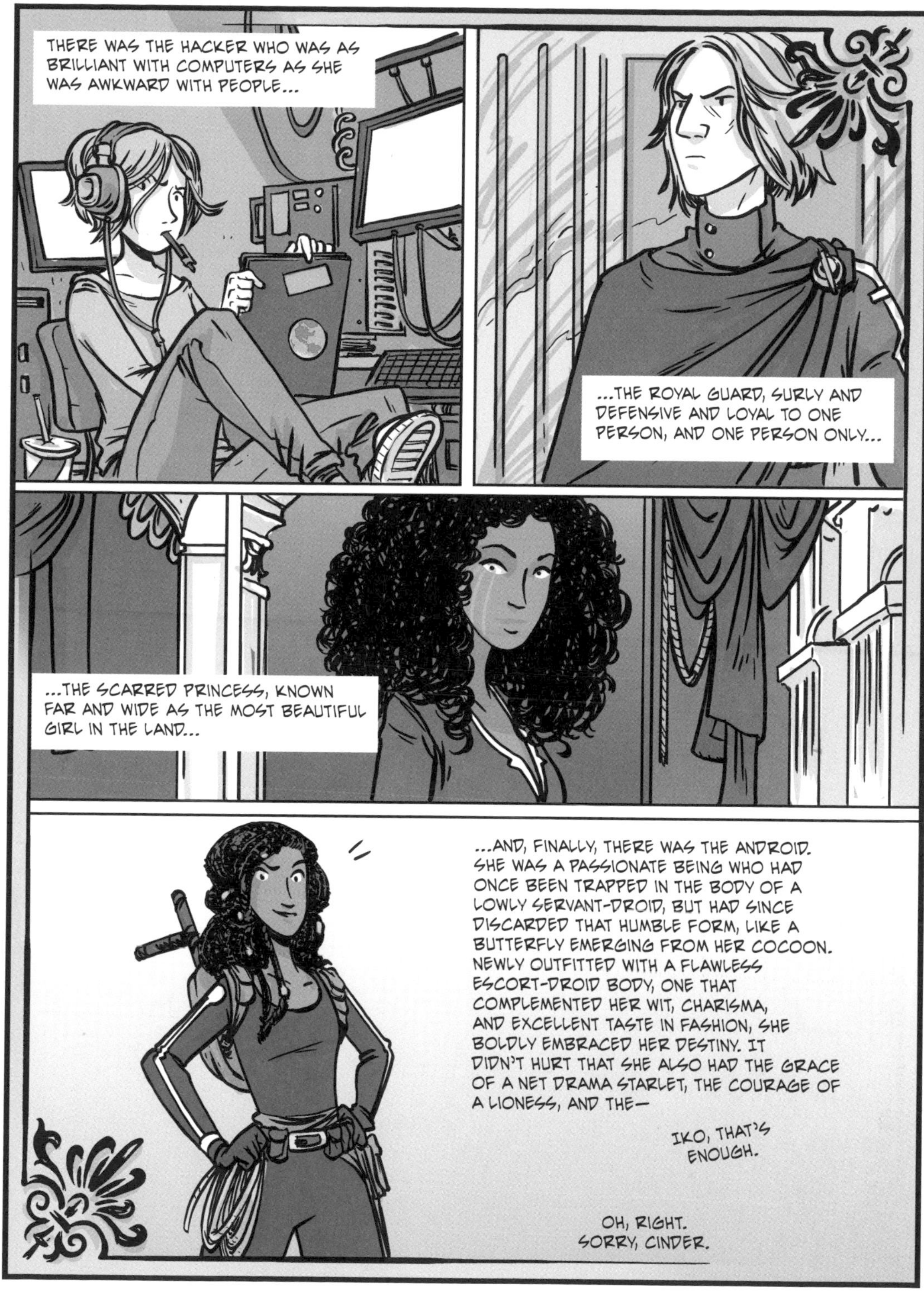
THERE WAS THE HACKER WHO WAS AS BRILLIANT WITH COMPUTERS AS SHE WAS AWKWARD WITH PEOPLE...
...THE ROYAL GUARD, SURLY AND DEFENSIVE AND LOYAL TO ONE PERSON, AND ONE PERSON ONLY...
...THE SCARRED PRINCESS, KNOWN FAR AND WIDE AS THE MOST BEAUTIFUL GIRL IN THE LAND...
...AND, FINALLY, THERE WAS THE ANDROID. SHE WAS A PASSIONATE BEING WHO HAD ONCE BEEN TRAPPED IN THE BODY OF A LOWLY SERVANT-DROID, BUT HAD SINCE DISCARDED THAT HUMBLE FORM, LIKE A BUTTERFLY EMERGING FROM HER COCOON. NEWLY OUTFITTED WITH A FLAWLESS ESCORT-DROID BODY, ONE THAT COMPLEMENTED HER WIT, CHARISMA, AND EXCELLENT TASTE IN FASHION, SHE BOLDLY EMBRACED HER DESTINY. IT DIDN'T HURT THAT SHE ALSO HAD THE GRACE OF A NET DRAMA STARLET, THE COURAGE OF A LIONESS, AND THE—
IKO, THAT'S ENOUGH.
OH, RIGHT. SORRY, CINDER.

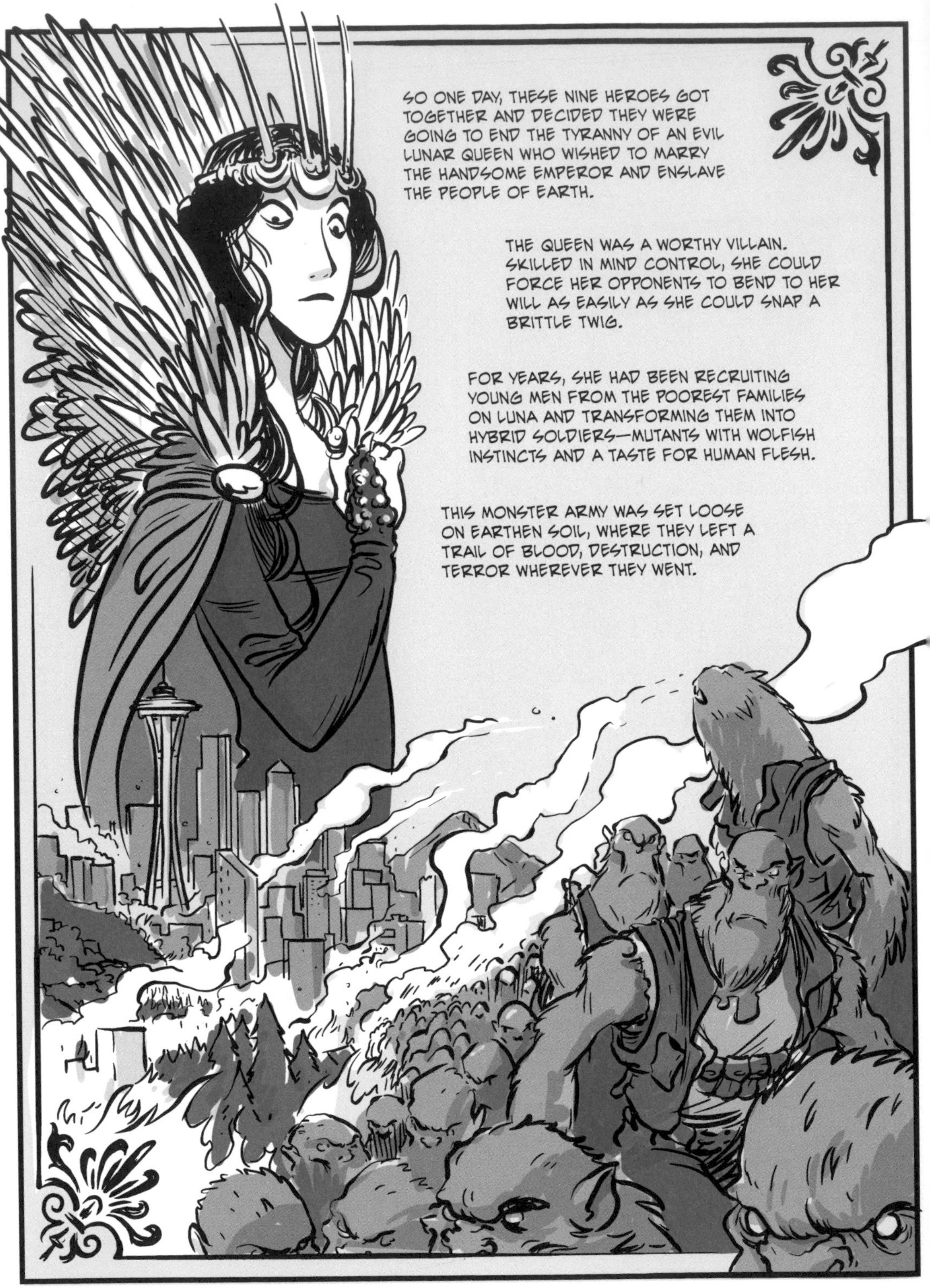
SO ONE DAY, THESE NINE HEROES GOT TOGETHER AND DECIDED THEY WERE GOING TO END THE TYRANNY OF AN EVIL LUNAR QUEEN WHO WISHED TO MARRY THE HANDSOME EMPEROR AND ENSLAVE THE PEOPLE OF EARTH.
THE QUEEN WAS A WORTHY VILLAIN. SKILLED IN MIND CONTROL, SHE COULD FORCE HER OPPONENTS TO BEND TO HER WILL AS EASILY AS SHE COULD SNAP A BRITTLE TWIG.
FOR YEARS, SHE HAD BEEN RECRUITING YOUNG MEN FROM THE POOREST FAMILIES ON LUNA AND TRANSFORMING THEM INTO HYBRID SOLDIERS—MUTANTS WITH WOLFISH INSTINCTS AND A TASTE FOR HUMAN FLESH.
THIS MONSTER ARMY WAS SET LOOSE ON EARTHEN SOIL, WHERE THEY LEFT A TRAIL OF BLOOD, DESTRUCTION, AND TERROR WHEREVER THEY WENT.

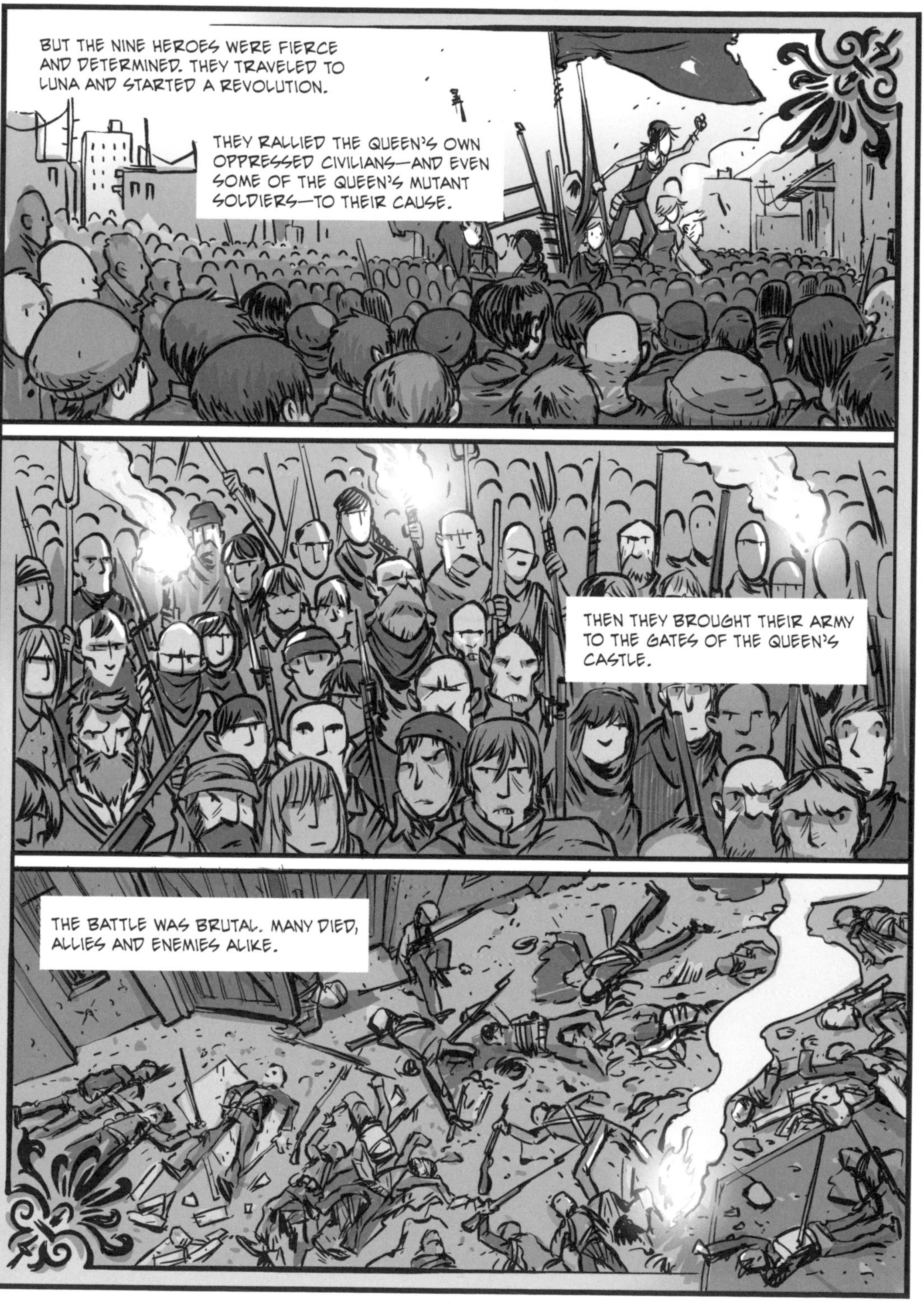
BUT THE NINE HEROES WERE FIERCE AND DETERMINED. THEY TRAVELED TO LUNA AND STARTED A REVOLUTION.
THEY RALLIED THE QUEEN'S OWN OPPRESSED CIVILIANS—AND EVEN SOME OF THE QUEEN'S MUTANT SOLDIERS—TO THEIR CAUSE.
THEN THEY BROUGHT THEIR ARMY TO THE GATES OF THE QUEEN'S CASTLE.
THE BATTLE WAS BRUTAL. MANY DIED, ALLIES AND ENEMIES ALIKE.

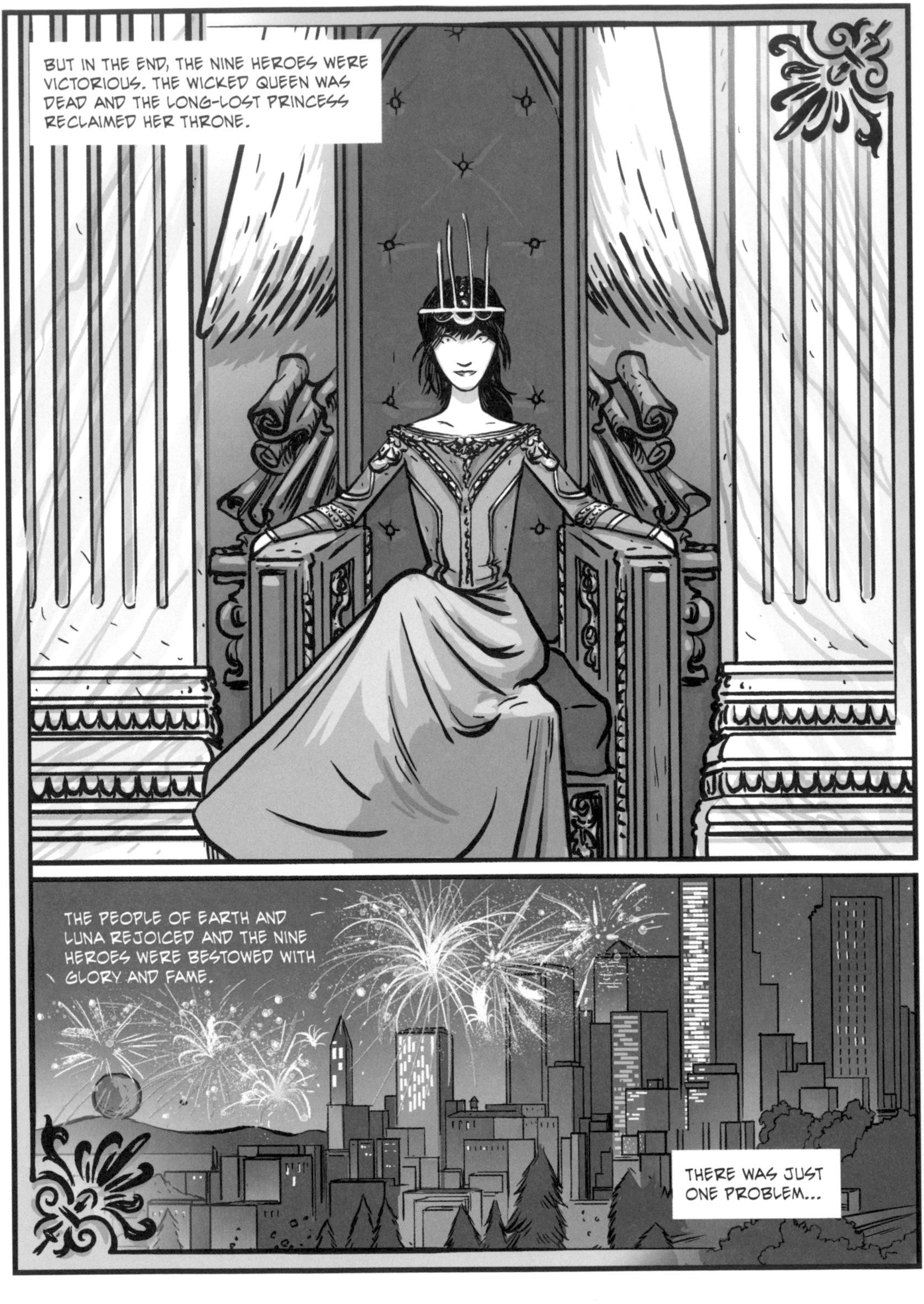
BUT IN THE END, THE NINE HEROES WERE VICTORIOUS. THE WICKED QUEEN WAS DEAD AND THE LONG-LOST PRINCESS RECLAIMED HER THRONE.
THE PEOPLE OF EARTH AND LUNA REJOICED AND THE NINE HEROES WERE BESTOWED WITH GLORY AND FAME.
THERE WAS JUST ONE PROBLEM...

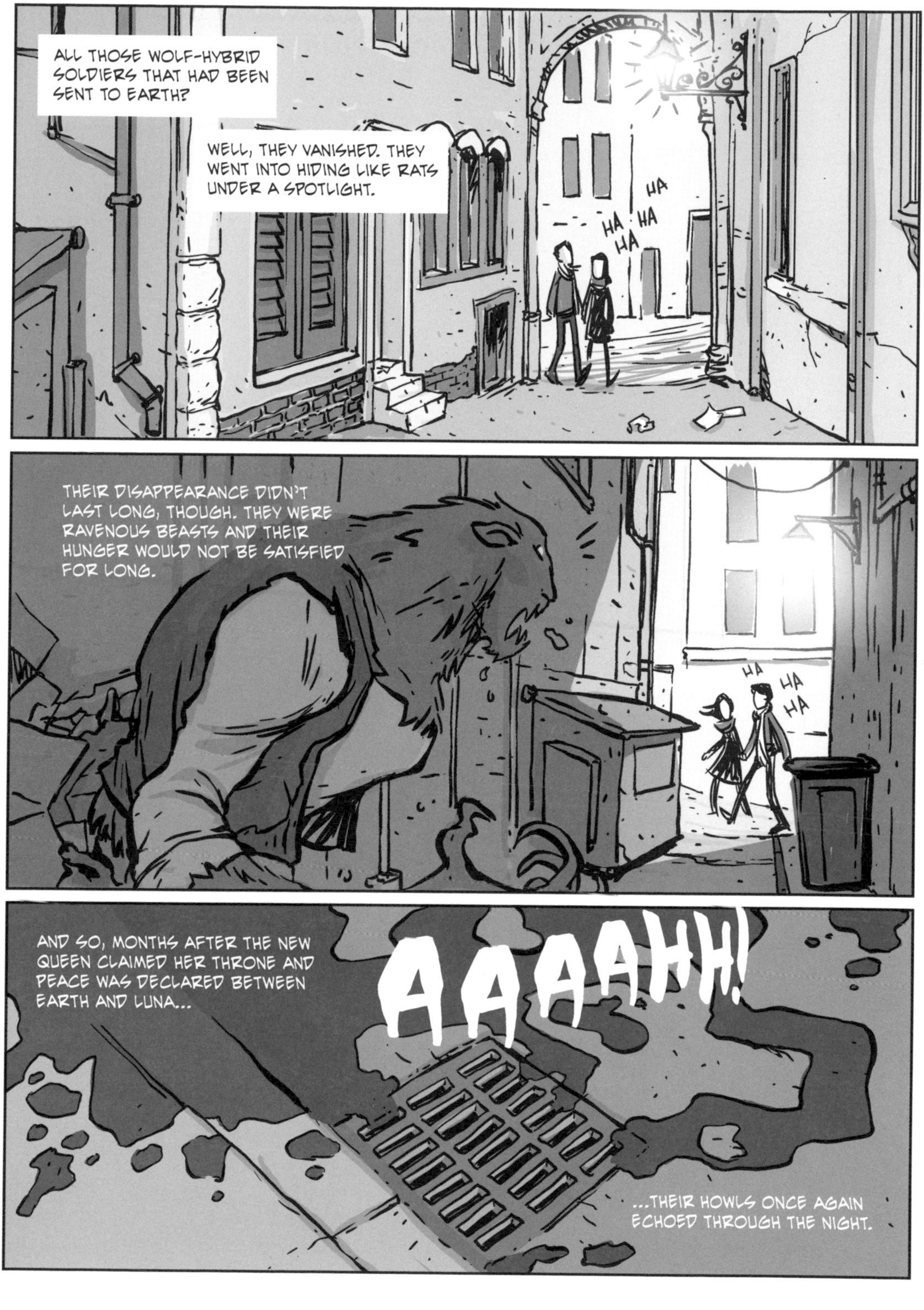
ALL THOSE WOLF-HYBRID SOLDIERS THAT HAD BEEN SENT TO EARTH?
WELL, THEY VANISHED. THEY WENT INTO HIDING LIKE RATS UNDER A SPOTLIGHT.
HA HA HA HA
THEIR DISAPPEARANCE DIDN'T LAST LONG, THOUGH. THEY WERE RAVENOUS BEASTS AND THEIR HUNGER WOULD NOT BE SATISFIED FOR LONG.
HA HA HA
AND SO, MONTHS AFTER THE NEW QUEEN CLAIMED HER THRONE AND PEACE WAS DECLARED BETWEEN EARTH AND LUNA...
AAAAHH!
...THEIR HOWLS ONCE AGAIN ECHOED THROUGH THE NIGHT.

For Leilani and Micaela

A FEIWEL AND FRIENDS BOOK
An imprint of Macmillan Publishing Group, LLC
WIRES AND NERVE. Copyright © 2017 by Rampion Books. All rights reserved. Printed in the United States.
For information, address Feiwel and Friends, 175 Fifth Avenue, New York, N.Y. 10010.

Our books may be purchased in bulk for promotional, educational, or business use. Please contact your
local bookseller or the Macmillan Corporate and Premium Sales Department at (800) 221-7945 ext. 5442
or by e-mail at MacmillanSpecialMarkets@macmillan.com.

Library of Congress Control Number: 2016939440
ISBN 978-1-250-07826-1 (hardcover)
Book design by Rich Deas and Doug Holgate
Feiwel and Friends logo designed by Filomena Tuosto
First Edition—January 2017
10 9 8 7 6 5 4 3 2 1
fiercereads.com

WIRES
AND
NERVE

VOLUME 1

MARISSA MEYER

art by
DOUG HOLGATE
with **STEPHEN GILPIN**

Feiwel and Friends
New York

CHAPTER 1

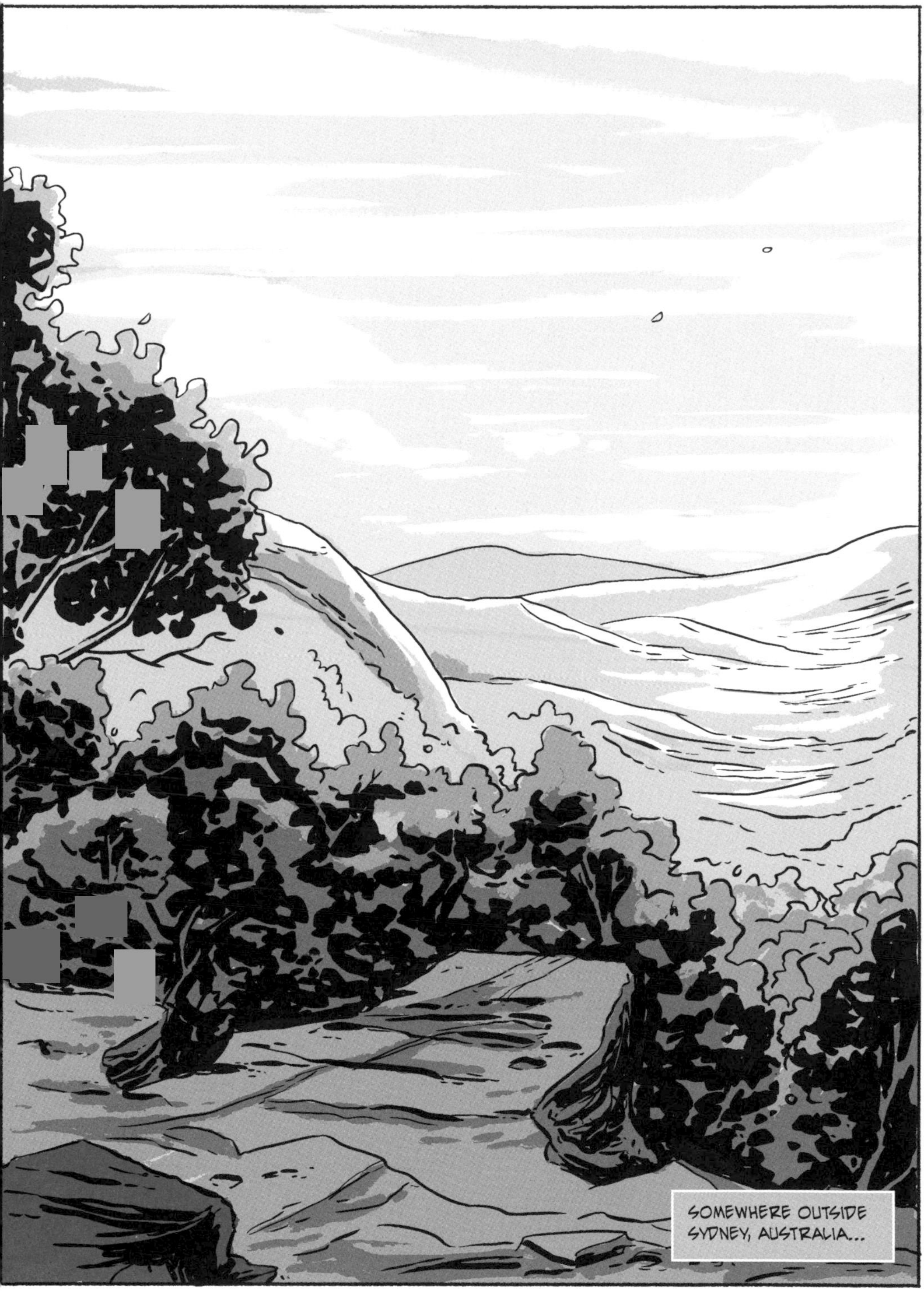
SOMEWHERE OUTSIDE
SYDNEY, AUSTRALIA...

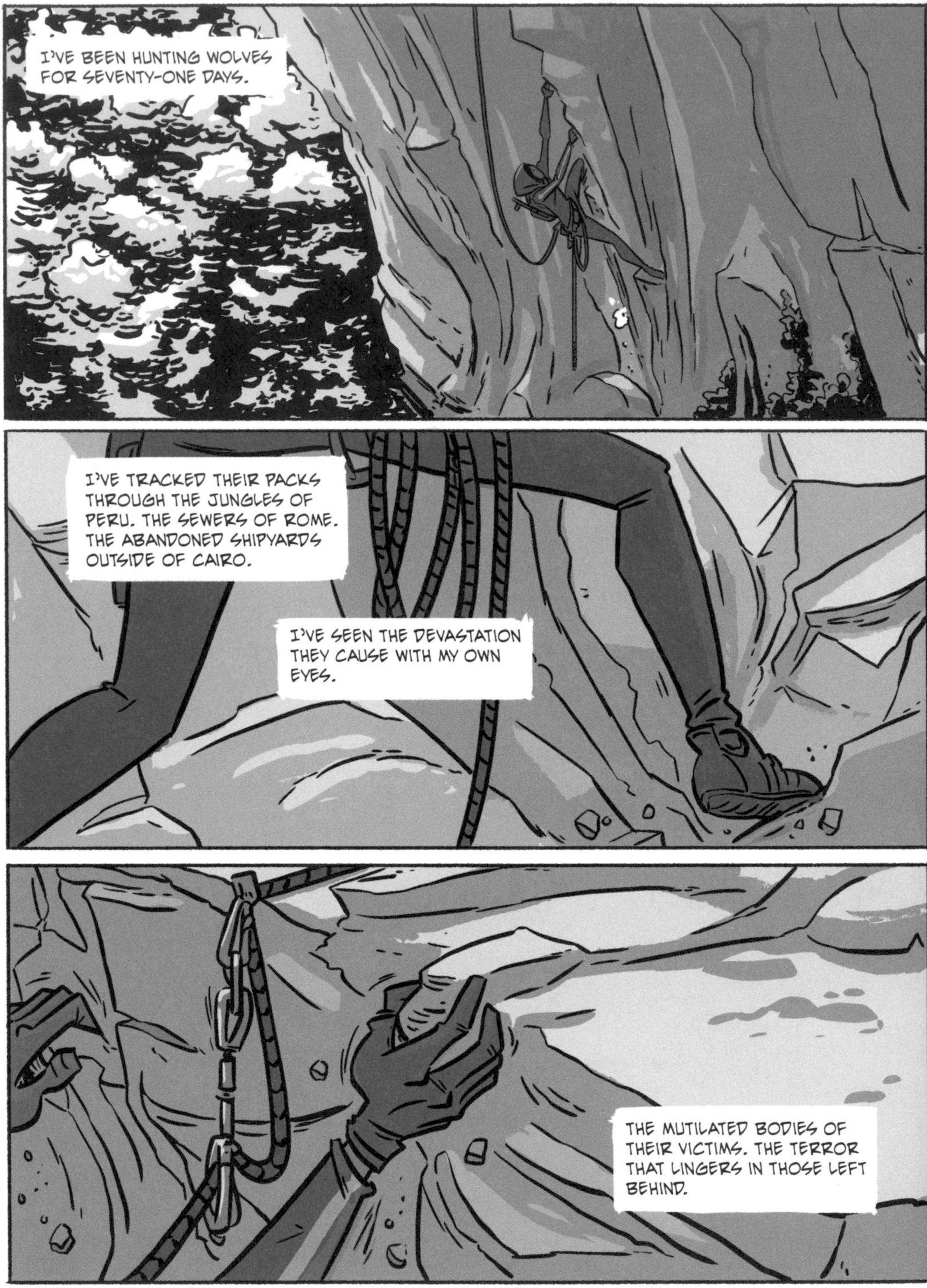
I'VE BEEN HUNTING WOLVES FOR SEVENTY-ONE DAYS.
I'VE TRACKED THEIR PACKS THROUGH THE JUNGLES OF PERU. THE SEWERS OF ROME. THE ABANDONED SHIPYARDS OUTSIDE OF CAIRO.
I'VE SEEN THE DEVASTATION THEY CAUSE WITH MY OWN EYES.
THE MUTILATED BODIES OF THEIR VICTIMS. THE TERROR THAT LINGERS IN THOSE LEFT BEHIND.

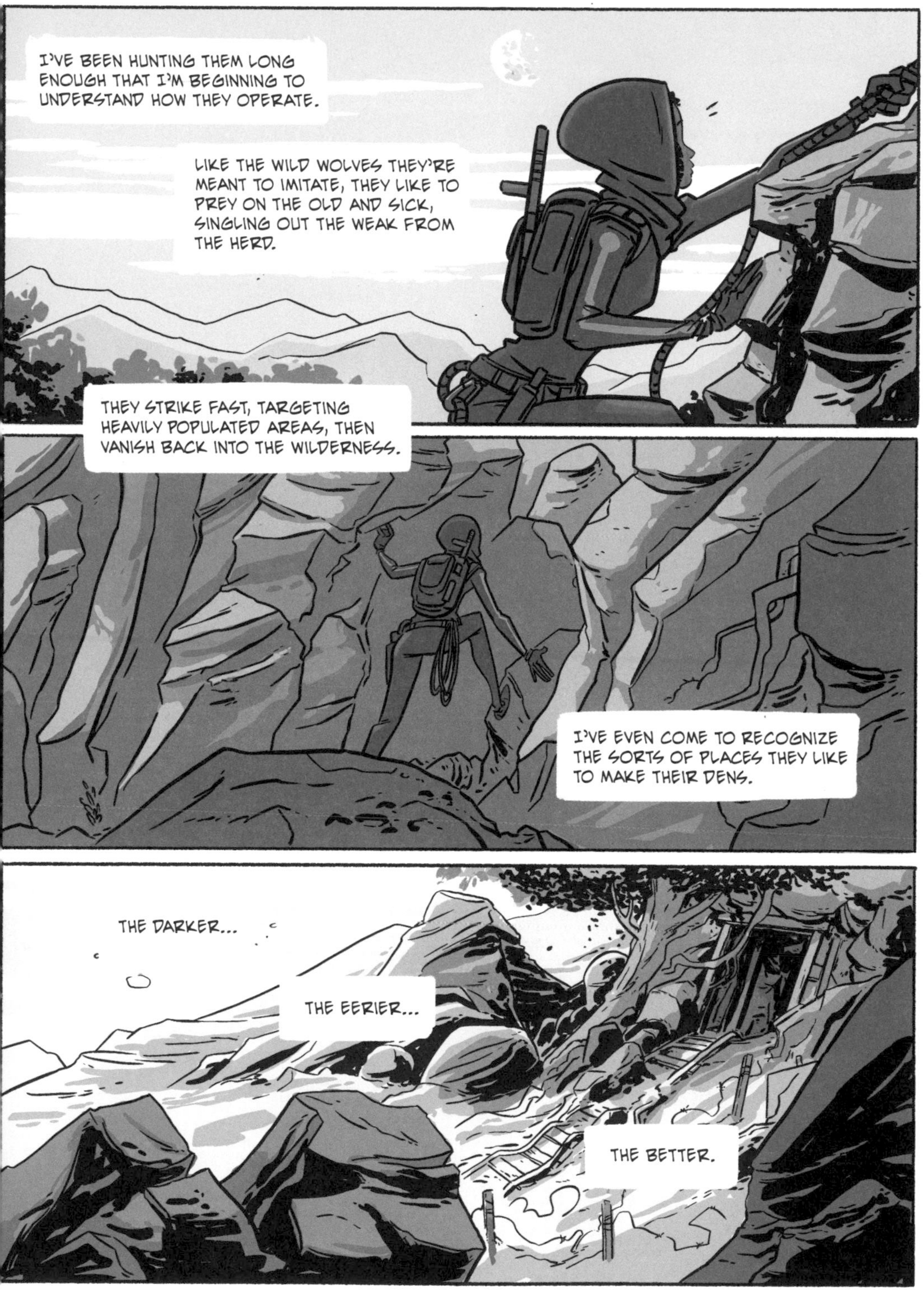
I'VE BEEN HUNTING THEM LONG ENOUGH THAT I'M BEGINNING TO UNDERSTAND HOW THEY OPERATE.
LIKE THE WILD WOLVES THEY'RE MEANT TO IMITATE, THEY LIKE TO PREY ON THE OLD AND SICK, SINGLING OUT THE WEAK FROM THE HERD.
THEY STRIKE FAST, TARGETING HEAVILY POPULATED AREAS, THEN VANISH BACK INTO THE WILDERNESS.
I'VE EVEN COME TO RECOGNIZE THE SORTS OF PLACES THEY LIKE TO MAKE THEIR DENS.
THE DARKER...
THE EERIER...
THE BETTER.

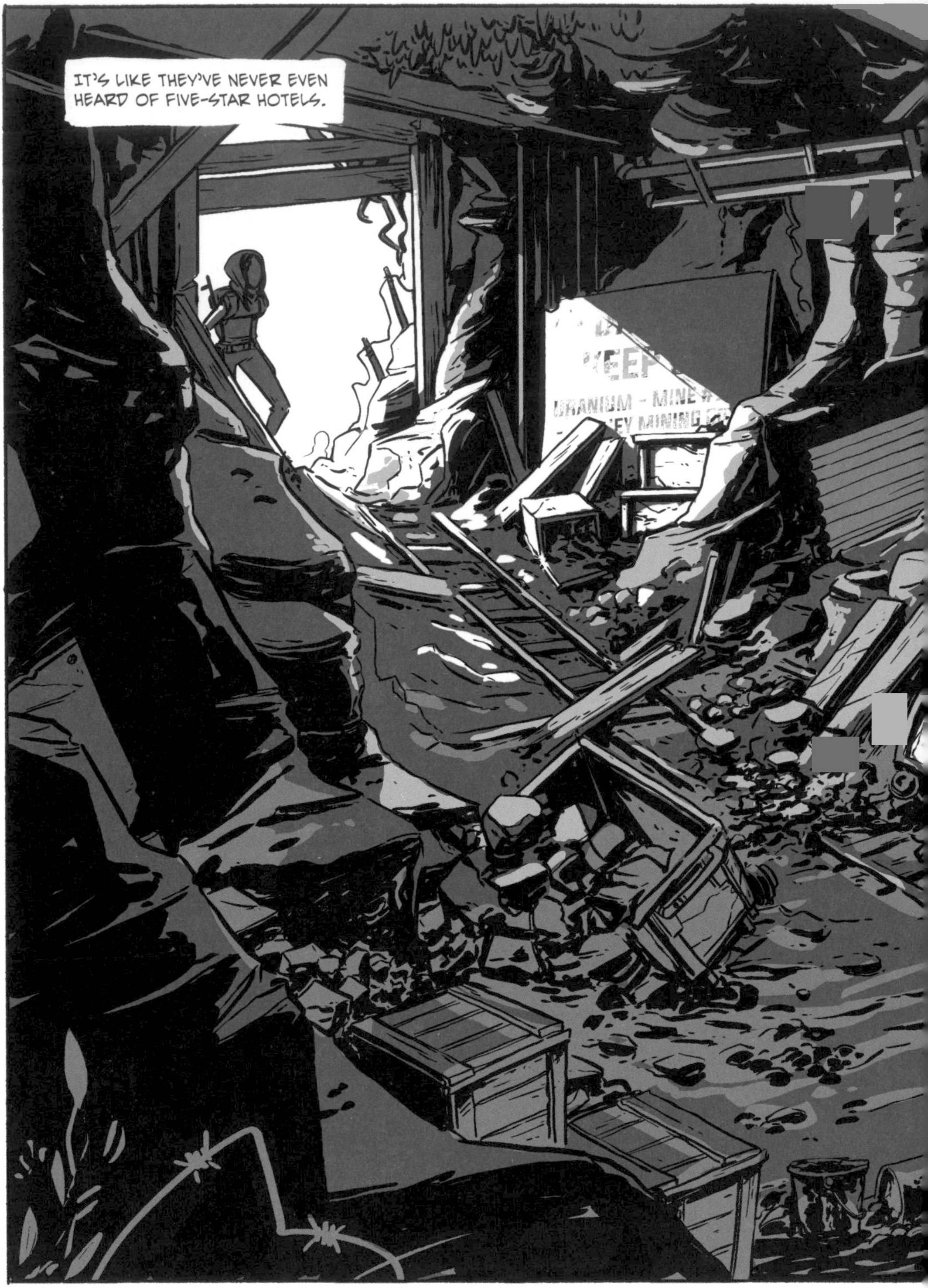
IT'S LIKE THEY'VE NEVER EVEN HEARD OF FIVE-STAR HOTELS.
URANIUM - MINE #

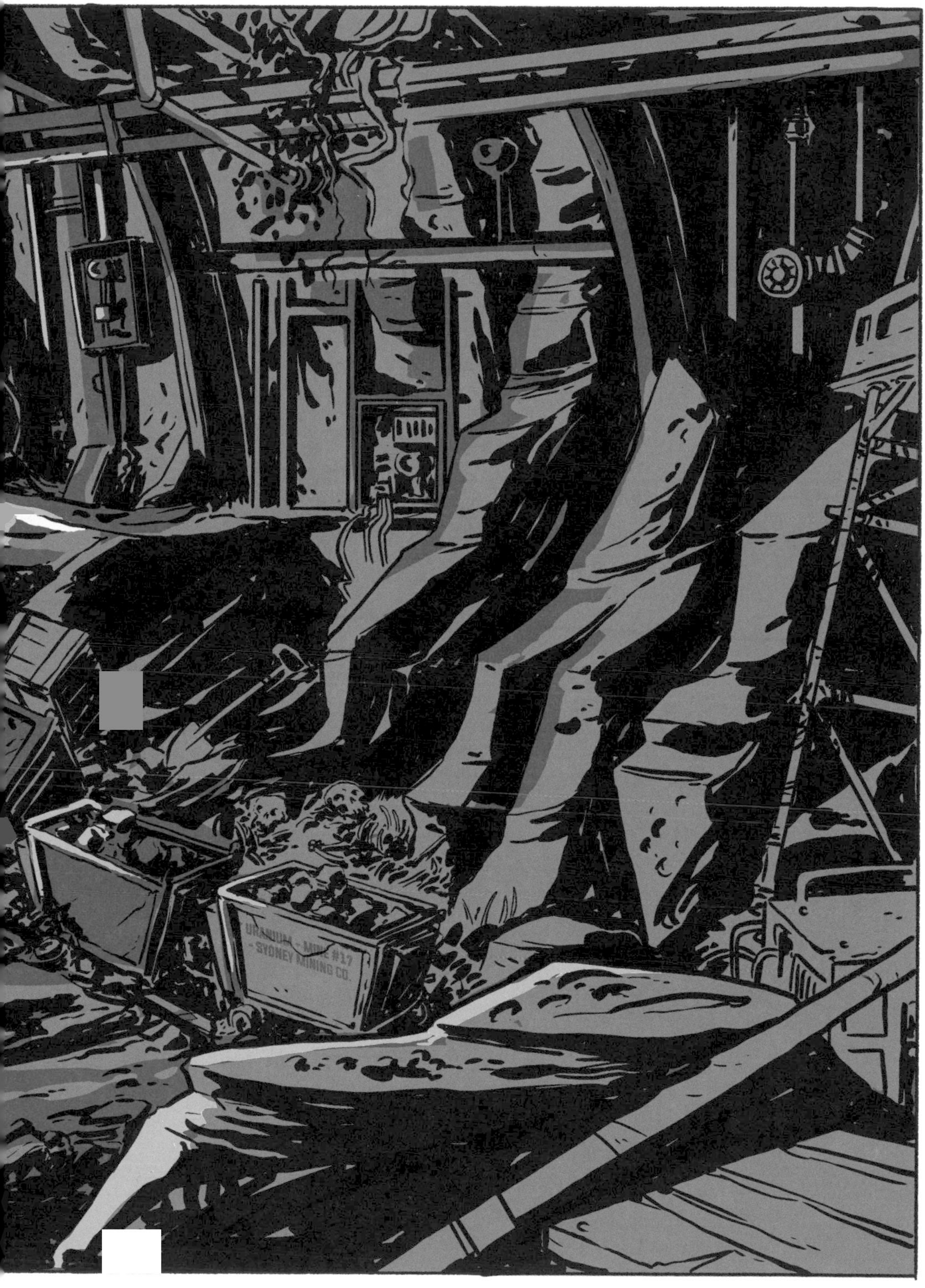
URANIUM - MINE #17
- SYDNEY MINING CO.

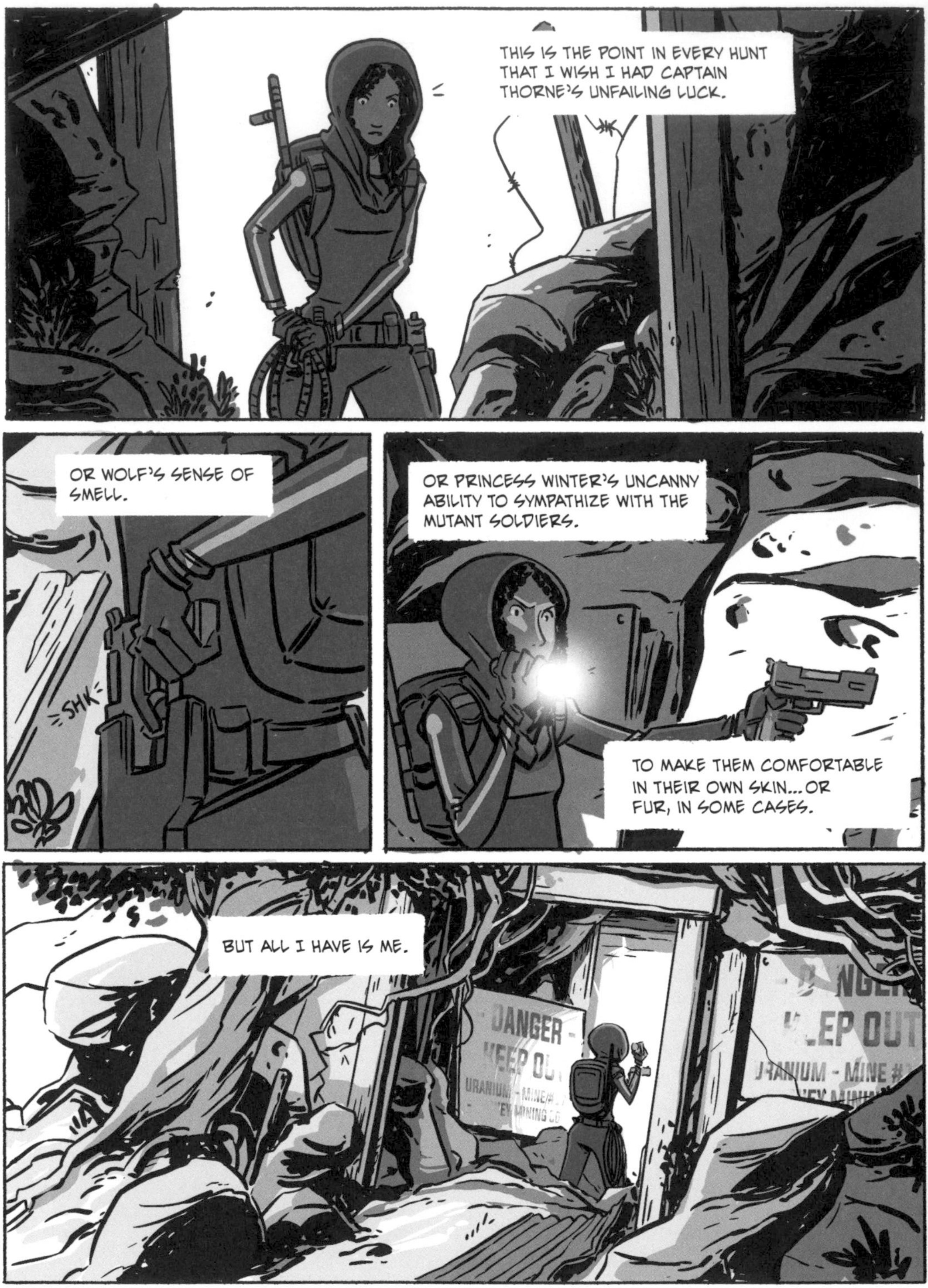
THIS IS THE POINT IN EVERY HUNT THAT I WISH I HAD CAPTAIN THORNE'S UNFAILING LUCK.
OR WOLF'S SENSE OF SMELL.
SHK
OR PRINCESS WINTER'S UNCANNY ABILITY TO SYMPATHIZE WITH THE MUTANT SOLDIERS.
TO MAKE THEM COMFORTABLE IN THEIR OWN SKIN... OR FUR, IN SOME CASES.
BUT ALL I HAVE IS ME.
DANGER -

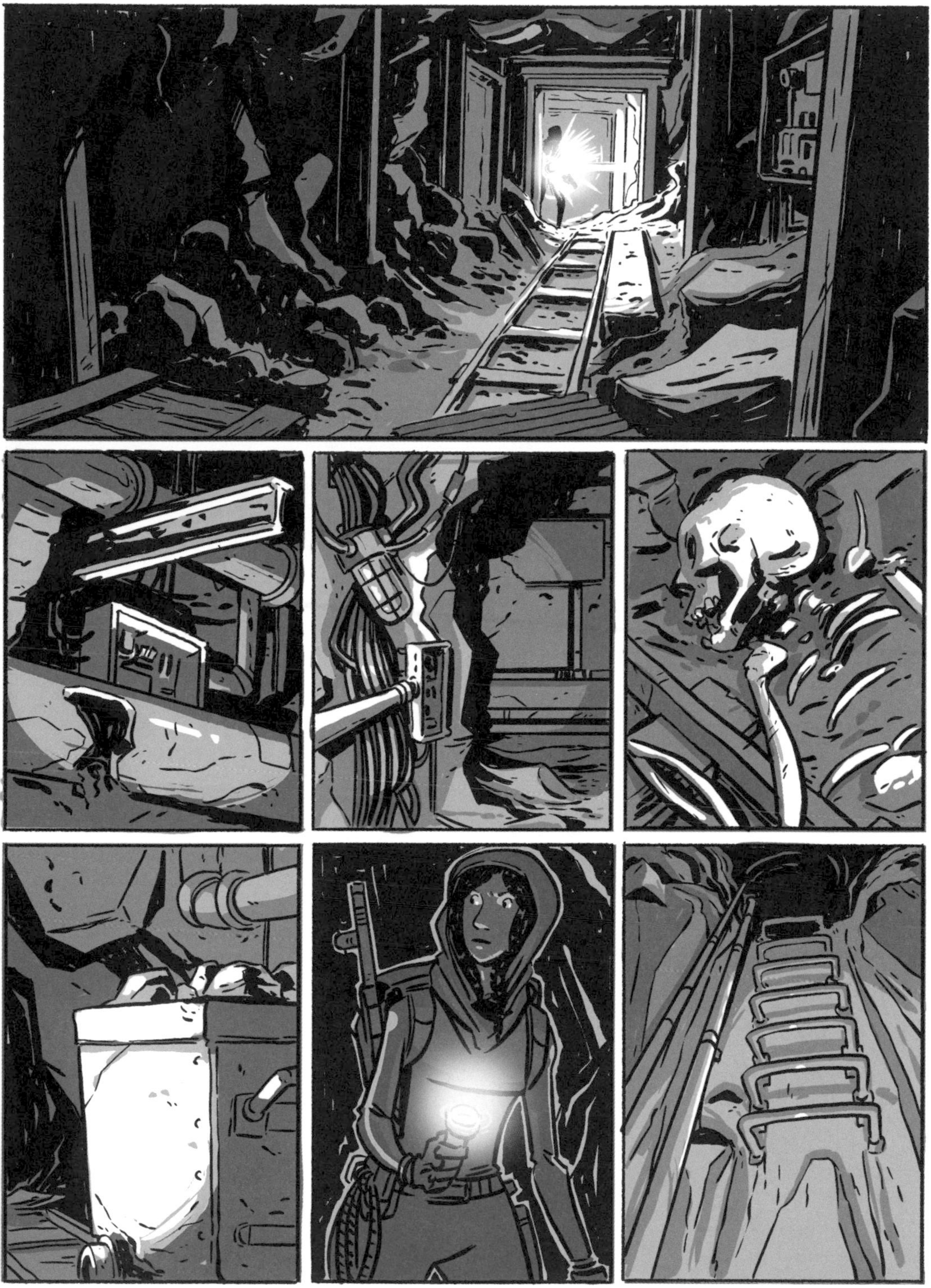

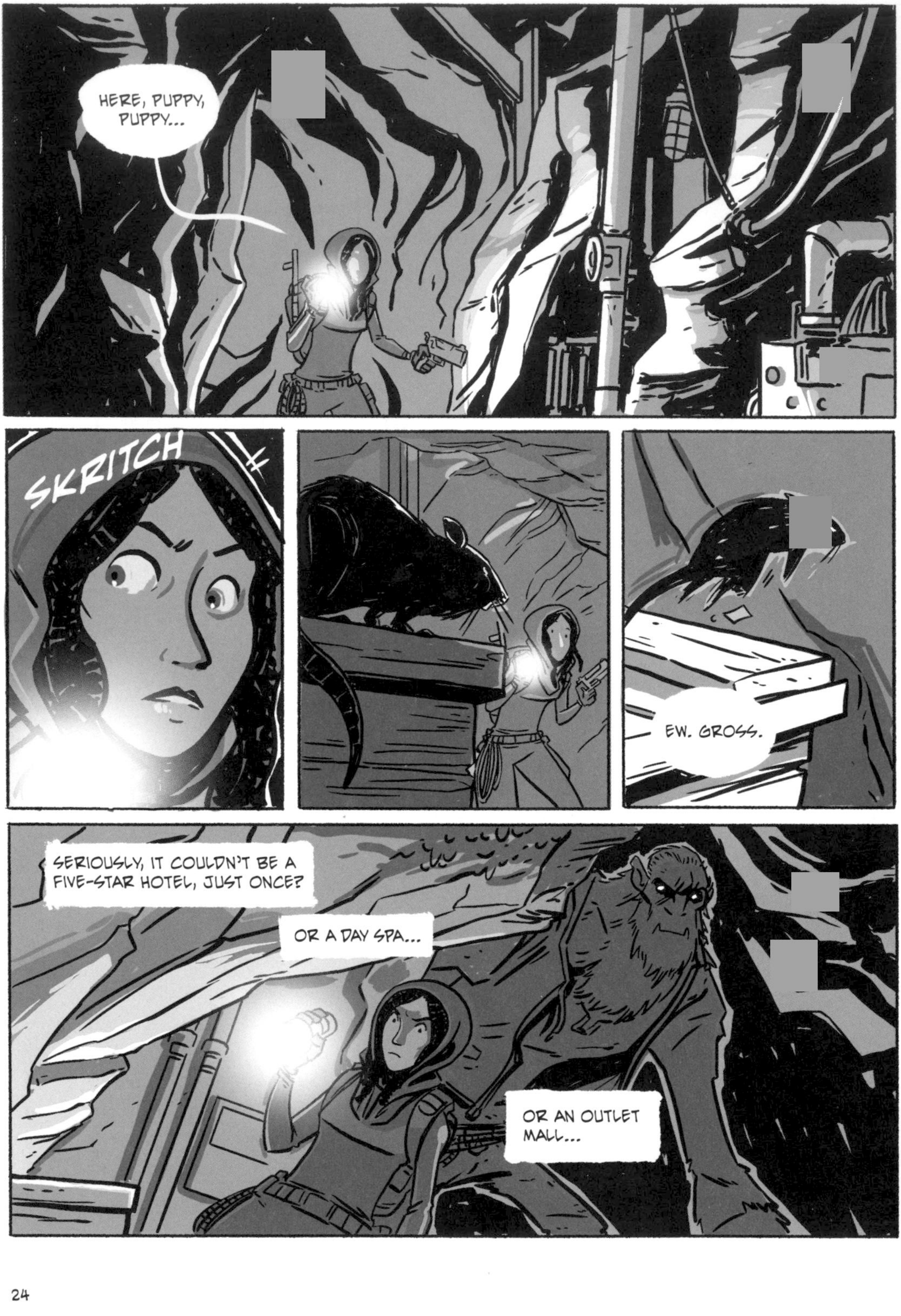

HERE, PUPPY, PUPPY...
SKRITCH
EW. GROSS.
SERIOUSLY, IT COULDN'T BE A FIVE-STAR HOTEL, JUST ONCE?
OR A DAY SPA...
OR AN OUTLET MALL...

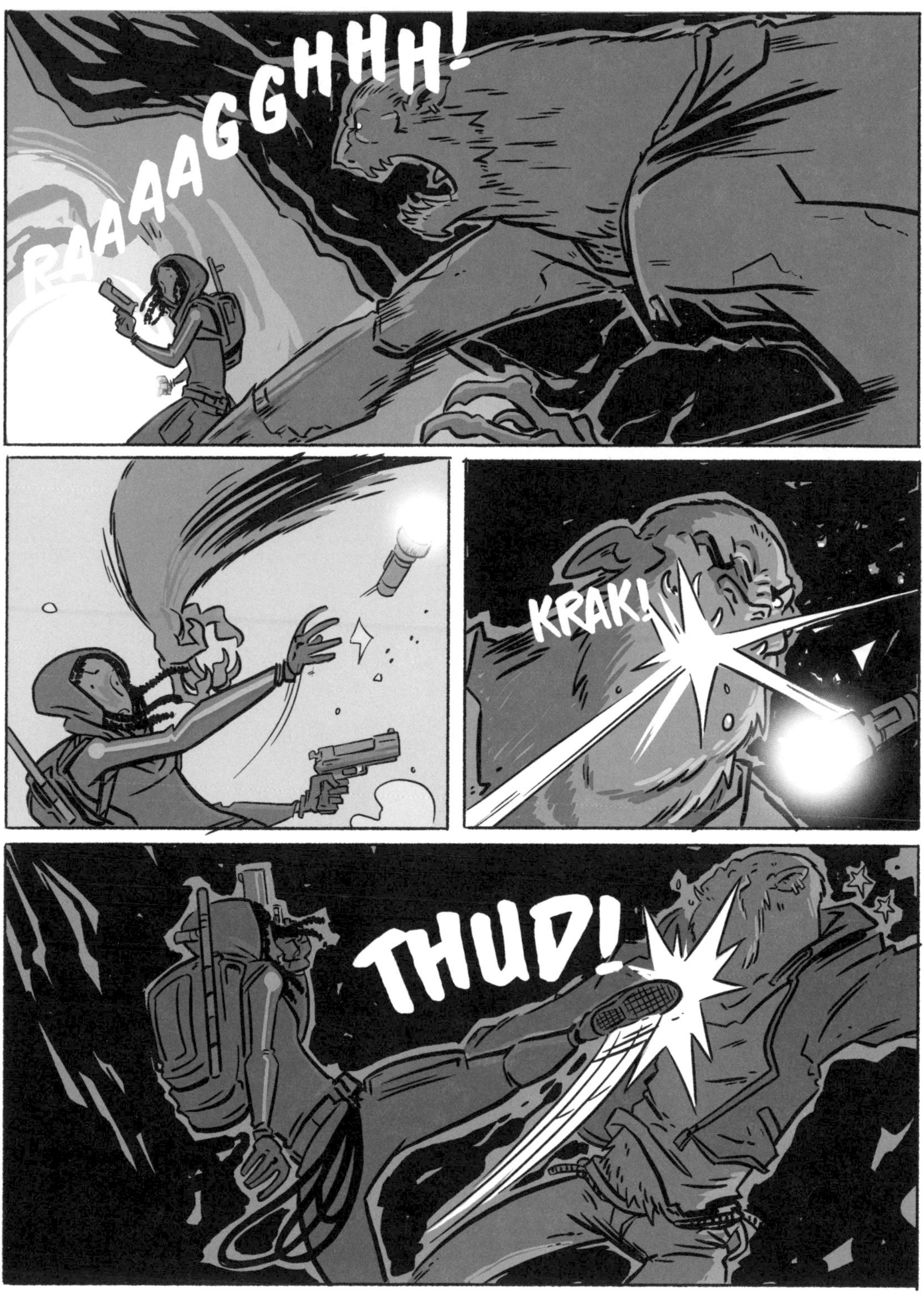
RAAAAGGHHHH!
KRAK!
THUD!

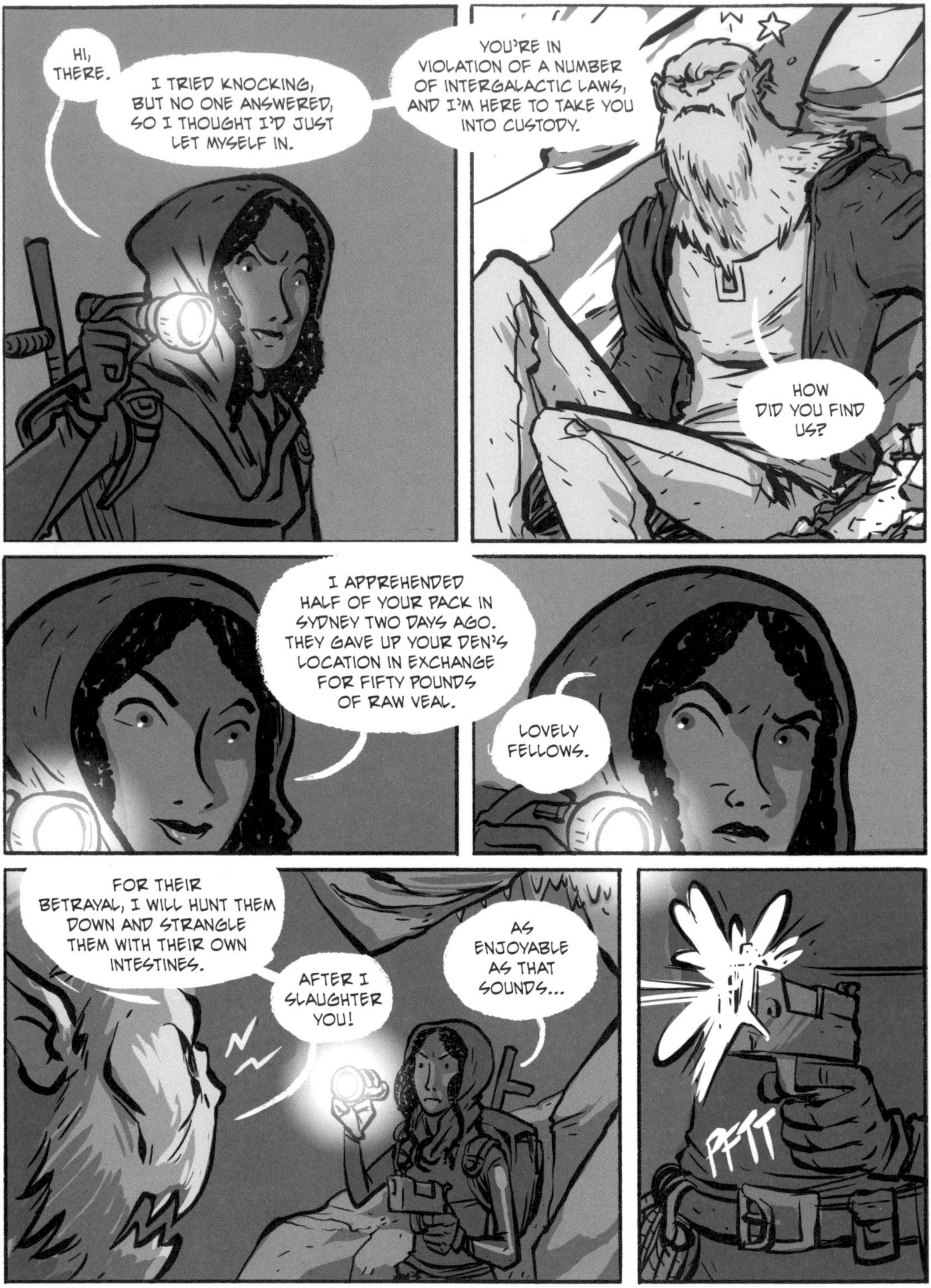
HI, THERE.
I TRIED KNOCKING, BUT NO ONE ANSWERED, SO I THOUGHT I'D JUST LET MYSELF IN.
YOU'RE IN VIOLATION OF A NUMBER OF INTERGALACTIC LAWS, AND I'M HERE TO TAKE YOU INTO CUSTODY.
HOW DID YOU FIND US?
I APPREHENDED HALF OF YOUR PACK IN SYDNEY TWO DAYS AGO. THEY GAVE UP YOUR DEN'S LOCATION IN EXCHANGE FOR FIFTY POUNDS OF RAW VEAL.
LOVELY FELLOWS.
FOR THEIR BETRAYAL, I WILL HUNT THEM DOWN AND STRANGLE THEM WITH THEIR OWN INTESTINES.
AFTER I SLAUGHTER YOU!
AS ENJOYABLE AS THAT SOUNDS...
PFTT

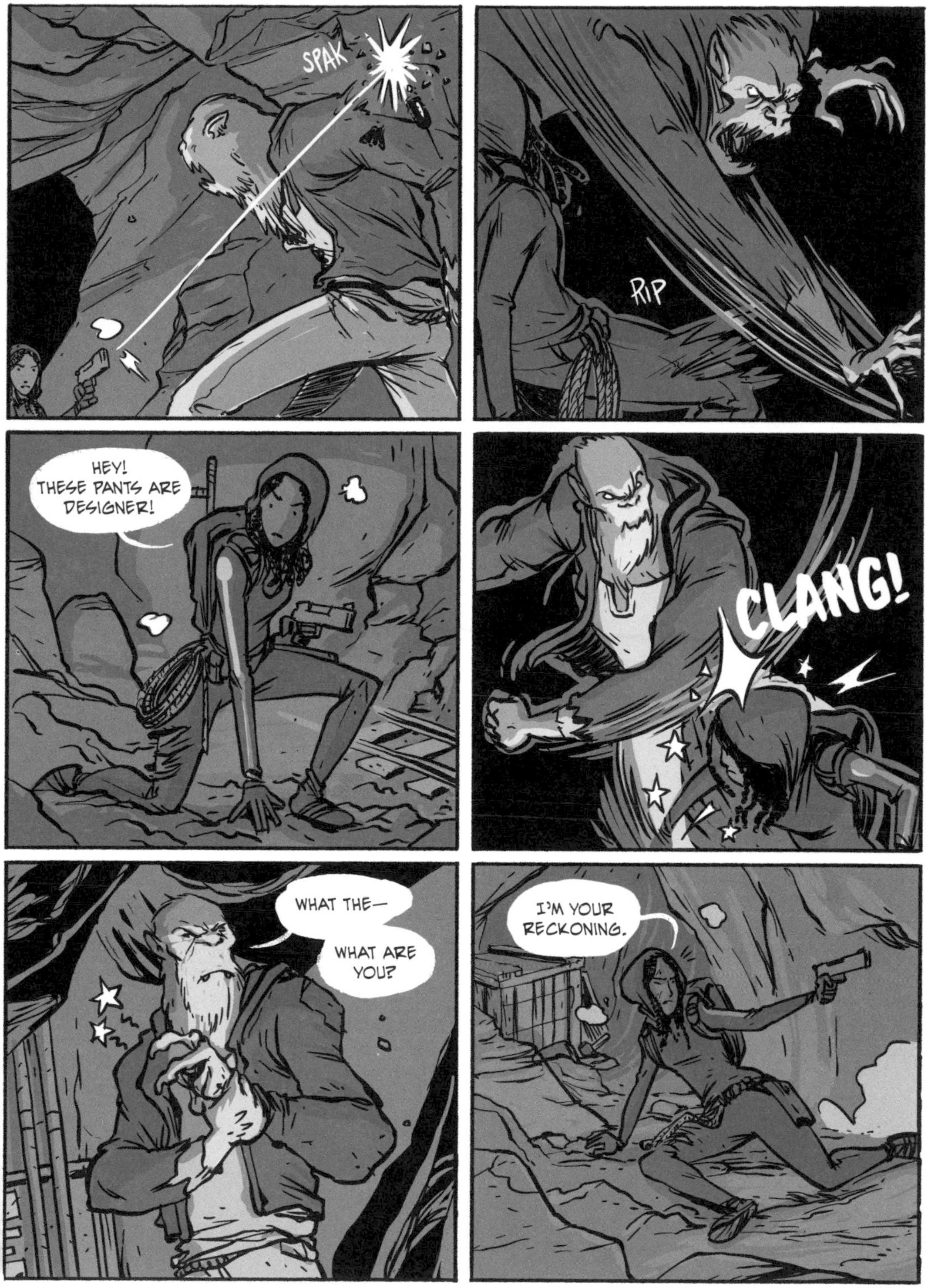
SPAK
RIP
HEY! THESE PANTS ARE DESIGNER!
CLANG!
WHAT THE—
WHAT ARE YOU?
I'M YOUR RECKONING.

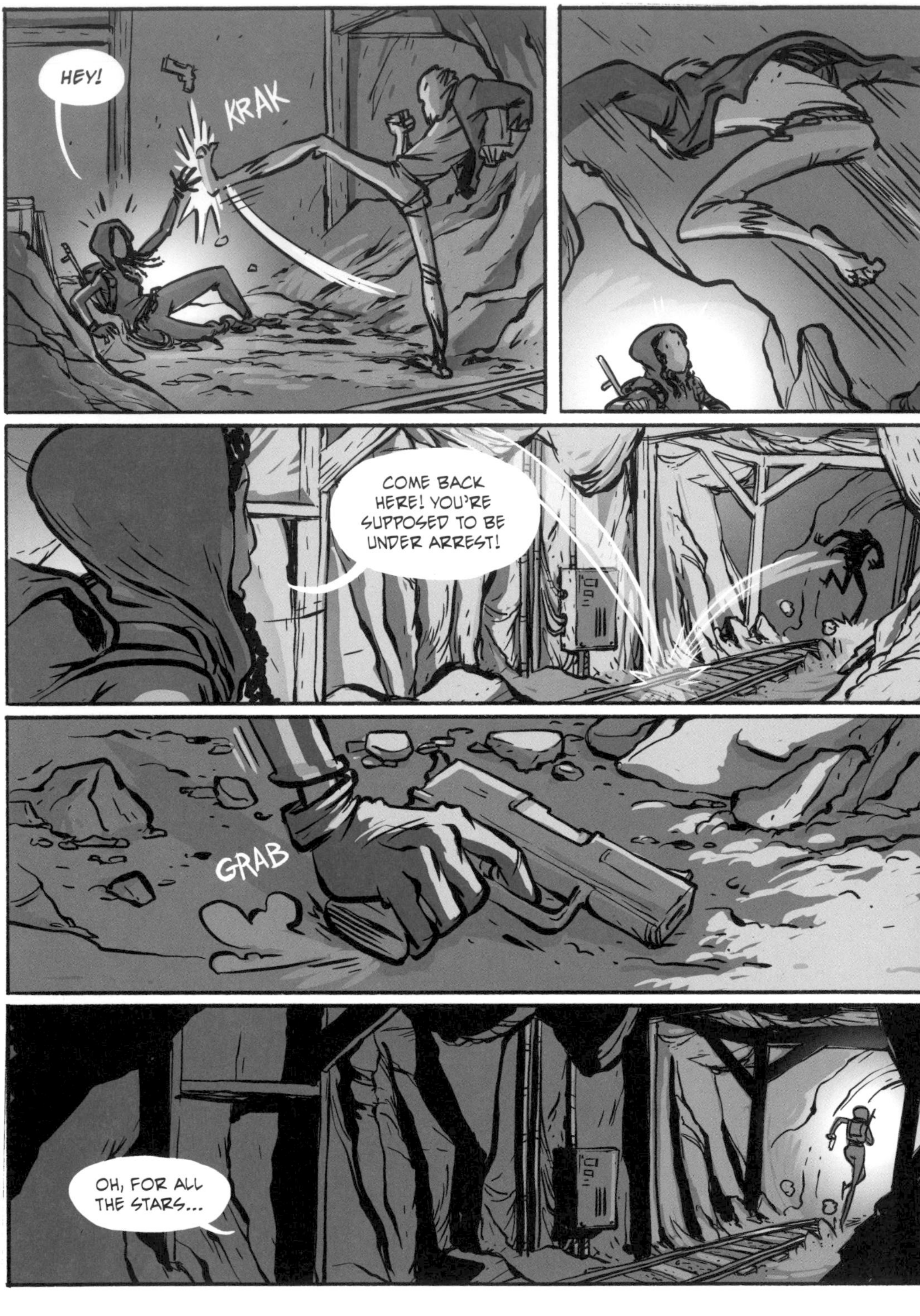
HEY!
KRAK
COME BACK HERE! YOU'RE SUPPOSED TO BE UNDER ARREST!
GRAB
OH, FOR ALL THE STARS...

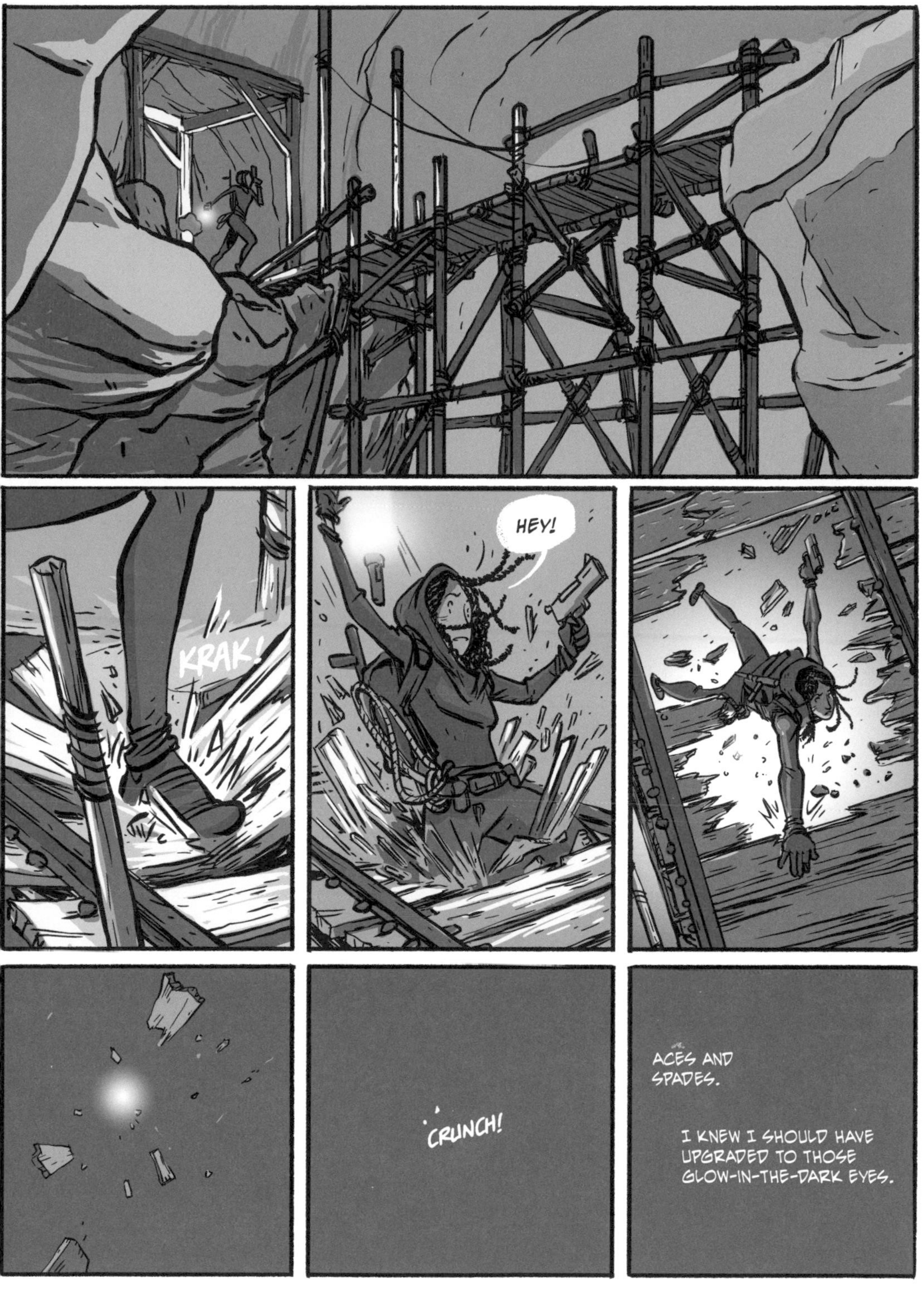
KRAK!
HEY!
CRUNCH!
ACES AND SPADES.
I KNEW I SHOULD HAVE UPGRADED TO THOSE GLOW-IN-THE-DARK EYES.

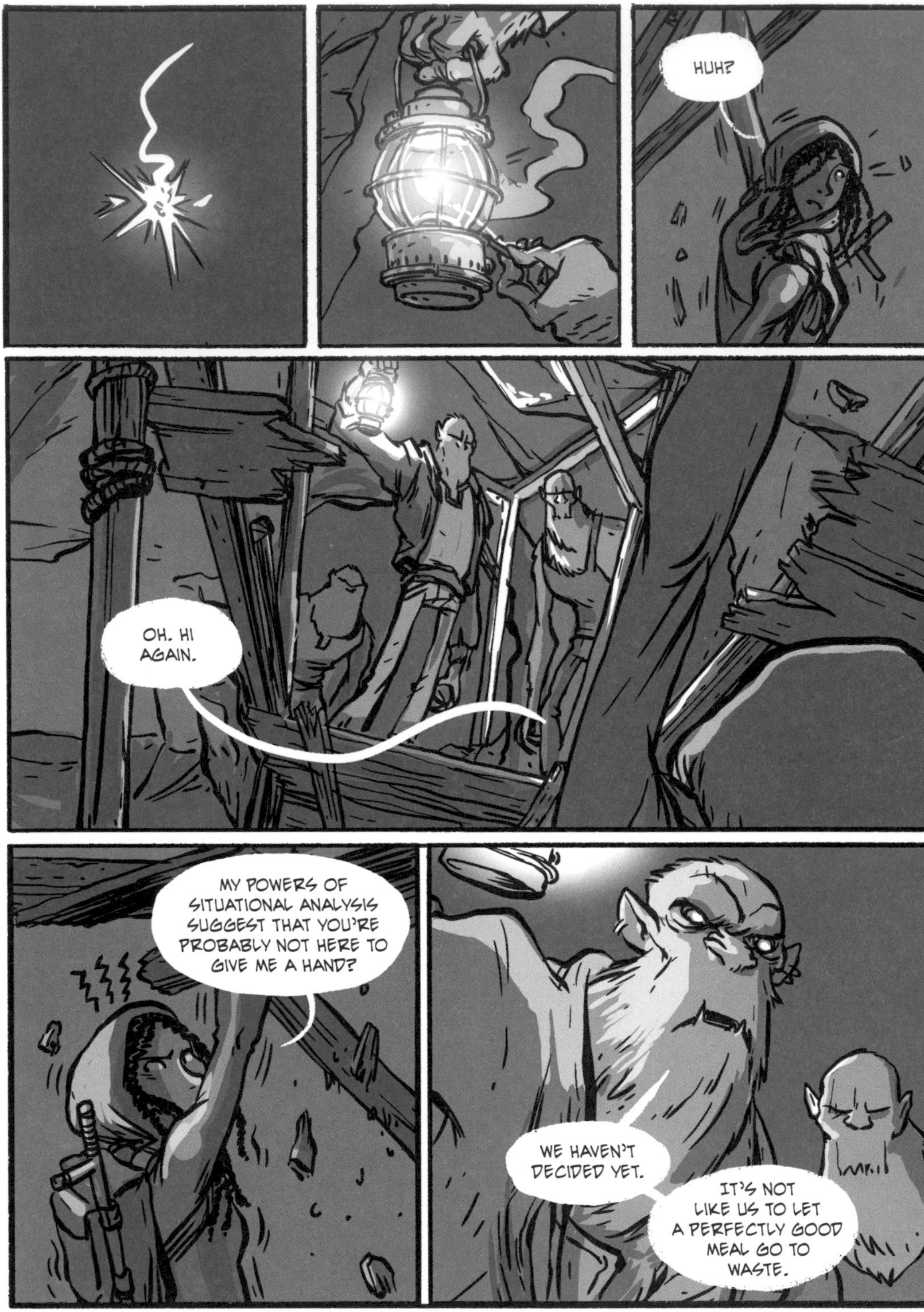
HUH?
OH. HI AGAIN.
MY POWERS OF SITUATIONAL ANALYSIS SUGGEST THAT YOU'RE PROBABLY NOT HERE TO GIVE ME A HAND?
WE HAVEN'T DECIDED YET.
IT'S NOT LIKE US TO LET A PERFECTLY GOOD MEAL GO TO WASTE.

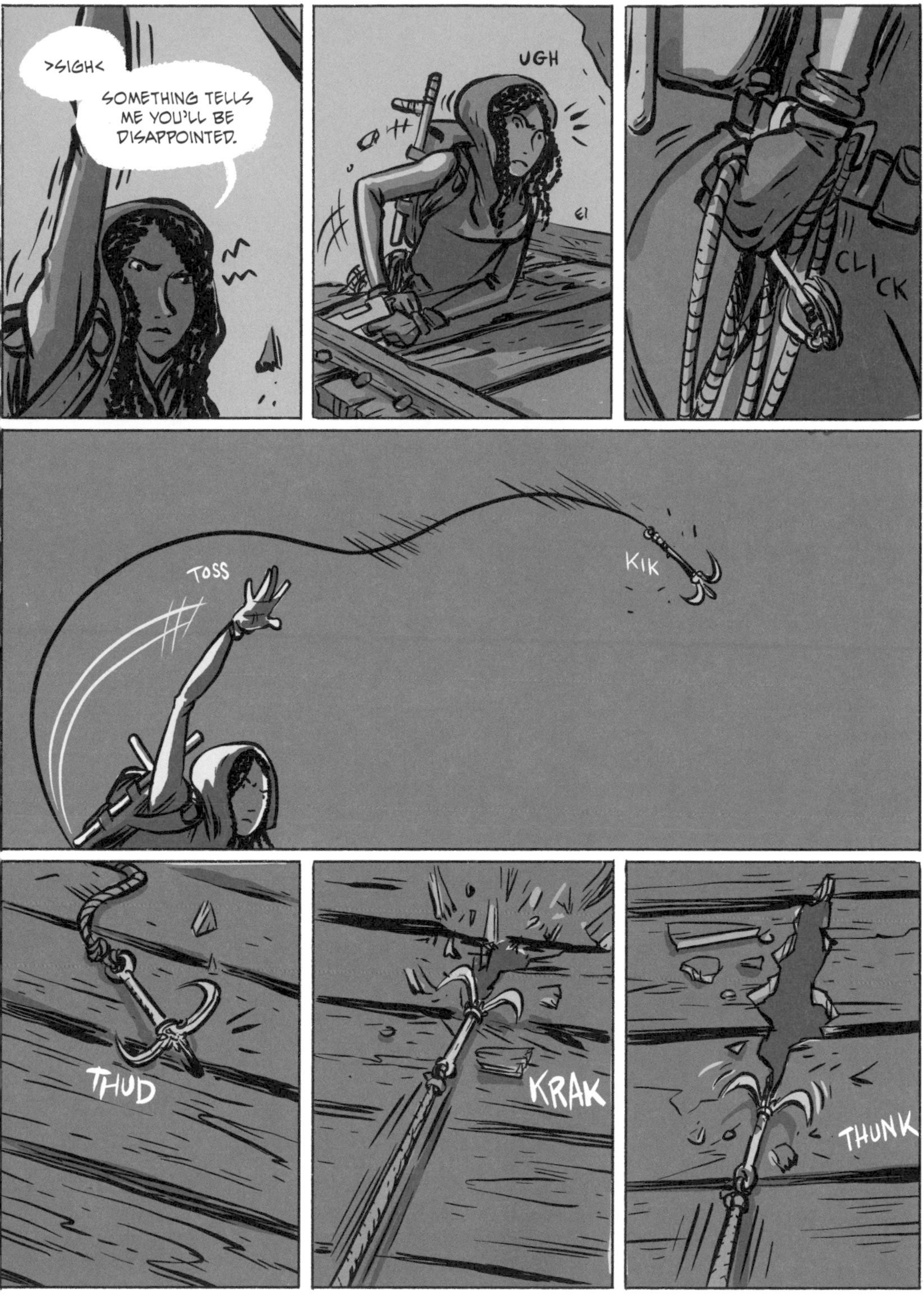
>SIGH<
SOMETHING TELLS ME YOU'LL BE DISAPPOINTED.
UGH
CLICK
TOSS
KIK
THUD
KRAK
THUNK

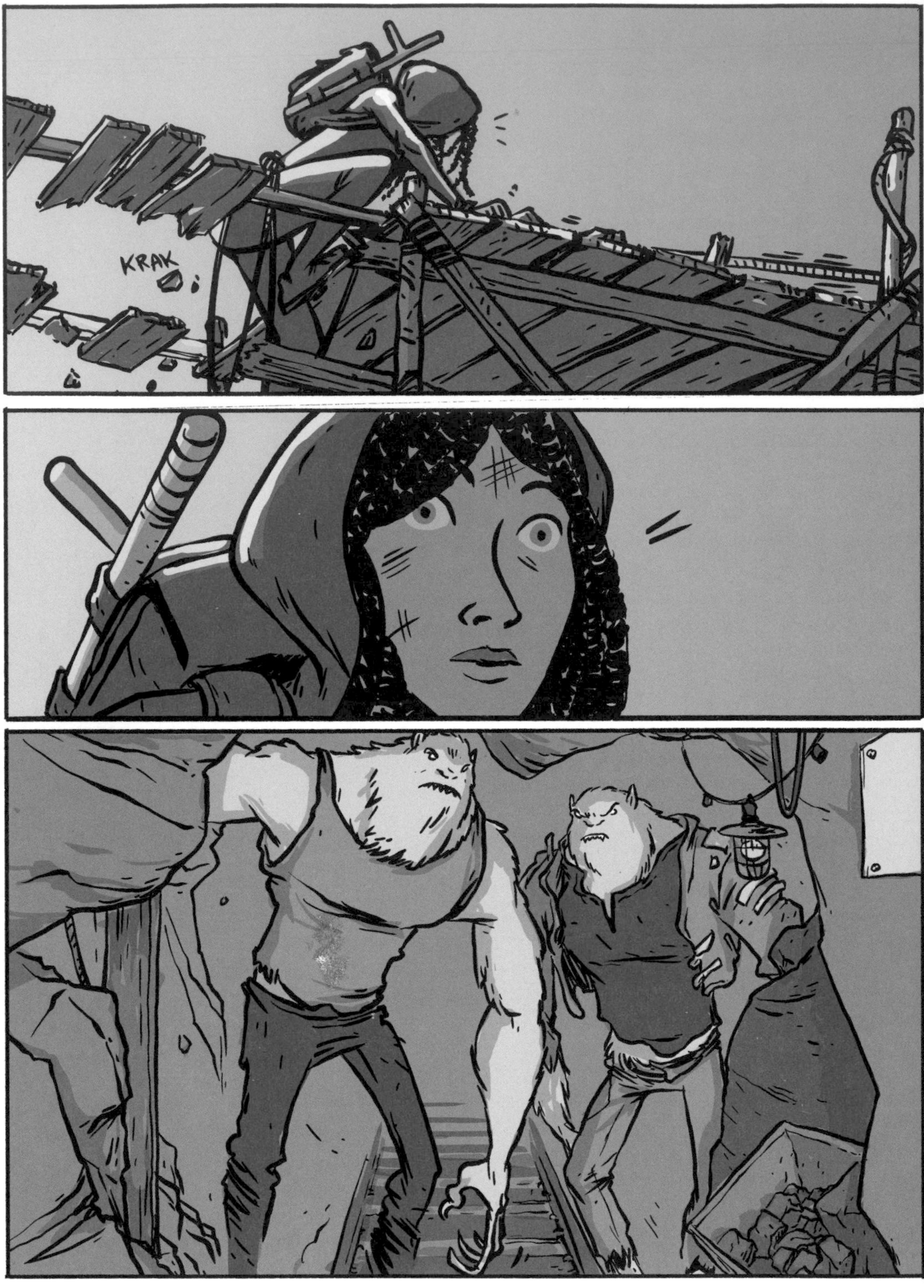
KRAK

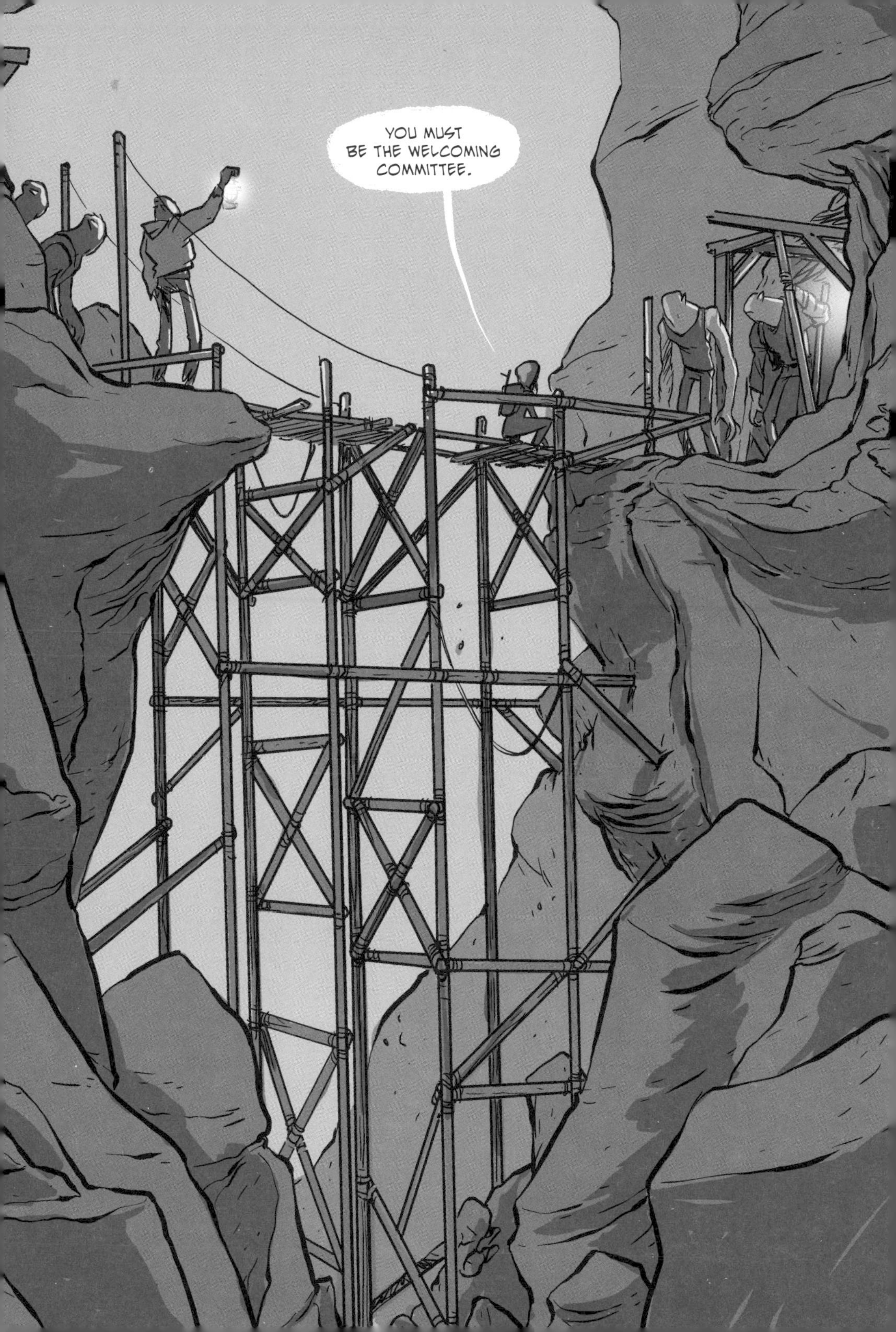
YOU MUST BE THE WELCOMING COMMITTEE.

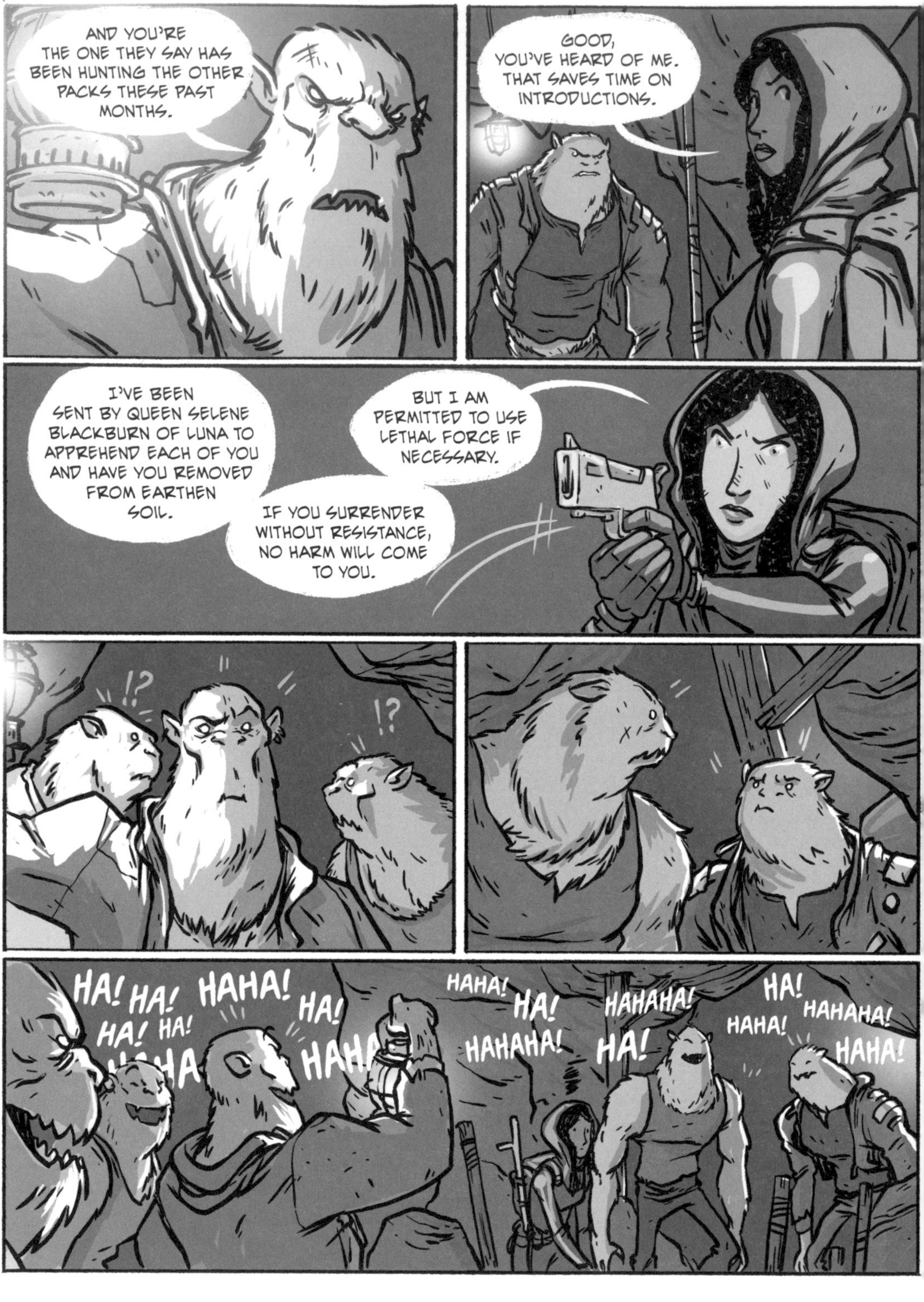
AND YOU'RE THE ONE THEY SAY HAS BEEN HUNTING THE OTHER PACKS THESE PAST MONTHS.
GOOD, YOU'VE HEARD OF ME. THAT SAVES TIME ON INTRODUCTIONS.
I'VE BEEN SENT BY QUEEN SELENE BLACKBURN OF LUNA TO APPREHEND EACH OF YOU AND HAVE YOU REMOVED FROM EARTHEN SOIL.
IF YOU SURRENDER WITHOUT RESISTANCE, NO HARM WILL COME TO YOU.
BUT I AM PERMITTED TO USE LETHAL FORCE IF NECESSARY.
!?
!?
HA! HA! HAHA! HA! HA! HA!
HAHA! HA! HAHAHA! HAHAHA! HA!
HA! HAHA! HAHAHA! HAHA!

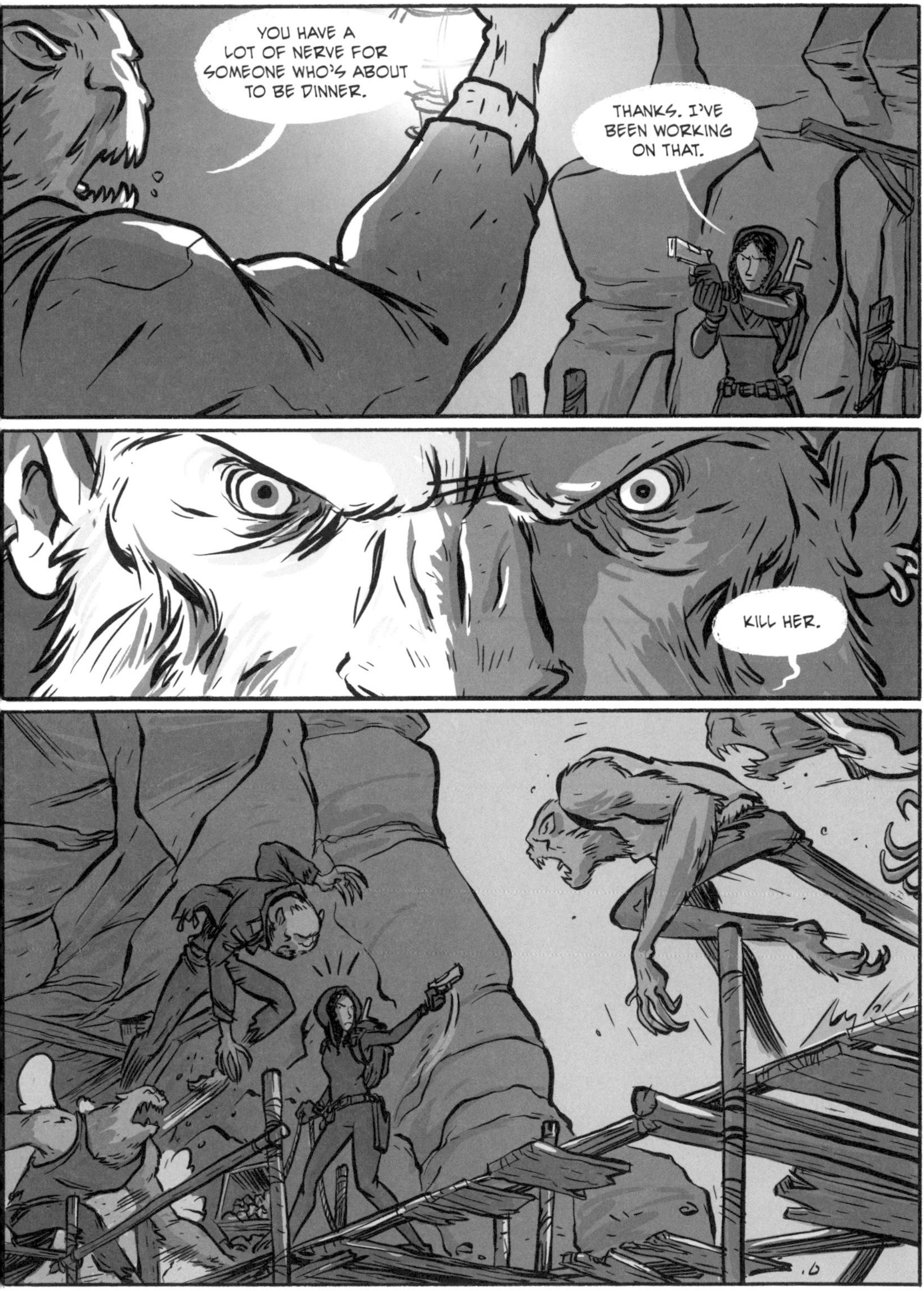
YOU HAVE A LOT OF NERVE FOR SOMEONE WHO'S ABOUT TO BE DINNER.
THANKS. I'VE BEEN WORKING ON THAT.
KILL HER.

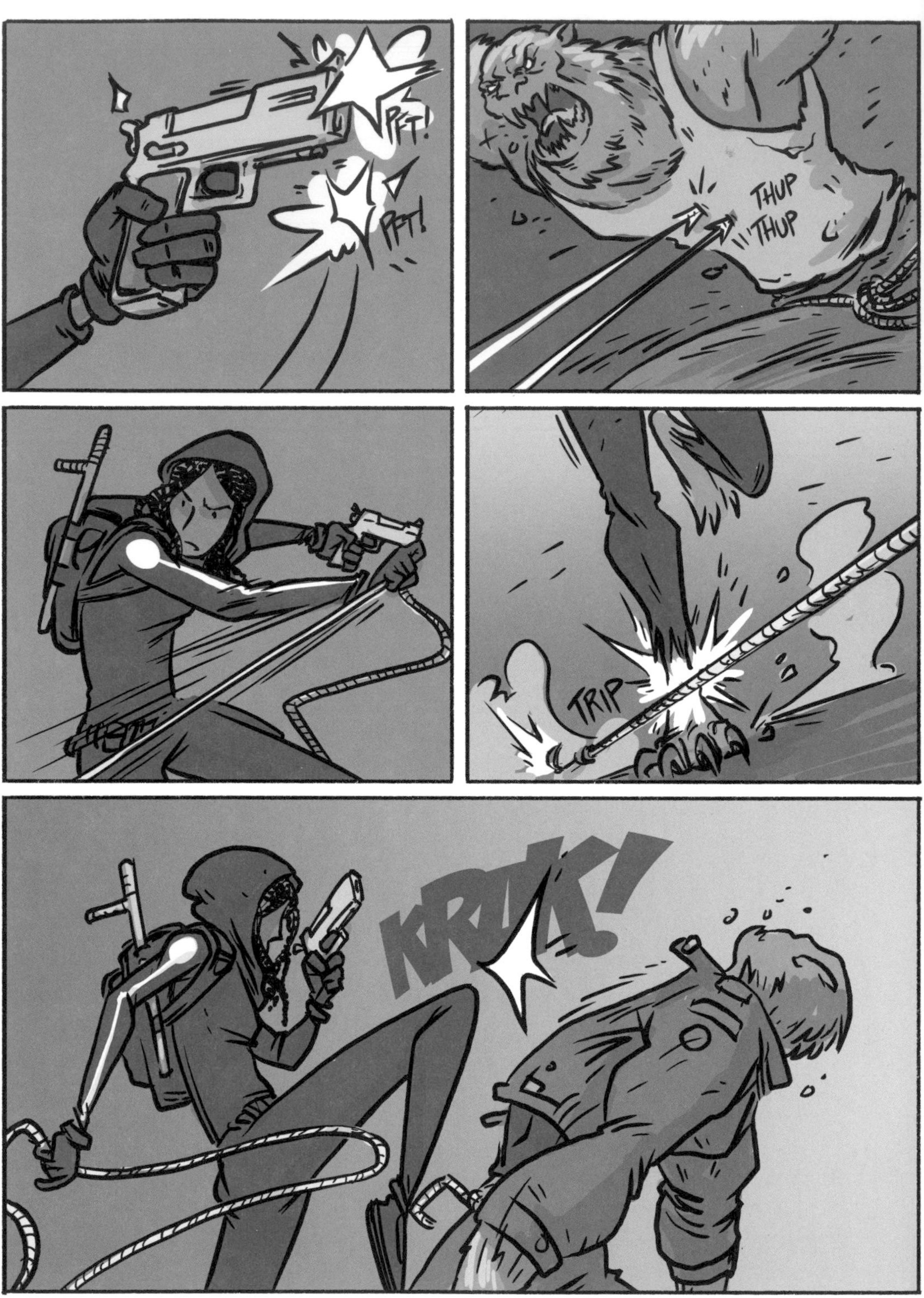
PFT!
PFT!
THUP
THUP
TRIP
KRAK!

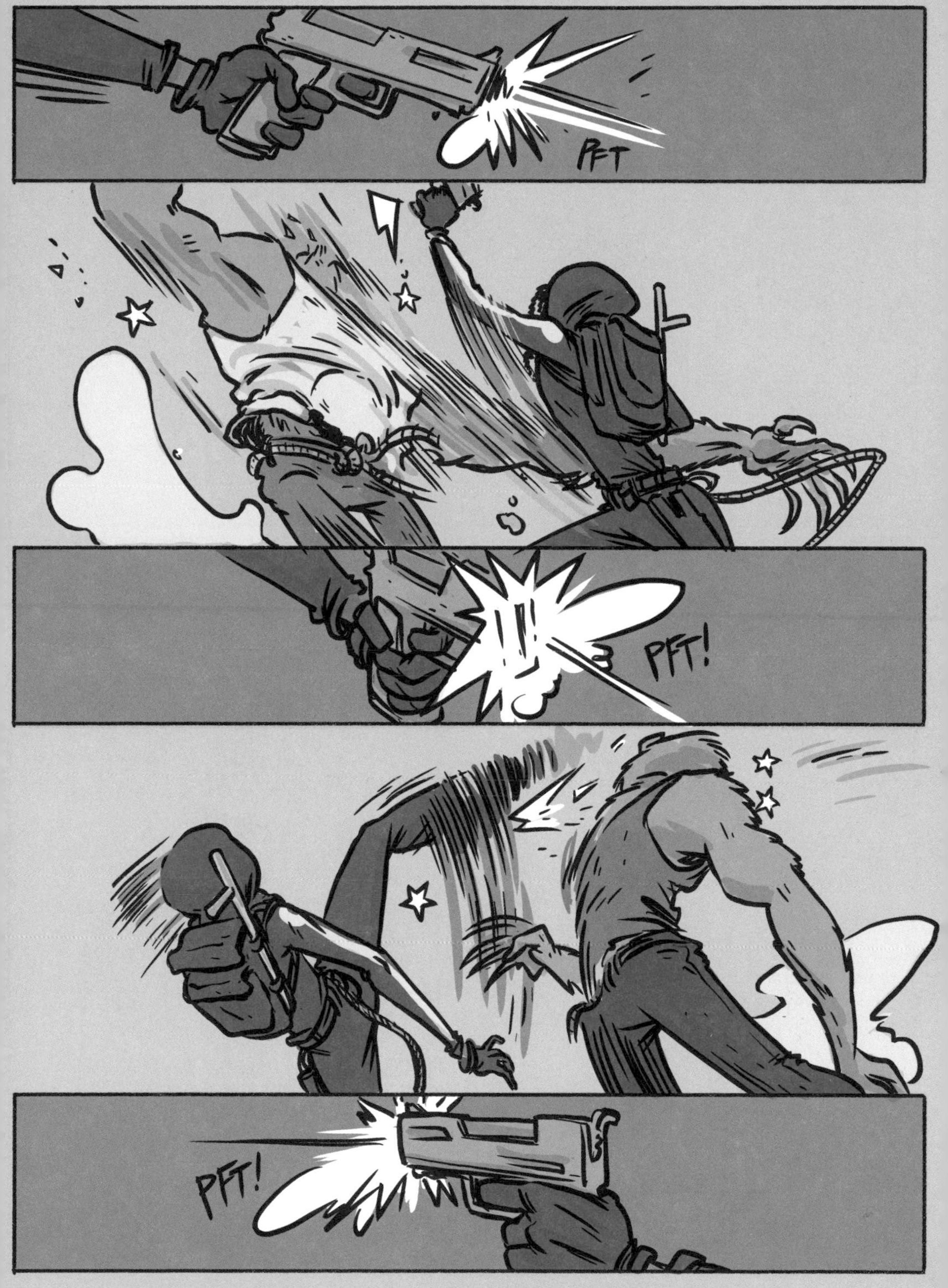
PFT
PFT!
PFT!

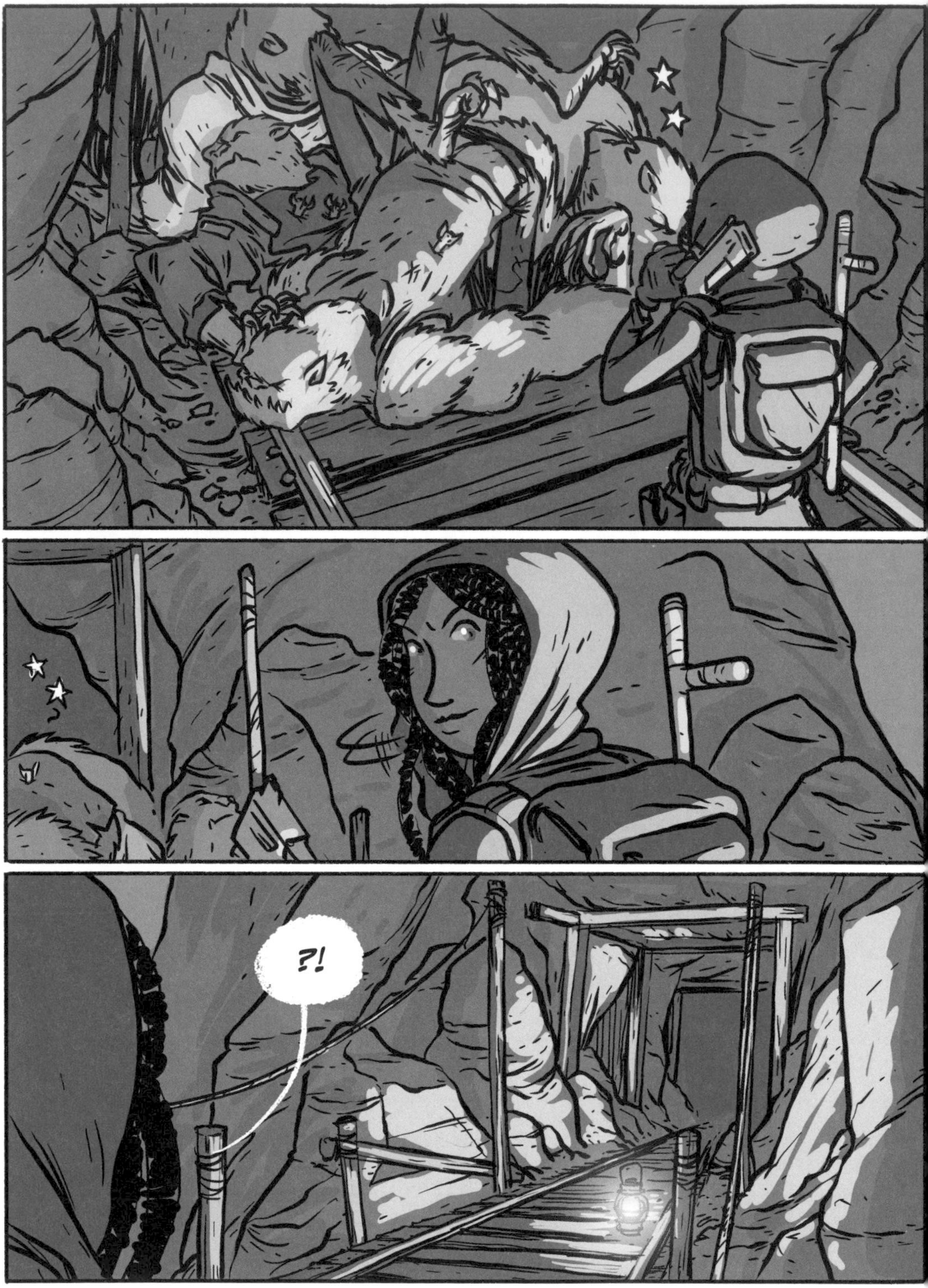
?!

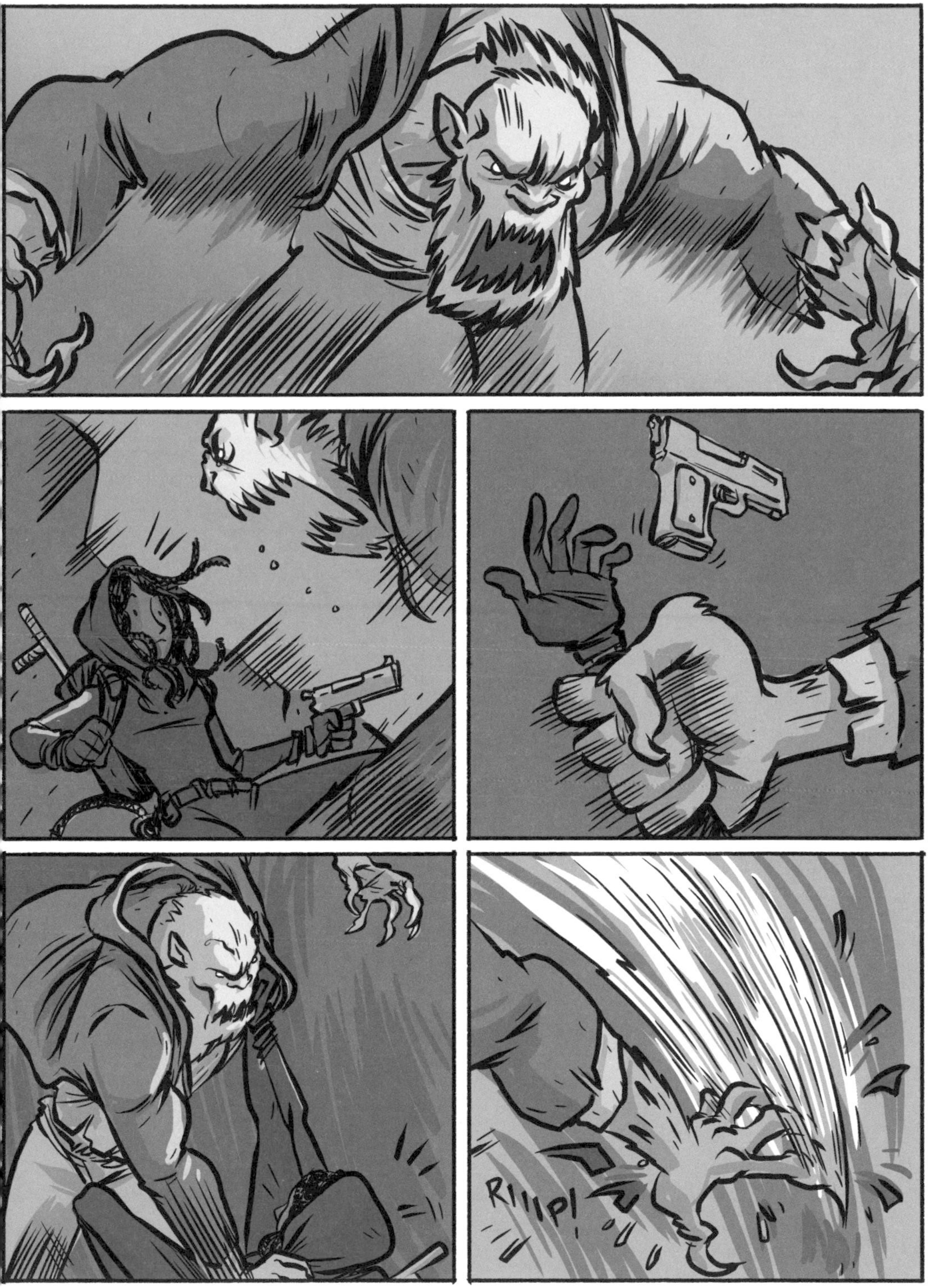
RIIIP!

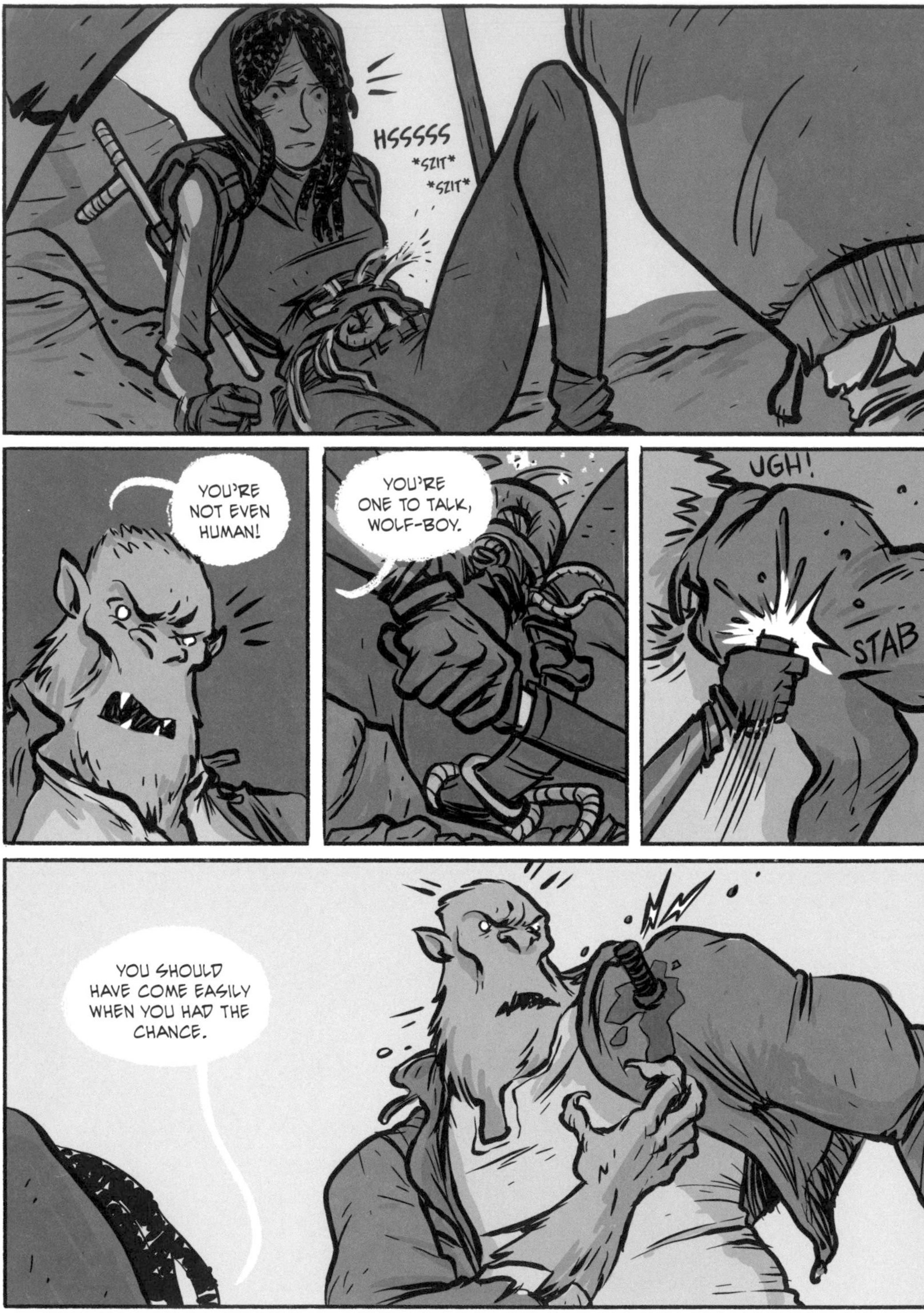
HSSSSS
SZIT
SZIT
YOU'RE NOT EVEN HUMAN!
YOU'RE ONE TO TALK, WOLF-BOY.
UGH!
STAB
YOU SHOULD HAVE COME EASILY WHEN YOU HAD THE CHANCE.

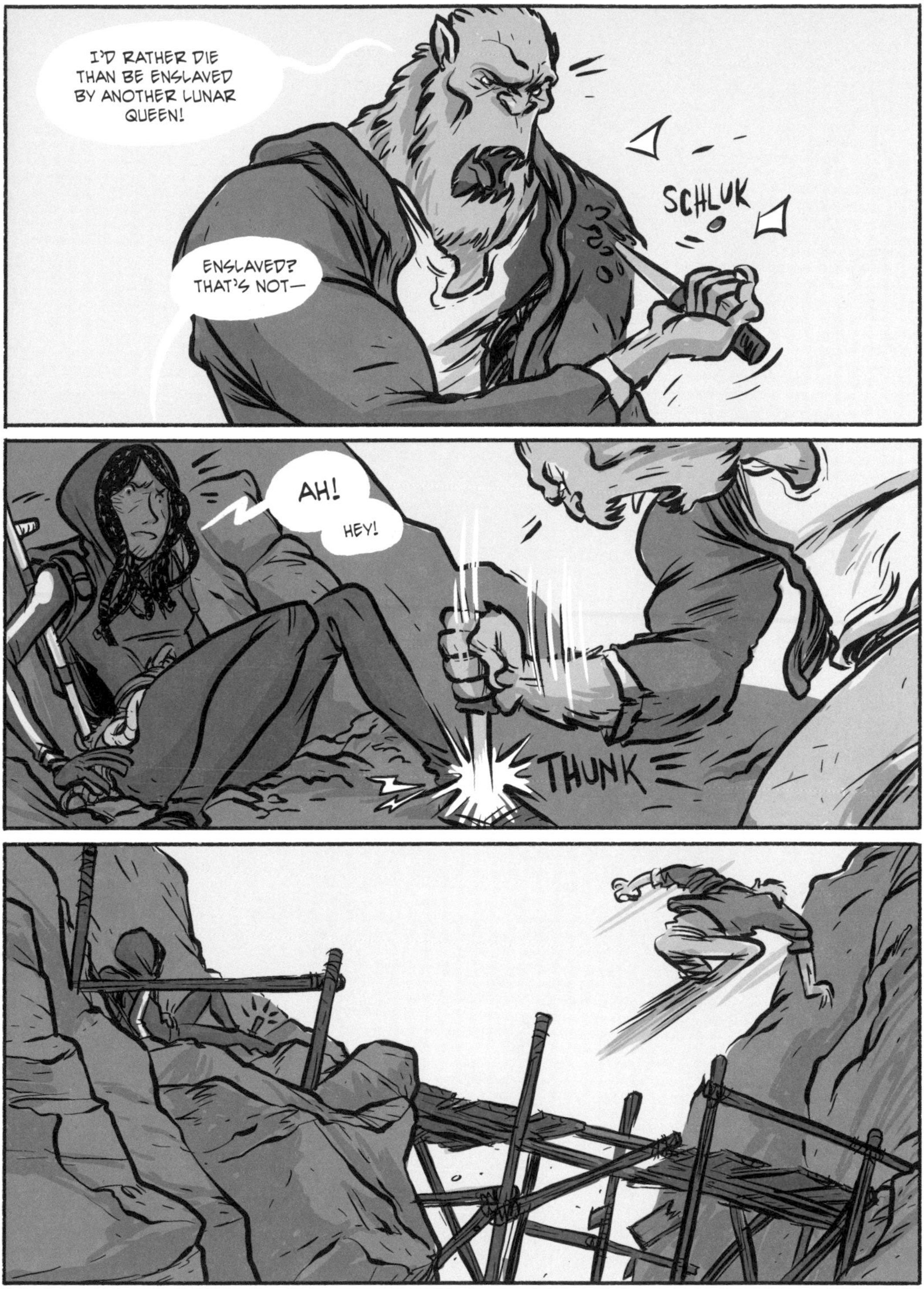
I'D RATHER DIE THAN BE ENSLAVED BY ANOTHER LUNAR QUEEN!
ENSLAVED? THAT'S NOT—
SCHLUK
AH!
HEY!
THUNK

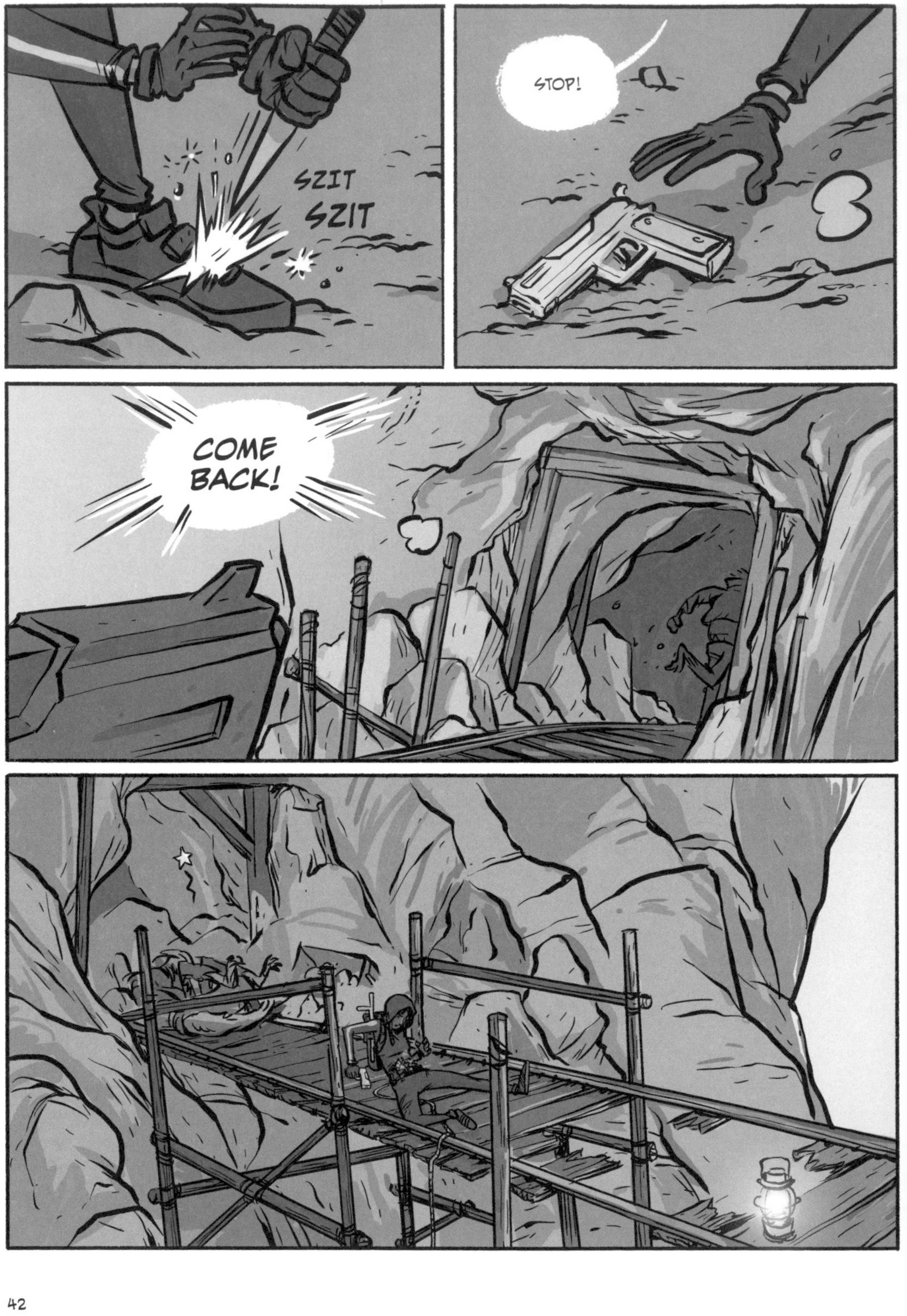
SZIT
SZIT
STOP!
COME BACK!

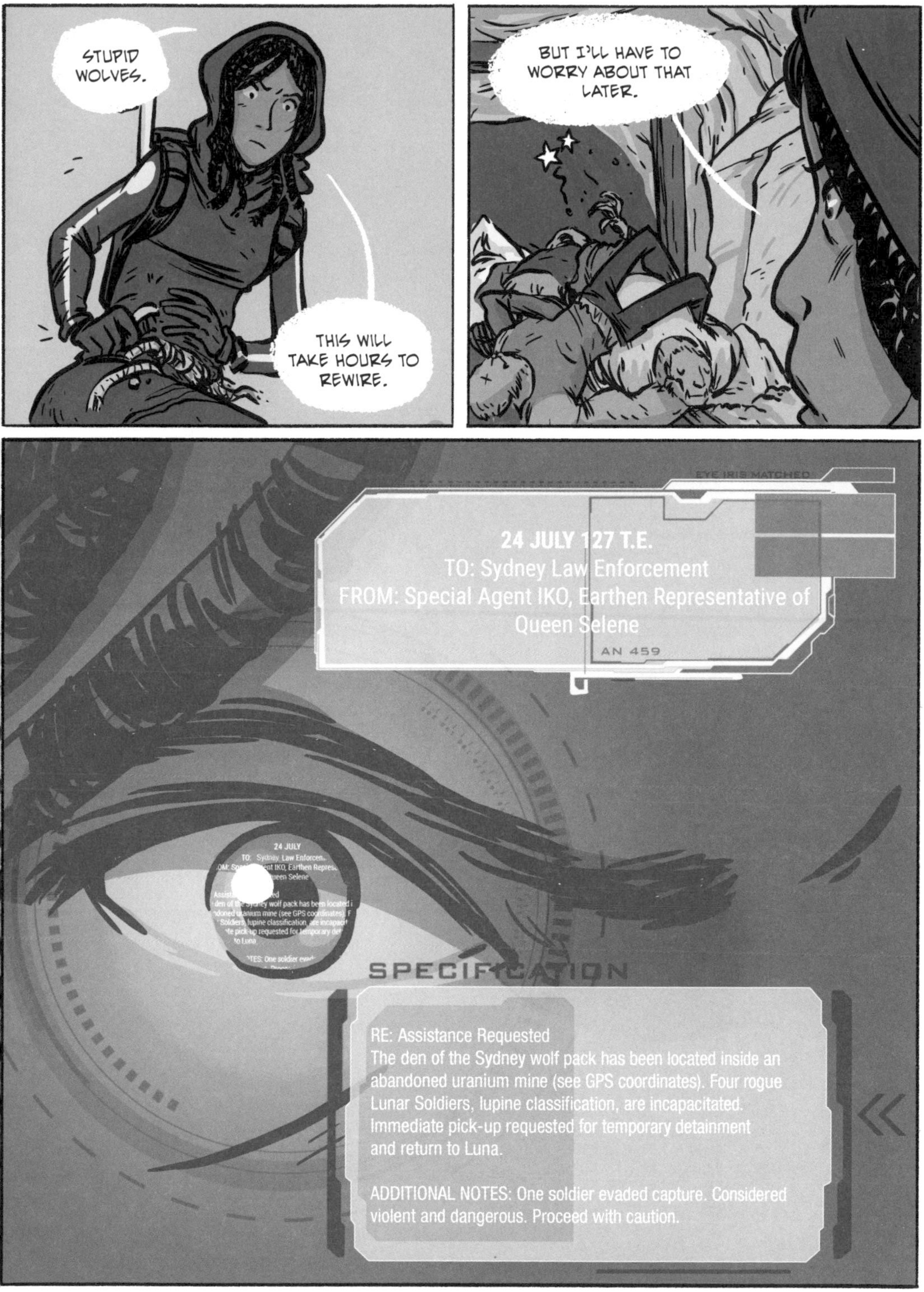
STUPID WOLVES.
THIS WILL TAKE HOURS TO REWIRE.
BUT I'LL HAVE TO WORRY ABOUT THAT LATER.
EYE IRIS MATCHED
24 JULY 127 T.E.
TO: Sydney Law Enforcement
FROM: Special Agent IKO, Earthen Representative of Queen Selene
AN 459
SPECIFICATION
RE: Assistance Requested
The den of the Sydney wolf pack has been located inside an abandoned uranium mine (see GPS coordinates). Four rogue Lunar Soldiers, lupine classification, are incapacitated. Immediate pick-up requested for temporary detainment and return to Luna.
ADDITIONAL NOTES: One soldier evaded capture. Considered violent and dangerous. Proceed with caution.

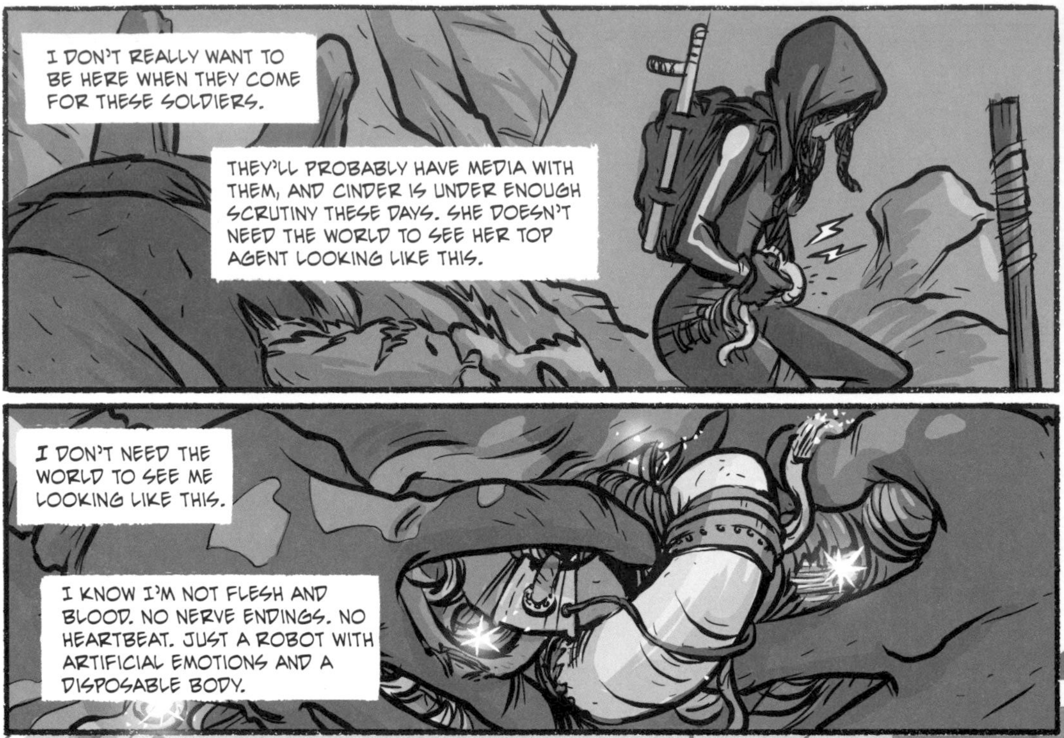
I DON'T REALLY WANT TO BE HERE WHEN THEY COME FOR THESE SOLDIERS.
THEY'LL PROBABLY HAVE MEDIA WITH THEM, AND CINDER IS UNDER ENOUGH SCRUTINY THESE DAYS. SHE DOESN'T NEED THE WORLD TO SEE HER TOP AGENT LOOKING LIKE THIS.
I DON'T NEED THE WORLD TO SEE ME LOOKING LIKE THIS.
I KNOW I'M NOT FLESH AND BLOOD. NO NERVE ENDINGS. NO HEARTBEAT. JUST A ROBOT WITH ARTIFICIAL EMOTIONS AND A DISPOSABLE BODY.

COMMLINK ESTABLISHED WITH USER: RAMPION

IKO: Hit a bit of a snag outside of Sydney. Don't suppose you could give me a lift?
RAMPION: Long time, no comms, Iko! Give us a second.
...
...
...
RAMPION: Cress is confirming your coordinates. We'll be there soon.
IKO: Thanks, Captain.

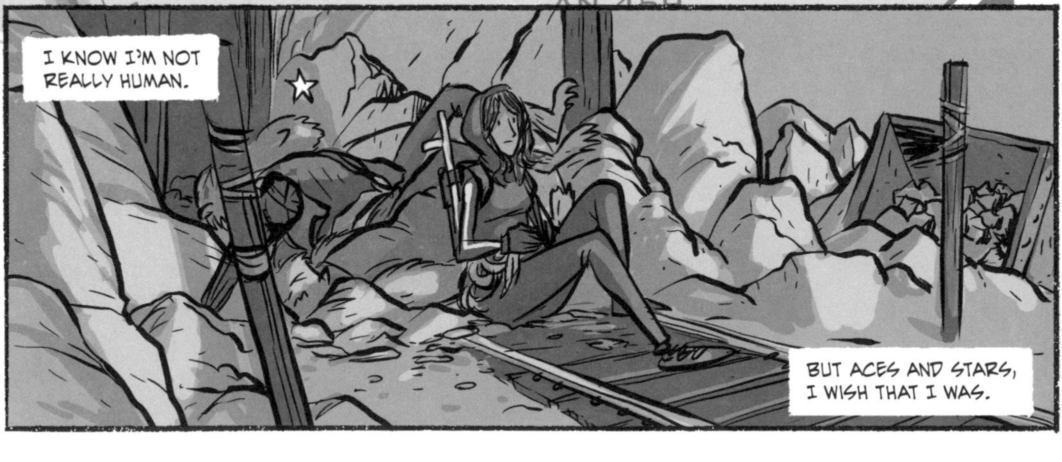
I KNOW I'M NOT REALLY HUMAN.
BUT ACES AND STARS, I WISH THAT I WAS.

CHAPTER 11

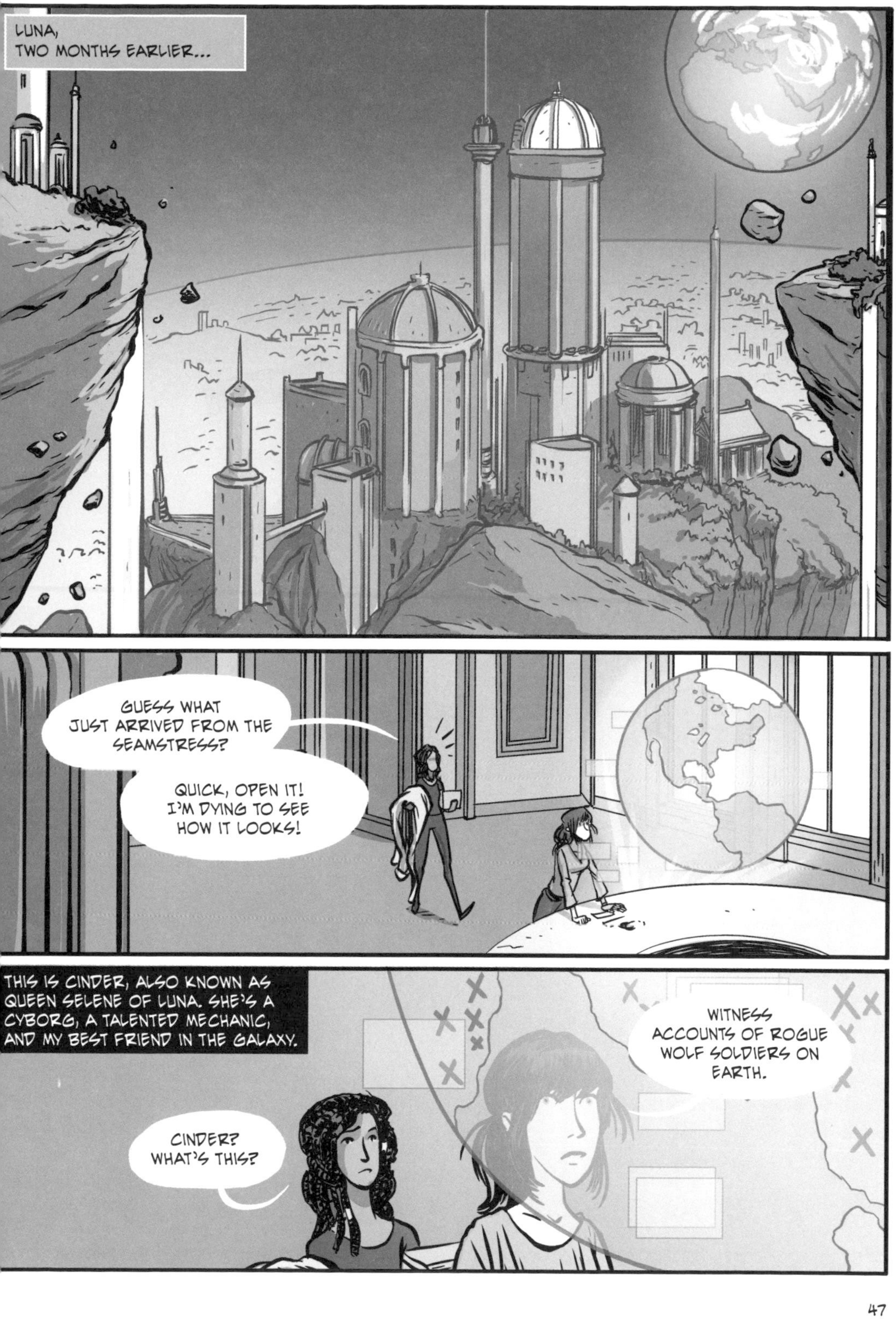
LUNA,
TWO MONTHS EARLIER...
GUESS WHAT JUST ARRIVED FROM THE SEAMSTRESS?
QUICK, OPEN IT! I'M DYING TO SEE HOW IT LOOKS!
THIS IS CINDER, ALSO KNOWN AS QUEEN SELENE OF LUNA. SHE'S A CYBORG, A TALENTED MECHANIC, AND MY BEST FRIEND IN THE GALAXY.
WITNESS ACCOUNTS OF ROGUE WOLF SOLDIERS ON EARTH.
CINDER? WHAT'S THIS?

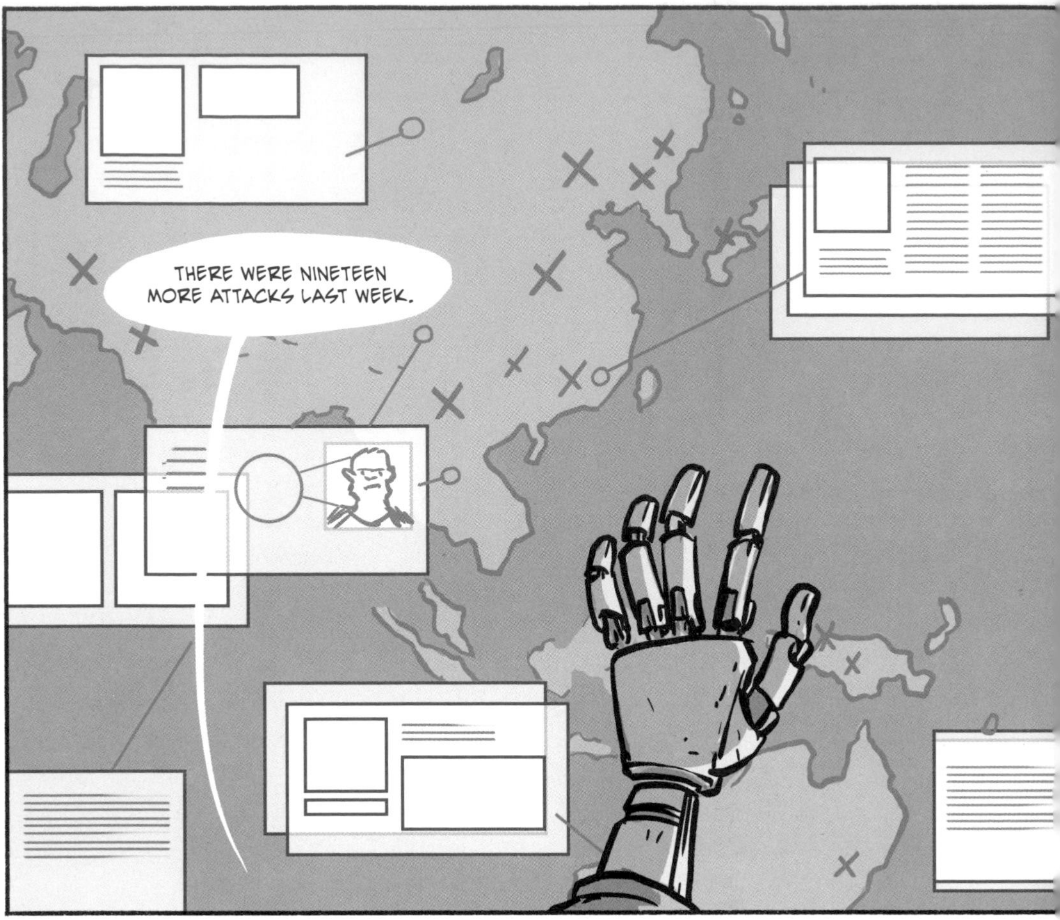
THERE WERE NINETEEN MORE ATTACKS LAST WEEK.

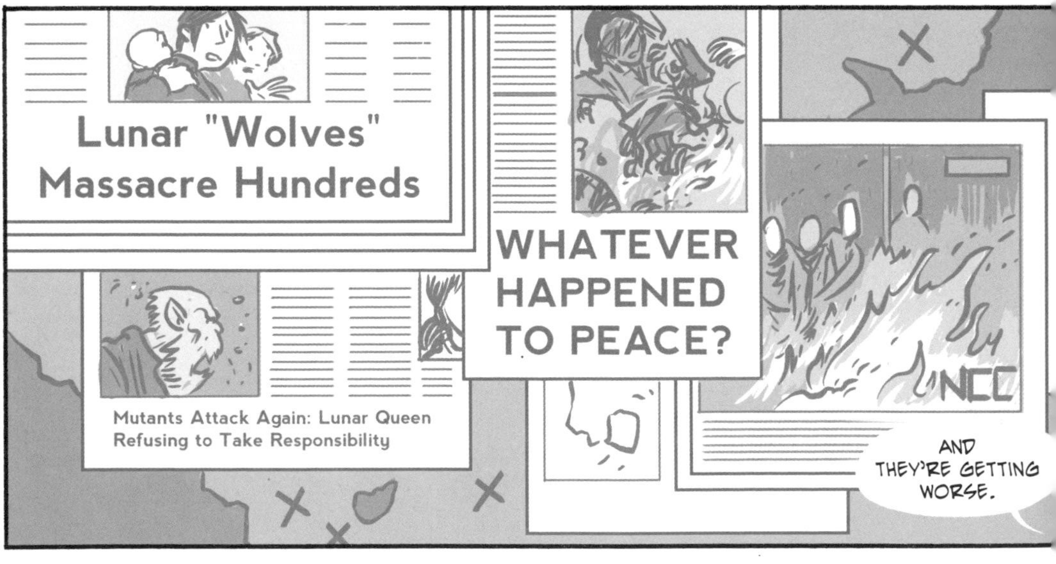
Lunar "Wolves" Massacre Hundreds
WHATEVER HAPPENED TO PEACE?
Mutants Attack Again: Lunar Queen Refusing to Take Responsibility
NCC
AND THEY'RE GETTING WORSE.

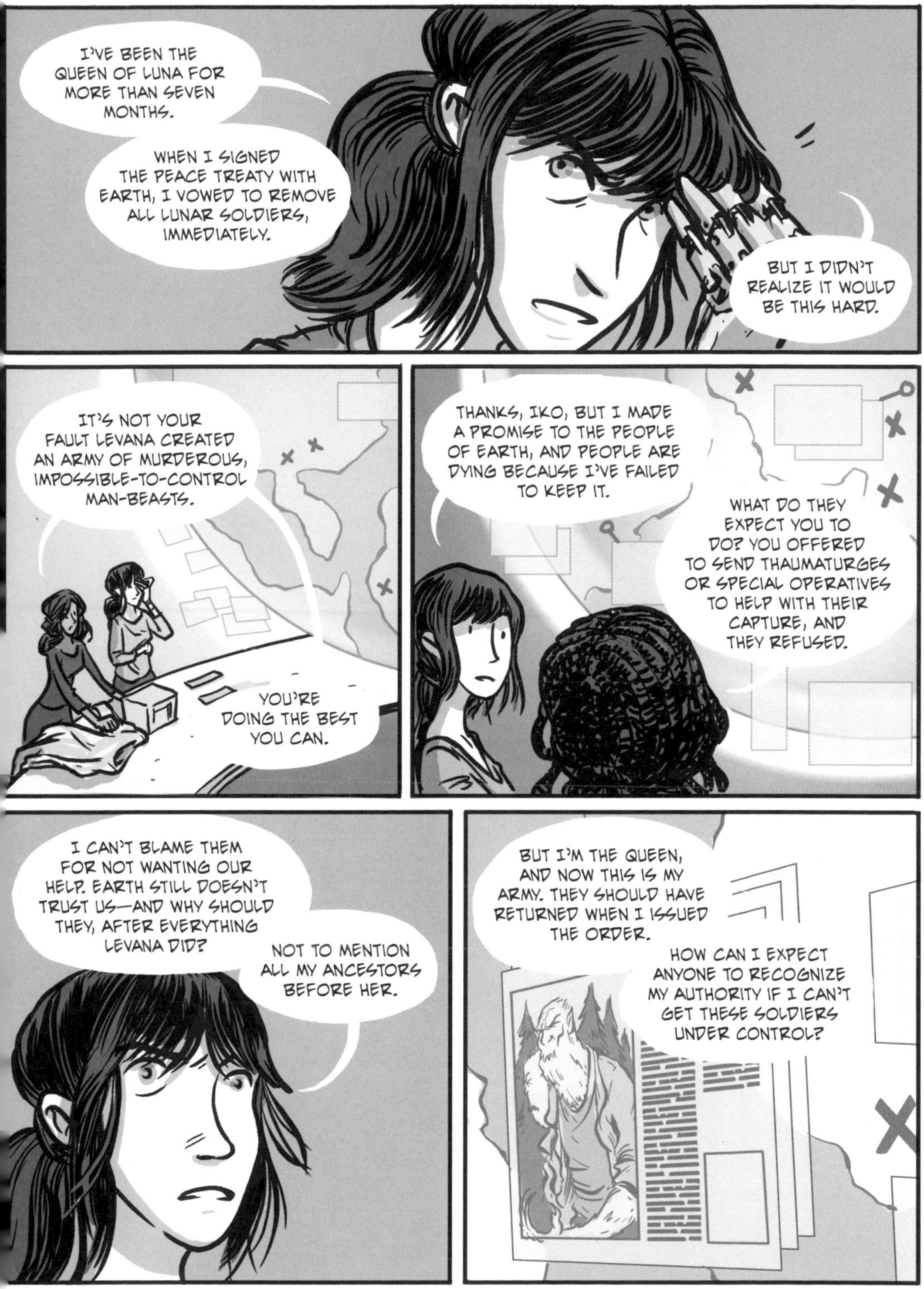
I'VE BEEN THE QUEEN OF LUNA FOR MORE THAN SEVEN MONTHS.
WHEN I SIGNED THE PEACE TREATY WITH EARTH, I VOWED TO REMOVE ALL LUNAR SOLDIERS, IMMEDIATELY.
BUT I DIDN'T REALIZE IT WOULD BE THIS HARD.
IT'S NOT YOUR FAULT LEVANA CREATED AN ARMY OF MURDEROUS, IMPOSSIBLE-TO-CONTROL MAN-BEASTS.
YOU'RE DOING THE BEST YOU CAN.
THANKS, IKO, BUT I MADE A PROMISE TO THE PEOPLE OF EARTH, AND PEOPLE ARE DYING BECAUSE I'VE FAILED TO KEEP IT.
WHAT DO THEY EXPECT YOU TO DO? YOU OFFERED TO SEND THAUMATURGES OR SPECIAL OPERATIVES TO HELP WITH THEIR CAPTURE, AND THEY REFUSED.
I CAN'T BLAME THEM FOR NOT WANTING OUR HELP. EARTH STILL DOESN'T TRUST US—AND WHY SHOULD THEY, AFTER EVERYTHING LEVANA DID?
NOT TO MENTION ALL MY ANCESTORS BEFORE HER.
BUT I'M THE QUEEN, AND NOW THIS IS MY ARMY. THEY SHOULD HAVE RETURNED WHEN I ISSUED THE ORDER.
HOW CAN I EXPECT ANYONE TO RECOGNIZE MY AUTHORITY IF I CAN'T GET THESE SOLDIERS UNDER CONTROL?

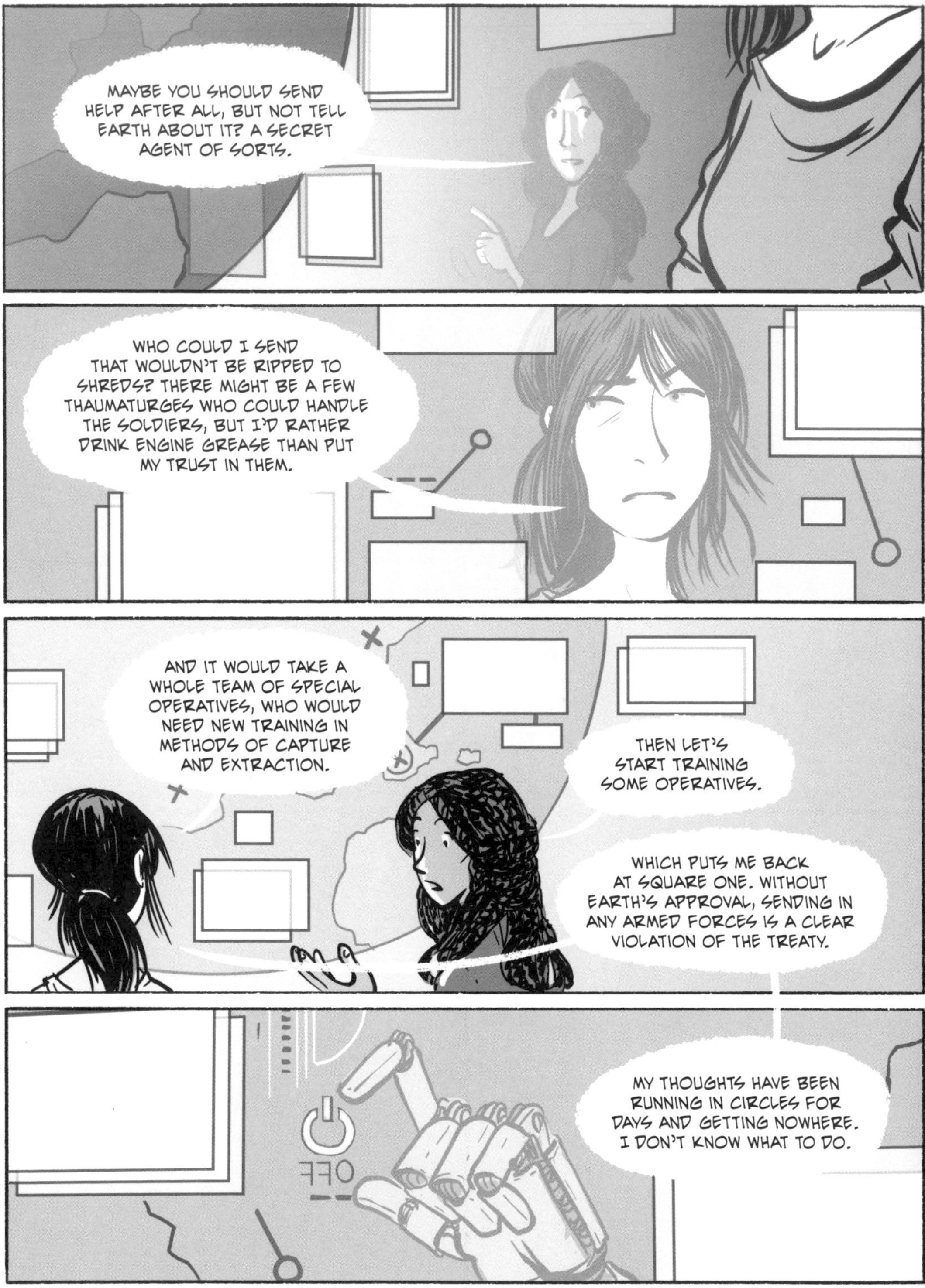
MAYBE YOU SHOULD SEND HELP AFTER ALL, BUT NOT TELL EARTH ABOUT IT? A SECRET AGENT OF SORTS.
WHO COULD I SEND THAT WOULDN'T BE RIPPED TO SHREDS? THERE MIGHT BE A FEW THAUMATURGES WHO COULD HANDLE THE SOLDIERS, BUT I'D RATHER DRINK ENGINE GREASE THAN PUT MY TRUST IN THEM.
AND IT WOULD TAKE A WHOLE TEAM OF SPECIAL OPERATIVES, WHO WOULD NEED NEW TRAINING IN METHODS OF CAPTURE AND EXTRACTION.
THEN LET'S START TRAINING SOME OPERATIVES.
WHICH PUTS ME BACK AT SQUARE ONE. WITHOUT EARTH'S APPROVAL, SENDING IN ANY ARMED FORCES IS A CLEAR VIOLATION OF THE TREATY.
OFF
MY THOUGHTS HAVE BEEN RUNNING IN CIRCLES FOR DAYS AND GETTING NOWHERE. I DON'T KNOW WHAT TO DO.

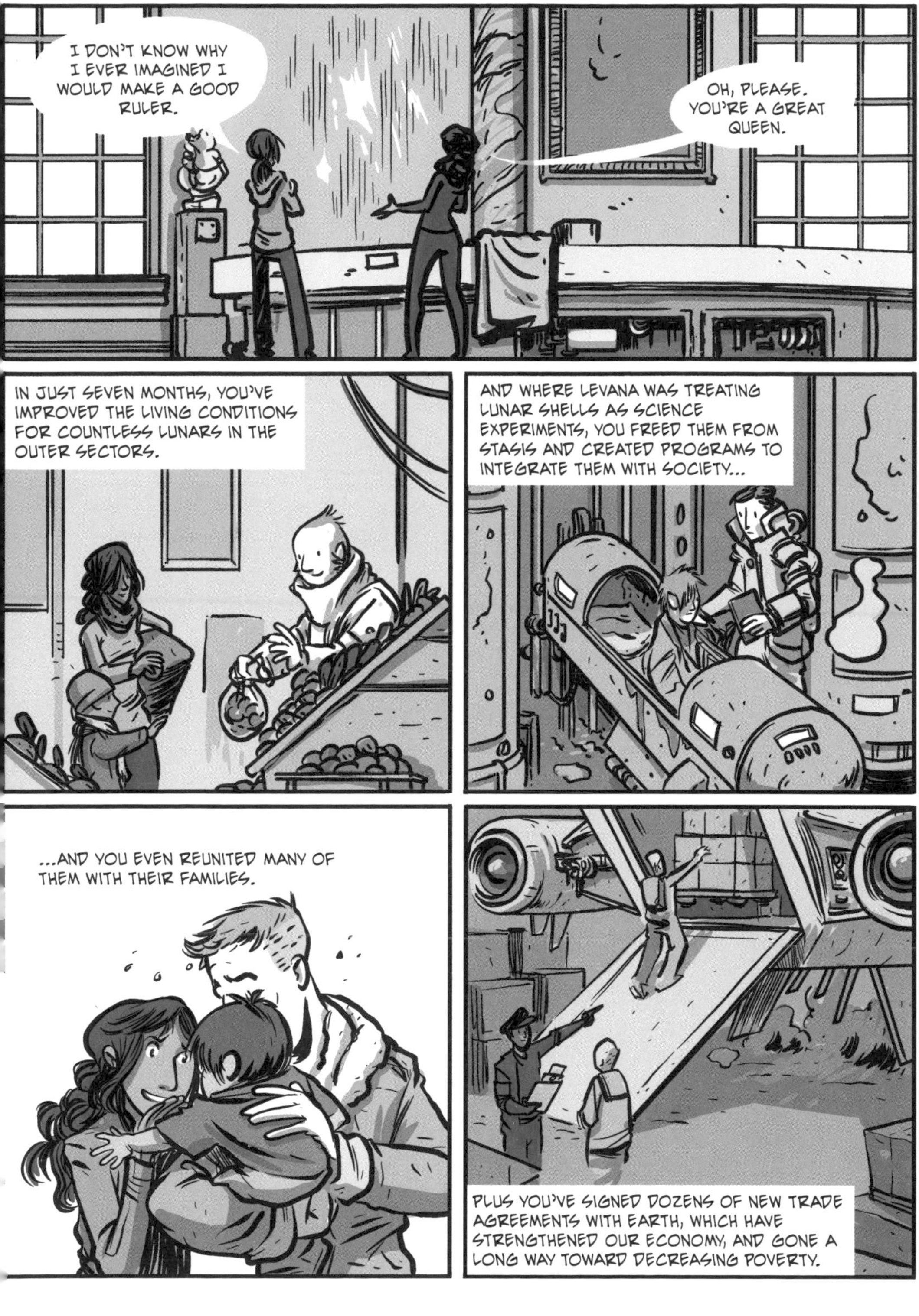
I DON'T KNOW WHY I EVER IMAGINED I WOULD MAKE A GOOD RULER.
OH, PLEASE. YOU'RE A GREAT QUEEN.
IN JUST SEVEN MONTHS, YOU'VE IMPROVED THE LIVING CONDITIONS FOR COUNTLESS LUNARS IN THE OUTER SECTORS.
AND WHERE LEVANA WAS TREATING LUNAR SHELLS AS SCIENCE EXPERIMENTS, YOU FREED THEM FROM STASIS AND CREATED PROGRAMS TO INTEGRATE THEM WITH SOCIETY...
...AND YOU EVEN REUNITED MANY OF THEM WITH THEIR FAMILIES.
PLUS YOU'VE SIGNED DOZENS OF NEW TRADE AGREEMENTS WITH EARTH, WHICH HAVE STRENGTHENED OUR ECONOMY, AND GONE A LONG WAY TOWARD DECREASING POVERTY.

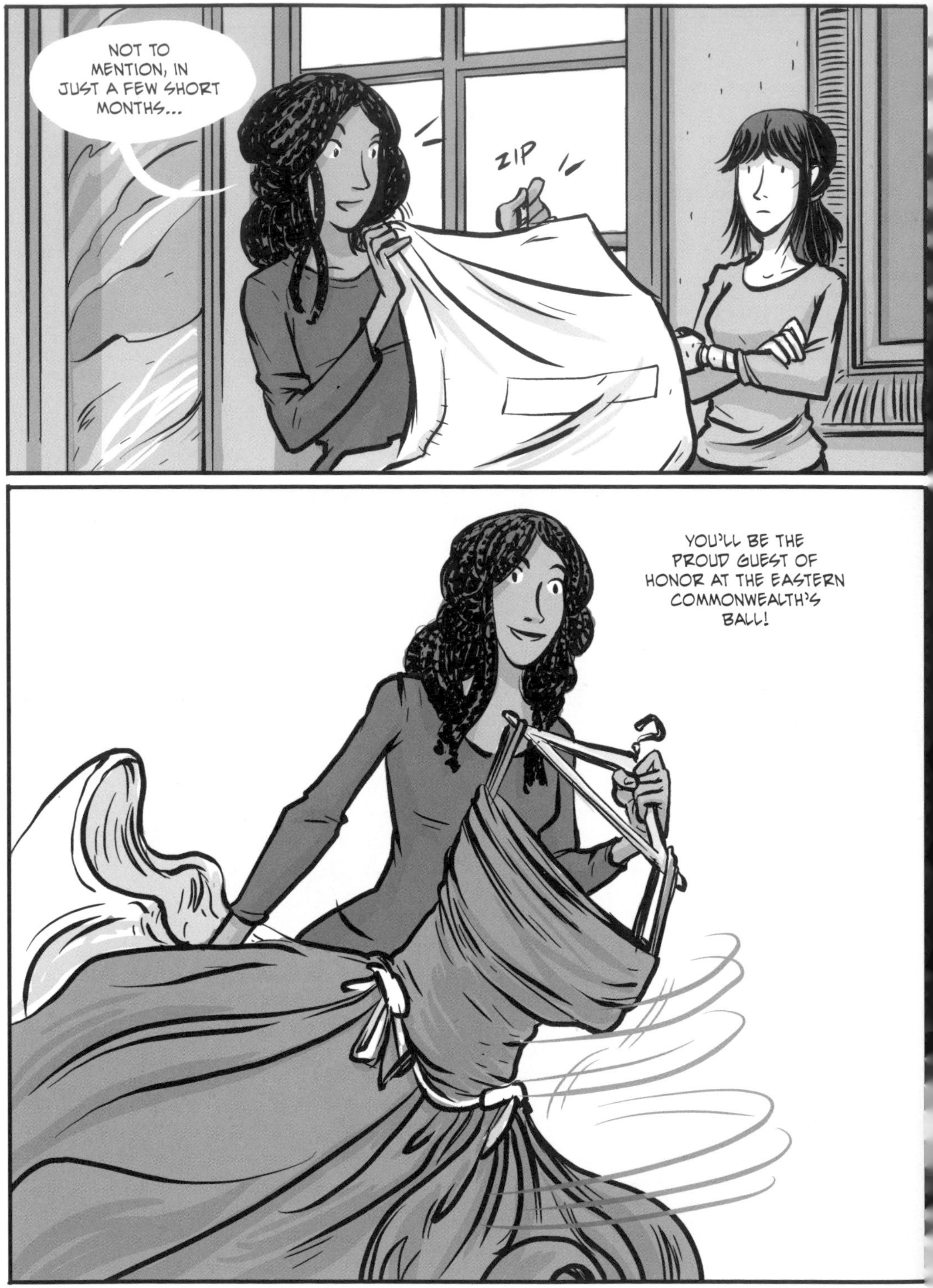
NOT TO MENTION, IN JUST A FEW SHORT MONTHS...
ZIP
YOU'LL BE THE PROUD GUEST OF HONOR AT THE EASTERN COMMONWEALTH'S BALL!

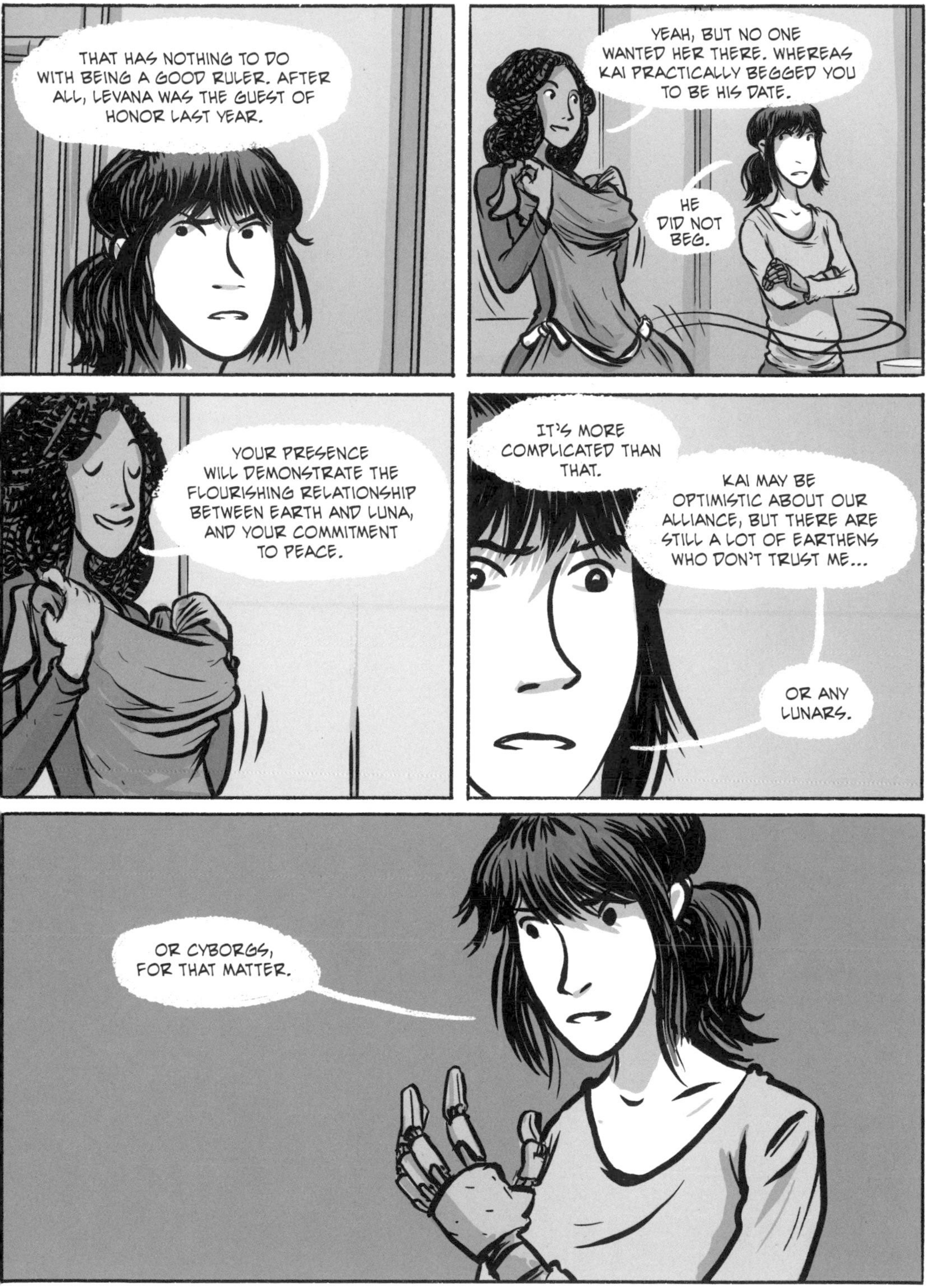
THAT HAS NOTHING TO DO WITH BEING A GOOD RULER. AFTER ALL, LEVANA WAS THE GUEST OF HONOR LAST YEAR.
YEAH, BUT NO ONE WANTED HER THERE. WHEREAS KAI PRACTICALLY BEGGED YOU TO BE HIS DATE.
HE DID NOT BEG.
YOUR PRESENCE WILL DEMONSTRATE THE FLOURISHING RELATIONSHIP BETWEEN EARTH AND LUNA, AND YOUR COMMITMENT TO PEACE.
IT'S MORE COMPLICATED THAN THAT.
KAI MAY BE OPTIMISTIC ABOUT OUR ALLIANCE, BUT THERE ARE STILL A LOT OF EARTHENS WHO DON'T TRUST ME...
OR ANY LUNARS.
OR CYBORGS, FOR THAT MATTER.

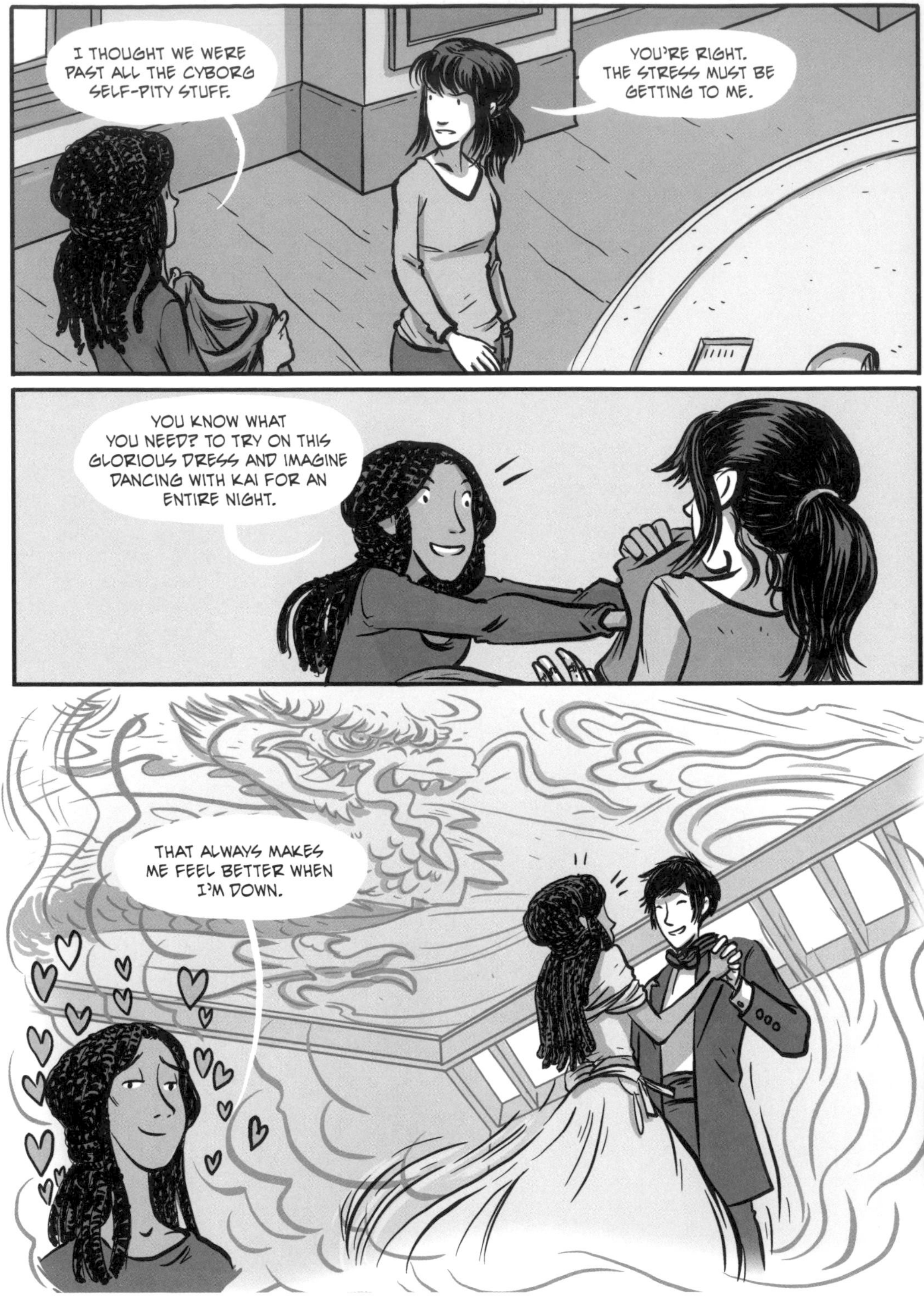
I THOUGHT WE WERE PAST ALL THE CYBORG SELF-PITY STUFF.
YOU'RE RIGHT. THE STRESS MUST BE GETTING TO ME.
YOU KNOW WHAT YOU NEED? TO TRY ON THIS GLORIOUS DRESS AND IMAGINE DANCING WITH KAI FOR AN ENTIRE NIGHT.
THAT ALWAYS MAKES ME FEEL BETTER WHEN I'M DOWN.

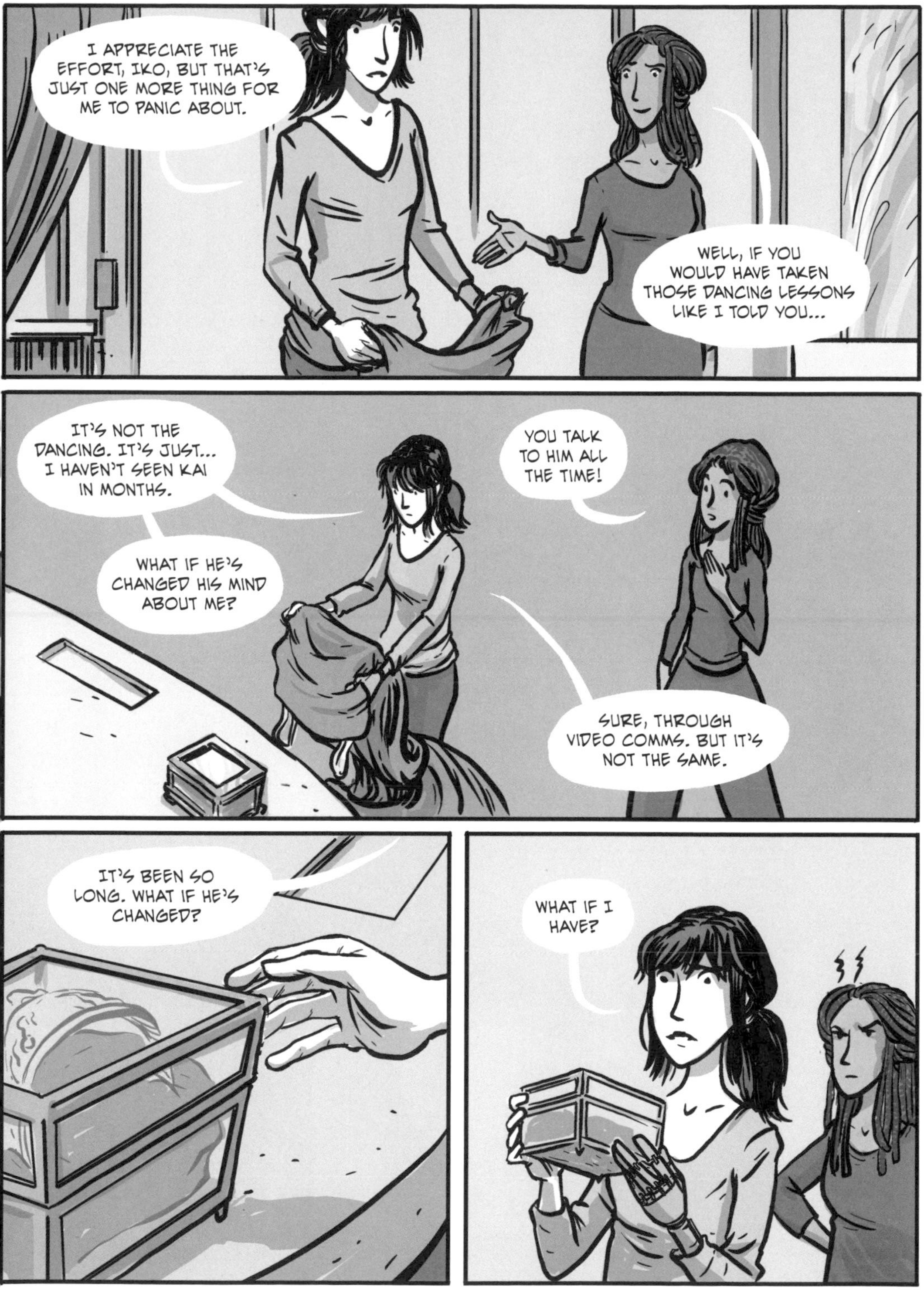
I APPRECIATE THE EFFORT, IKO, BUT THAT'S JUST ONE MORE THING FOR ME TO PANIC ABOUT.
WELL, IF YOU WOULD HAVE TAKEN THOSE DANCING LESSONS LIKE I TOLD YOU...
IT'S NOT THE DANCING. IT'S JUST... I HAVEN'T SEEN KAI IN MONTHS.
WHAT IF HE'S CHANGED HIS MIND ABOUT ME?
YOU TALK TO HIM ALL THE TIME!
SURE, THROUGH VIDEO COMMS. BUT IT'S NOT THE SAME.
IT'S BEEN SO LONG. WHAT IF HE'S CHANGED?
WHAT IF I HAVE?

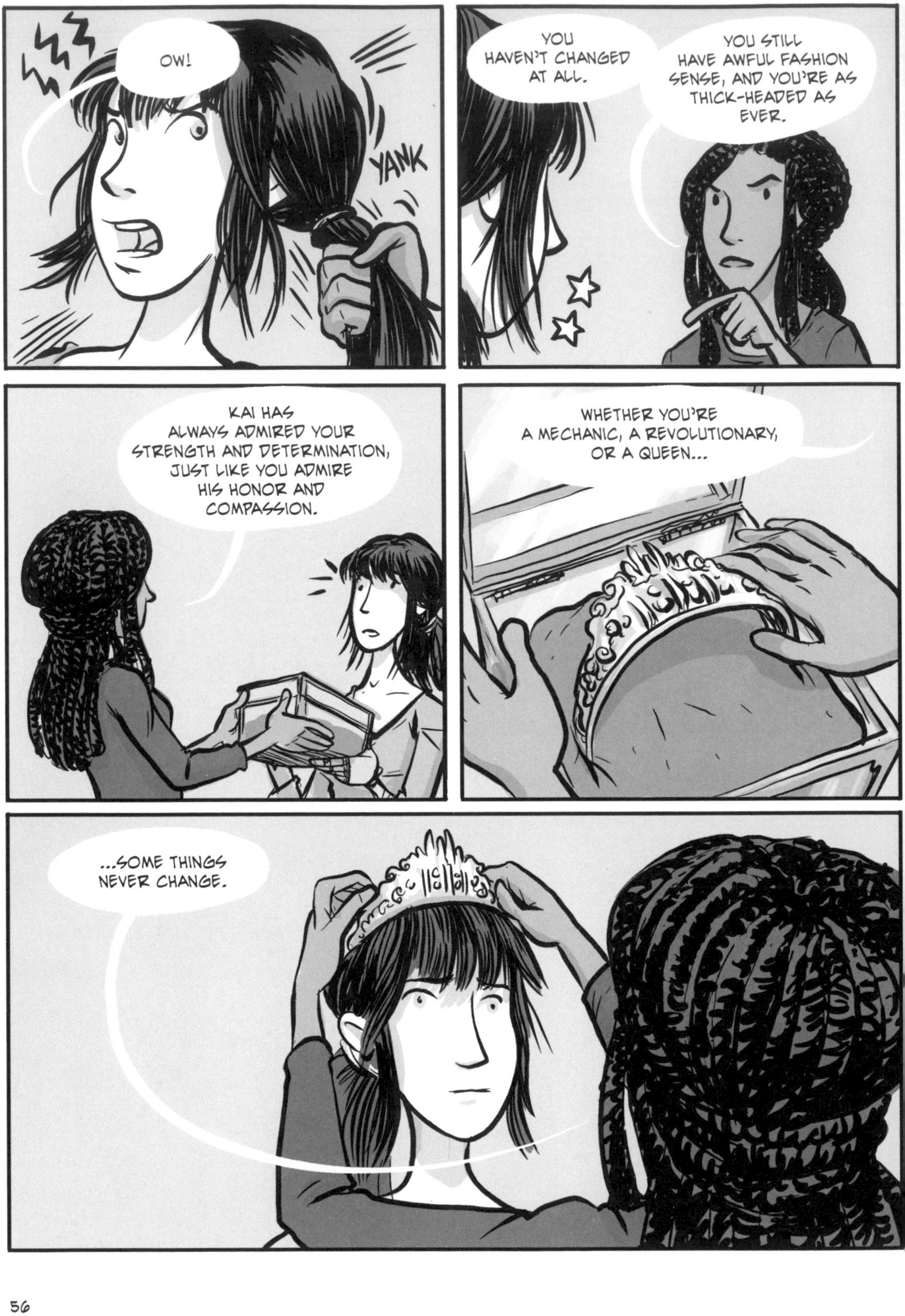
OW!
YANK
YOU HAVEN'T CHANGED AT ALL.
YOU STILL HAVE AWFUL FASHION SENSE, AND YOU'RE AS THICK-HEADED AS EVER.
KAI HAS ALWAYS ADMIRED YOUR STRENGTH AND DETERMINATION, JUST LIKE YOU ADMIRE HIS HONOR AND COMPASSION.
WHETHER YOU'RE A MECHANIC, A REVOLUTIONARY, OR A QUEEN...
...SOME THINGS NEVER CHANGE.

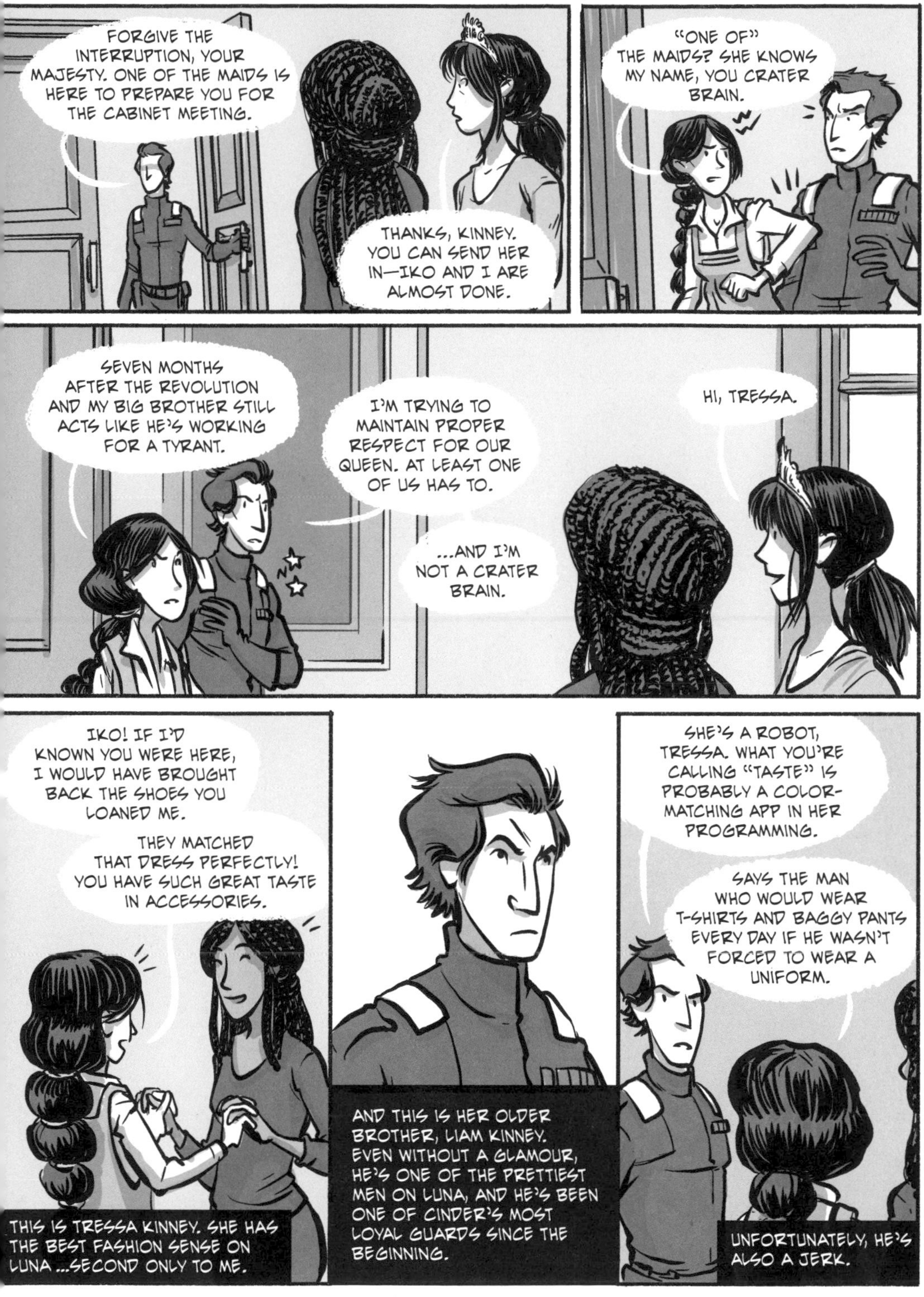
FORGIVE THE INTERRUPTION, YOUR MAJESTY. ONE OF THE MAIDS IS HERE TO PREPARE YOU FOR THE CABINET MEETING.
THANKS, KINNEY. YOU CAN SEND HER IN—IKO AND I ARE ALMOST DONE.
"ONE OF" THE MAIDS? SHE KNOWS MY NAME, YOU CRATER BRAIN.
SEVEN MONTHS AFTER THE REVOLUTION AND MY BIG BROTHER STILL ACTS LIKE HE'S WORKING FOR A TYRANT.
I'M TRYING TO MAINTAIN PROPER RESPECT FOR OUR QUEEN. AT LEAST ONE OF US HAS TO.
...AND I'M NOT A CRATER BRAIN.
HI, TRESSA.
IKO! IF I'D KNOWN YOU WERE HERE, I WOULD HAVE BROUGHT BACK THE SHOES YOU LOANED ME.
THEY MATCHED THAT DRESS PERFECTLY! YOU HAVE SUCH GREAT TASTE IN ACCESSORIES.
THIS IS TRESSA KINNEY. SHE HAS THE BEST FASHION SENSE ON LUNA ...SECOND ONLY TO ME.
AND THIS IS HER OLDER BROTHER, LIAM KINNEY. EVEN WITHOUT A GLAMOUR, HE'S ONE OF THE PRETTIEST MEN ON LUNA, AND HE'S BEEN ONE OF CINDER'S MOST LOYAL GUARDS SINCE THE BEGINNING.
SHE'S A ROBOT, TRESSA. WHAT YOU'RE CALLING "TASTE" IS PROBABLY A COLOR-MATCHING APP IN HER PROGRAMMING.
SAYS THE MAN WHO WOULD WEAR T-SHIRTS AND BAGGY PANTS EVERY DAY IF HE WASN'T FORCED TO WEAR A UNIFORM.
UNFORTUNATELY, HE'S ALSO A JERK.

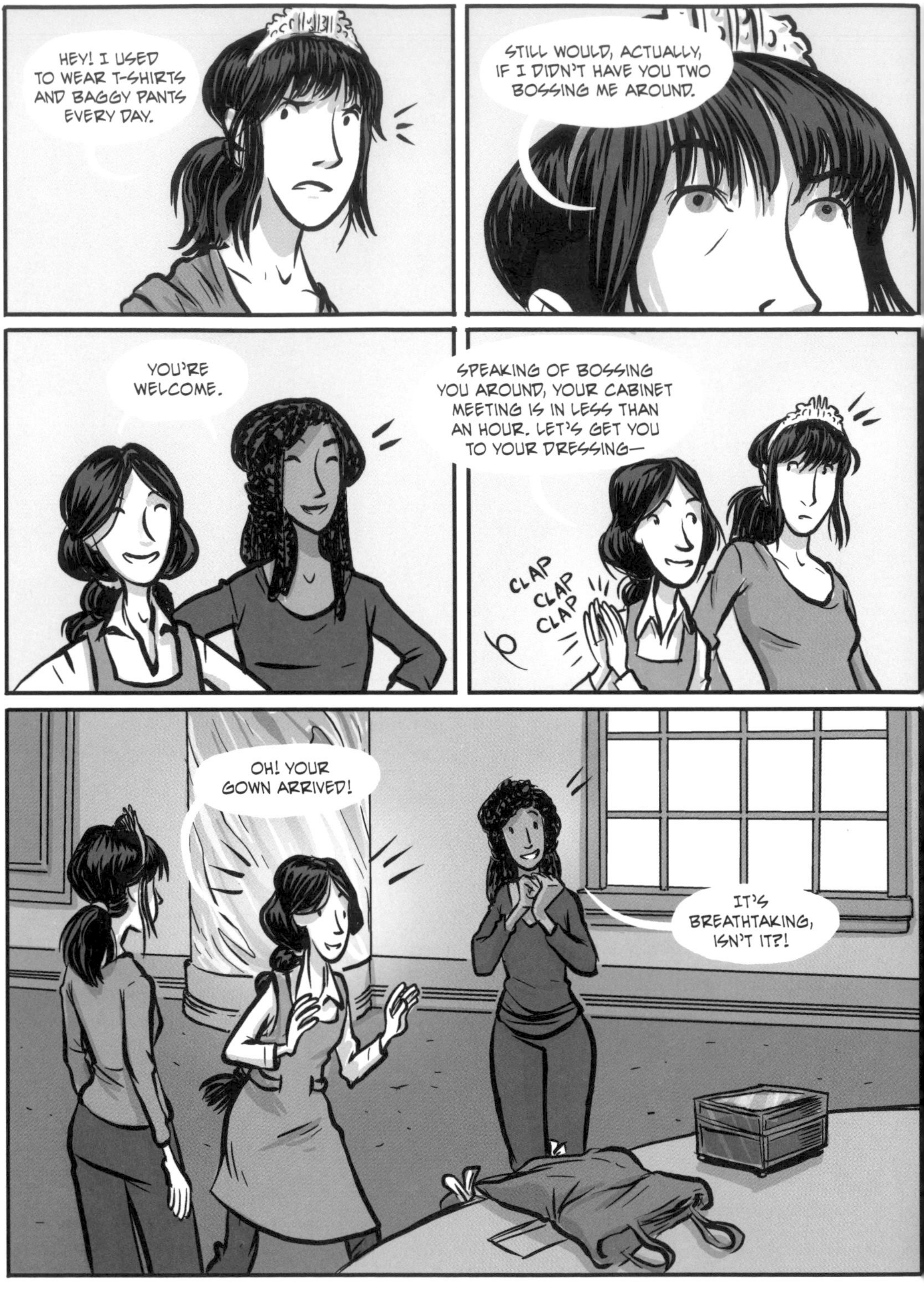
HEY! I USED TO WEAR T-SHIRTS AND BAGGY PANTS EVERY DAY.
STILL WOULD, ACTUALLY, IF I DIDN'T HAVE YOU TWO BOSSING ME AROUND.
YOU'RE WELCOME.
SPEAKING OF BOSSING YOU AROUND, YOUR CABINET MEETING IS IN LESS THAN AN HOUR. LET'S GET YOU TO YOUR DRESSING—
CLAP CLAP CLAP
OH! YOUR GOWN ARRIVED!
IT'S BREATHTAKING, ISN'T IT?!

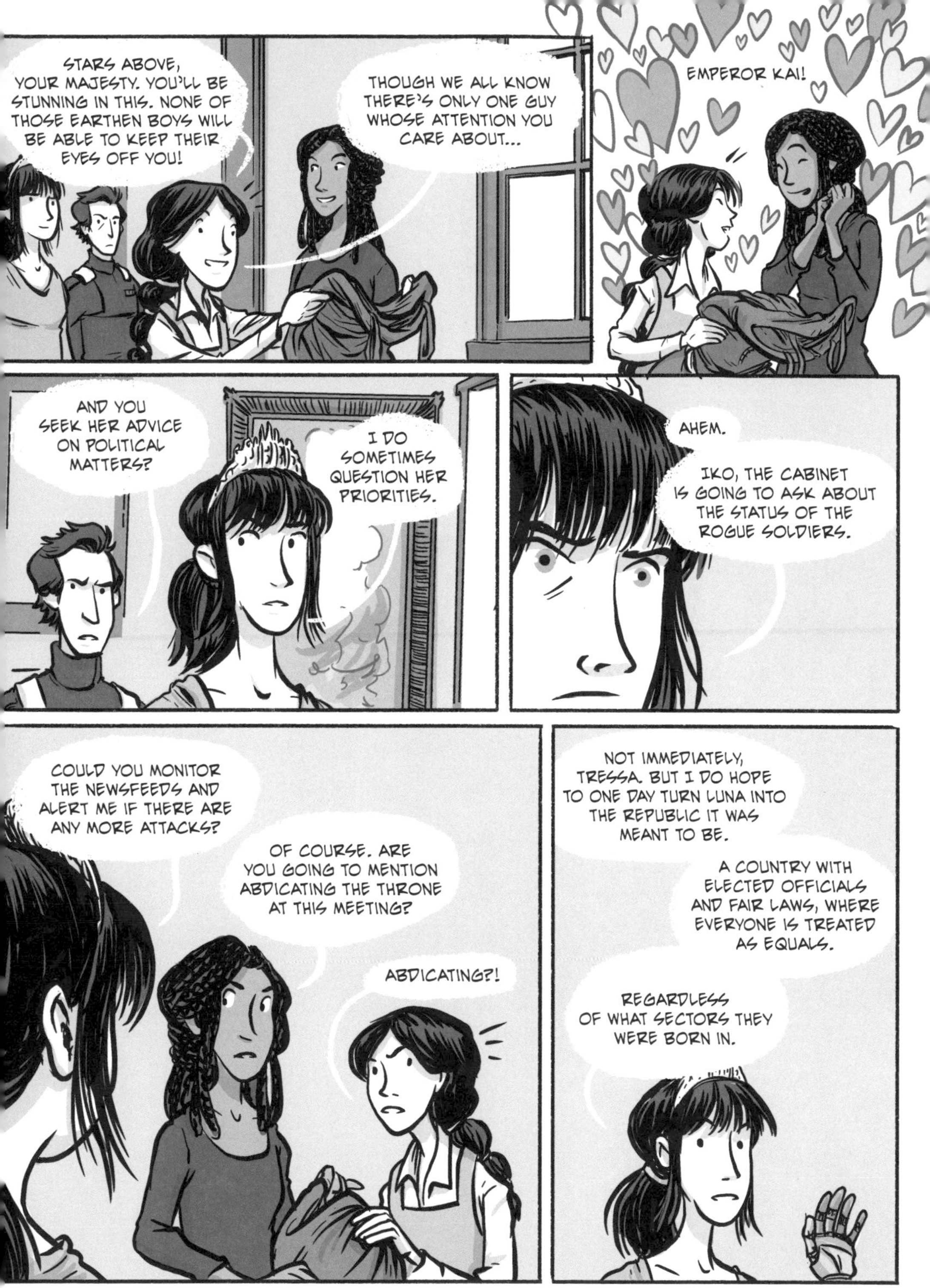
STARS ABOVE, YOUR MAJESTY. YOU'LL BE STUNNING IN THIS. NONE OF THOSE EARTHEN BOYS WILL BE ABLE TO KEEP THEIR EYES OFF YOU!
THOUGH WE ALL KNOW THERE'S ONLY ONE GUY WHOSE ATTENTION YOU CARE ABOUT...
EMPEROR KAI!
AND YOU SEEK HER ADVICE ON POLITICAL MATTERS?
I DO SOMETIMES QUESTION HER PRIORITIES.
AHEM.
IKO, THE CABINET IS GOING TO ASK ABOUT THE STATUS OF THE ROGUE SOLDIERS.
COULD YOU MONITOR THE NEWSFEEDS AND ALERT ME IF THERE ARE ANY MORE ATTACKS?
OF COURSE. ARE YOU GOING TO MENTION ABDICATING THE THRONE AT THIS MEETING?
ABDICATING?!
NOT IMMEDIATELY, TRESSA. BUT I DO HOPE TO ONE DAY TURN LUNA INTO THE REPUBLIC IT WAS MEANT TO BE.
A COUNTRY WITH ELECTED OFFICIALS AND FAIR LAWS, WHERE EVERYONE IS TREATED AS EQUALS.
REGARDLESS OF WHAT SECTORS THEY WERE BORN IN.

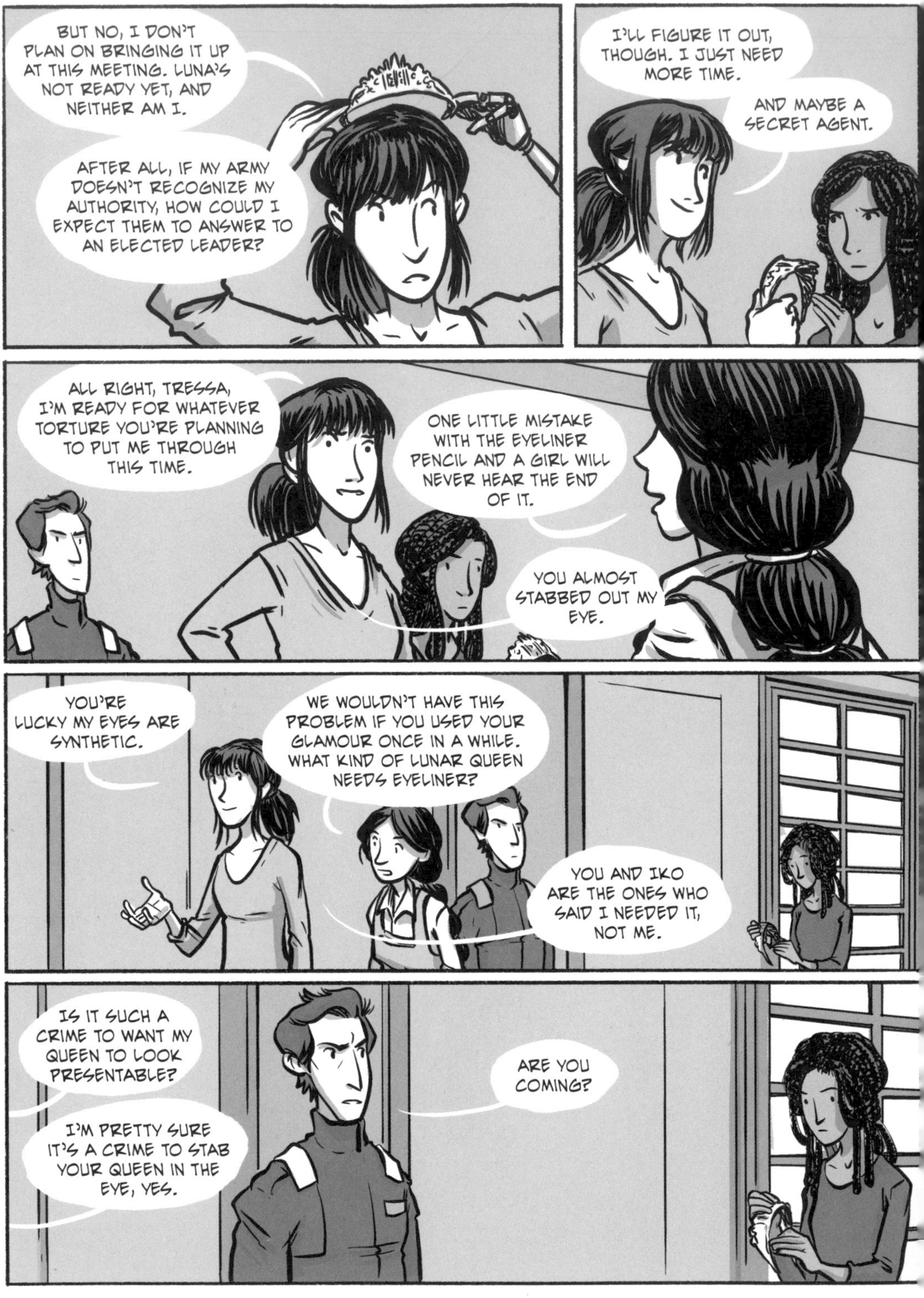
BUT NO, I DON'T PLAN ON BRINGING IT UP AT THIS MEETING. LUNA'S NOT READY YET, AND NEITHER AM I.
AFTER ALL, IF MY ARMY DOESN'T RECOGNIZE MY AUTHORITY, HOW COULD I EXPECT THEM TO ANSWER TO AN ELECTED LEADER?
I'LL FIGURE IT OUT, THOUGH. I JUST NEED MORE TIME.
AND MAYBE A SECRET AGENT.
ALL RIGHT, TRESSA, I'M READY FOR WHATEVER TORTURE YOU'RE PLANNING TO PUT ME THROUGH THIS TIME.
ONE LITTLE MISTAKE WITH THE EYELINER PENCIL AND A GIRL WILL NEVER HEAR THE END OF IT.
YOU ALMOST STABBED OUT MY EYE.
YOU'RE LUCKY MY EYES ARE SYNTHETIC.
WE WOULDN'T HAVE THIS PROBLEM IF YOU USED YOUR GLAMOUR ONCE IN A WHILE. WHAT KIND OF LUNAR QUEEN NEEDS EYELINER?
YOU AND IKO ARE THE ONES WHO SAID I NEEDED IT, NOT ME.
IS IT SUCH A CRIME TO WANT MY QUEEN TO LOOK PRESENTABLE?
I'M PRETTY SURE IT'S A CRIME TO STAB YOUR QUEEN IN THE EYE, YES.
ARE YOU COMING?

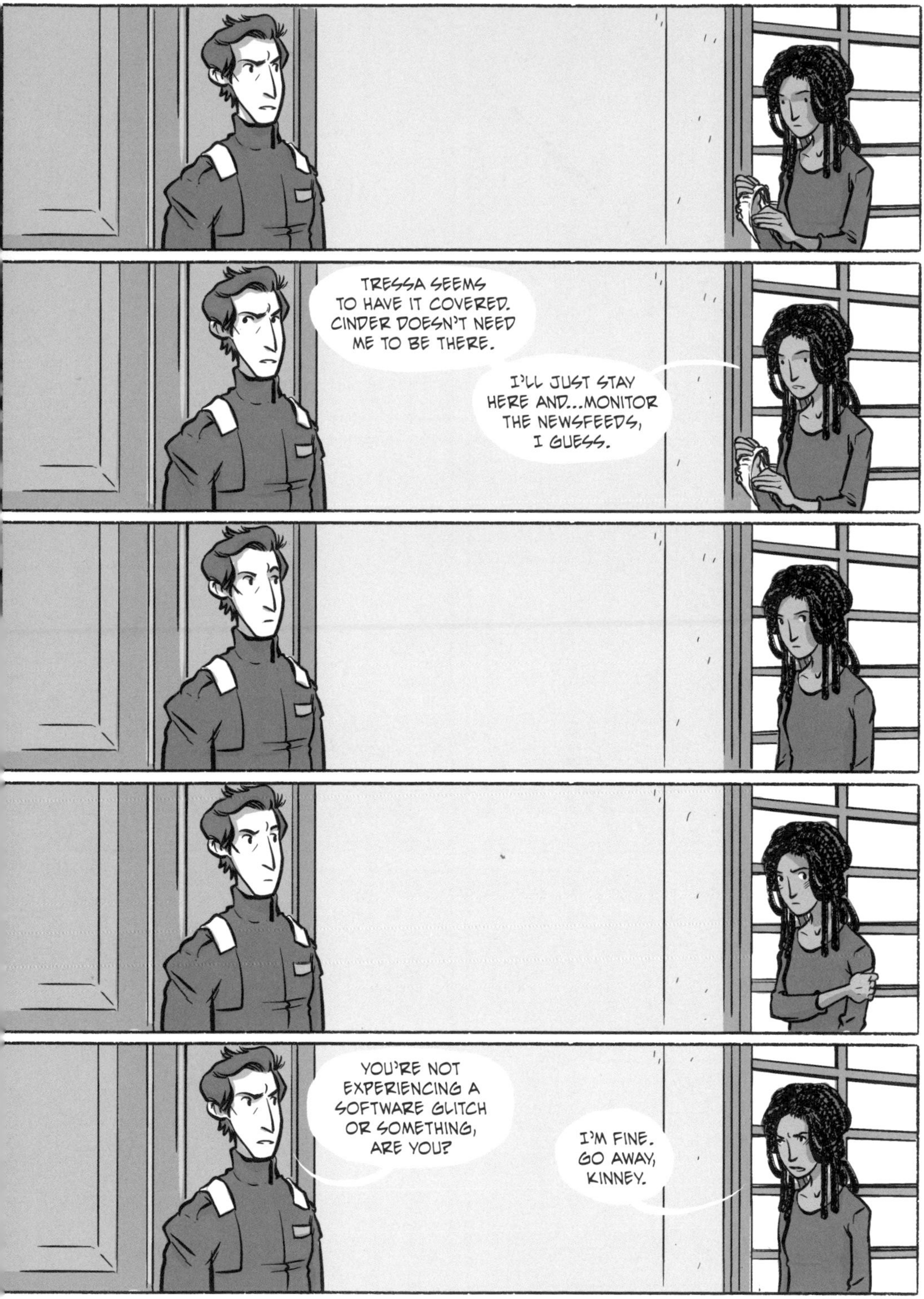
TRESSA SEEMS TO HAVE IT COVERED. CINDER DOESN'T NEED ME TO BE THERE.
I'LL JUST STAY HERE AND...MONITOR THE NEWSFEEDS, I GUESS.
YOU'RE NOT EXPERIENCING A SOFTWARE GLITCH OR SOMETHING, ARE YOU?
I'M FINE. GO AWAY, KINNEY.

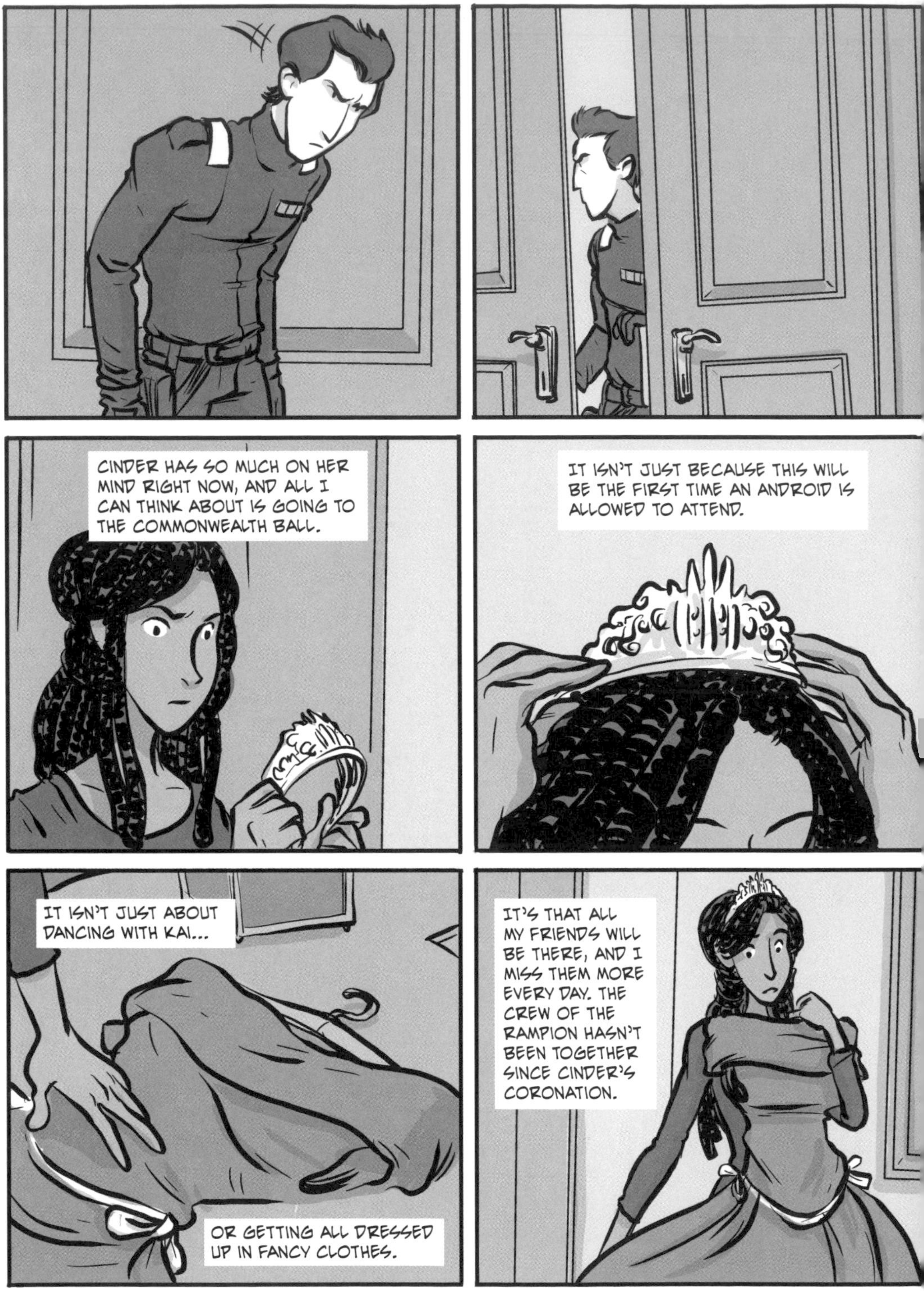
CINDER HAS SO MUCH ON HER MIND RIGHT NOW, AND ALL I CAN THINK ABOUT IS GOING TO THE COMMONWEALTH BALL.
IT ISN'T JUST BECAUSE THIS WILL BE THE FIRST TIME AN ANDROID IS ALLOWED TO ATTEND.
IT ISN'T JUST ABOUT DANCING WITH KAI...
OR GETTING ALL DRESSED UP IN FANCY CLOTHES.
IT'S THAT ALL MY FRIENDS WILL BE THERE, AND I MISS THEM MORE EVERY DAY. THE CREW OF THE RAMPION HASN'T BEEN TOGETHER SINCE CINDER'S CORONATION.

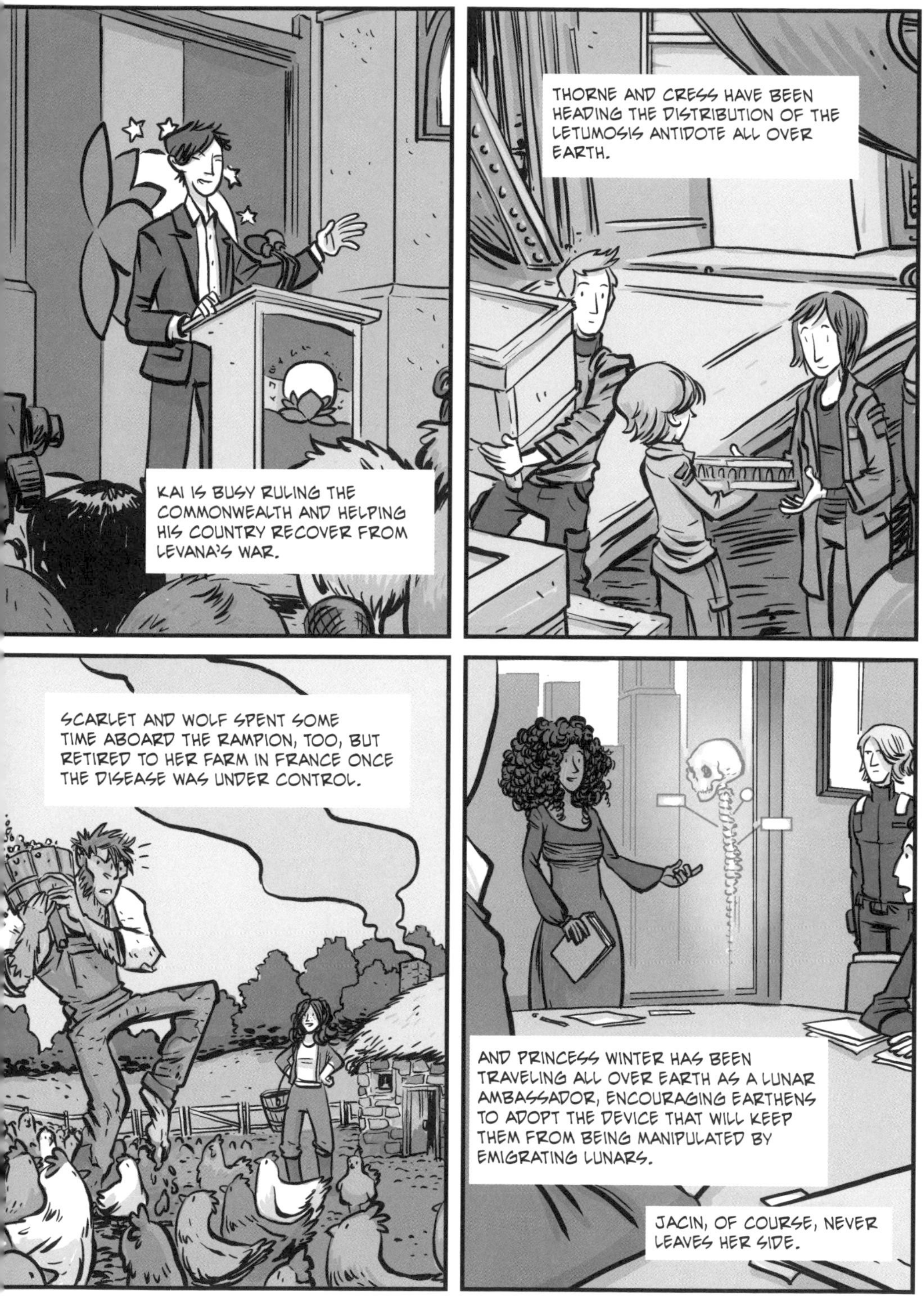
KAI IS BUSY RULING THE COMMONWEALTH AND HELPING HIS COUNTRY RECOVER FROM LEVANA'S WAR.
THORNE AND CRESS HAVE BEEN HEADING THE DISTRIBUTION OF THE LETUMOSIS ANTIDOTE ALL OVER EARTH.
SCARLET AND WOLF SPENT SOME TIME ABOARD THE RAMPION, TOO, BUT RETIRED TO HER FARM IN FRANCE ONCE THE DISEASE WAS UNDER CONTROL.
AND PRINCESS WINTER HAS BEEN TRAVELING ALL OVER EARTH AS A LUNAR AMBASSADOR, ENCOURAGING EARTHENS TO ADOPT THE DEVICE THAT WILL KEEP THEM FROM BEING MANIPULATED BY EMIGRATING LUNARS.
JACIN, OF COURSE, NEVER LEAVES HER SIDE.

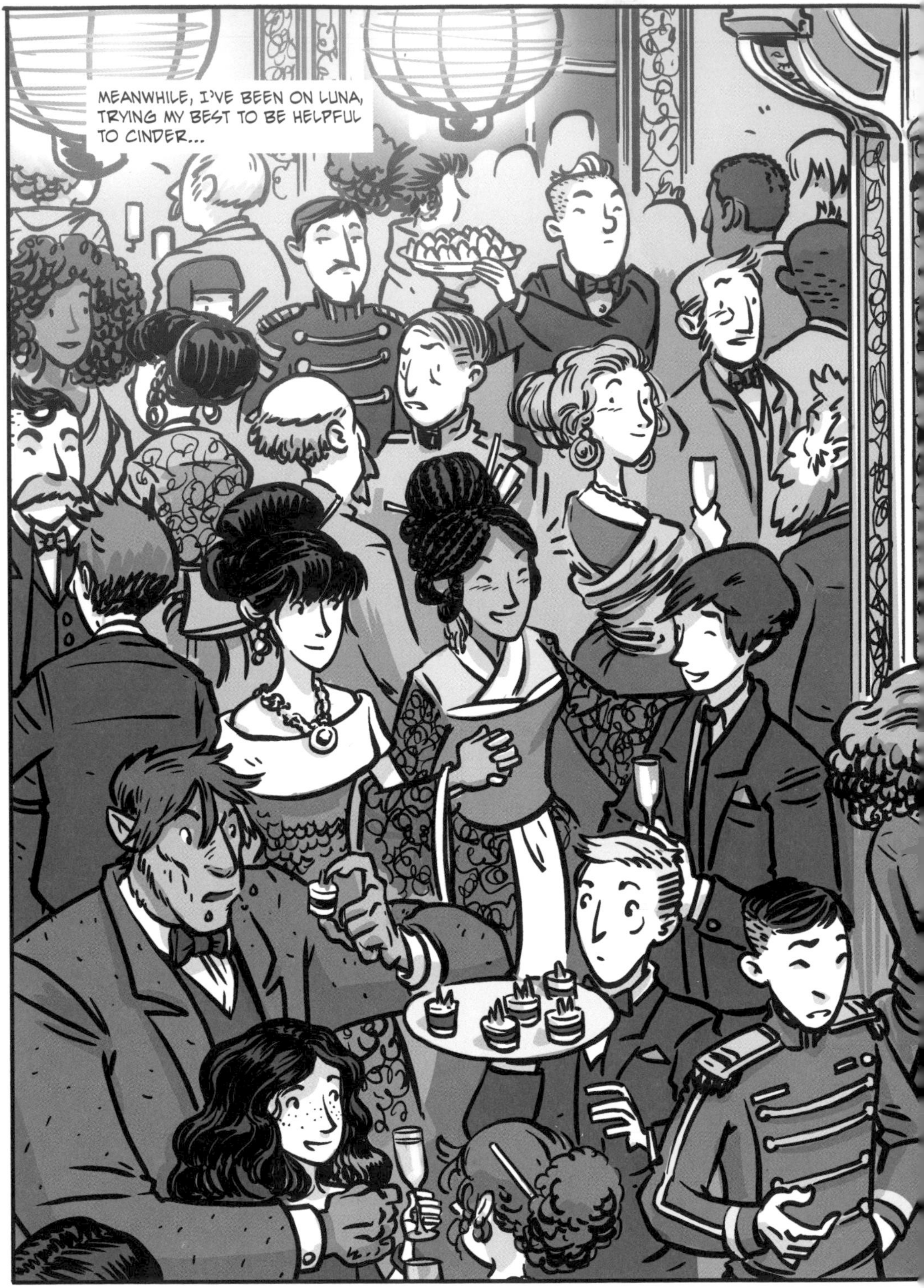
MEANWHILE, I'VE BEEN ON LUNA, TRYING MY BEST TO BE HELPFUL TO CINDER...

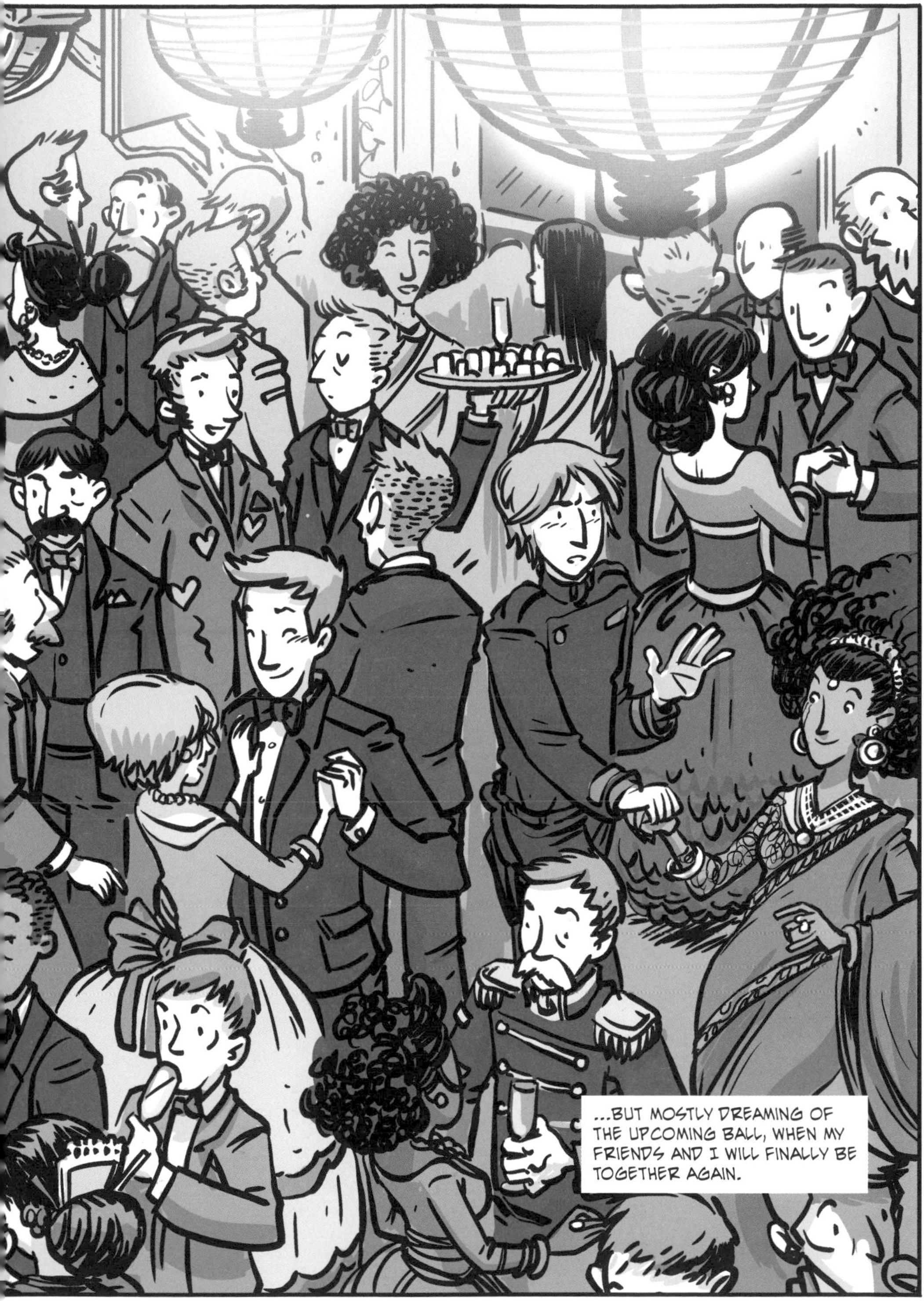
...BUT MOSTLY DREAMING OF THE UPCOMING BALL, WHEN MY FRIENDS AND I WILL FINALLY BE TOGETHER AGAIN.

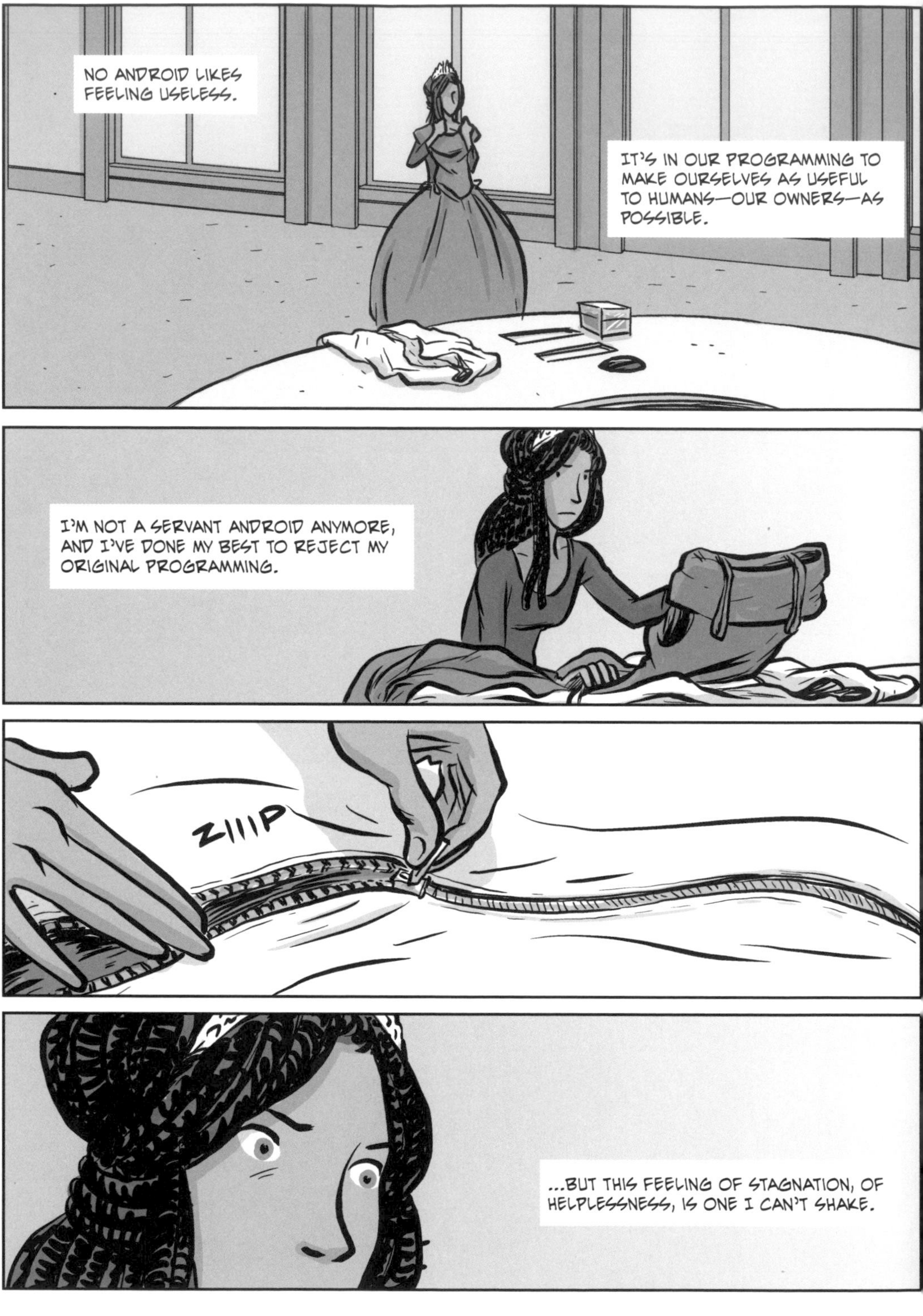
NO ANDROID LIKES FEELING USELESS.
IT'S IN OUR PROGRAMMING TO MAKE OURSELVES AS USEFUL TO HUMANS—OUR OWNERS—AS POSSIBLE.
I'M NOT A SERVANT ANDROID ANYMORE, AND I'VE DONE MY BEST TO REJECT MY ORIGINAL PROGRAMMING.
ZIIIP
...BUT THIS FEELING OF STAGNATION, OF HELPLESSNESS, IS ONE I CAN'T SHAKE.

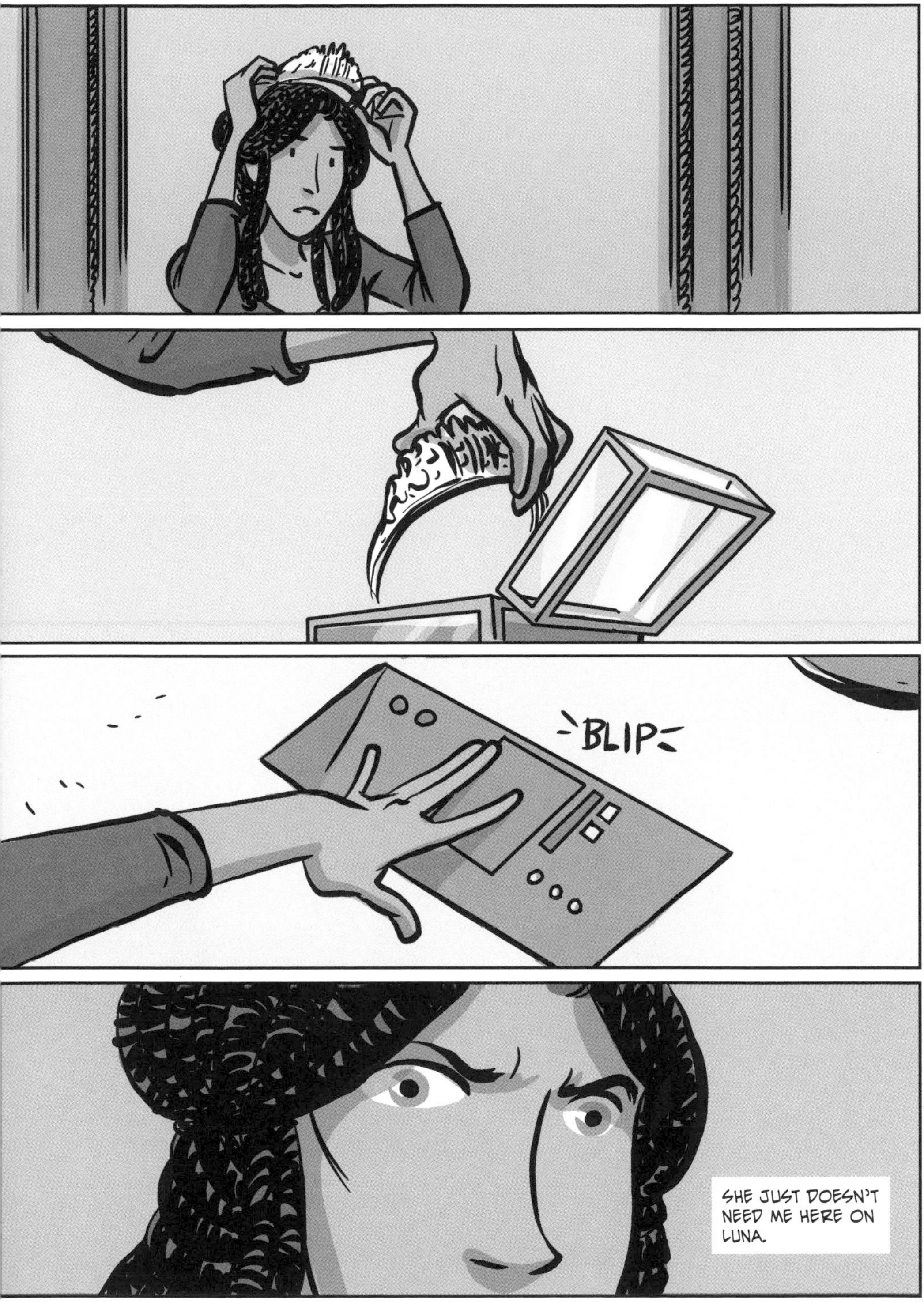
BLIP
SHE JUST DOESN'T NEED ME HERE ON LUNA.

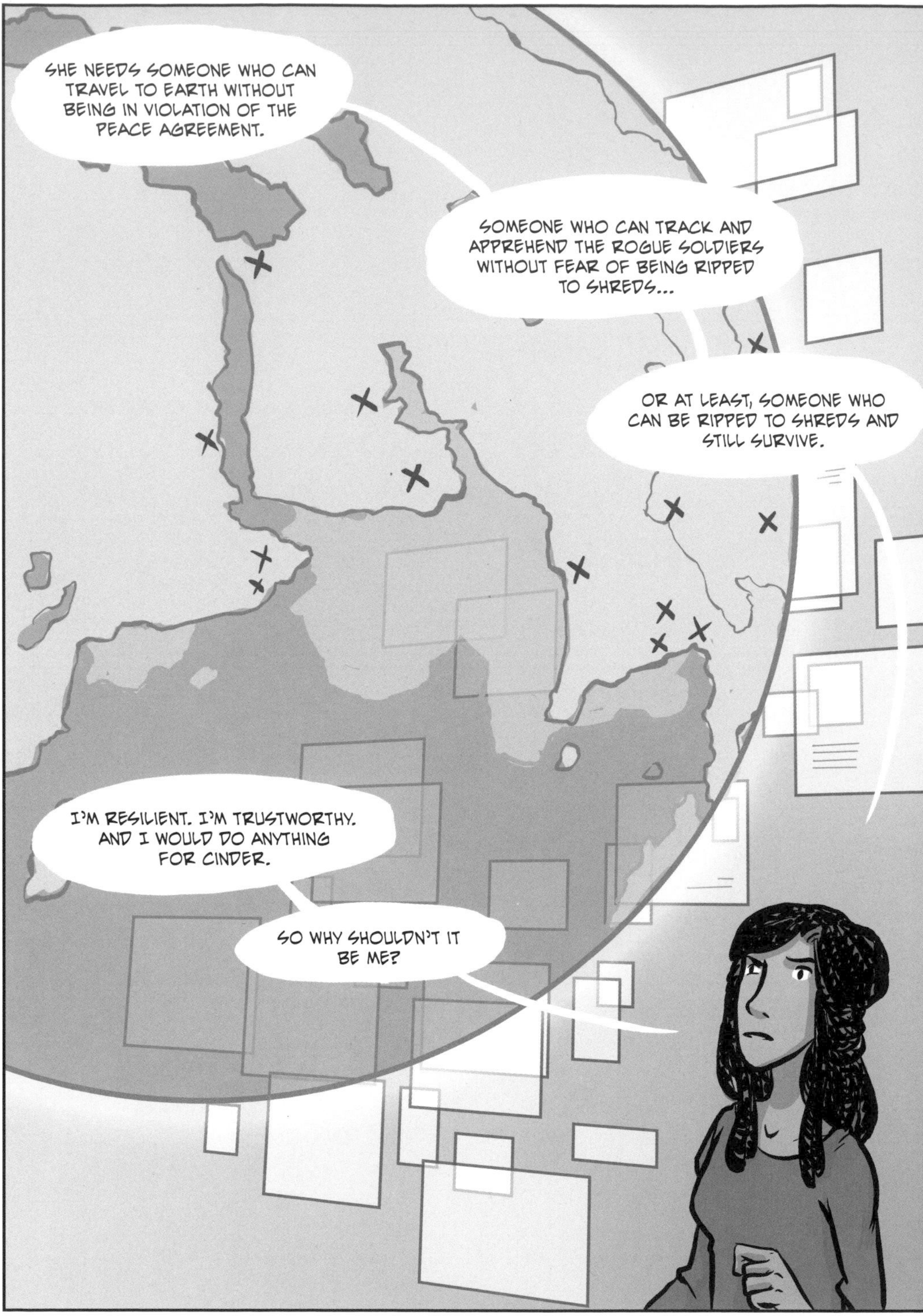
SHE NEEDS SOMEONE WHO CAN TRAVEL TO EARTH WITHOUT BEING IN VIOLATION OF THE PEACE AGREEMENT.
SOMEONE WHO CAN TRACK AND APPREHEND THE ROGUE SOLDIERS WITHOUT FEAR OF BEING RIPPED TO SHREDS...
OR AT LEAST, SOMEONE WHO CAN BE RIPPED TO SHREDS AND STILL SURVIVE.
I'M RESILIENT. I'M TRUSTWORTHY. AND I WOULD DO ANYTHING FOR CINDER.
SO WHY SHOULDN'T IT BE ME?

CHAPTER III

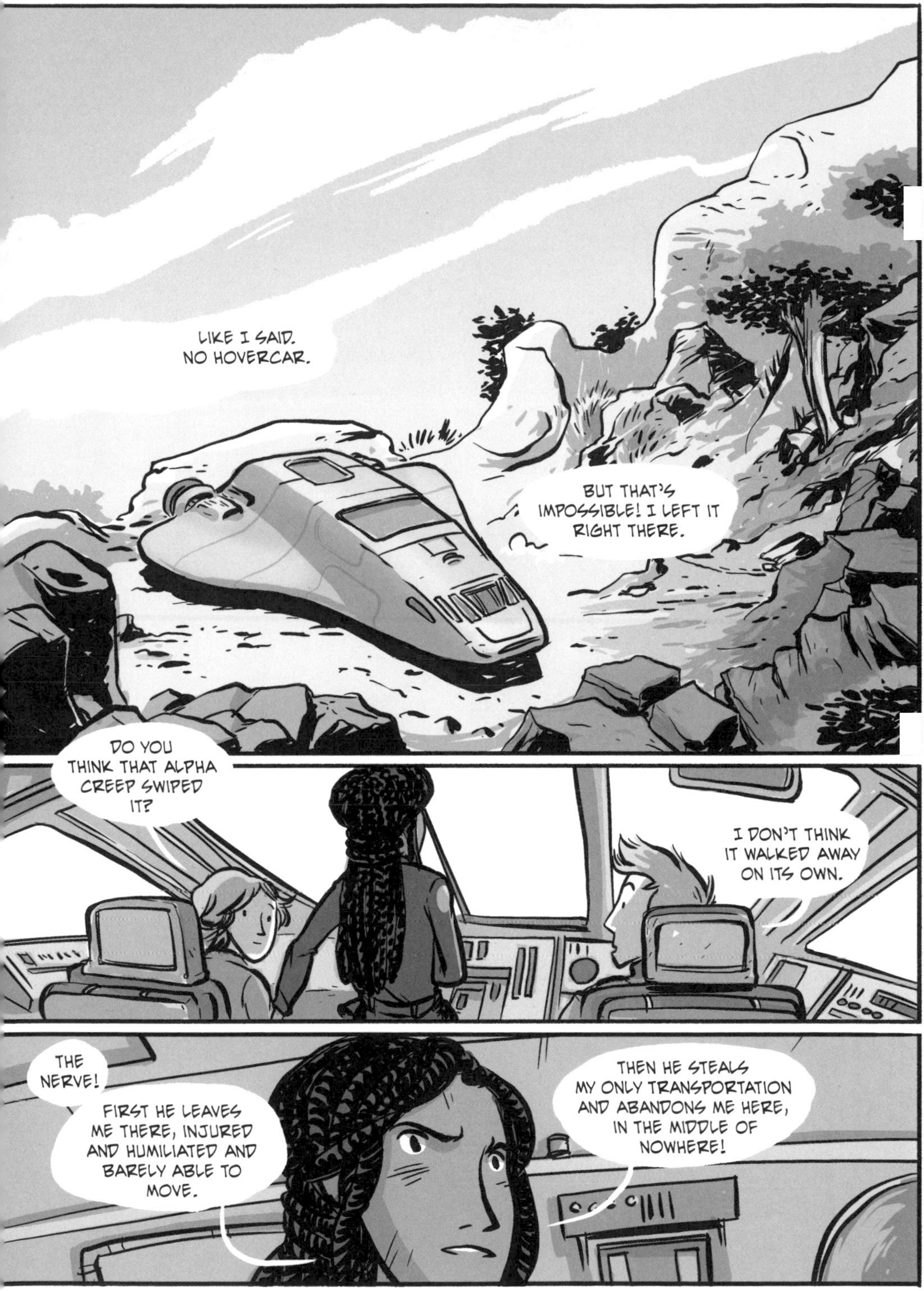
LIKE I SAID. NO HOVERCAR.
BUT THAT'S IMPOSSIBLE! I LEFT IT RIGHT THERE.
DO YOU THINK THAT ALPHA CREEP SWIPED IT?
I DON'T THINK IT WALKED AWAY ON ITS OWN.
THE NERVE!
FIRST HE LEAVES ME THERE, INJURED AND HUMILIATED AND BARELY ABLE TO MOVE.
THEN HE STEALS MY ONLY TRANSPORTATION AND ABANDONS ME HERE, IN THE MIDDLE OF NOWHERE!

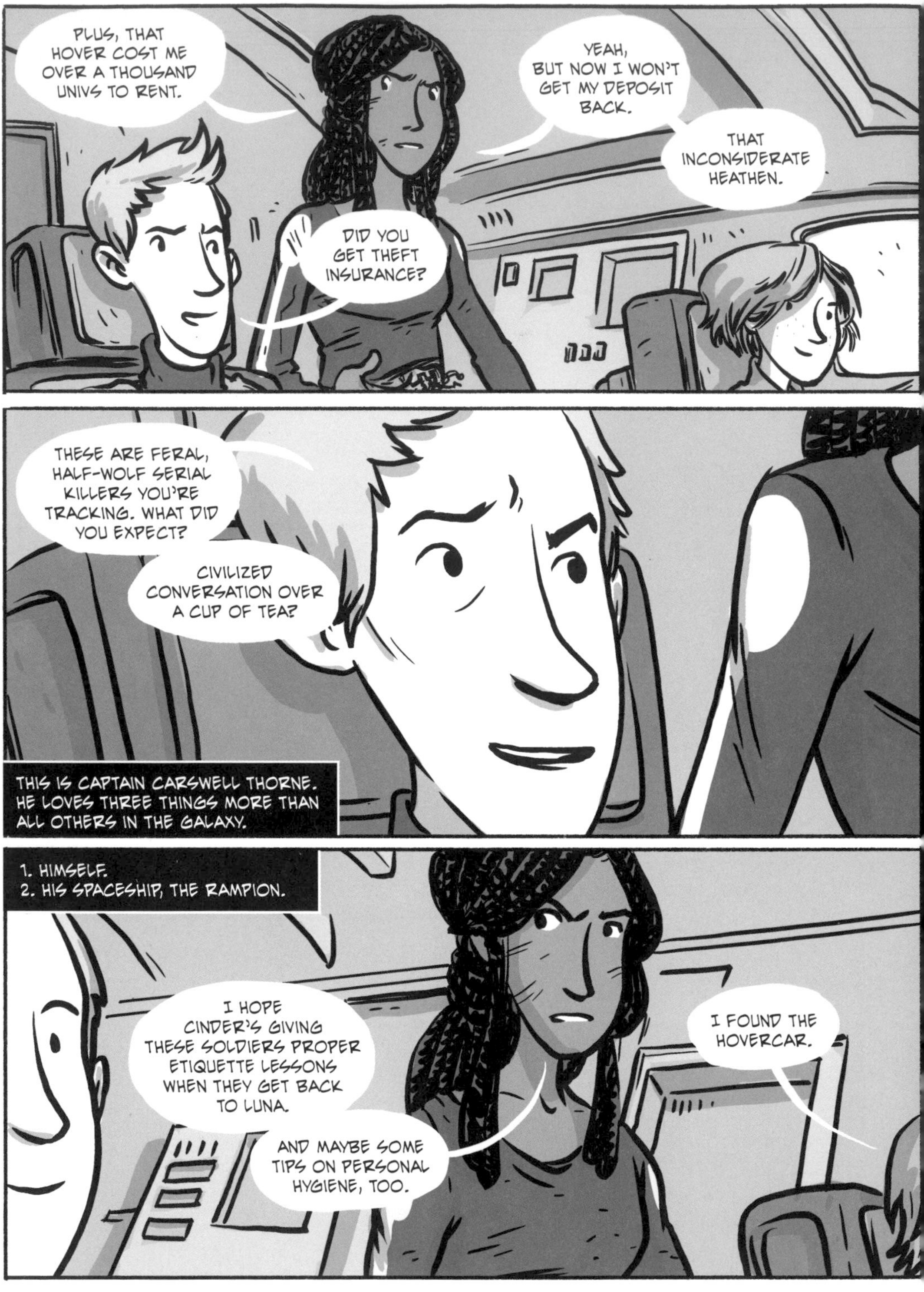
PLUS, THAT HOVER COST ME OVER A THOUSAND UNIVS TO RENT.
YEAH, BUT NOW I WON'T GET MY DEPOSIT BACK.
THAT INCONSIDERATE HEATHEN.
DID YOU GET THEFT INSURANCE?
THESE ARE FERAL, HALF-WOLF SERIAL KILLERS YOU'RE TRACKING. WHAT DID YOU EXPECT?
CIVILIZED CONVERSATION OVER A CUP OF TEA?
THIS IS CAPTAIN CARSWELL THORNE. HE LOVES THREE THINGS MORE THAN ALL OTHERS IN THE GALAXY.
1. HIMSELF.
2. HIS SPACESHIP, THE RAMPION.
I HOPE CINDER'S GIVING THESE SOLDIERS PROPER ETIQUETTE LESSONS WHEN THEY GET BACK TO LUNA.
AND MAYBE SOME TIPS ON PERSONAL HYGIENE, TOO.
I FOUND THE HOVERCAR.

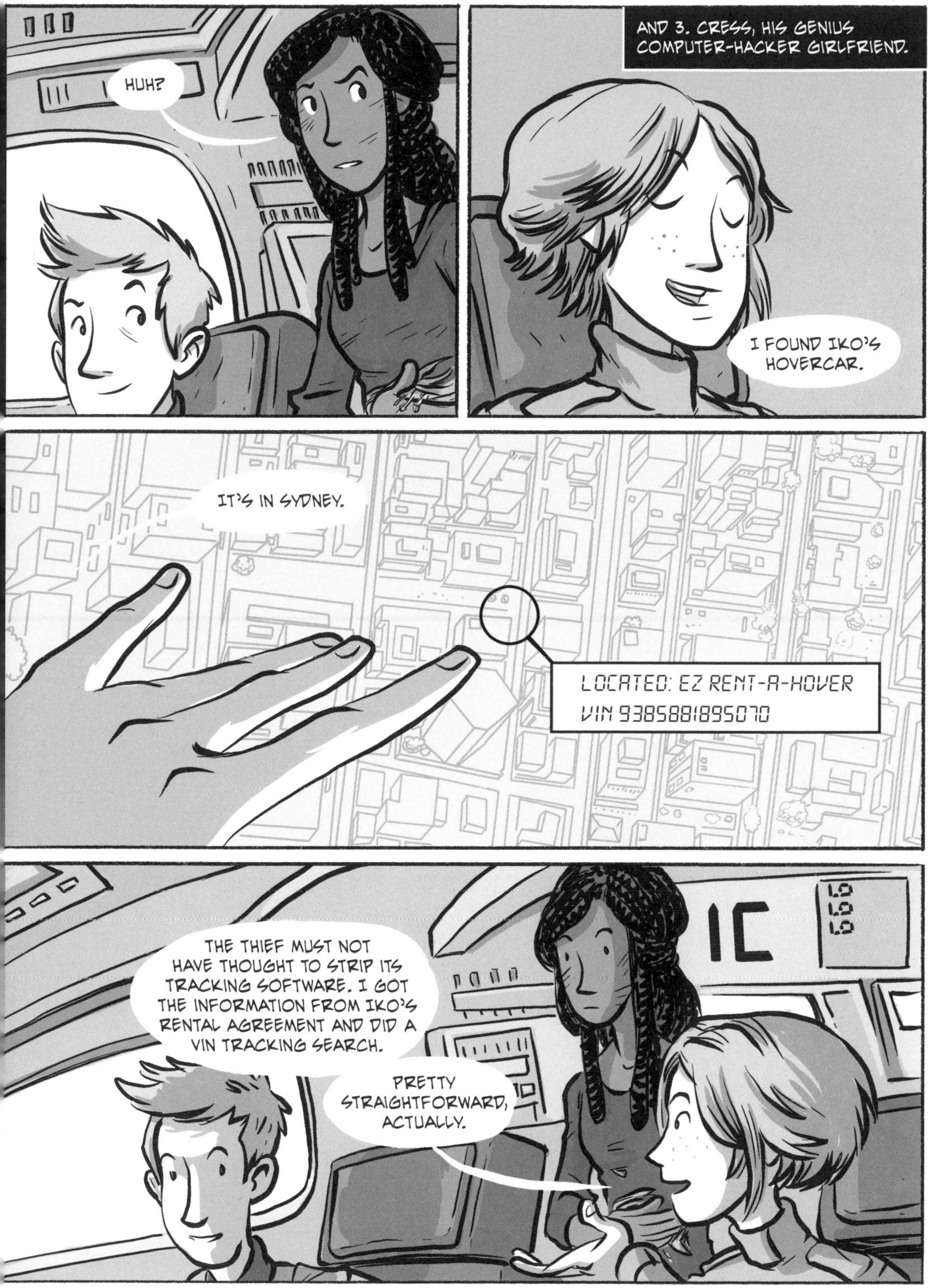
HUH?
AND 3. CRESS, HIS GENIUS COMPUTER-HACKER GIRLFRIEND.
I FOUND IKO'S HOVERCAR.
IT'S IN SYDNEY.
LOCATED: EZ RENT-A-HOVER
VIN 9385881895070
IC
THE THIEF MUST NOT HAVE THOUGHT TO STRIP ITS TRACKING SOFTWARE. I GOT THE INFORMATION FROM IKO'S RENTAL AGREEMENT AND DID A VIN TRACKING SEARCH.
PRETTY STRAIGHTFORWARD, ACTUALLY.

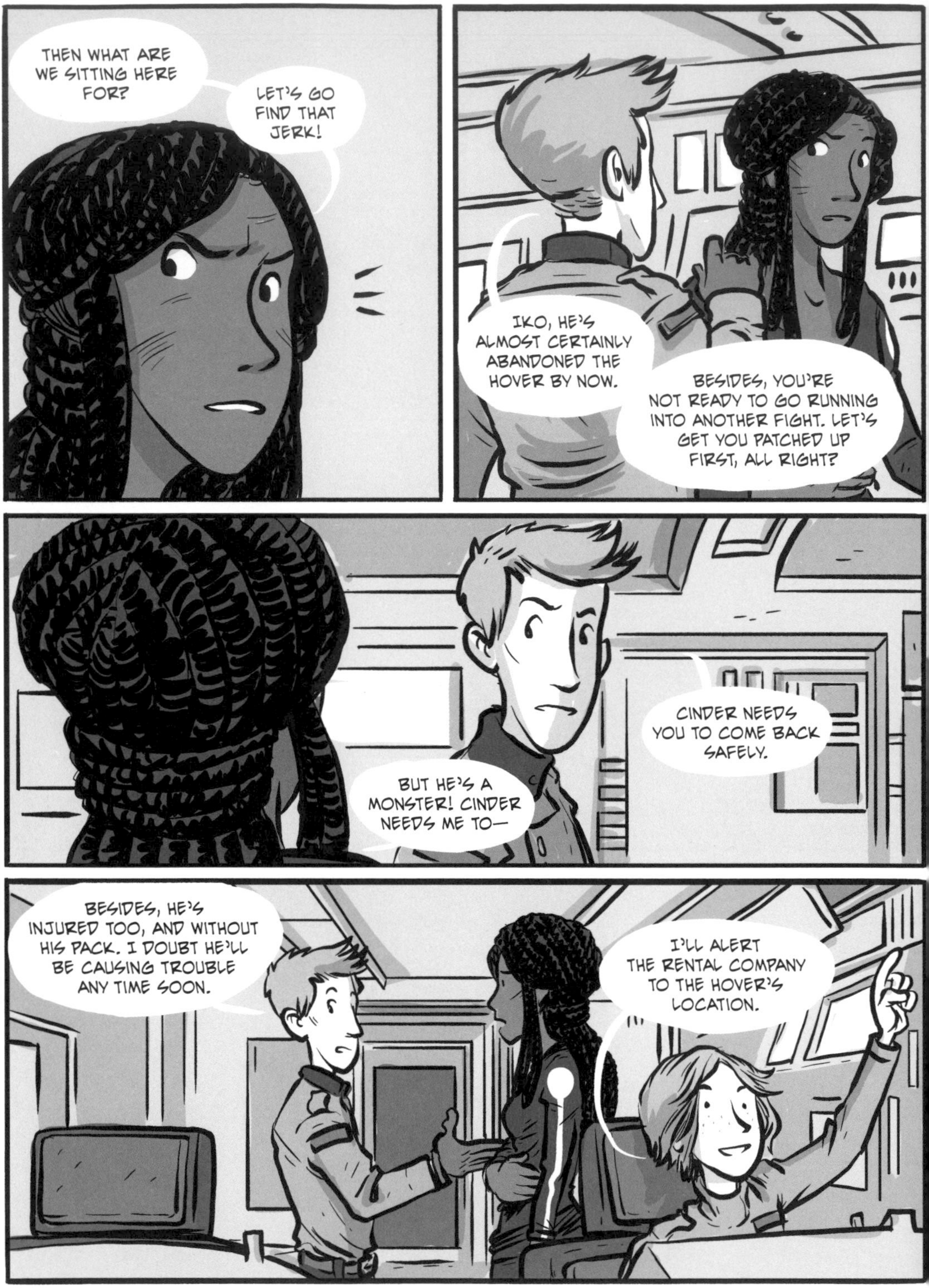
THEN WHAT ARE WE SITTING HERE FOR?
LET'S GO FIND THAT JERK!
IKO, HE'S ALMOST CERTAINLY ABANDONED THE HOVER BY NOW.
BESIDES, YOU'RE NOT READY TO GO RUNNING INTO ANOTHER FIGHT. LET'S GET YOU PATCHED UP FIRST, ALL RIGHT?
BUT HE'S A MONSTER! CINDER NEEDS ME TO—
CINDER NEEDS YOU TO COME BACK SAFELY.
BESIDES, HE'S INJURED TOO, AND WITHOUT HIS PACK. I DOUBT HE'LL BE CAUSING TROUBLE ANY TIME SOON.
I'LL ALERT THE RENTAL COMPANY TO THE HOVER'S LOCATION.

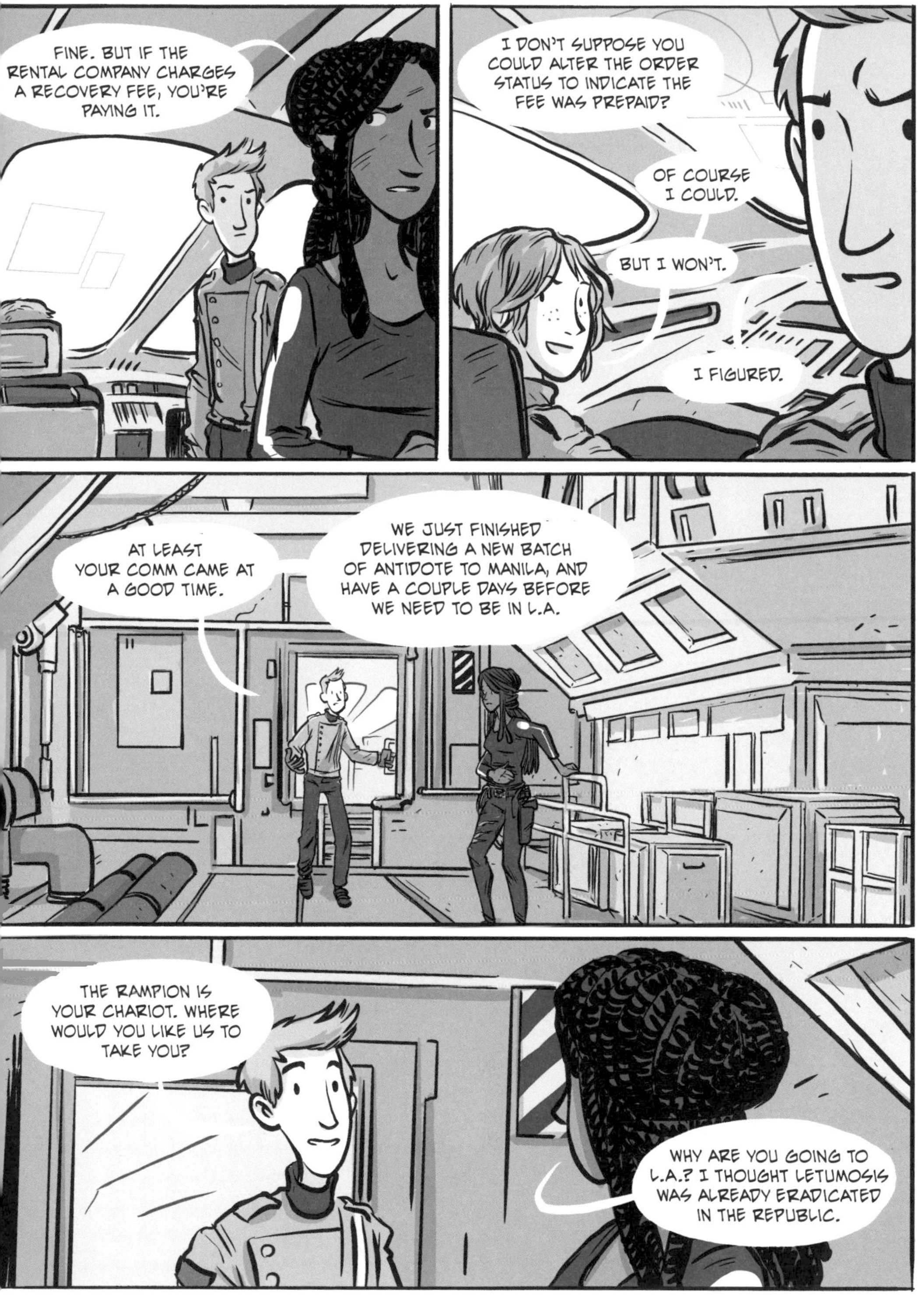
FINE. BUT IF THE RENTAL COMPANY CHARGES A RECOVERY FEE, YOU'RE PAYING IT.
I DON'T SUPPOSE YOU COULD ALTER THE ORDER STATUS TO INDICATE THE FEE WAS PREPAID?
OF COURSE I COULD.
BUT I WON'T.
I FIGURED.
AT LEAST YOUR COMM CAME AT A GOOD TIME.
WE JUST FINISHED DELIVERING A NEW BATCH OF ANTIDOTE TO MANILA, AND HAVE A COUPLE DAYS BEFORE WE NEED TO BE IN L.A.
THE RAMPION IS YOUR CHARIOT. WHERE WOULD YOU LIKE US TO TAKE YOU?
WHY ARE YOU GOING TO L.A.? I THOUGHT LETUMOSIS WAS ALREADY ERADICATED IN THE REPUBLIC.

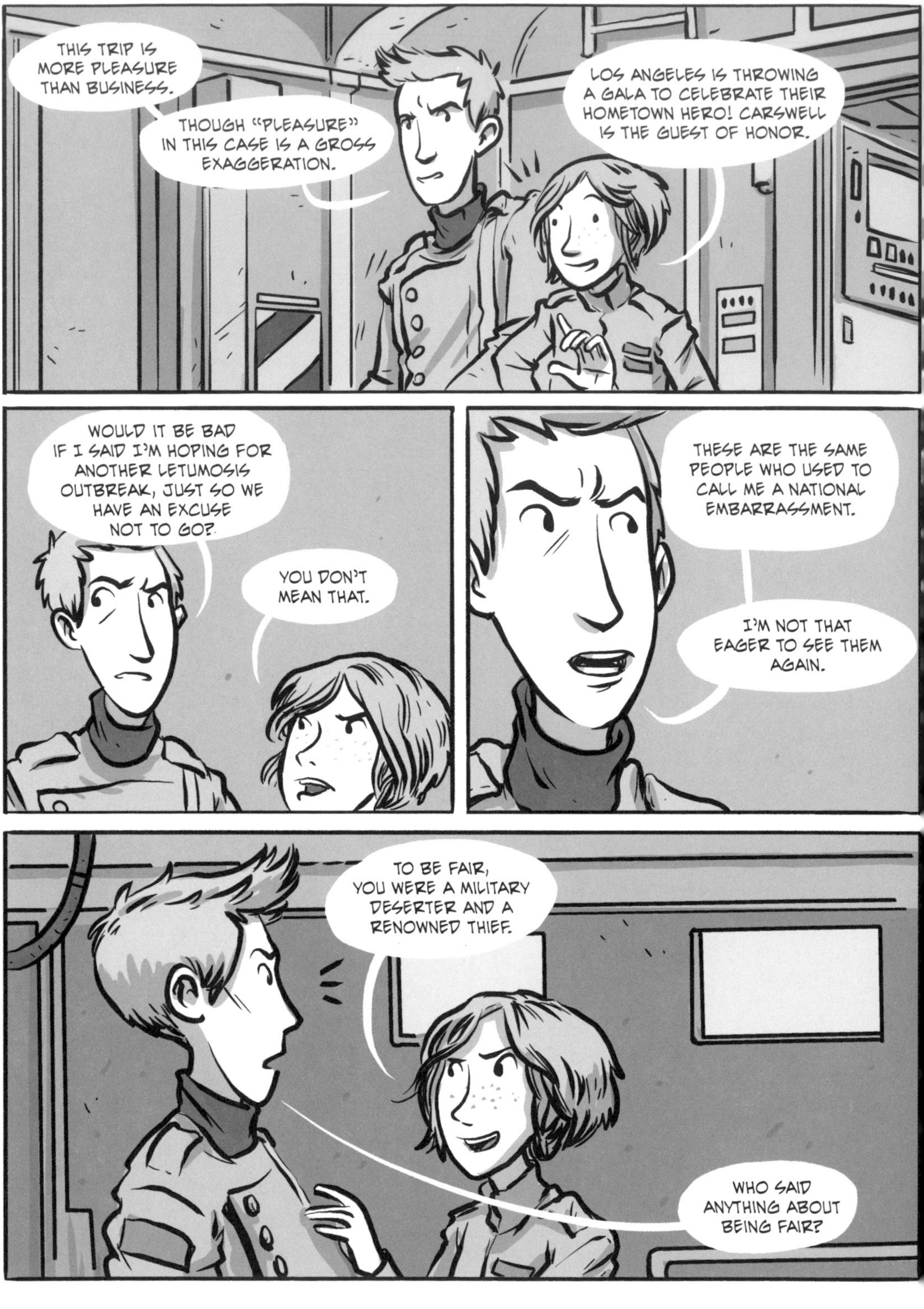
THIS TRIP IS MORE PLEASURE THAN BUSINESS.
THOUGH "PLEASURE" IN THIS CASE IS A GROSS EXAGGERATION.
LOS ANGELES IS THROWING A GALA TO CELEBRATE THEIR HOMETOWN HERO! CARSWELL IS THE GUEST OF HONOR.
WOULD IT BE BAD IF I SAID I'M HOPING FOR ANOTHER LETUMOSIS OUTBREAK, JUST SO WE HAVE AN EXCUSE NOT TO GO?
YOU DON'T MEAN THAT.
THESE ARE THE SAME PEOPLE WHO USED TO CALL ME A NATIONAL EMBARRASSMENT.
I'M NOT THAT EAGER TO SEE THEM AGAIN.
TO BE FAIR, YOU WERE A MILITARY DESERTER AND A RENOWNED THIEF.
WHO SAID ANYTHING ABOUT BEING FAIR?

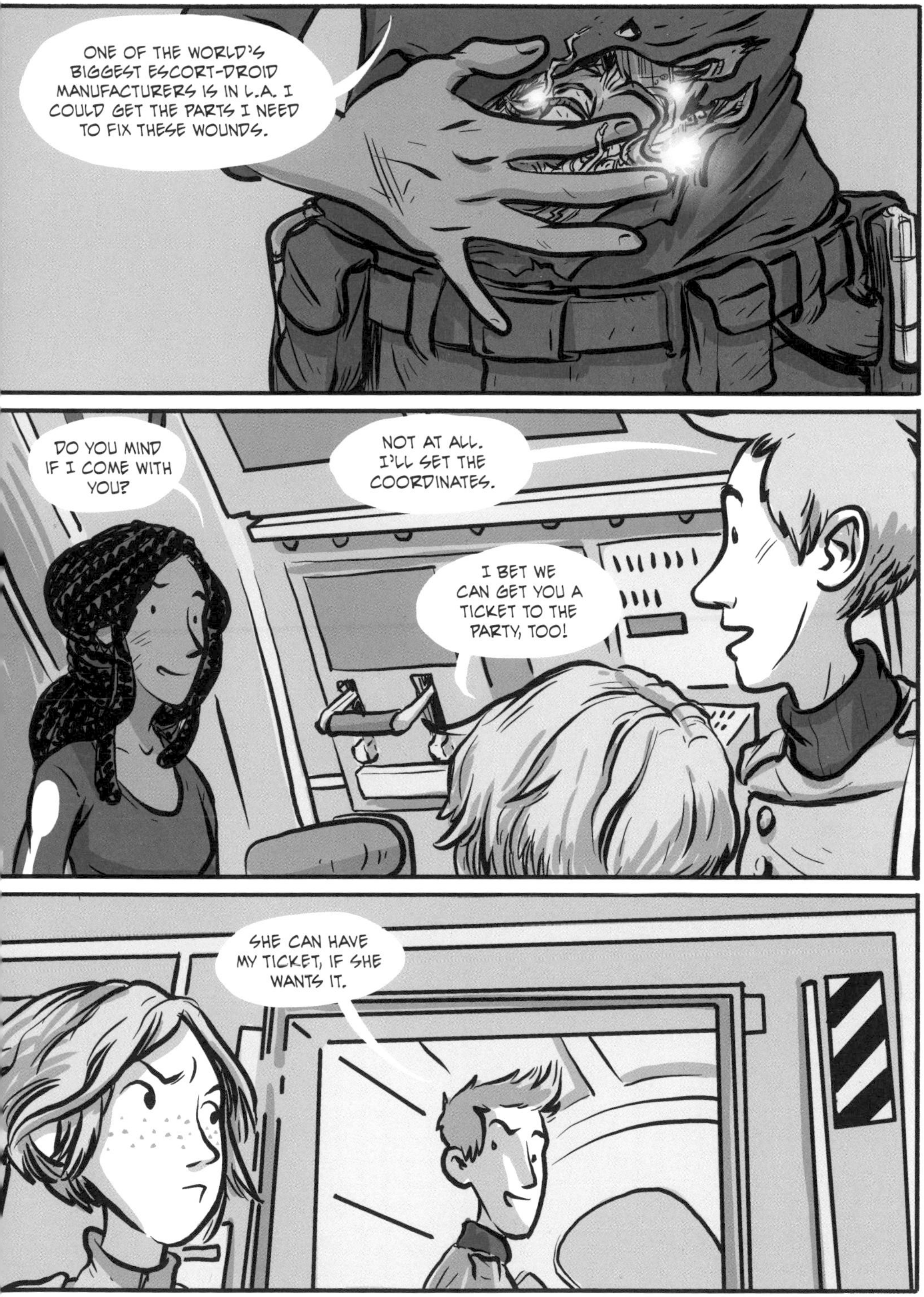
ONE OF THE WORLD'S BIGGEST ESCORT-DROID MANUFACTURERS IS IN L.A. I COULD GET THE PARTS I NEED TO FIX THESE WOUNDS.
DO YOU MIND IF I COME WITH YOU?
NOT AT ALL. I'LL SET THE COORDINATES.
I BET WE CAN GET YOU A TICKET TO THE PARTY, TOO!
SHE CAN HAVE MY TICKET, IF SHE WANTS IT.

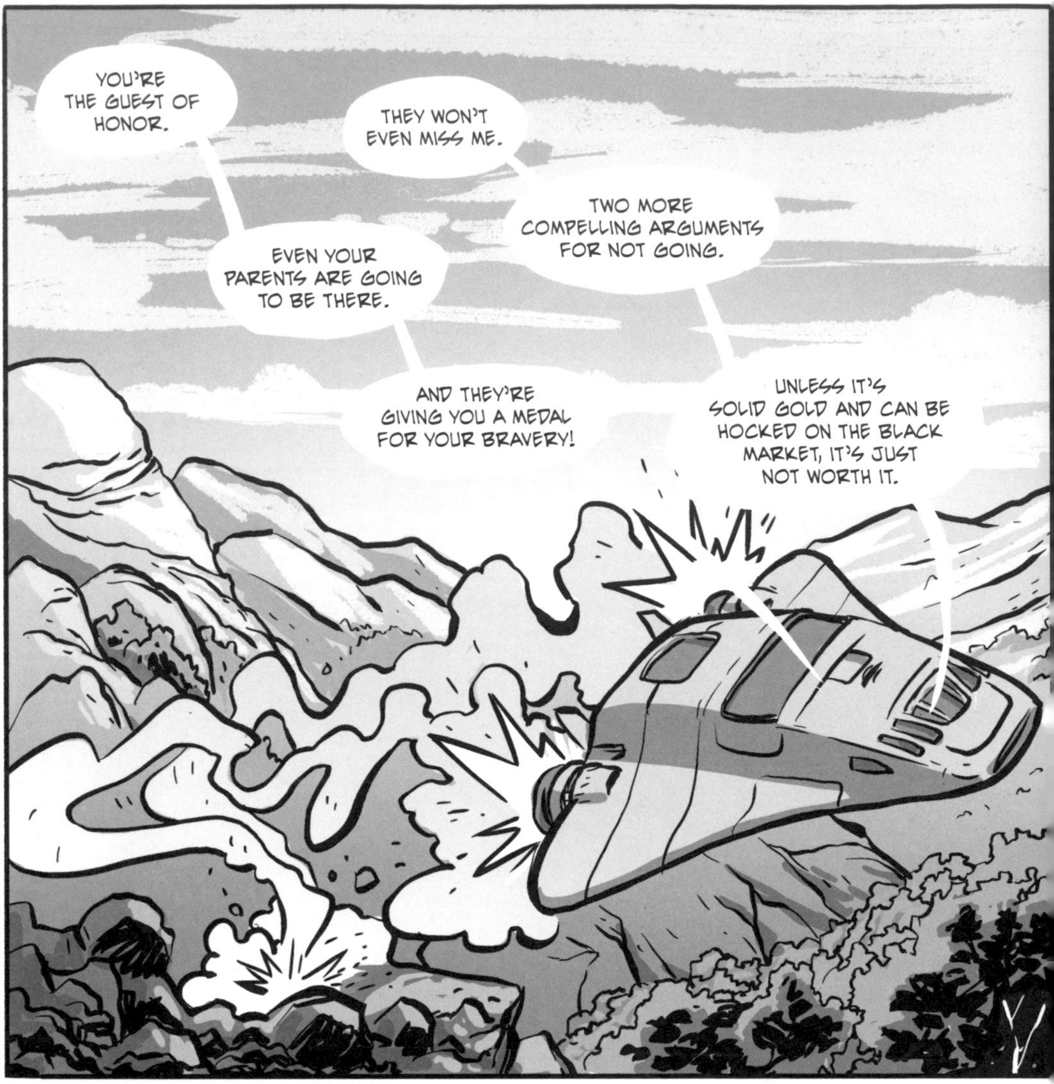
YOU'RE THE GUEST OF HONOR.
THEY WON'T EVEN MISS ME.
EVEN YOUR PARENTS ARE GOING TO BE THERE.
TWO MORE COMPELLING ARGUMENTS FOR NOT GOING.
AND THEY'RE GIVING YOU A MEDAL FOR YOUR BRAVERY!
UNLESS IT'S SOLID GOLD AND CAN BE HOCKED ON THE BLACK MARKET, IT'S JUST NOT WORTH IT.

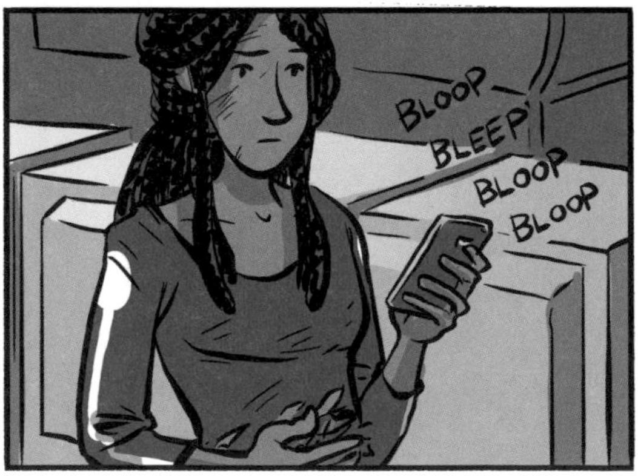
BLOOP
BLEEP
BLOOP
BLOOP

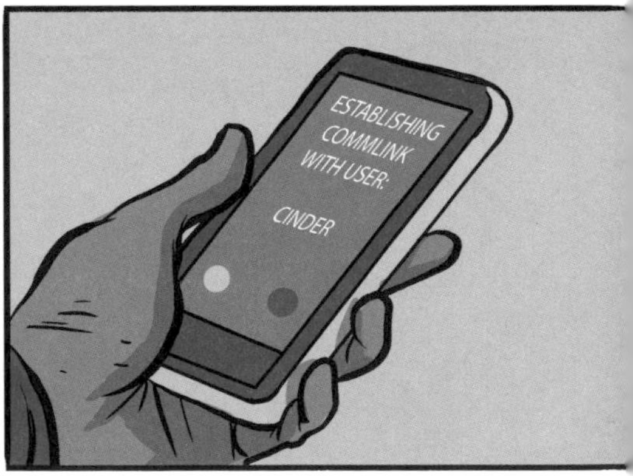
ESTABLISHING COMMLINK WITH USER:
CINDER

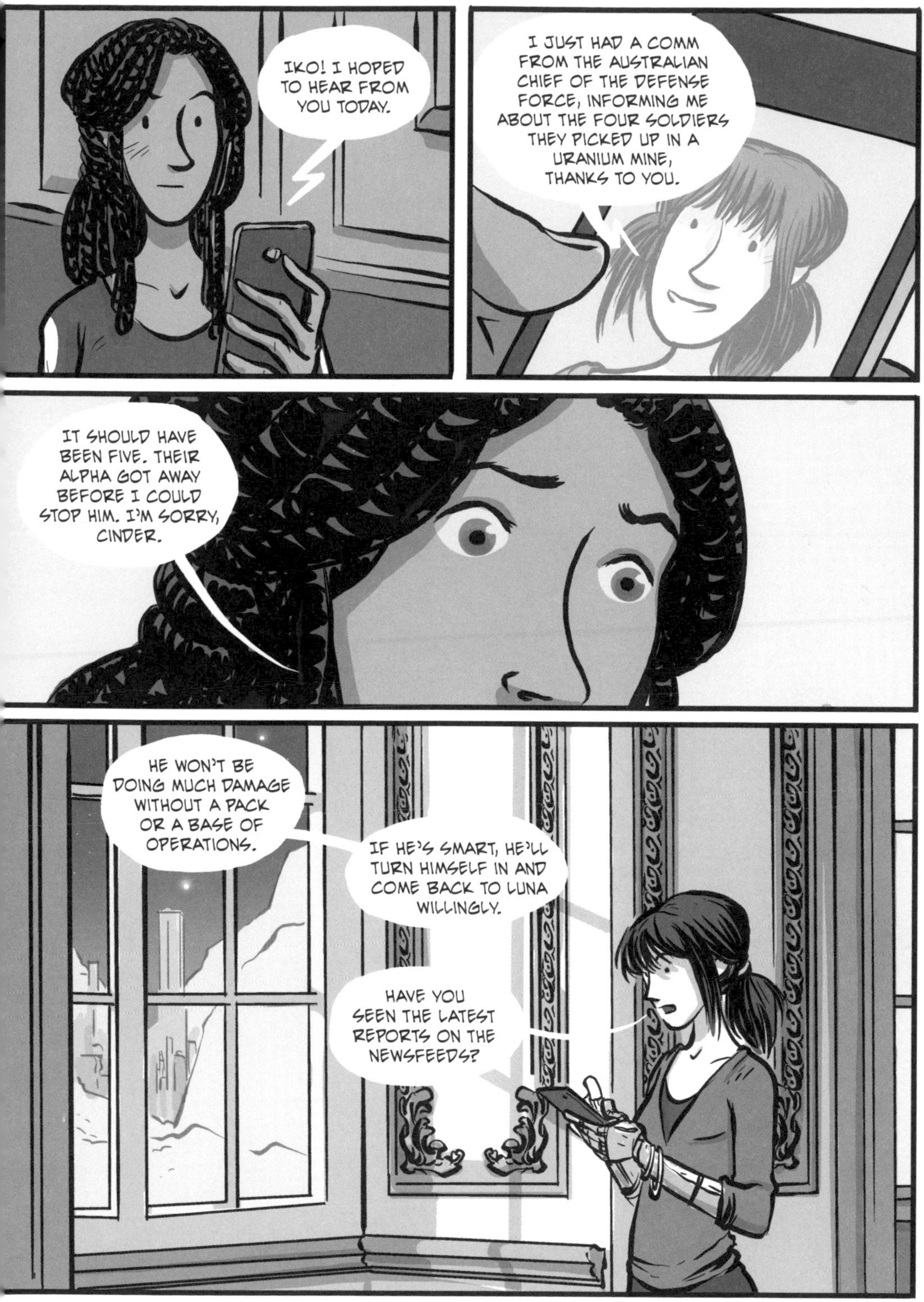
IKO! I HOPED TO HEAR FROM YOU TODAY.
I JUST HAD A COMM FROM THE AUSTRALIAN CHIEF OF THE DEFENSE FORCE, INFORMING ME ABOUT THE FOUR SOLDIERS THEY PICKED UP IN A URANIUM MINE, THANKS TO YOU.
IT SHOULD HAVE BEEN FIVE. THEIR ALPHA GOT AWAY BEFORE I COULD STOP HIM. I'M SORRY, CINDER.
HE WON'T BE DOING MUCH DAMAGE WITHOUT A PACK OR A BASE OF OPERATIONS.
IF HE'S SMART, HE'LL TURN HIMSELF IN AND COME BACK TO LUNA WILLINGLY.
HAVE YOU SEEN THE LATEST REPORTS ON THE NEWSFEEDS?

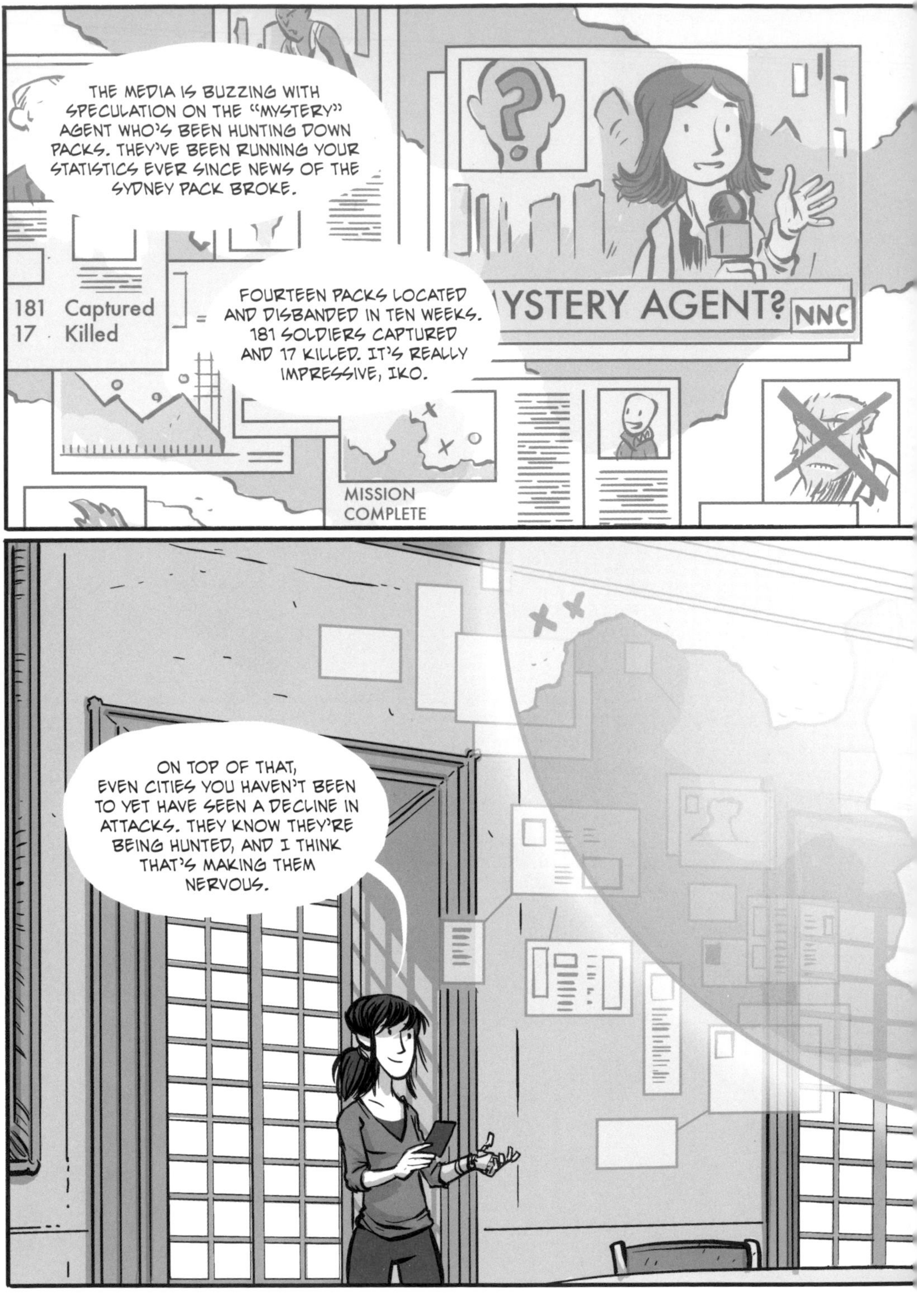
THE MEDIA IS BUZZING WITH SPECULATION ON THE "MYSTERY" AGENT WHO'S BEEN HUNTING DOWN PACKS. THEY'VE BEEN RUNNING YOUR STATISTICS EVER SINCE NEWS OF THE SYDNEY PACK BROKE.
MYSTERY AGENT?
NNC
181 Captured
17 Killed
FOURTEEN PACKS LOCATED AND DISBANDED IN TEN WEEKS. 181 SOLDIERS CAPTURED AND 17 KILLED. IT'S REALLY IMPRESSIVE, IKO.
MISSION COMPLETE
ON TOP OF THAT, EVEN CITIES YOU HAVEN'T BEEN TO YET HAVE SEEN A DECLINE IN ATTACKS. THEY KNOW THEY'RE BEING HUNTED, AND I THINK THAT'S MAKING THEM NERVOUS.

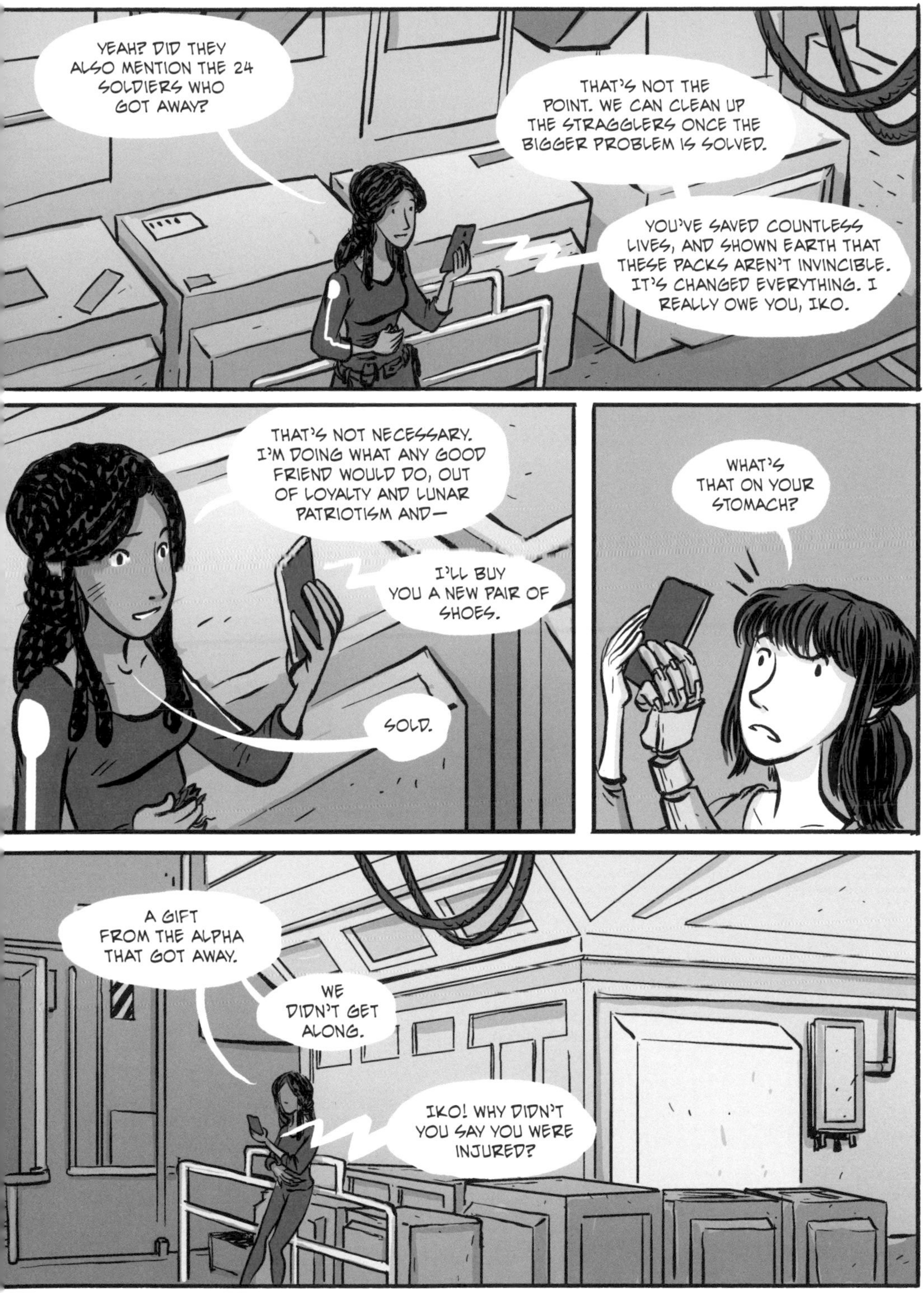
YEAH? DID THEY ALSO MENTION THE 24 SOLDIERS WHO GOT AWAY?
THAT'S NOT THE POINT. WE CAN CLEAN UP THE STRAGGLERS ONCE THE BIGGER PROBLEM IS SOLVED.
YOU'VE SAVED COUNTLESS LIVES, AND SHOWN EARTH THAT THESE PACKS AREN'T INVINCIBLE. IT'S CHANGED EVERYTHING. I REALLY OWE YOU, IKO.
THAT'S NOT NECESSARY. I'M DOING WHAT ANY GOOD FRIEND WOULD DO, OUT OF LOYALTY AND LUNAR PATRIOTISM AND—
I'LL BUY YOU A NEW PAIR OF SHOES.
SOLD.
WHAT'S THAT ON YOUR STOMACH?
A GIFT FROM THE ALPHA THAT GOT AWAY.
WE DIDN'T GET ALONG.
IKO! WHY DIDN'T YOU SAY YOU WERE INJURED?

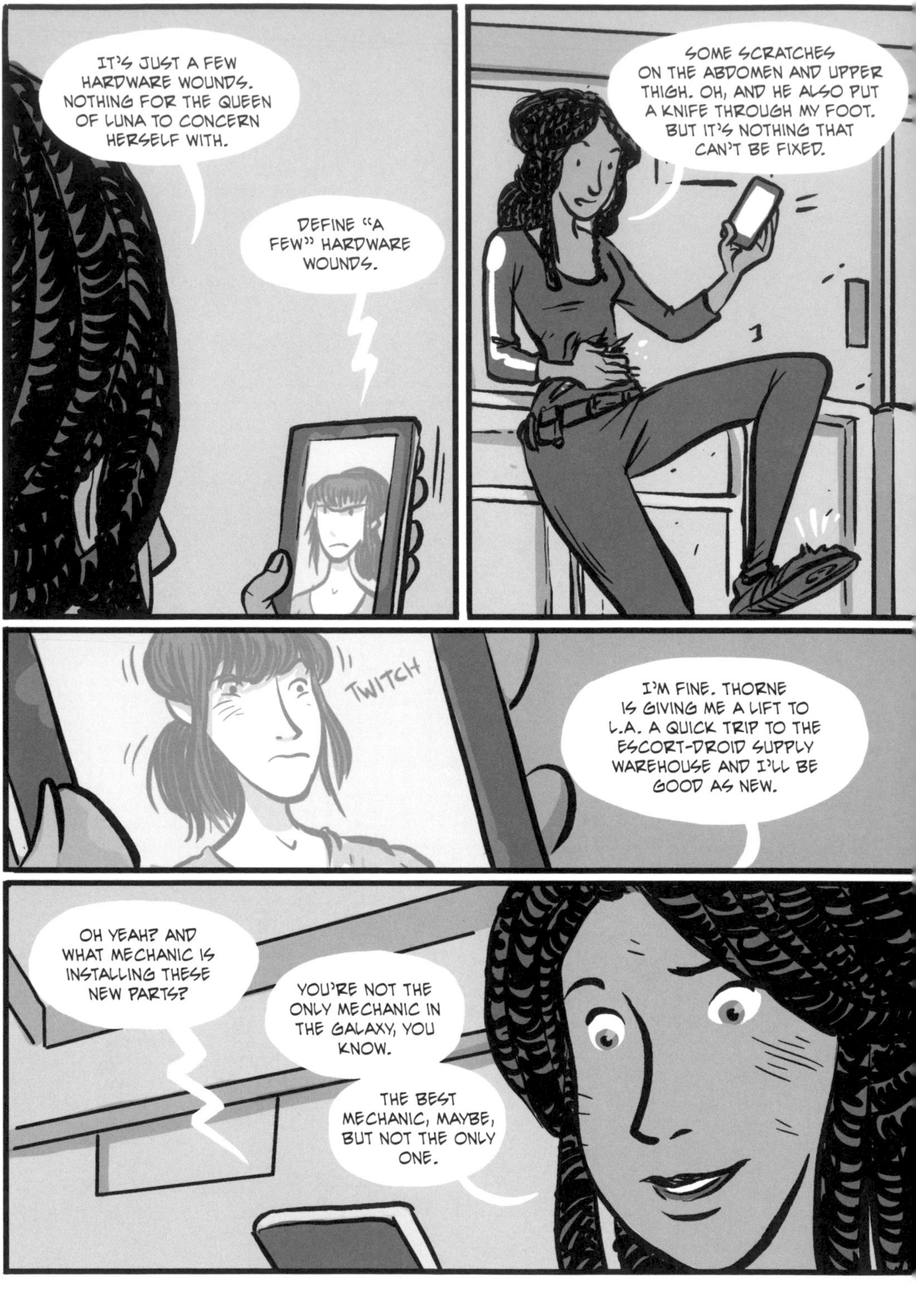
IT'S JUST A FEW HARDWARE WOUNDS. NOTHING FOR THE QUEEN OF LUNA TO CONCERN HERSELF WITH.
DEFINE "A FEW" HARDWARE WOUNDS.
SOME SCRATCHES ON THE ABDOMEN AND UPPER THIGH. OH, AND HE ALSO PUT A KNIFE THROUGH MY FOOT. BUT IT'S NOTHING THAT CAN'T BE FIXED.
TWITCH
I'M FINE. THORNE IS GIVING ME A LIFT TO L.A. A QUICK TRIP TO THE ESCORT-DROID SUPPLY WAREHOUSE AND I'LL BE GOOD AS NEW.
OH YEAH? AND WHAT MECHANIC IS INSTALLING THESE NEW PARTS?
YOU'RE NOT THE ONLY MECHANIC IN THE GALAXY, YOU KNOW.
THE BEST MECHANIC, MAYBE, BUT NOT THE ONLY ONE.

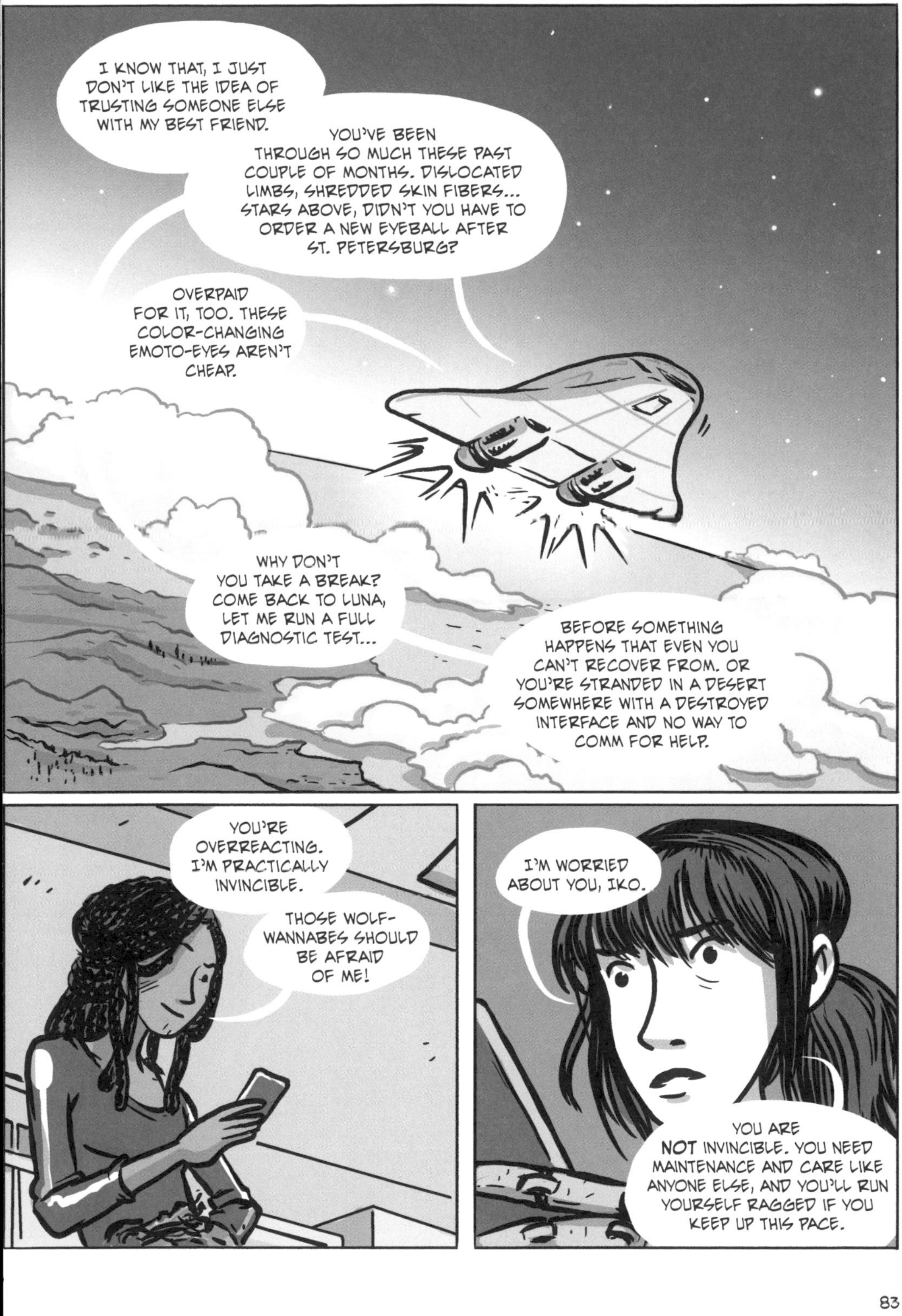
I KNOW THAT, I JUST DON'T LIKE THE IDEA OF TRUSTING SOMEONE ELSE WITH MY BEST FRIEND.
YOU'VE BEEN THROUGH SO MUCH THESE PAST COUPLE OF MONTHS. DISLOCATED LIMBS, SHREDDED SKIN FIBERS... STARS ABOVE, DIDN'T YOU HAVE TO ORDER A NEW EYEBALL AFTER ST. PETERSBURG?
OVERPAID FOR IT, TOO. THESE COLOR-CHANGING EMOTO-EYES AREN'T CHEAP.
WHY DON'T YOU TAKE A BREAK? COME BACK TO LUNA, LET ME RUN A FULL DIAGNOSTIC TEST...
BEFORE SOMETHING HAPPENS THAT EVEN YOU CAN'T RECOVER FROM. OR YOU'RE STRANDED IN A DESERT SOMEWHERE WITH A DESTROYED INTERFACE AND NO WAY TO COMM FOR HELP.
YOU'RE OVERREACTING. I'M PRACTICALLY INVINCIBLE.
THOSE WOLF-WANNABES SHOULD BE AFRAID OF ME!
I'M WORRIED ABOUT YOU, IKO.
YOU ARE **NOT** INVINCIBLE. YOU NEED MAINTENANCE AND CARE LIKE ANYONE ELSE, AND YOU'LL RUN YOURSELF RAGGED IF YOU KEEP UP THIS PACE.

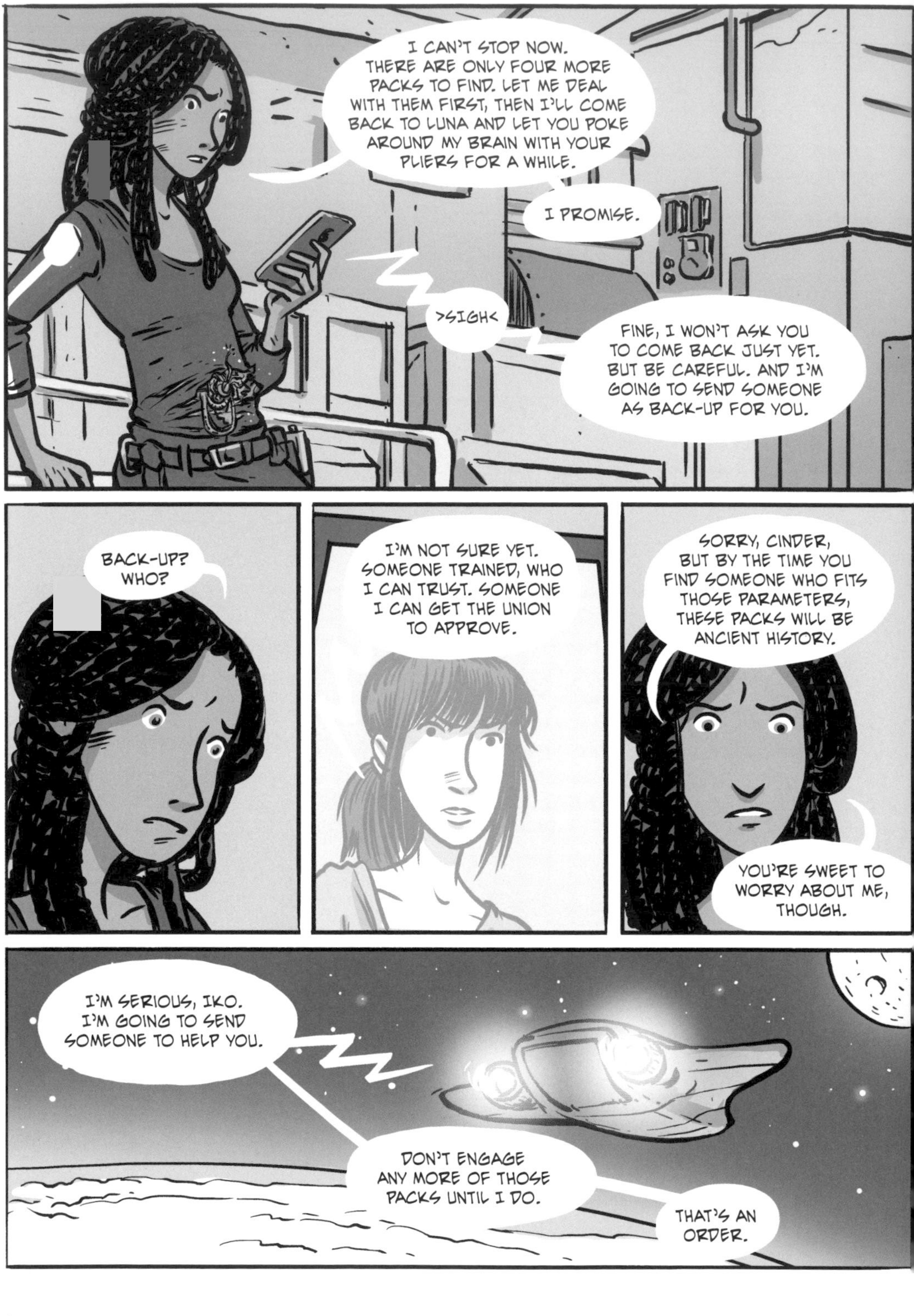
I CAN'T STOP NOW. THERE ARE ONLY FOUR MORE PACKS TO FIND. LET ME DEAL WITH THEM FIRST, THEN I'LL COME BACK TO LUNA AND LET YOU POKE AROUND MY BRAIN WITH YOUR PLIERS FOR A WHILE.
I PROMISE.
>SIGH<
FINE, I WON'T ASK YOU TO COME BACK JUST YET. BUT BE CAREFUL. AND I'M GOING TO SEND SOMEONE AS BACK-UP FOR YOU.
BACK-UP? WHO?
I'M NOT SURE YET. SOMEONE TRAINED, WHO I CAN TRUST. SOMEONE I CAN GET THE UNION TO APPROVE.
SORRY, CINDER, BUT BY THE TIME YOU FIND SOMEONE WHO FITS THOSE PARAMETERS, THESE PACKS WILL BE ANCIENT HISTORY.
YOU'RE SWEET TO WORRY ABOUT ME, THOUGH.
I'M SERIOUS, IKO. I'M GOING TO SEND SOMEONE TO HELP YOU.
DON'T ENGAGE ANY MORE OF THOSE PACKS UNTIL I DO.
THAT'S AN ORDER.

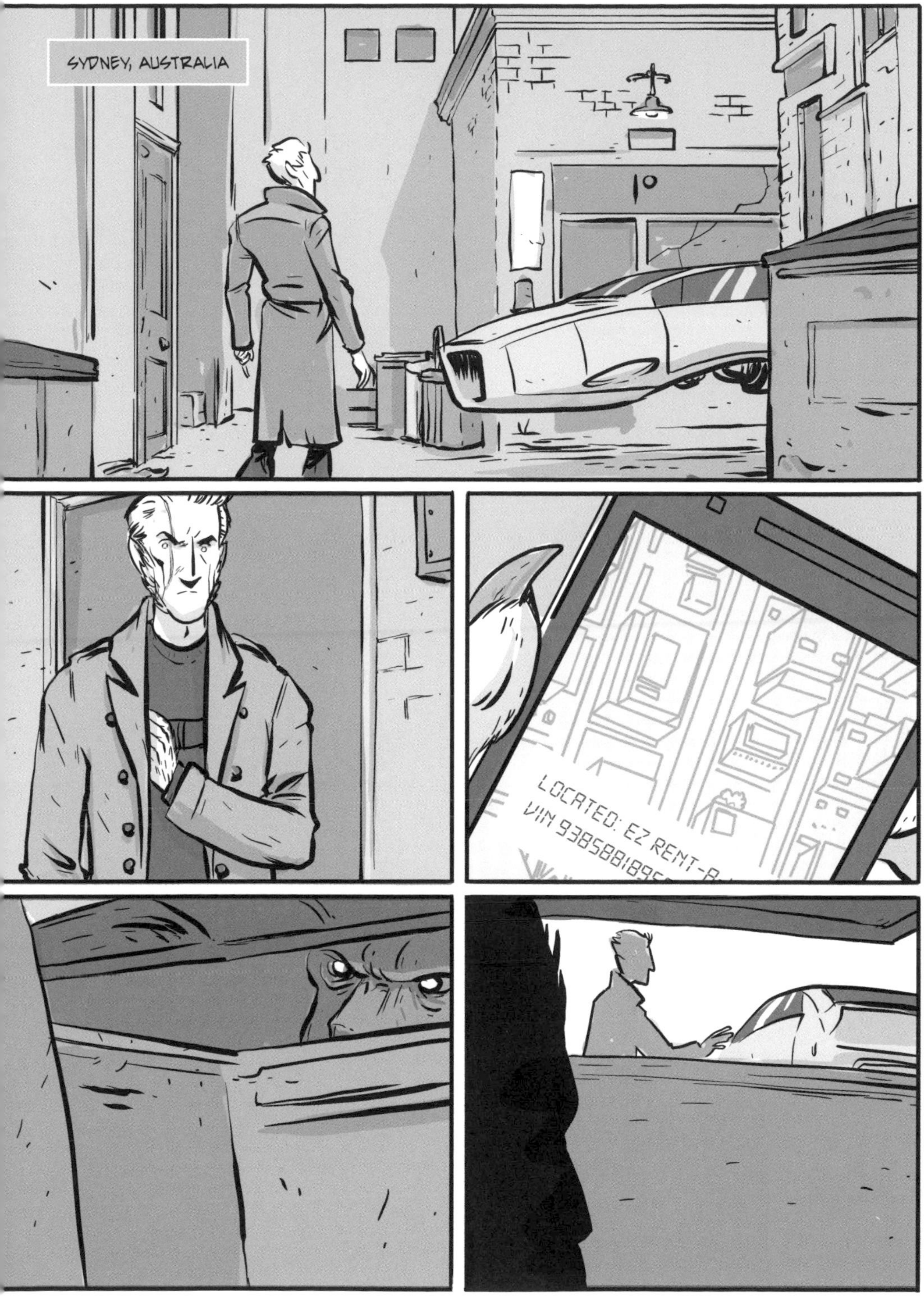
SYDNEY, AUSTRALIA
LOCATED: EZ RENT-A
VIN 93858818895

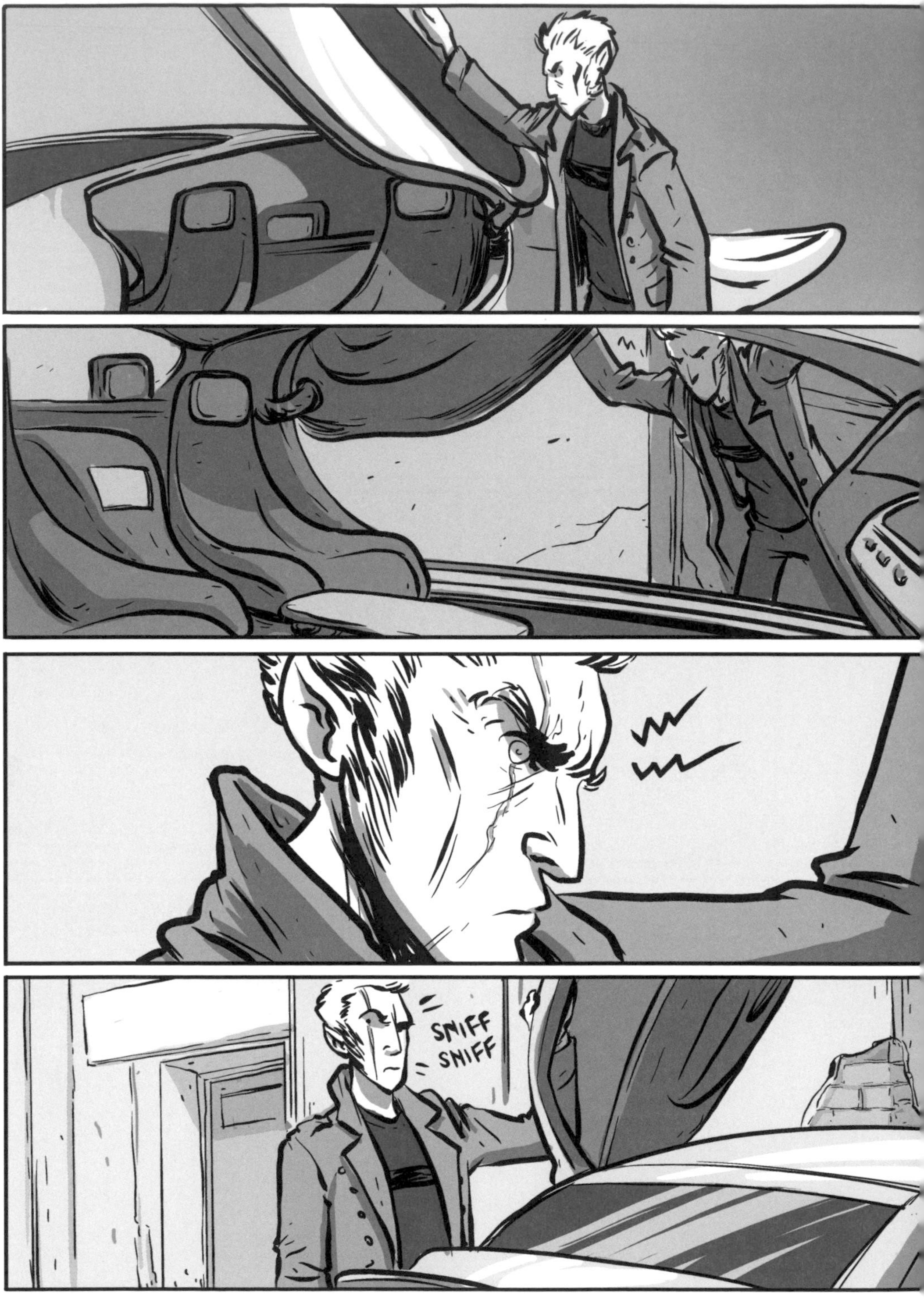
SNIFF
SNIFF

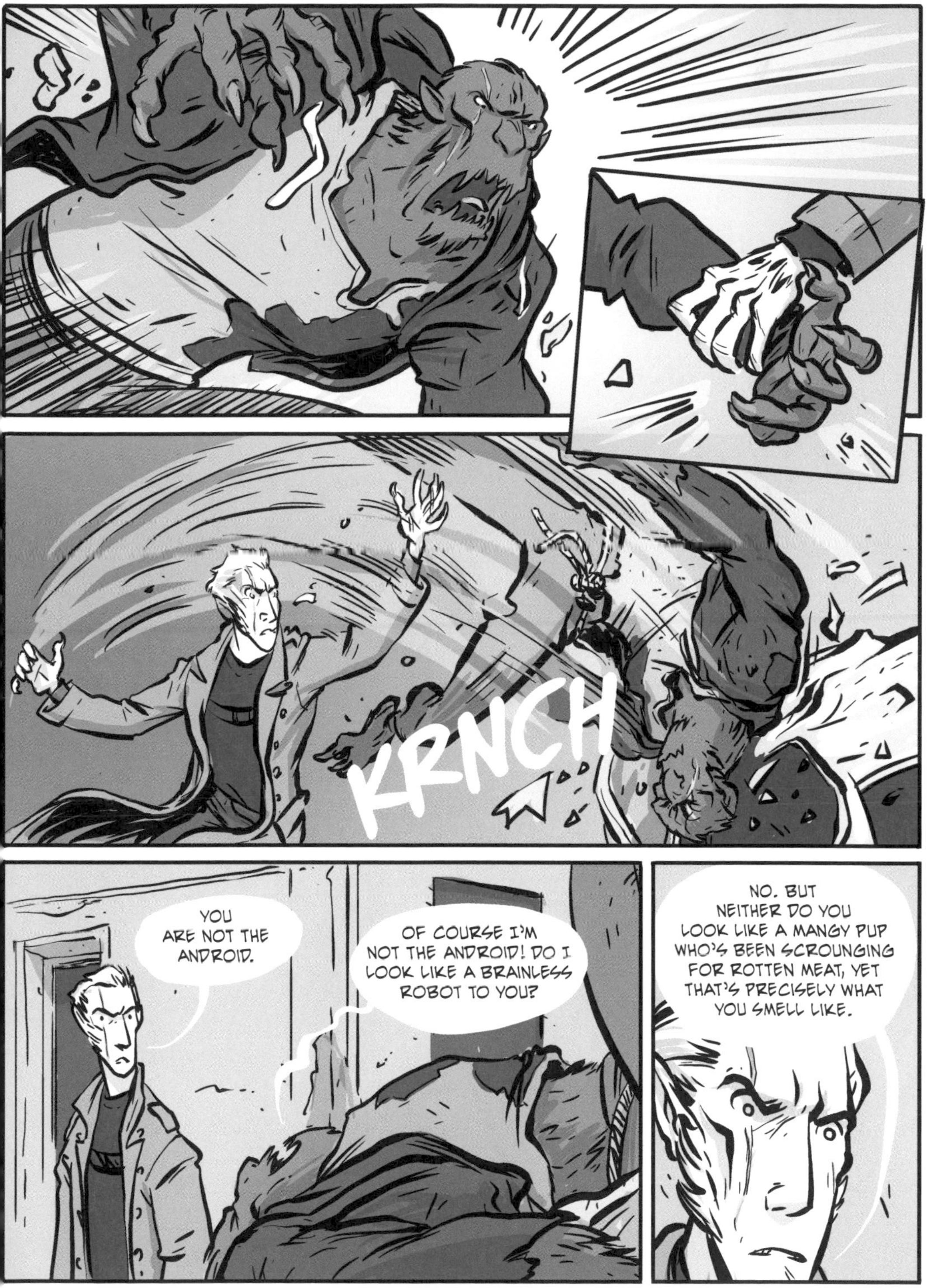
KRNCH
YOU ARE NOT THE ANDROID.
OF COURSE I'M NOT THE ANDROID! DO I LOOK LIKE A BRAINLESS ROBOT TO YOU?
NO. BUT NEITHER DO YOU LOOK LIKE A MANGY PUP WHO'S BEEN SCROUNGING FOR ROTTEN MEAT, YET THAT'S PRECISELY WHAT YOU SMELL LIKE.

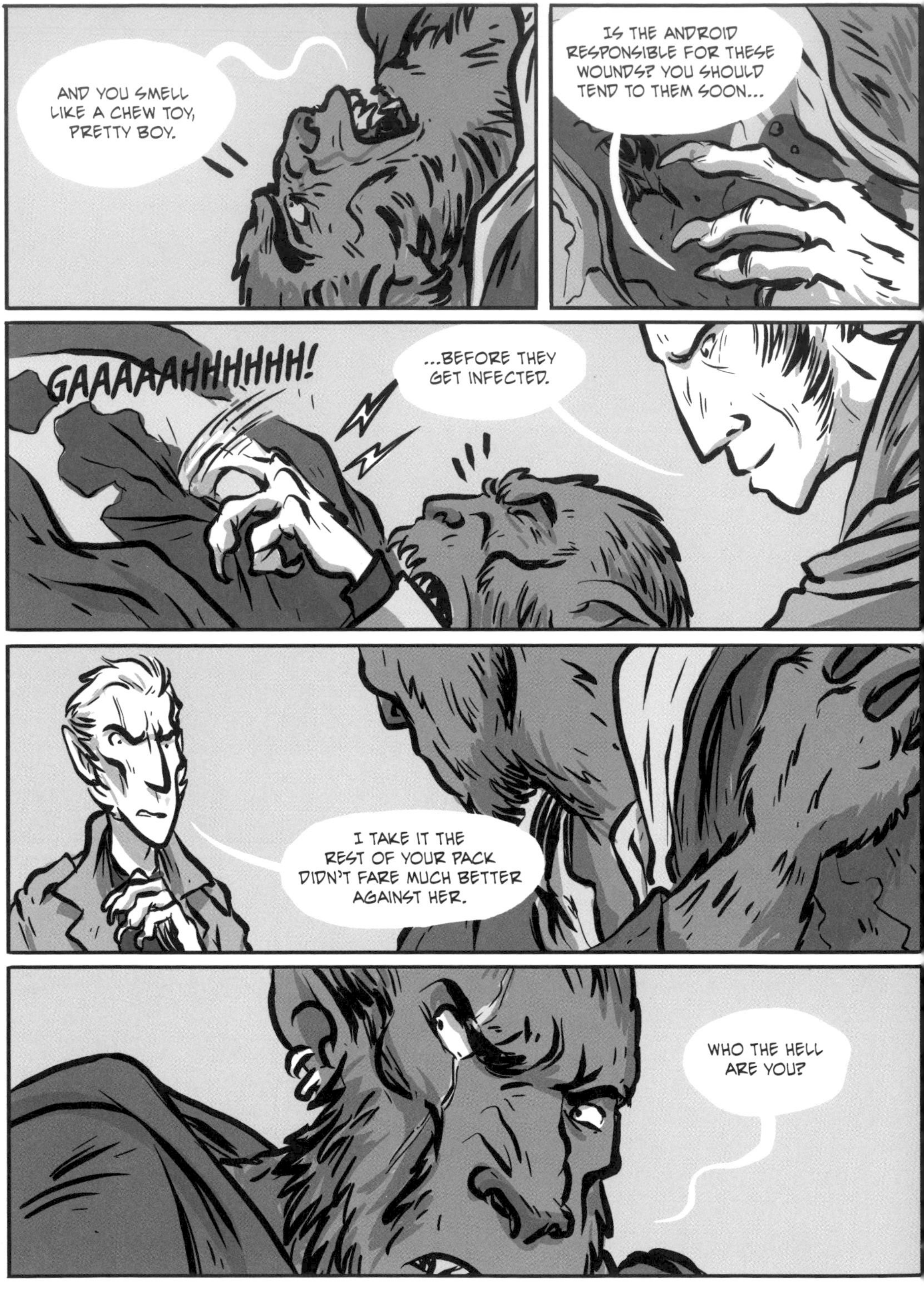
AND YOU SMELL LIKE A CHEW TOY, PRETTY BOY.
IS THE ANDROID RESPONSIBLE FOR THESE WOUNDS? YOU SHOULD TEND TO THEM SOON...
GAAAAAHHHHHH!
...BEFORE THEY GET INFECTED.
I TAKE IT THE REST OF YOUR PACK DIDN'T FARE MUCH BETTER AGAINST HER.
WHO THE HELL ARE YOU?

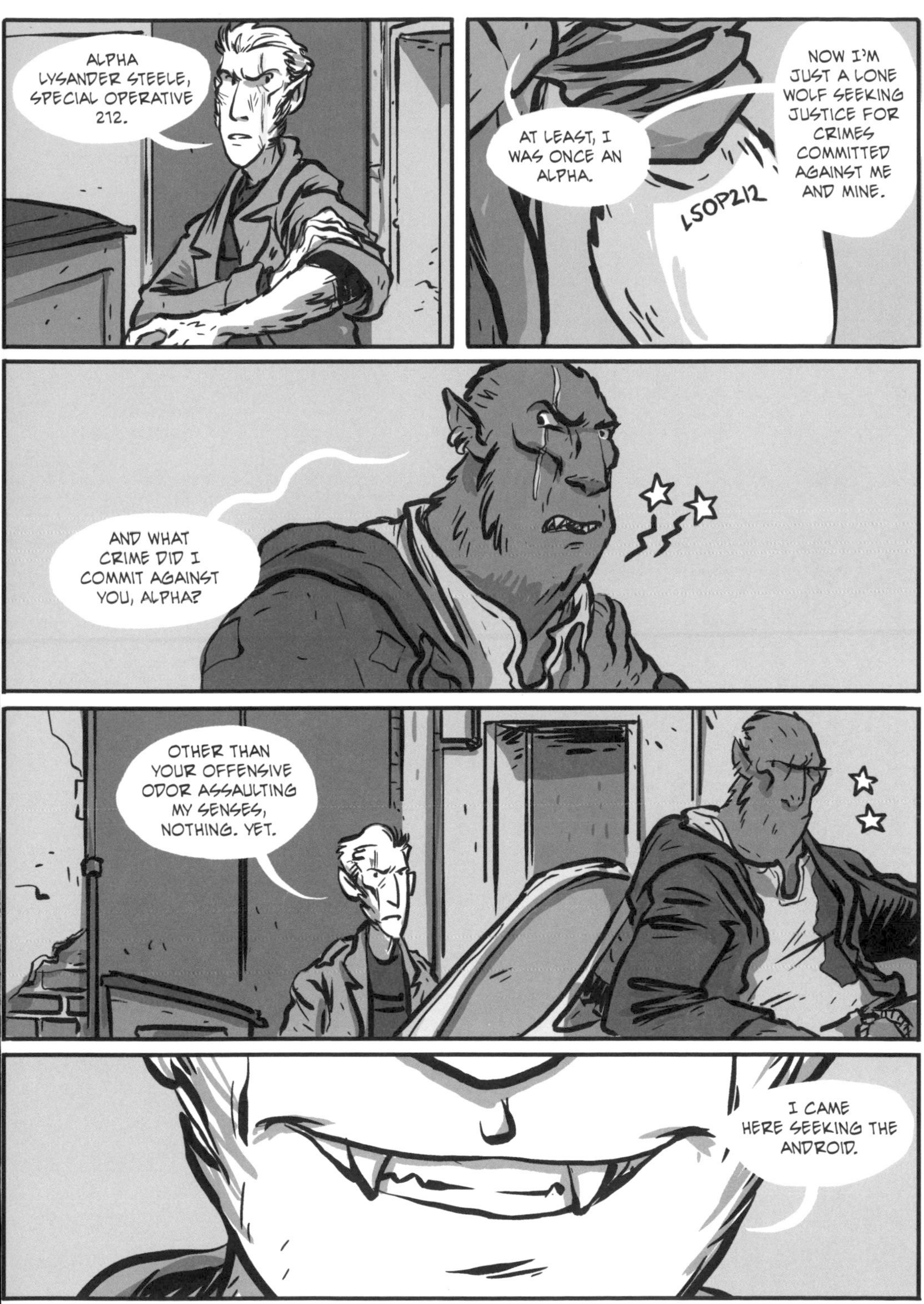
ALPHA LYSANDER STEELE, SPECIAL OPERATIVE 212.
AT LEAST, I WAS ONCE AN ALPHA.
NOW I'M JUST A LONE WOLF SEEKING JUSTICE FOR CRIMES COMMITTED AGAINST ME AND MINE.
LSOP212
AND WHAT CRIME DID I COMMIT AGAINST YOU, ALPHA?
OTHER THAN YOUR OFFENSIVE ODOR ASSAULTING MY SENSES, NOTHING. YET.
I CAME HERE SEEKING THE ANDROID.

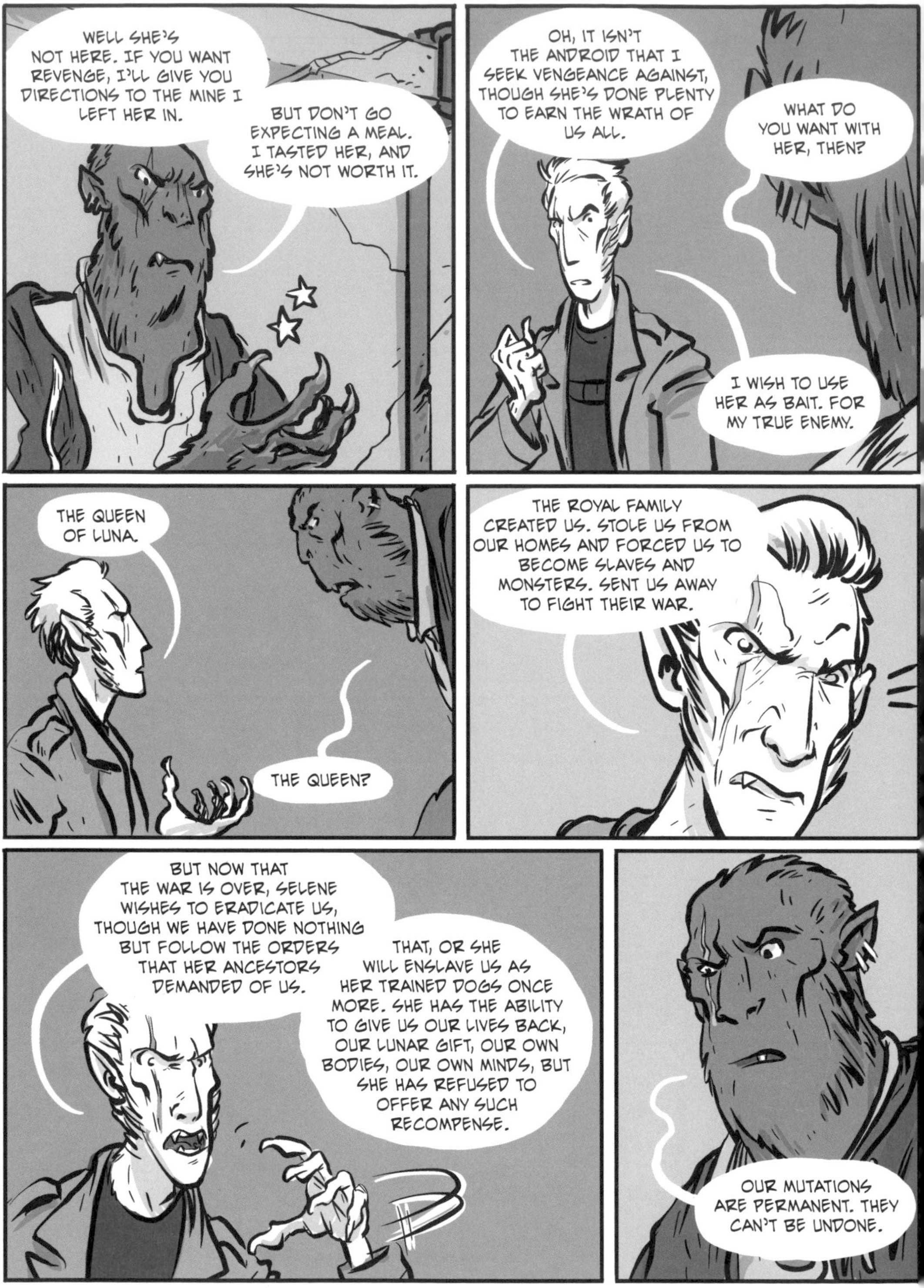
WELL SHE'S NOT HERE. IF YOU WANT REVENGE, I'LL GIVE YOU DIRECTIONS TO THE MINE I LEFT HER IN.
BUT DON'T GO EXPECTING A MEAL. I TASTED HER, AND SHE'S NOT WORTH IT.
OH, IT ISN'T THE ANDROID THAT I SEEK VENGEANCE AGAINST, THOUGH SHE'S DONE PLENTY TO EARN THE WRATH OF US ALL.
WHAT DO YOU WANT WITH HER, THEN?
I WISH TO USE HER AS BAIT. FOR MY TRUE ENEMY.
THE QUEEN OF LUNA.
THE QUEEN?
THE ROYAL FAMILY CREATED US. STOLE US FROM OUR HOMES AND FORCED US TO BECOME SLAVES AND MONSTERS. SENT US AWAY TO FIGHT THEIR WAR.
BUT NOW THAT THE WAR IS OVER, SELENE WISHES TO ERADICATE US, THOUGH WE HAVE DONE NOTHING BUT FOLLOW THE ORDERS THAT HER ANCESTORS DEMANDED OF US.
THAT, OR SHE WILL ENSLAVE US AS HER TRAINED DOGS ONCE MORE. SHE HAS THE ABILITY TO GIVE US OUR LIVES BACK, OUR LUNAR GIFT, OUR OWN BODIES, OUR OWN MINDS, BUT SHE HAS REFUSED TO OFFER ANY SUCH RECOMPENSE.
OUR MUTATIONS ARE PERMANENT. THEY CAN'T BE UNDONE.

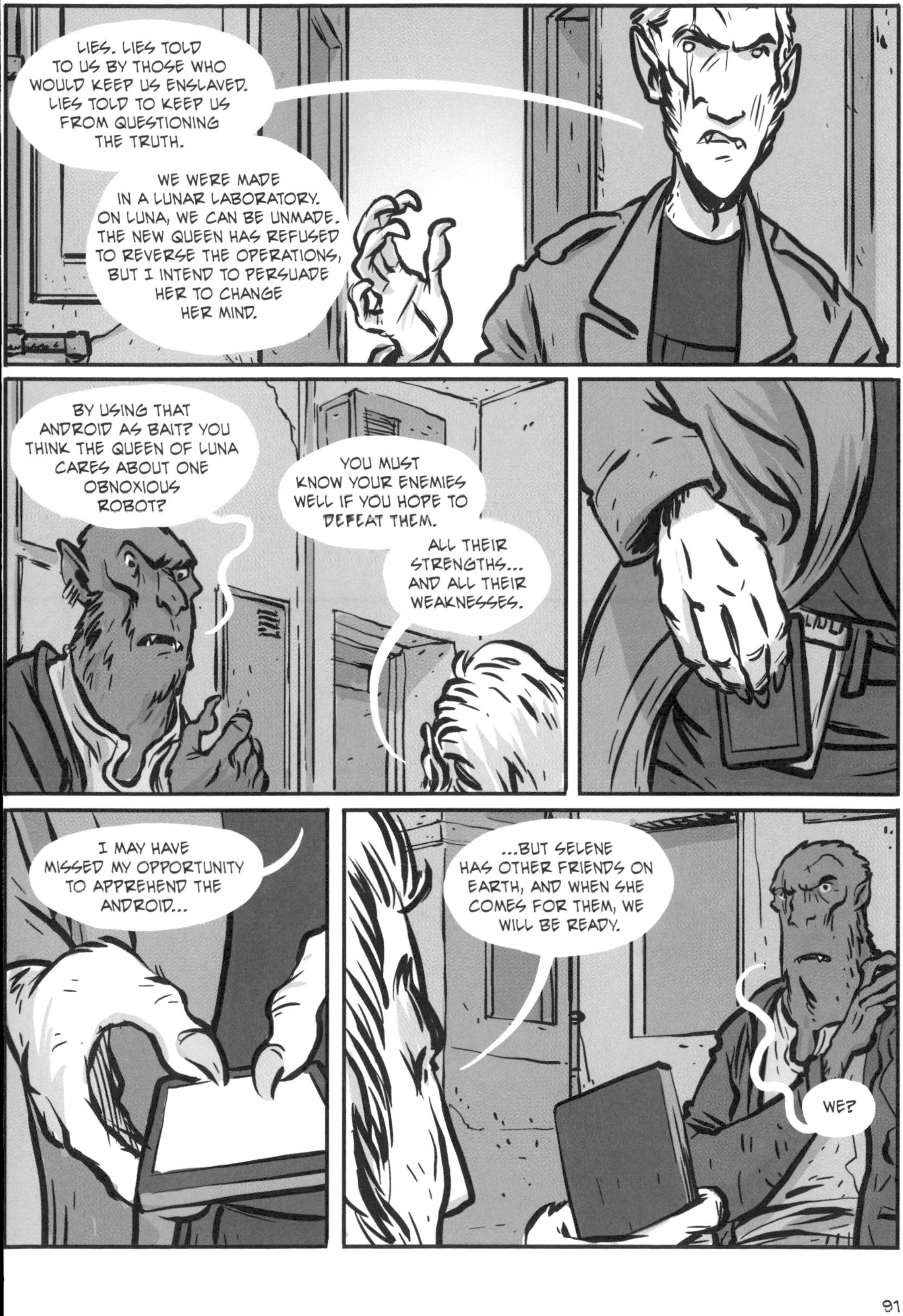
LIES. LIES TOLD TO US BY THOSE WHO WOULD KEEP US ENSLAVED. LIES TOLD TO KEEP US FROM QUESTIONING THE TRUTH.
WE WERE MADE IN A LUNAR LABORATORY. ON LUNA, WE CAN BE UNMADE. THE NEW QUEEN HAS REFUSED TO REVERSE THE OPERATIONS, BUT I INTEND TO PERSUADE HER TO CHANGE HER MIND.
BY USING THAT ANDROID AS BAIT? YOU THINK THE QUEEN OF LUNA CARES ABOUT ONE OBNOXIOUS ROBOT?
YOU MUST KNOW YOUR ENEMIES WELL IF YOU HOPE TO DEFEAT THEM.
ALL THEIR STRENGTHS... AND ALL THEIR WEAKNESSES.
I MAY HAVE MISSED MY OPPORTUNITY TO APPREHEND THE ANDROID...
...BUT SELENE HAS OTHER FRIENDS ON EARTH, AND WHEN SHE COMES FOR THEM, WE WILL BE READY.
WE?

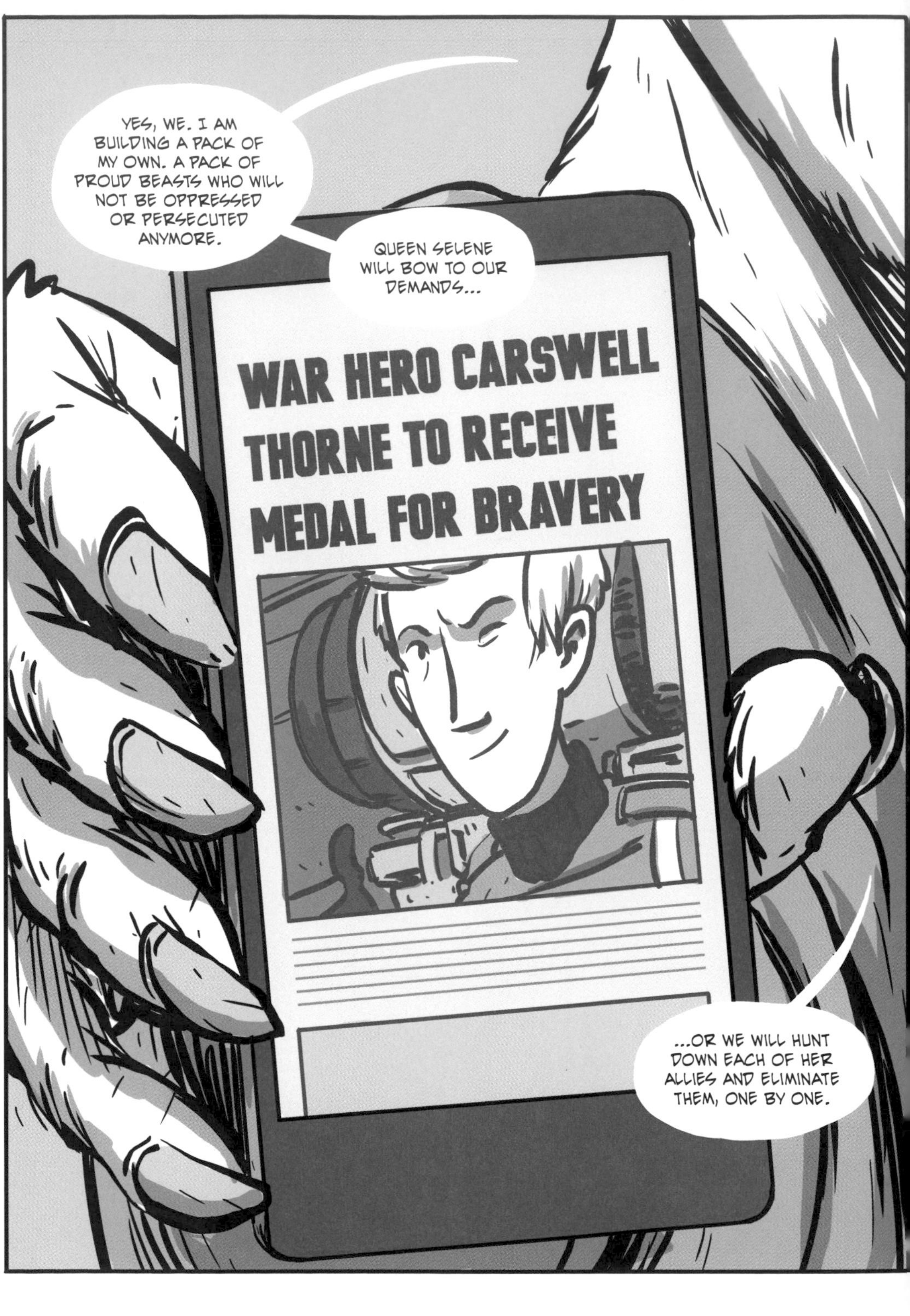
YES, WE. I AM BUILDING A PACK OF MY OWN. A PACK OF PROUD BEASTS WHO WILL NOT BE OPPRESSED OR PERSECUTED ANYMORE.
QUEEN SELENE WILL BOW TO OUR DEMANDS...
WAR HERO CARSWELL THORNE TO RECEIVE MEDAL FOR BRAVERY
...OR WE WILL HUNT DOWN EACH OF HER ALLIES AND ELIMINATE THEM, ONE BY ONE.

CHAPTER IV

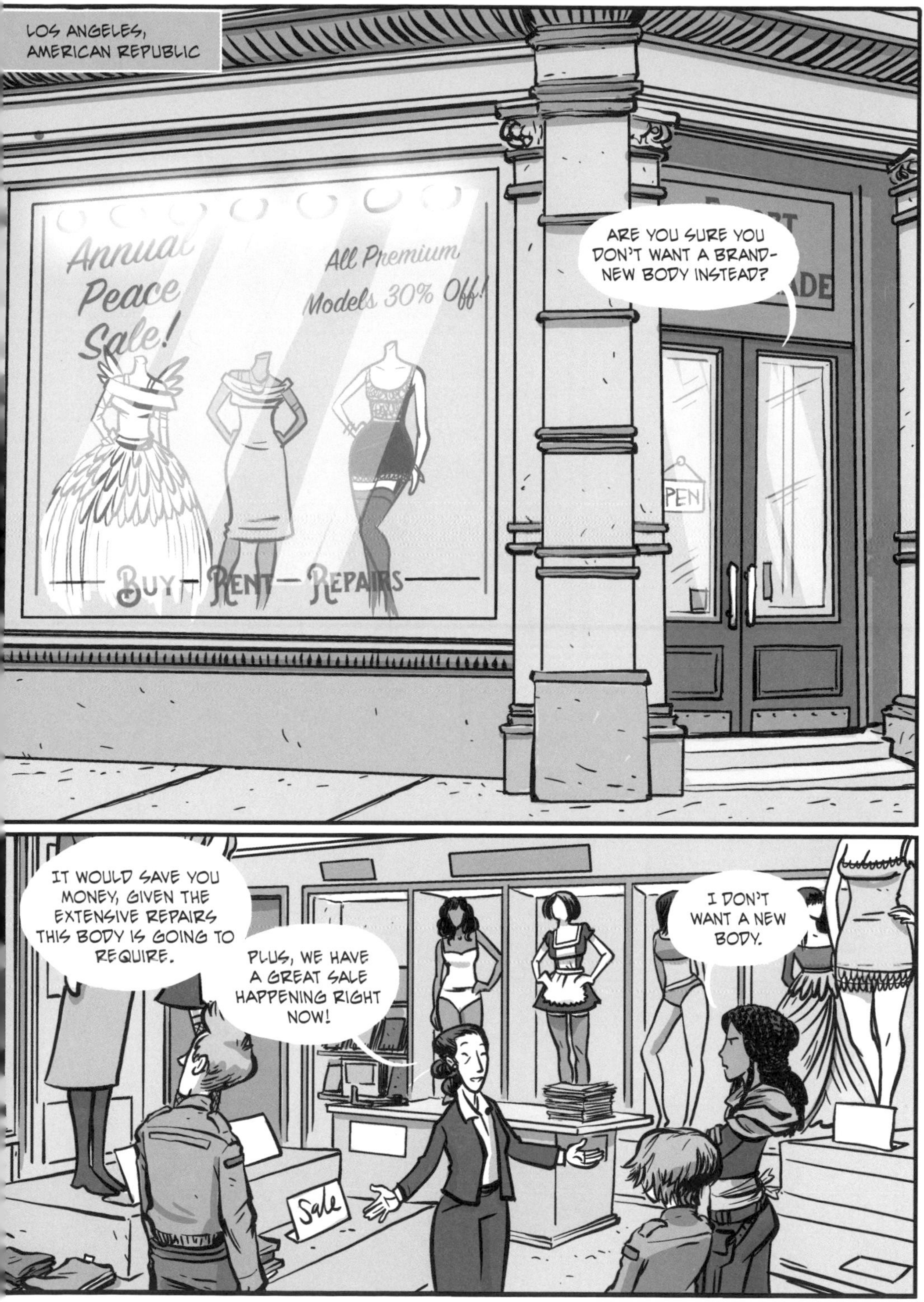
LOS ANGELES, AMERICAN REPUBLIC
Annual Peace Sale!
All Premium Models 30% Off!
Buy — Rent — Repairs
ARE YOU SURE YOU DON'T WANT A BRAND-NEW BODY INSTEAD?
IT WOULD SAVE YOU MONEY, GIVEN THE EXTENSIVE REPAIRS THIS BODY IS GOING TO REQUIRE.
PLUS, WE HAVE A GREAT SALE HAPPENING RIGHT NOW!
I DON'T WANT A NEW BODY.
Sale

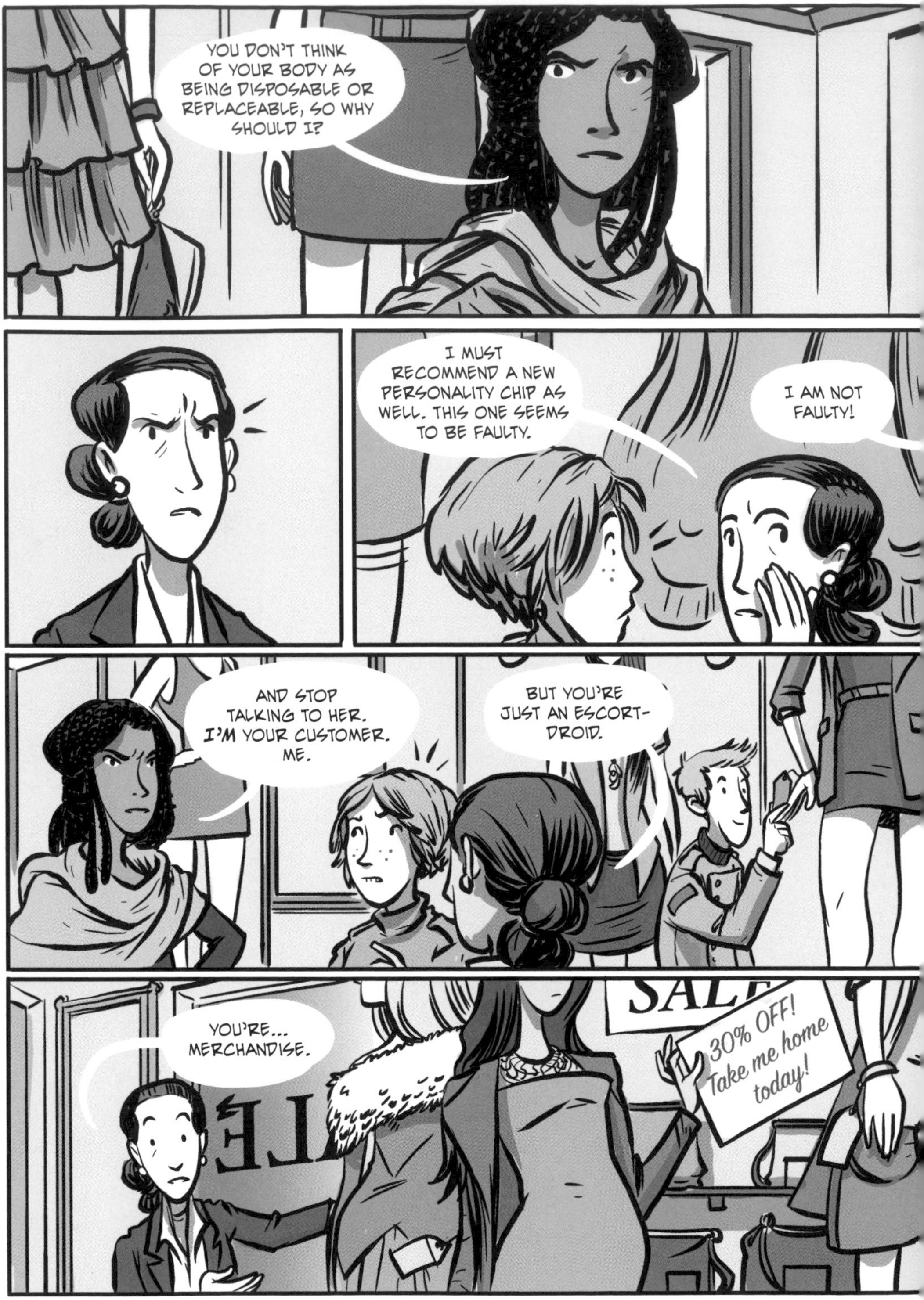
YOU DON'T THINK OF YOUR BODY AS BEING DISPOSABLE OR REPLACEABLE, SO WHY SHOULD I?
I MUST RECOMMEND A NEW PERSONALITY CHIP AS WELL. THIS ONE SEEMS TO BE FAULTY.
I AM NOT FAULTY!
AND STOP TALKING TO HER. I'M YOUR CUSTOMER. ME.
BUT YOU'RE JUST AN ESCORT-DROID.
YOU'RE... MERCHANDISE.
SALE
30% OFF! Take me home today!

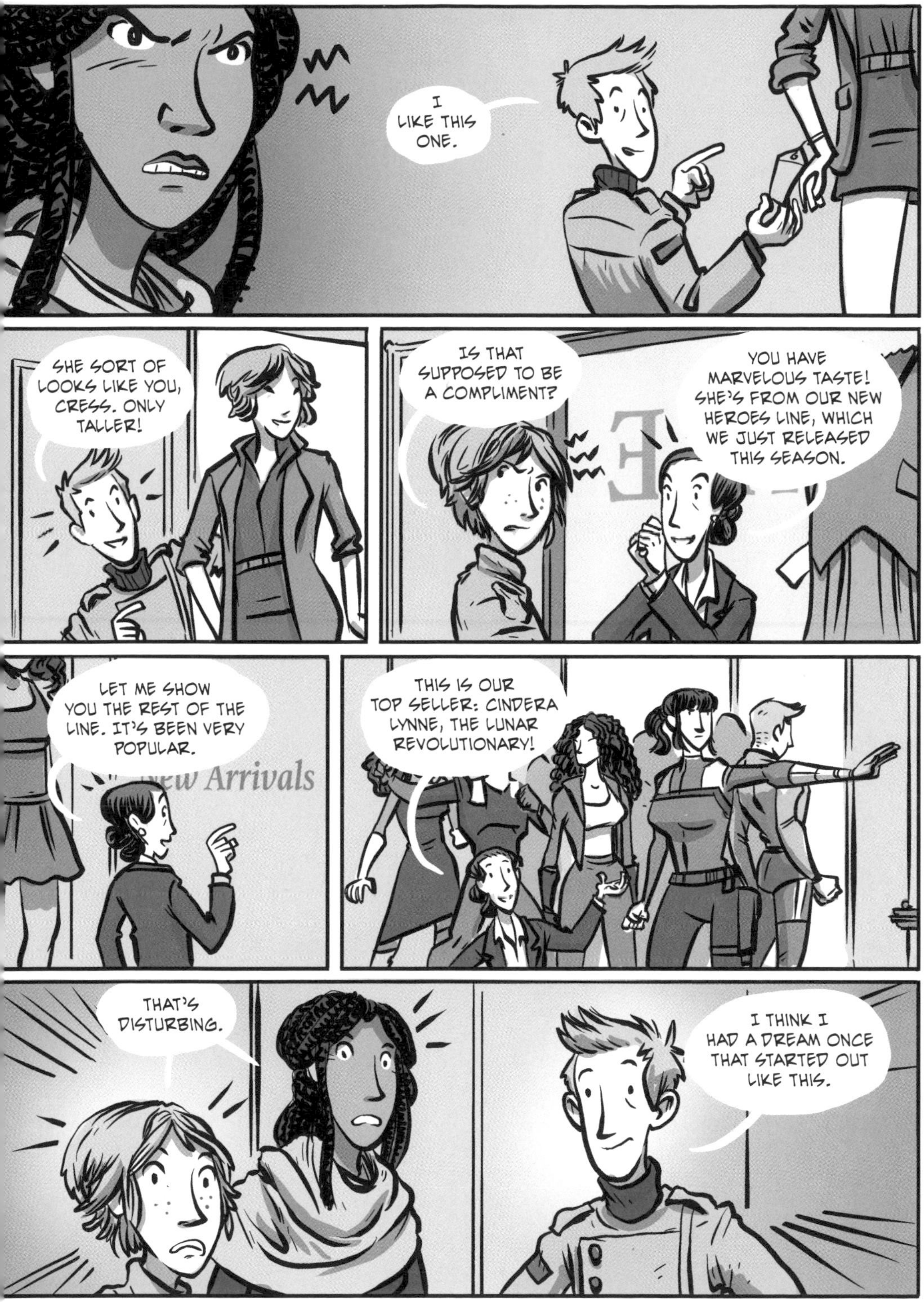
I LIKE THIS ONE.
SHE SORT OF LOOKS LIKE YOU, CRESS. ONLY TALLER!
IS THAT SUPPOSED TO BE A COMPLIMENT?
YOU HAVE MARVELOUS TASTE! SHE'S FROM OUR NEW HEROES LINE, WHICH WE JUST RELEASED THIS SEASON.
LET ME SHOW YOU THE REST OF THE LINE. IT'S BEEN VERY POPULAR.
New Arrivals
THIS IS OUR TOP SELLER: CINDERA LYNNE, THE LUNAR REVOLUTIONARY!
THAT'S DISTURBING.
I THINK I HAD A DREAM ONCE THAT STARTED OUT LIKE THIS.

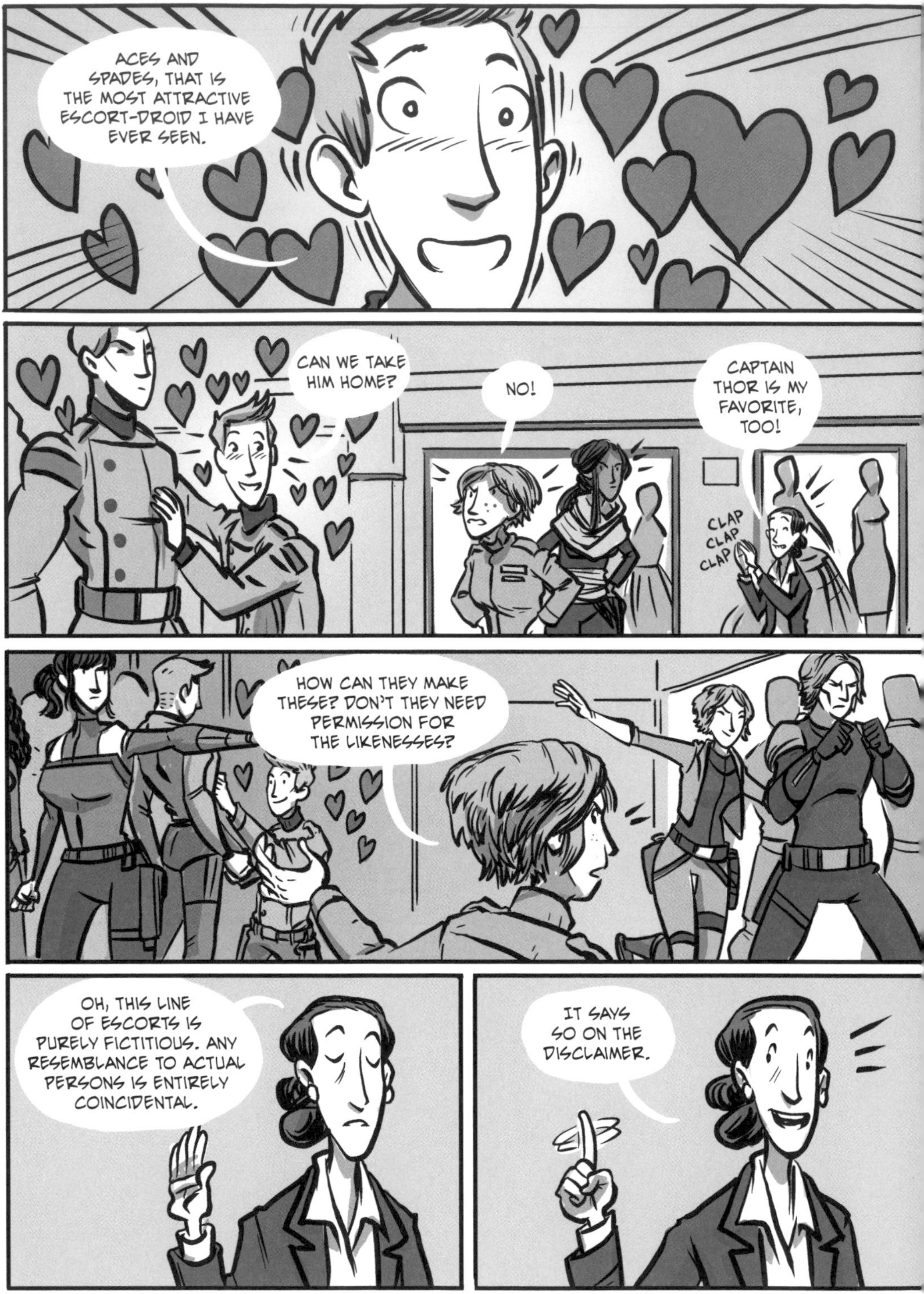
ACES AND SPADES, THAT IS THE MOST ATTRACTIVE ESCORT-DROID I HAVE EVER SEEN.
CAN WE TAKE HIM HOME?
NO!
CAPTAIN THOR IS MY FAVORITE, TOO!
CLAP CLAP CLAP
HOW CAN THEY MAKE THESE? DON'T THEY NEED PERMISSION FOR THE LIKENESSES?
OH, THIS LINE OF ESCORTS IS PURELY FICTITIOUS. ANY RESEMBLANCE TO ACTUAL PERSONS IS ENTIRELY COINCIDENTAL.
IT SAYS SO ON THE DISCLAIMER.

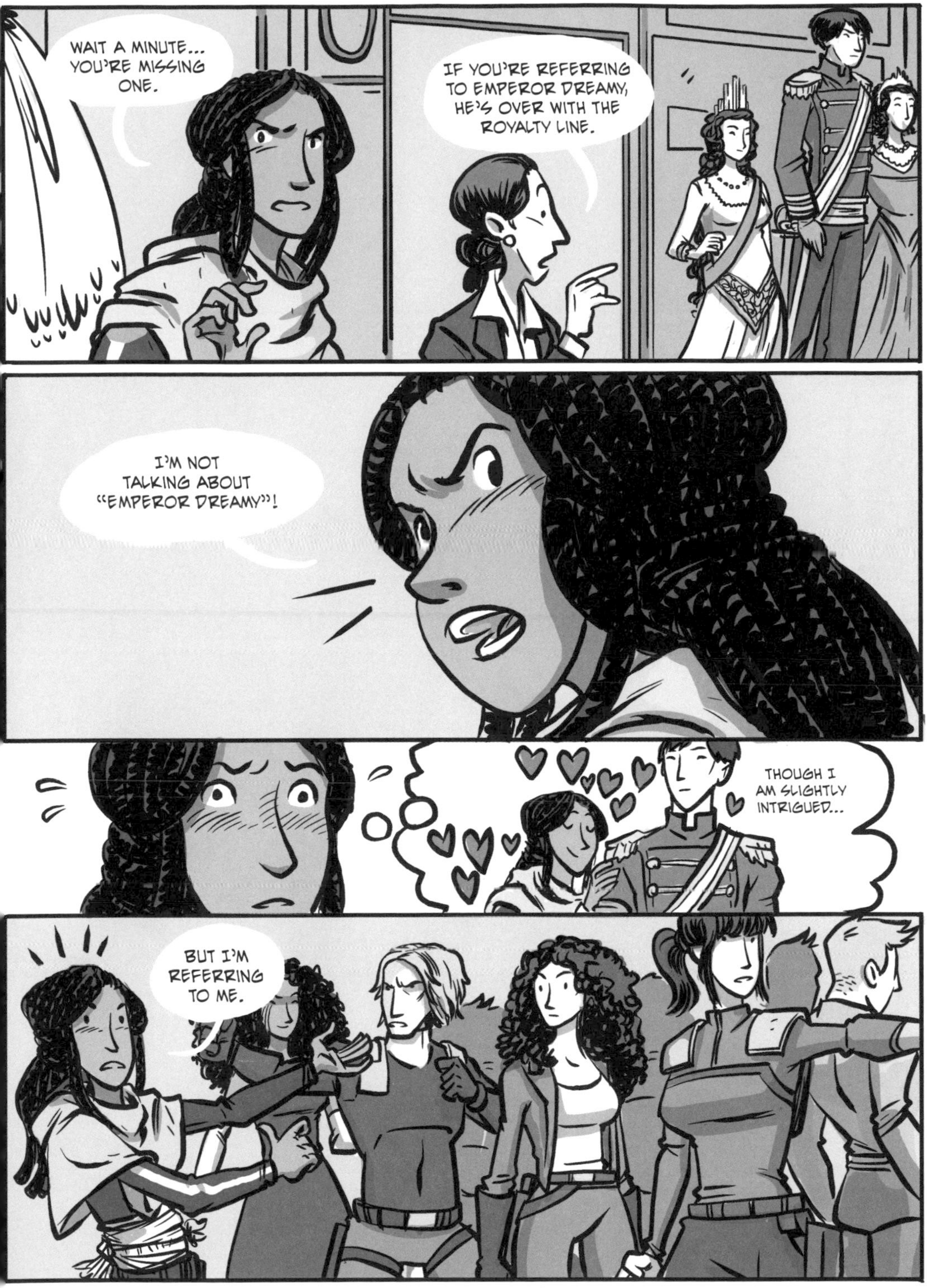
WAIT A MINUTE... YOU'RE MISSING ONE.
IF YOU'RE REFERRING TO EMPEROR DREAMY, HE'S OVER WITH THE ROYALTY LINE.
I'M NOT TALKING ABOUT "EMPEROR DREAMY"!
THOUGH I AM SLIGHTLY INTRIGUED...
BUT I'M REFERRING TO ME.

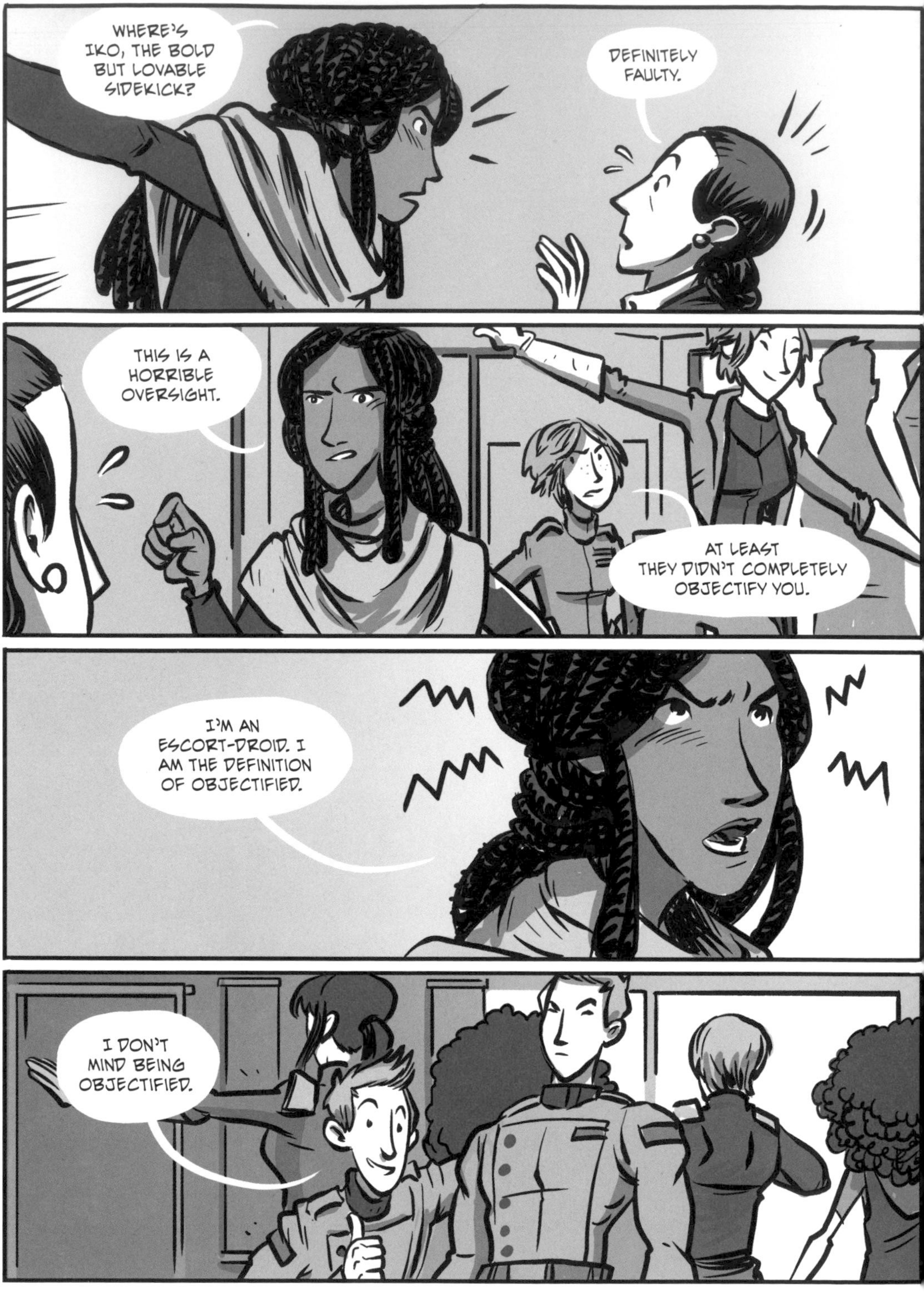
WHERE'S IKO, THE BOLD BUT LOVABLE SIDEKICK?
DEFINITELY FAULTY.
THIS IS A HORRIBLE OVERSIGHT.
AT LEAST THEY DIDN'T COMPLETELY OBJECTIFY YOU.
I'M AN ESCORT-DROID. I AM THE DEFINITION OF OBJECTIFIED.
I DON'T MIND BEING OBJECTIFIED.

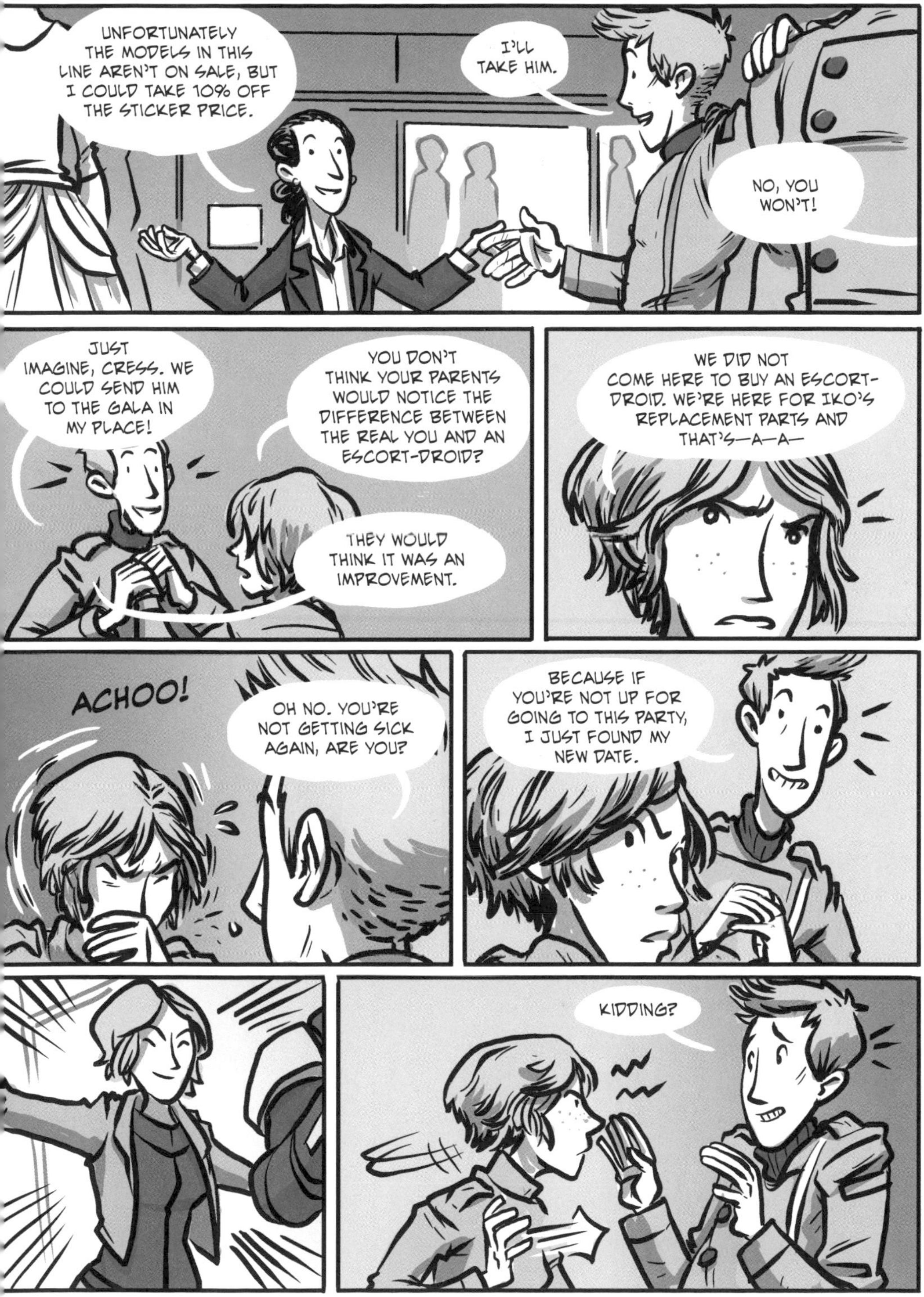
UNFORTUNATELY THE MODELS IN THIS LINE AREN'T ON SALE, BUT I COULD TAKE 10% OFF THE STICKER PRICE.
I'LL TAKE HIM.
NO, YOU WON'T!
JUST IMAGINE, CRESS. WE COULD SEND HIM TO THE GALA IN MY PLACE!
YOU DON'T THINK YOUR PARENTS WOULD NOTICE THE DIFFERENCE BETWEEN THE REAL YOU AND AN ESCORT-DROID?
THEY WOULD THINK IT WAS AN IMPROVEMENT.
WE DID NOT COME HERE TO BUY AN ESCORT-DROID. WE'RE HERE FOR IKO'S REPLACEMENT PARTS AND THAT'S—A—A—
ACHOO!
OH NO. YOU'RE NOT GETTING SICK AGAIN, ARE YOU?
BECAUSE IF YOU'RE NOT UP FOR GOING TO THIS PARTY, I JUST FOUND MY NEW DATE.
KIDDING?

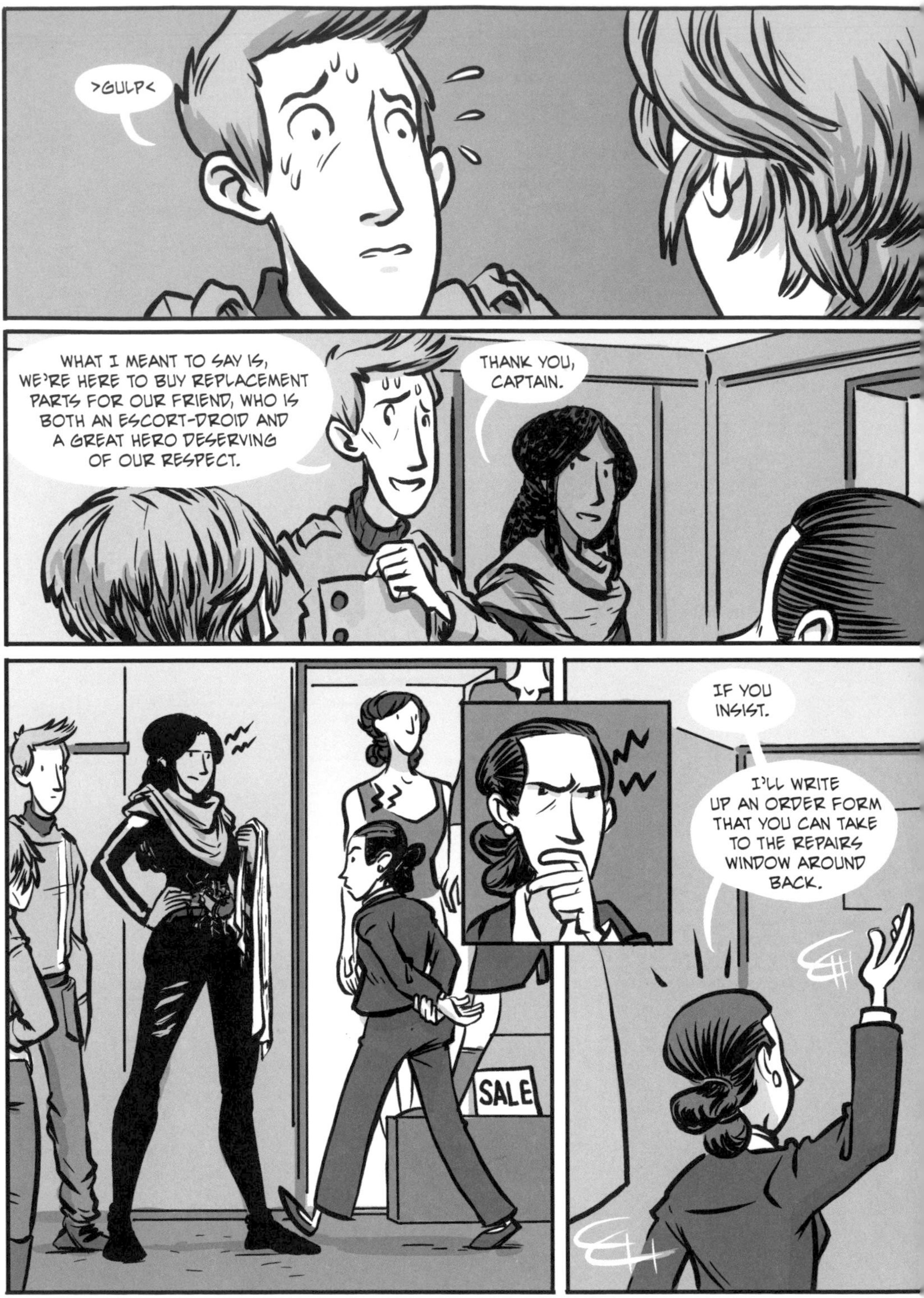
>GULP<
WHAT I MEANT TO SAY IS, WE'RE HERE TO BUY REPLACEMENT PARTS FOR OUR FRIEND, WHO IS BOTH AN ESCORT-DROID AND A GREAT HERO DESERVING OF OUR RESPECT.
THANK YOU, CAPTAIN.
SALE
IF YOU INSIST.
I'LL WRITE UP AN ORDER FORM THAT YOU CAN TAKE TO THE REPAIRS WINDOW AROUND BACK.

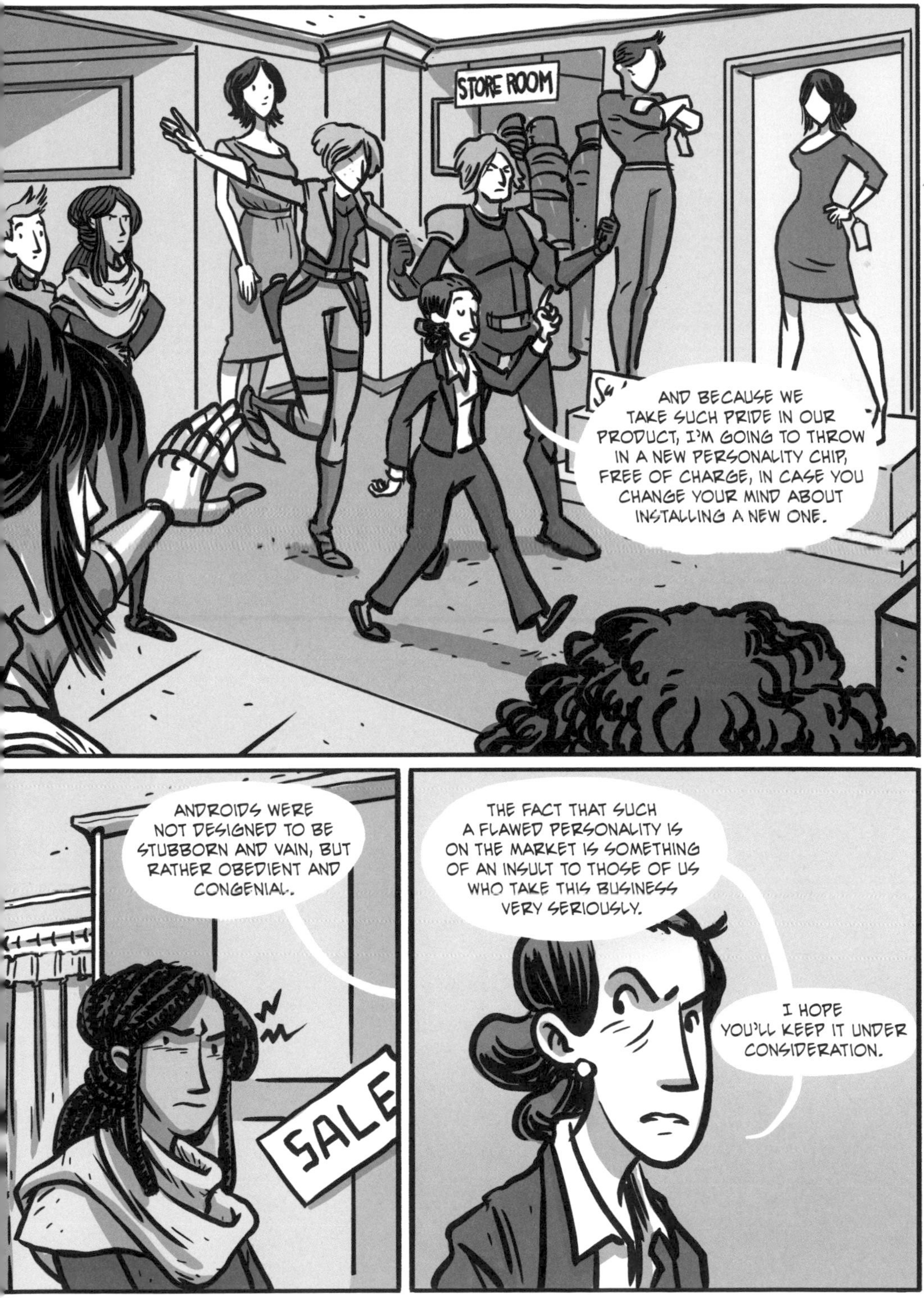
STORE ROOM
AND BECAUSE WE TAKE SUCH PRIDE IN OUR PRODUCT, I'M GOING TO THROW IN A NEW PERSONALITY CHIP, FREE OF CHARGE, IN CASE YOU CHANGE YOUR MIND ABOUT INSTALLING A NEW ONE.
ANDROIDS WERE NOT DESIGNED TO BE STUBBORN AND VAIN, BUT RATHER OBEDIENT AND CONGENIAL.
SALE
THE FACT THAT SUCH A FLAWED PERSONALITY IS ON THE MARKET IS SOMETHING OF AN INSULT TO THOSE OF US WHO TAKE THIS BUSINESS VERY SERIOUSLY.
I HOPE YOU'LL KEEP IT UNDER CONSIDERATION.

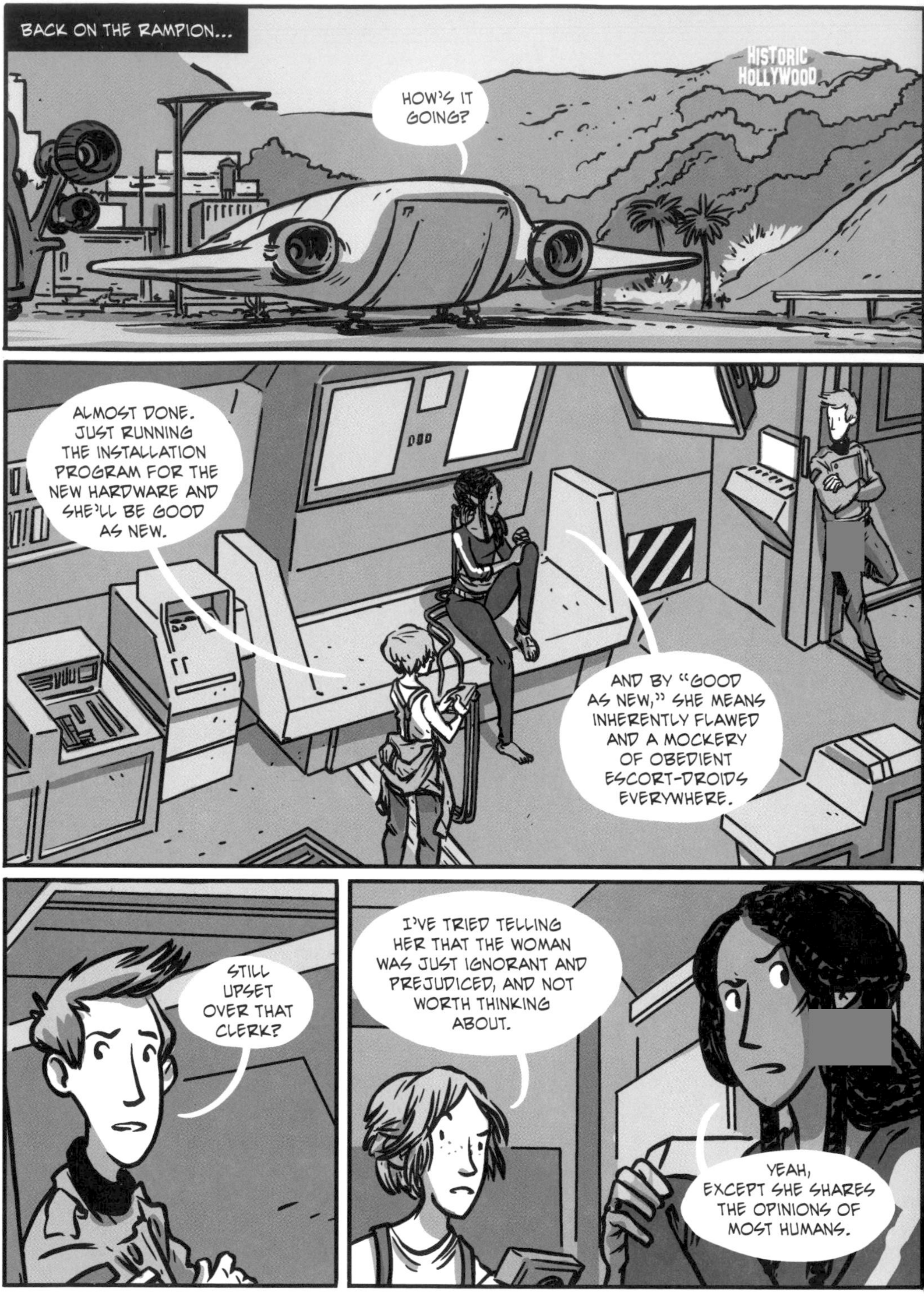
BACK ON THE RAMPION...
HISTORIC HOLLYWOOD
HOW'S IT GOING?
ALMOST DONE. JUST RUNNING THE INSTALLATION PROGRAM FOR THE NEW HARDWARE AND SHE'LL BE GOOD AS NEW.
AND BY "GOOD AS NEW," SHE MEANS INHERENTLY FLAWED AND A MOCKERY OF OBEDIENT ESCORT-DROIDS EVERYWHERE.
STILL UPSET OVER THAT CLERK?
I'VE TRIED TELLING HER THAT THE WOMAN WAS JUST IGNORANT AND PREJUDICED, AND NOT WORTH THINKING ABOUT.
YEAH, EXCEPT SHE SHARES THE OPINIONS OF MOST HUMANS.

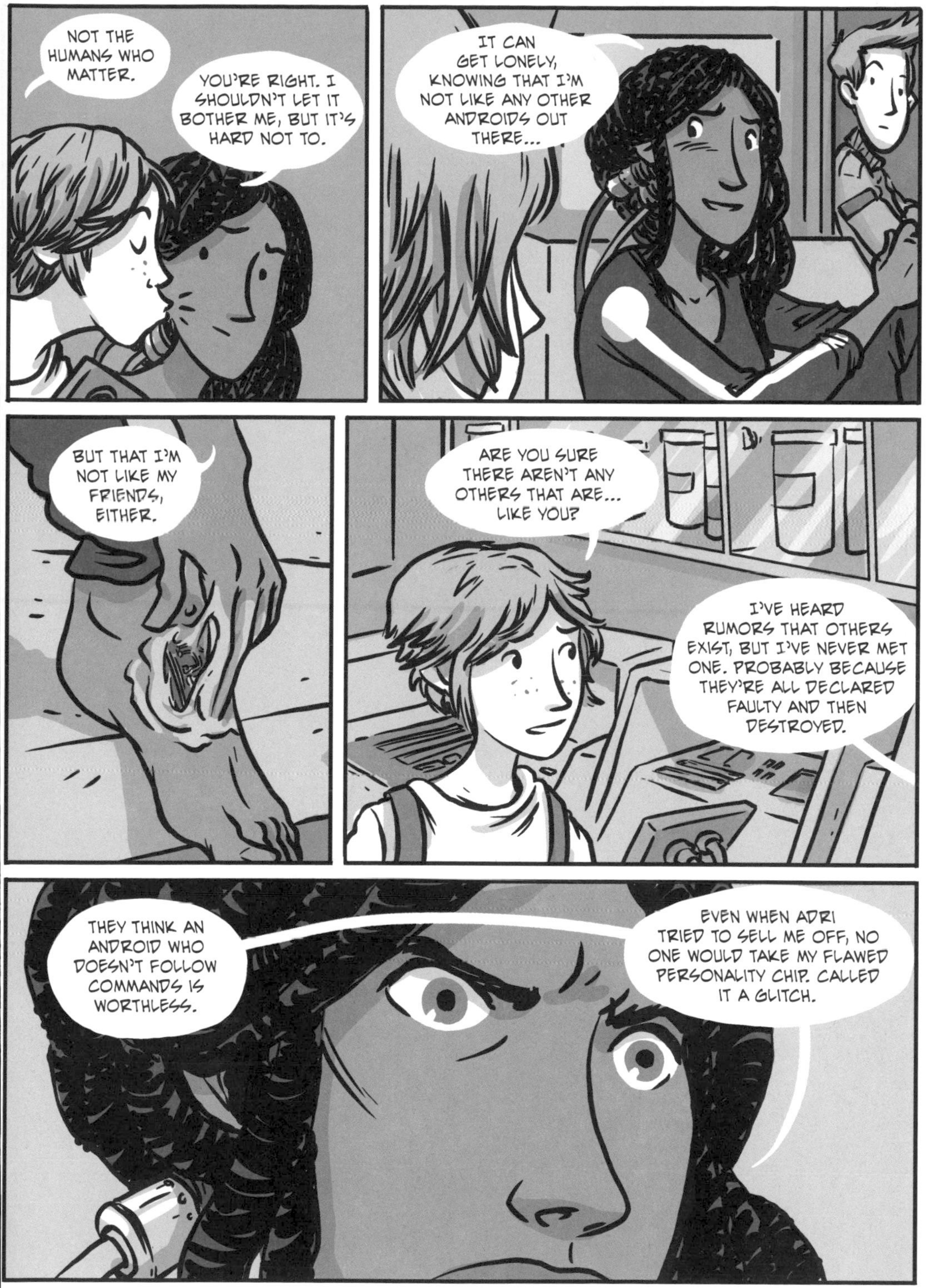
NOT THE HUMANS WHO MATTER.
YOU'RE RIGHT. I SHOULDN'T LET IT BOTHER ME, BUT IT'S HARD NOT TO.
IT CAN GET LONELY, KNOWING THAT I'M NOT LIKE ANY OTHER ANDROIDS OUT THERE...
BUT THAT I'M NOT LIKE MY FRIENDS, EITHER.
ARE YOU SURE THERE AREN'T ANY OTHERS THAT ARE... LIKE YOU?
I'VE HEARD RUMORS THAT OTHERS EXIST, BUT I'VE NEVER MET ONE. PROBABLY BECAUSE THEY'RE ALL DECLARED FAULTY AND THEN DESTROYED.
THEY THINK AN ANDROID WHO DOESN'T FOLLOW COMMANDS IS WORTHLESS.
EVEN WHEN ADRI TRIED TO SELL ME OFF, NO ONE WOULD TAKE MY FLAWED PERSONALITY CHIP. CALLED IT A GLITCH.

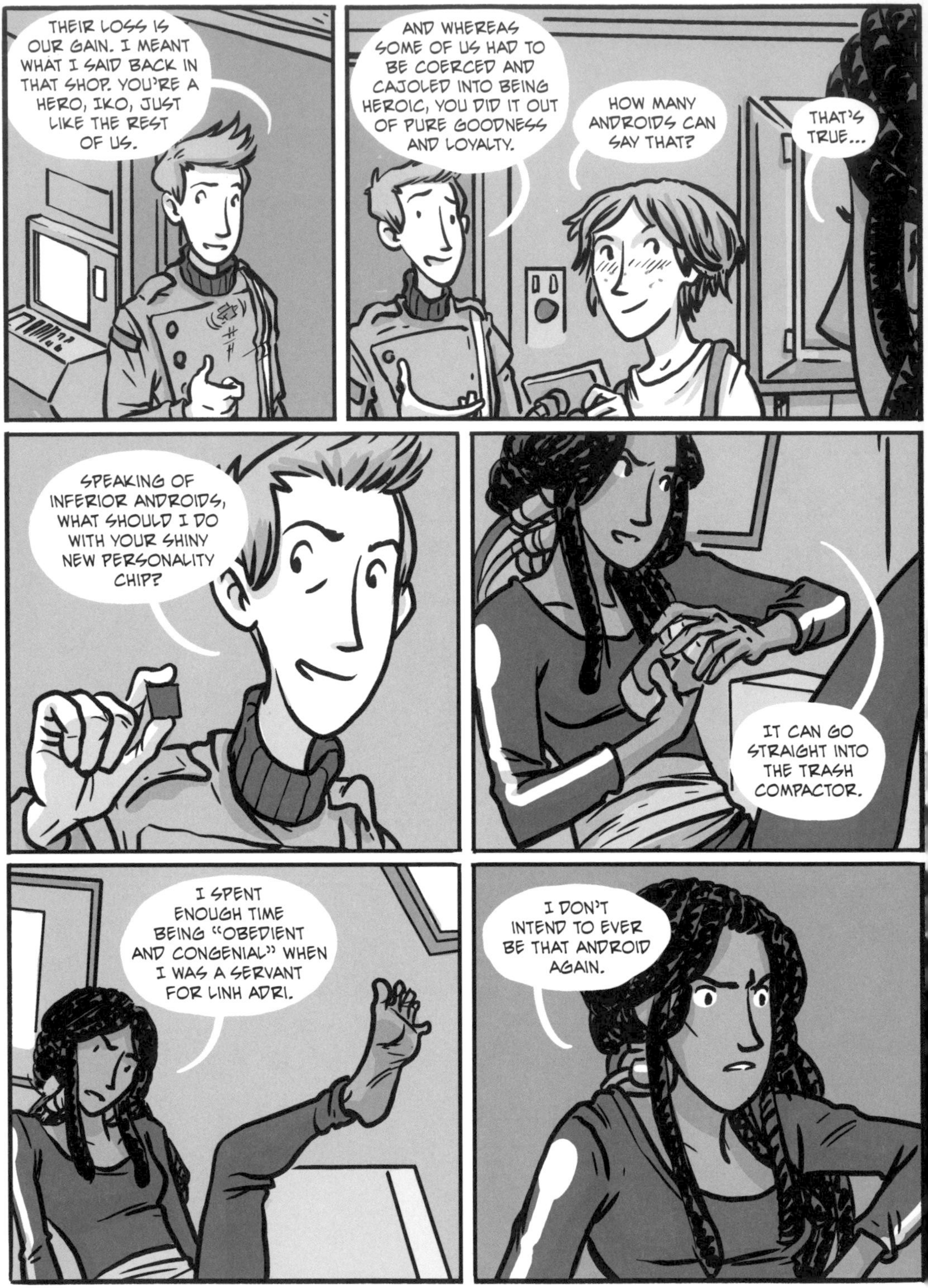
THEIR LOSS IS OUR GAIN. I MEANT WHAT I SAID BACK IN THAT SHOP. YOU'RE A HERO, IKO, JUST LIKE THE REST OF US.
AND WHEREAS SOME OF US HAD TO BE COERCED AND CAJOLED INTO BEING HEROIC, YOU DID IT OUT OF PURE GOODNESS AND LOYALTY.
HOW MANY ANDROIDS CAN SAY THAT?
THAT'S TRUE...
SPEAKING OF INFERIOR ANDROIDS, WHAT SHOULD I DO WITH YOUR SHINY NEW PERSONALITY CHIP?
IT CAN GO STRAIGHT INTO THE TRASH COMPACTOR.
I SPENT ENOUGH TIME BEING "OBEDIENT AND CONGENIAL" WHEN I WAS A SERVANT FOR LINH ADRI.
I DON'T INTEND TO EVER BE THAT ANDROID AGAIN.

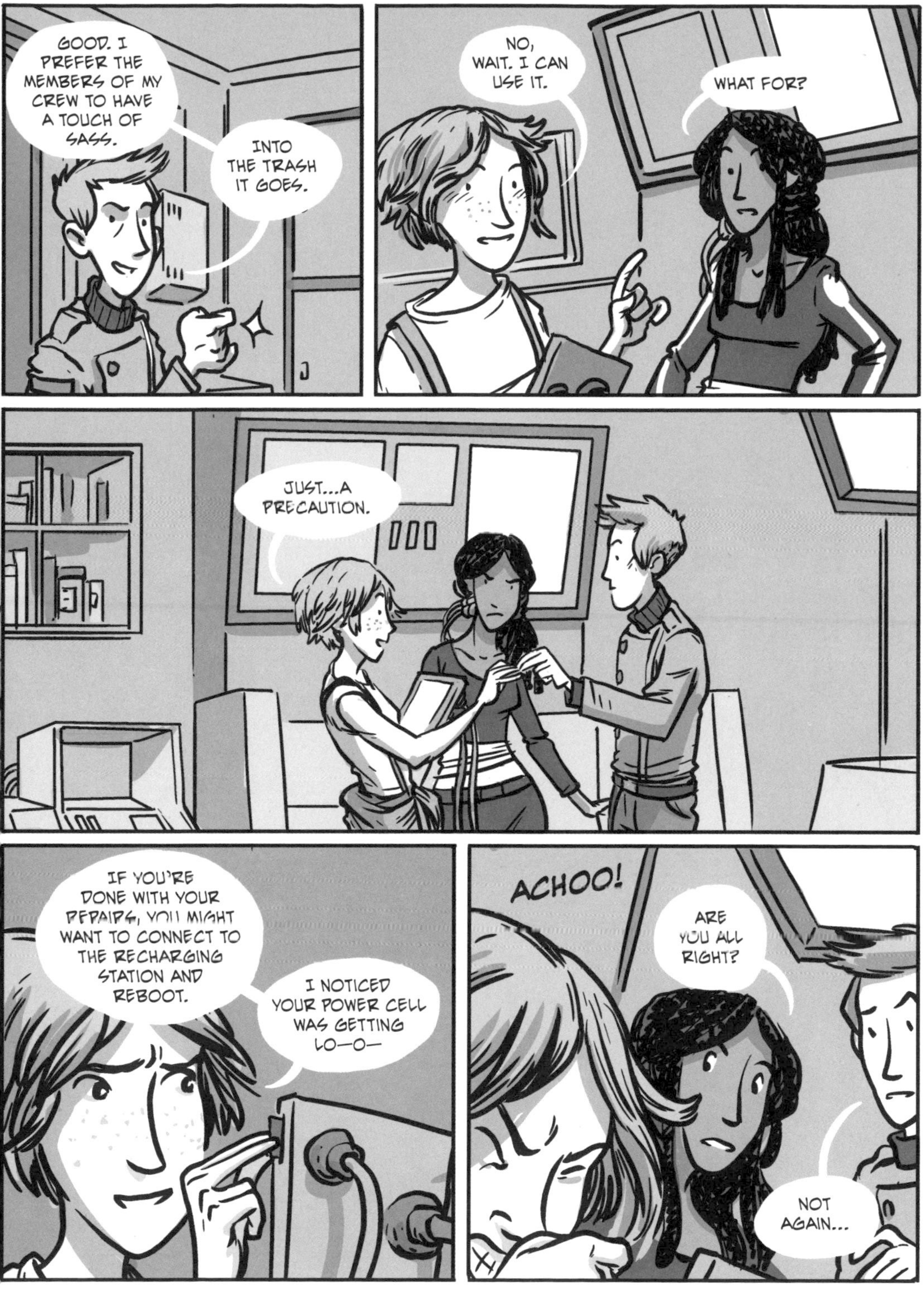
GOOD. I PREFER THE MEMBERS OF MY CREW TO HAVE A TOUCH OF SASS.
INTO THE TRASH IT GOES.
NO, WAIT. I CAN USE IT.
WHAT FOR?
JUST...A PRECAUTION.
IF YOU'RE DONE WITH YOUR REPAIRS, YOU MIGHT WANT TO CONNECT TO THE RECHARGING STATION AND REBOOT.
I NOTICED YOUR POWER CELL WAS GETTING LO—O—
ACHOO!
ARE YOU ALL RIGHT?
NOT AGAIN...

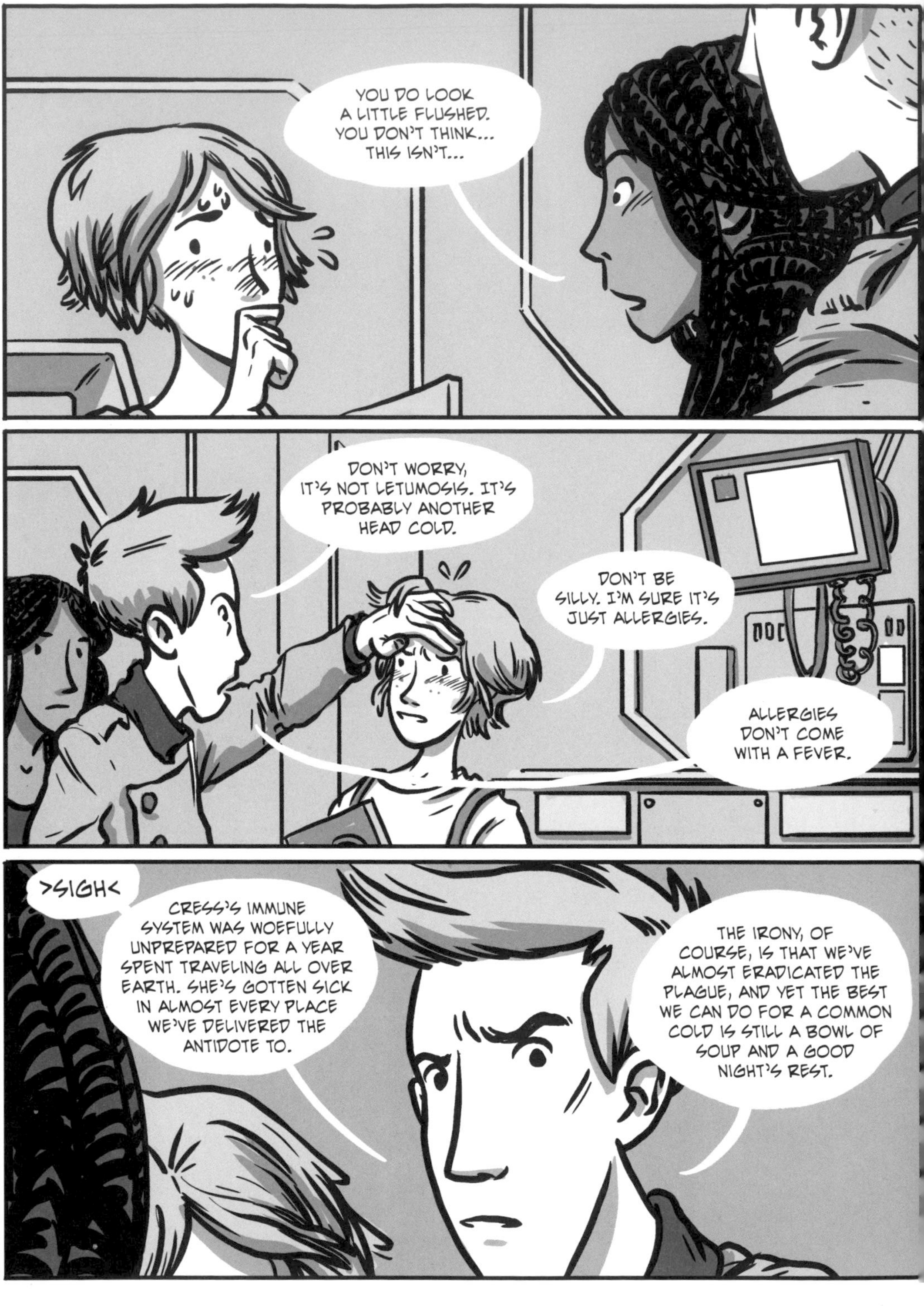
YOU DO LOOK A LITTLE FLUSHED. YOU DON'T THINK... THIS ISN'T...
DON'T WORRY, IT'S NOT LETUMOSIS. IT'S PROBABLY ANOTHER HEAD COLD.
DON'T BE SILLY. I'M SURE IT'S JUST ALLERGIES.
ALLERGIES DON'T COME WITH A FEVER.
>SIGH<
CRESS'S IMMUNE SYSTEM WAS WOEFULLY UNPREPARED FOR A YEAR SPENT TRAVELING ALL OVER EARTH. SHE'S GOTTEN SICK IN ALMOST EVERY PLACE WE'VE DELIVERED THE ANTIDOTE TO.
THE IRONY, OF COURSE, IS THAT WE'VE ALMOST ERADICATED THE PLAGUE, AND YET THE BEST WE CAN DO FOR A COMMON COLD IS STILL A BOWL OF SOUP AND A GOOD NIGHT'S REST.

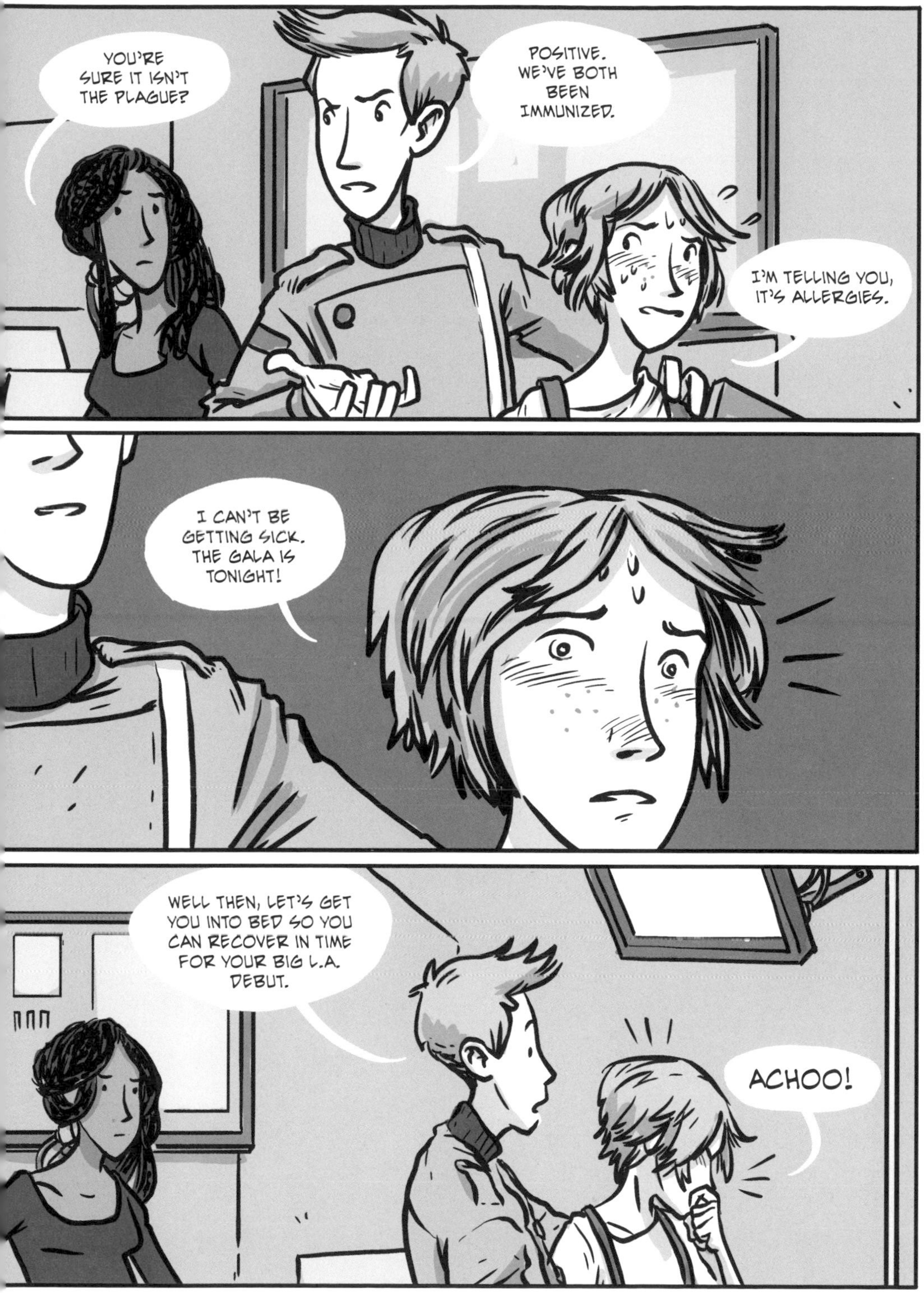
YOU'RE SURE IT ISN'T THE PLAGUE?
POSITIVE. WE'VE BOTH BEEN IMMUNIZED.
I'M TELLING YOU, IT'S ALLERGIES.
I CAN'T BE GETTING SICK. THE GALA IS TONIGHT!
WELL THEN, LET'S GET YOU INTO BED SO YOU CAN RECOVER IN TIME FOR YOUR BIG L.A. DEBUT.
ACHOO!

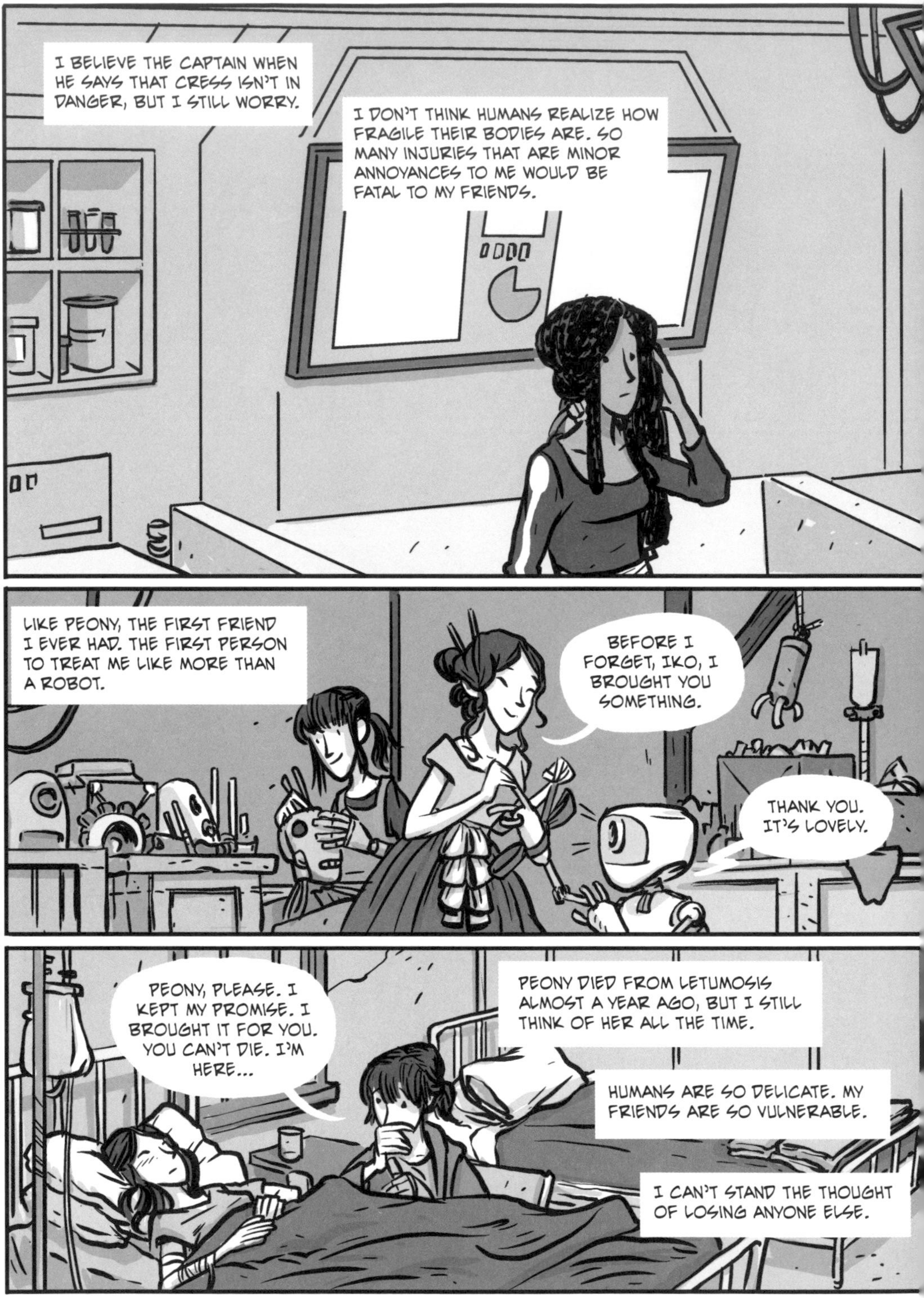
I BELIEVE THE CAPTAIN WHEN HE SAYS THAT CRESS ISN'T IN DANGER, BUT I STILL WORRY.
I DON'T THINK HUMANS REALIZE HOW FRAGILE THEIR BODIES ARE. SO MANY INJURIES THAT ARE MINOR ANNOYANCES TO ME WOULD BE FATAL TO MY FRIENDS.
LIKE PEONY, THE FIRST FRIEND I EVER HAD. THE FIRST PERSON TO TREAT ME LIKE MORE THAN A ROBOT.
BEFORE I FORGET, IKO, I BROUGHT YOU SOMETHING.
THANK YOU. IT'S LOVELY.
PEONY, PLEASE. I KEPT MY PROMISE. I BROUGHT IT FOR YOU. YOU CAN'T DIE. I'M HERE...
PEONY DIED FROM LETUMOSIS ALMOST A YEAR AGO, BUT I STILL THINK OF HER ALL THE TIME.
HUMANS ARE SO DELICATE. MY FRIENDS ARE SO VULNERABLE.
I CAN'T STAND THE THOUGHT OF LOSING ANYONE ELSE.

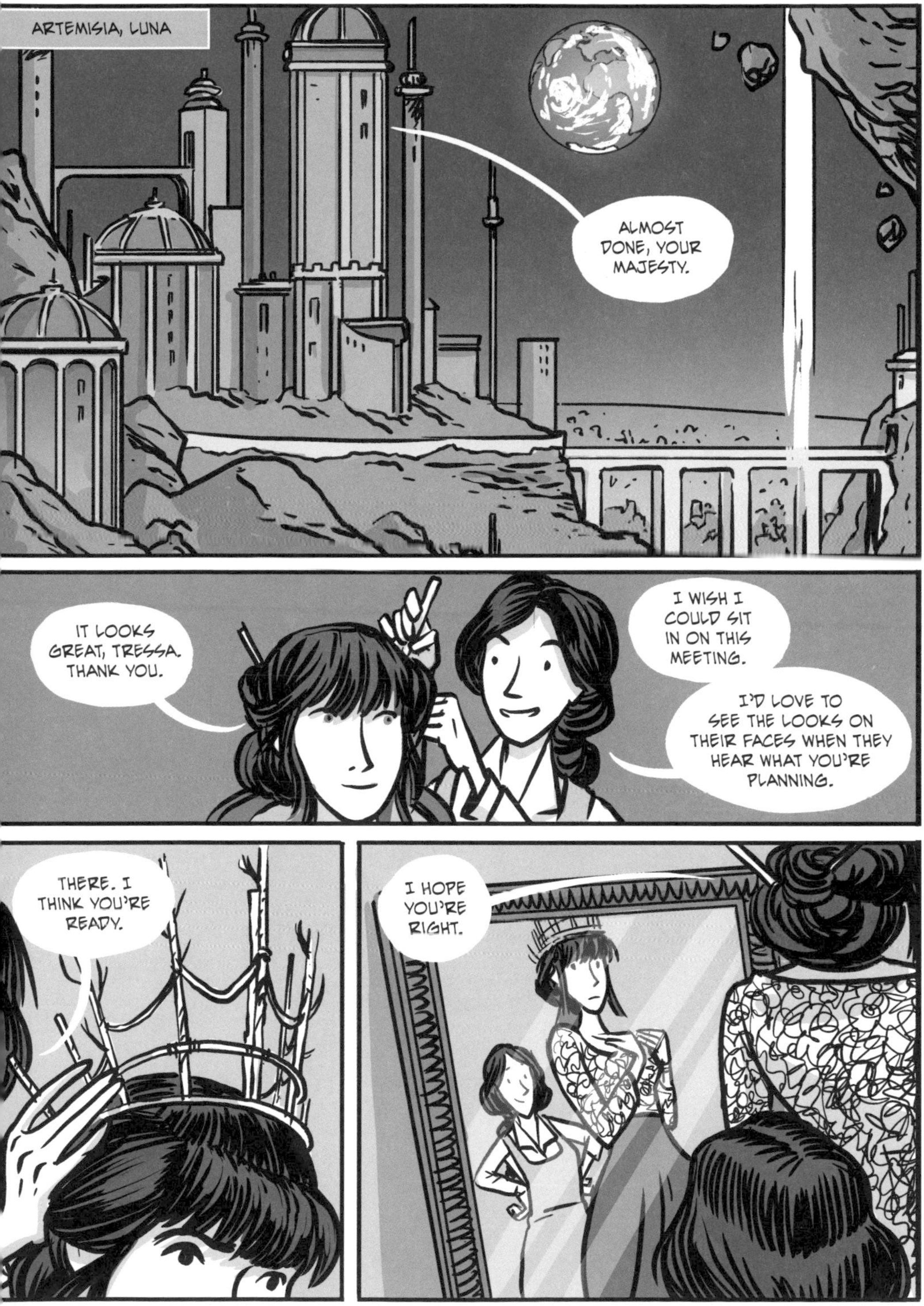
ARTEMISIA, LUNA
ALMOST DONE, YOUR MAJESTY.
IT LOOKS GREAT, TRESSA. THANK YOU.
I WISH I COULD SIT IN ON THIS MEETING.
I'D LOVE TO SEE THE LOOKS ON THEIR FACES WHEN THEY HEAR WHAT YOU'RE PLANNING.
THERE. I THINK YOU'RE READY.
I HOPE YOU'RE RIGHT.

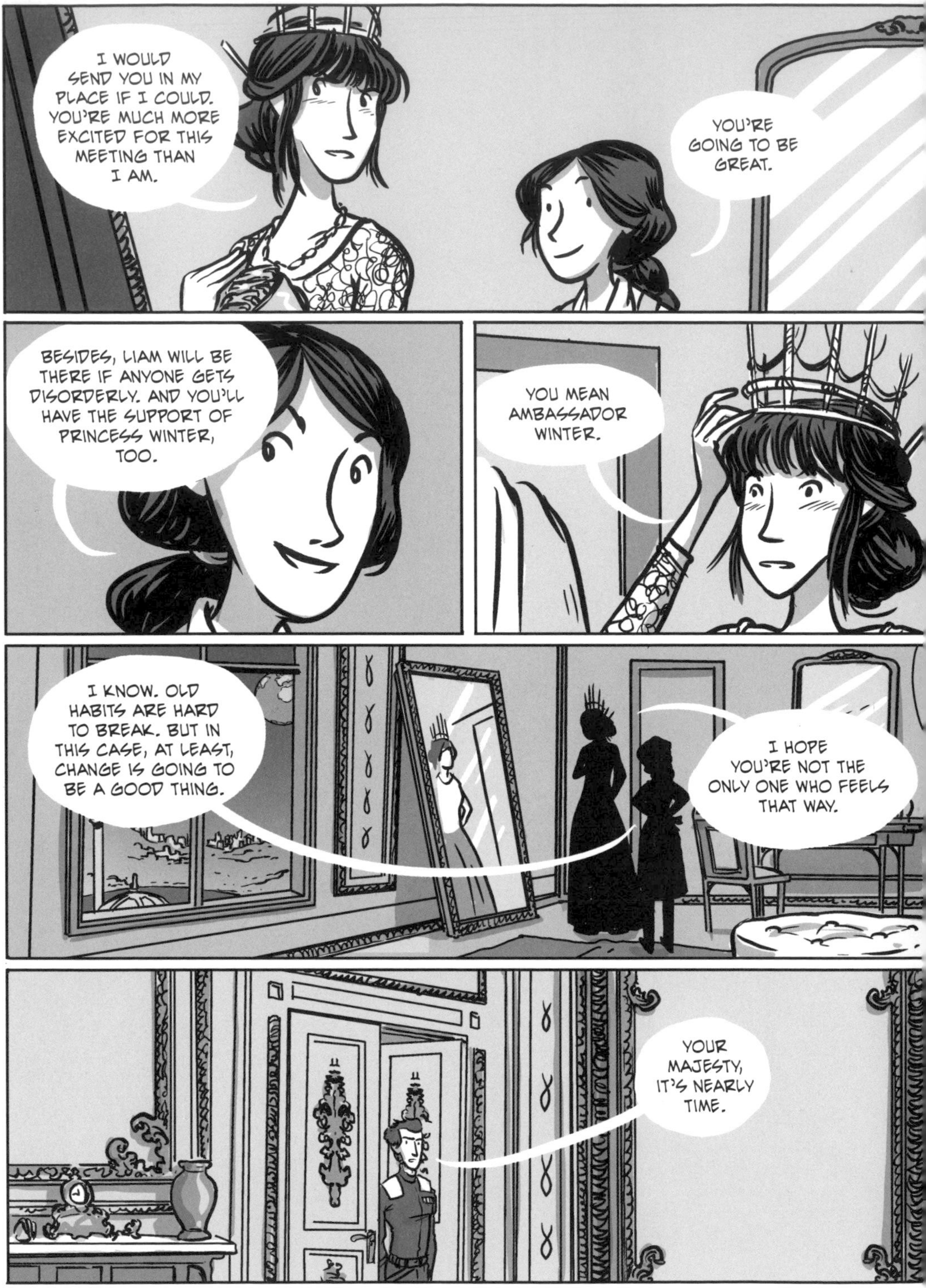
I WOULD SEND YOU IN MY PLACE IF I COULD. YOU'RE MUCH MORE EXCITED FOR THIS MEETING THAN I AM.
YOU'RE GOING TO BE GREAT.
BESIDES, LIAM WILL BE THERE IF ANYONE GETS DISORDERLY. AND YOU'LL HAVE THE SUPPORT OF PRINCESS WINTER, TOO.
YOU MEAN AMBASSADOR WINTER.
I KNOW. OLD HABITS ARE HARD TO BREAK. BUT IN THIS CASE, AT LEAST, CHANGE IS GOING TO BE A GOOD THING.
I HOPE YOU'RE NOT THE ONLY ONE WHO FEELS THAT WAY.
YOUR MAJESTY, IT'S NEARLY TIME.

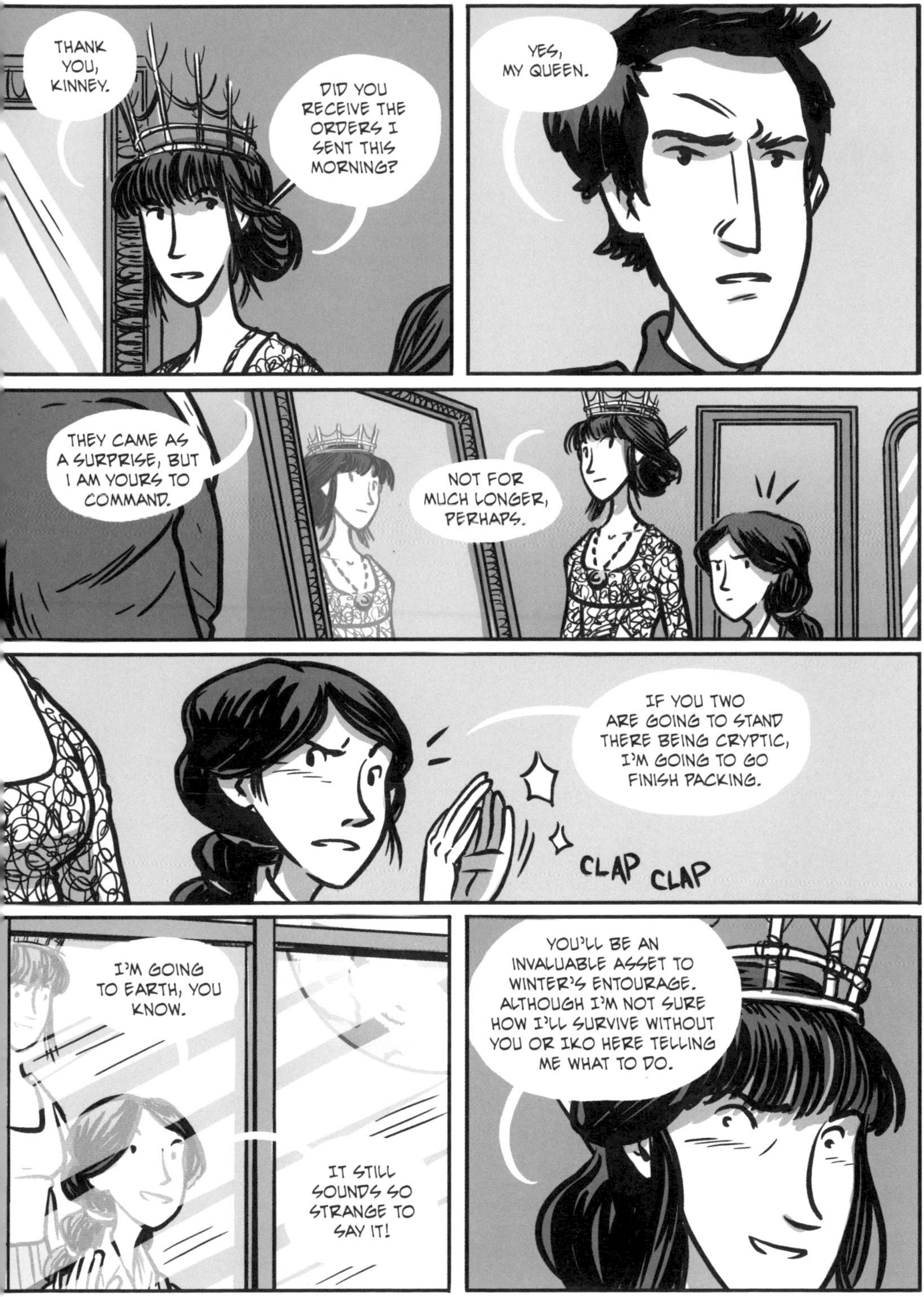
THANK YOU, KINNEY.
DID YOU RECEIVE THE ORDERS I SENT THIS MORNING?
YES, MY QUEEN.
THEY CAME AS A SURPRISE, BUT I AM YOURS TO COMMAND.
NOT FOR MUCH LONGER, PERHAPS.
IF YOU TWO ARE GOING TO STAND THERE BEING CRYPTIC, I'M GOING TO GO FINISH PACKING.
CLAP CLAP
I'M GOING TO EARTH, YOU KNOW.
IT STILL SOUNDS SO STRANGE TO SAY IT!
YOU'LL BE AN INVALUABLE ASSET TO WINTER'S ENTOURAGE. ALTHOUGH I'M NOT SURE HOW I'LL SURVIVE WITHOUT YOU OR IKO HERE TELLING ME WHAT TO DO.

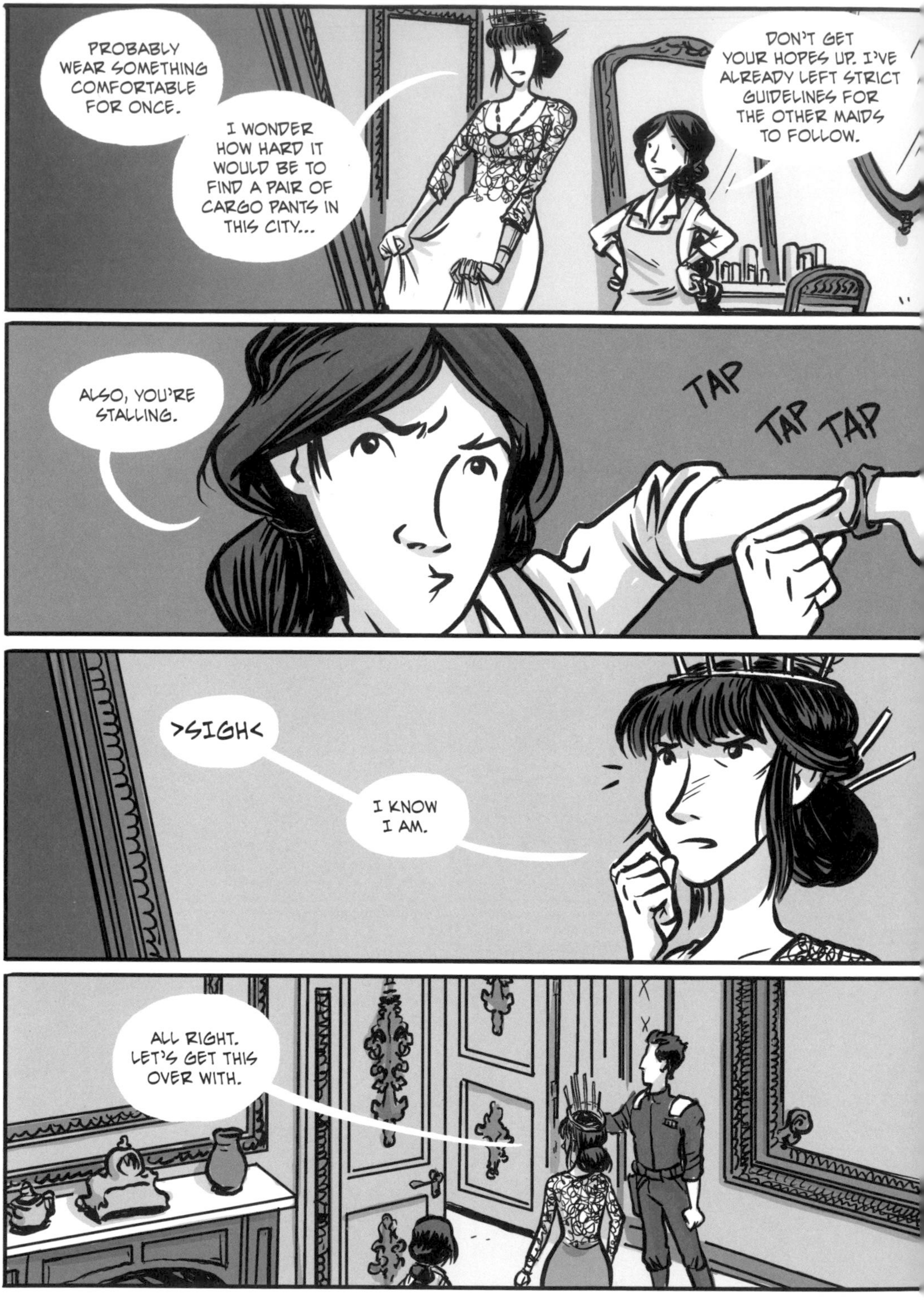
PROBABLY WEAR SOMETHING COMFORTABLE FOR ONCE.
I WONDER HOW HARD IT WOULD BE TO FIND A PAIR OF CARGO PANTS IN THIS CITY...
DON'T GET YOUR HOPES UP. I'VE ALREADY LEFT STRICT GUIDELINES FOR THE OTHER MAIDS TO FOLLOW.
ALSO, YOU'RE STALLING.
TAP TAP TAP
>SIGH<
I KNOW I AM.
ALL RIGHT. LET'S GET THIS OVER WITH.

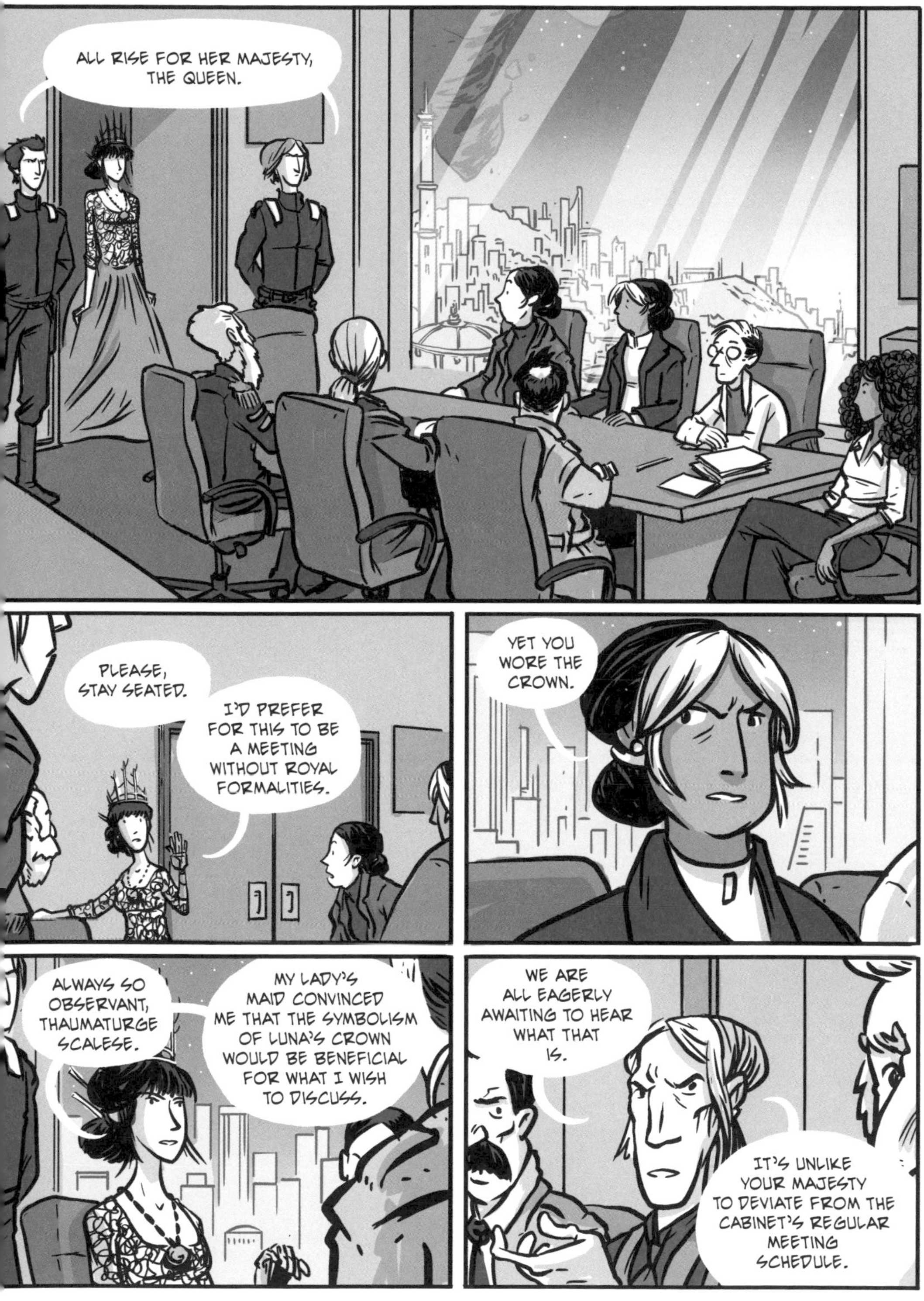
ALL RISE FOR HER MAJESTY, THE QUEEN.
PLEASE, STAY SEATED.
I'D PREFER FOR THIS TO BE A MEETING WITHOUT ROYAL FORMALITIES.
YET YOU WORE THE CROWN.
ALWAYS SO OBSERVANT, THAUMATURGE SCALESE.
MY LADY'S MAID CONVINCED ME THAT THE SYMBOLISM OF LUNA'S CROWN WOULD BE BENEFICIAL FOR WHAT I WISH TO DISCUSS.
WE ARE ALL EAGERLY AWAITING TO HEAR WHAT THAT IS.
IT'S UNLIKE YOUR MAJESTY TO DEVIATE FROM THE CABINET'S REGULAR MEETING SCHEDULE.

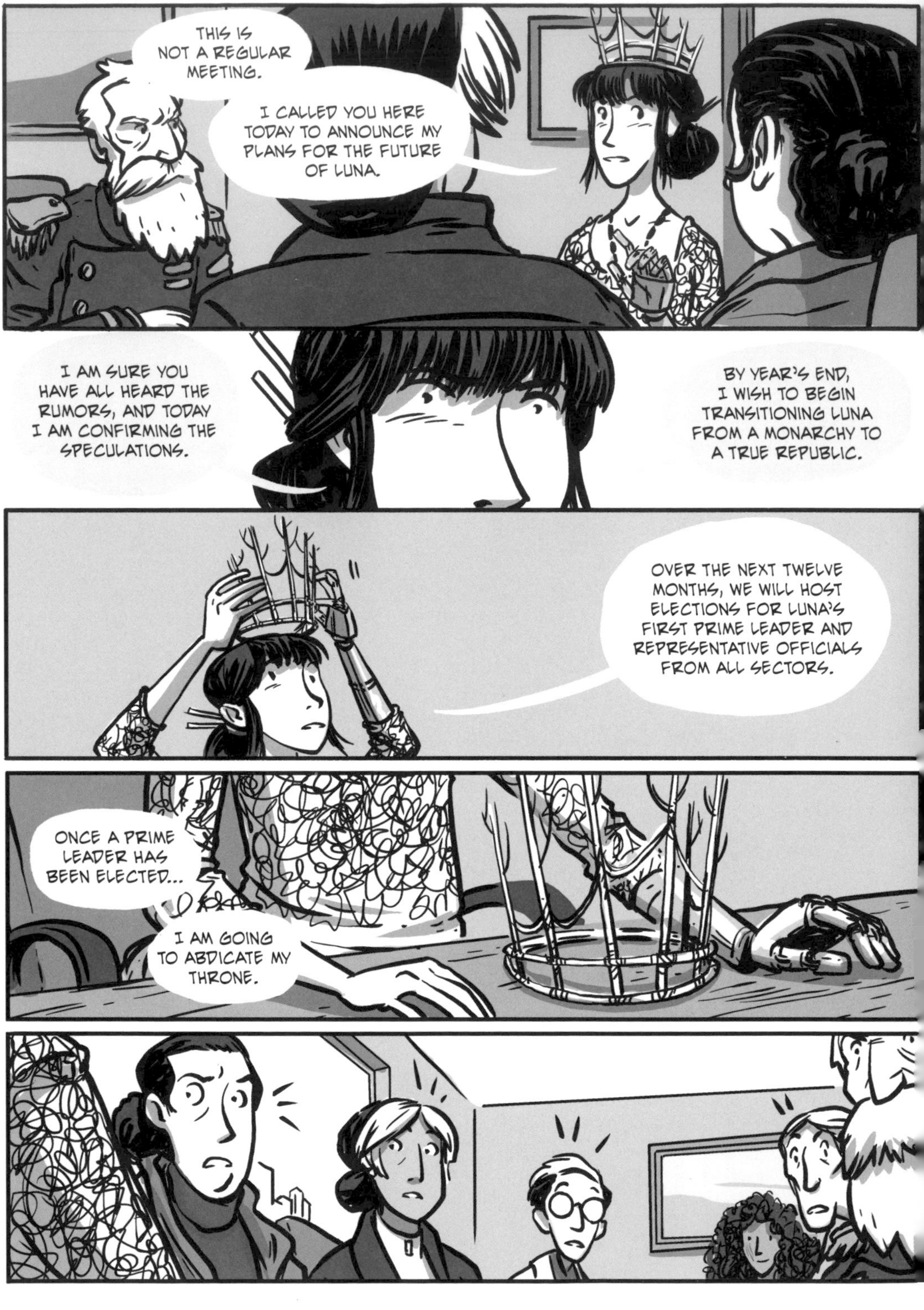
THIS IS NOT A REGULAR MEETING.
I CALLED YOU HERE TODAY TO ANNOUNCE MY PLANS FOR THE FUTURE OF LUNA.
I AM SURE YOU HAVE ALL HEARD THE RUMORS, AND TODAY I AM CONFIRMING THE SPECULATIONS.
BY YEAR'S END, I WISH TO BEGIN TRANSITIONING LUNA FROM A MONARCHY TO A TRUE REPUBLIC.
OVER THE NEXT TWELVE MONTHS, WE WILL HOST ELECTIONS FOR LUNA'S FIRST PRIME LEADER AND REPRESENTATIVE OFFICIALS FROM ALL SECTORS.
ONCE A PRIME LEADER HAS BEEN ELECTED...
I AM GOING TO ABDICATE MY THRONE.

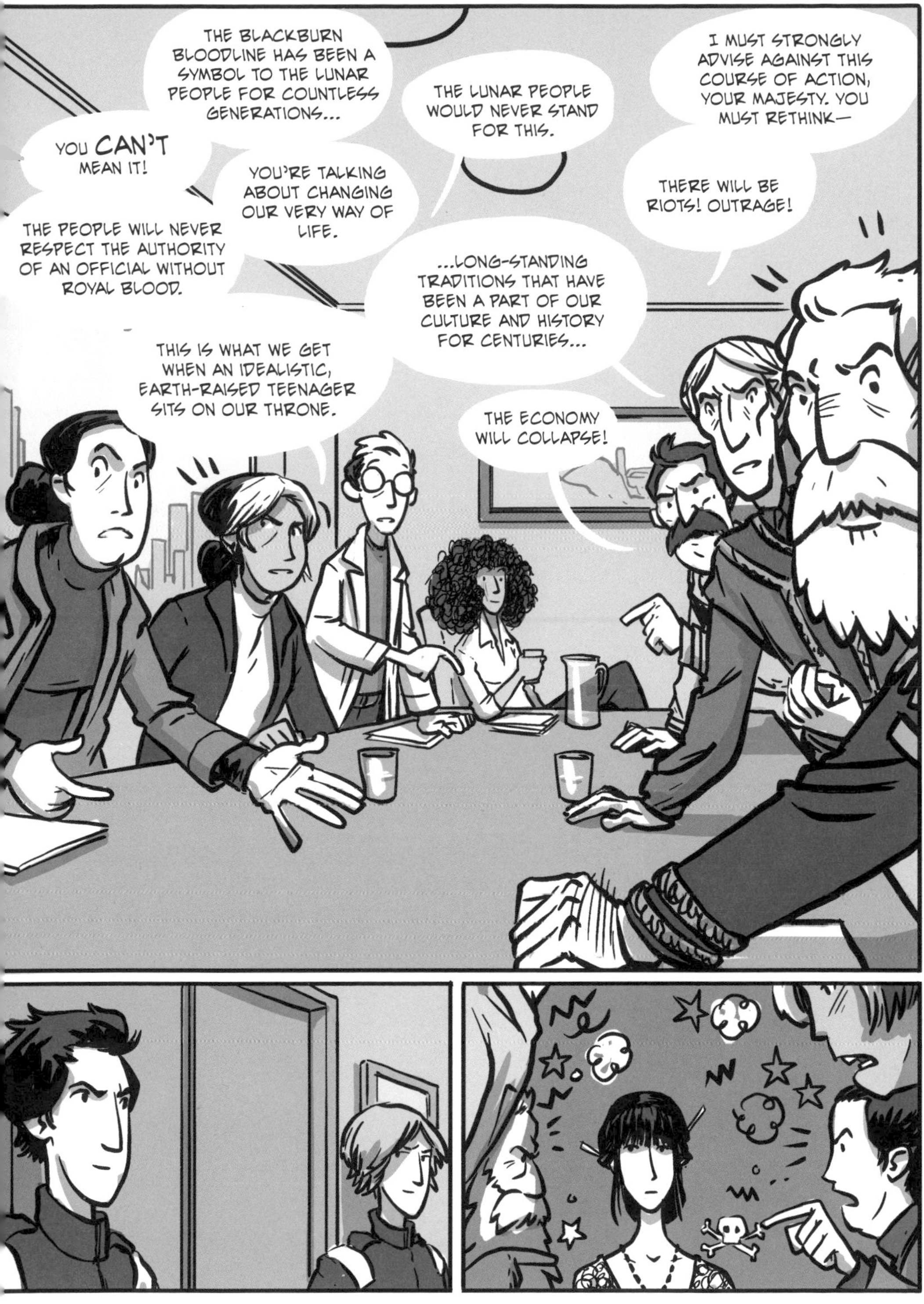
THE BLACKBURN BLOODLINE HAS BEEN A SYMBOL TO THE LUNAR PEOPLE FOR COUNTLESS GENERATIONS...
YOU CAN'T MEAN IT!
THE LUNAR PEOPLE WOULD NEVER STAND FOR THIS.
I MUST STRONGLY ADVISE AGAINST THIS COURSE OF ACTION, YOUR MAJESTY. YOU MUST RETHINK—
YOU'RE TALKING ABOUT CHANGING OUR VERY WAY OF LIFE.
THERE WILL BE RIOTS! OUTRAGE!
THE PEOPLE WILL NEVER RESPECT THE AUTHORITY OF AN OFFICIAL WITHOUT ROYAL BLOOD.
...LONG-STANDING TRADITIONS THAT HAVE BEEN A PART OF OUR CULTURE AND HISTORY FOR CENTURIES...
THIS IS WHAT WE GET WHEN AN IDEALISTIC, EARTH-RAISED TEENAGER SITS ON OUR THRONE.
THE ECONOMY WILL COLLAPSE!

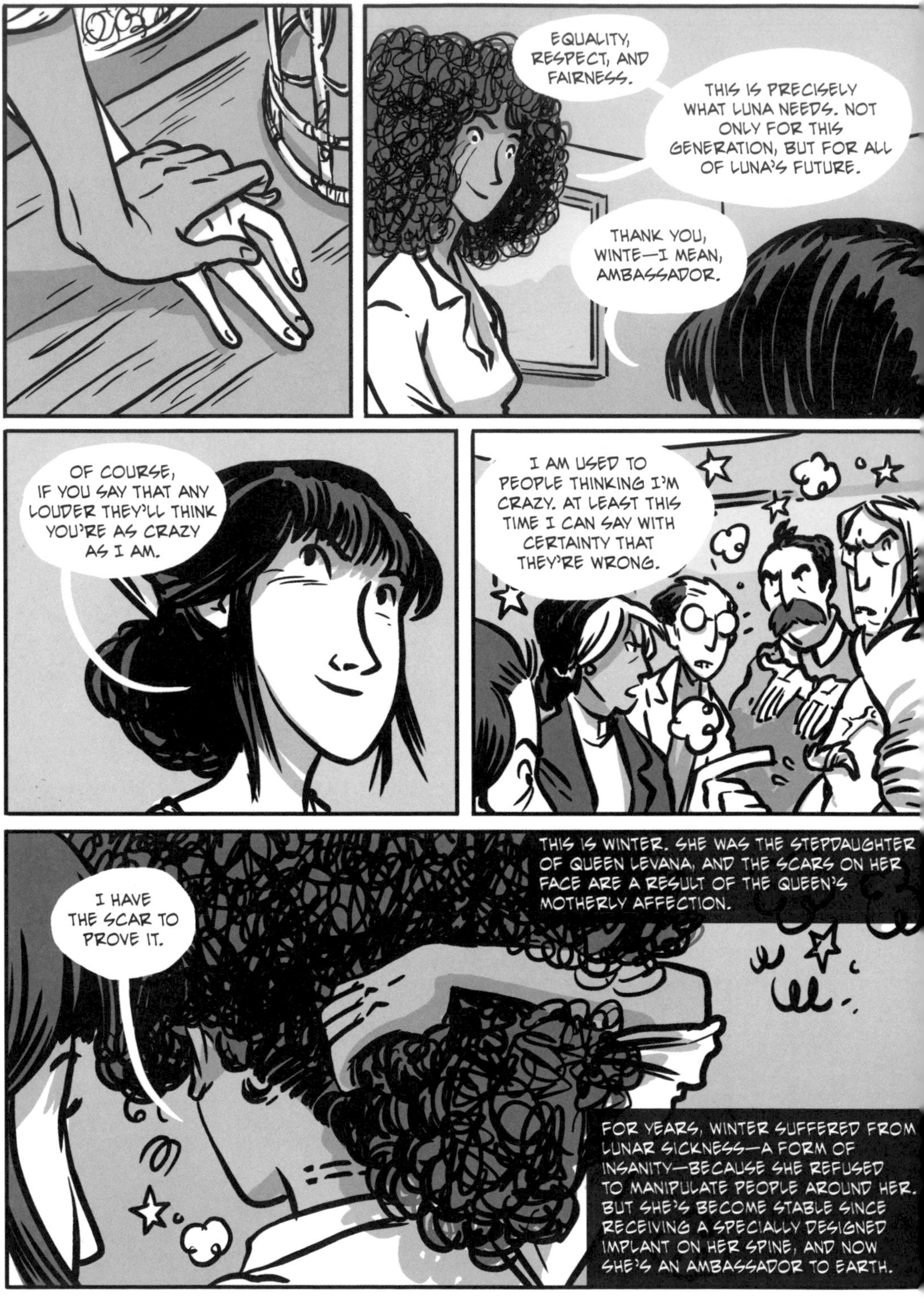
EQUALITY, RESPECT, AND FAIRNESS.
THIS IS PRECISELY WHAT LUNA NEEDS. NOT ONLY FOR THIS GENERATION, BUT FOR ALL OF LUNA'S FUTURE.
THANK YOU, WINTE—I MEAN, AMBASSADOR.
OF COURSE, IF YOU SAY THAT ANY LOUDER THEY'LL THINK YOU'RE AS CRAZY AS I AM.
I AM USED TO PEOPLE THINKING I'M CRAZY. AT LEAST THIS TIME I CAN SAY WITH CERTAINTY THAT THEY'RE WRONG.
I HAVE THE SCAR TO PROVE IT.
THIS IS WINTER. SHE WAS THE STEPDAUGHTER OF QUEEN LEVANA, AND THE SCARS ON HER FACE ARE A RESULT OF THE QUEEN'S MOTHERLY AFFECTION.
FOR YEARS, WINTER SUFFERED FROM LUNAR SICKNESS—A FORM OF INSANITY—BECAUSE SHE REFUSED TO MANIPULATE PEOPLE AROUND HER. BUT SHE'S BECOME STABLE SINCE RECEIVING A SPECIALLY DESIGNED IMPLANT ON HER SPINE, AND NOW SHE'S AN AMBASSADOR TO EARTH.

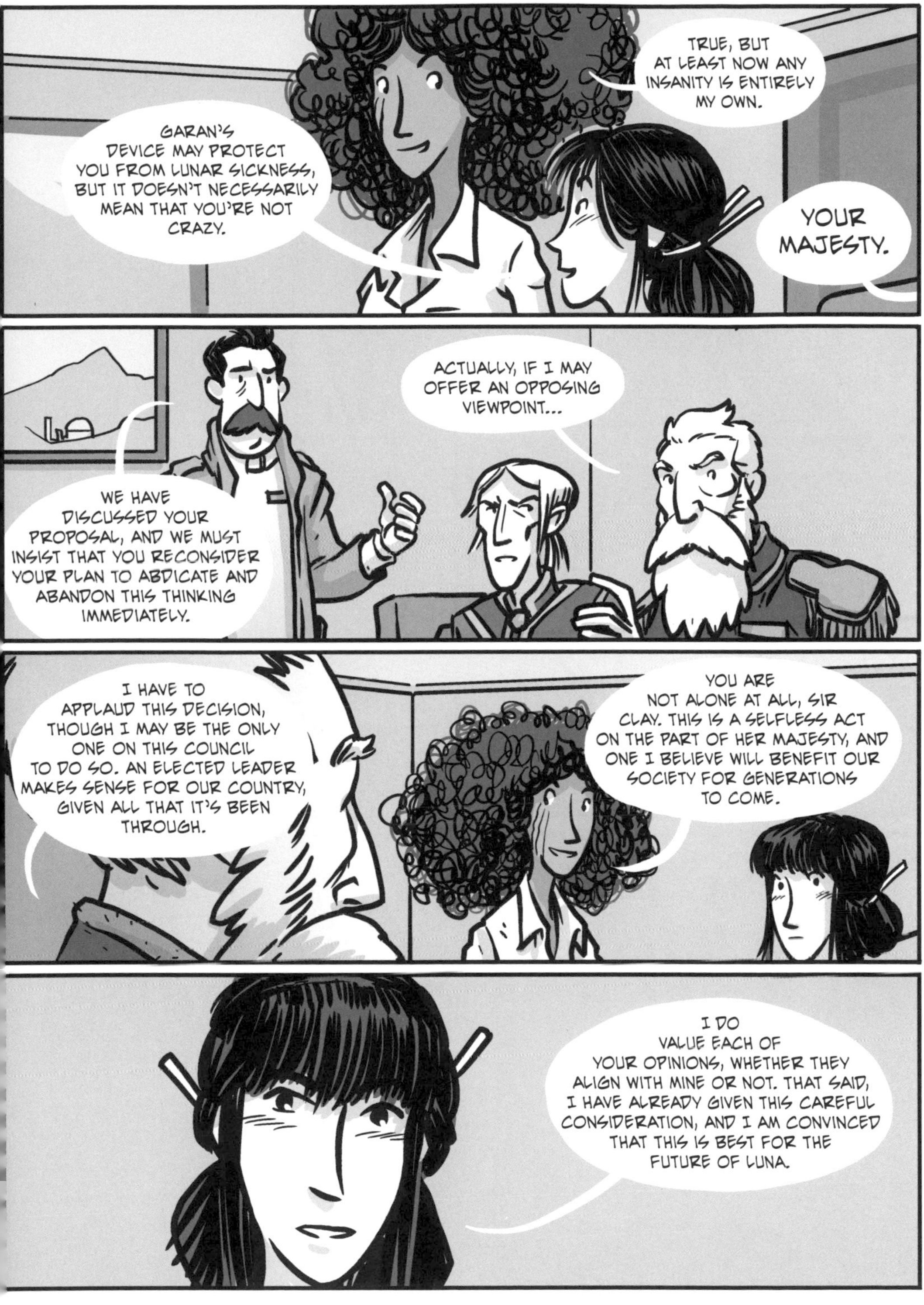
GARAN'S DEVICE MAY PROTECT YOU FROM LUNAR SICKNESS, BUT IT DOESN'T NECESSARILY MEAN THAT YOU'RE NOT CRAZY.
TRUE, BUT AT LEAST NOW ANY INSANITY IS ENTIRELY MY OWN.
YOUR MAJESTY.
WE HAVE DISCUSSED YOUR PROPOSAL, AND WE MUST INSIST THAT YOU RECONSIDER YOUR PLAN TO ABDICATE AND ABANDON THIS THINKING IMMEDIATELY.
ACTUALLY, IF I MAY OFFER AN OPPOSING VIEWPOINT...
I HAVE TO APPLAUD THIS DECISION, THOUGH I MAY BE THE ONLY ONE ON THIS COUNCIL TO DO SO. AN ELECTED LEADER MAKES SENSE FOR OUR COUNTRY, GIVEN ALL THAT IT'S BEEN THROUGH.
YOU ARE NOT ALONE AT ALL, SIR CLAY. THIS IS A SELFLESS ACT ON THE PART OF HER MAJESTY, AND ONE I BELIEVE WILL BENEFIT OUR SOCIETY FOR GENERATIONS TO COME.
I DO VALUE EACH OF YOUR OPINIONS, WHETHER THEY ALIGN WITH MINE OR NOT. THAT SAID, I HAVE ALREADY GIVEN THIS CAREFUL CONSIDERATION, AND I AM CONVINCED THAT THIS IS BEST FOR THE FUTURE OF LUNA.

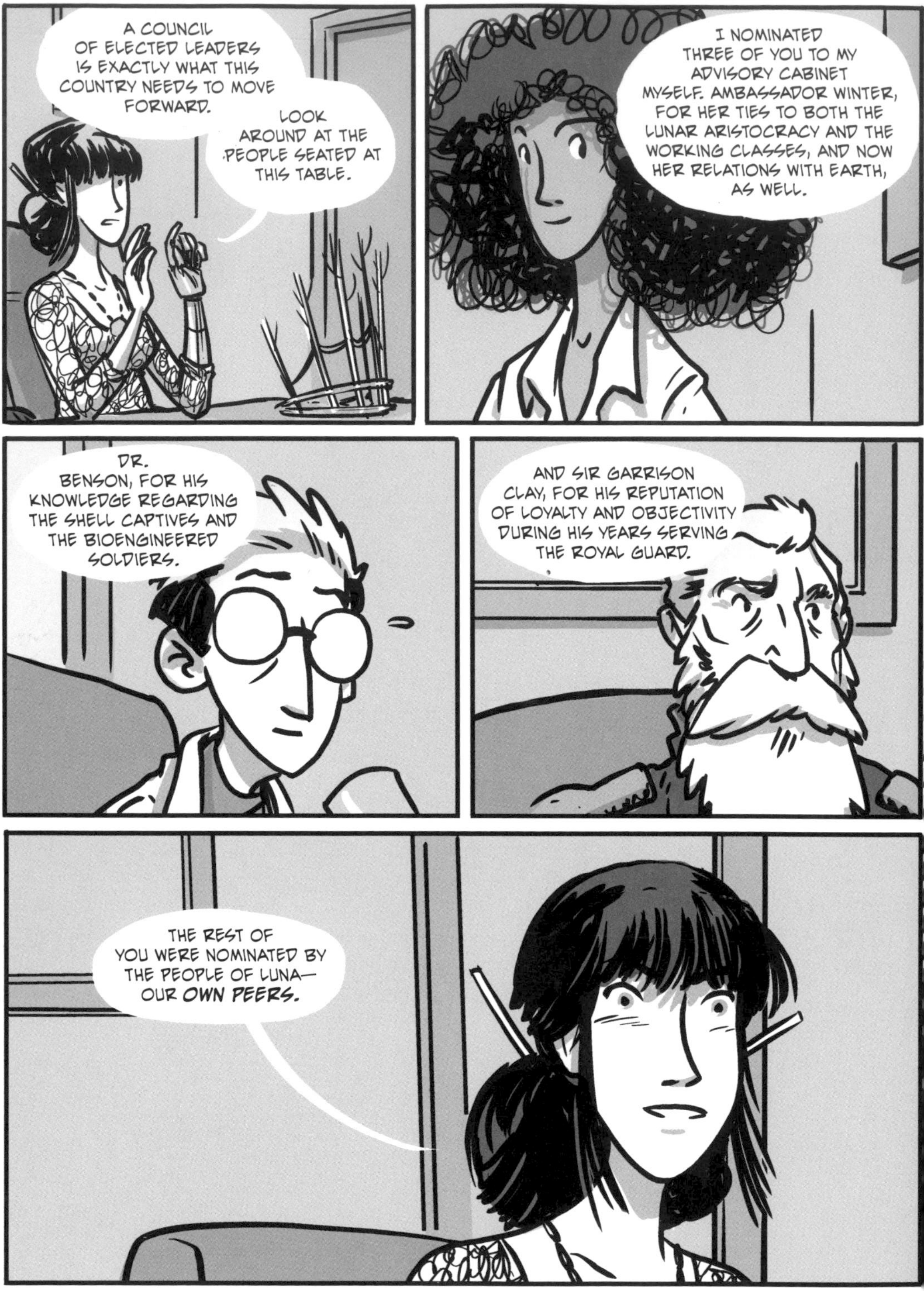
A COUNCIL OF ELECTED LEADERS IS EXACTLY WHAT THIS COUNTRY NEEDS TO MOVE FORWARD.
LOOK AROUND AT THE PEOPLE SEATED AT THIS TABLE.
I NOMINATED THREE OF YOU TO MY ADVISORY CABINET MYSELF. AMBASSADOR WINTER, FOR HER TIES TO BOTH THE LUNAR ARISTOCRACY AND THE WORKING CLASSES, AND NOW HER RELATIONS WITH EARTH, AS WELL.
DR. BENSON, FOR HIS KNOWLEDGE REGARDING THE SHELL CAPTIVES AND THE BIOENGINEERED SOLDIERS.
AND SIR GARRISON CLAY, FOR HIS REPUTATION OF LOYALTY AND OBJECTIVITY DURING HIS YEARS SERVING THE ROYAL GUARD.
THE REST OF YOU WERE NOMINATED BY THE PEOPLE OF LUNA—OUR **OWN PEERS.**

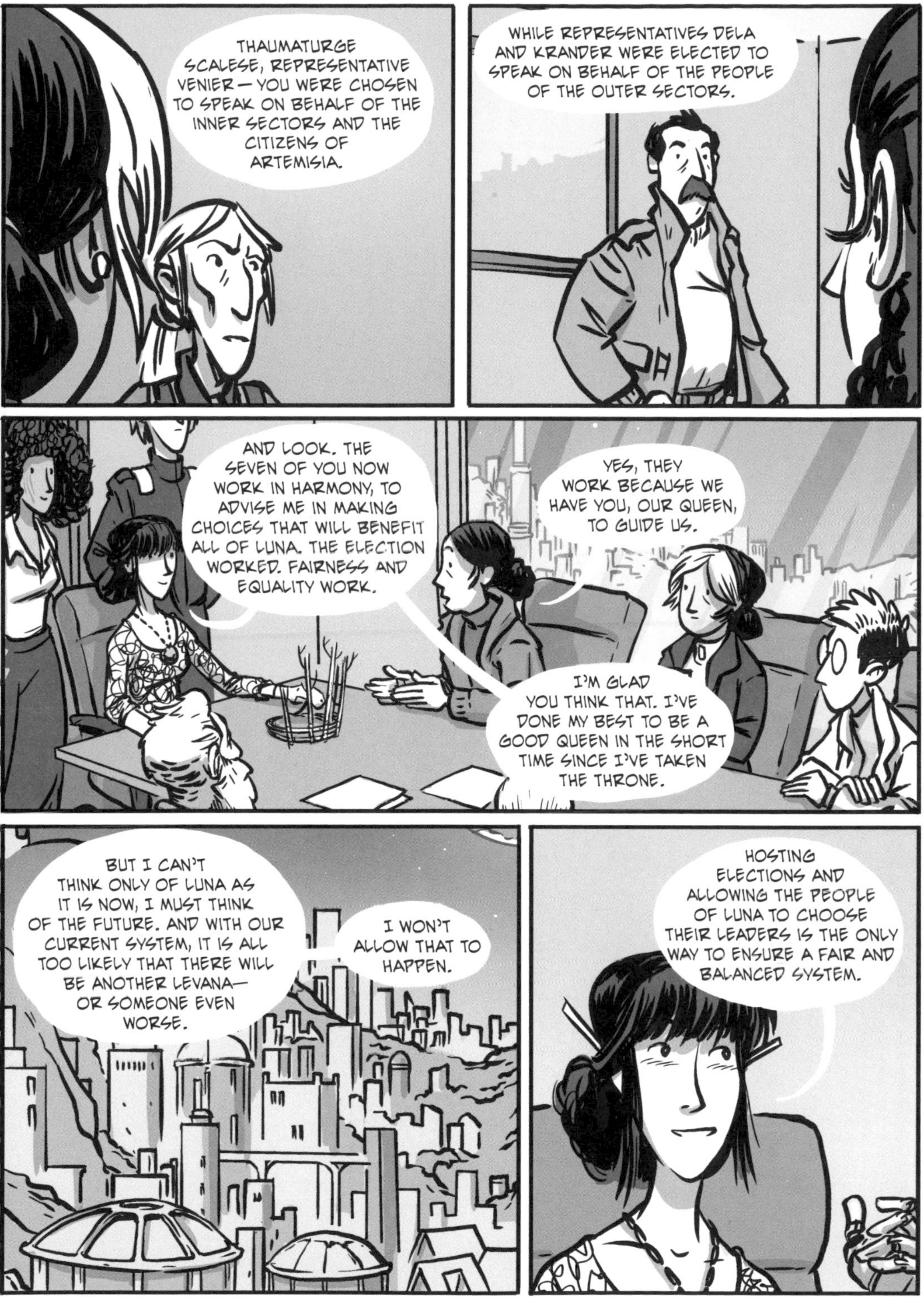
THAUMATURGE SCALESE, REPRESENTATIVE VENIER — YOU WERE CHOSEN TO SPEAK ON BEHALF OF THE INNER SECTORS AND THE CITIZENS OF ARTEMISIA.
WHILE REPRESENTATIVES DELA AND KRANDER WERE ELECTED TO SPEAK ON BEHALF OF THE PEOPLE OF THE OUTER SECTORS.
AND LOOK. THE SEVEN OF YOU NOW WORK IN HARMONY, TO ADVISE ME IN MAKING CHOICES THAT WILL BENEFIT ALL OF LUNA. THE ELECTION WORKED. FAIRNESS AND EQUALITY WORK.
YES, THEY WORK BECAUSE WE HAVE YOU, OUR QUEEN, TO GUIDE US.
I'M GLAD YOU THINK THAT. I'VE DONE MY BEST TO BE A GOOD QUEEN IN THE SHORT TIME SINCE I'VE TAKEN THE THRONE.
BUT I CAN'T THINK ONLY OF LUNA AS IT IS NOW, I MUST THINK OF THE FUTURE. AND WITH OUR CURRENT SYSTEM, IT IS ALL TOO LIKELY THAT THERE WILL BE ANOTHER LEVANA— OR SOMEONE EVEN WORSE.
I WON'T ALLOW THAT TO HAPPEN.
HOSTING ELECTIONS AND ALLOWING THE PEOPLE OF LUNA TO CHOOSE THEIR LEADERS IS THE ONLY WAY TO ENSURE A FAIR AND BALANCED SYSTEM.

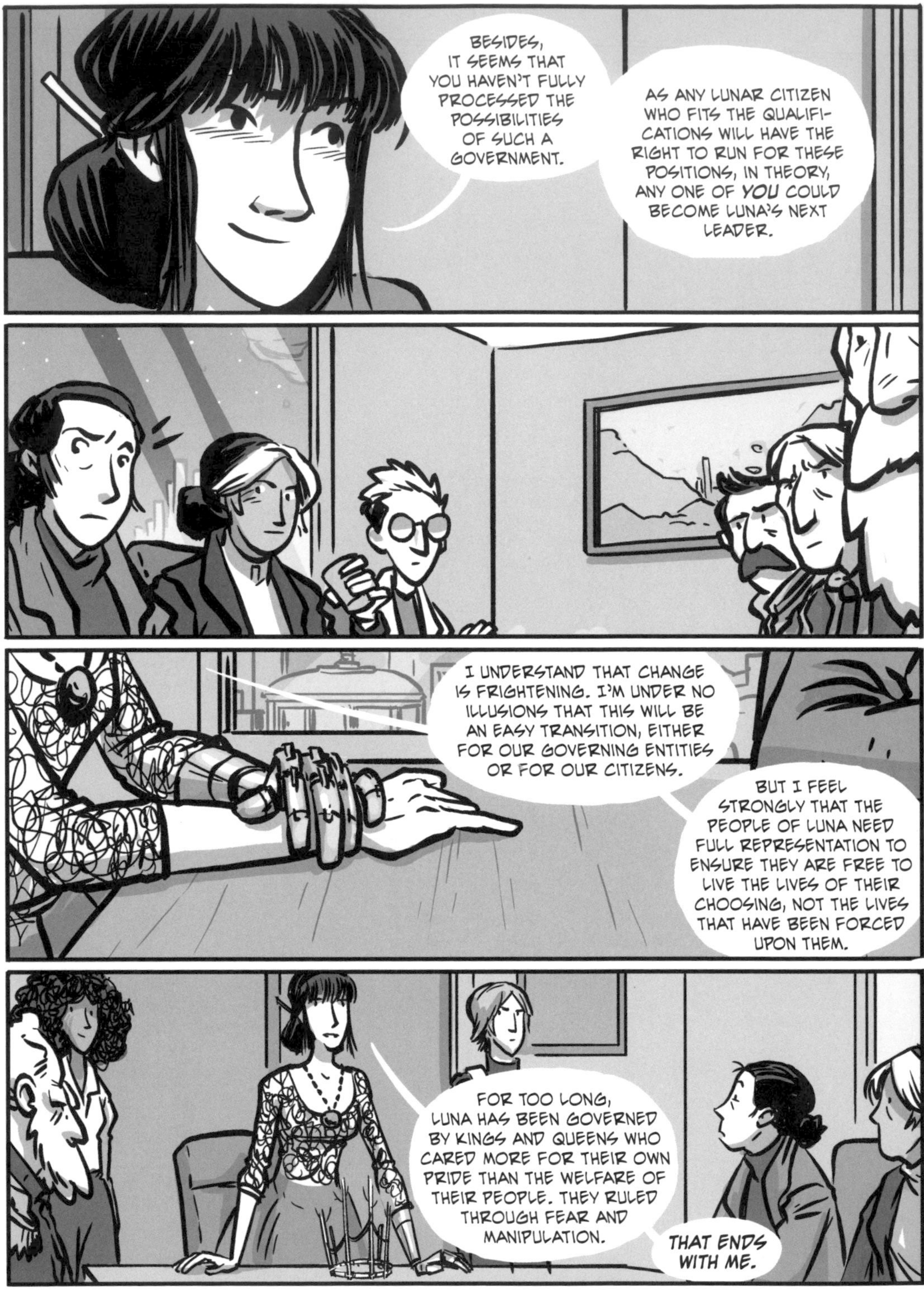
BESIDES, IT SEEMS THAT YOU HAVEN'T FULLY PROCESSED THE POSSIBILITIES OF SUCH A GOVERNMENT.
AS ANY LUNAR CITIZEN WHO FITS THE QUALIFI-CATIONS WILL HAVE THE RIGHT TO RUN FOR THESE POSITIONS, IN THEORY, ANY ONE OF *YOU* COULD BECOME LUNA'S NEXT LEADER.
I UNDERSTAND THAT CHANGE IS FRIGHTENING. I'M UNDER NO ILLUSIONS THAT THIS WILL BE AN EASY TRANSITION, EITHER FOR OUR GOVERNING ENTITIES OR FOR OUR CITIZENS.
BUT I FEEL STRONGLY THAT THE PEOPLE OF LUNA NEED FULL REPRESENTATION TO ENSURE THEY ARE FREE TO LIVE THE LIVES OF THEIR CHOOSING, NOT THE LIVES THAT HAVE BEEN FORCED UPON THEM.
FOR TOO LONG, LUNA HAS BEEN GOVERNED BY KINGS AND QUEENS WHO CARED MORE FOR THEIR OWN PRIDE THAN THE WELFARE OF THEIR PEOPLE. THEY RULED THROUGH FEAR AND MANIPULATION.
THAT ENDS WITH ME.

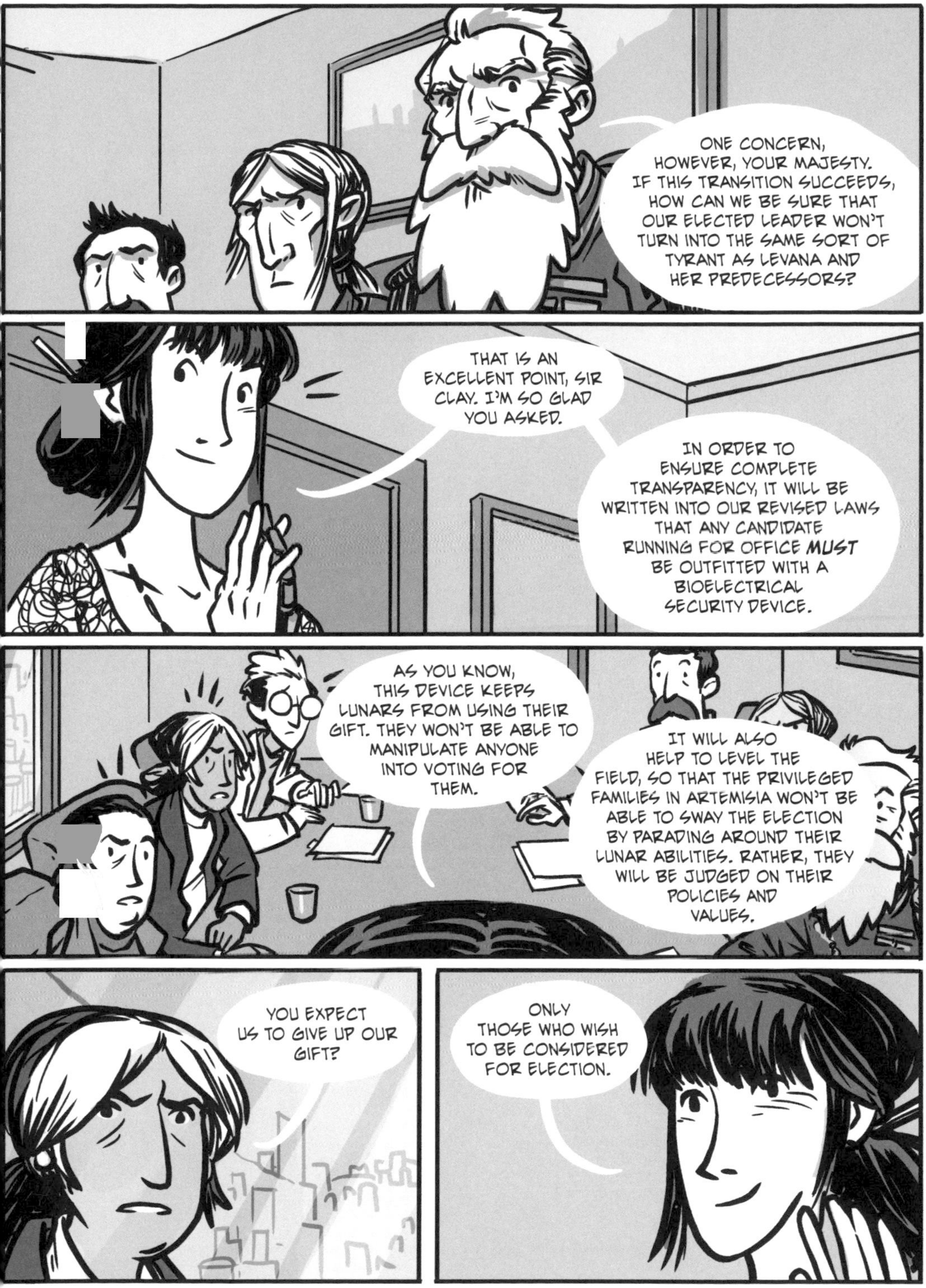
ONE CONCERN, HOWEVER, YOUR MAJESTY. IF THIS TRANSITION SUCCEEDS, HOW CAN WE BE SURE THAT OUR ELECTED LEADER WON'T TURN INTO THE SAME SORT OF TYRANT AS LEVANA AND HER PREDECESSORS?
THAT IS AN EXCELLENT POINT, SIR CLAY. I'M SO GLAD YOU ASKED.
IN ORDER TO ENSURE COMPLETE TRANSPARENCY, IT WILL BE WRITTEN INTO OUR REVISED LAWS THAT ANY CANDIDATE RUNNING FOR OFFICE **MUST** BE OUTFITTED WITH A BIOELECTRICAL SECURITY DEVICE.
AS YOU KNOW, THIS DEVICE KEEPS LUNARS FROM USING THEIR GIFT. THEY WON'T BE ABLE TO MANIPULATE ANYONE INTO VOTING FOR THEM.
IT WILL ALSO HELP TO LEVEL THE FIELD, SO THAT THE PRIVILEGED FAMILIES IN ARTEMISIA WON'T BE ABLE TO SWAY THE ELECTION BY PARADING AROUND THEIR LUNAR ABILITIES. RATHER, THEY WILL BE JUDGED ON THEIR POLICIES AND VALUES.
YOU EXPECT US TO GIVE UP OUR GIFT?
ONLY THOSE WHO WISH TO BE CONSIDERED FOR ELECTION.

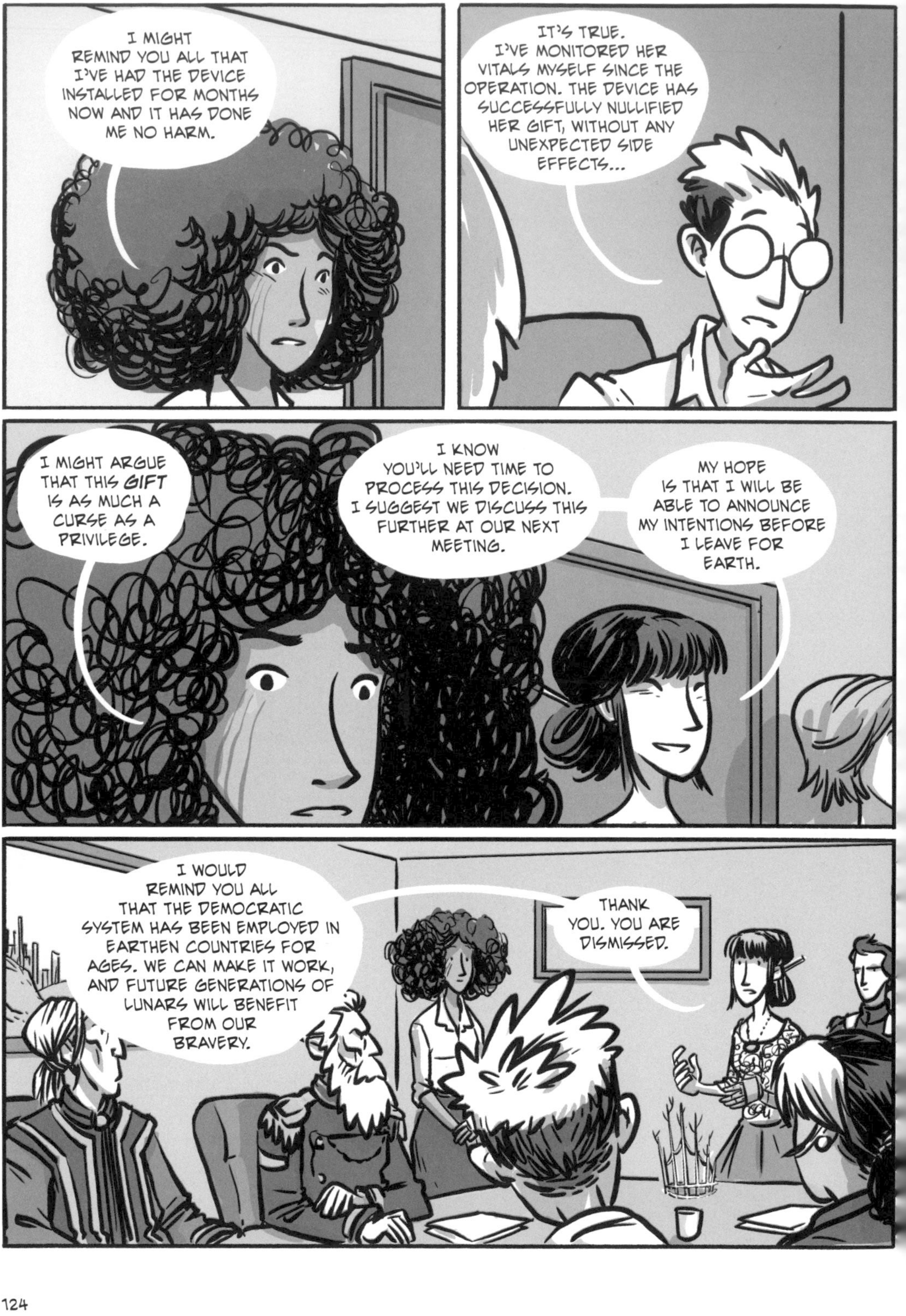
I MIGHT REMIND YOU ALL THAT I'VE HAD THE DEVICE INSTALLED FOR MONTHS NOW AND IT HAS DONE ME NO HARM.
IT'S TRUE. I'VE MONITORED HER VITALS MYSELF SINCE THE OPERATION. THE DEVICE HAS SUCCESSFULLY NULLIFIED HER GIFT, WITHOUT ANY UNEXPECTED SIDE EFFECTS...
I MIGHT ARGUE THAT THIS **GIFT** IS AS MUCH A CURSE AS A PRIVILEGE.
I KNOW YOU'LL NEED TIME TO PROCESS THIS DECISION. I SUGGEST WE DISCUSS THIS FURTHER AT OUR NEXT MEETING.
MY HOPE IS THAT I WILL BE ABLE TO ANNOUNCE MY INTENTIONS BEFORE I LEAVE FOR EARTH.
I WOULD REMIND YOU ALL THAT THE DEMOCRATIC SYSTEM HAS BEEN EMPLOYED IN EARTHEN COUNTRIES FOR AGES. WE CAN MAKE IT WORK, AND FUTURE GENERATIONS OF LUNARS WILL BENEFIT FROM OUR BRAVERY.
THANK YOU. YOU ARE DISMISSED.

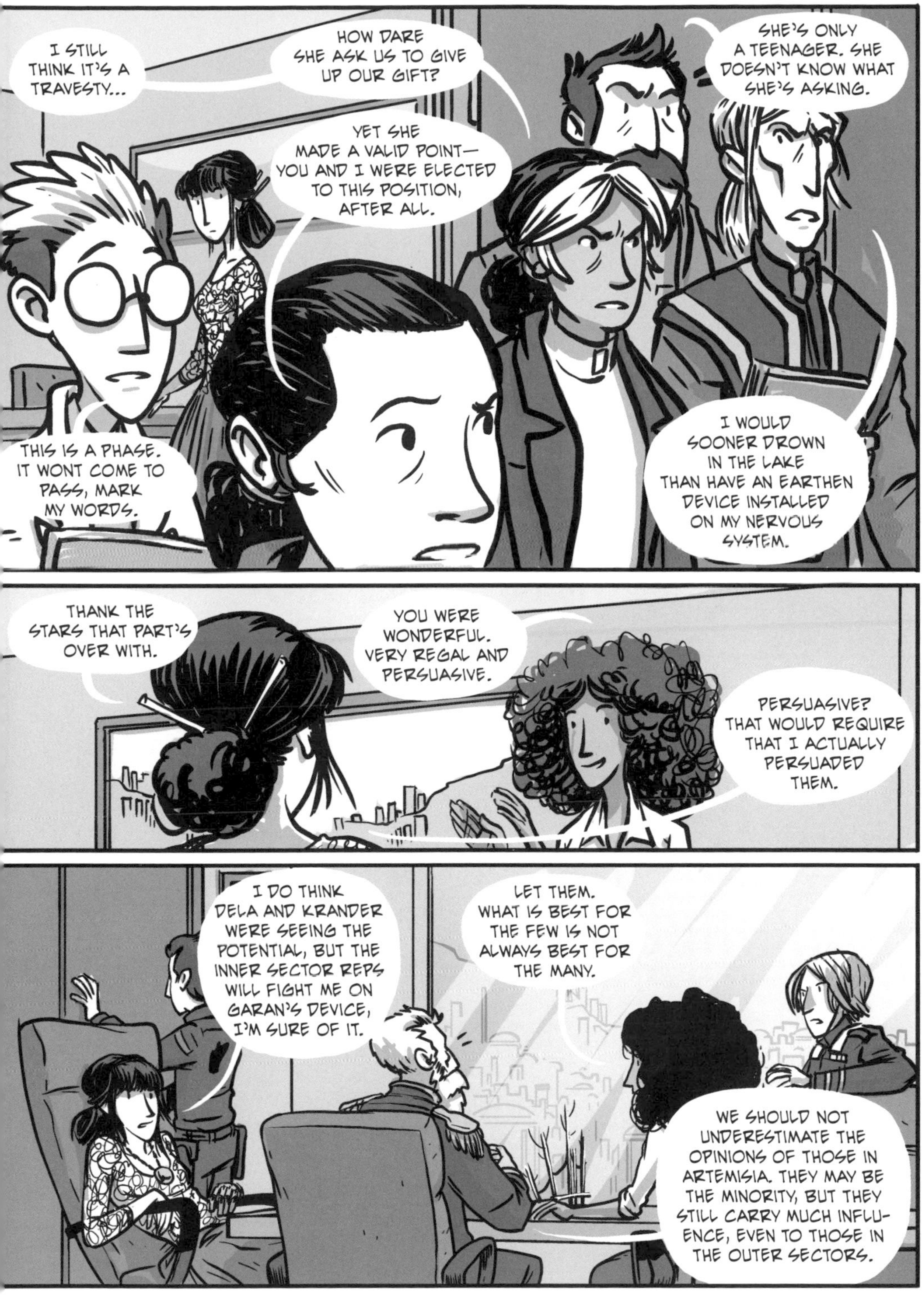
I STILL THINK IT'S A TRAVESTY...
HOW DARE SHE ASK US TO GIVE UP OUR GIFT?
SHE'S ONLY A TEENAGER. SHE DOESN'T KNOW WHAT SHE'S ASKING.
YET SHE MADE A VALID POINT— YOU AND I WERE ELECTED TO THIS POSITION, AFTER ALL.
THIS IS A PHASE. IT WONT COME TO PASS, MARK MY WORDS.
I WOULD SOONER DROWN IN THE LAKE THAN HAVE AN EARTHEN DEVICE INSTALLED ON MY NERVOUS SYSTEM.
THANK THE STARS THAT PART'S OVER WITH.
YOU WERE WONDERFUL. VERY REGAL AND PERSUASIVE.
PERSUASIVE? THAT WOULD REQUIRE THAT I ACTUALLY PERSUADED THEM.
I DO THINK DELA AND KRANDER WERE SEEING THE POTENTIAL, BUT THE INNER SECTOR REPS WILL FIGHT ME ON GARAN'S DEVICE, I'M SURE OF IT.
LET THEM. WHAT IS BEST FOR THE FEW IS NOT ALWAYS BEST FOR THE MANY.
WE SHOULD NOT UNDERESTIMATE THE OPINIONS OF THOSE IN ARTEMISIA. THEY MAY BE THE MINORITY, BUT THEY STILL CARRY MUCH INFLU-ENCE, EVEN TO THOSE IN THE OUTER SECTORS.

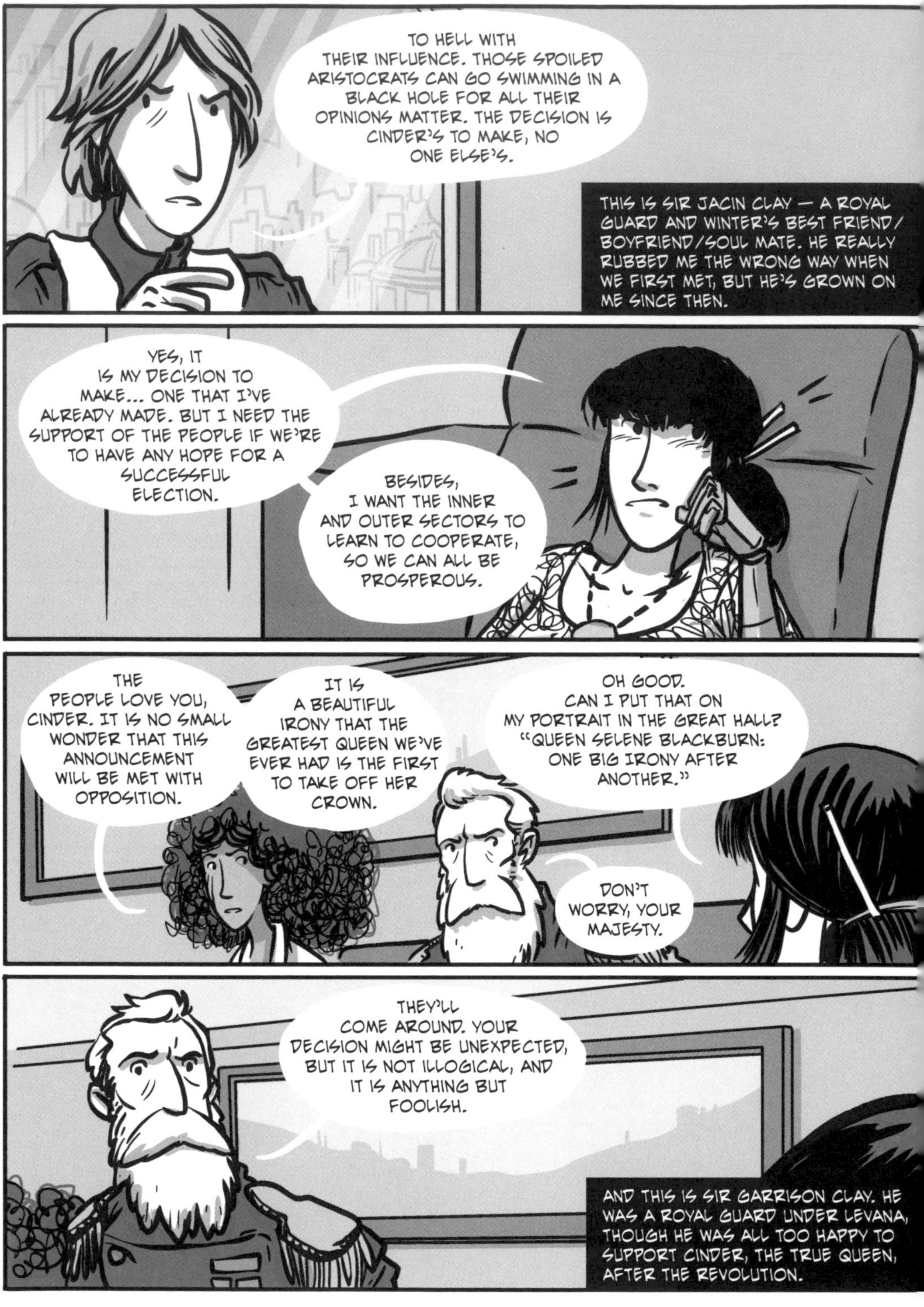
TO HELL WITH THEIR INFLUENCE. THOSE SPOILED ARISTOCRATS CAN GO SWIMMING IN A BLACK HOLE FOR ALL THEIR OPINIONS MATTER. THE DECISION IS CINDER'S TO MAKE, NO ONE ELSE'S.
THIS IS SIR JACIN CLAY — A ROYAL GUARD AND WINTER'S BEST FRIEND/BOYFRIEND/SOUL MATE. HE REALLY RUBBED ME THE WRONG WAY WHEN WE FIRST MET, BUT HE'S GROWN ON ME SINCE THEN.
YES, IT IS MY DECISION TO MAKE... ONE THAT I'VE ALREADY MADE. BUT I NEED THE SUPPORT OF THE PEOPLE IF WE'RE TO HAVE ANY HOPE FOR A SUCCESSFUL ELECTION.
BESIDES, I WANT THE INNER AND OUTER SECTORS TO LEARN TO COOPERATE, SO WE CAN ALL BE PROSPEROUS.
THE PEOPLE LOVE YOU, CINDER. IT IS NO SMALL WONDER THAT THIS ANNOUNCEMENT WILL BE MET WITH OPPOSITION.
IT IS A BEAUTIFUL IRONY THAT THE GREATEST QUEEN WE'VE EVER HAD IS THE FIRST TO TAKE OFF HER CROWN.
OH GOOD. CAN I PUT THAT ON MY PORTRAIT IN THE GREAT HALL? "QUEEN SELENE BLACKBURN: ONE BIG IRONY AFTER ANOTHER."
DON'T WORRY, YOUR MAJESTY.
THEY'LL COME AROUND. YOUR DECISION MIGHT BE UNEXPECTED, BUT IT IS NOT ILLOGICAL, AND IT IS ANYTHING BUT FOOLISH.
AND THIS IS SIR GARRISON CLAY. HE WAS A ROYAL GUARD UNDER LEVANA, THOUGH HE WAS ALL TOO HAPPY TO SUPPORT CINDER, THE TRUE QUEEN, AFTER THE REVOLUTION.

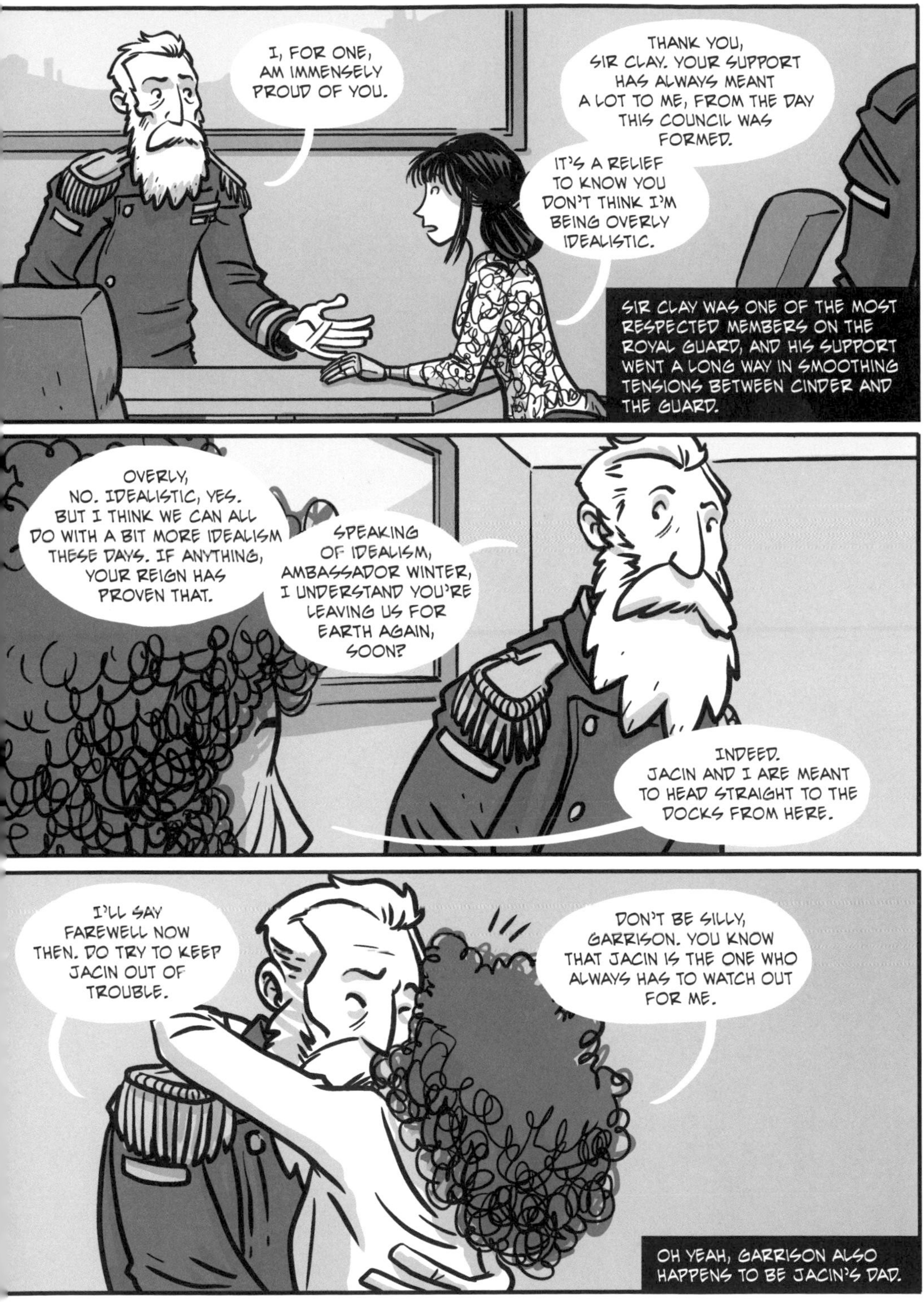
I, FOR ONE, AM IMMENSELY PROUD OF YOU.
THANK YOU, SIR CLAY. YOUR SUPPORT HAS ALWAYS MEANT A LOT TO ME, FROM THE DAY THIS COUNCIL WAS FORMED.
IT'S A RELIEF TO KNOW YOU DON'T THINK I'M BEING OVERLY IDEALISTIC.
SIR CLAY WAS ONE OF THE MOST RESPECTED MEMBERS ON THE ROYAL GUARD, AND HIS SUPPORT WENT A LONG WAY IN SMOOTHING TENSIONS BETWEEN CINDER AND THE GUARD.
OVERLY, NO. IDEALISTIC, YES. BUT I THINK WE CAN ALL DO WITH A BIT MORE IDEALISM THESE DAYS. IF ANYTHING, YOUR REIGN HAS PROVEN THAT.
SPEAKING OF IDEALISM, AMBASSADOR WINTER, I UNDERSTAND YOU'RE LEAVING US FOR EARTH AGAIN, SOON?
INDEED. JACIN AND I ARE MEANT TO HEAD STRAIGHT TO THE DOCKS FROM HERE.
I'LL SAY FAREWELL NOW THEN. DO TRY TO KEEP JACIN OUT OF TROUBLE.
DON'T BE SILLY, GARRISON. YOU KNOW THAT JACIN IS THE ONE WHO ALWAYS HAS TO WATCH OUT FOR ME.
OH YEAH, GARRISON ALSO HAPPENS TO BE JACIN'S DAD.

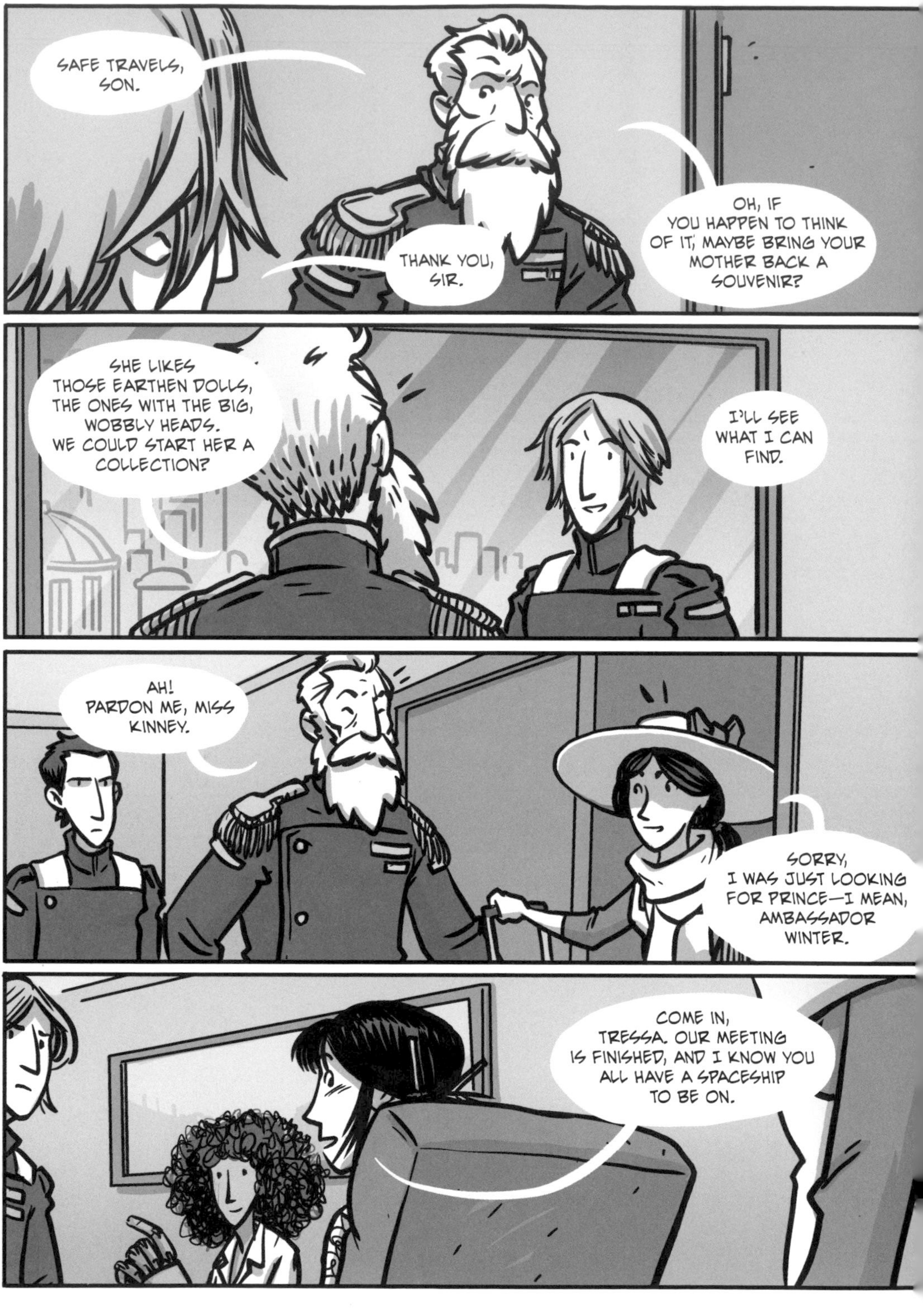
SAFE TRAVELS, SON.
THANK YOU, SIR.
OH, IF YOU HAPPEN TO THINK OF IT, MAYBE BRING YOUR MOTHER BACK A SOUVENIR?
SHE LIKES THOSE EARTHEN DOLLS, THE ONES WITH THE BIG, WOBBLY HEADS. WE COULD START HER A COLLECTION?
I'LL SEE WHAT I CAN FIND.
AH! PARDON ME, MISS KINNEY.
SORRY, I WAS JUST LOOKING FOR PRINCE—I MEAN, AMBASSADOR WINTER.
COME IN, TRESSA. OUR MEETING IS FINISHED, AND I KNOW YOU ALL HAVE A SPACESHIP TO BE ON.

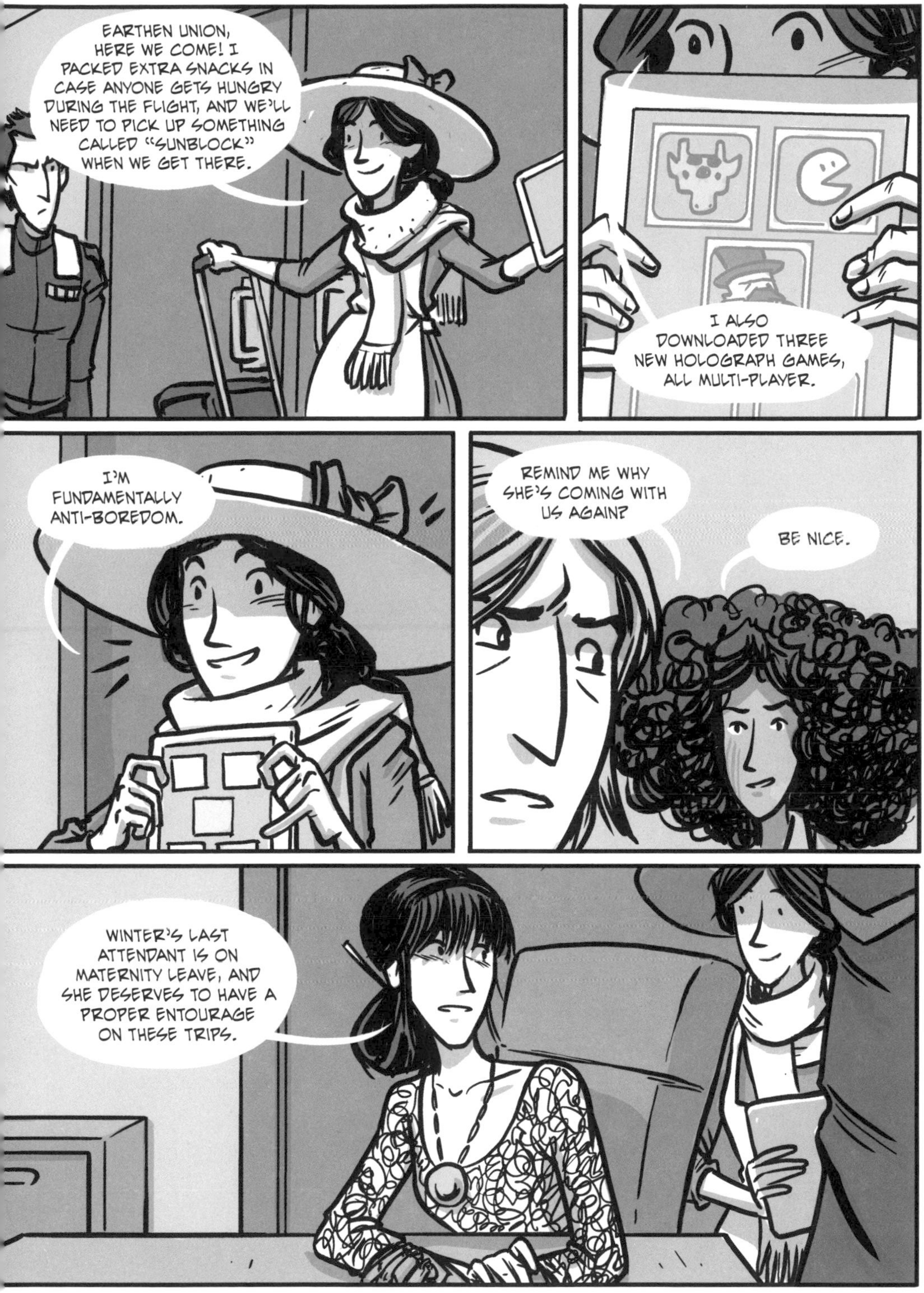
EARTHEN UNION, HERE WE COME! I PACKED EXTRA SNACKS IN CASE ANYONE GETS HUNGRY DURING THE FLIGHT, AND WE'LL NEED TO PICK UP SOMETHING CALLED "SUNBLOCK" WHEN WE GET THERE.
I ALSO DOWNLOADED THREE NEW HOLOGRAPH GAMES, ALL MULTI-PLAYER.
I'M FUNDAMENTALLY ANTI-BOREDOM.
REMIND ME WHY SHE'S COMING WITH US AGAIN?
BE NICE.
WINTER'S LAST ATTENDANT IS ON MATERNITY LEAVE, AND SHE DESERVES TO HAVE A PROPER ENTOURAGE ON THESE TRIPS.

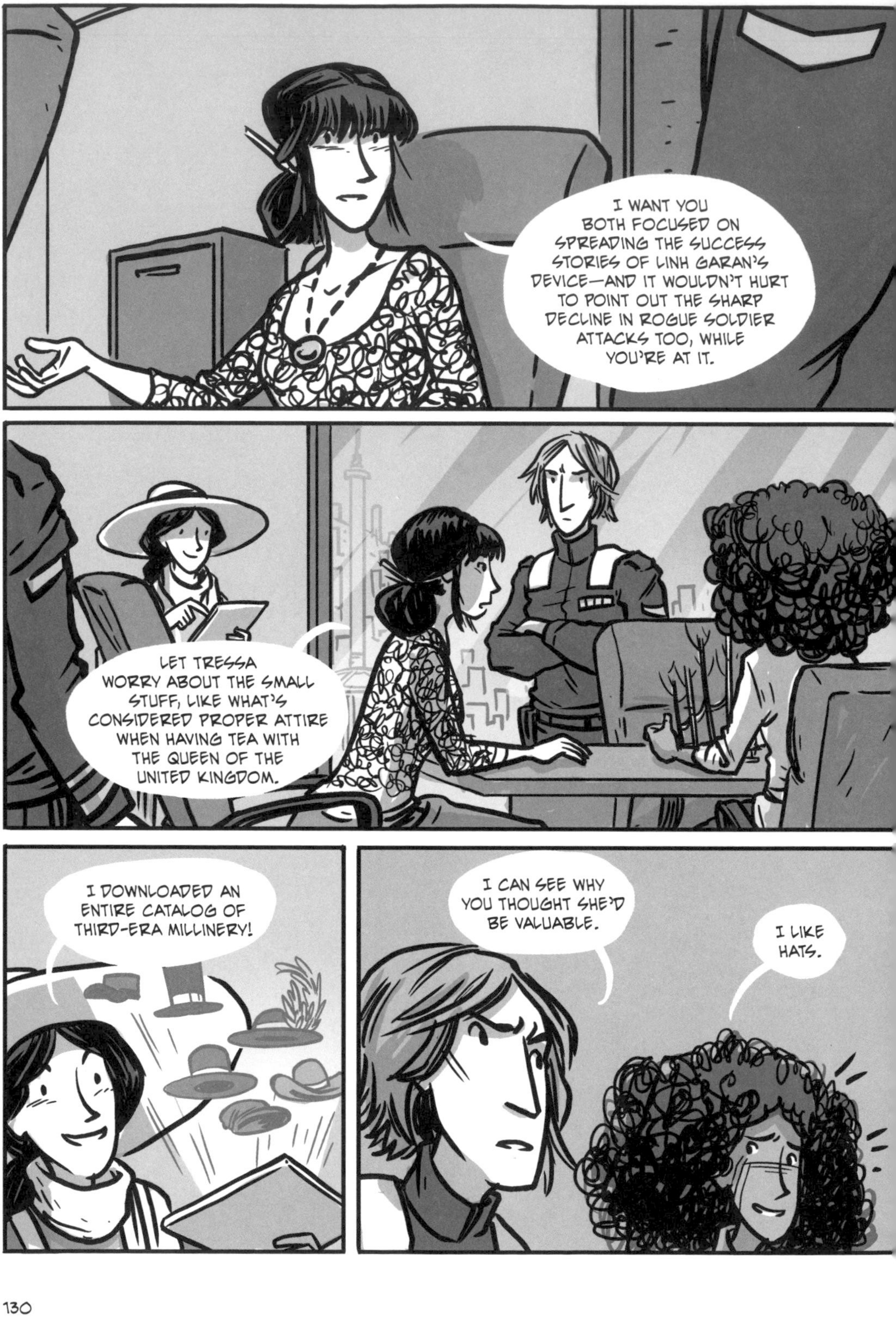
I WANT YOU BOTH FOCUSED ON SPREADING THE SUCCESS STORIES OF LINH GARAN'S DEVICE—AND IT WOULDN'T HURT TO POINT OUT THE SHARP DECLINE IN ROGUE SOLDIER ATTACKS TOO, WHILE YOU'RE AT IT.
LET TRESSA WORRY ABOUT THE SMALL STUFF, LIKE WHAT'S CONSIDERED PROPER ATTIRE WHEN HAVING TEA WITH THE QUEEN OF THE UNITED KINGDOM.
I DOWNLOADED AN ENTIRE CATALOG OF THIRD-ERA MILLINERY!
I CAN SEE WHY YOU THOUGHT SHE'D BE VALUABLE.
I LIKE HATS.

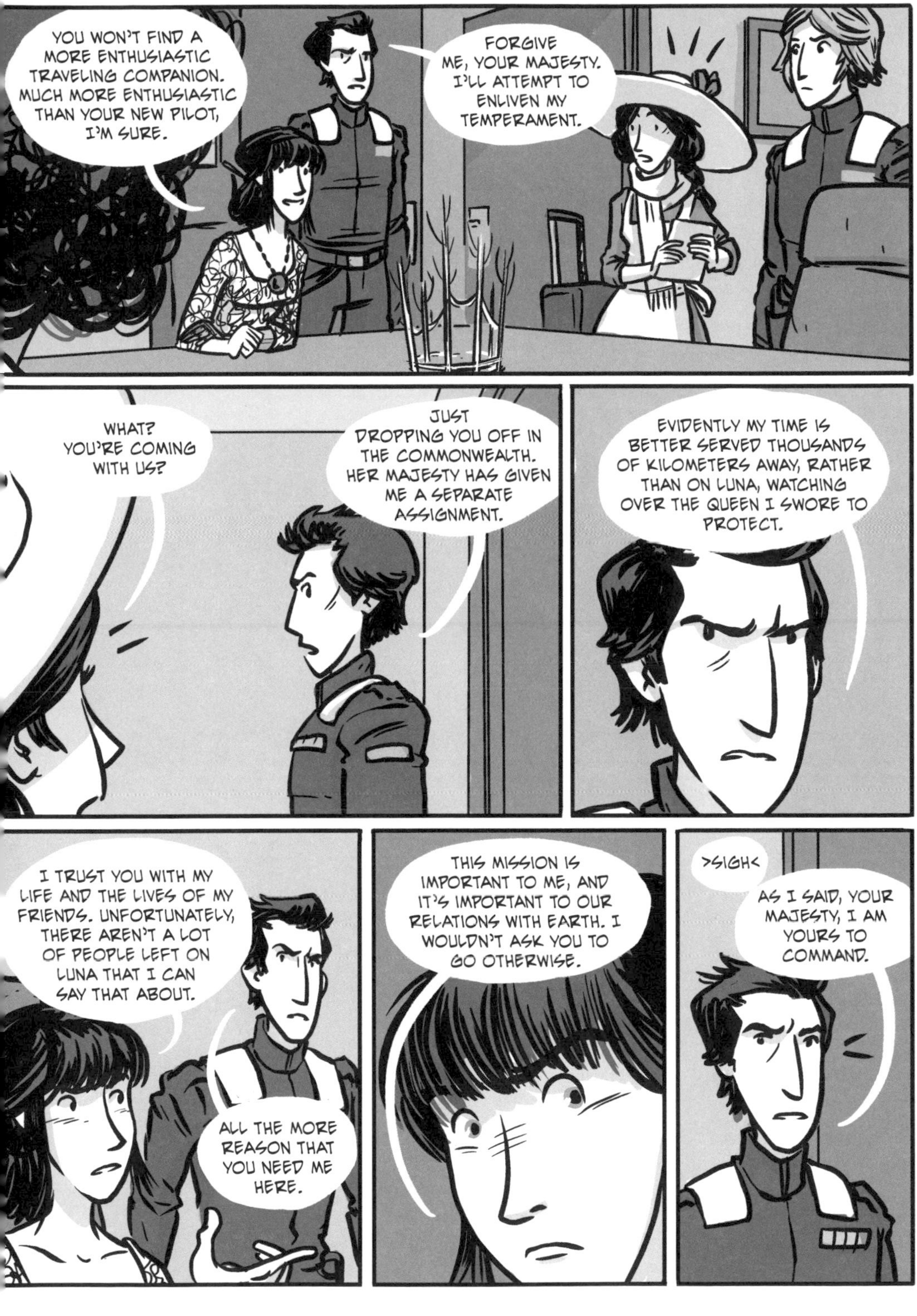
YOU WON'T FIND A MORE ENTHUSIASTIC TRAVELING COMPANION. MUCH MORE ENTHUSIASTIC THAN YOUR NEW PILOT, I'M SURE.
FORGIVE ME, YOUR MAJESTY. I'LL ATTEMPT TO ENLIVEN MY TEMPERAMENT.
WHAT? YOU'RE COMING WITH US?
JUST DROPPING YOU OFF IN THE COMMONWEALTH. HER MAJESTY HAS GIVEN ME A SEPARATE ASSIGNMENT.
EVIDENTLY MY TIME IS BETTER SERVED THOUSANDS OF KILOMETERS AWAY, RATHER THAN ON LUNA, WATCHING OVER THE QUEEN I SWORE TO PROTECT.
I TRUST YOU WITH MY LIFE AND THE LIVES OF MY FRIENDS. UNFORTUNATELY, THERE AREN'T A LOT OF PEOPLE LEFT ON LUNA THAT I CAN SAY THAT ABOUT.
ALL THE MORE REASON THAT YOU NEED ME HERE.
THIS MISSION IS IMPORTANT TO ME, AND IT'S IMPORTANT TO OUR RELATIONS WITH EARTH. I WOULDN'T ASK YOU TO GO OTHERWISE.
>SIGH<
AS I SAID, YOUR MAJESTY, I AM YOURS TO COMMAND.

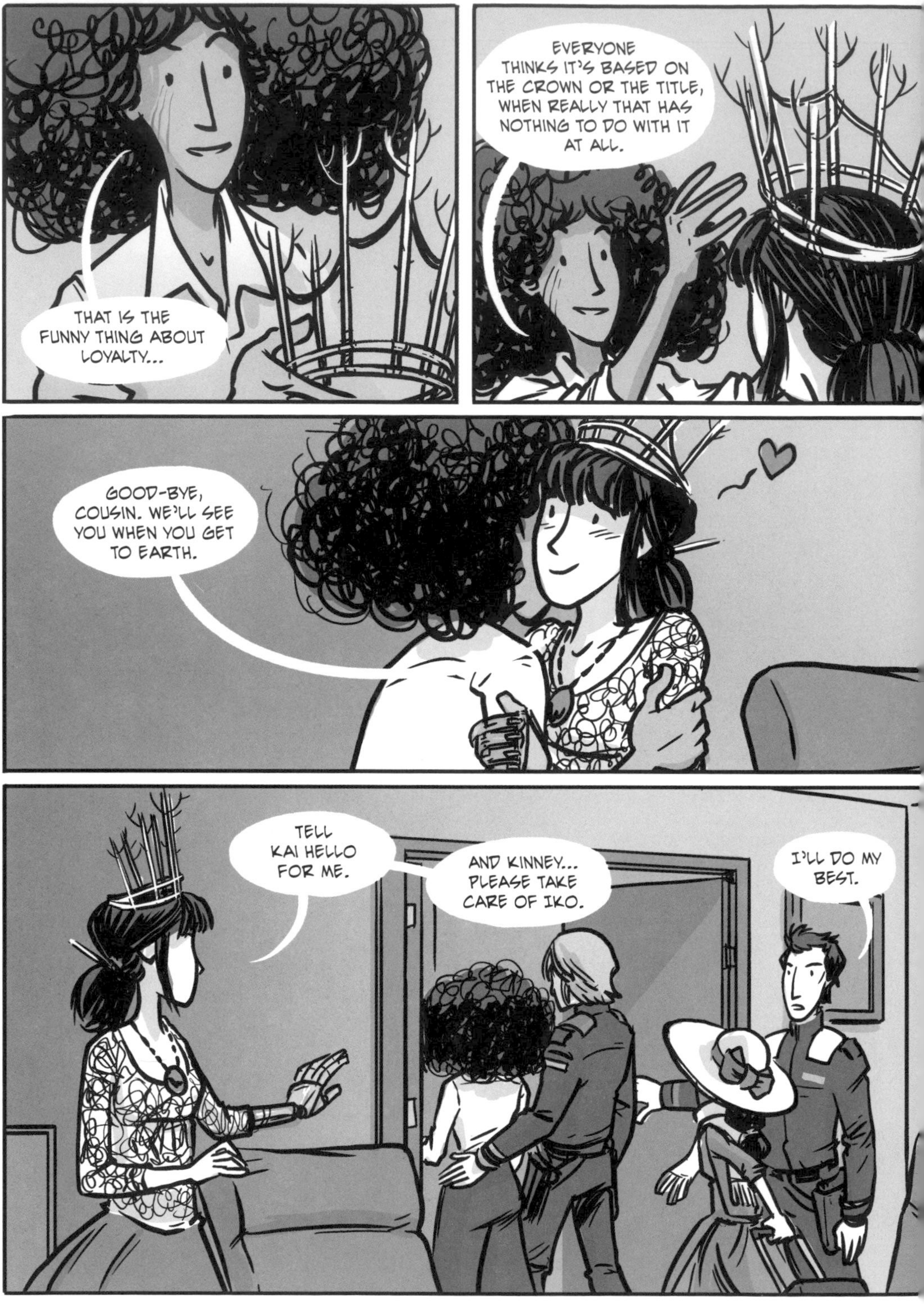
THAT IS THE FUNNY THING ABOUT LOYALTY...
EVERYONE THINKS IT'S BASED ON THE CROWN OR THE TITLE, WHEN REALLY THAT HAS NOTHING TO DO WITH IT AT ALL.
GOOD-BYE, COUSIN. WE'LL SEE YOU WHEN YOU GET TO EARTH.
TELL KAI HELLO FOR ME.
AND KINNEY... PLEASE TAKE CARE OF IKO.
I'LL DO MY BEST.

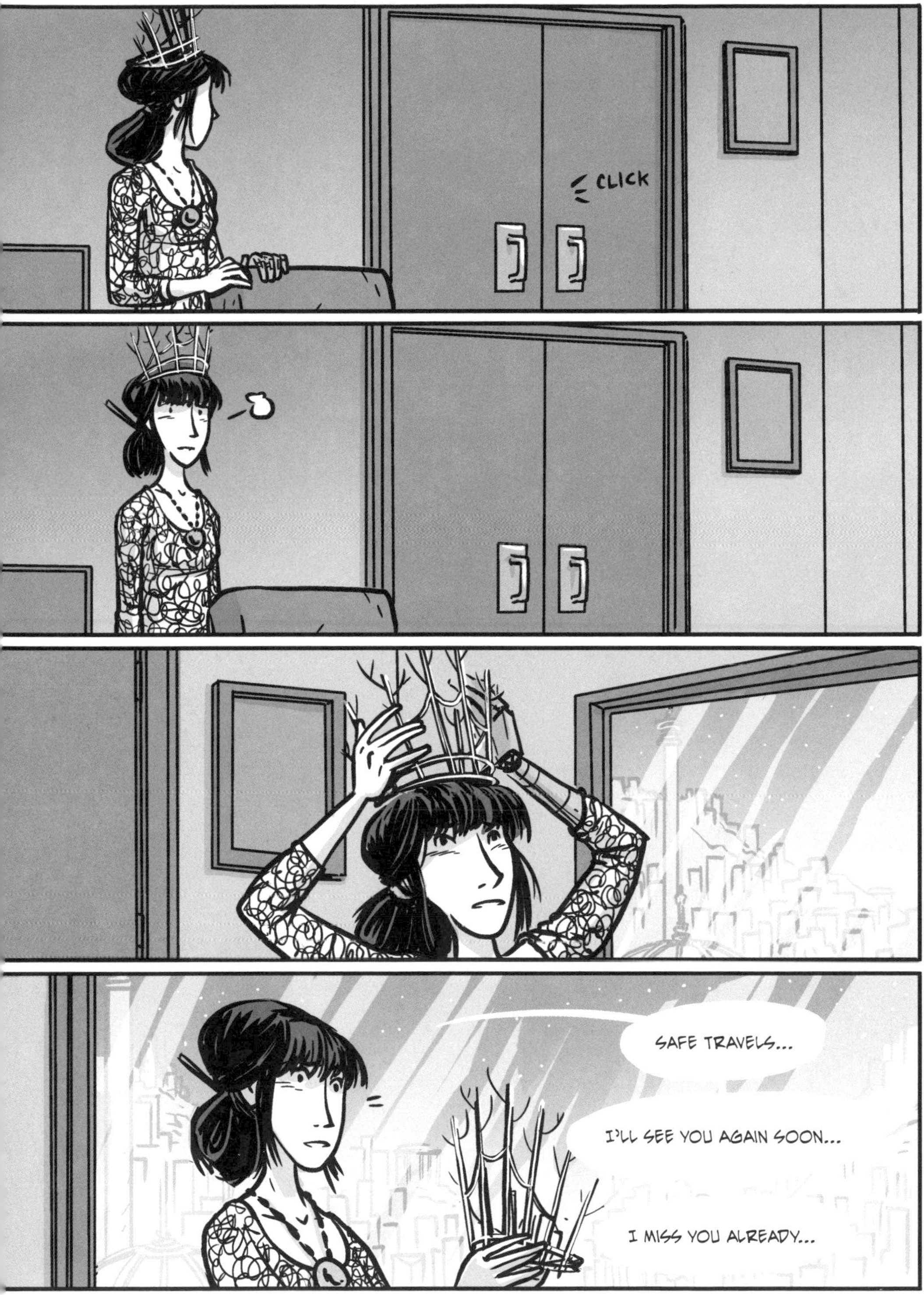
CLICK
SAFE TRAVELS...
I'LL SEE YOU AGAIN SOON...
I MISS YOU ALREADY...

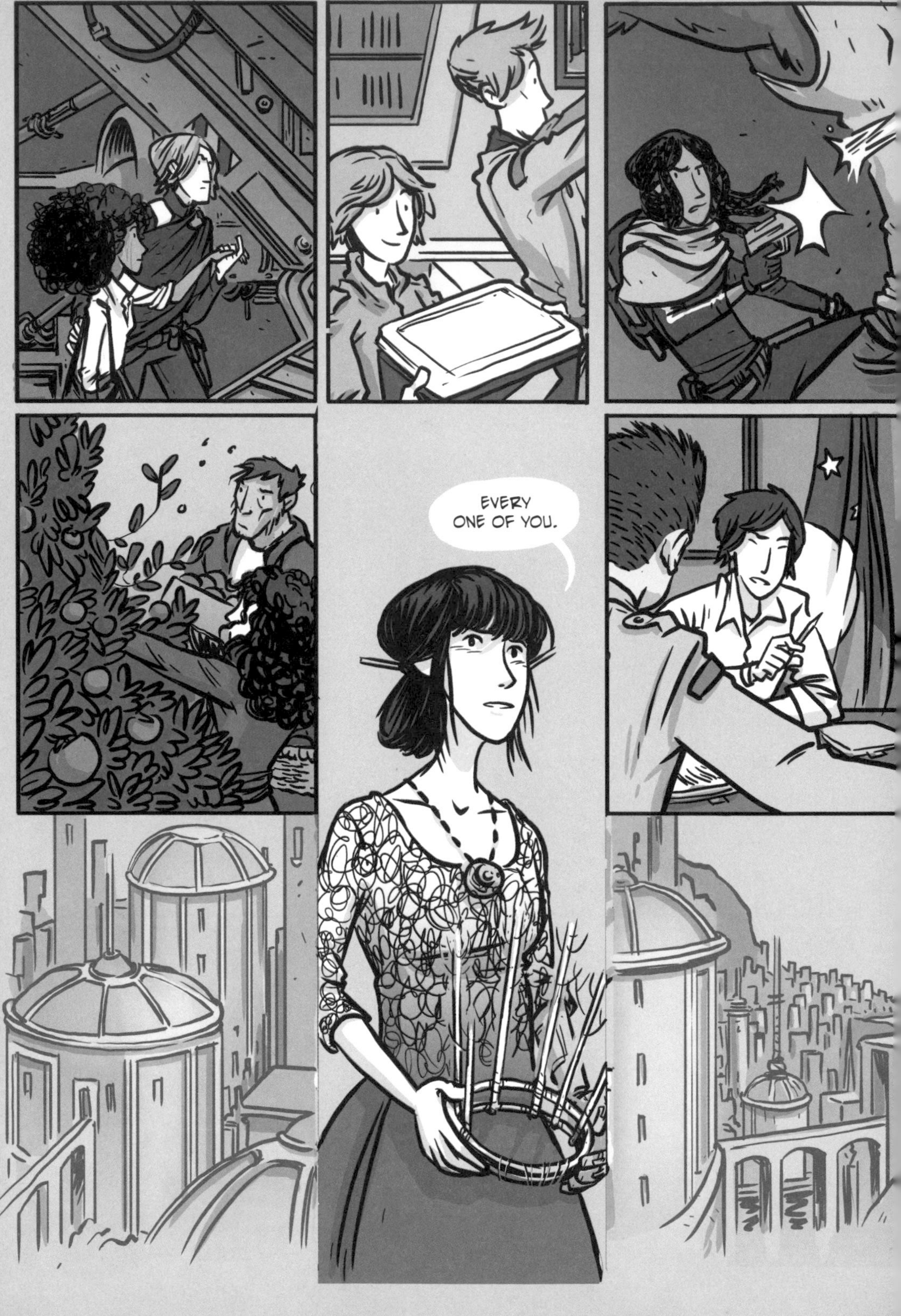
EVERY ONE OF YOU.

CHAPTER V

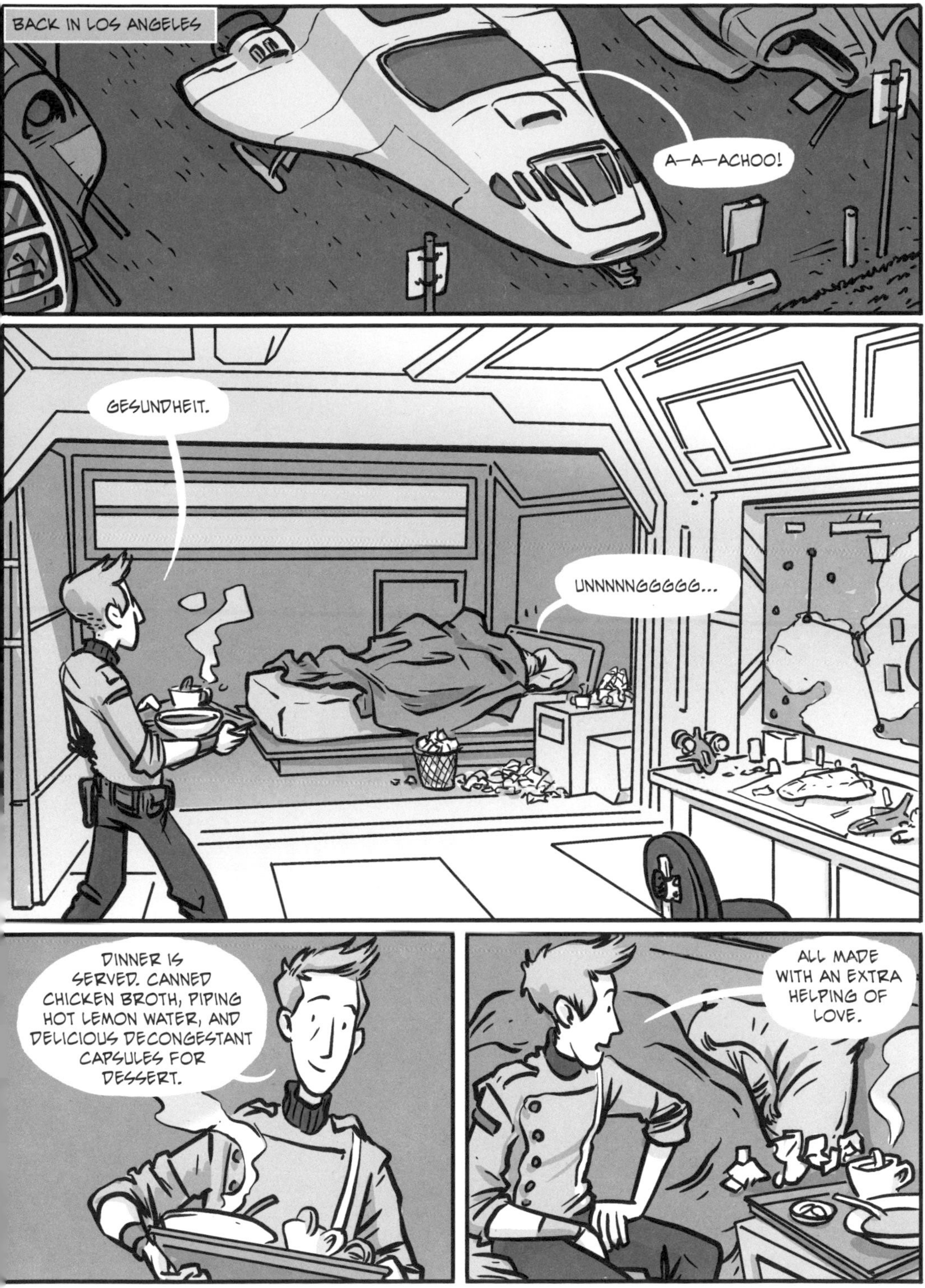
BACK IN LOS ANGELES
A—A—ACHOO!
GESUNDHEIT.
UNNNNNGGGGG...
DINNER IS SERVED. CANNED CHICKEN BROTH, PIPING HOT LEMON WATER, AND DELICIOUS DECONGESTANT CAPSULES FOR DESSERT.
ALL MADE WITH AN EXTRA HELPING OF LOVE.

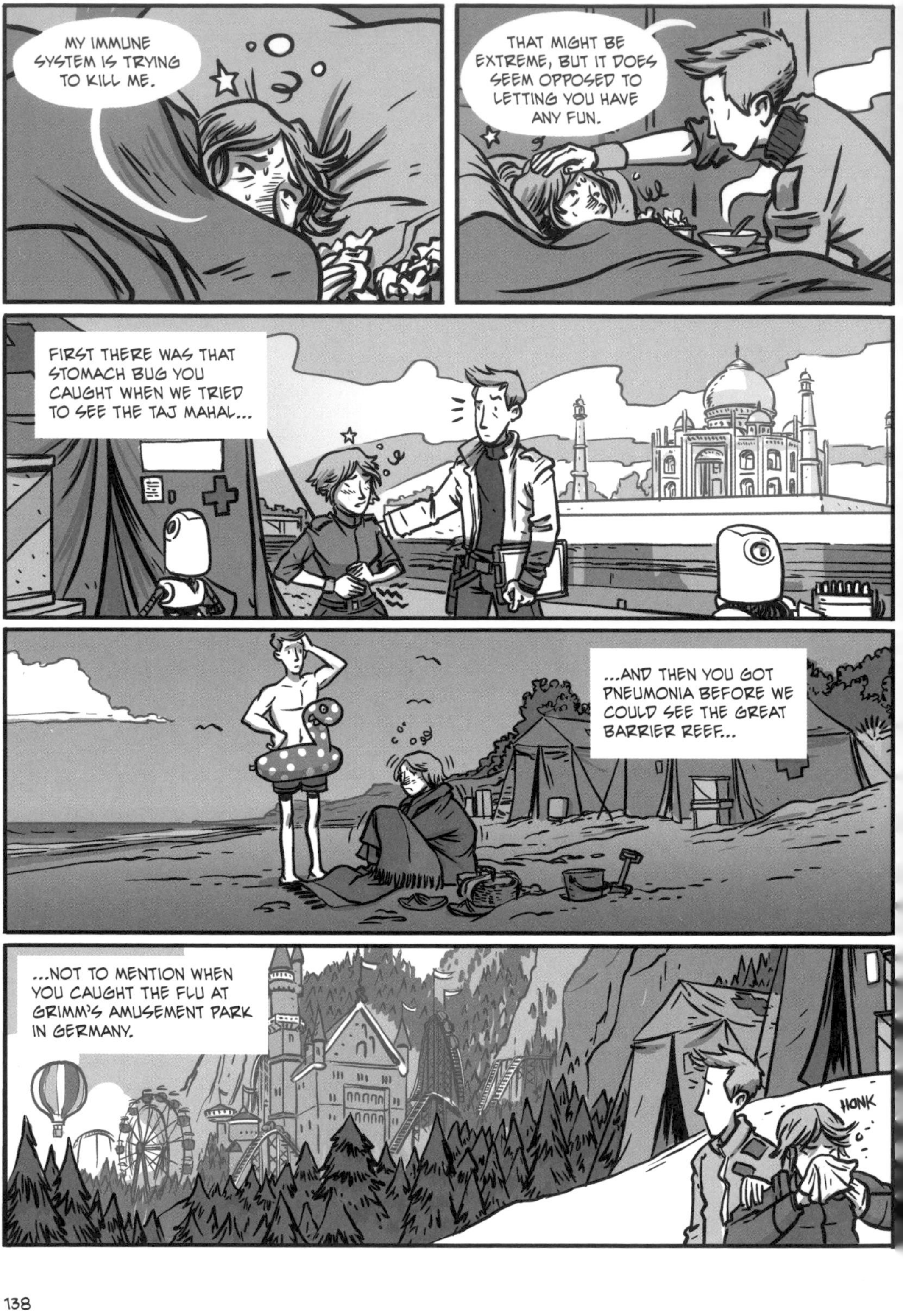

MY IMMUNE SYSTEM IS TRYING TO KILL ME.
THAT MIGHT BE EXTREME, BUT IT DOES SEEM OPPOSED TO LETTING YOU HAVE ANY FUN.
FIRST THERE WAS THAT STOMACH BUG YOU CAUGHT WHEN WE TRIED TO SEE THE TAJ MAHAL...
...AND THEN YOU GOT PNEUMONIA BEFORE WE COULD SEE THE GREAT BARRIER REEF...
...NOT TO MENTION WHEN YOU CAUGHT THE FLU AT GRIMM'S AMUSEMENT PARK IN GERMANY.
HONK

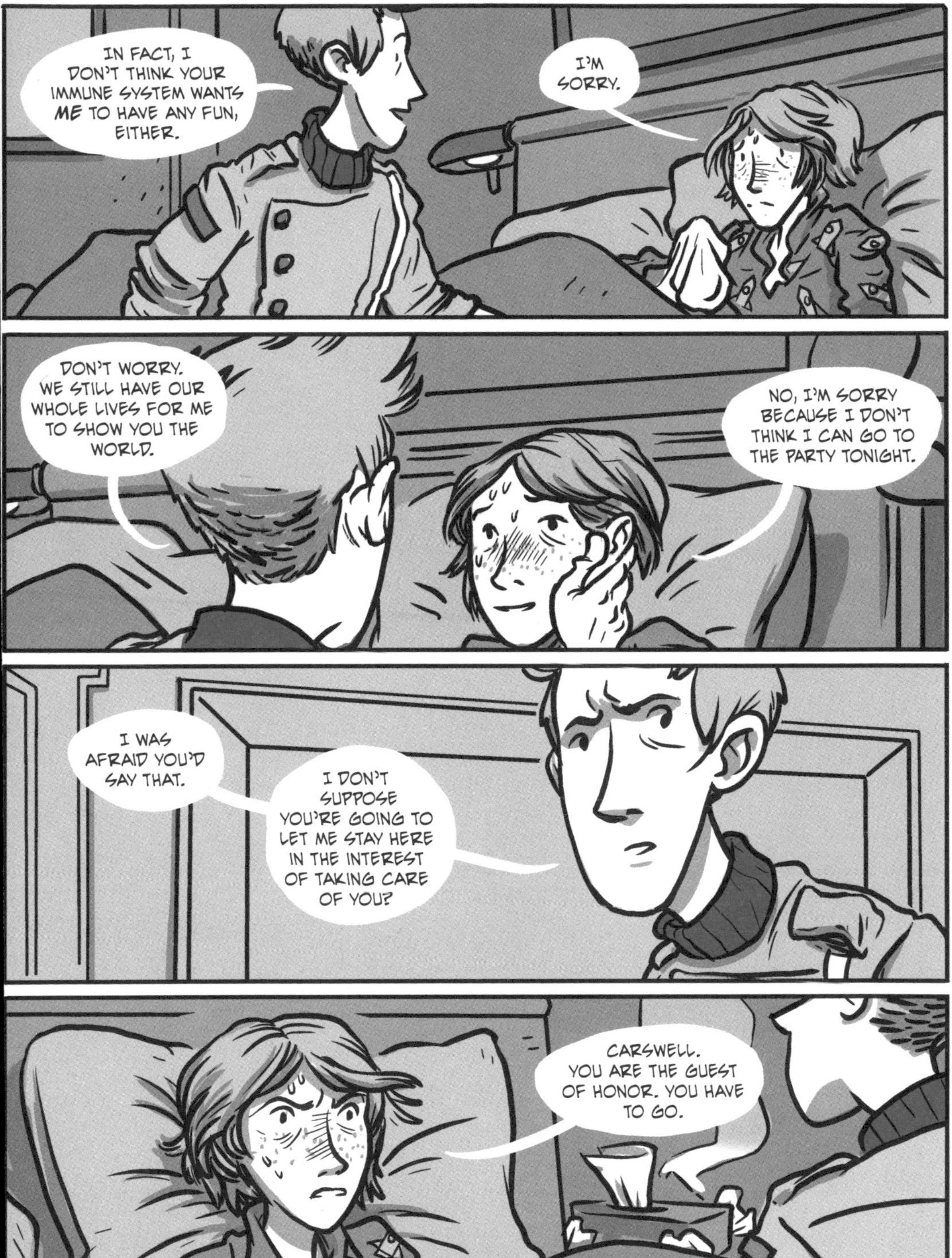
IN FACT, I DON'T THINK YOUR IMMUNE SYSTEM WANTS *ME* TO HAVE ANY FUN, EITHER.
I'M SORRY.
DON'T WORRY. WE STILL HAVE OUR WHOLE LIVES FOR ME TO SHOW YOU THE WORLD.
NO, I'M SORRY BECAUSE I DON'T THINK I CAN GO TO THE PARTY TONIGHT.
I WAS AFRAID YOU'D SAY THAT.
I DON'T SUPPOSE YOU'RE GOING TO LET ME STAY HERE IN THE INTEREST OF TAKING CARE OF YOU?
CARSWELL. YOU ARE THE GUEST OF HONOR. YOU HAVE TO GO.

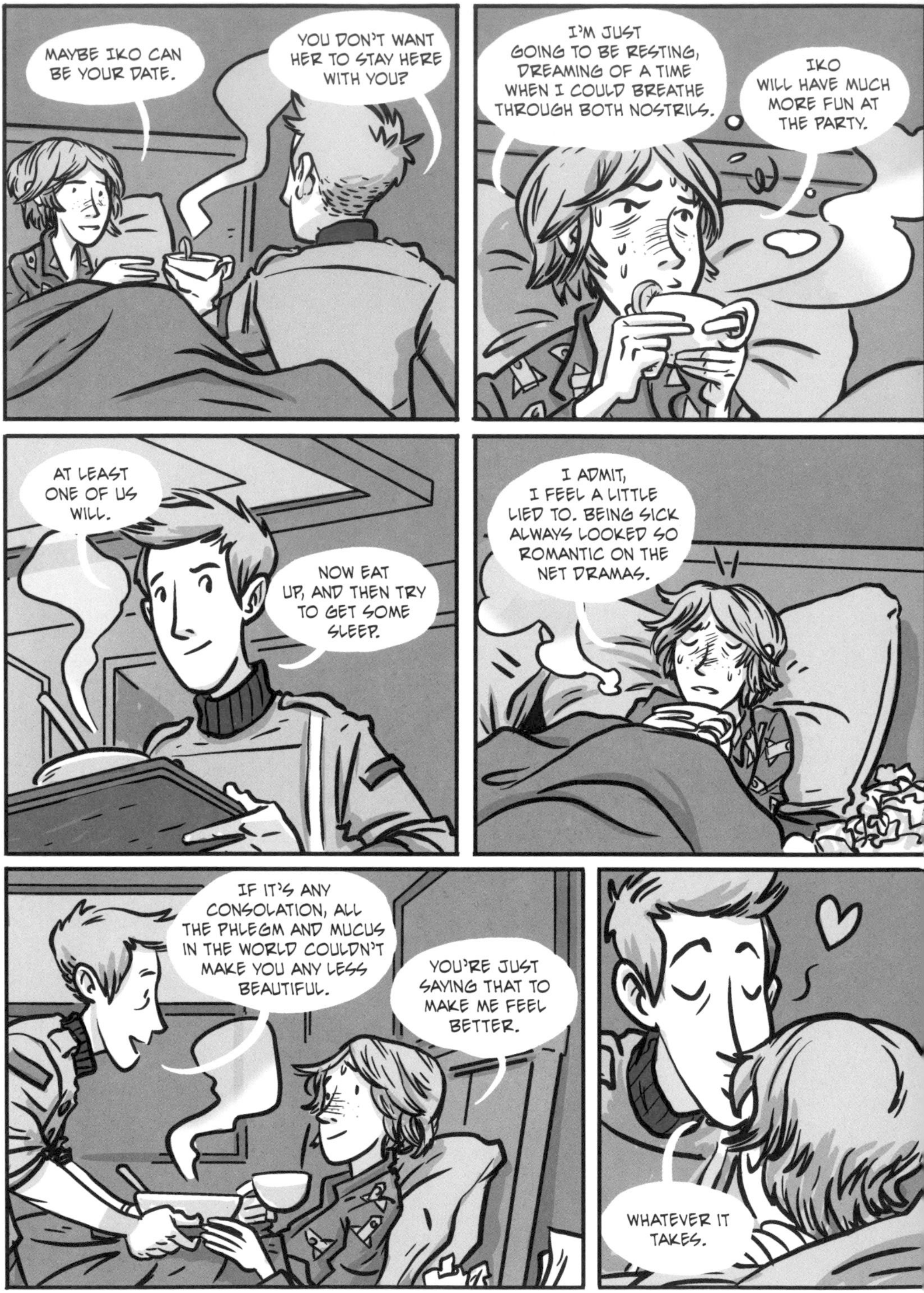
MAYBE IKO CAN BE YOUR DATE.
YOU DON'T WANT HER TO STAY HERE WITH YOU?
I'M JUST GOING TO BE RESTING, DREAMING OF A TIME WHEN I COULD BREATHE THROUGH BOTH NOSTRILS.
IKO WILL HAVE MUCH MORE FUN AT THE PARTY.
AT LEAST ONE OF US WILL.
NOW EAT UP, AND THEN TRY TO GET SOME SLEEP.
I ADMIT, I FEEL A LITTLE LIED TO. BEING SICK ALWAYS LOOKED SO ROMANTIC ON THE NET DRAMAS.
IF IT'S ANY CONSOLATION, ALL THE PHLEGM AND MUCUS IN THE WORLD COULDN'T MAKE YOU ANY LESS BEAUTIFUL.
YOU'RE JUST SAYING THAT TO MAKE ME FEEL BETTER.
WHATEVER IT TAKES.

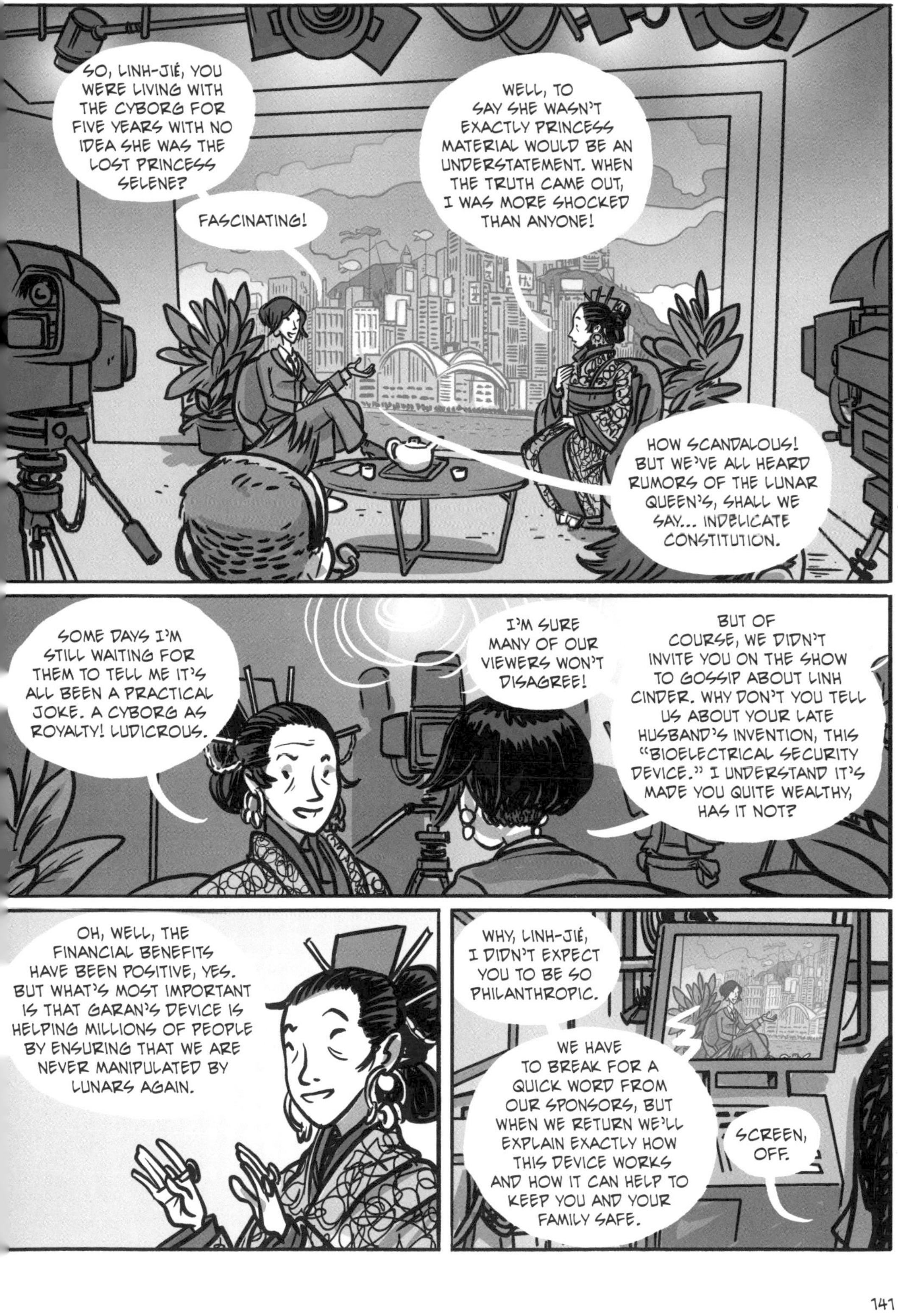
SO, LINH-JIÉ, YOU WERE LIVING WITH THE CYBORG FOR FIVE YEARS WITH NO IDEA SHE WAS THE LOST PRINCESS SELENE?
FASCINATING!
WELL, TO SAY SHE WASN'T EXACTLY PRINCESS MATERIAL WOULD BE AN UNDERSTATEMENT. WHEN THE TRUTH CAME OUT, I WAS MORE SHOCKED THAN ANYONE!
HOW SCANDALOUS! BUT WE'VE ALL HEARD RUMORS OF THE LUNAR QUEEN'S, SHALL WE SAY... INDELICATE CONSTITUTION.
SOME DAYS I'M STILL WAITING FOR THEM TO TELL ME IT'S ALL BEEN A PRACTICAL JOKE. A CYBORG AS ROYALTY! LUDICROUS.
I'M SURE MANY OF OUR VIEWERS WON'T DISAGREE!
BUT OF COURSE, WE DIDN'T INVITE YOU ON THE SHOW TO GOSSIP ABOUT LINH CINDER. WHY DON'T YOU TELL US ABOUT YOUR LATE HUSBAND'S INVENTION, THIS "BIOELECTRICAL SECURITY DEVICE." I UNDERSTAND IT'S MADE YOU QUITE WEALTHY, HAS IT NOT?
OH, WELL, THE FINANCIAL BENEFITS HAVE BEEN POSITIVE, YES. BUT WHAT'S MOST IMPORTANT IS THAT GARAN'S DEVICE IS HELPING MILLIONS OF PEOPLE BY ENSURING THAT WE ARE NEVER MANIPULATED BY LUNARS AGAIN.
WHY, LINH-JIÉ, I DIDN'T EXPECT YOU TO BE SO PHILANTHROPIC.
WE HAVE TO BREAK FOR A QUICK WORD FROM OUR SPONSORS, BUT WHEN WE RETURN WE'LL EXPLAIN EXACTLY HOW THIS DEVICE WORKS AND HOW IT CAN HELP TO KEEP YOU AND YOUR FAMILY SAFE.
SCREEN, OFF.

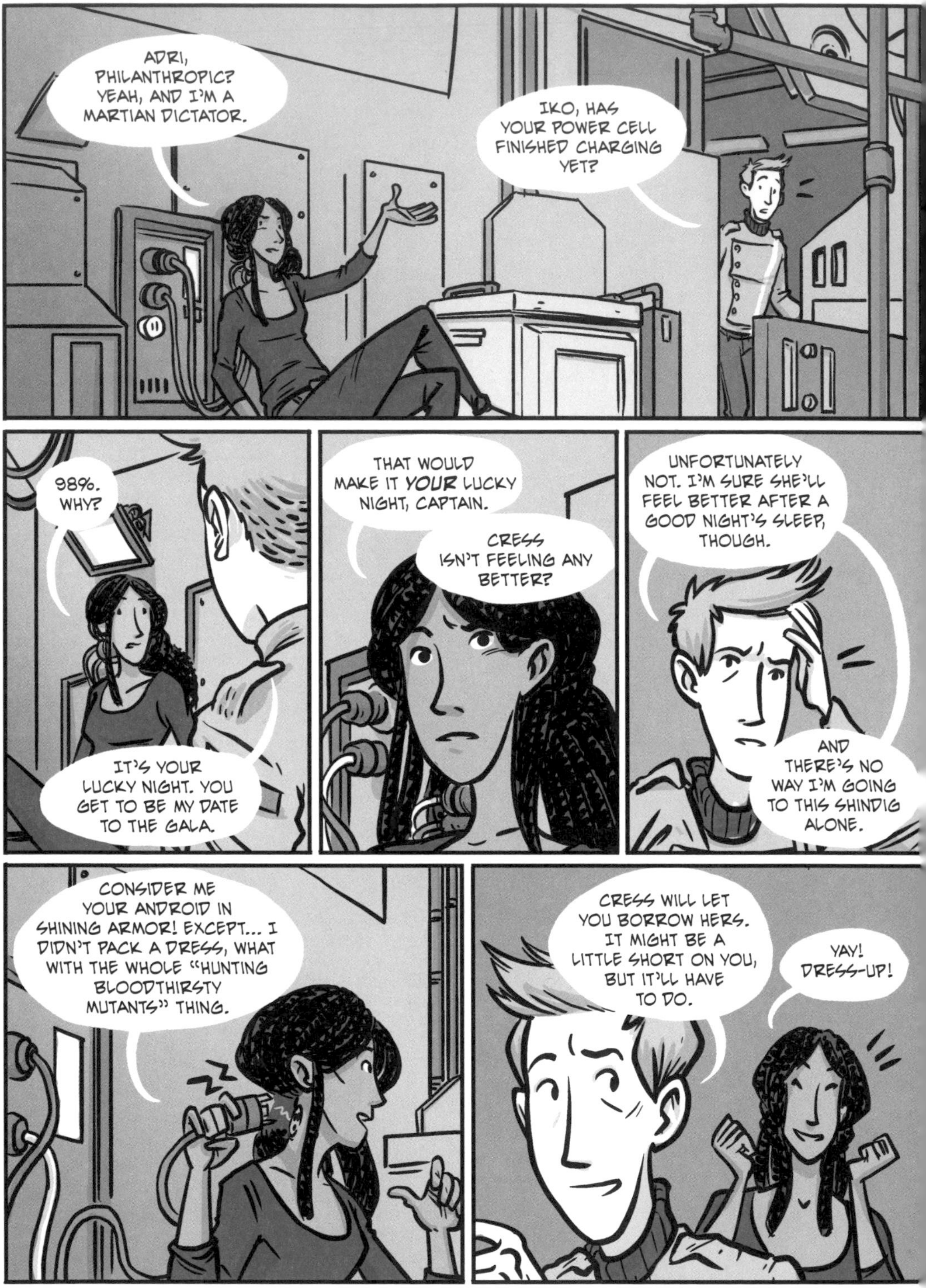
ADRI, PHILANTHROPIC? YEAH, AND I'M A MARTIAN DICTATOR.
IKO, HAS YOUR POWER CELL FINISHED CHARGING YET?
98%. WHY?
IT'S YOUR LUCKY NIGHT. YOU GET TO BE MY DATE TO THE GALA.
THAT WOULD MAKE IT *YOUR* LUCKY NIGHT, CAPTAIN.
CRESS ISN'T FEELING ANY BETTER?
UNFORTUNATELY NOT. I'M SURE SHE'LL FEEL BETTER AFTER A GOOD NIGHT'S SLEEP, THOUGH.
AND THERE'S NO WAY I'M GOING TO THIS SHINDIG ALONE.
CONSIDER ME YOUR ANDROID IN SHINING ARMOR! EXCEPT... I DIDN'T PACK A DRESS, WHAT WITH THE WHOLE "HUNTING BLOODTHIRSTY MUTANTS" THING.
CRESS WILL LET YOU BORROW HERS. IT MIGHT BE A LITTLE SHORT ON YOU, BUT IT'LL HAVE TO DO.
YAY! DRESS-UP!

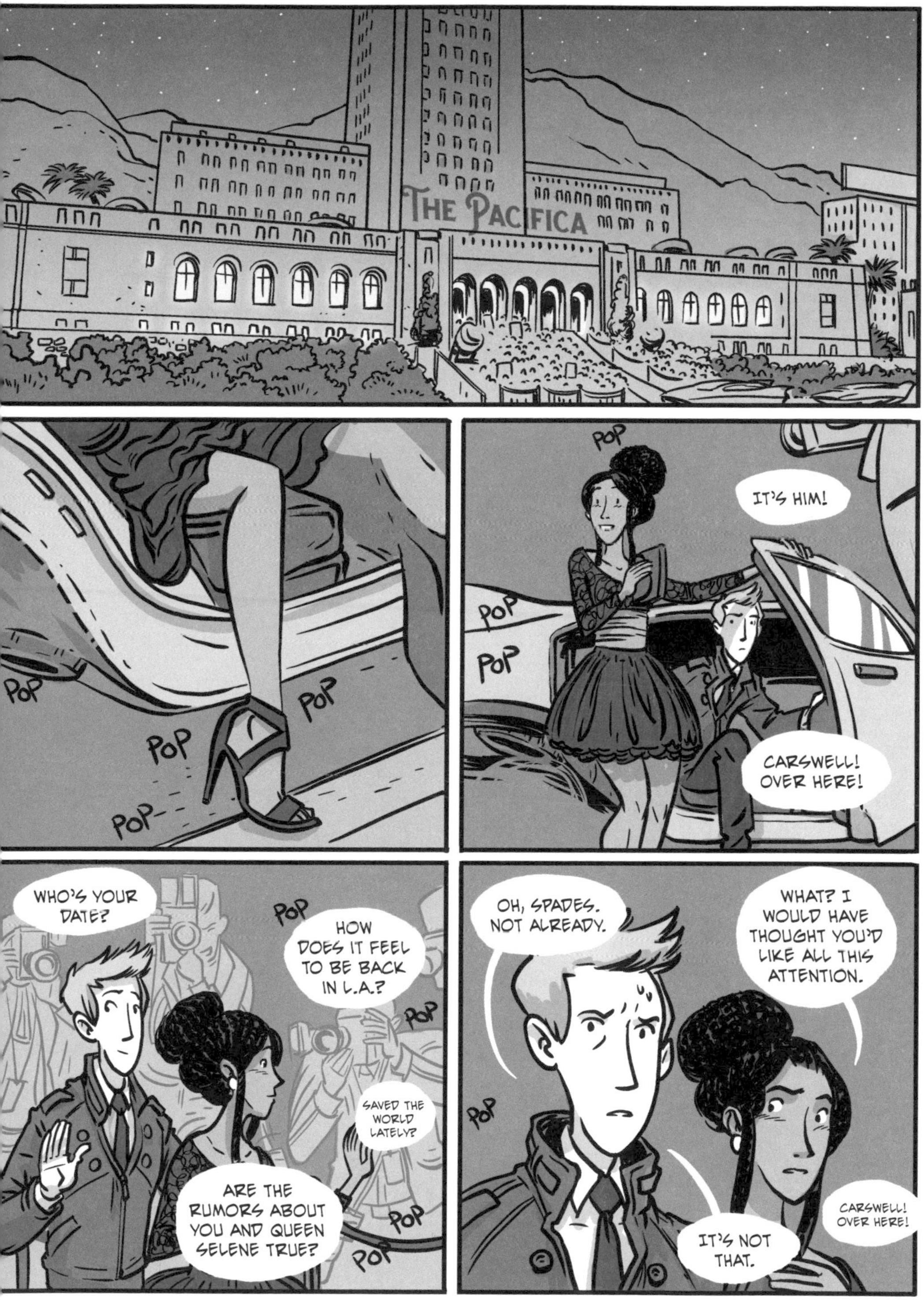
THE PACIFICA
POP
POP
POP
POP
POP
IT'S HIM!
POP
POP
CARSWELL! OVER HERE!
WHO'S YOUR DATE?
POP
HOW DOES IT FEEL TO BE BACK IN L.A.?
POP
SAVED THE WORLD LATELY?
ARE THE RUMORS ABOUT YOU AND QUEEN SELENE TRUE?
POP
POP
OH, SPADES. NOT ALREADY.
WHAT? I WOULD HAVE THOUGHT YOU'D LIKE ALL THIS ATTENTION.
POP
IT'S NOT THAT.
CARSWELL! OVER HERE!

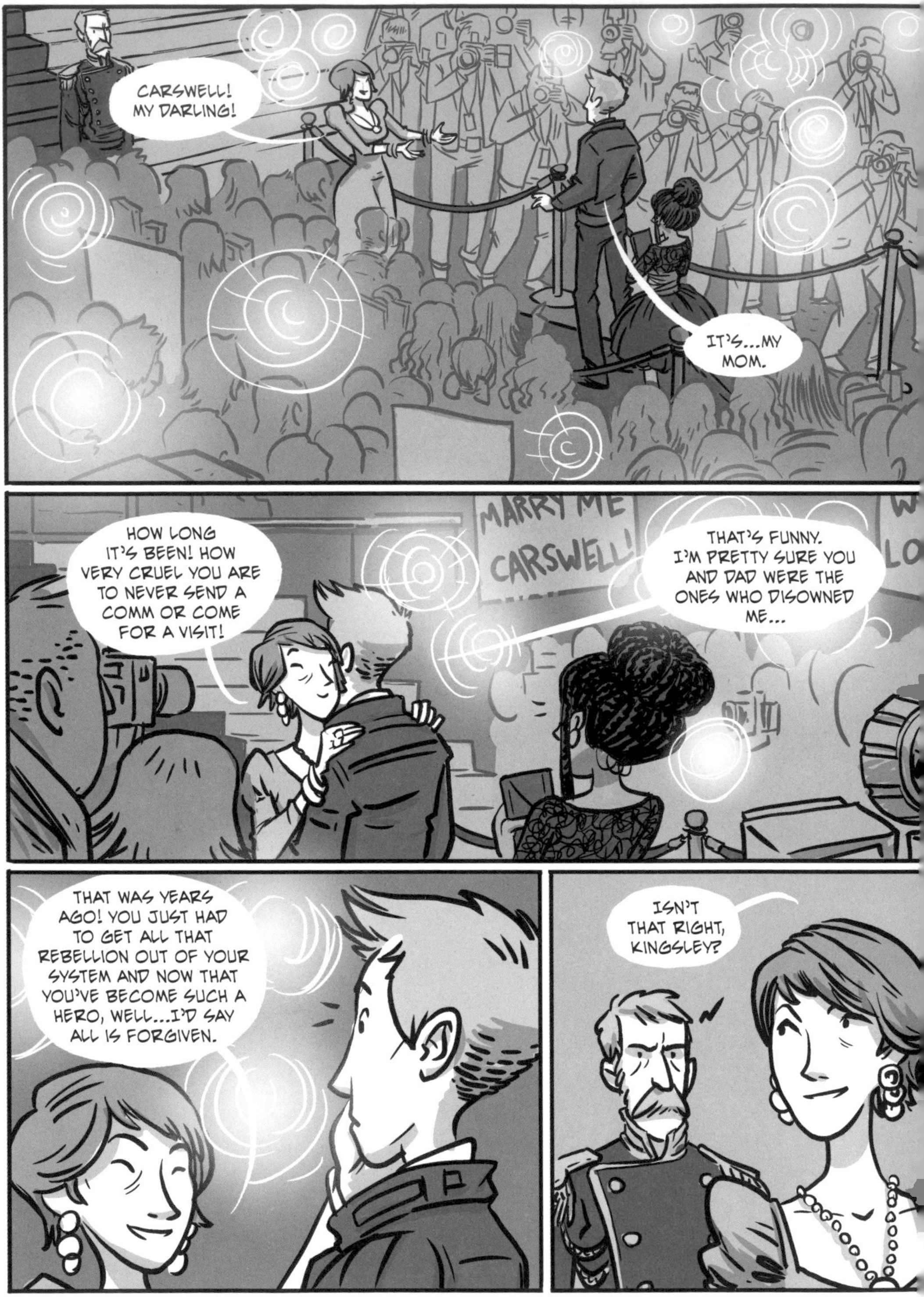
CARSWELL! MY DARLING!
IT'S...MY MOM.
HOW LONG IT'S BEEN! HOW VERY CRUEL YOU ARE TO NEVER SEND A COMM OR COME FOR A VISIT!
MARRY ME CARSWELL!
THAT'S FUNNY. I'M PRETTY SURE YOU AND DAD WERE THE ONES WHO DISOWNED ME...
THAT WAS YEARS AGO! YOU JUST HAD TO GET ALL THAT REBELLION OUT OF YOUR SYSTEM AND NOW THAT YOU'VE BECOME SUCH A HERO, WELL...I'D SAY ALL IS FORGIVEN.
ISN'T THAT RIGHT, KINGSLEY?

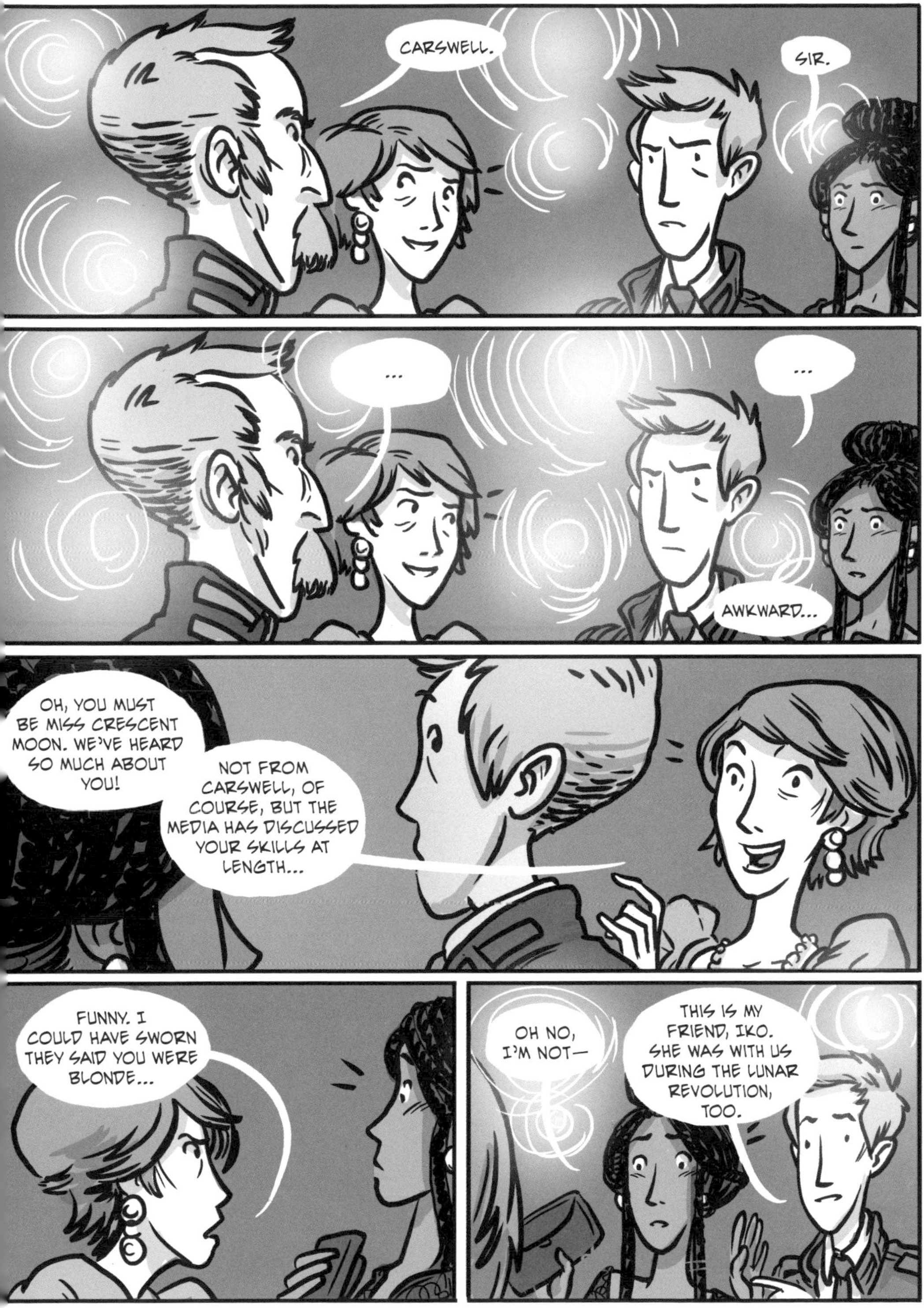
CARSWELL.
SIR.
...
...
AWKWARD...
OH, YOU MUST BE MISS CRESCENT MOON. WE'VE HEARD SO MUCH ABOUT YOU!
NOT FROM CARSWELL, OF COURSE, BUT THE MEDIA HAS DISCUSSED YOUR SKILLS AT LENGTH...
FUNNY. I COULD HAVE SWORN THEY SAID YOU WERE BLONDE...
OH NO, I'M NOT—
THIS IS MY FRIEND, IKO. SHE WAS WITH US DURING THE LUNAR REVOLUTION, TOO.

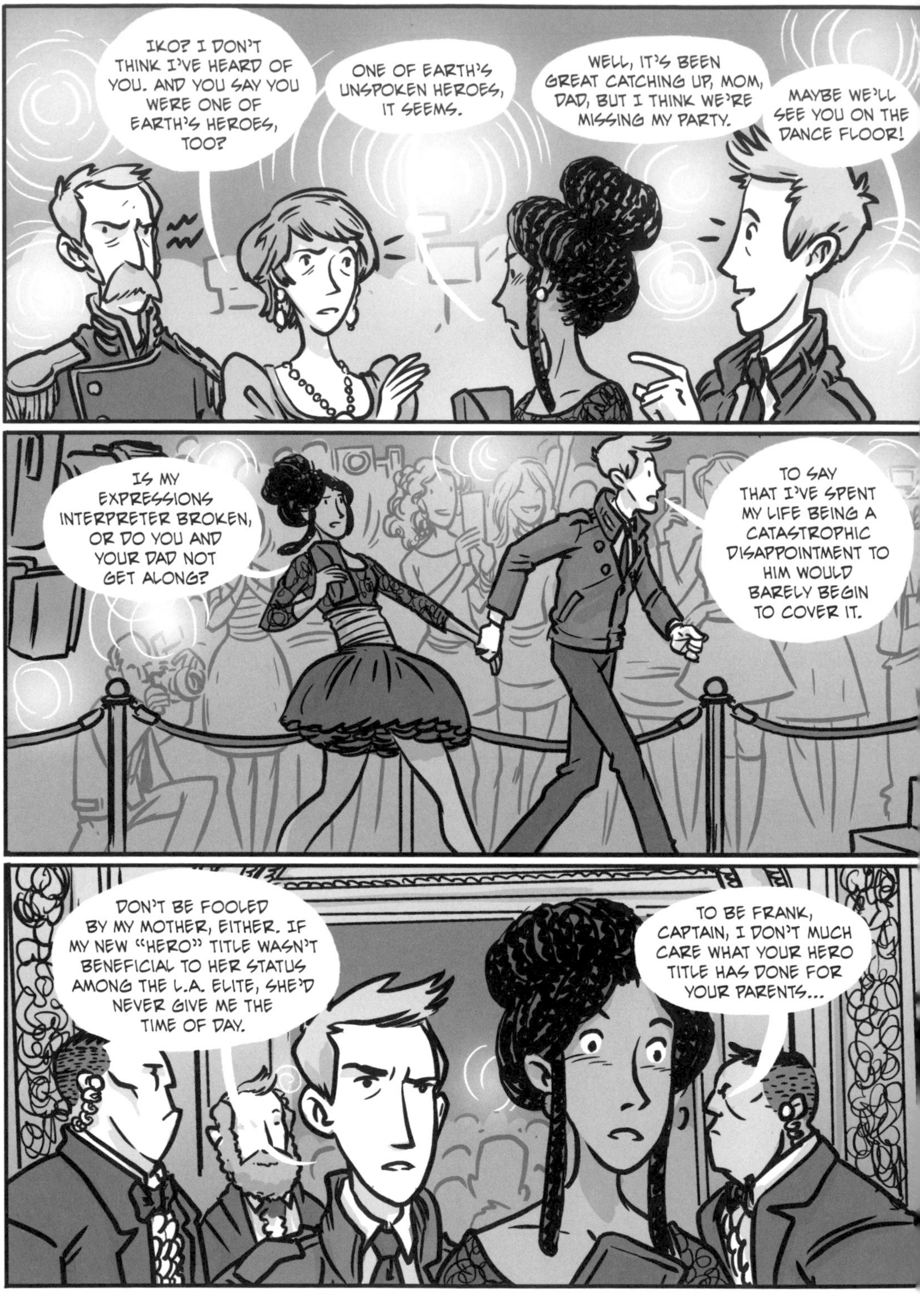
IKO? I DON'T THINK I'VE HEARD OF YOU. AND YOU SAY YOU WERE ONE OF EARTH'S HEROES, TOO?
ONE OF EARTH'S UNSPOKEN HEROES, IT SEEMS.
WELL, IT'S BEEN GREAT CATCHING UP, MOM, DAD, BUT I THINK WE'RE MISSING MY PARTY.
MAYBE WE'LL SEE YOU ON THE DANCE FLOOR!
IS MY EXPRESSIONS INTERPRETER BROKEN, OR DO YOU AND YOUR DAD NOT GET ALONG?
TO SAY THAT I'VE SPENT MY LIFE BEING A CATASTROPHIC DISAPPOINTMENT TO HIM WOULD BARELY BEGIN TO COVER IT.
DON'T BE FOOLED BY MY MOTHER, EITHER. IF MY NEW "HERO" TITLE WASN'T BENEFICIAL TO HER STATUS AMONG THE L.A. ELITE, SHE'D NEVER GIVE ME THE TIME OF DAY.
TO BE FRANK, CAPTAIN, I DON'T MUCH CARE WHAT YOUR HERO TITLE HAS DONE FOR YOUR PARENTS...

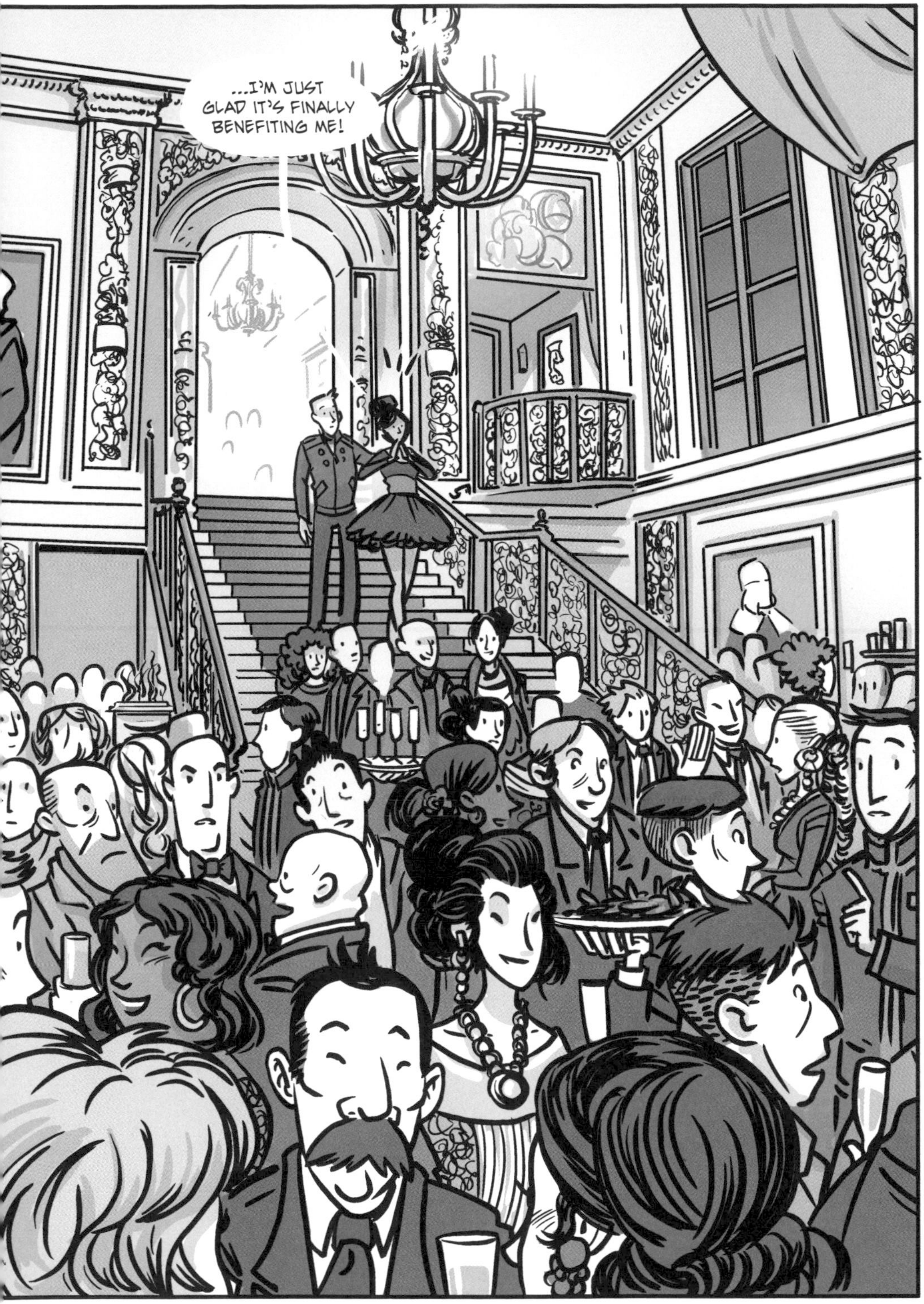
...I'M JUST GLAD IT'S FINALLY BENEFITING ME!

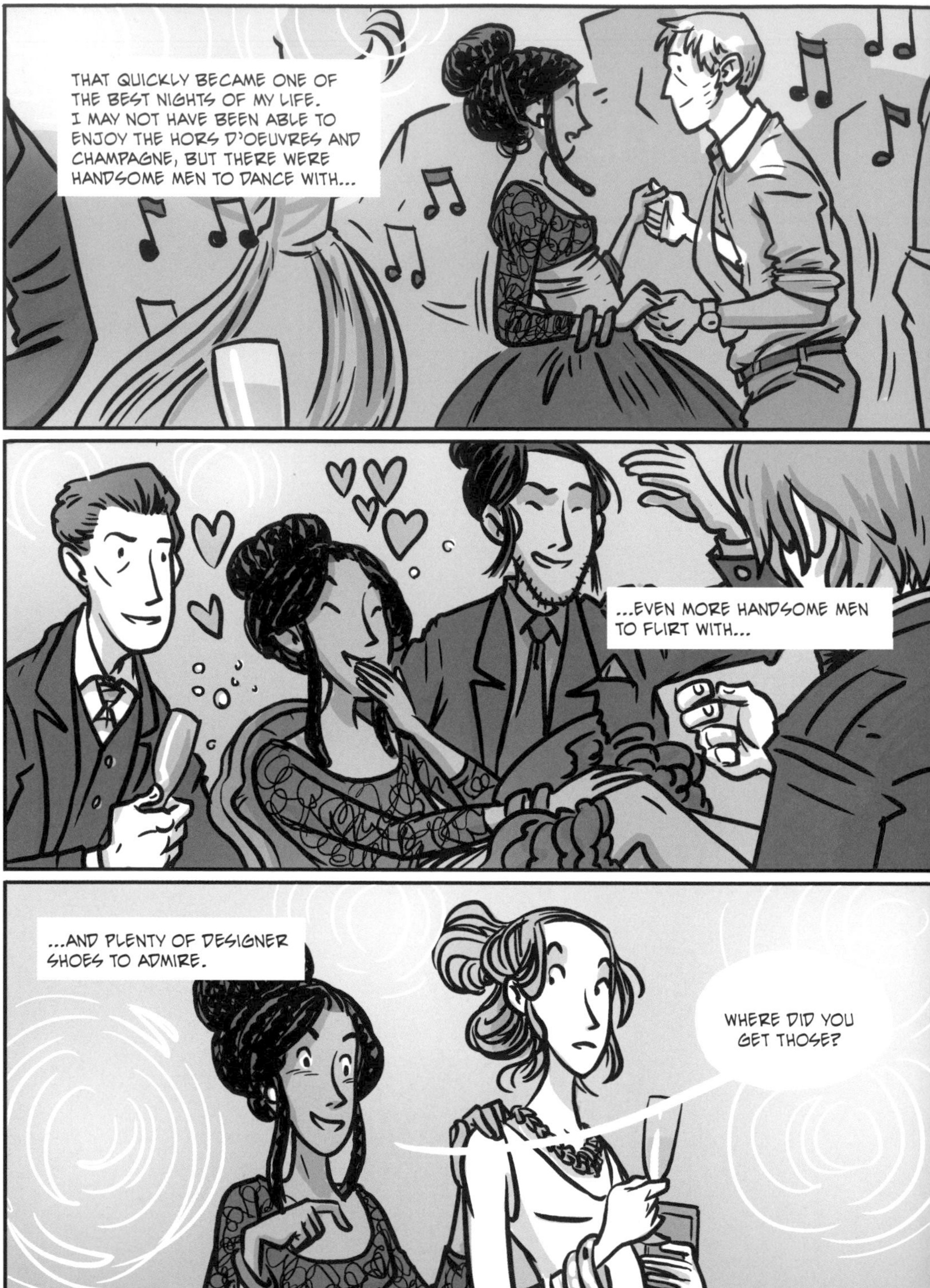
THAT QUICKLY BECAME ONE OF THE BEST NIGHTS OF MY LIFE. I MAY NOT HAVE BEEN ABLE TO ENJOY THE HORS D'OEUVRES AND CHAMPAGNE, BUT THERE WERE HANDSOME MEN TO DANCE WITH...
...EVEN MORE HANDSOME MEN TO FLIRT WITH...
...AND PLENTY OF DESIGNER SHOES TO ADMIRE.
WHERE DID YOU GET THOSE?

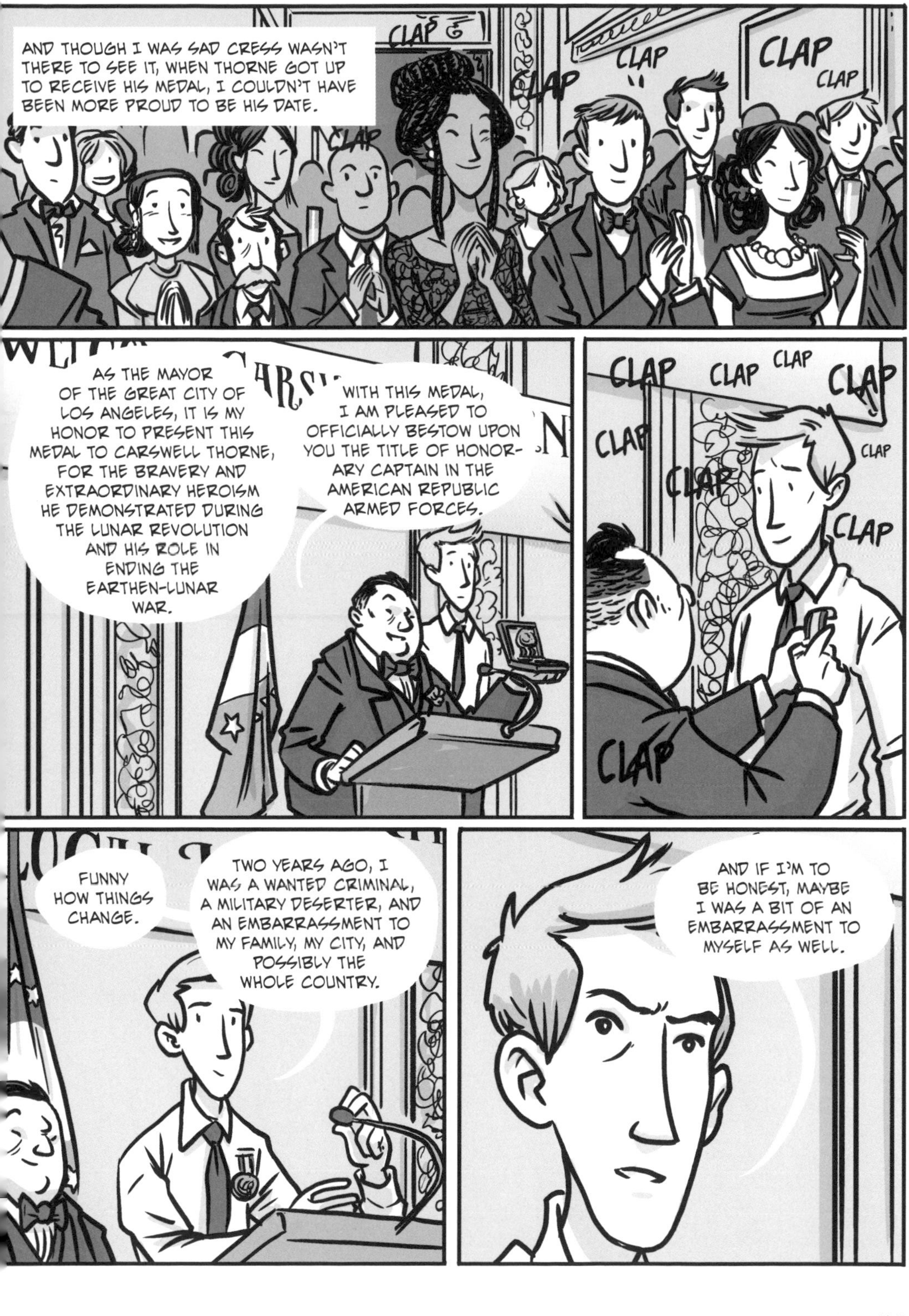
AND THOUGH I WAS SAD CRESS WASN'T THERE TO SEE IT, WHEN THORNE GOT UP TO RECEIVE HIS MEDAL, I COULDN'T HAVE BEEN MORE PROUD TO BE HIS DATE.
CLAP
CLAP
CLAP
CLAP
CLAP
CLAP
AS THE MAYOR OF THE GREAT CITY OF LOS ANGELES, IT IS MY HONOR TO PRESENT THIS MEDAL TO CARSWELL THORNE, FOR THE BRAVERY AND EXTRAORDINARY HEROISM HE DEMONSTRATED DURING THE LUNAR REVOLUTION AND HIS ROLE IN ENDING THE EARTHEN-LUNAR WAR.
WITH THIS MEDAL, I AM PLEASED TO OFFICIALLY BESTOW UPON YOU THE TITLE OF HONORARY CAPTAIN IN THE AMERICAN REPUBLIC ARMED FORCES.
CLAP
CLAP
CLAP
CLAP
CLAP
CLAP
CLAP
CLAP
CLAP
FUNNY HOW THINGS CHANGE.
TWO YEARS AGO, I WAS A WANTED CRIMINAL, A MILITARY DESERTER, AND AN EMBARRASSMENT TO MY FAMILY, MY CITY, AND POSSIBLY THE WHOLE COUNTRY.
AND IF I'M TO BE HONEST, MAYBE I WAS A BIT OF AN EMBARRASSMENT TO MYSELF AS WELL.

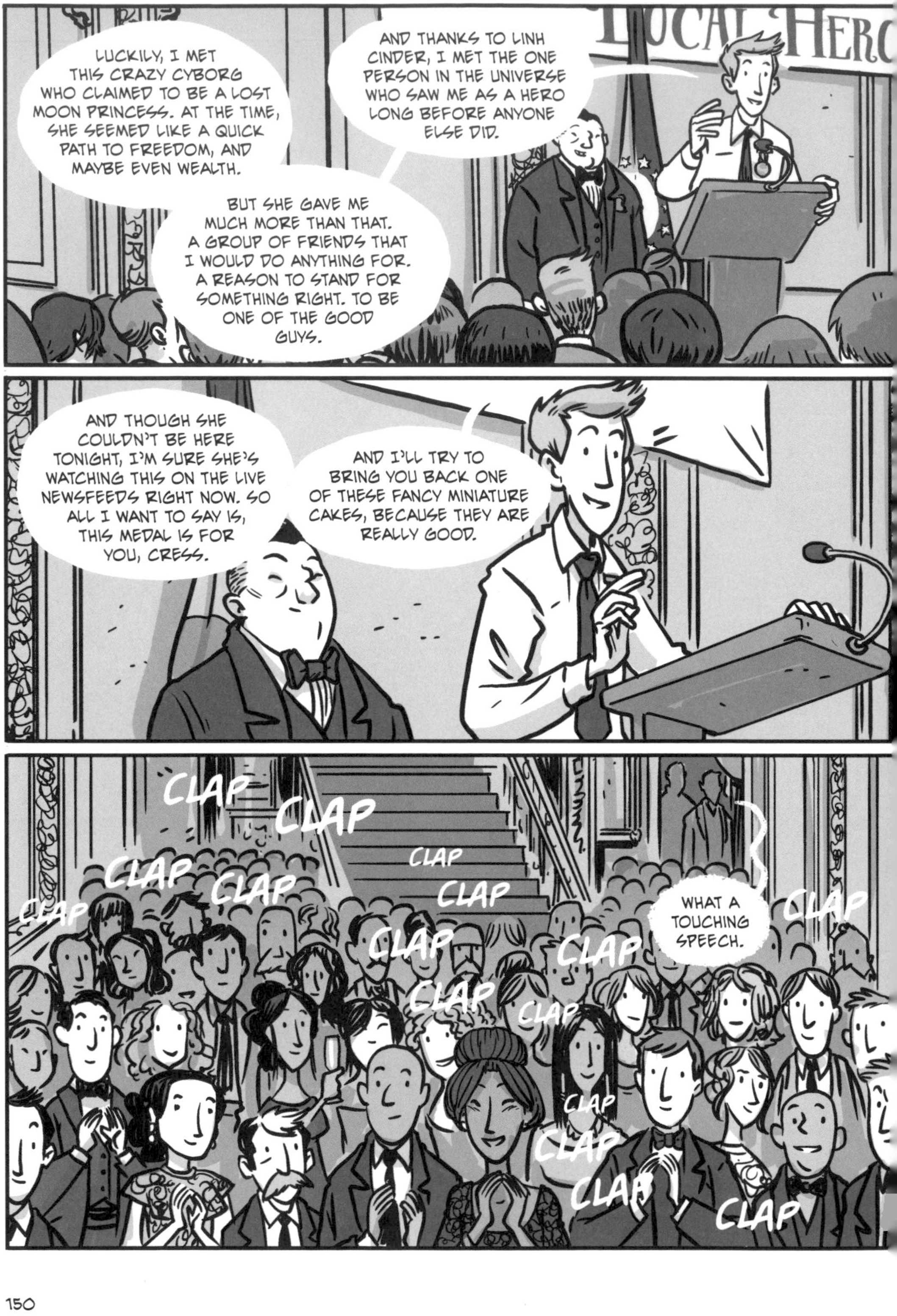
LOCAL HERO
LUCKILY, I MET THIS CRAZY CYBORG WHO CLAIMED TO BE A LOST MOON PRINCESS. AT THE TIME, SHE SEEMED LIKE A QUICK PATH TO FREEDOM, AND MAYBE EVEN WEALTH.
AND THANKS TO LINH CINDER, I MET THE ONE PERSON IN THE UNIVERSE WHO SAW ME AS A HERO LONG BEFORE ANYONE ELSE DID.
BUT SHE GAVE ME MUCH MORE THAN THAT. A GROUP OF FRIENDS THAT I WOULD DO ANYTHING FOR. A REASON TO STAND FOR SOMETHING RIGHT. TO BE ONE OF THE GOOD GUYS.
AND THOUGH SHE COULDN'T BE HERE TONIGHT, I'M SURE SHE'S WATCHING THIS ON THE LIVE NEWSFEEDS RIGHT NOW. SO ALL I WANT TO SAY IS, THIS MEDAL IS FOR YOU, CRESS.
AND I'LL TRY TO BRING YOU BACK ONE OF THESE FANCY MINIATURE CAKES, BECAUSE THEY ARE REALLY GOOD.
CLAP CLAP CLAP CLAP CLAP CLAP CLAP
WHAT A TOUCHING SPEECH.
CLAP CLAP CLAP CLAP CLAP CLAP CLAP CLAP CLAP

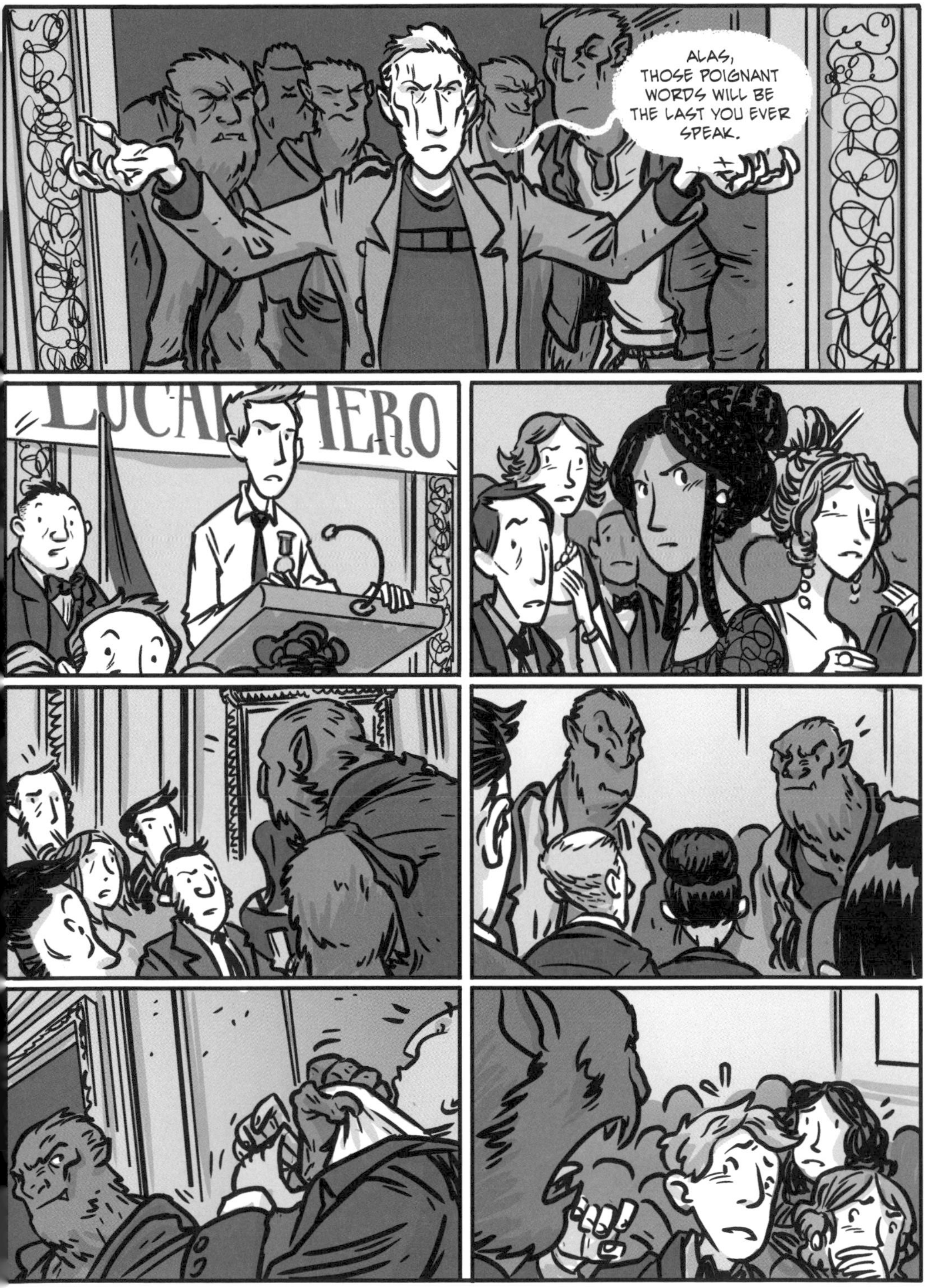
ALAS, THOSE POIGNANT WORDS WILL BE THE LAST YOU EVER SPEAK.
LOCAL HERO

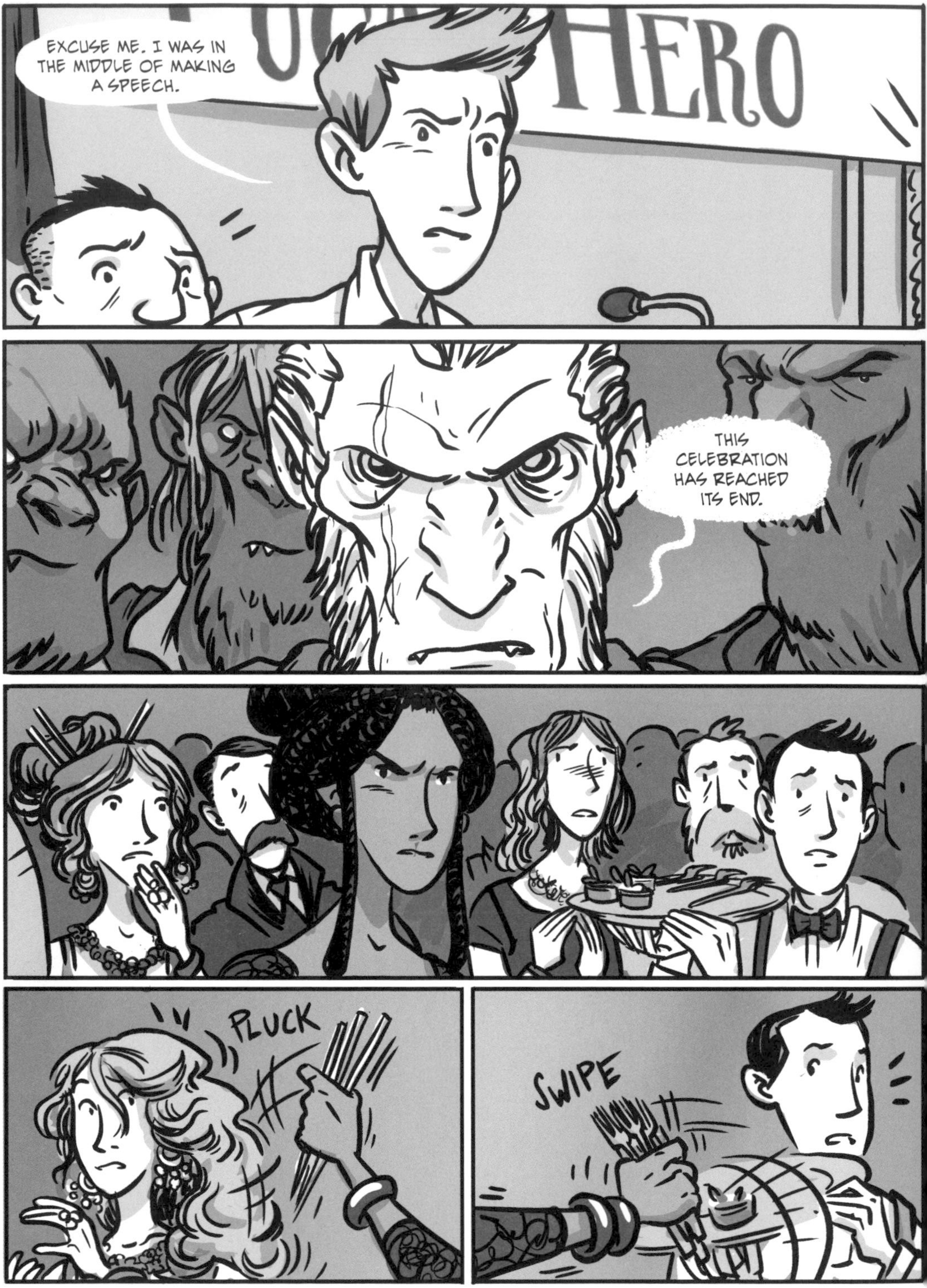
HERO
EXCUSE ME. I WAS IN THE MIDDLE OF MAKING A SPEECH.
THIS CELEBRATION HAS REACHED ITS END.
PLUCK
SWIPE

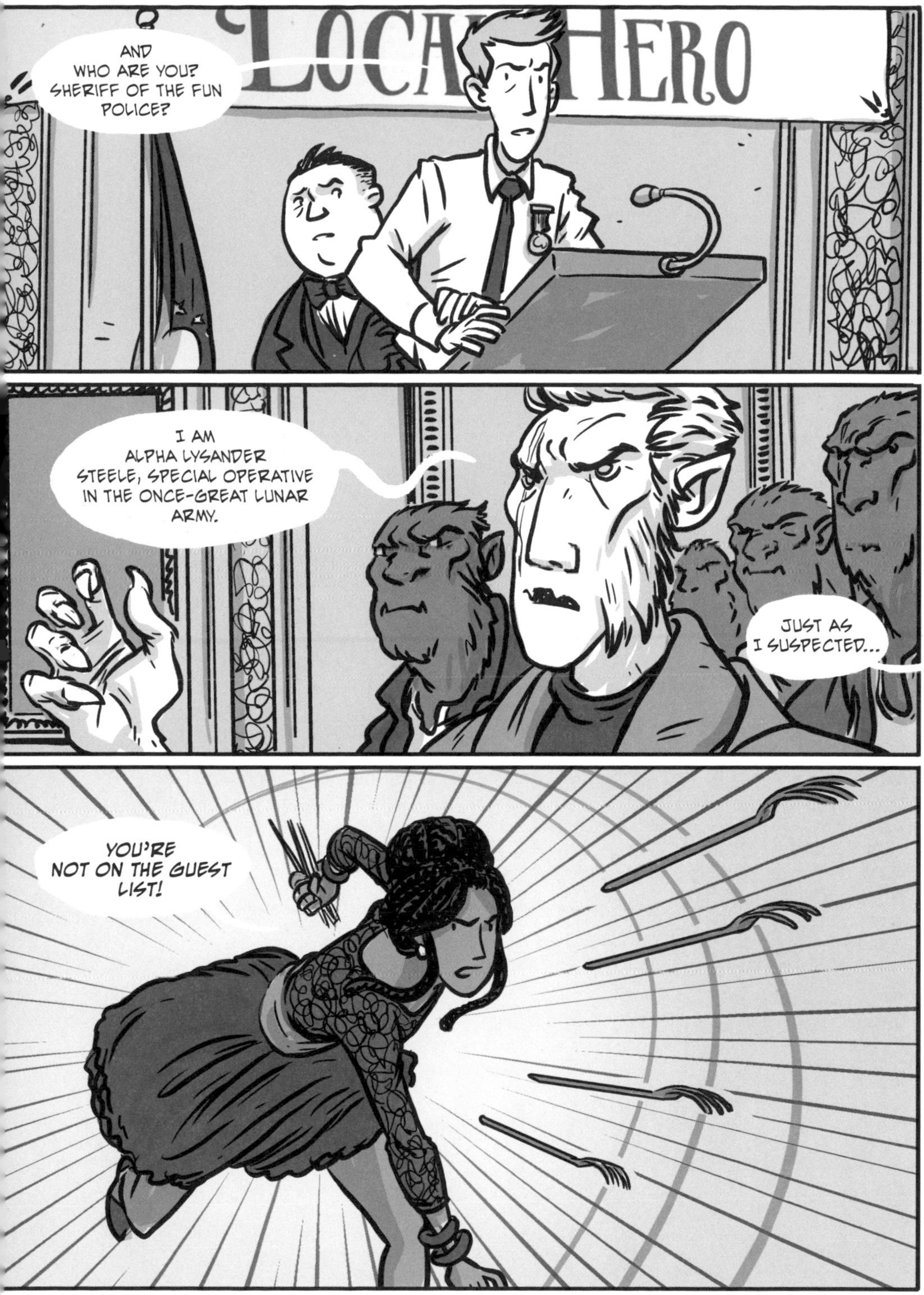
LOCAL HERO
AND WHO ARE YOU? SHERIFF OF THE FUN POLICE?
I AM ALPHA LYSANDER STEELE, SPECIAL OPERATIVE IN THE ONCE-GREAT LUNAR ARMY.
JUST AS I SUSPECTED...
YOU'RE NOT ON THE GUEST LIST!

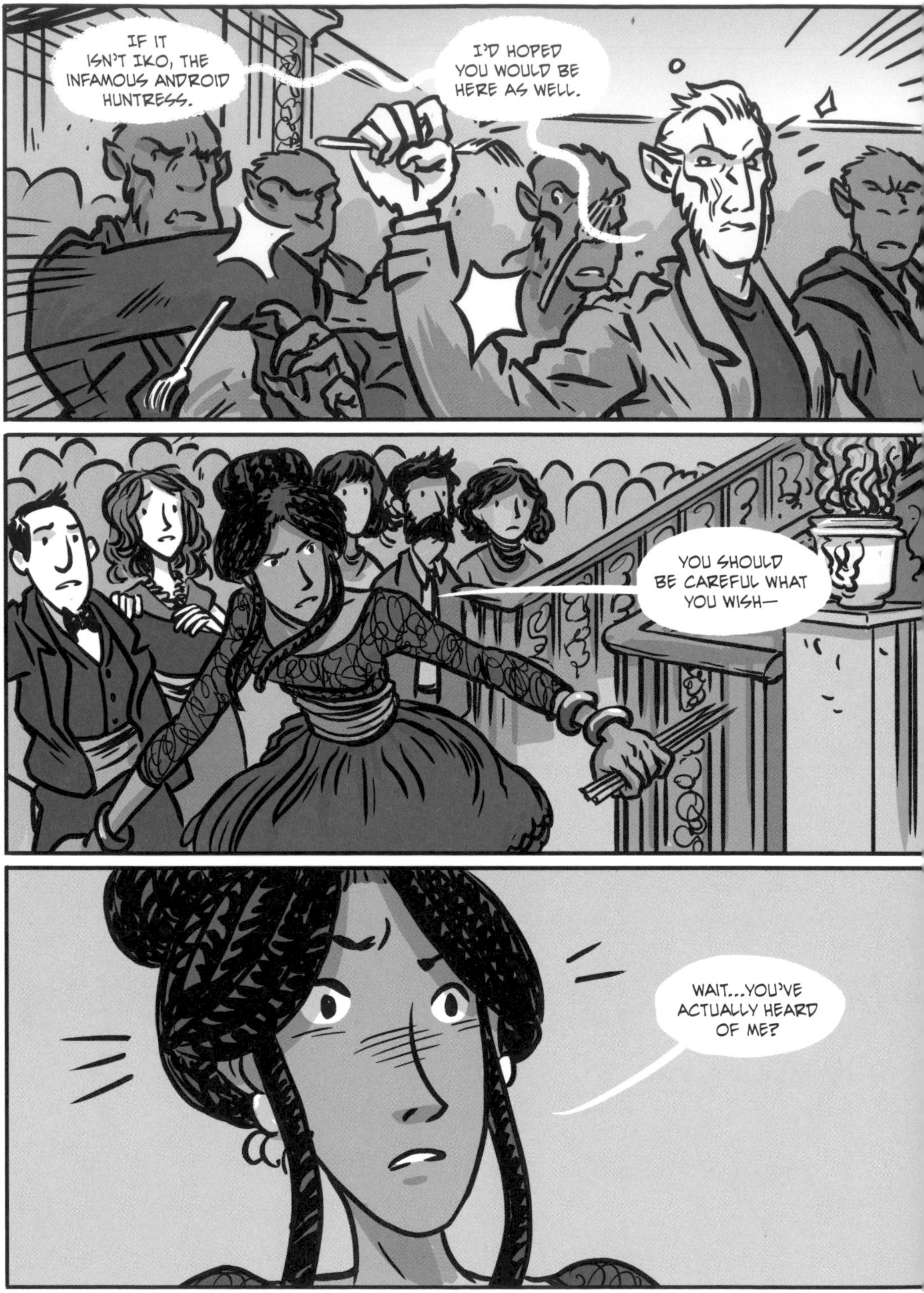
IF IT ISN'T IKO, THE INFAMOUS ANDROID HUNTRESS.
I'D HOPED YOU WOULD BE HERE AS WELL.
YOU SHOULD BE CAREFUL WHAT YOU WISH—
WAIT...YOU'VE ACTUALLY HEARD OF ME?

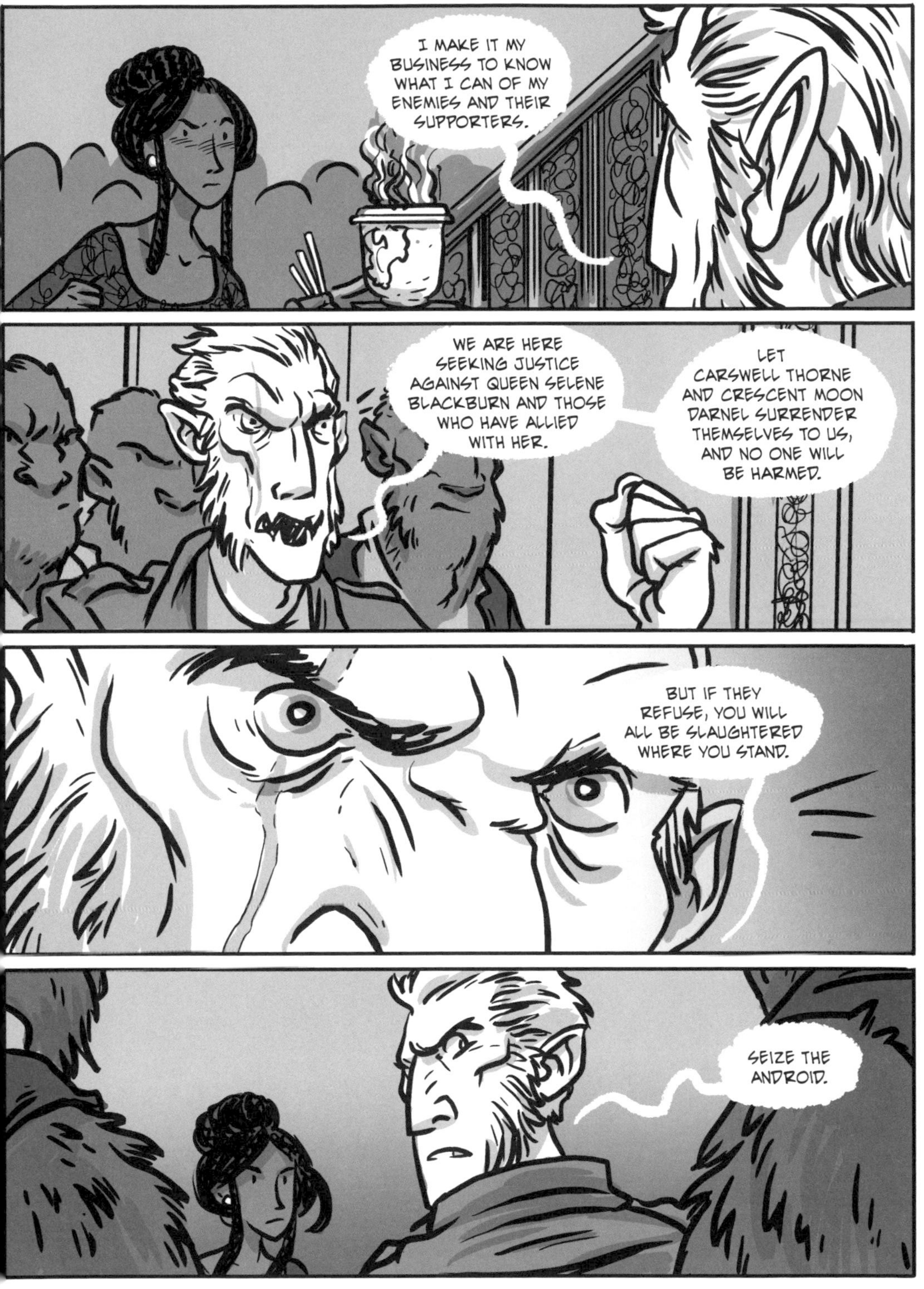
I MAKE IT MY BUSINESS TO KNOW WHAT I CAN OF MY ENEMIES AND THEIR SUPPORTERS.
WE ARE HERE SEEKING JUSTICE AGAINST QUEEN SELENE BLACKBURN AND THOSE WHO HAVE ALLIED WITH HER.
LET CARSWELL THORNE AND CRESCENT MOON DARNEL SURRENDER THEMSELVES TO US, AND NO ONE WILL BE HARMED.
BUT IF THEY REFUSE, YOU WILL ALL BE SLAUGHTERED WHERE YOU STAND.
SEIZE THE ANDROID.

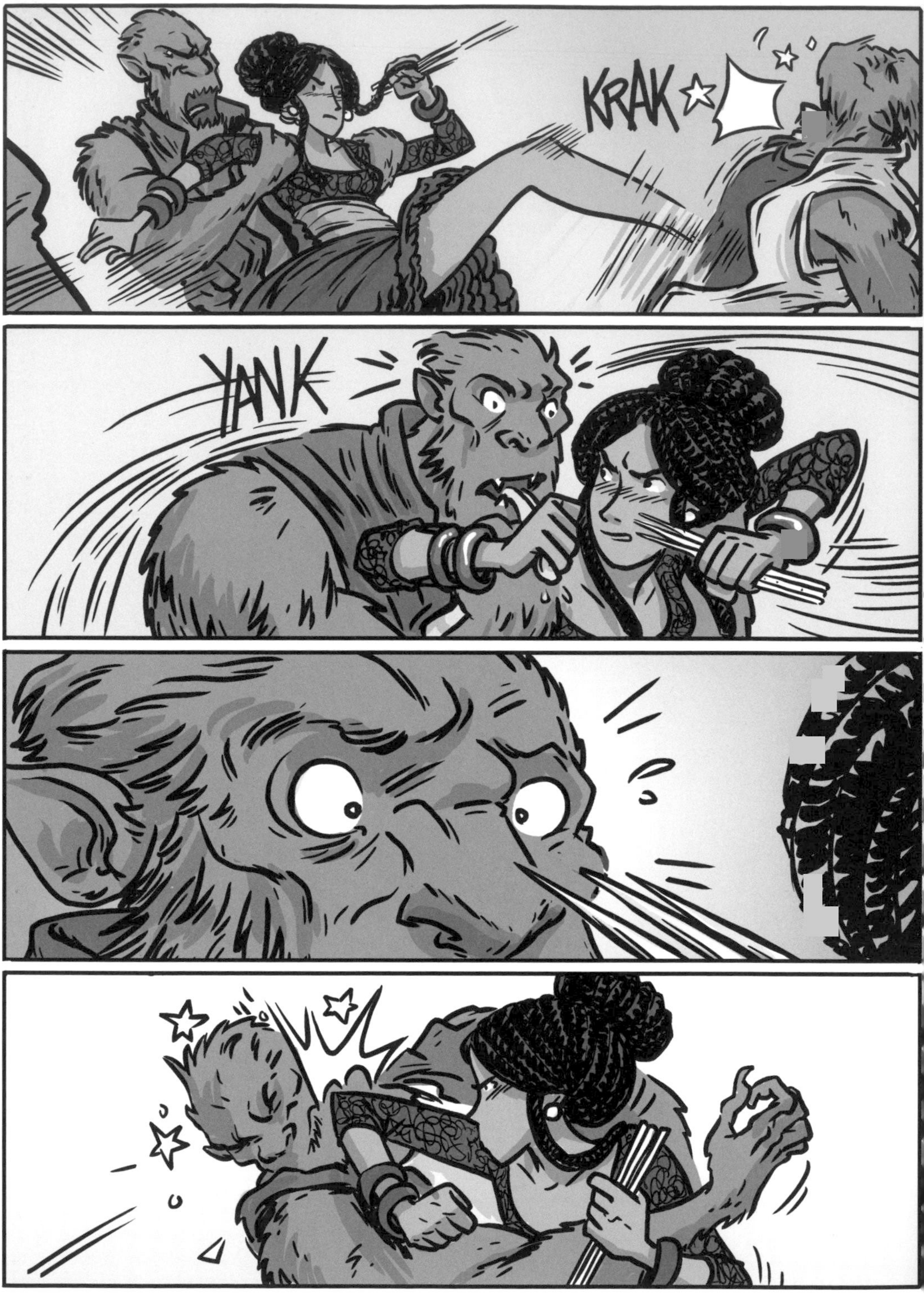
KRAK
YANK

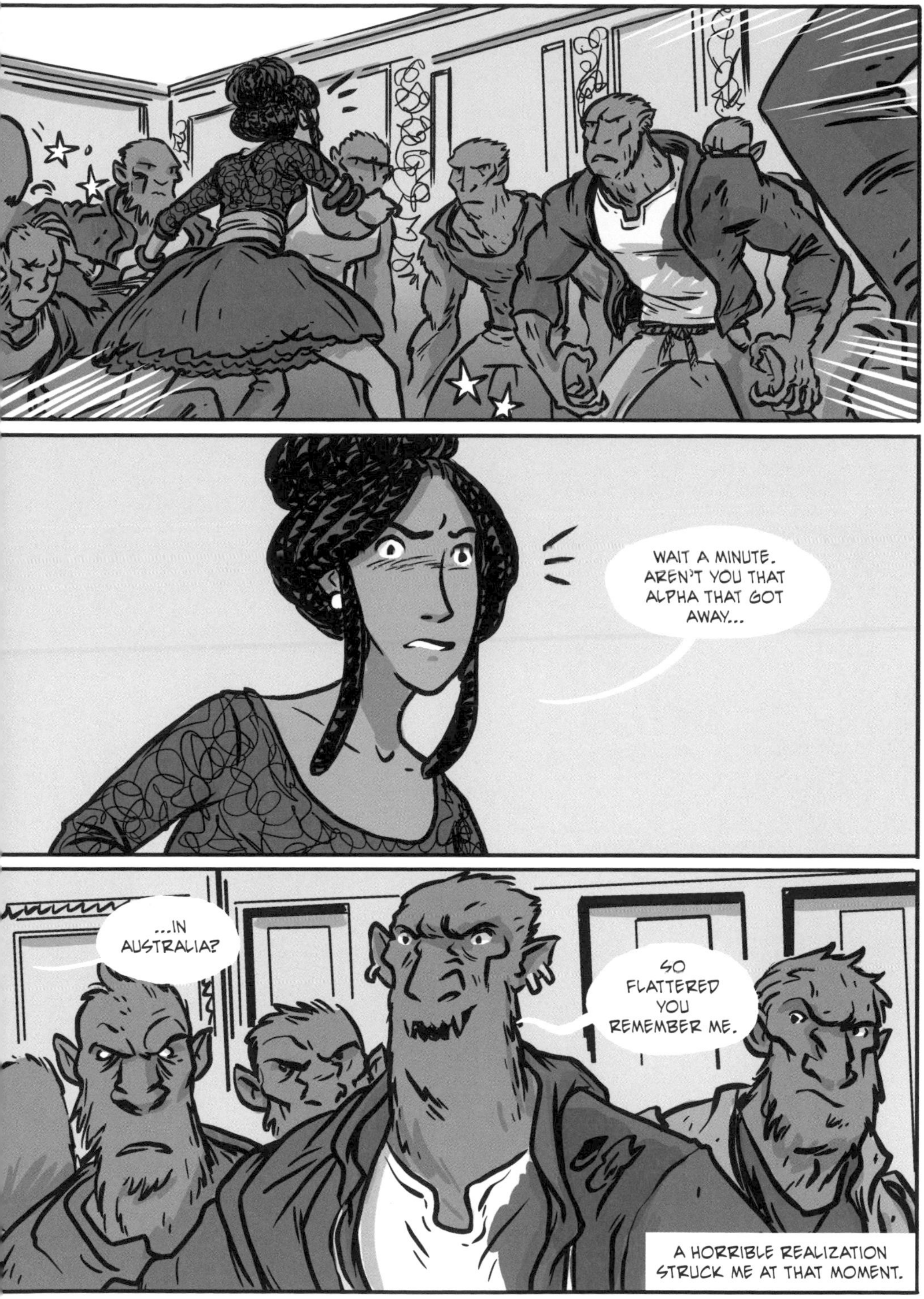
WAIT A MINUTE. AREN'T YOU THAT ALPHA THAT GOT AWAY...
...IN AUSTRALIA?
SO FLATTERED YOU REMEMBER ME.
A HORRIBLE REALIZATION STRUCK ME AT THAT MOMENT.

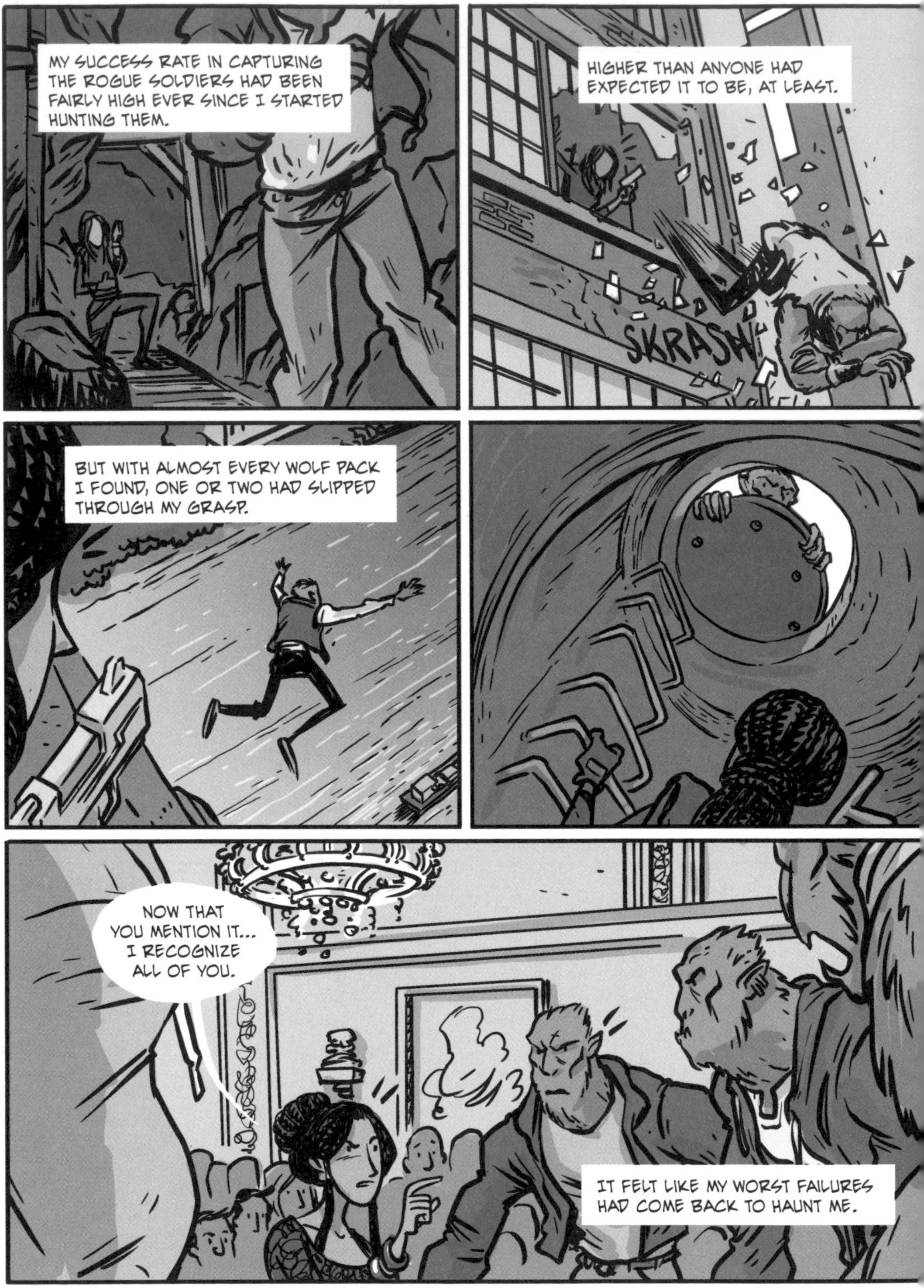
MY SUCCESS RATE IN CAPTURING THE ROGUE SOLDIERS HAD BEEN FAIRLY HIGH EVER SINCE I STARTED HUNTING THEM.
HIGHER THAN ANYONE HAD EXPECTED IT TO BE, AT LEAST.
SKRASH
BUT WITH ALMOST EVERY WOLF PACK I FOUND, ONE OR TWO HAD SLIPPED THROUGH MY GRASP.
NOW THAT YOU MENTION IT... I RECOGNIZE ALL OF YOU.
IT FELT LIKE MY WORST FAILURES HAD COME BACK TO HAUNT ME.

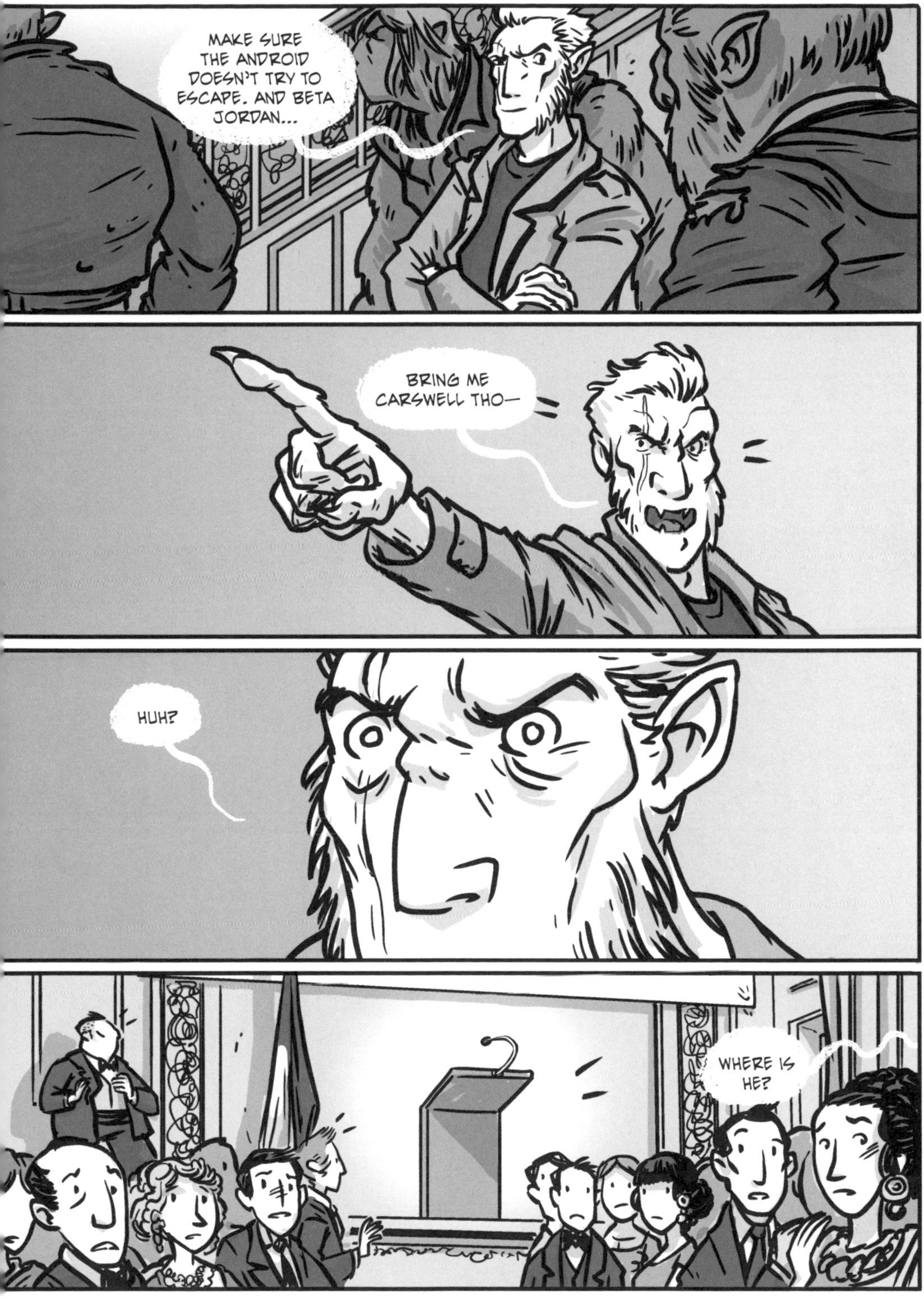
MAKE SURE THE ANDROID DOESN'T TRY TO ESCAPE. AND BETA JORDAN...
BRING ME CARSWELL THO—
HUH?
WHERE IS HE?

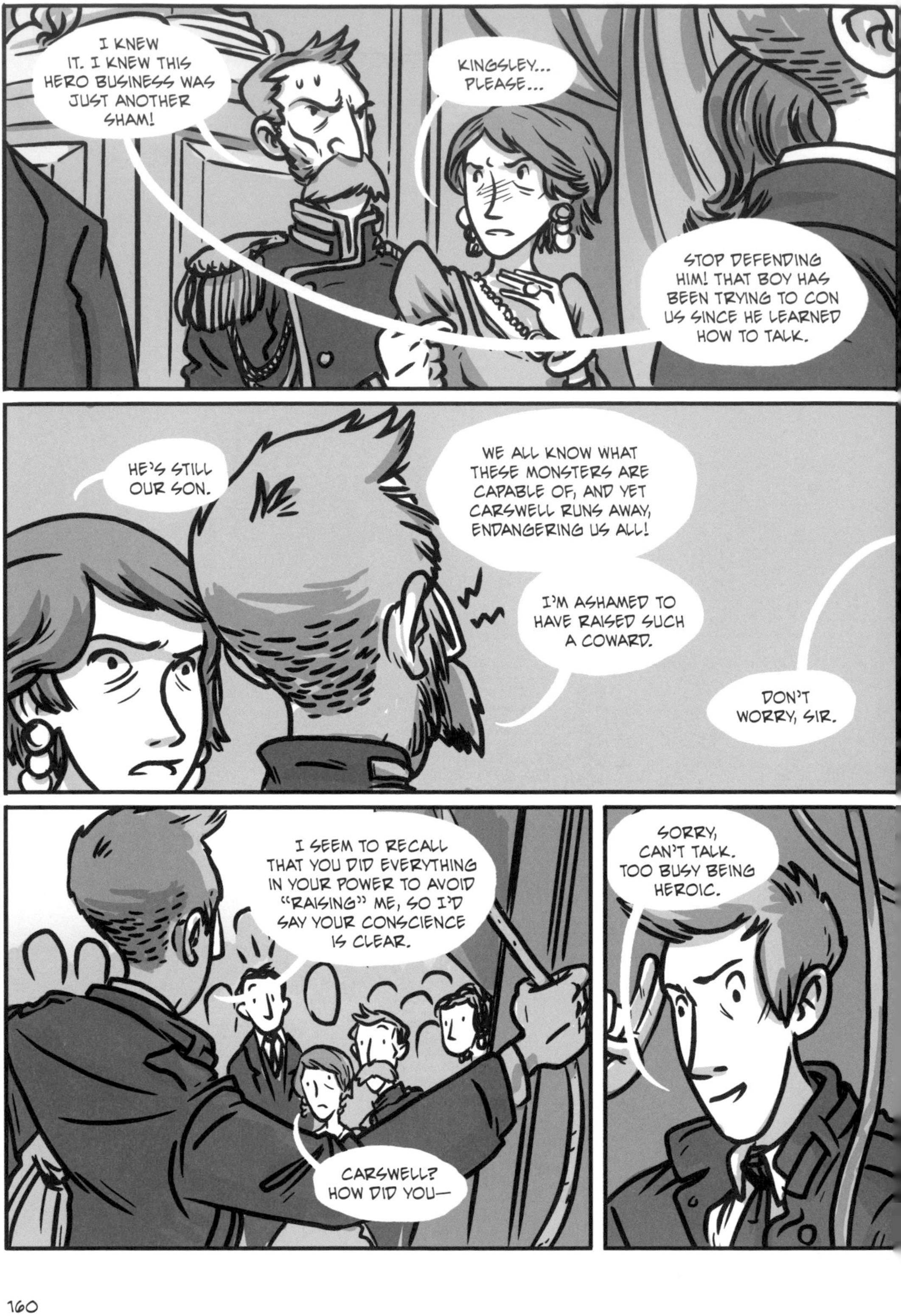
I KNEW IT. I KNEW THIS HERO BUSINESS WAS JUST ANOTHER SHAM!
KINGSLEY... PLEASE...
STOP DEFENDING HIM! THAT BOY HAS BEEN TRYING TO CON US SINCE HE LEARNED HOW TO TALK.
HE'S STILL OUR SON.
WE ALL KNOW WHAT THESE MONSTERS ARE CAPABLE OF, AND YET CARSWELL RUNS AWAY, ENDANGERING US ALL!
I'M ASHAMED TO HAVE RAISED SUCH A COWARD.
DON'T WORRY, SIR.
I SEEM TO RECALL THAT YOU DID EVERYTHING IN YOUR POWER TO AVOID "RAISING" ME, SO I'D SAY YOUR CONSCIENCE IS CLEAR.
CARSWELL? HOW DID YOU—
SORRY, CAN'T TALK. TOO BUSY BEING HEROIC.

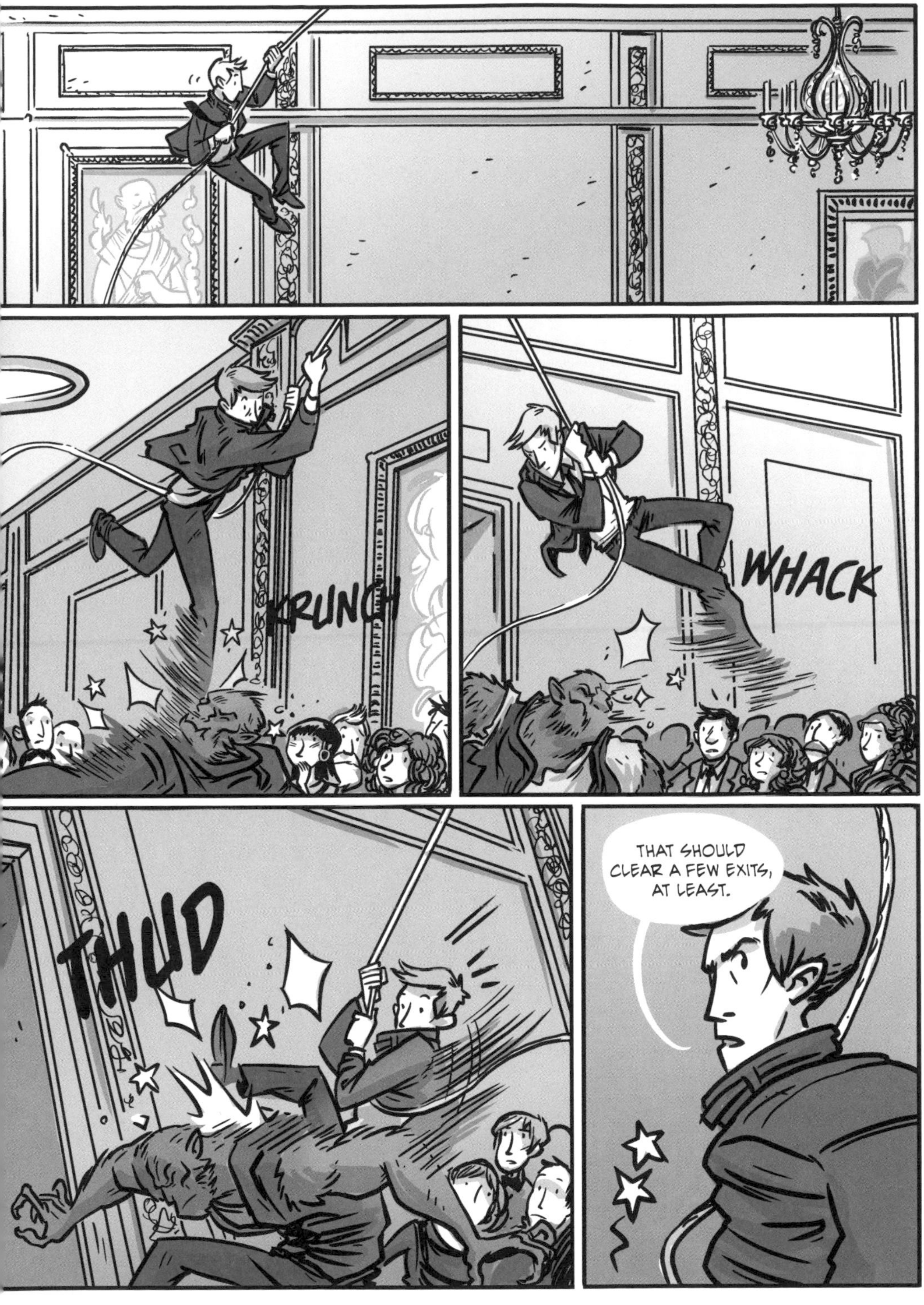
KRUNCH
WHACK
THUD
THAT SHOULD CLEAR A FEW EXITS, AT LEAST.

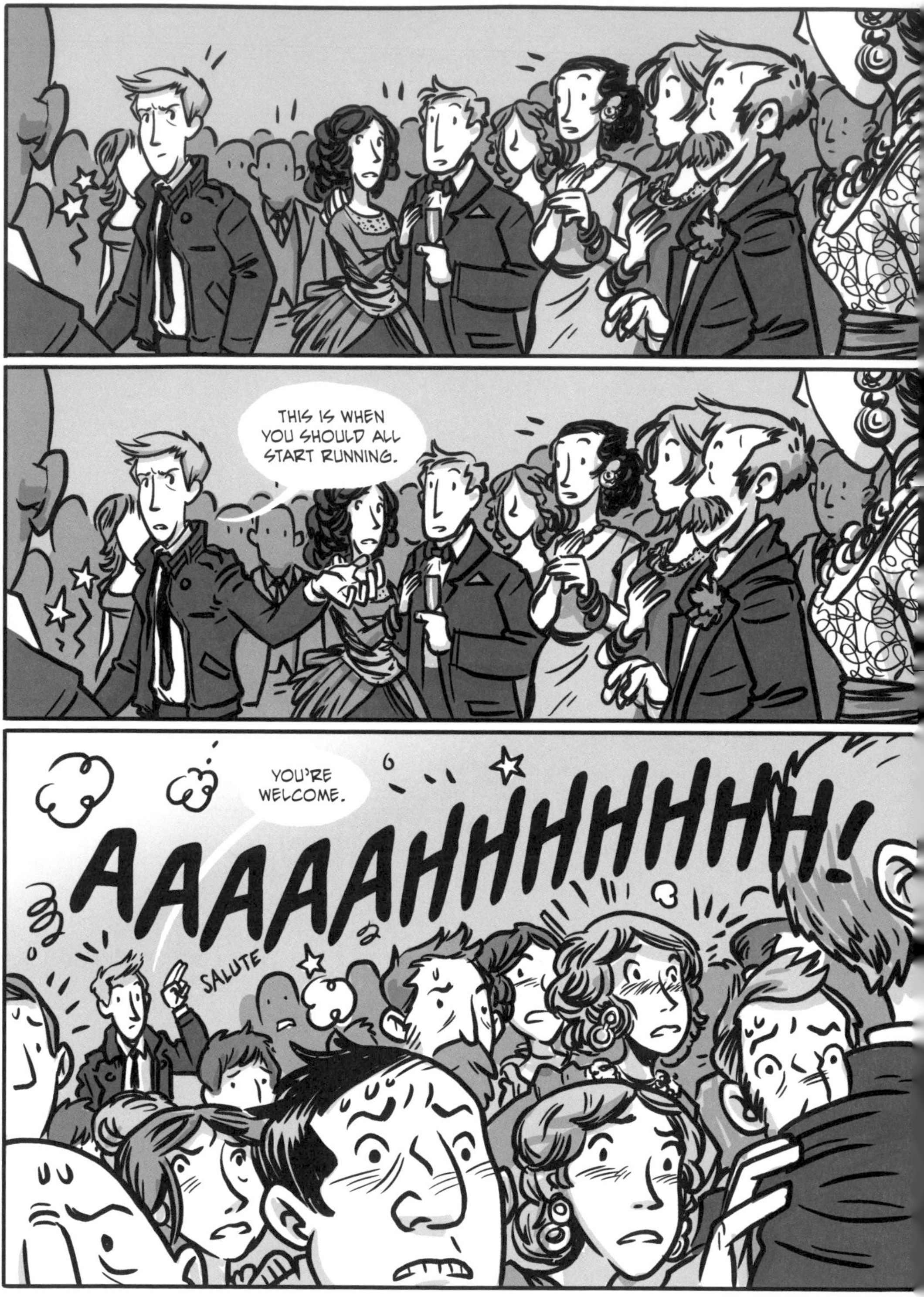
THIS IS WHEN YOU SHOULD ALL START RUNNING.
YOU'RE WELCOME.
AAAAAHHHHHHHHH!
SALUTE

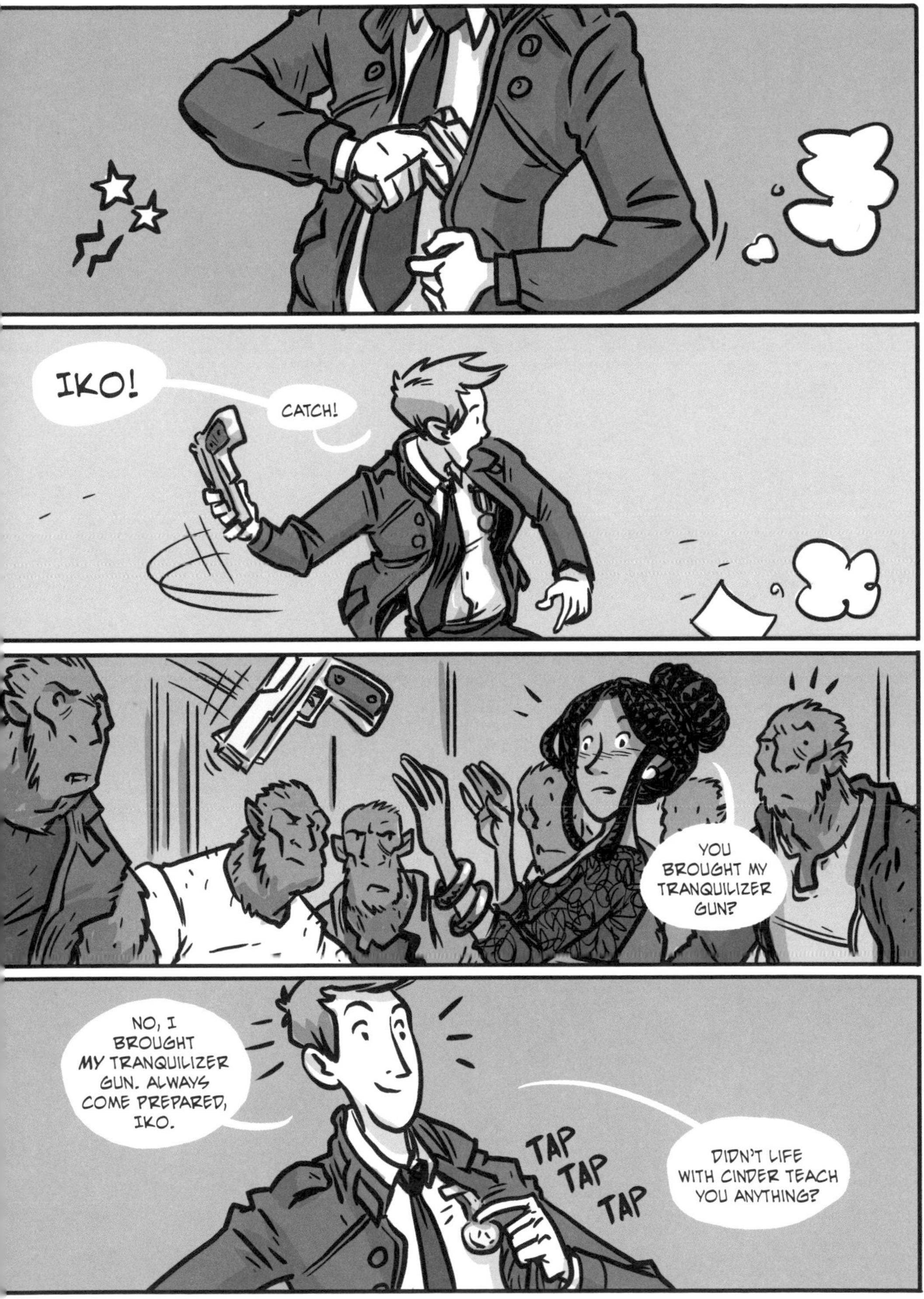
IKO!
CATCH!
YOU BROUGHT MY TRANQUILIZER GUN?
NO, I BROUGHT MY TRANQUILIZER GUN. ALWAYS COME PREPARED, IKO.
TAP TAP TAP
DIDN'T LIFE WITH CINDER TEACH YOU ANYTHING?

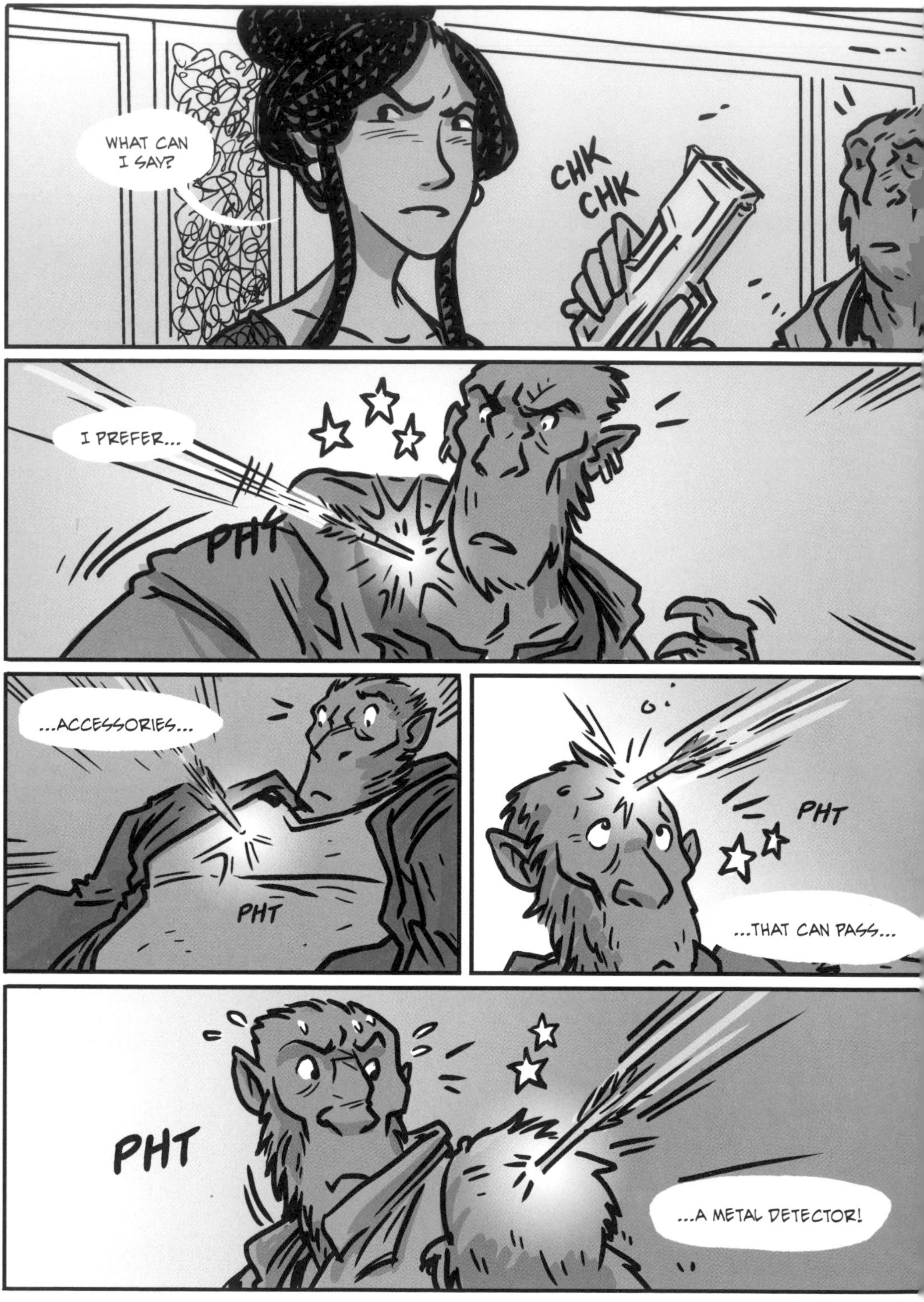
WHAT CAN I SAY?
CHK CHK
I PREFER...
PHT
...ACCESSORIES...
PHT
PHT
...THAT CAN PASS...
PHT
...A METAL DETECTOR!

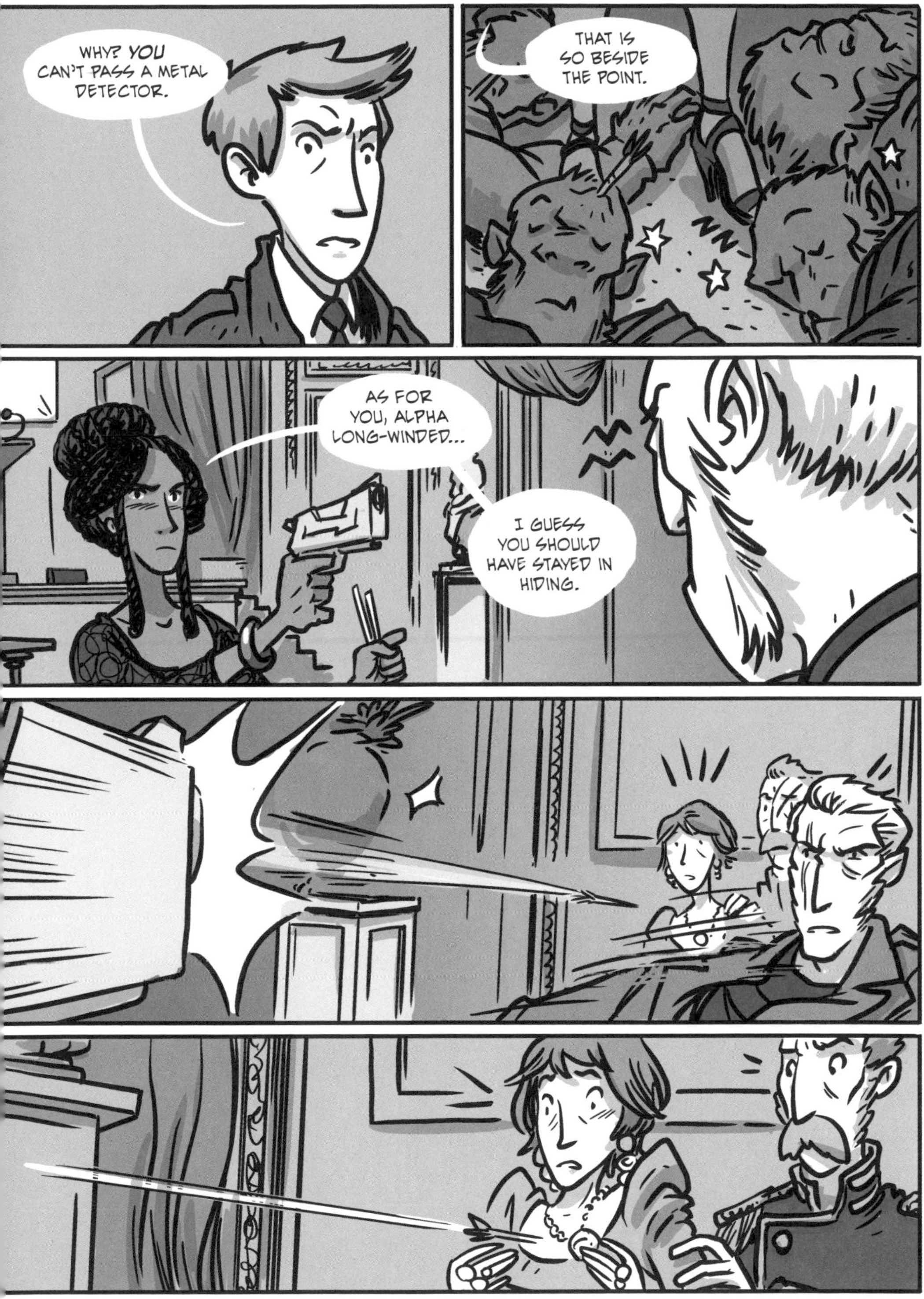
WHY? YOU CAN'T PASS A METAL DETECTOR.
THAT IS SO BESIDE THE POINT.
AS FOR YOU, ALPHA LONG-WINDED...
I GUESS YOU SHOULD HAVE STAYED IN HIDING.

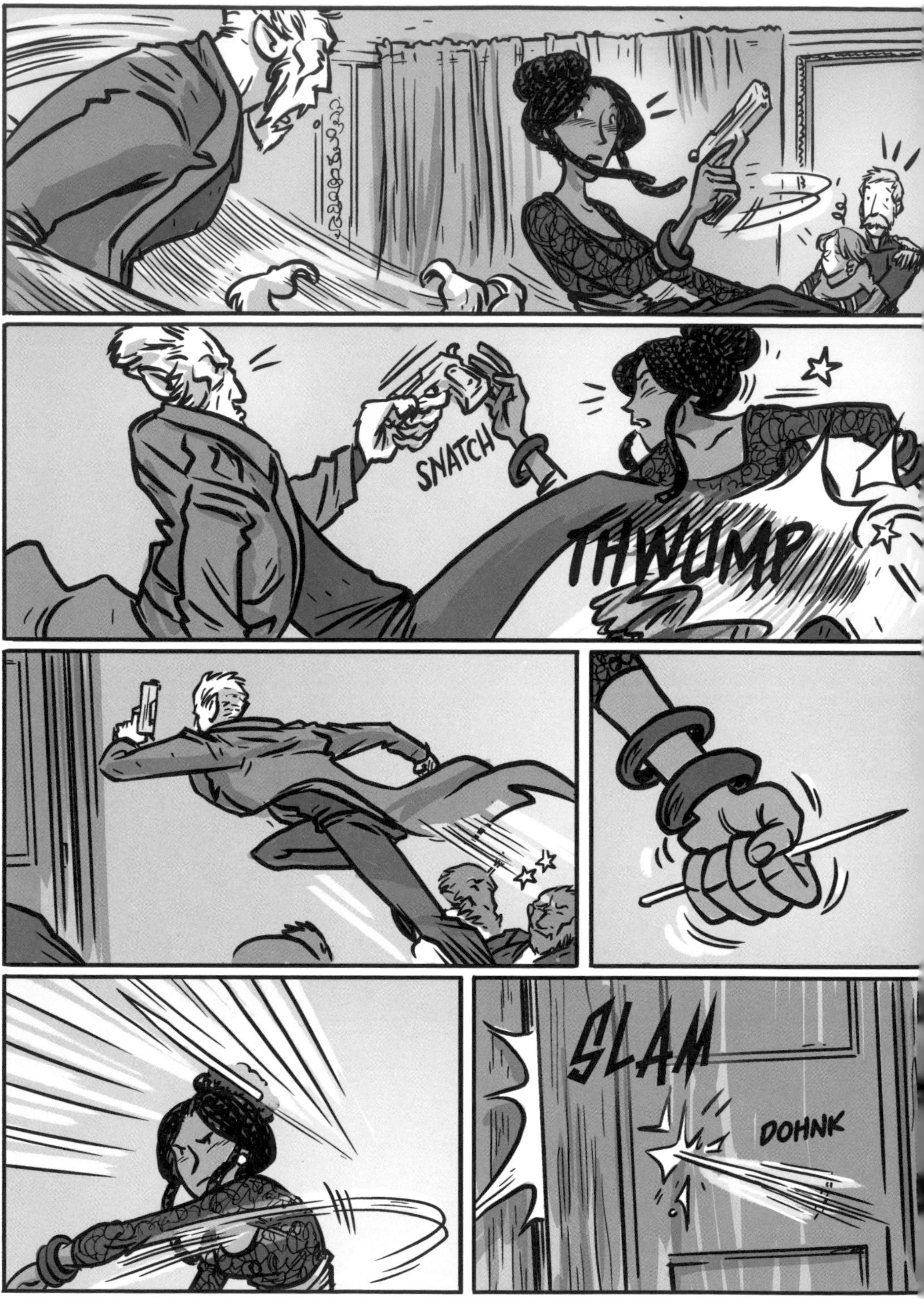
SNATCH
THWUMP
SLAM
DOHNK

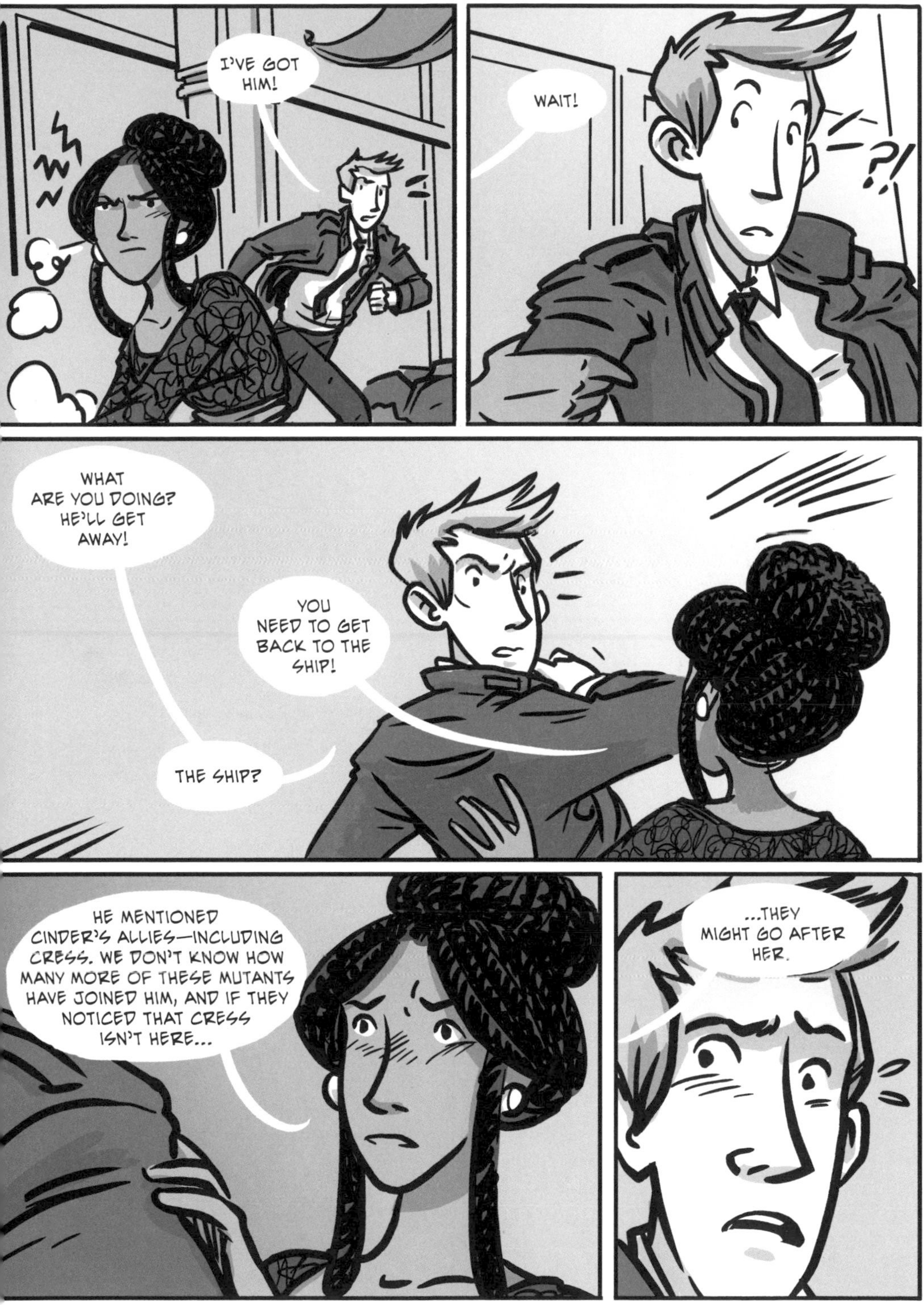

I'VE GOT HIM!
WAIT!
?!
WHAT ARE YOU DOING? HE'LL GET AWAY!
YOU NEED TO GET BACK TO THE SHIP!
THE SHIP?
HE MENTIONED CINDER'S ALLIES—INCLUDING CRESS. WE DON'T KNOW HOW MANY MORE OF THESE MUTANTS HAVE JOINED HIM, AND IF THEY NOTICED THAT CRESS ISN'T HERE...
...THEY MIGHT GO AFTER HER.

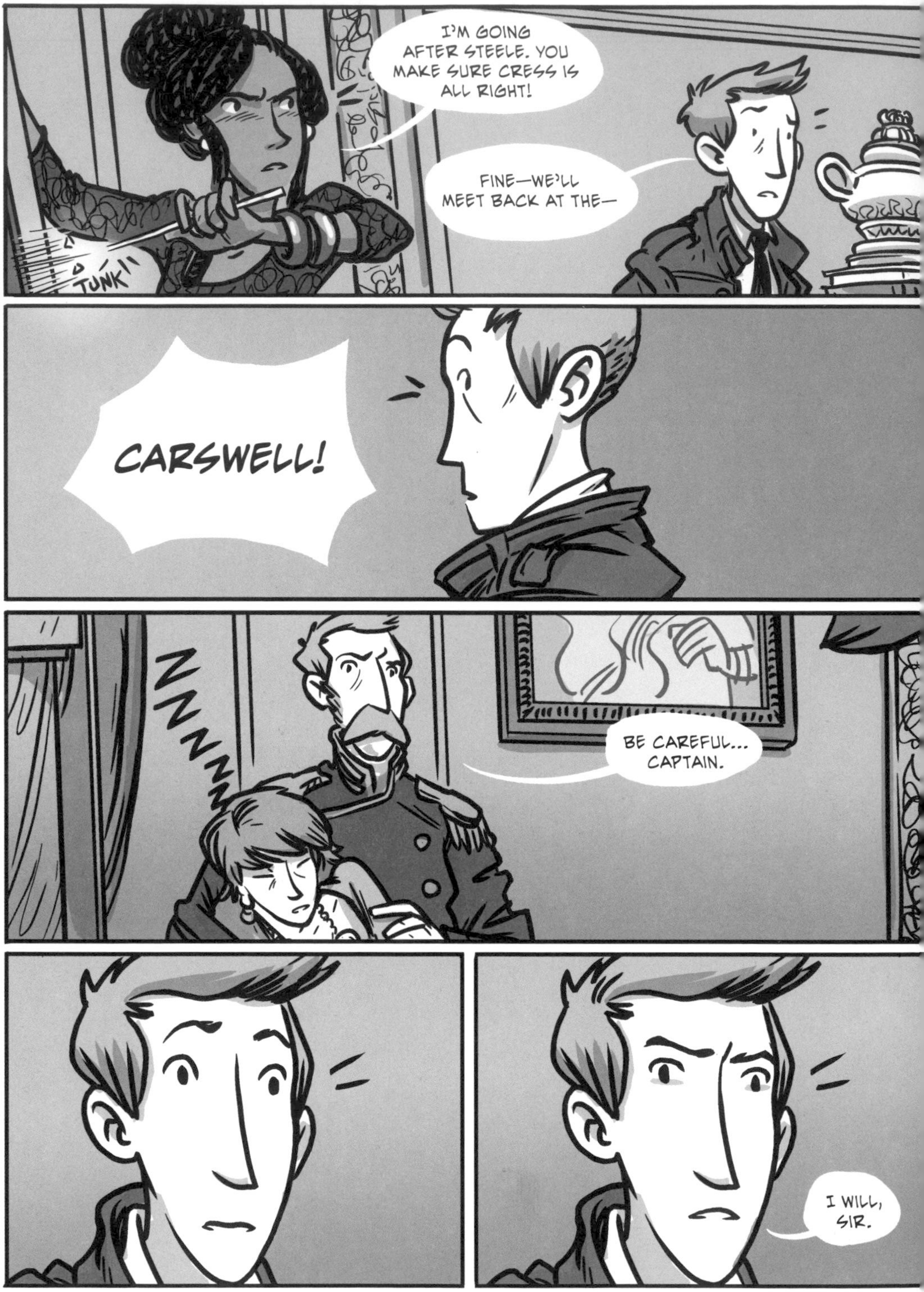
I'M GOING AFTER STEELE. YOU MAKE SURE CRESS IS ALL RIGHT!
TUNK
FINE—WE'LL MEET BACK AT THE—
CARSWELL!
ZZZZZ
BE CAREFUL... CAPTAIN.
I WILL, SIR.

CHAPTER VI

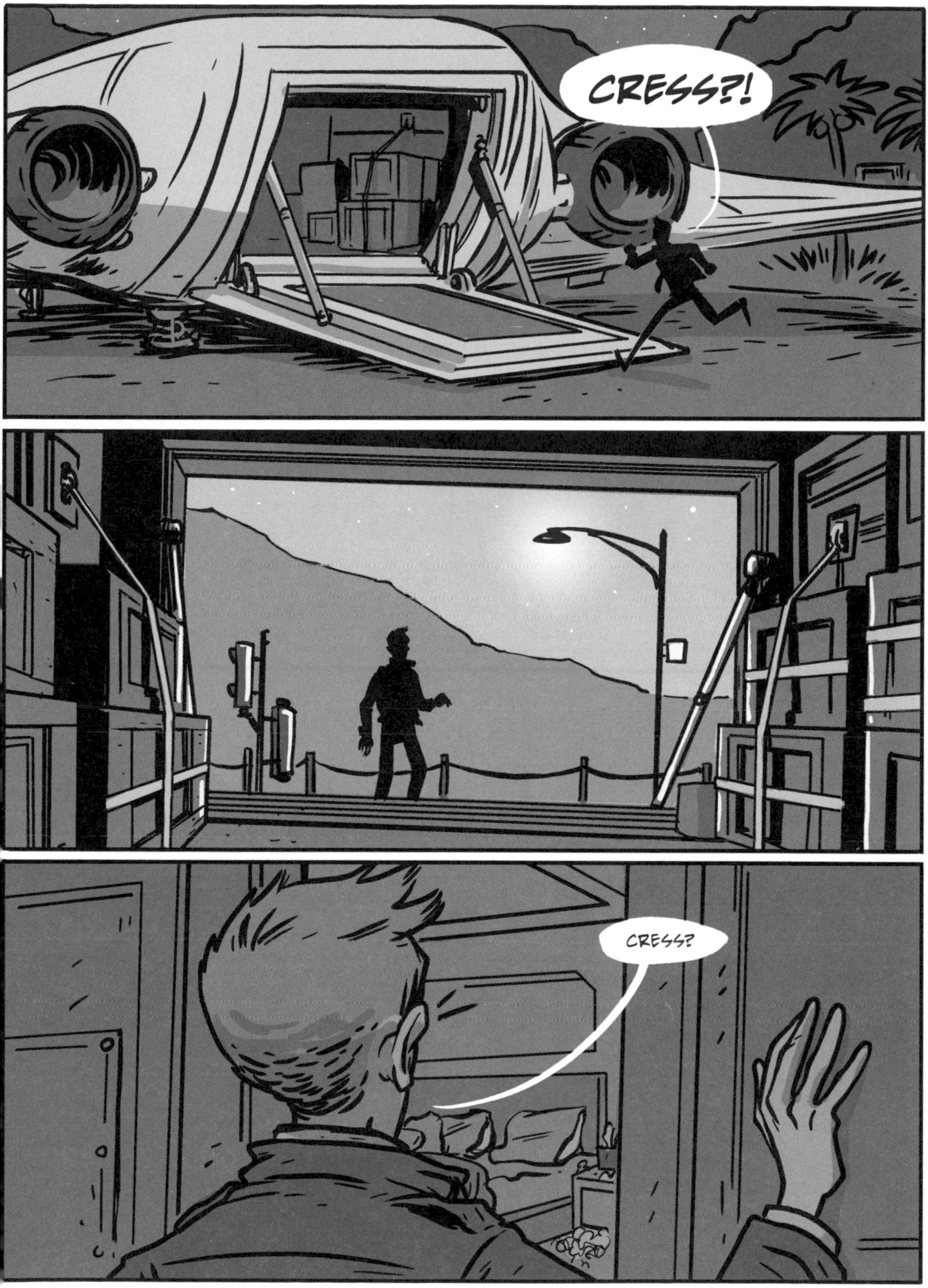
CRESS?!
CRESS?

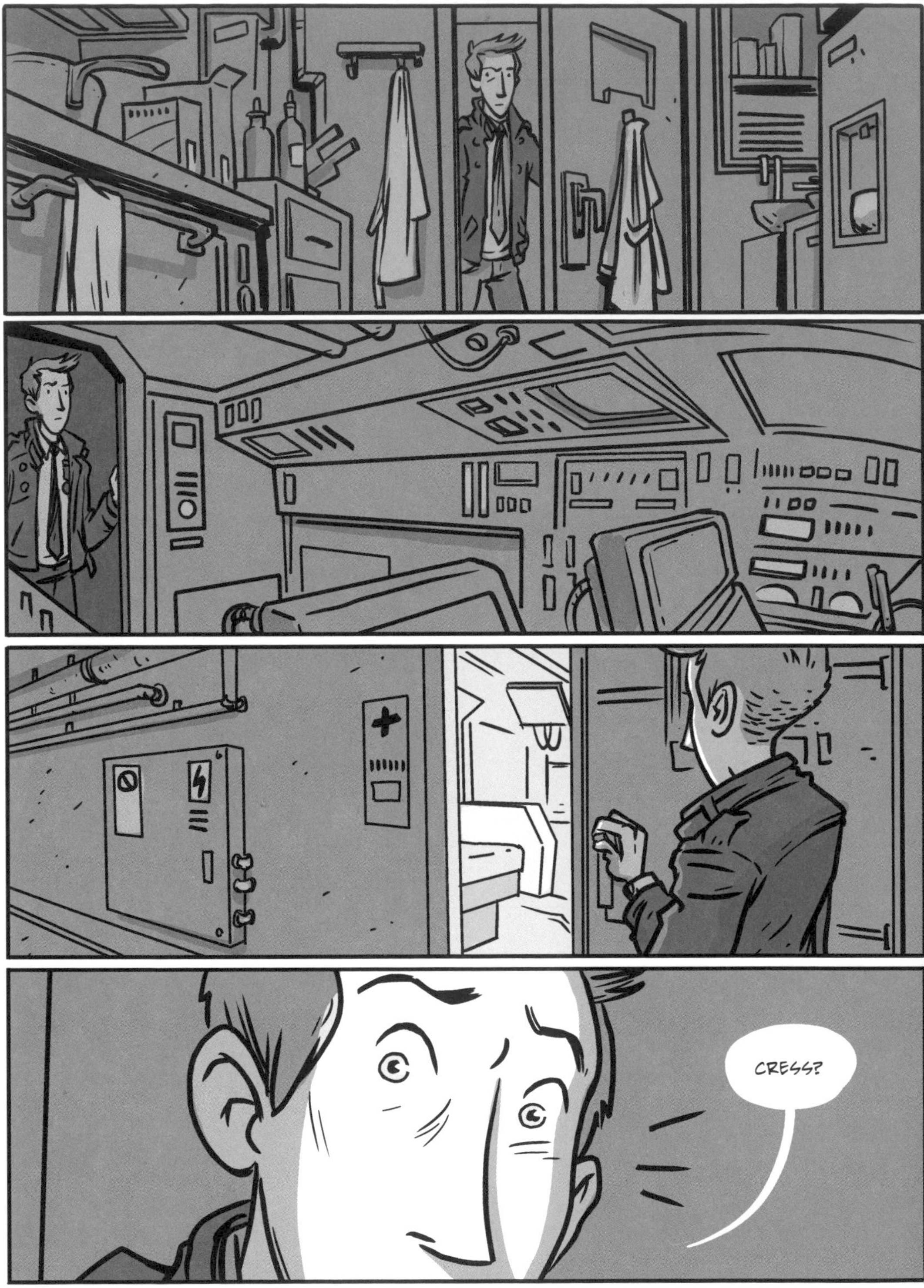
CRESS?

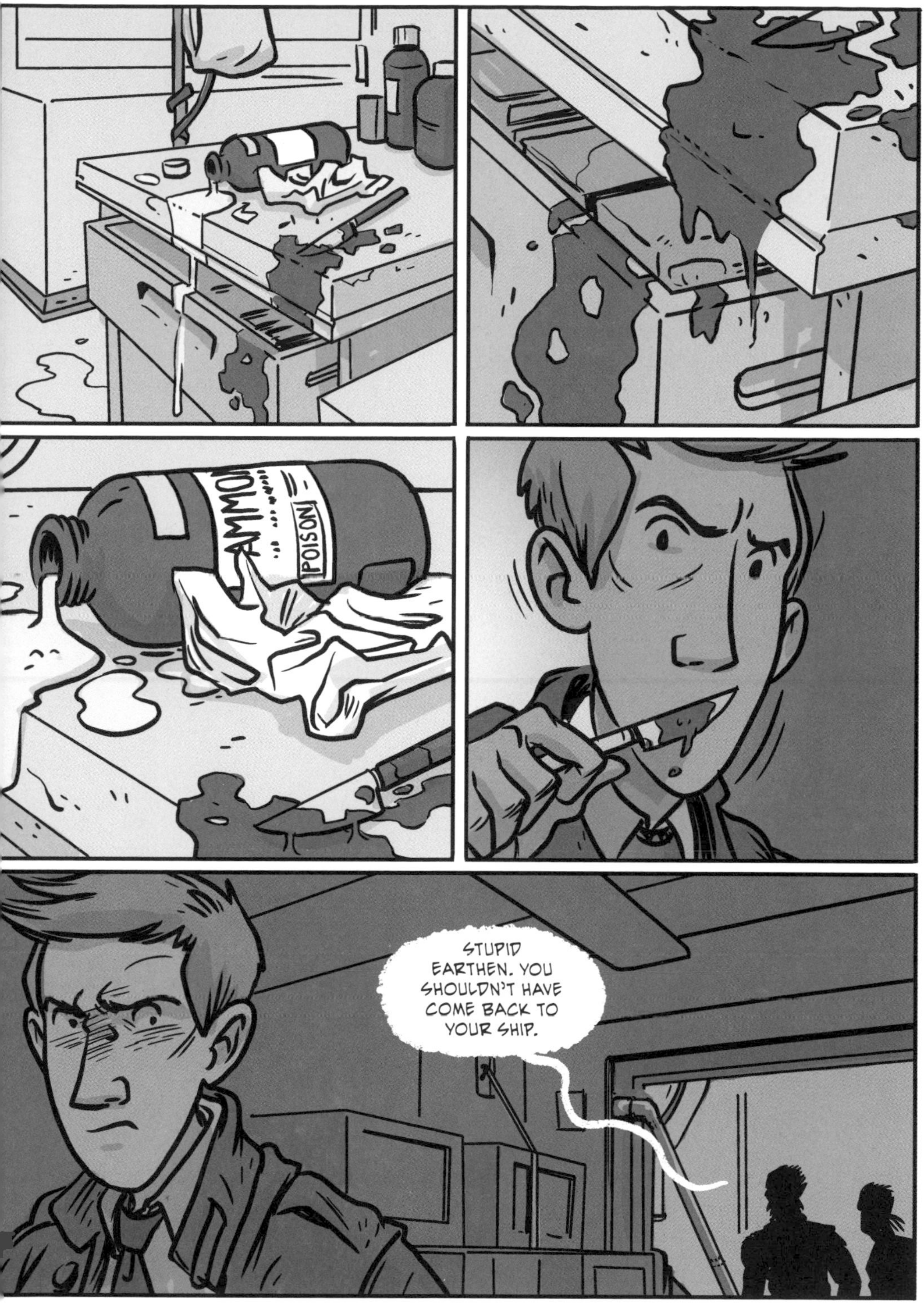
AMMO
POISON
STUPID EARTHEN. YOU SHOULDN'T HAVE COME BACK TO YOUR SHIP.

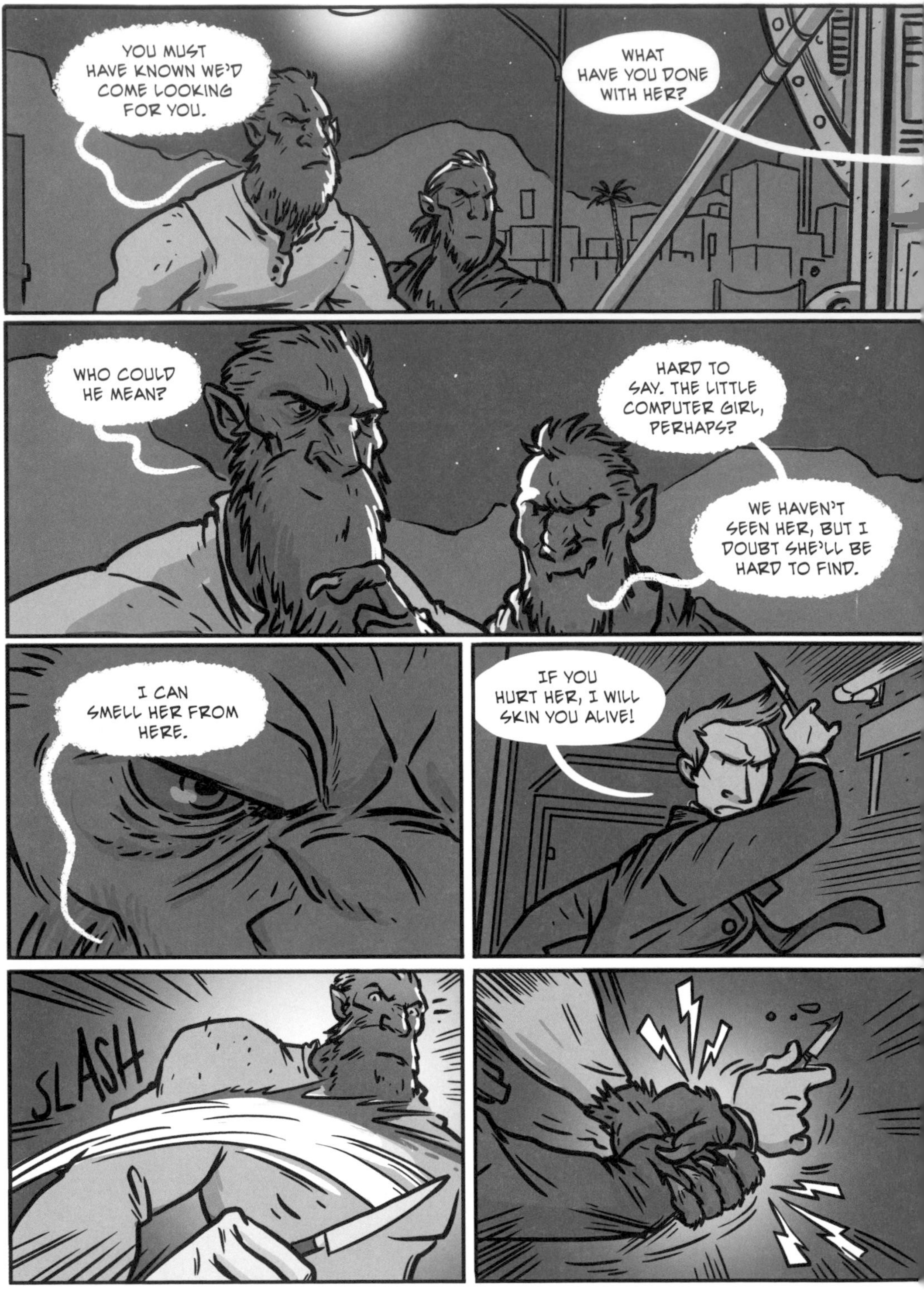
YOU MUST HAVE KNOWN WE'D COME LOOKING FOR YOU.
WHAT HAVE YOU DONE WITH HER?
WHO COULD HE MEAN?
HARD TO SAY. THE LITTLE COMPUTER GIRL, PERHAPS?
WE HAVEN'T SEEN HER, BUT I DOUBT SHE'LL BE HARD TO FIND.
I CAN SMELL HER FROM HERE.
IF YOU HURT HER, I WILL SKIN YOU ALIVE!
SLASH

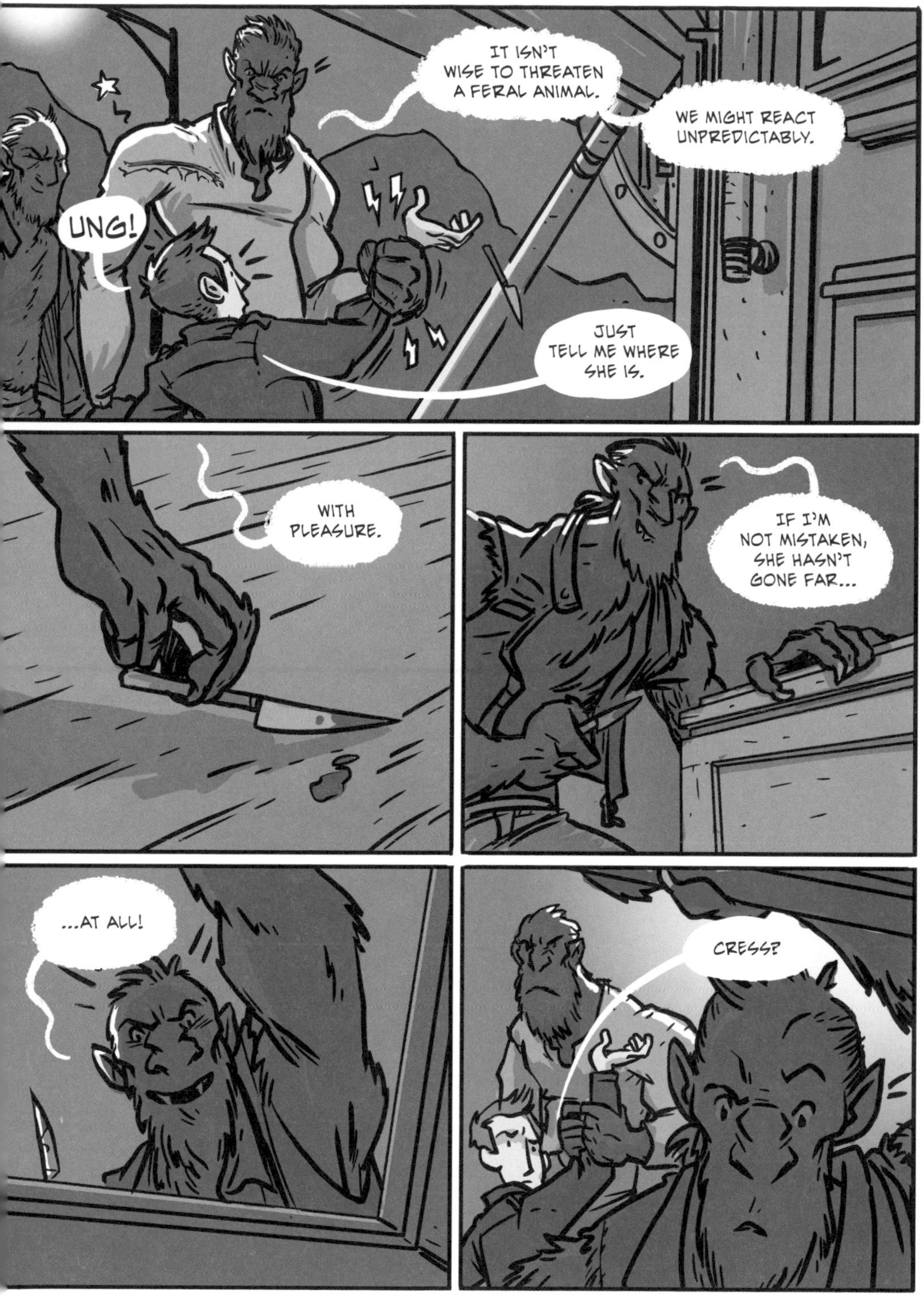
IT ISN'T WISE TO THREATEN A FERAL ANIMAL.
WE MIGHT REACT UNPREDICTABLY.
UNG!
JUST TELL ME WHERE SHE IS.
WITH PLEASURE.
IF I'M NOT MISTAKEN, SHE HASN'T GONE FAR...
...AT ALL!
CRESS?

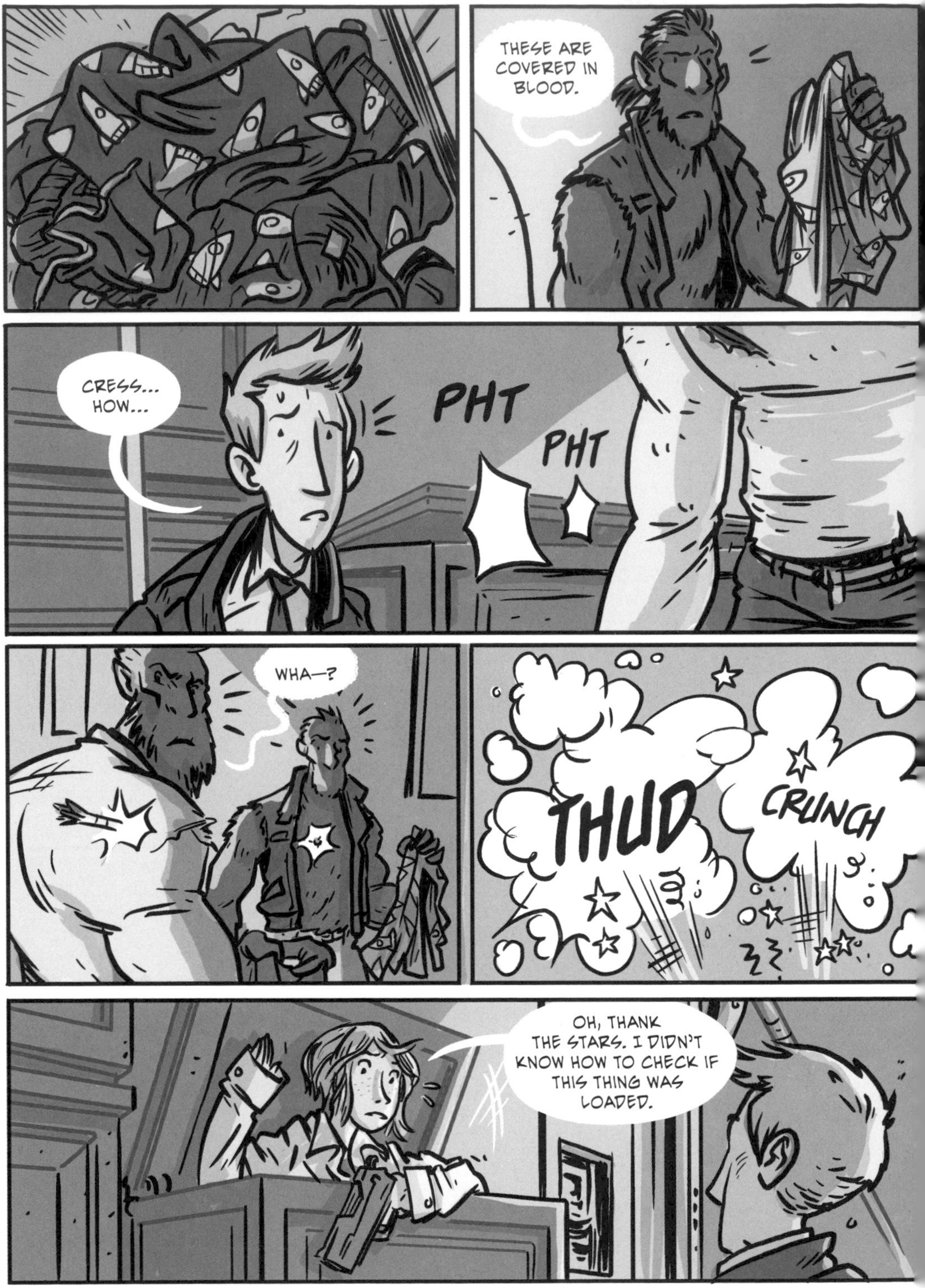
THESE ARE COVERED IN BLOOD.
CRESS... HOW...
PHT
PHT
WHA—?
THUD
CRUNCH
OH, THANK THE STARS. I DIDN'T KNOW HOW TO CHECK IF THIS THING WAS LOADED.

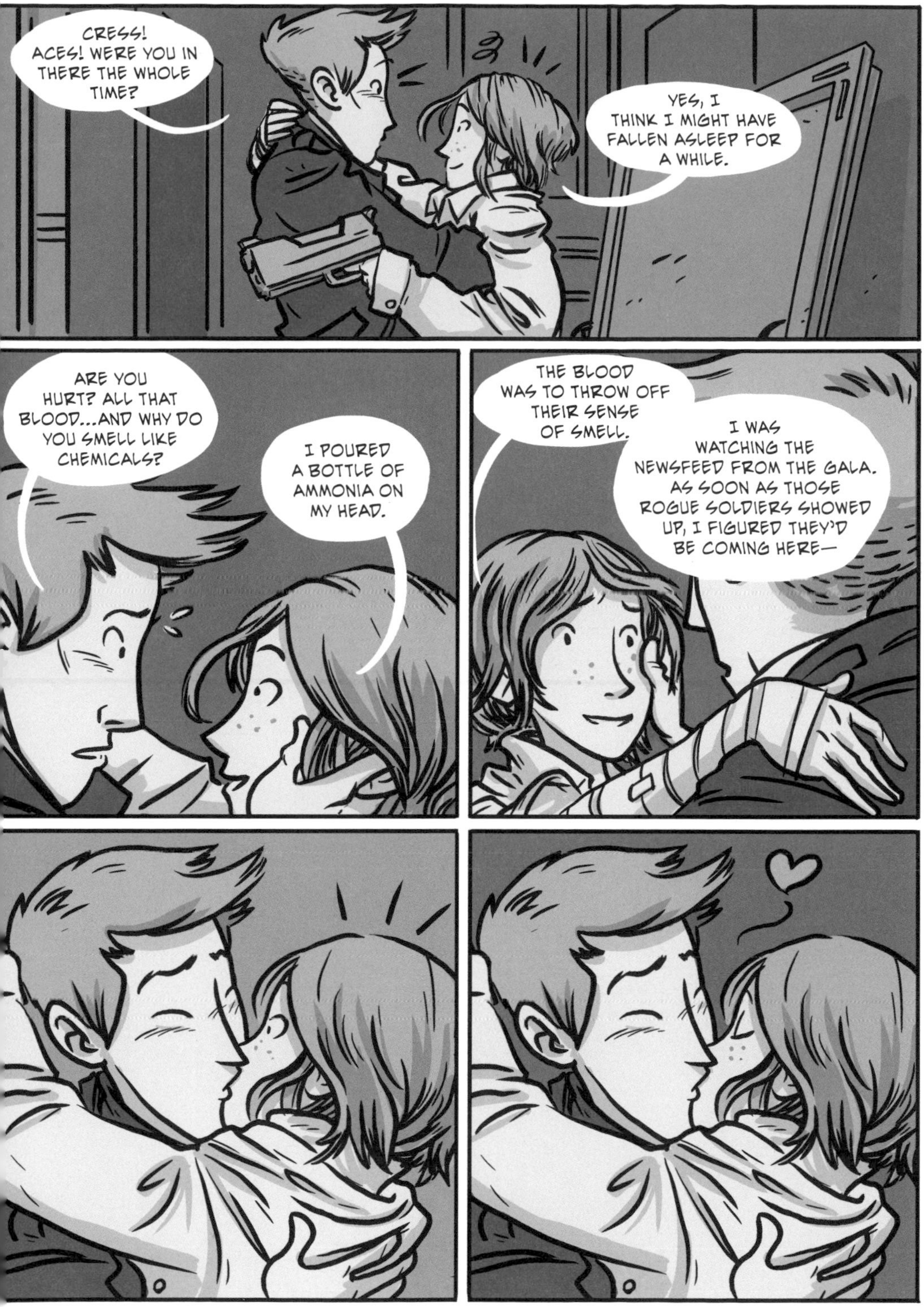
CRESS! ACES! WERE YOU IN THERE THE WHOLE TIME?
YES, I THINK I MIGHT HAVE FALLEN ASLEEP FOR A WHILE.
ARE YOU HURT? ALL THAT BLOOD...AND WHY DO YOU SMELL LIKE CHEMICALS?
I POURED A BOTTLE OF AMMONIA ON MY HEAD.
THE BLOOD WAS TO THROW OFF THEIR SENSE OF SMELL.
I WAS WATCHING THE NEWSFEED FROM THE GALA. AS SOON AS THOSE ROGUE SOLDIERS SHOWED UP, I FIGURED THEY'D BE COMING HERE—

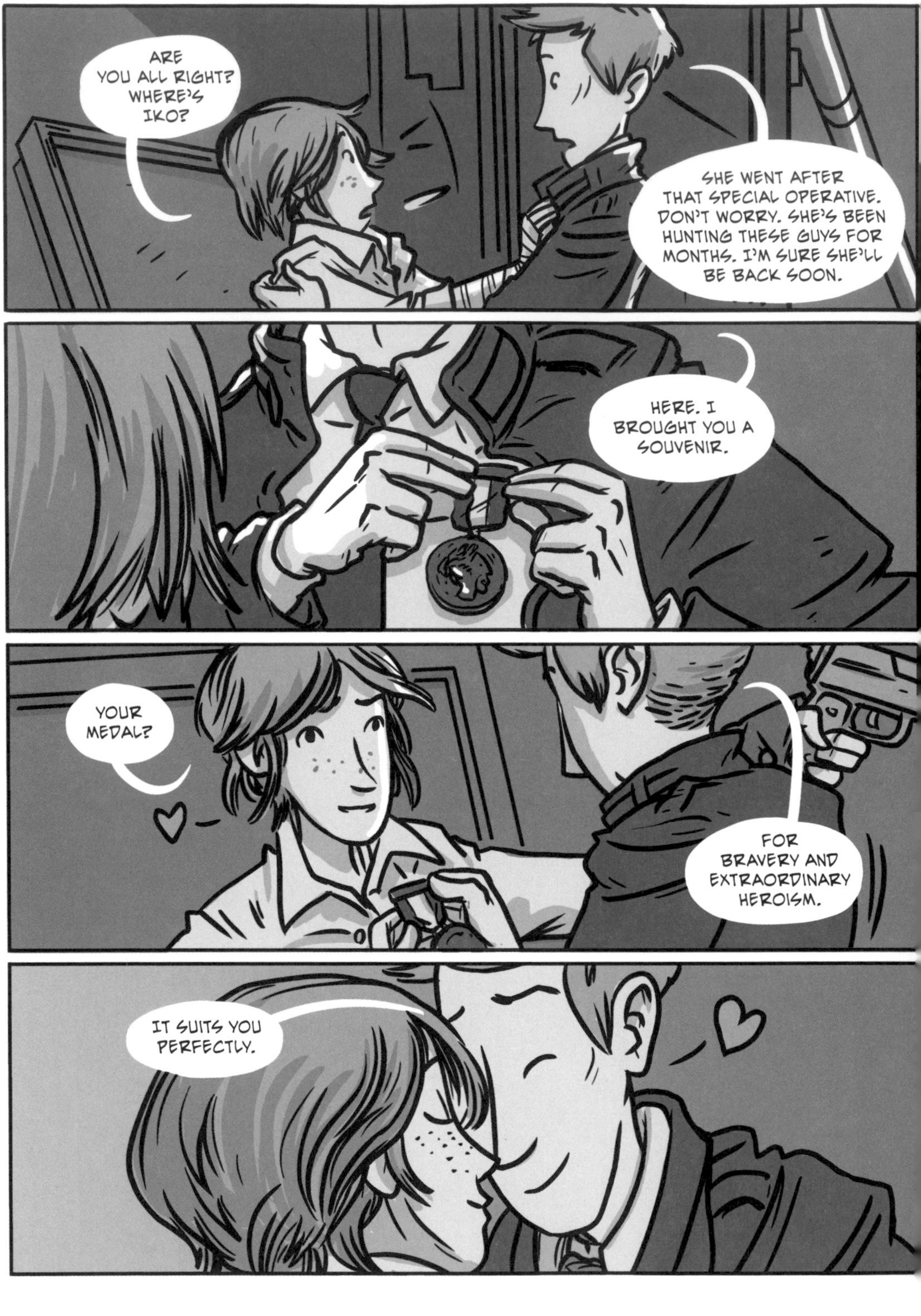
ARE YOU ALL RIGHT? WHERE'S IKO?
SHE WENT AFTER THAT SPECIAL OPERATIVE. DON'T WORRY. SHE'S BEEN HUNTING THESE GUYS FOR MONTHS. I'M SURE SHE'LL BE BACK SOON.
HERE. I BROUGHT YOU A SOUVENIR.
YOUR MEDAL?
FOR BRAVERY AND EXTRAORDINARY HEROISM.
IT SUITS YOU PERFECTLY.

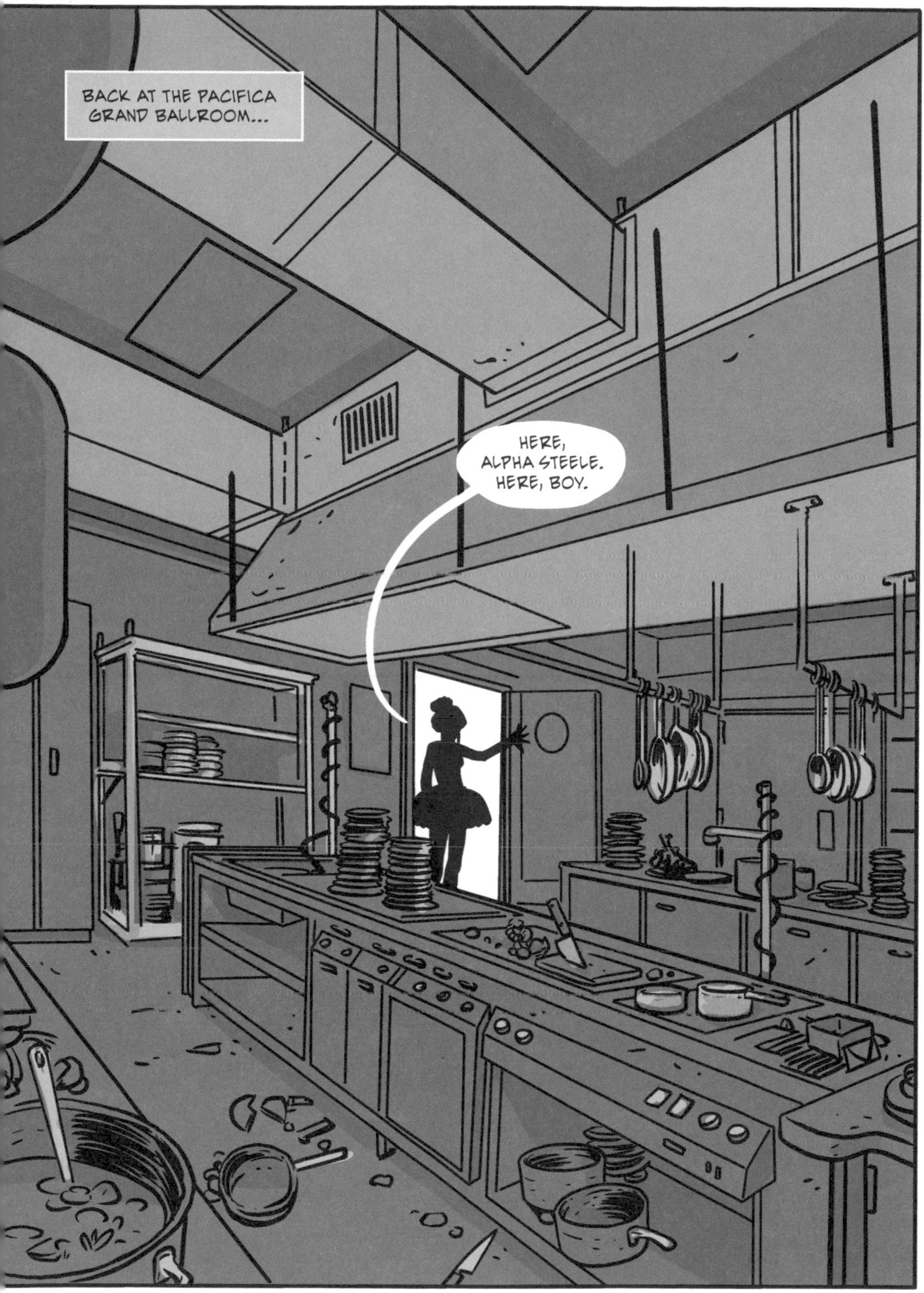
BACK AT THE PACIFICA GRAND BALLROOM...
HERE, ALPHA STEELE. HERE, BOY.

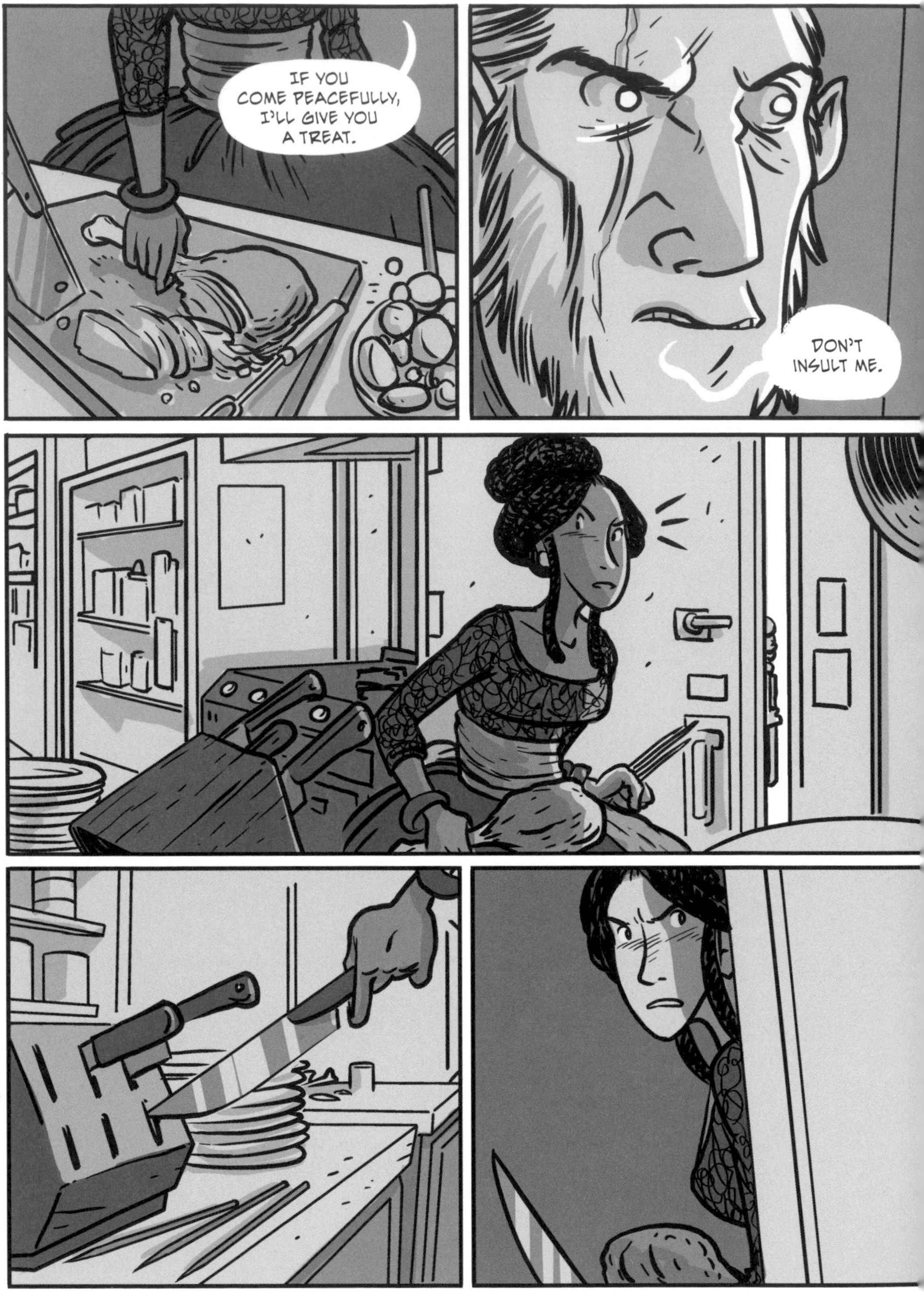
IF YOU COME PEACEFULLY, I'LL GIVE YOU A TREAT.
DON'T INSULT ME.

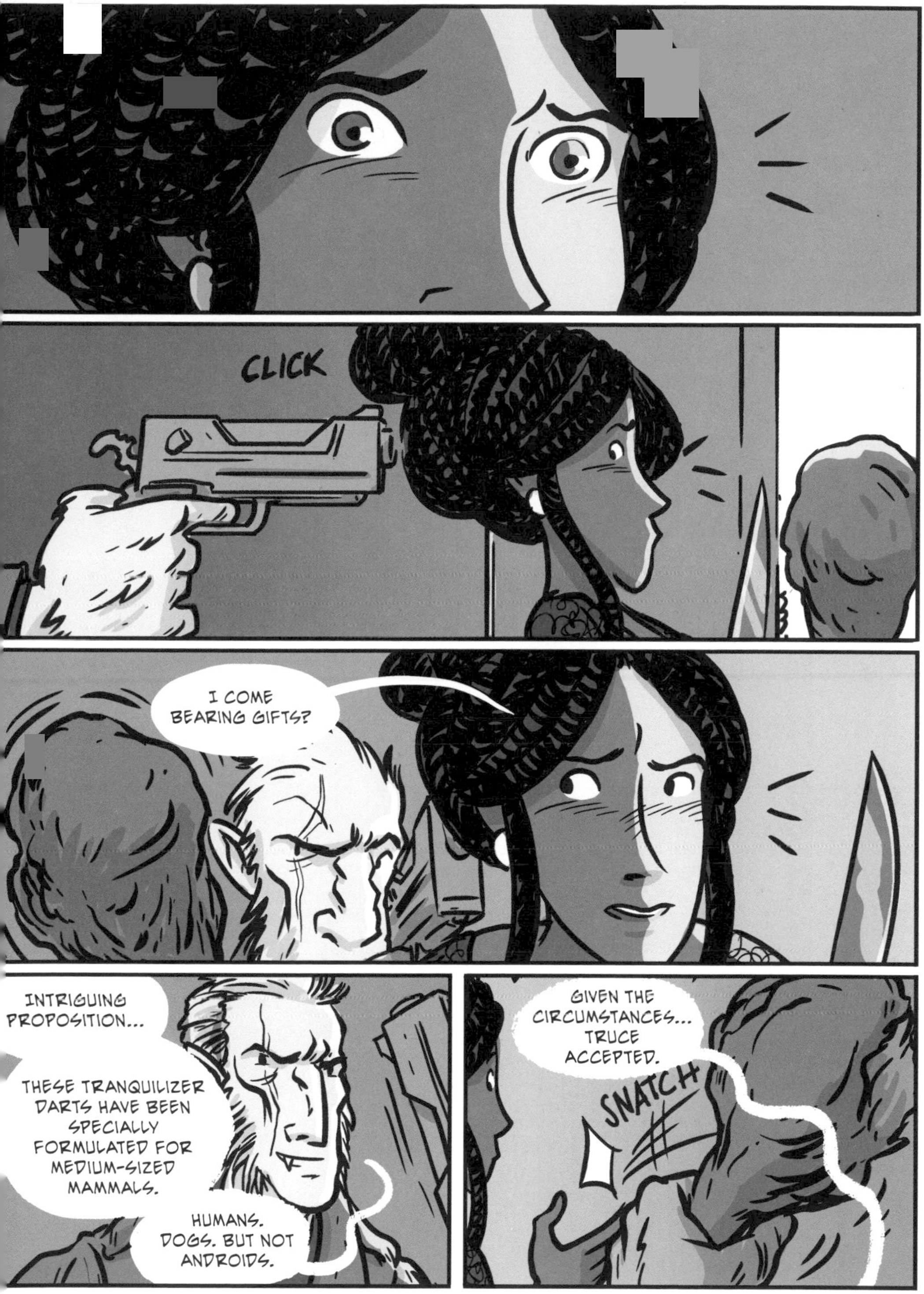
CLICK
I COME BEARING GIFTS?
INTRIGUING PROPOSITION...
THESE TRANQUILIZER DARTS HAVE BEEN SPECIALLY FORMULATED FOR MEDIUM-SIZED MAMMALS.
HUMANS. DOGS. BUT NOT ANDROIDS.
GIVEN THE CIRCUMSTANCES... TRUCE ACCEPTED.
SNATCH

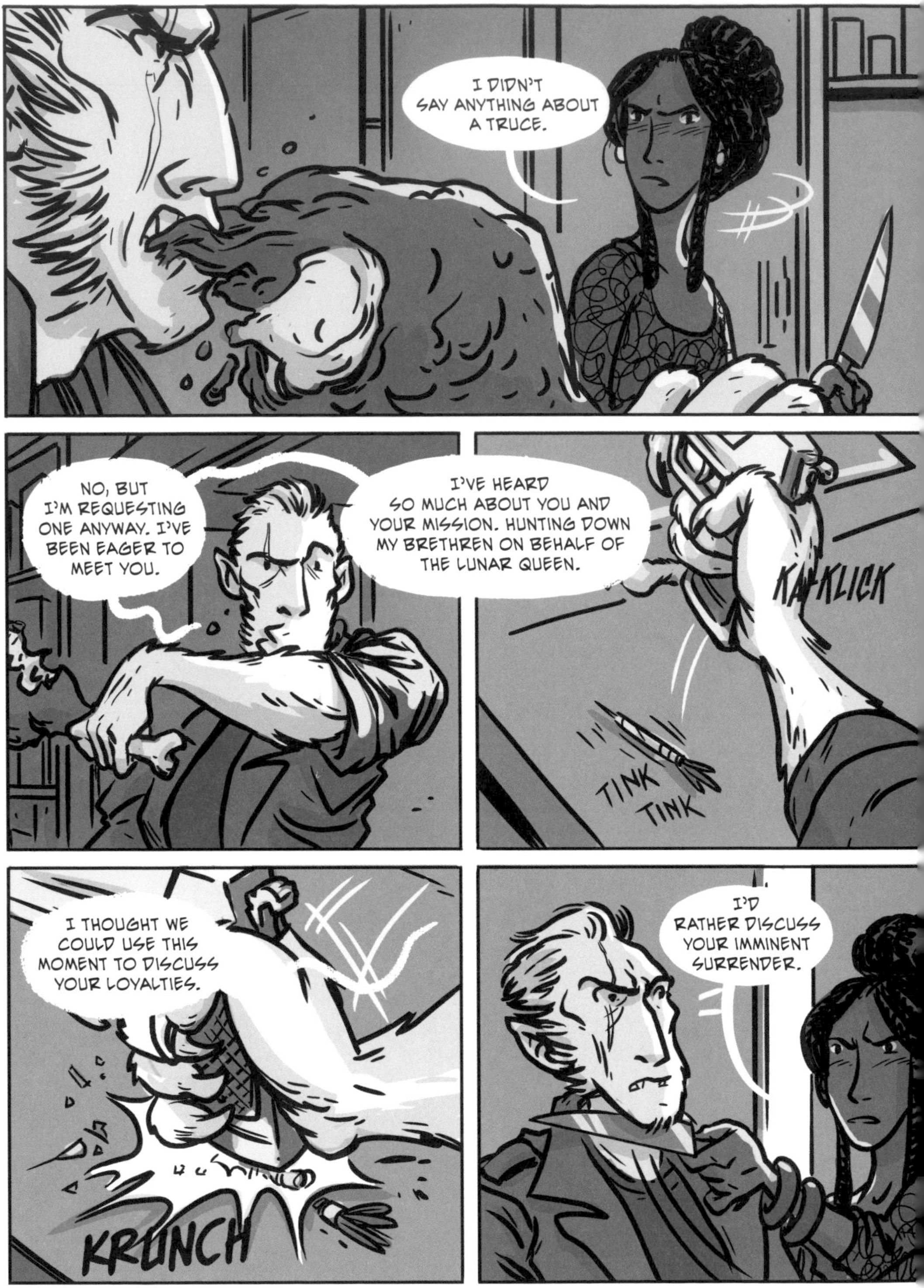
I DIDN'T SAY ANYTHING ABOUT A TRUCE.
NO, BUT I'M REQUESTING ONE ANYWAY. I'VE BEEN EAGER TO MEET YOU.
I'VE HEARD SO MUCH ABOUT YOU AND YOUR MISSION. HUNTING DOWN MY BRETHREN ON BEHALF OF THE LUNAR QUEEN.
KA-KLICK
TINK
TINK
I THOUGHT WE COULD USE THIS MOMENT TO DISCUSS YOUR LOYALTIES.
KRUNCH
I'D RATHER DISCUSS YOUR IMMINENT SURRENDER.

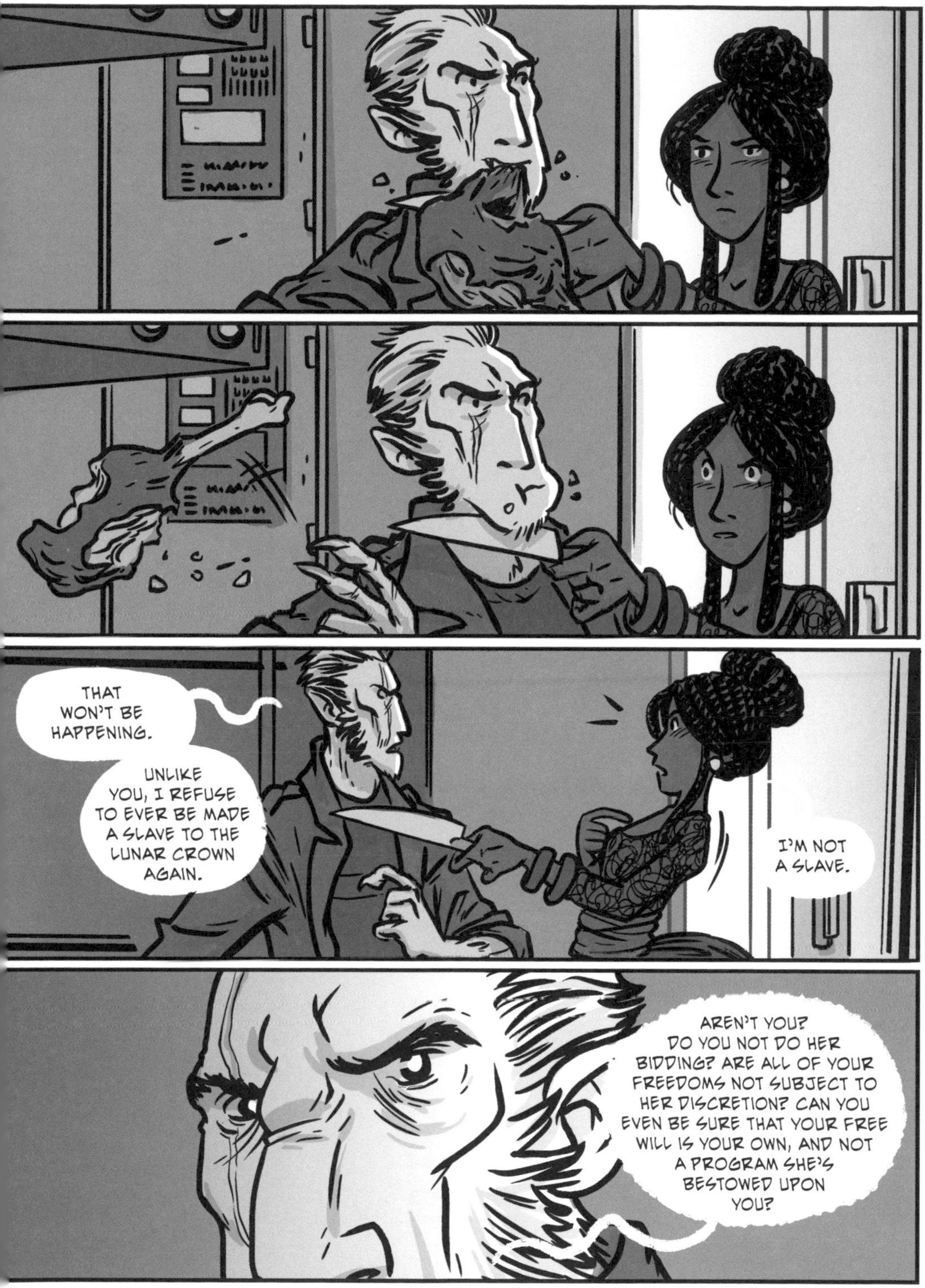
THAT WON'T BE HAPPENING.
UNLIKE YOU, I REFUSE TO EVER BE MADE A SLAVE TO THE LUNAR CROWN AGAIN.
I'M NOT A SLAVE.
AREN'T YOU? DO YOU NOT DO HER BIDDING? ARE ALL OF YOUR FREEDOMS NOT SUBJECT TO HER DISCRETION? CAN YOU EVEN BE SURE THAT YOUR FREE WILL IS YOUR OWN, AND NOT A PROGRAM SHE'S BESTOWED UPON YOU?

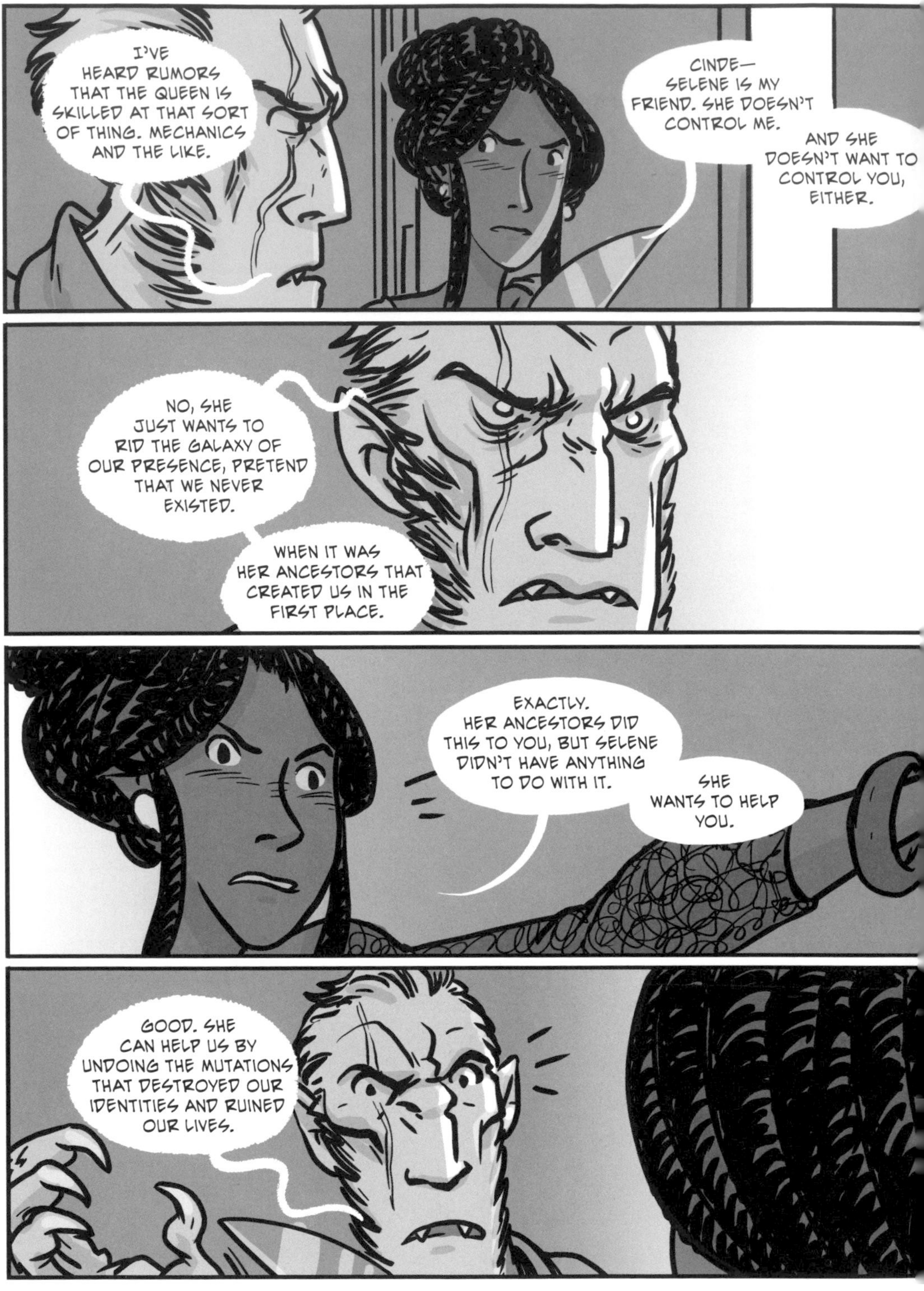
I'VE HEARD RUMORS THAT THE QUEEN IS SKILLED AT THAT SORT OF THING. MECHANICS AND THE LIKE.
CINDE— SELENE IS MY FRIEND. SHE DOESN'T CONTROL ME.
AND SHE DOESN'T WANT TO CONTROL YOU, EITHER.
NO, SHE JUST WANTS TO RID THE GALAXY OF OUR PRESENCE, PRETEND THAT WE NEVER EXISTED.
WHEN IT WAS HER ANCESTORS THAT CREATED US IN THE FIRST PLACE.
EXACTLY. HER ANCESTORS DID THIS TO YOU, BUT SELENE DIDN'T HAVE ANYTHING TO DO WITH IT.
SHE WANTS TO HELP YOU.
GOOD. SHE CAN HELP US BY UNDOING THE MUTATIONS THAT DESTROYED OUR IDENTITIES AND RUINED OUR LIVES.

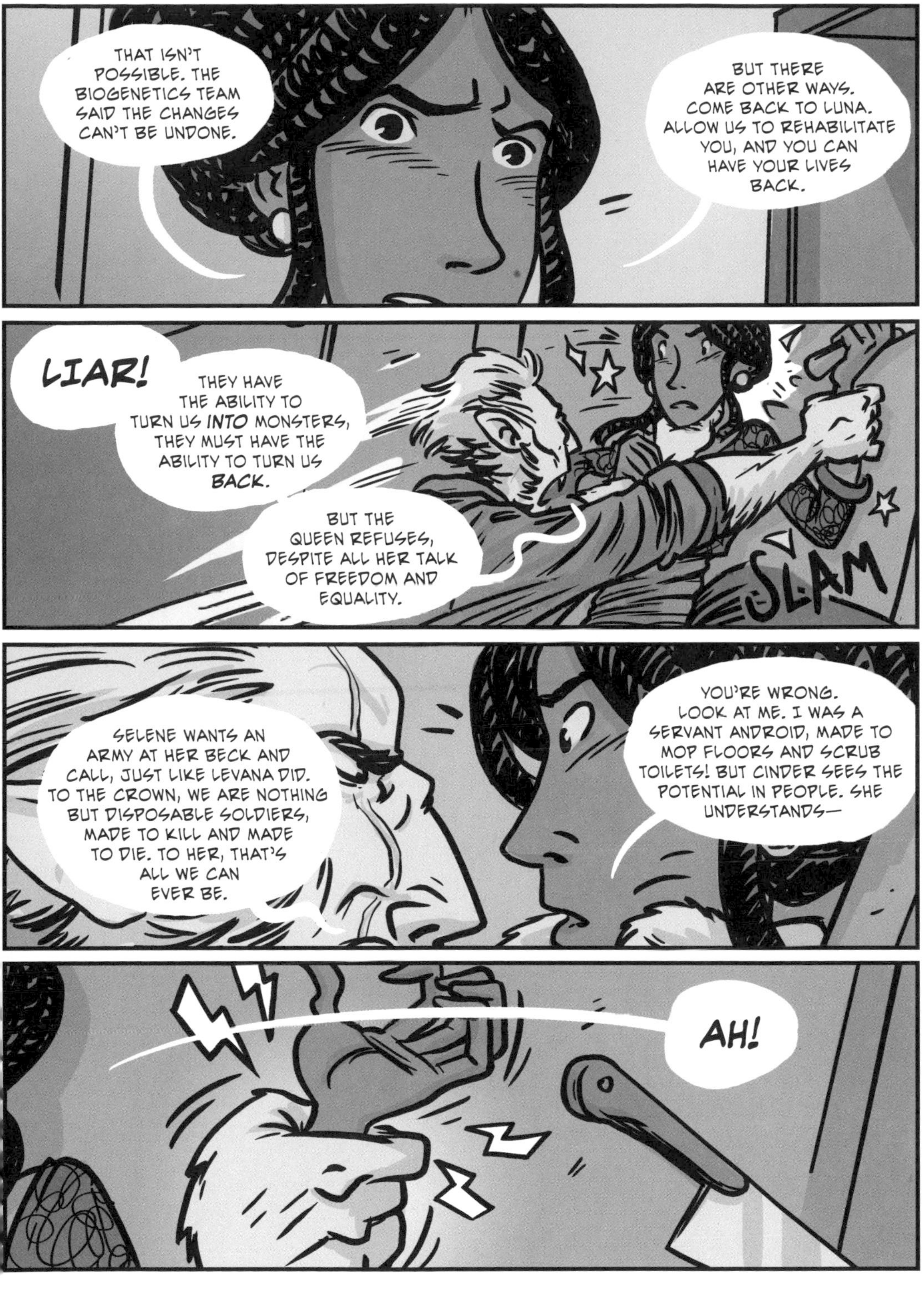
THAT ISN'T POSSIBLE. THE BIOGENETICS TEAM SAID THE CHANGES CAN'T BE UNDONE.
BUT THERE ARE OTHER WAYS. COME BACK TO LUNA. ALLOW US TO REHABILITATE YOU, AND YOU CAN HAVE YOUR LIVES BACK.
LIAR!
THEY HAVE THE ABILITY TO TURN US *INTO* MONSTERS, THEY MUST HAVE THE ABILITY TO TURN US *BACK*.
BUT THE QUEEN REFUSES, DESPITE ALL HER TALK OF FREEDOM AND EQUALITY.
SLAM
SELENE WANTS AN ARMY AT HER BECK AND CALL, JUST LIKE LEVANA DID. TO THE CROWN, WE ARE NOTHING BUT DISPOSABLE SOLDIERS, MADE TO KILL AND MADE TO DIE. TO HER, THAT'S ALL WE CAN EVER BE.
YOU'RE WRONG. LOOK AT ME. I WAS A SERVANT ANDROID, MADE TO MOP FLOORS AND SCRUB TOILETS! BUT CINDER SEES THE POTENTIAL IN PEOPLE. SHE UNDERSTANDS—
AH!

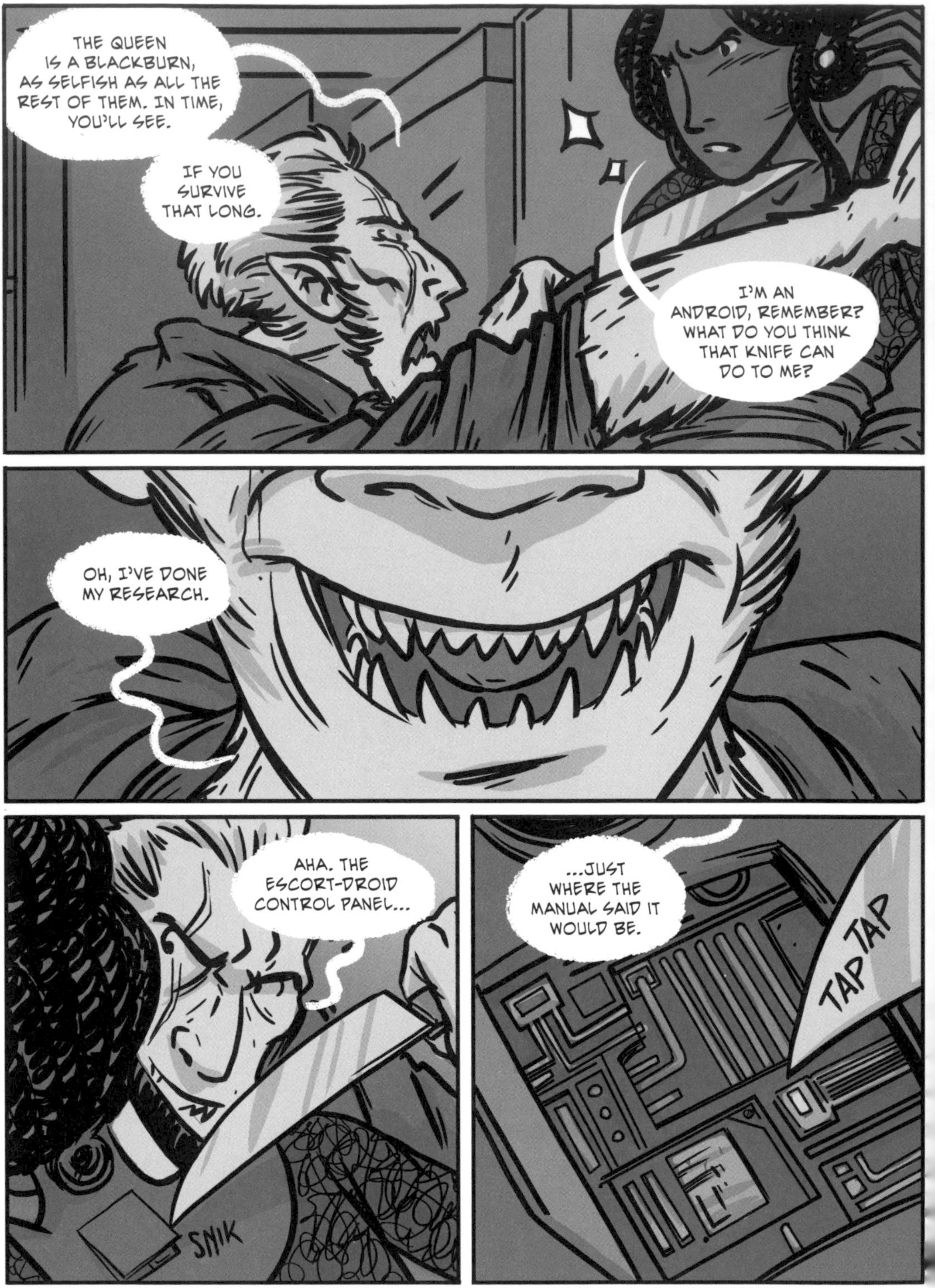
THE QUEEN IS A BLACKBURN, AS SELFISH AS ALL THE REST OF THEM. IN TIME, YOU'LL SEE.
IF YOU SURVIVE THAT LONG.
I'M AN ANDROID, REMEMBER? WHAT DO YOU THINK THAT KNIFE CAN DO TO ME?
OH, I'VE DONE MY RESEARCH.
AHA. THE ESCORT-DROID CONTROL PANEL...
SNIK
...JUST WHERE THE MANUAL SAID IT WOULD BE.
TAP TAP

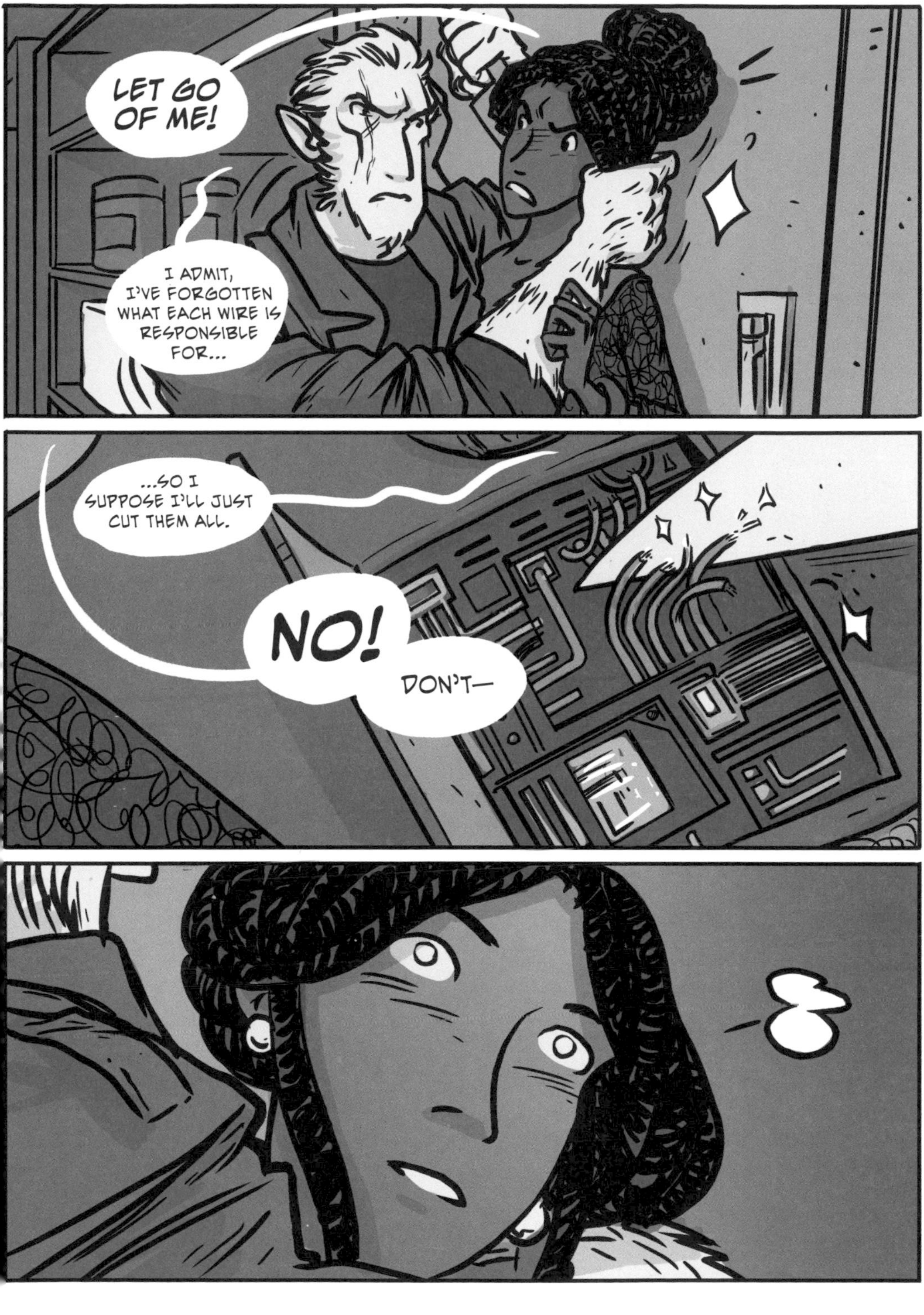
LET GO OF ME!
I ADMIT, I'VE FORGOTTEN WHAT EACH WIRE IS RESPONSIBLE FOR...
...SO I SUPPOSE I'LL JUST CUT THEM ALL.
NO!
DON'T—

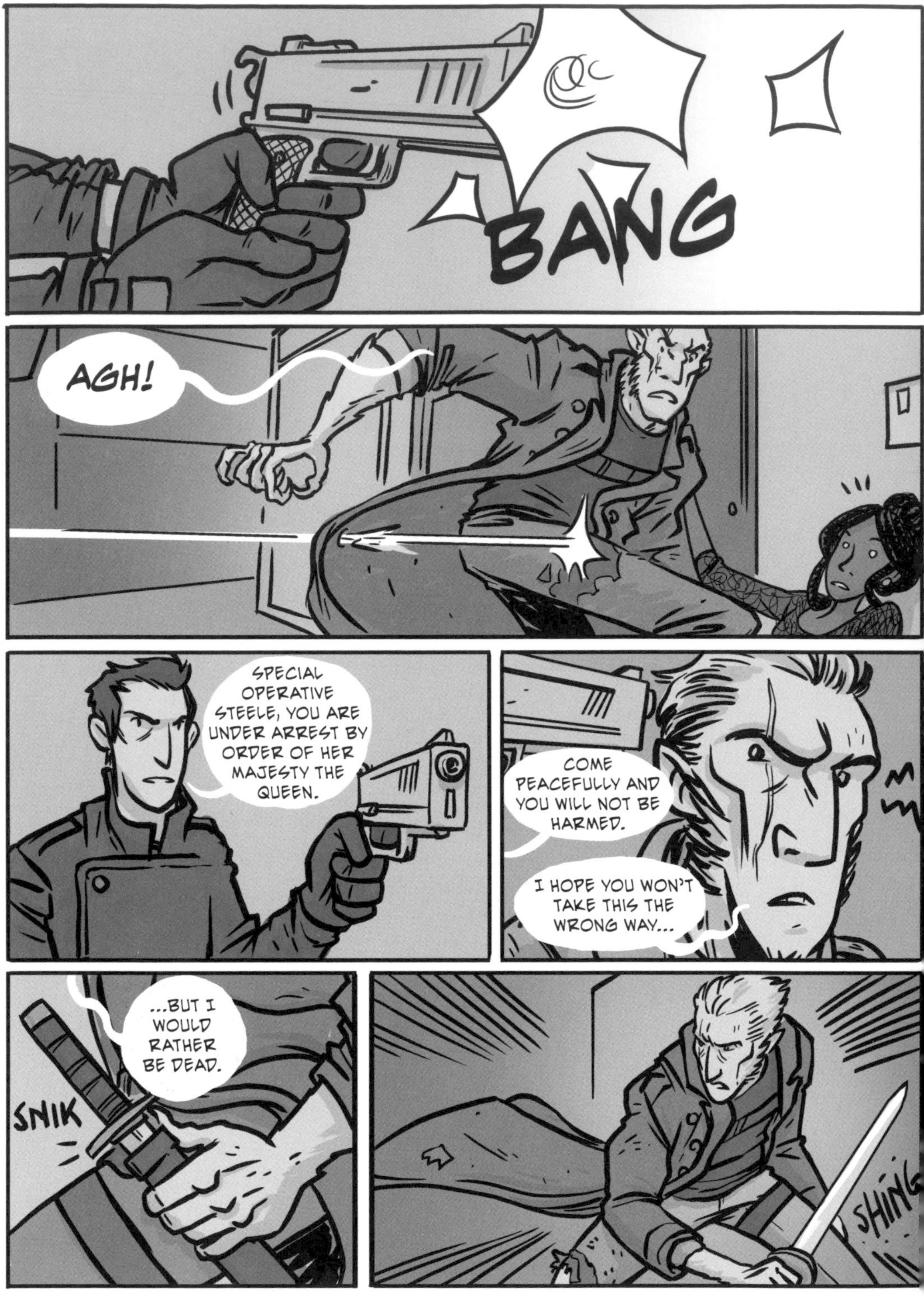
BANG
AGH!
SPECIAL OPERATIVE STEELE, YOU ARE UNDER ARREST BY ORDER OF HER MAJESTY THE QUEEN.
COME PEACEFULLY AND YOU WILL NOT BE HARMED.
I HOPE YOU WON'T TAKE THIS THE WRONG WAY...
...BUT I WOULD RATHER BE DEAD.
SNIK
SHING

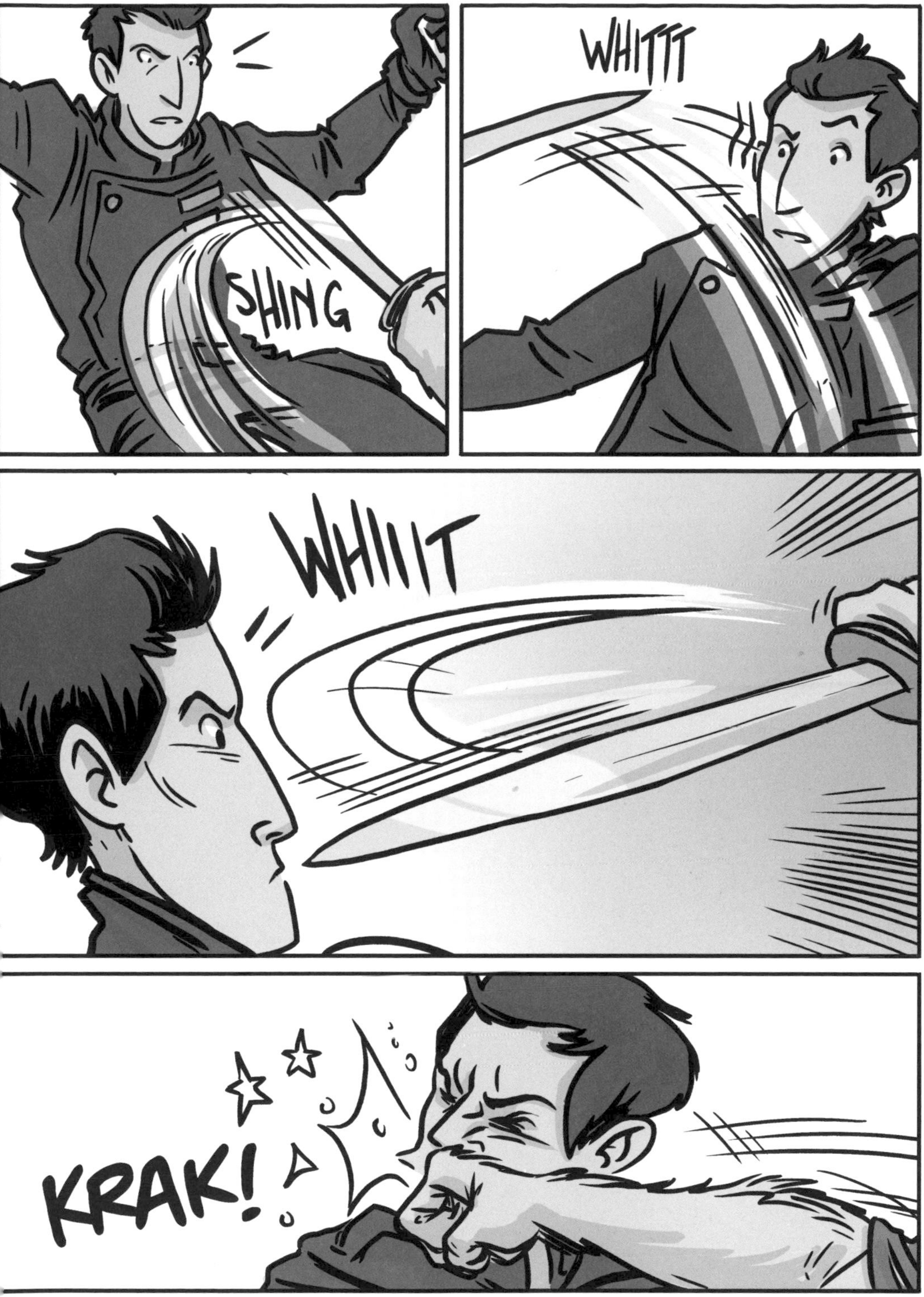
SHING
WHITTT
WHIIIT
KRAK!

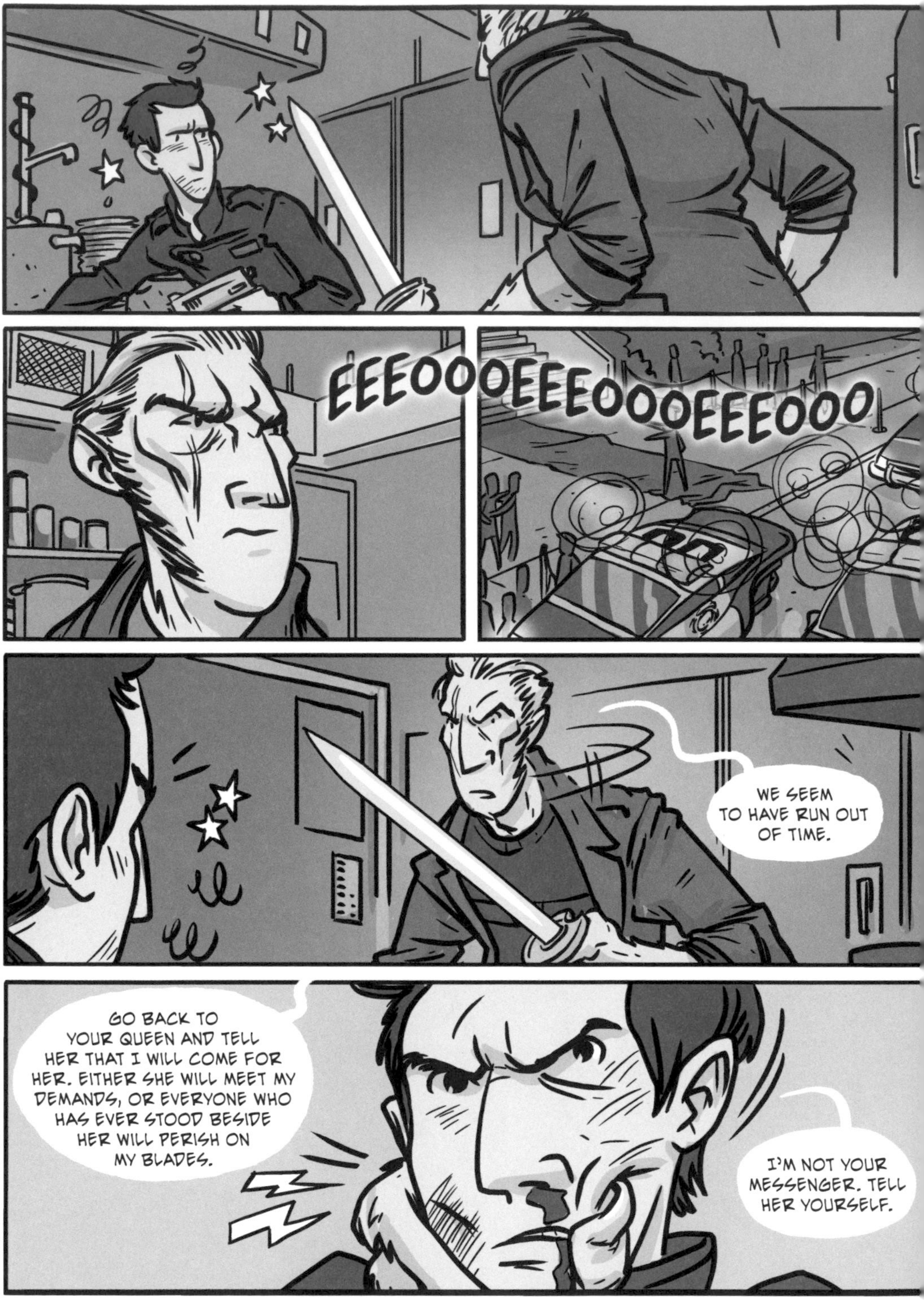
EEEOOOEEEOOOEEEOOO
WE SEEM TO HAVE RUN OUT OF TIME.
GO BACK TO YOUR QUEEN AND TELL HER THAT I WILL COME FOR HER. EITHER SHE WILL MEET MY DEMANDS, OR EVERYONE WHO HAS EVER STOOD BESIDE HER WILL PERISH ON MY BLADES.
I'M NOT YOUR MESSENGER. TELL HER YOURSELF.

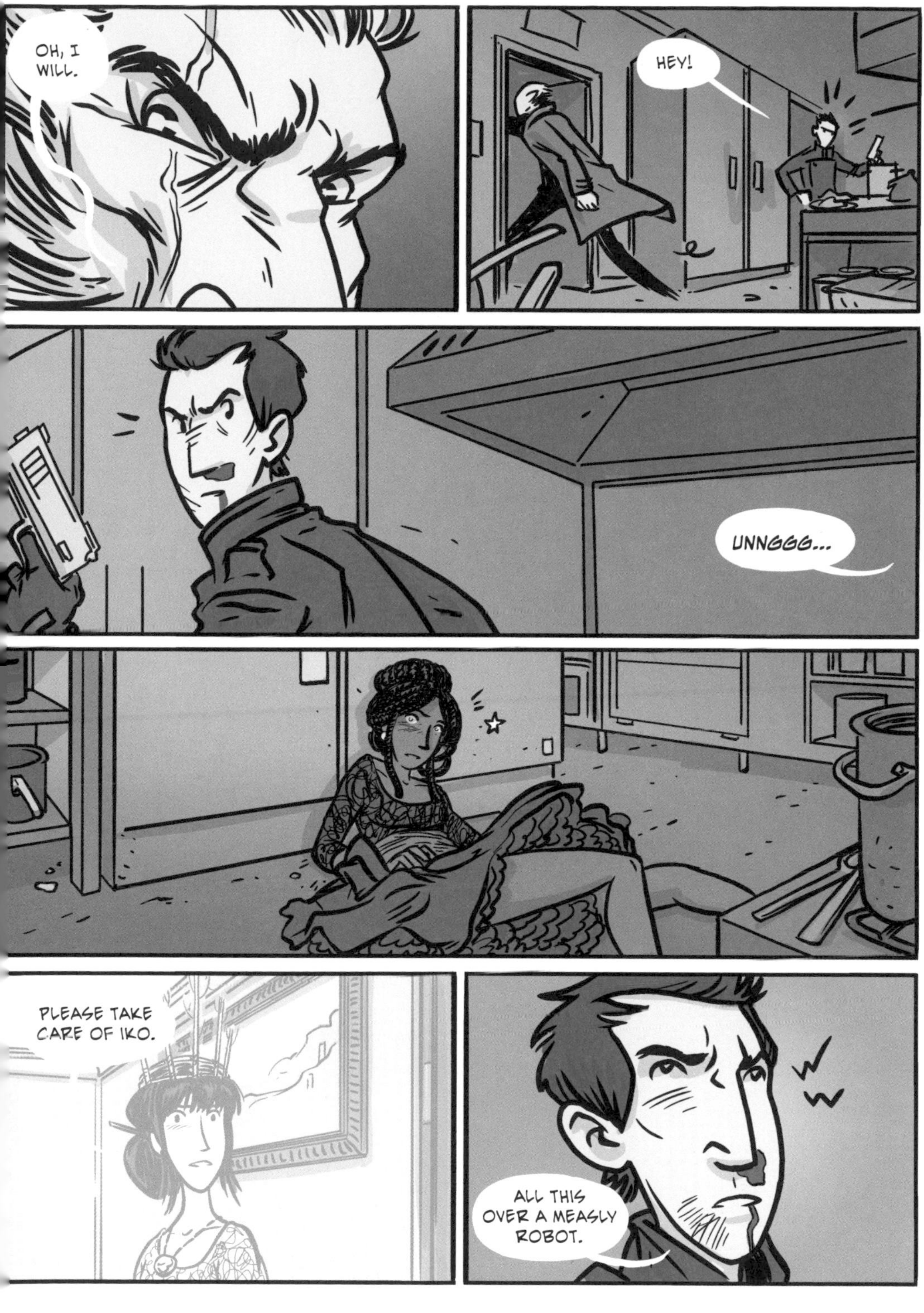
OH, I WILL.
HEY!
UNNGGG...
PLEASE TAKE CARE OF IKO.
ALL THIS OVER A MEASLY ROBOT.

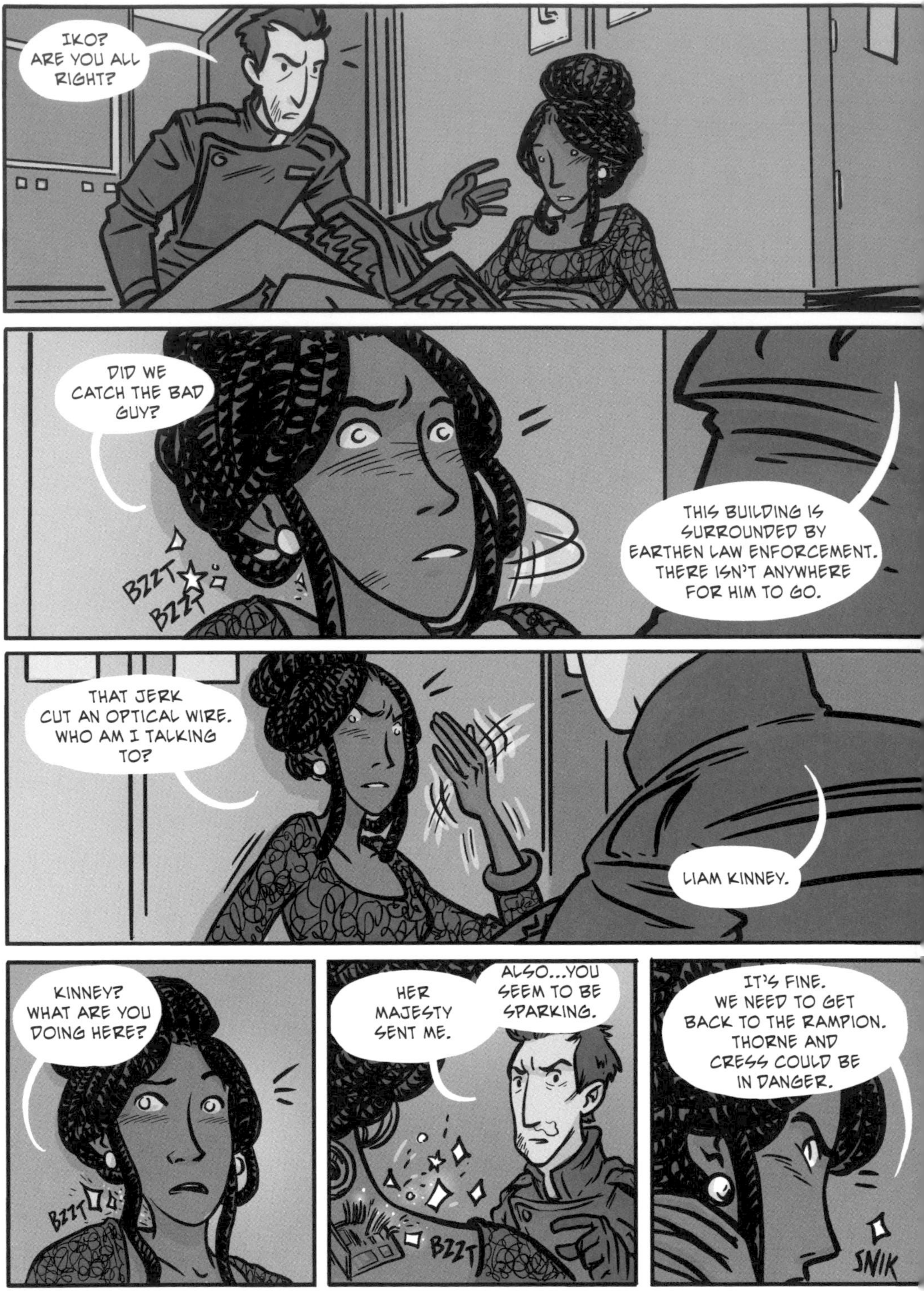
IKO? ARE YOU ALL RIGHT?
DID WE CATCH THE BAD GUY?
BZZT BZZT
THIS BUILDING IS SURROUNDED BY EARTHEN LAW ENFORCEMENT. THERE ISN'T ANYWHERE FOR HIM TO GO.
THAT JERK CUT AN OPTICAL WIRE. WHO AM I TALKING TO?
LIAM KINNEY.
KINNEY? WHAT ARE YOU DOING HERE?
BZZT
HER MAJESTY SENT ME.
ALSO...YOU SEEM TO BE SPARKING.
BZZT
IT'S FINE. WE NEED TO GET BACK TO THE RAMPION. THORNE AND CRESS COULD BE IN DANGER.
SNIK

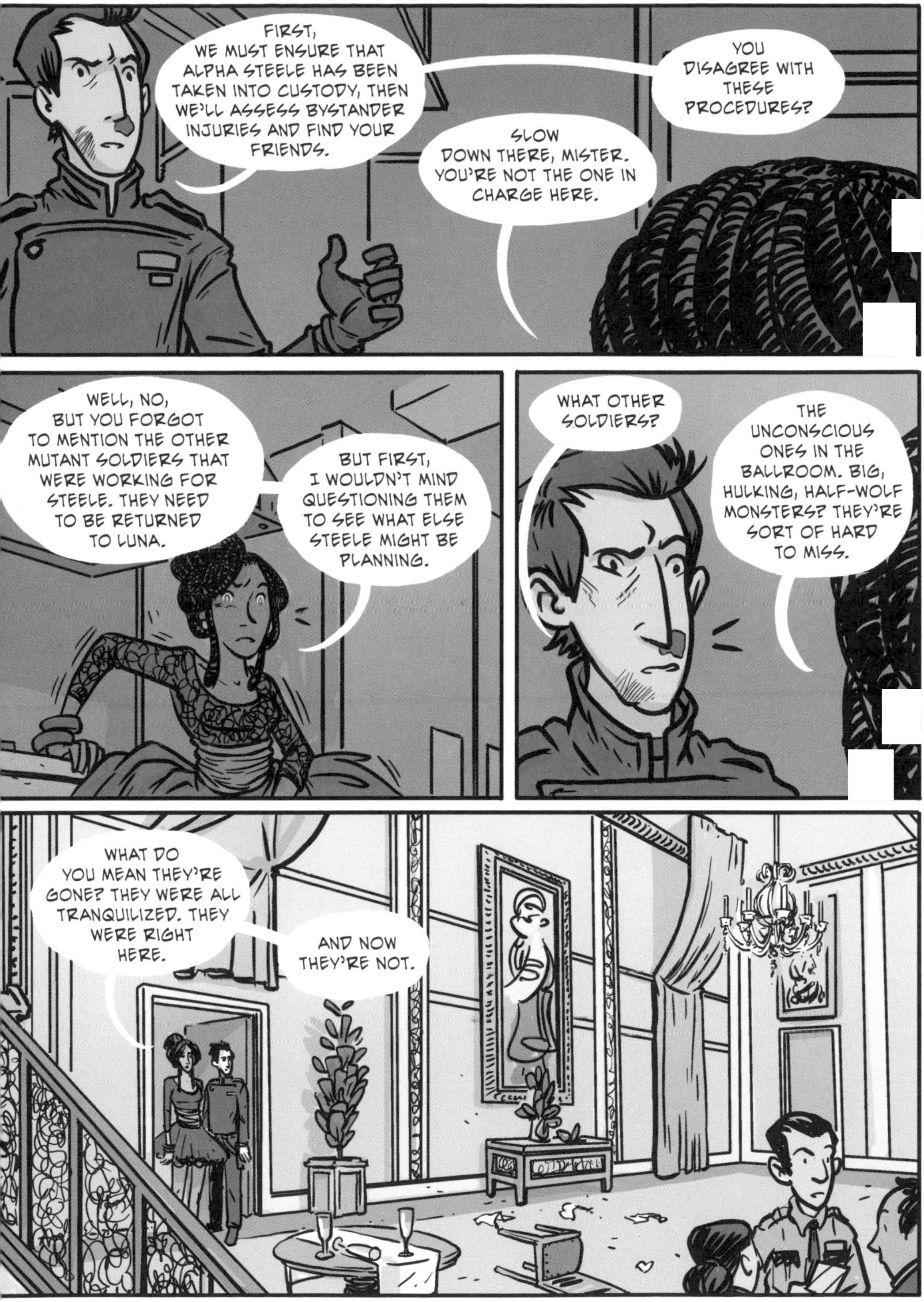
FIRST, WE MUST ENSURE THAT ALPHA STEELE HAS BEEN TAKEN INTO CUSTODY, THEN WE'LL ASSESS BYSTANDER INJURIES AND FIND YOUR FRIENDS.
YOU DISAGREE WITH THESE PROCEDURES?
SLOW DOWN THERE, MISTER. YOU'RE NOT THE ONE IN CHARGE HERE.
WELL, NO, BUT YOU FORGOT TO MENTION THE OTHER MUTANT SOLDIERS THAT WERE WORKING FOR STEELE. THEY NEED TO BE RETURNED TO LUNA.
BUT FIRST, I WOULDN'T MIND QUESTIONING THEM TO SEE WHAT ELSE STEELE MIGHT BE PLANNING.
WHAT OTHER SOLDIERS?
THE UNCONSCIOUS ONES IN THE BALLROOM. BIG, HULKING, HALF-WOLF MONSTERS? THEY'RE SORT OF HARD TO MISS.
WHAT DO YOU MEAN THEY'RE GONE? THEY WERE ALL TRANQUILIZED. THEY WERE RIGHT HERE.
AND NOW THEY'RE NOT.

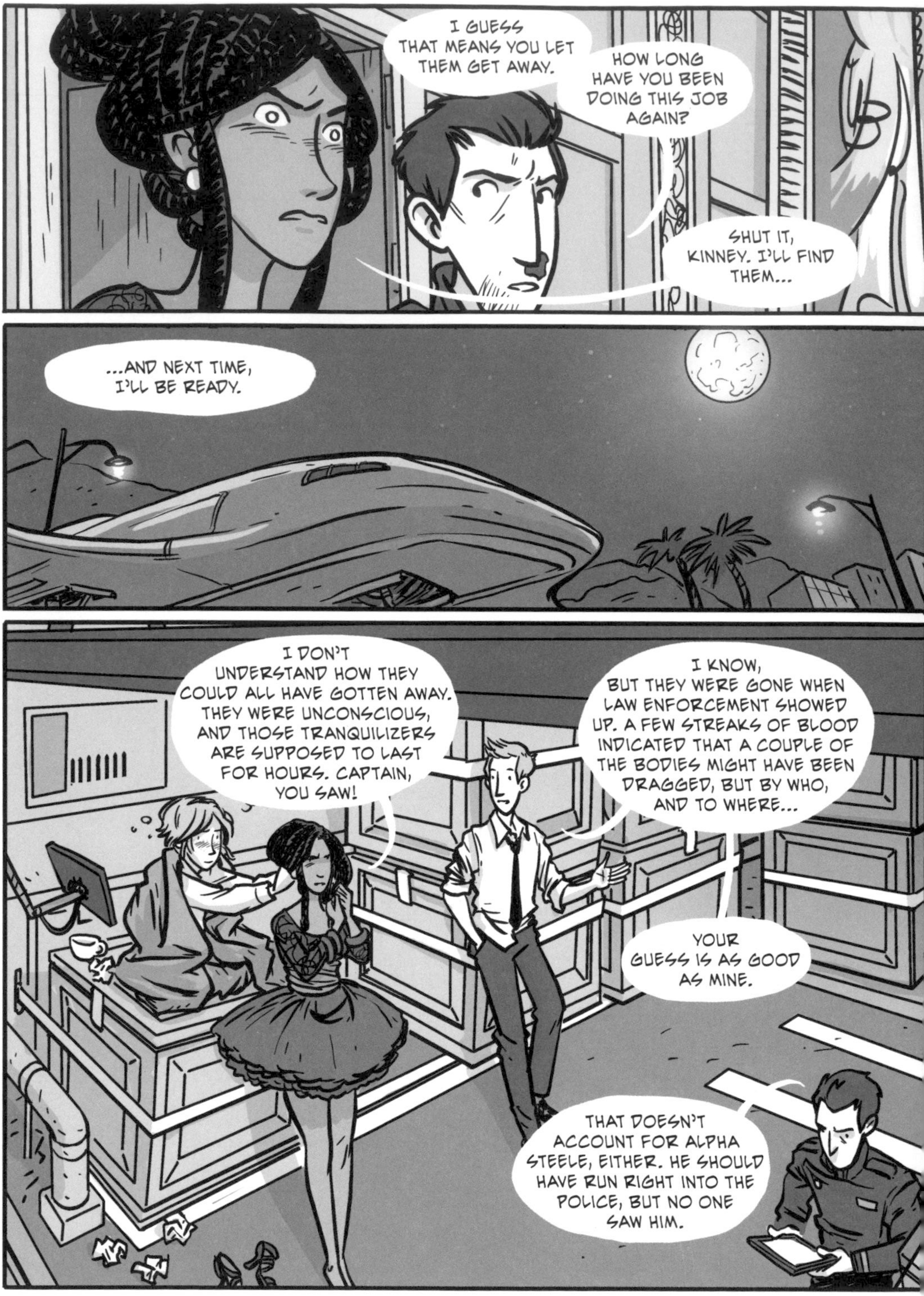
I GUESS THAT MEANS YOU LET THEM GET AWAY.
HOW LONG HAVE YOU BEEN DOING THIS JOB AGAIN?
SHUT IT, KINNEY. I'LL FIND THEM...
...AND NEXT TIME, I'LL BE READY.
I DON'T UNDERSTAND HOW THEY COULD ALL HAVE GOTTEN AWAY. THEY WERE UNCONSCIOUS, AND THOSE TRANQUILIZERS ARE SUPPOSED TO LAST FOR HOURS. CAPTAIN, YOU SAW!
I KNOW, BUT THEY WERE GONE WHEN LAW ENFORCEMENT SHOWED UP. A FEW STREAKS OF BLOOD INDICATED THAT A COUPLE OF THE BODIES MIGHT HAVE BEEN DRAGGED, BUT BY WHO, AND TO WHERE...
YOUR GUESS IS AS GOOD AS MINE.
THAT DOESN'T ACCOUNT FOR ALPHA STEELE, EITHER. HE SHOULD HAVE RUN RIGHT INTO THE POLICE, BUT NO ONE SAW HIM.

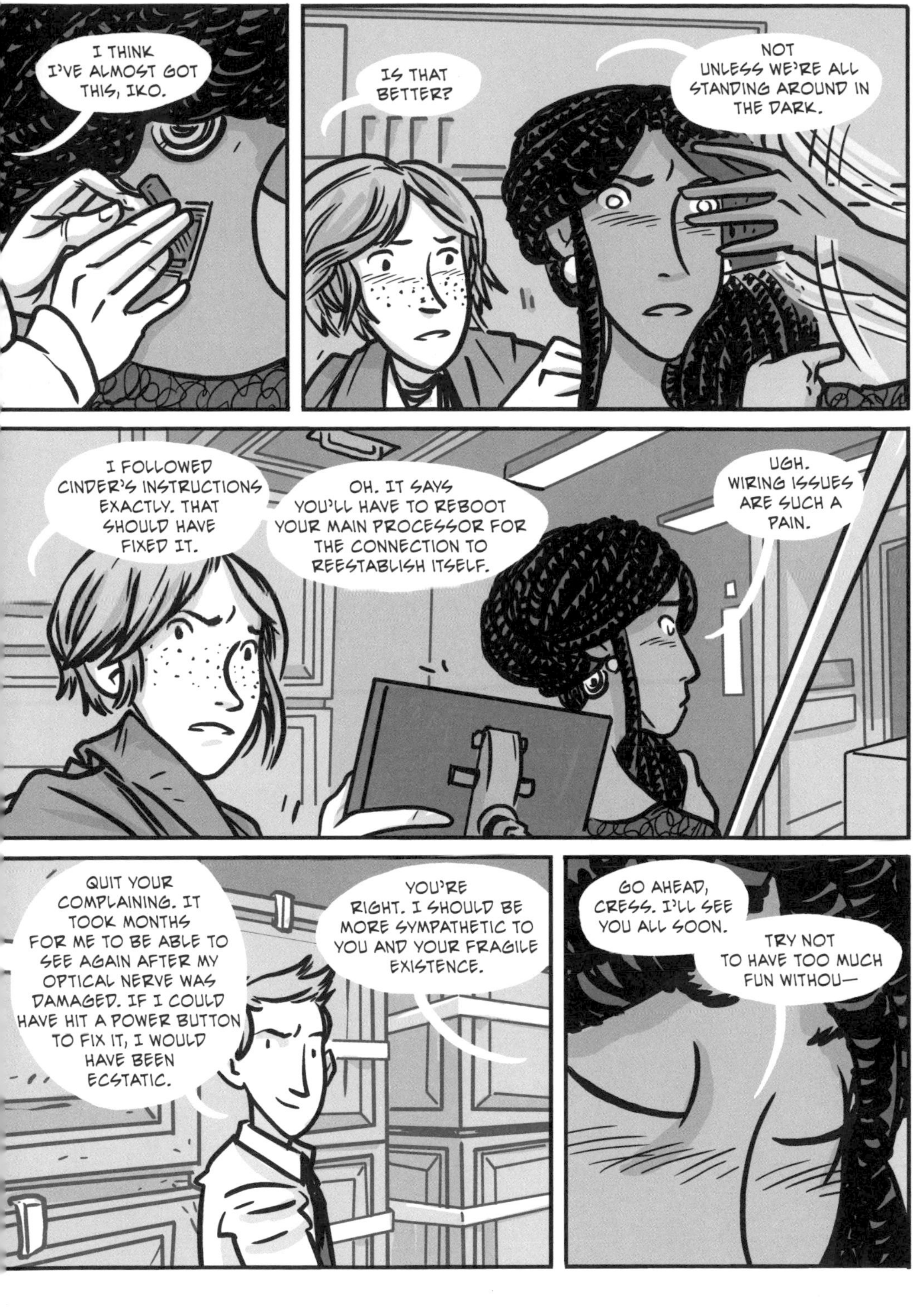
I THINK I'VE ALMOST GOT THIS, IKO.
IS THAT BETTER?
NOT UNLESS WE'RE ALL STANDING AROUND IN THE DARK.
I FOLLOWED CINDER'S INSTRUCTIONS EXACTLY. THAT SHOULD HAVE FIXED IT.
OH. IT SAYS YOU'LL HAVE TO REBOOT YOUR MAIN PROCESSOR FOR THE CONNECTION TO REESTABLISH ITSELF.
UGH. WIRING ISSUES ARE SUCH A PAIN.
QUIT YOUR COMPLAINING. IT TOOK MONTHS FOR ME TO BE ABLE TO SEE AGAIN AFTER MY OPTICAL NERVE WAS DAMAGED. IF I COULD HAVE HIT A POWER BUTTON TO FIX IT, I WOULD HAVE BEEN ECSTATIC.
YOU'RE RIGHT. I SHOULD BE MORE SYMPATHETIC TO YOU AND YOUR FRAGILE EXISTENCE.
GO AHEAD, CRESS. I'LL SEE YOU ALL SOON.
TRY NOT TO HAVE TOO MUCH FUN WITHOU—

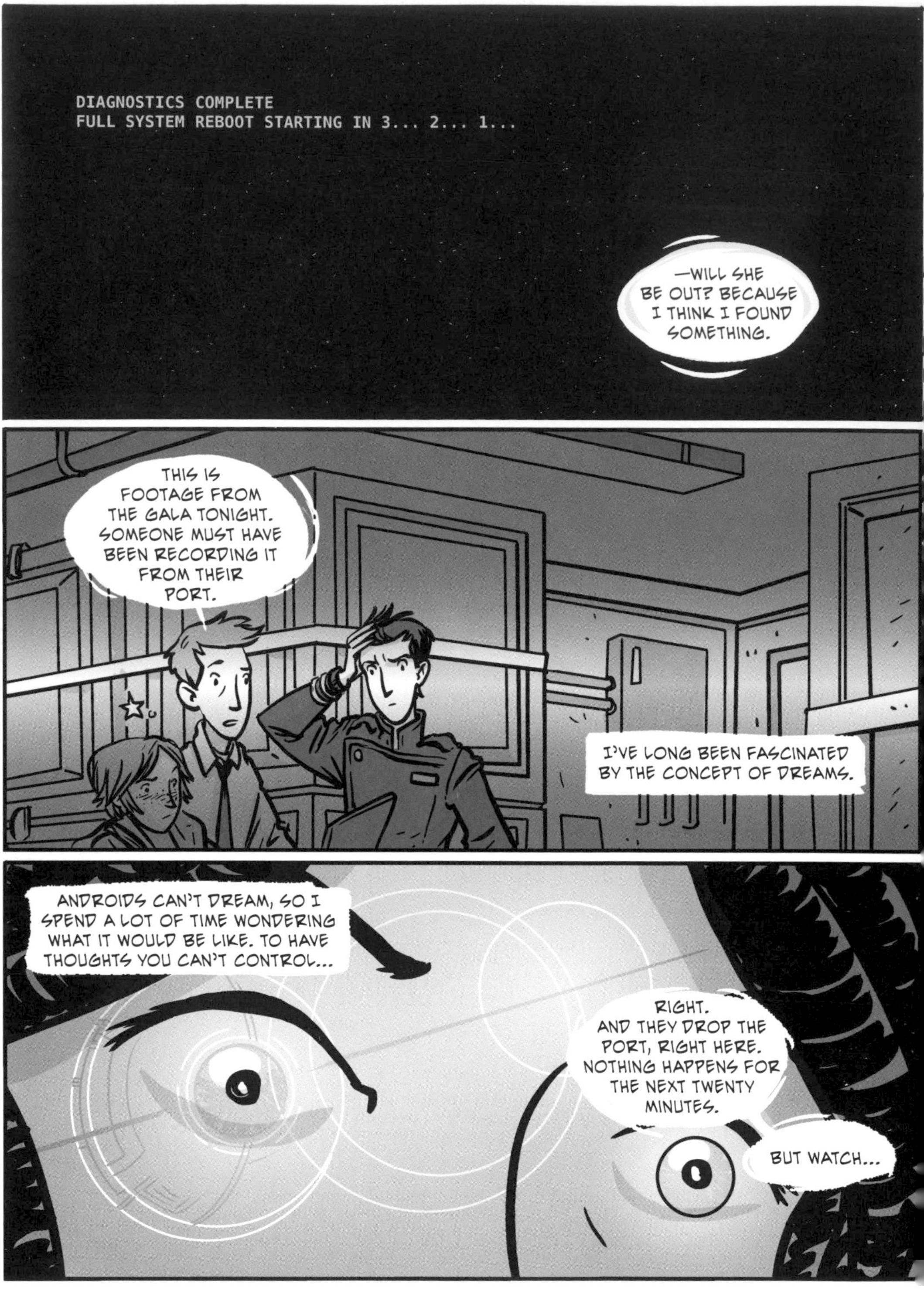
DIAGNOSTICS COMPLETE
FULL SYSTEM REBOOT STARTING IN 3... 2... 1...
—WILL SHE BE OUT? BECAUSE I THINK I FOUND SOMETHING.
THIS IS FOOTAGE FROM THE GALA TONIGHT. SOMEONE MUST HAVE BEEN RECORDING IT FROM THEIR PORT.
I'VE LONG BEEN FASCINATED BY THE CONCEPT OF DREAMS.
ANDROIDS CAN'T DREAM, SO I SPEND A LOT OF TIME WONDERING WHAT IT WOULD BE LIKE. TO HAVE THOUGHTS YOU CAN'T CONTROL...
RIGHT. AND THEY DROP THE PORT, RIGHT HERE. NOTHING HAPPENS FOR THE NEXT TWENTY MINUTES.
BUT WATCH...

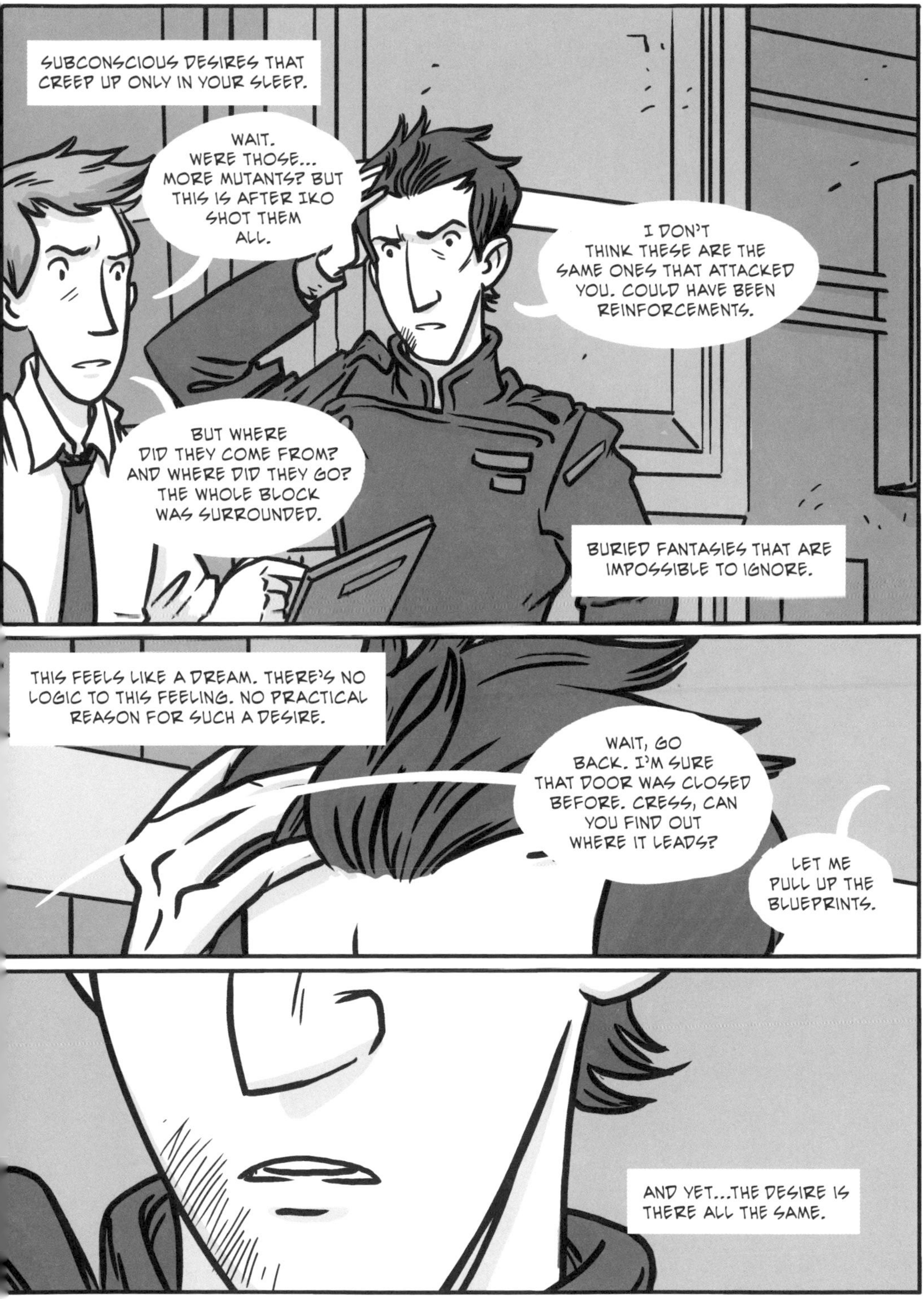
SUBCONSCIOUS DESIRES THAT CREEP UP ONLY IN YOUR SLEEP.
WAIT. WERE THOSE... MORE MUTANTS? BUT THIS IS AFTER IKO SHOT THEM ALL.
I DON'T THINK THESE ARE THE SAME ONES THAT ATTACKED YOU. COULD HAVE BEEN REINFORCEMENTS.
BUT WHERE DID THEY COME FROM? AND WHERE DID THEY GO? THE WHOLE BLOCK WAS SURROUNDED.
BURIED FANTASIES THAT ARE IMPOSSIBLE TO IGNORE.
THIS FEELS LIKE A DREAM. THERE'S NO LOGIC TO THIS FEELING. NO PRACTICAL REASON FOR SUCH A DESIRE.
WAIT, GO BACK. I'M SURE THAT DOOR WAS CLOSED BEFORE. CRESS, CAN YOU FIND OUT WHERE IT LEADS?
LET ME PULL UP THE BLUEPRINTS.
AND YET...THE DESIRE IS THERE ALL THE SAME.

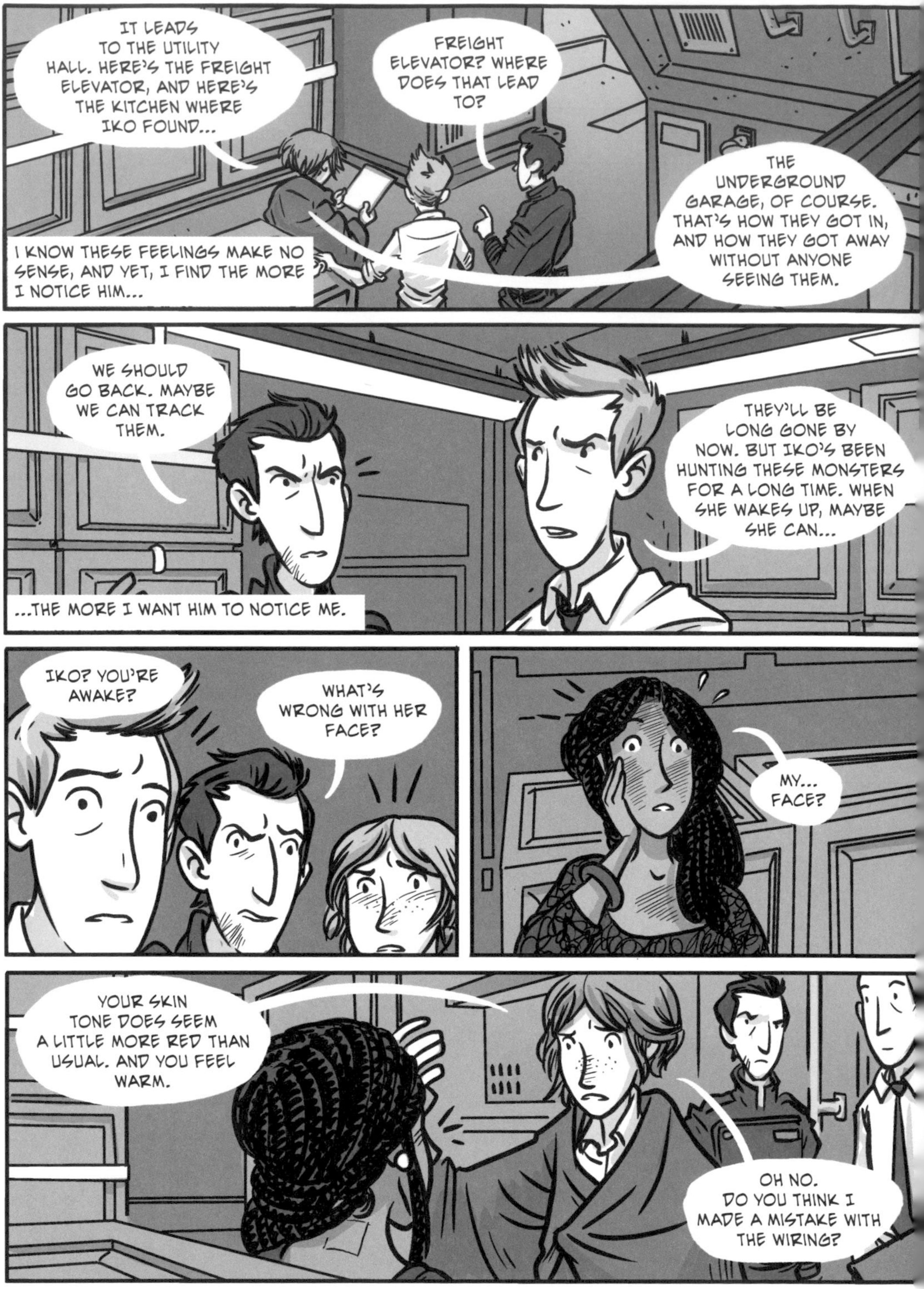
IT LEADS TO THE UTILITY HALL. HERE'S THE FREIGHT ELEVATOR, AND HERE'S THE KITCHEN WHERE IKO FOUND...
FREIGHT ELEVATOR? WHERE DOES THAT LEAD TO?
I KNOW THESE FEELINGS MAKE NO SENSE, AND YET, I FIND THE MORE I NOTICE HIM...
THE UNDERGROUND GARAGE, OF COURSE. THAT'S HOW THEY GOT IN, AND HOW THEY GOT AWAY WITHOUT ANYONE SEEING THEM.
WE SHOULD GO BACK. MAYBE WE CAN TRACK THEM.
THEY'LL BE LONG GONE BY NOW. BUT IKO'S BEEN HUNTING THESE MONSTERS FOR A LONG TIME. WHEN SHE WAKES UP, MAYBE SHE CAN...
...THE MORE I WANT HIM TO NOTICE ME.
IKO? YOU'RE AWAKE?
WHAT'S WRONG WITH HER FACE?
MY... FACE?
YOUR SKIN TONE DOES SEEM A LITTLE MORE RED THAN USUAL. AND YOU FEEL WARM.
OH NO. DO YOU THINK I MADE A MISTAKE WITH THE WIRING?

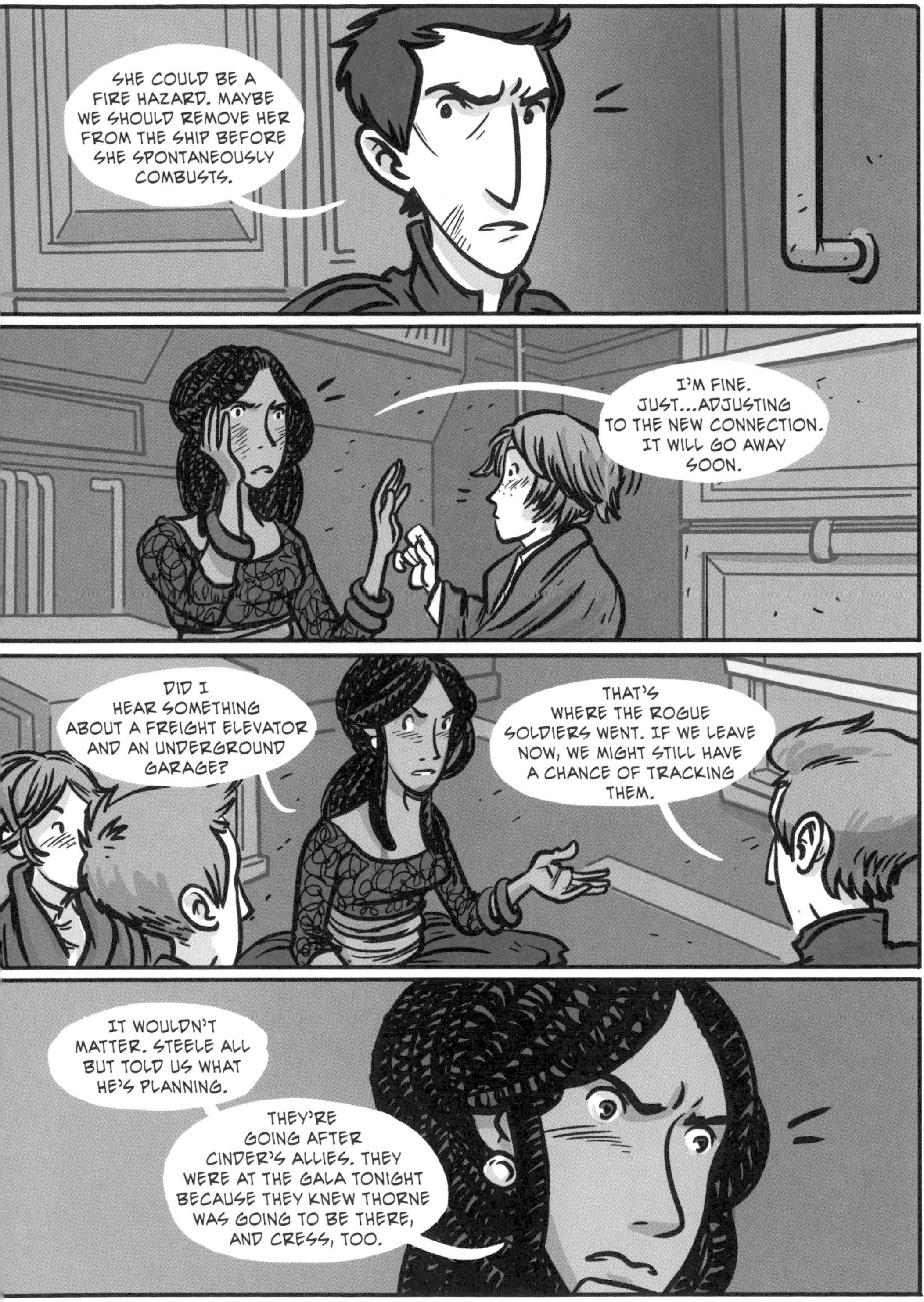
SHE COULD BE A FIRE HAZARD. MAYBE WE SHOULD REMOVE HER FROM THE SHIP BEFORE SHE SPONTANEOUSLY COMBUSTS.
I'M FINE. JUST...ADJUSTING TO THE NEW CONNECTION. IT WILL GO AWAY SOON.
DID I HEAR SOMETHING ABOUT A FREIGHT ELEVATOR AND AN UNDERGROUND GARAGE?
THAT'S WHERE THE ROGUE SOLDIERS WENT. IF WE LEAVE NOW, WE MIGHT STILL HAVE A CHANCE OF TRACKING THEM.
IT WOULDN'T MATTER. STEELE ALL BUT TOLD US WHAT HE'S PLANNING.
THEY'RE GOING AFTER CINDER'S ALLIES. THEY WERE AT THE GALA TONIGHT BECAUSE THEY KNEW THORNE WAS GOING TO BE THERE, AND CRESS, TOO.

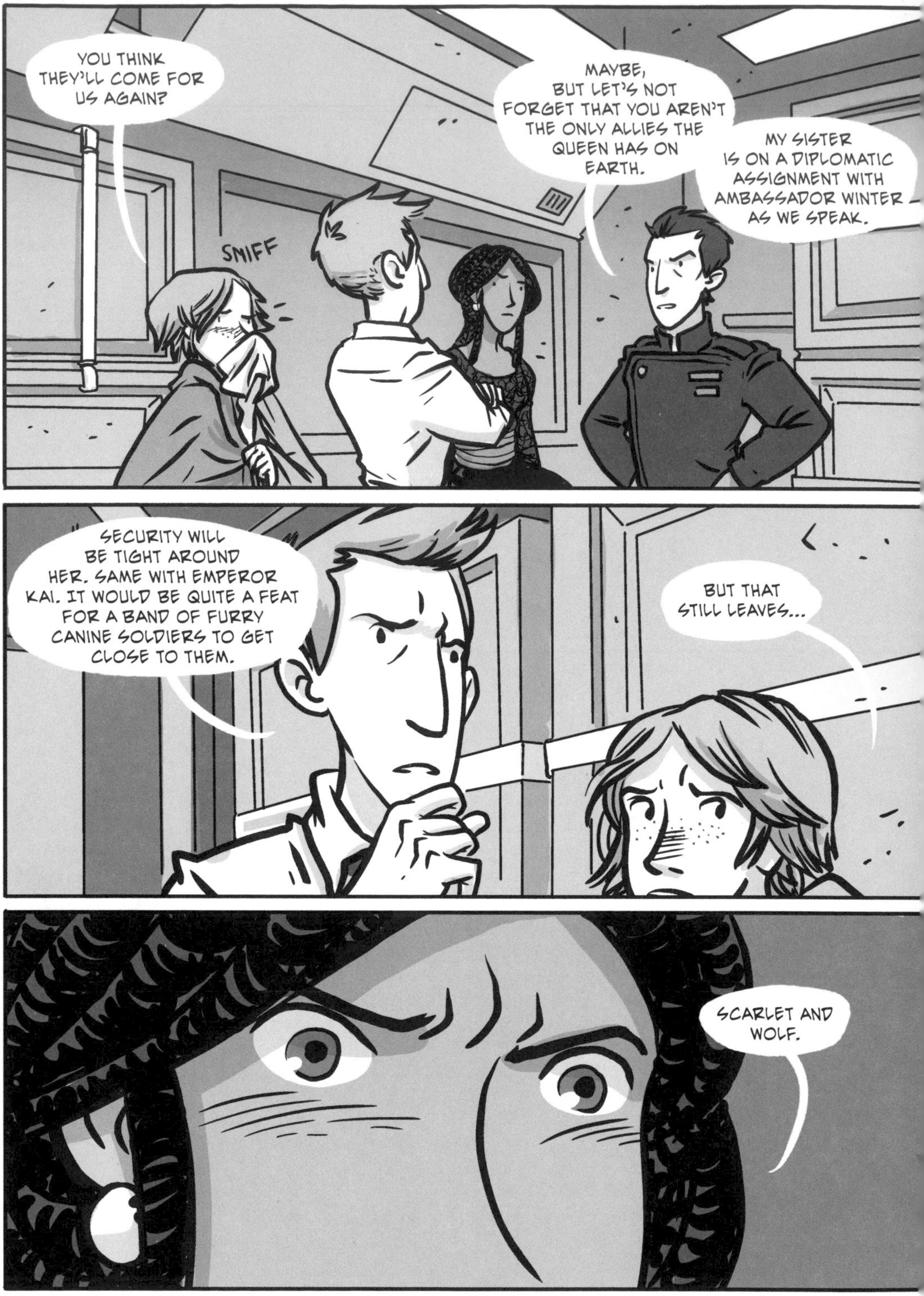
YOU THINK THEY'LL COME FOR US AGAIN?
SMIFF
MAYBE, BUT LET'S NOT FORGET THAT YOU AREN'T THE ONLY ALLIES THE QUEEN HAS ON EARTH.
MY SISTER IS ON A DIPLOMATIC ASSIGNMENT WITH AMBASSADOR WINTER AS WE SPEAK.
SECURITY WILL BE TIGHT AROUND HER. SAME WITH EMPEROR KAI. IT WOULD BE QUITE A FEAT FOR A BAND OF FURRY CANINE SOLDIERS TO GET CLOSE TO THEM.
BUT THAT STILL LEAVES...
SCARLET AND WOLF.

CHAPTER VII

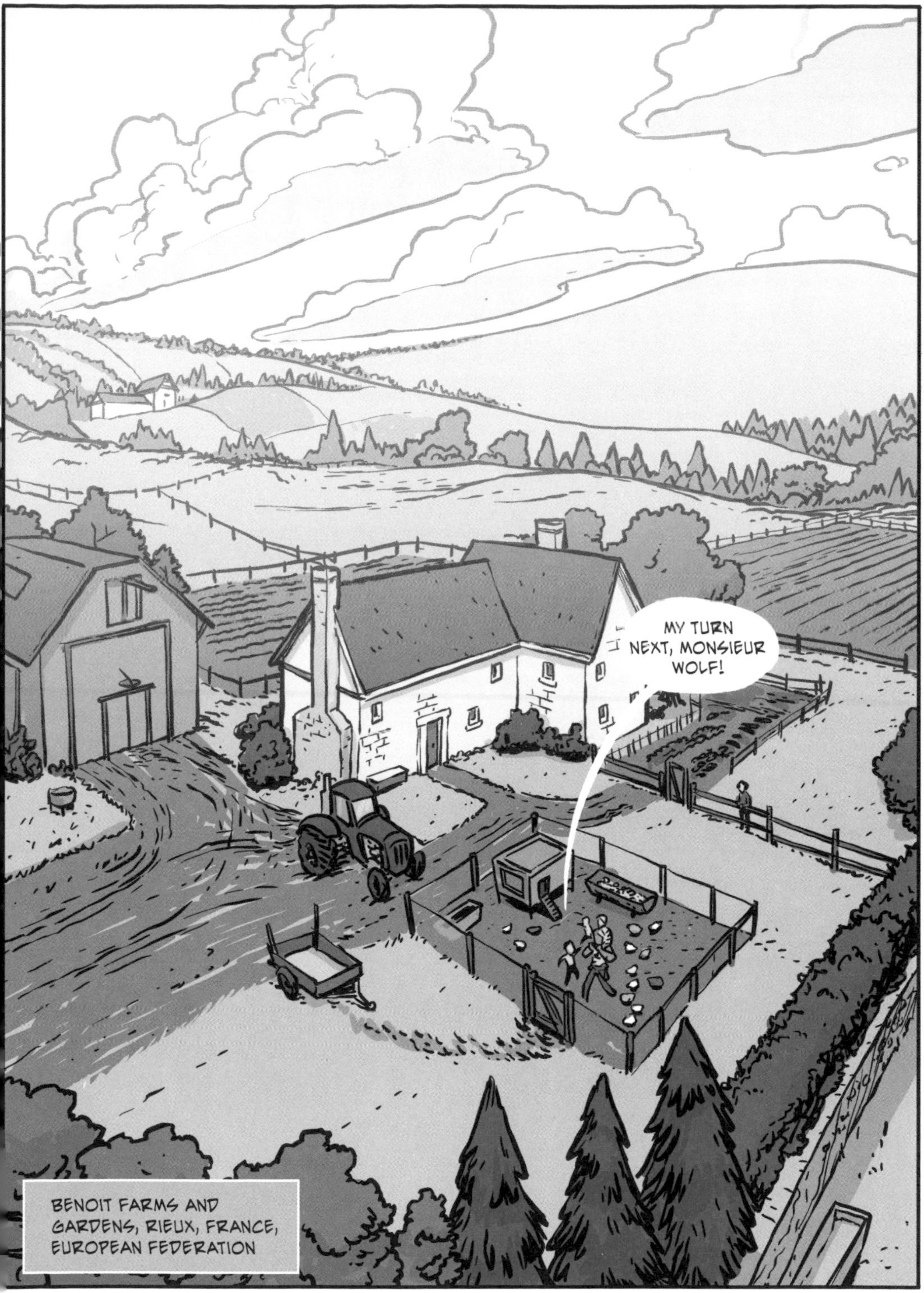

MY TURN NEXT, MONSIEUR WOLF!
BENOIT FARMS AND GARDENS, RIEUX, FRANCE, EUROPEAN FEDERATION

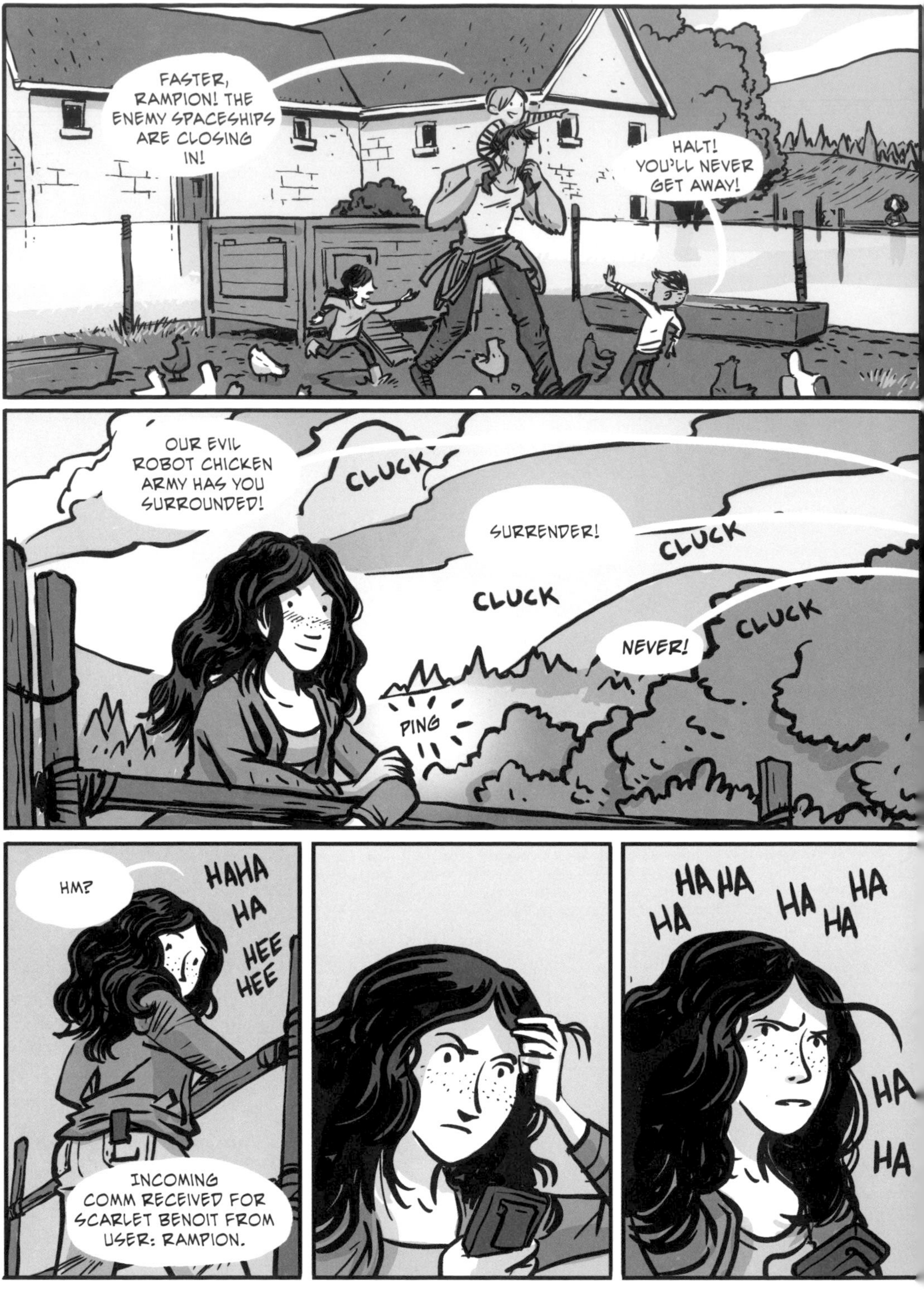
FASTER, RAMPION! THE ENEMY SPACESHIPS ARE CLOSING IN!
HALT! YOU'LL NEVER GET AWAY!
OUR EVIL ROBOT CHICKEN ARMY HAS YOU SURROUNDED!
CLUCK
SURRENDER!
CLUCK
CLUCK
CLUCK
NEVER!
PING
HM?
HAHA HA HEE HEE
INCOMING COMM RECEIVED FOR SCARLET BENOIT FROM USER: RAMPION.
HA HAHA HA HA HA HA
HA HA

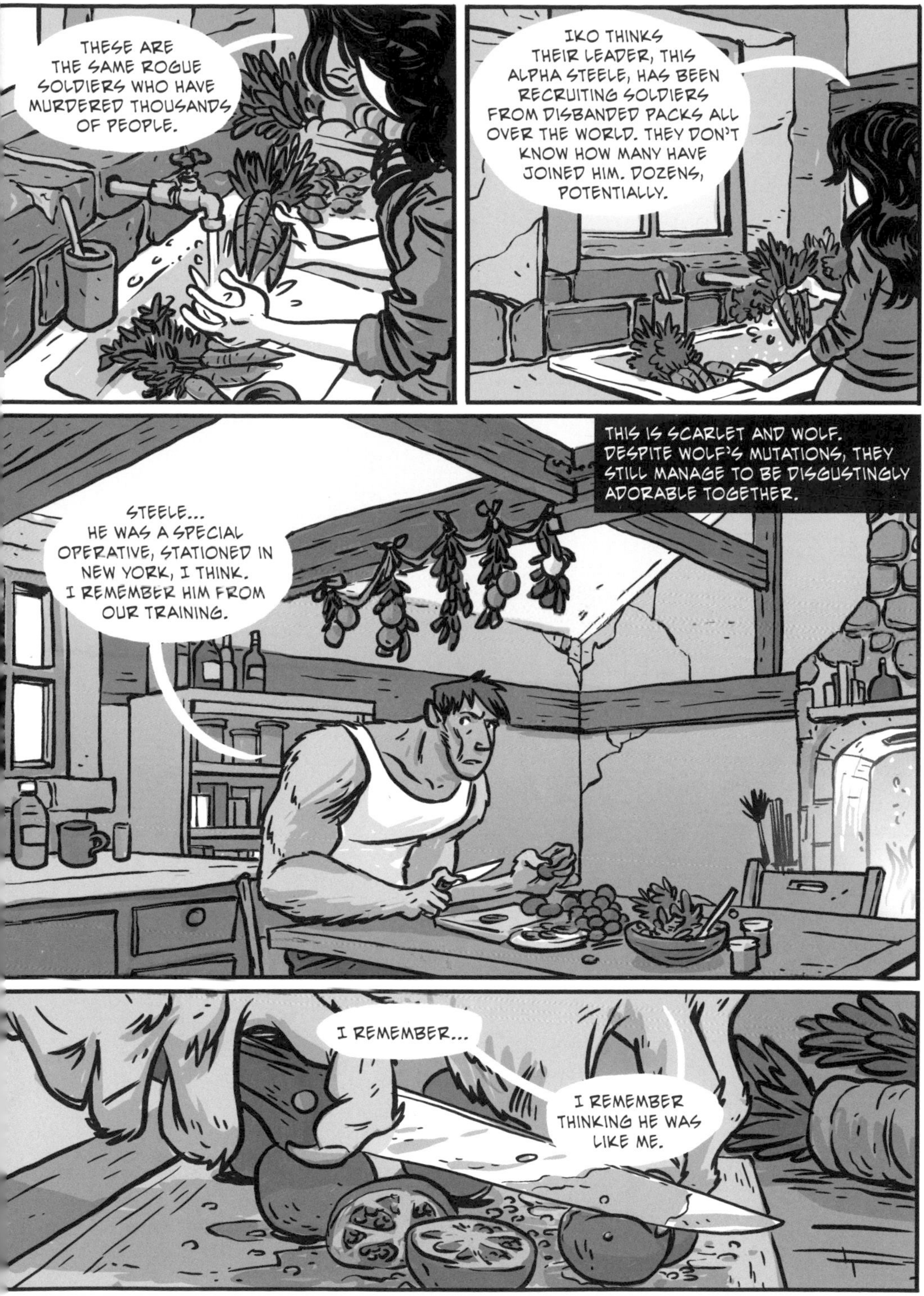
THESE ARE THE SAME ROGUE SOLDIERS WHO HAVE MURDERED THOUSANDS OF PEOPLE.
IKO THINKS THEIR LEADER, THIS ALPHA STEELE, HAS BEEN RECRUITING SOLDIERS FROM DISBANDED PACKS ALL OVER THE WORLD. THEY DON'T KNOW HOW MANY HAVE JOINED HIM. DOZENS, POTENTIALLY.
THIS IS SCARLET AND WOLF. DESPITE WOLF'S MUTATIONS, THEY STILL MANAGE TO BE DISGUSTINGLY ADORABLE TOGETHER.
STEELE... HE WAS A SPECIAL OPERATIVE, STATIONED IN NEW YORK, I THINK. I REMEMBER HIM FROM OUR TRAINING.
I REMEMBER...
I REMEMBER THINKING HE WAS LIKE ME.

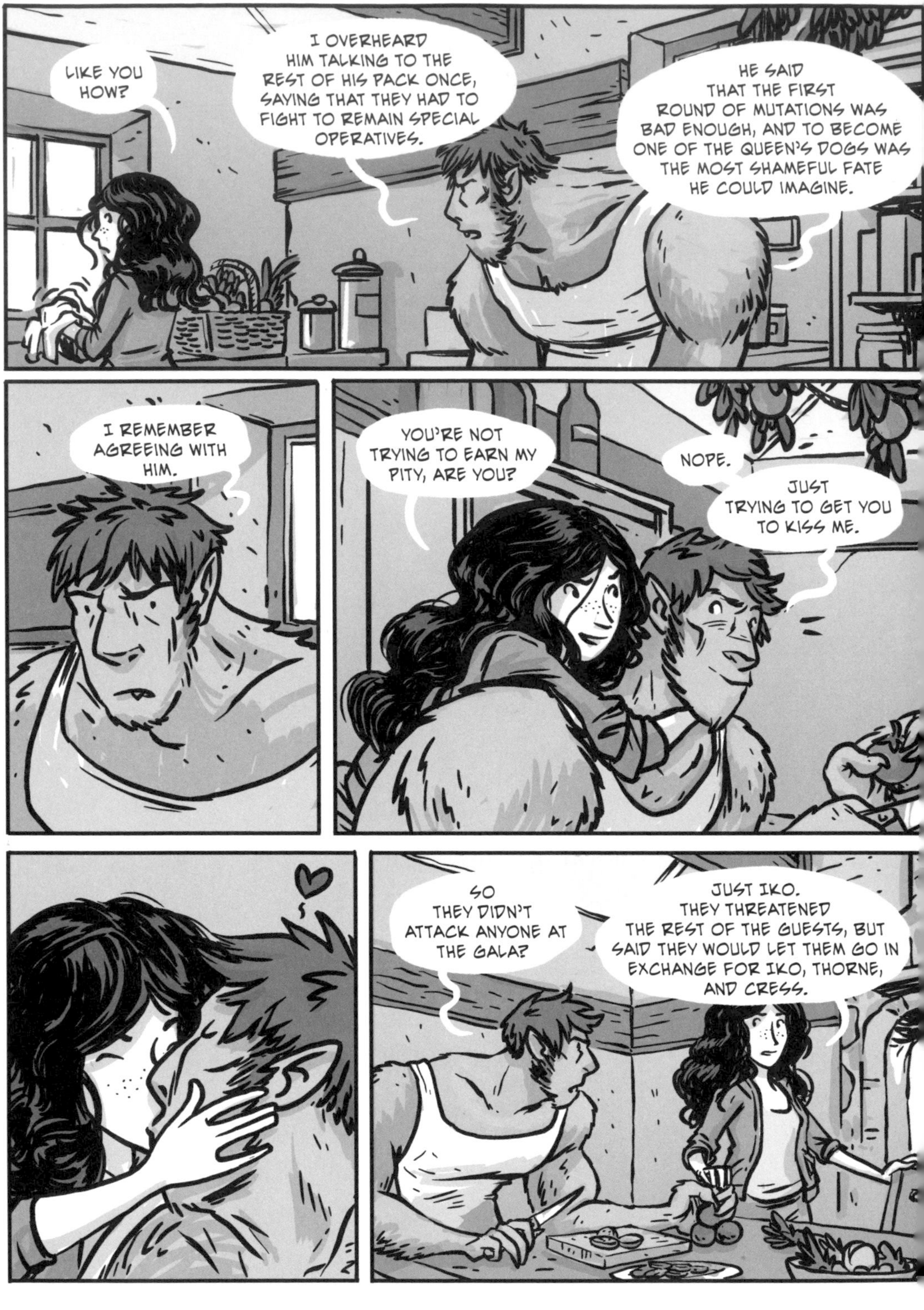
LIKE YOU HOW?
I OVERHEARD HIM TALKING TO THE REST OF HIS PACK ONCE, SAYING THAT THEY HAD TO FIGHT TO REMAIN SPECIAL OPERATIVES.
HE SAID THAT THE FIRST ROUND OF MUTATIONS WAS BAD ENOUGH, AND TO BECOME ONE OF THE QUEEN'S DOGS WAS THE MOST SHAMEFUL FATE HE COULD IMAGINE.
I REMEMBER AGREEING WITH HIM.
YOU'RE NOT TRYING TO EARN MY PITY, ARE YOU?
NOPE.
JUST TRYING TO GET YOU TO KISS ME.
SO THEY DIDN'T ATTACK ANYONE AT THE GALA?
JUST IKO. THEY THREATENED THE REST OF THE GUESTS, BUT SAID THEY WOULD LET THEM GO IN EXCHANGE FOR IKO, THORNE, AND CRESS.

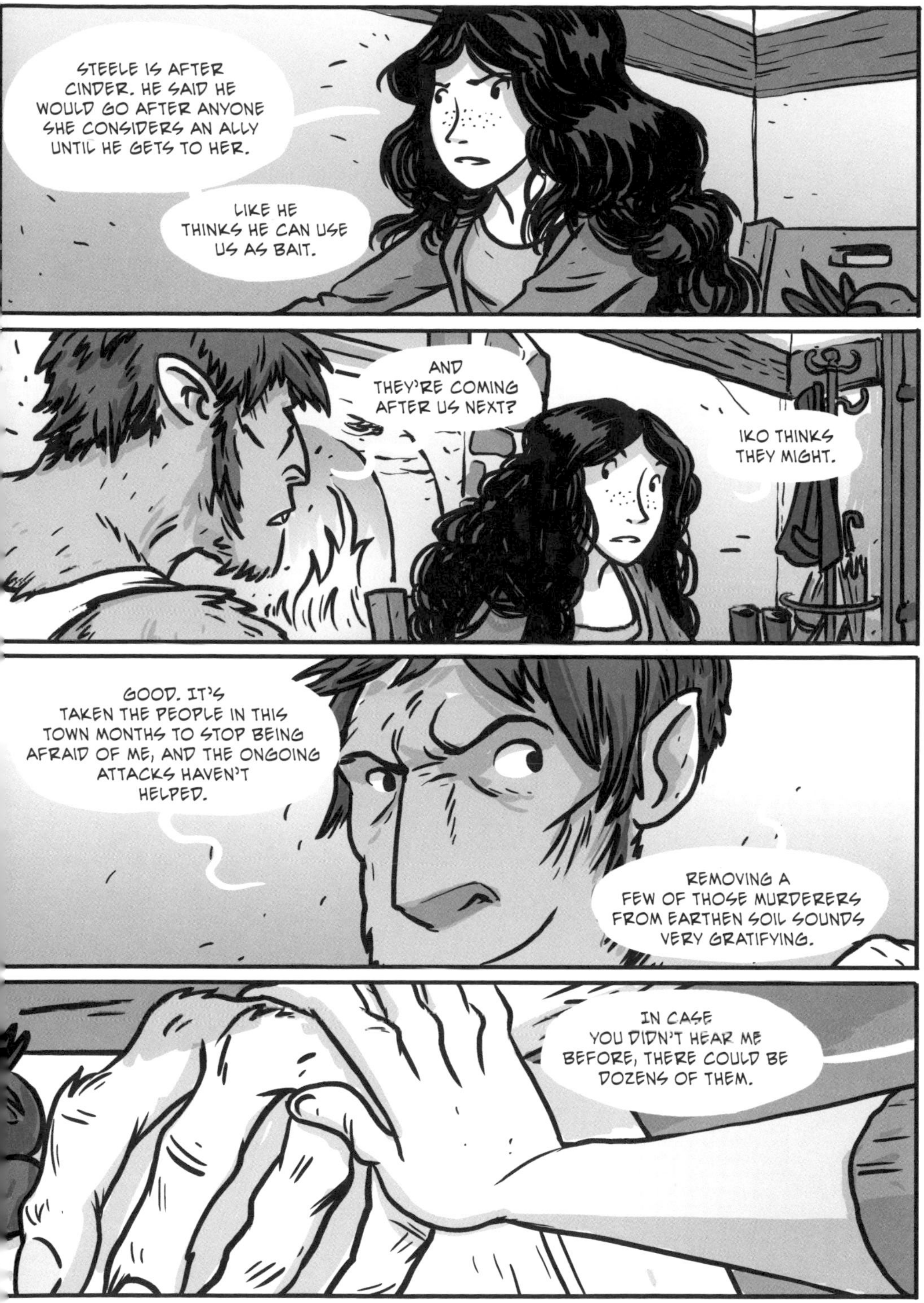
STEELE IS AFTER CINDER. HE SAID HE WOULD GO AFTER ANYONE SHE CONSIDERS AN ALLY UNTIL HE GETS TO HER.
LIKE HE THINKS HE CAN USE US AS BAIT.
AND THEY'RE COMING AFTER US NEXT?
IKO THINKS THEY MIGHT.
GOOD. IT'S TAKEN THE PEOPLE IN THIS TOWN MONTHS TO STOP BEING AFRAID OF ME, AND THE ONGOING ATTACKS HAVEN'T HELPED.
REMOVING A FEW OF THOSE MURDERERS FROM EARTHEN SOIL SOUNDS VERY GRATIFYING.
IN CASE YOU DIDN'T HEAR ME BEFORE, THERE COULD BE DOZENS OF THEM.

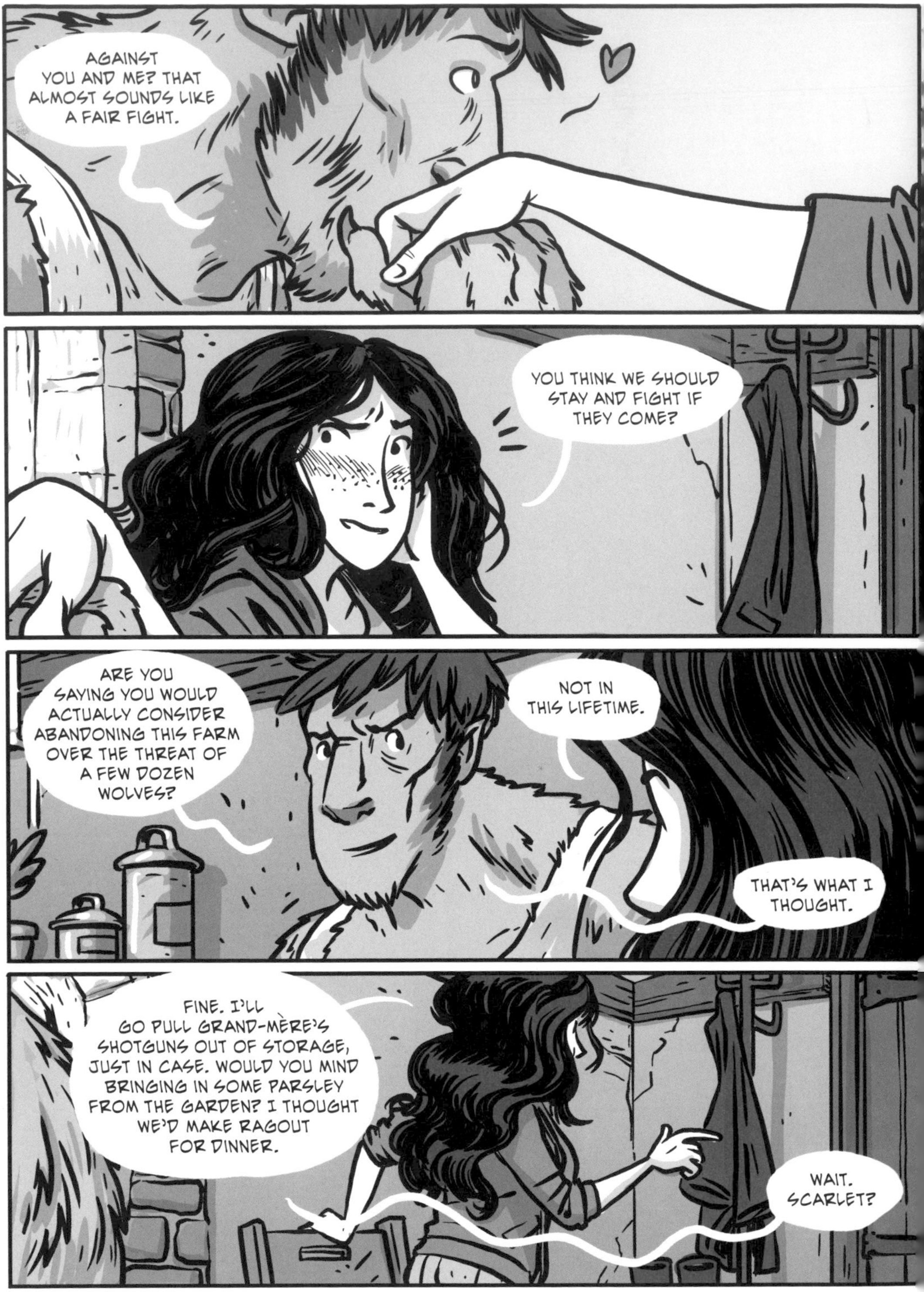
AGAINST YOU AND ME? THAT ALMOST SOUNDS LIKE A FAIR FIGHT.
YOU THINK WE SHOULD STAY AND FIGHT IF THEY COME?
ARE YOU SAYING YOU WOULD ACTUALLY CONSIDER ABANDONING THIS FARM OVER THE THREAT OF A FEW DOZEN WOLVES?
NOT IN THIS LIFETIME.
THAT'S WHAT I THOUGHT.
FINE. I'LL GO PULL GRAND-MÈRE'S SHOTGUNS OUT OF STORAGE, JUST IN CASE. WOULD YOU MIND BRINGING IN SOME PARSLEY FROM THE GARDEN? I THOUGHT WE'D MAKE RAGOUT FOR DINNER.
WAIT. SCARLET?

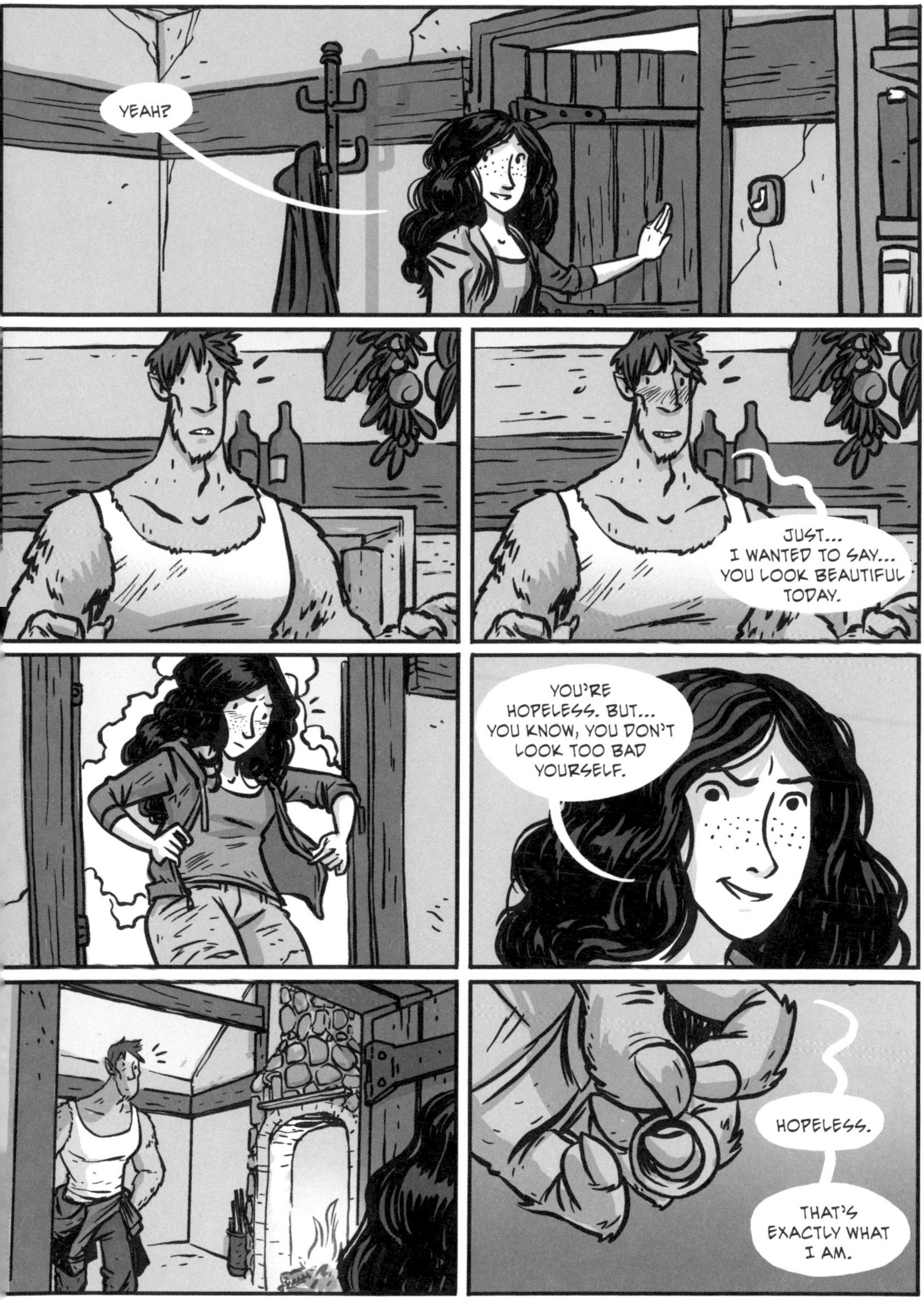
YEAH?
JUST... I WANTED TO SAY... YOU LOOK BEAUTIFUL TODAY.
YOU'RE HOPELESS. BUT... YOU KNOW, YOU DON'T LOOK TOO BAD YOURSELF.
HOPELESS.
THAT'S EXACTLY WHAT I AM.

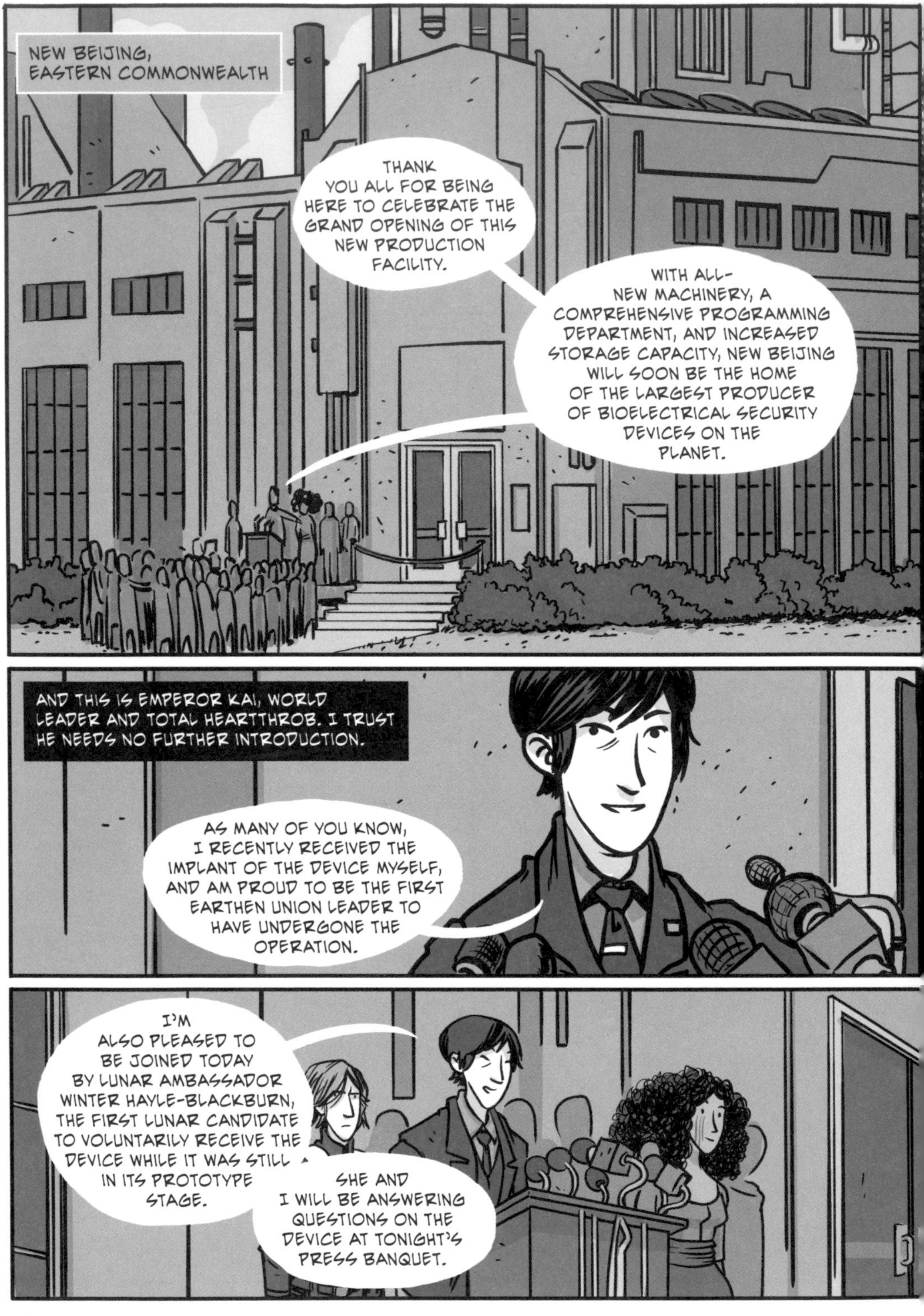
NEW BEIJING, EASTERN COMMONWEALTH
THANK YOU ALL FOR BEING HERE TO CELEBRATE THE GRAND OPENING OF THIS NEW PRODUCTION FACILITY.
WITH ALL-NEW MACHINERY, A COMPREHENSIVE PROGRAMMING DEPARTMENT, AND INCREASED STORAGE CAPACITY, NEW BEIJING WILL SOON BE THE HOME OF THE LARGEST PRODUCER OF BIOELECTRICAL SECURITY DEVICES ON THE PLANET.
AND THIS IS EMPEROR KAI, WORLD LEADER AND TOTAL HEARTTHROB. I TRUST HE NEEDS NO FURTHER INTRODUCTION.
AS MANY OF YOU KNOW, I RECENTLY RECEIVED THE IMPLANT OF THE DEVICE MYSELF, AND AM PROUD TO BE THE FIRST EARTHEN UNION LEADER TO HAVE UNDERGONE THE OPERATION.
I'M ALSO PLEASED TO BE JOINED TODAY BY LUNAR AMBASSADOR WINTER HAYLE-BLACKBURN, THE FIRST LUNAR CANDIDATE TO VOLUNTARILY RECEIVE THE DEVICE WHILE IT WAS STILL IN ITS PROTOTYPE STAGE.
SHE AND I WILL BE ANSWERING QUESTIONS ON THE DEVICE AT TONIGHT'S PRESS BANQUET.

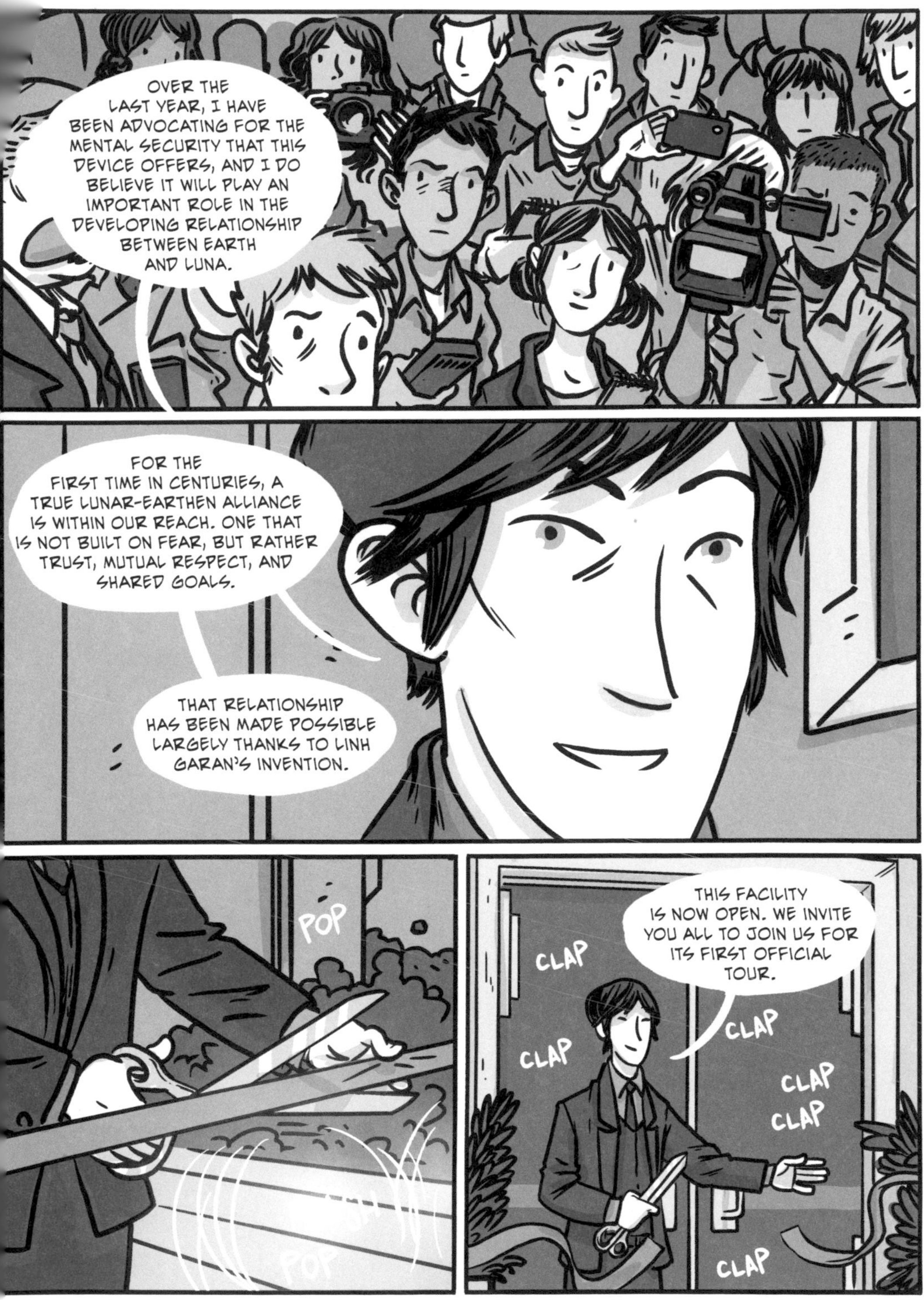
OVER THE LAST YEAR, I HAVE BEEN ADVOCATING FOR THE MENTAL SECURITY THAT THIS DEVICE OFFERS, AND I DO BELIEVE IT WILL PLAY AN IMPORTANT ROLE IN THE DEVELOPING RELATIONSHIP BETWEEN EARTH AND LUNA.
FOR THE FIRST TIME IN CENTURIES, A TRUE LUNAR-EARTHEN ALLIANCE IS WITHIN OUR REACH. ONE THAT IS NOT BUILT ON FEAR, BUT RATHER TRUST, MUTUAL RESPECT, AND SHARED GOALS.
THAT RELATIONSHIP HAS BEEN MADE POSSIBLE LARGELY THANKS TO LINH GARAN'S INVENTION.
POP
POP
THIS FACILITY IS NOW OPEN. WE INVITE YOU ALL TO JOIN US FOR ITS FIRST OFFICIAL TOUR.
CLAP
CLAP
CLAP
CLAP
CLAP
CLAP

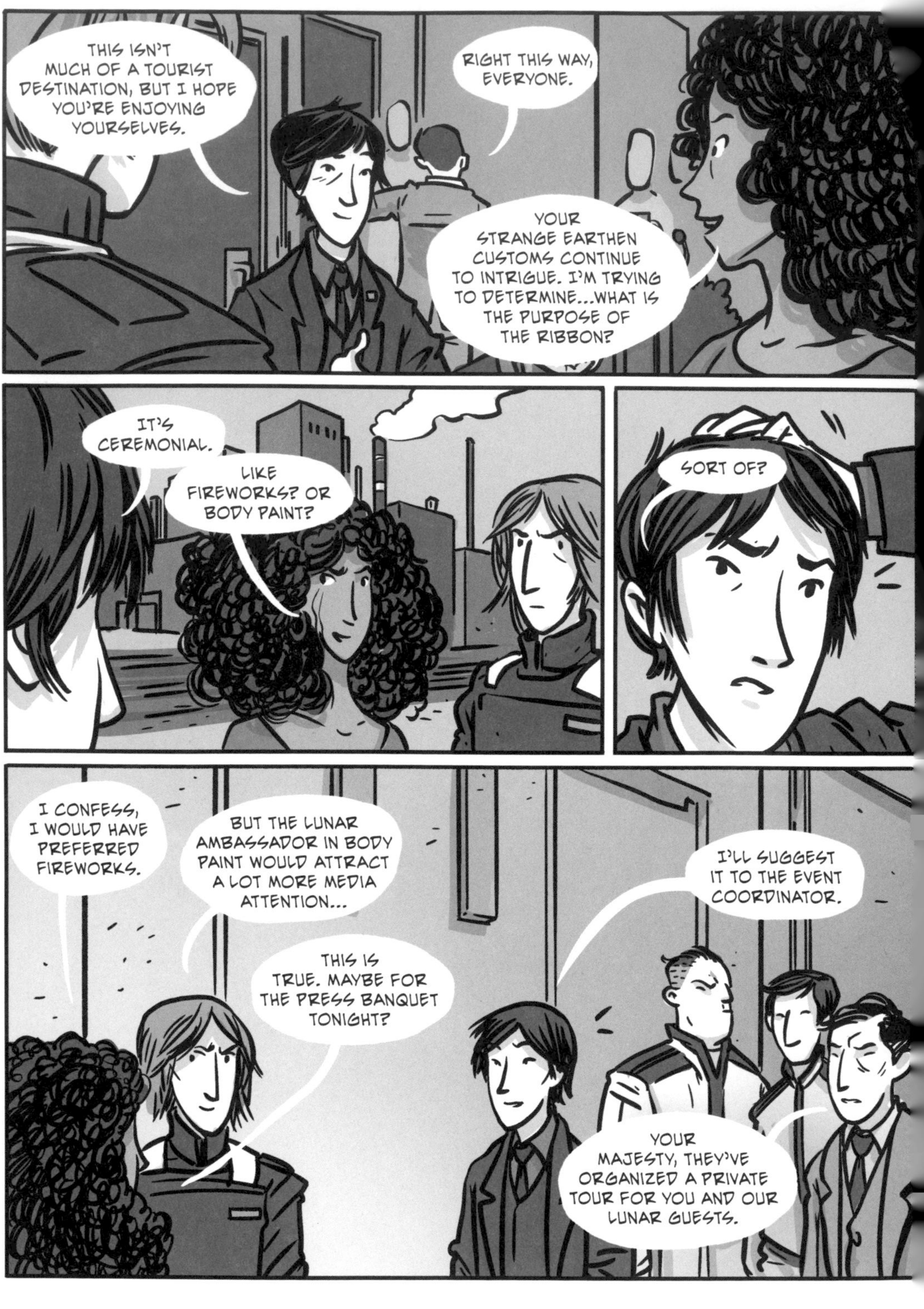
THIS ISN'T MUCH OF A TOURIST DESTINATION, BUT I HOPE YOU'RE ENJOYING YOURSELVES.
RIGHT THIS WAY, EVERYONE.
YOUR STRANGE EARTHEN CUSTOMS CONTINUE TO INTRIGUE. I'M TRYING TO DETERMINE...WHAT IS THE PURPOSE OF THE RIBBON?
IT'S CEREMONIAL.
LIKE FIREWORKS? OR BODY PAINT?
SORT OF?
I CONFESS, I WOULD HAVE PREFERRED FIREWORKS.
BUT THE LUNAR AMBASSADOR IN BODY PAINT WOULD ATTRACT A LOT MORE MEDIA ATTENTION...
THIS IS TRUE. MAYBE FOR THE PRESS BANQUET TONIGHT?
I'LL SUGGEST IT TO THE EVENT COORDINATOR.
YOUR MAJESTY, THEY'VE ORGANIZED A PRIVATE TOUR FOR YOU AND OUR LUNAR GUESTS.

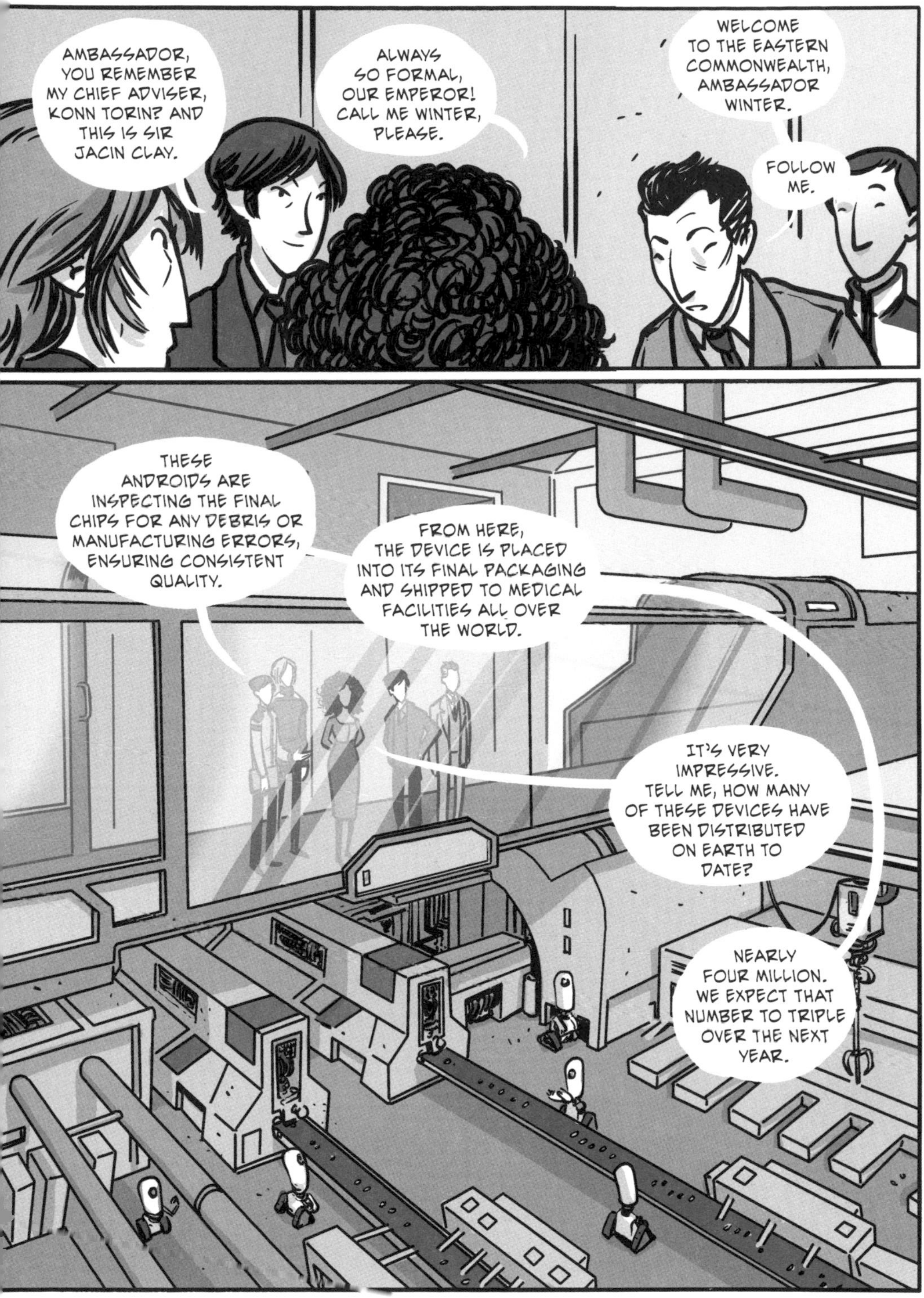
AMBASSADOR, YOU REMEMBER MY CHIEF ADVISER, KONN TORIN? AND THIS IS SIR JACIN CLAY.
ALWAYS SO FORMAL, OUR EMPEROR! CALL ME WINTER, PLEASE.
WELCOME TO THE EASTERN COMMONWEALTH, AMBASSADOR WINTER.
FOLLOW ME.
THESE ANDROIDS ARE INSPECTING THE FINAL CHIPS FOR ANY DEBRIS OR MANUFACTURING ERRORS, ENSURING CONSISTENT QUALITY.
FROM HERE, THE DEVICE IS PLACED INTO ITS FINAL PACKAGING AND SHIPPED TO MEDICAL FACILITIES ALL OVER THE WORLD.
IT'S VERY IMPRESSIVE. TELL ME, HOW MANY OF THESE DEVICES HAVE BEEN DISTRIBUTED ON EARTH TO DATE?
NEARLY FOUR MILLION. WE EXPECT THAT NUMBER TO TRIPLE OVER THE NEXT YEAR.

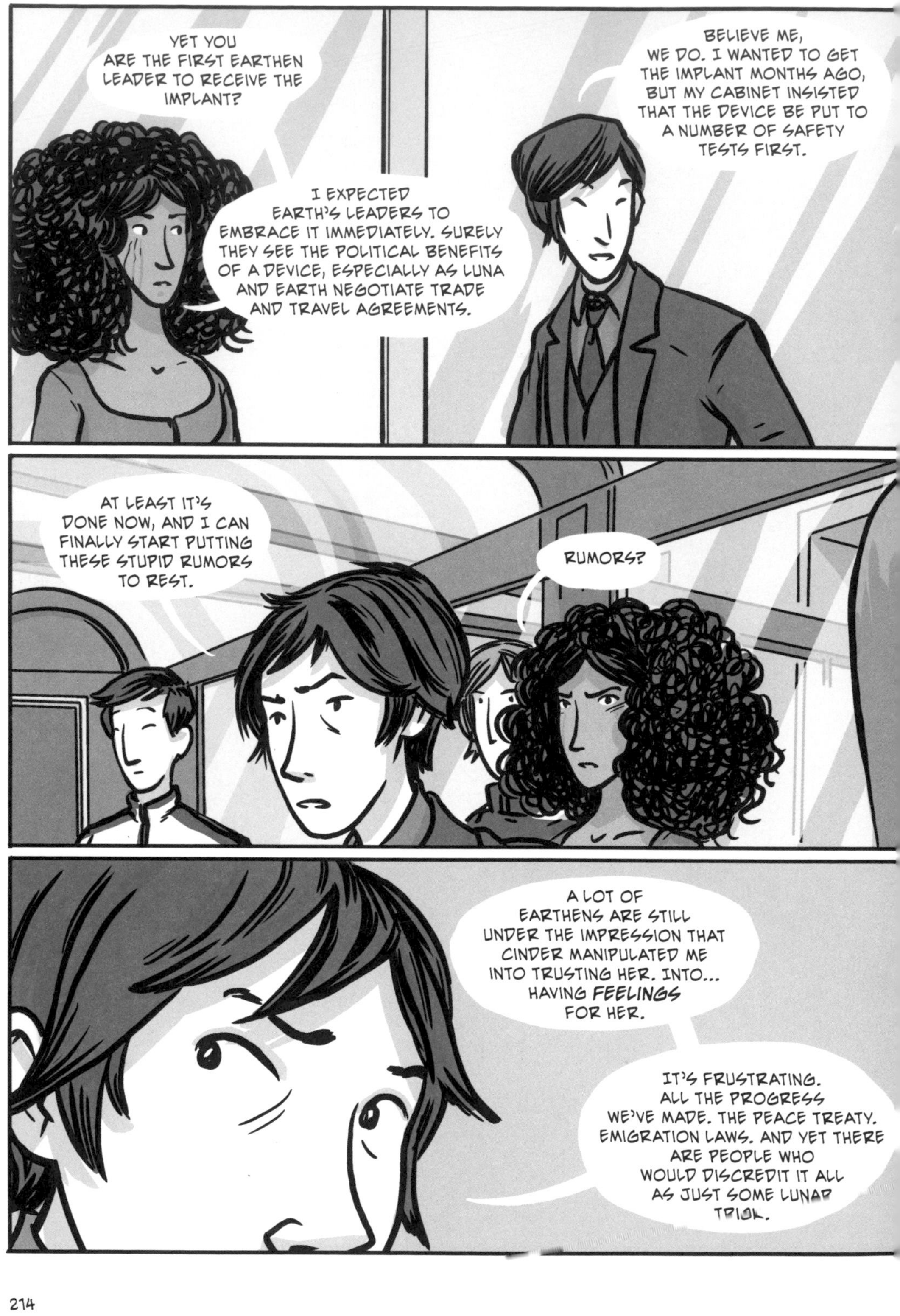
YET YOU ARE THE FIRST EARTHEN LEADER TO RECEIVE THE IMPLANT?
I EXPECTED EARTH'S LEADERS TO EMBRACE IT IMMEDIATELY. SURELY THEY SEE THE POLITICAL BENEFITS OF A DEVICE, ESPECIALLY AS LUNA AND EARTH NEGOTIATE TRADE AND TRAVEL AGREEMENTS.
BELIEVE ME, WE DO. I WANTED TO GET THE IMPLANT MONTHS AGO, BUT MY CABINET INSISTED THAT THE DEVICE BE PUT TO A NUMBER OF SAFETY TESTS FIRST.
AT LEAST IT'S DONE NOW, AND I CAN FINALLY START PUTTING THESE STUPID RUMORS TO REST.
RUMORS?
A LOT OF EARTHENS ARE STILL UNDER THE IMPRESSION THAT CINDER MANIPULATED ME INTO TRUSTING HER. INTO... HAVING ***FEELINGS*** FOR HER.
IT'S FRUSTRATING. ALL THE PROGRESS WE'VE MADE. THE PEACE TREATY. EMIGRATION LAWS. AND YET THERE ARE PEOPLE WHO WOULD DISCREDIT IT ALL AS JUST SOME LUNAR TRICK.

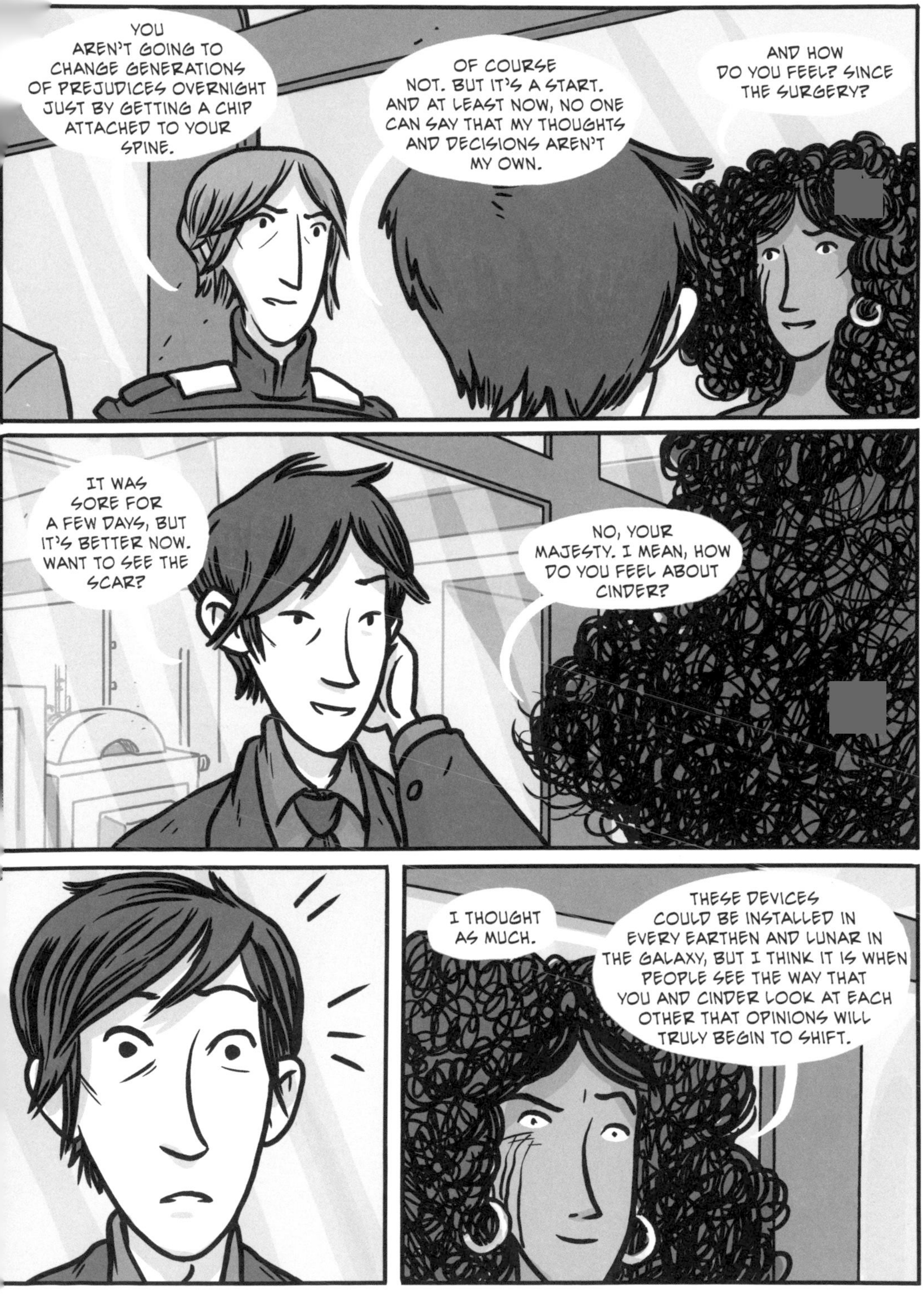
YOU AREN'T GOING TO CHANGE GENERATIONS OF PREJUDICES OVERNIGHT JUST BY GETTING A CHIP ATTACHED TO YOUR SPINE.
OF COURSE NOT. BUT IT'S A START. AND AT LEAST NOW, NO ONE CAN SAY THAT MY THOUGHTS AND DECISIONS AREN'T MY OWN.
AND HOW DO YOU FEEL? SINCE THE SURGERY?
IT WAS SORE FOR A FEW DAYS, BUT IT'S BETTER NOW. WANT TO SEE THE SCAR?
NO, YOUR MAJESTY. I MEAN, HOW DO YOU FEEL ABOUT CINDER?
I THOUGHT AS MUCH.
THESE DEVICES COULD BE INSTALLED IN EVERY EARTHEN AND LUNAR IN THE GALAXY, BUT I THINK IT IS WHEN PEOPLE SEE THE WAY THAT YOU AND CINDER LOOK AT EACH OTHER THAT OPINIONS WILL TRULY BEGIN TO SHIFT.

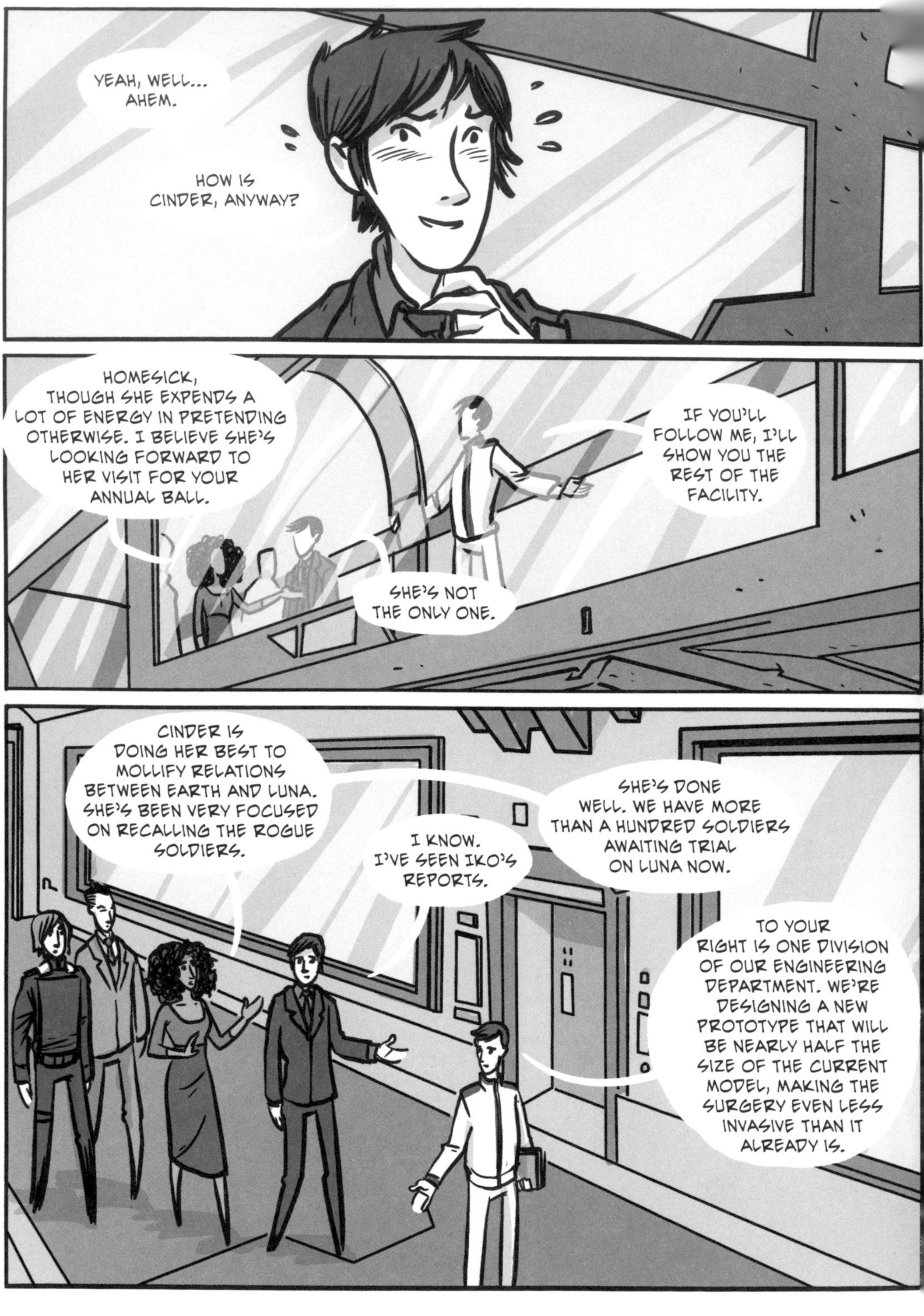
YEAH, WELL... AHEM.
HOW IS CINDER, ANYWAY?
HOMESICK, THOUGH SHE EXPENDS A LOT OF ENERGY IN PRETENDING OTHERWISE. I BELIEVE SHE'S LOOKING FORWARD TO HER VISIT FOR YOUR ANNUAL BALL.
IF YOU'LL FOLLOW ME, I'LL SHOW YOU THE REST OF THE FACILITY.
SHE'S NOT THE ONLY ONE.
CINDER IS DOING HER BEST TO MOLLIFY RELATIONS BETWEEN EARTH AND LUNA. SHE'S BEEN VERY FOCUSED ON RECALLING THE ROGUE SOLDIERS.
SHE'S DONE WELL. WE HAVE MORE THAN A HUNDRED SOLDIERS AWAITING TRIAL ON LUNA NOW.
I KNOW. I'VE SEEN IKO'S REPORTS.
TO YOUR RIGHT IS ONE DIVISION OF OUR ENGINEERING DEPARTMENT. WE'RE DESIGNING A NEW PROTOTYPE THAT WILL BE NEARLY HALF THE SIZE OF THE CURRENT MODEL, MAKING THE SURGERY EVEN LESS INVASIVE THAN IT ALREADY IS.

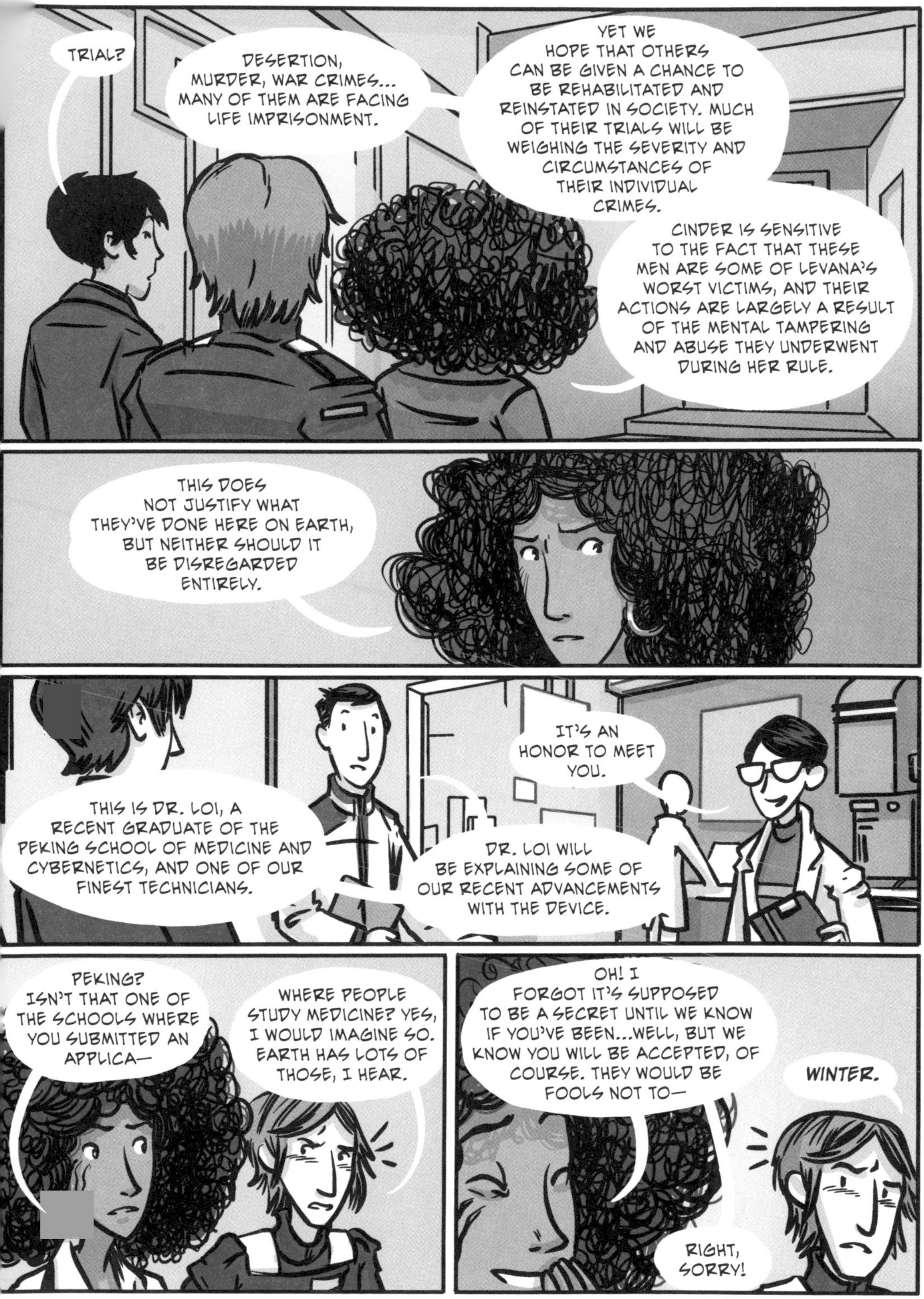
TRIAL?
DESERTION, MURDER, WAR CRIMES... MANY OF THEM ARE FACING LIFE IMPRISONMENT.
YET WE HOPE THAT OTHERS CAN BE GIVEN A CHANCE TO BE REHABILITATED AND REINSTATED IN SOCIETY. MUCH OF THEIR TRIALS WILL BE WEIGHING THE SEVERITY AND CIRCUMSTANCES OF THEIR INDIVIDUAL CRIMES.
CINDER IS SENSITIVE TO THE FACT THAT THESE MEN ARE SOME OF LEVANA'S WORST VICTIMS, AND THEIR ACTIONS ARE LARGELY A RESULT OF THE MENTAL TAMPERING AND ABUSE THEY UNDERWENT DURING HER RULE.
THIS DOES NOT JUSTIFY WHAT THEY'VE DONE HERE ON EARTH, BUT NEITHER SHOULD IT BE DISREGARDED ENTIRELY.
THIS IS DR. LOI, A RECENT GRADUATE OF THE PEKING SCHOOL OF MEDICINE AND CYBERNETICS, AND ONE OF OUR FINEST TECHNICIANS.
IT'S AN HONOR TO MEET YOU.
DR. LOI WILL BE EXPLAINING SOME OF OUR RECENT ADVANCEMENTS WITH THE DEVICE.
PEKING? ISN'T THAT ONE OF THE SCHOOLS WHERE YOU SUBMITTED AN APPLICA—
WHERE PEOPLE STUDY MEDICINE? YES, I WOULD IMAGINE SO. EARTH HAS LOTS OF THOSE, I HEAR.
OH! I FORGOT IT'S SUPPOSED TO BE A SECRET UNTIL WE KNOW IF YOU'VE BEEN...WELL, BUT WE KNOW YOU WILL BE ACCEPTED, OF COURSE. THEY WOULD BE FOOLS NOT TO—
WINTER.
RIGHT, SORRY!

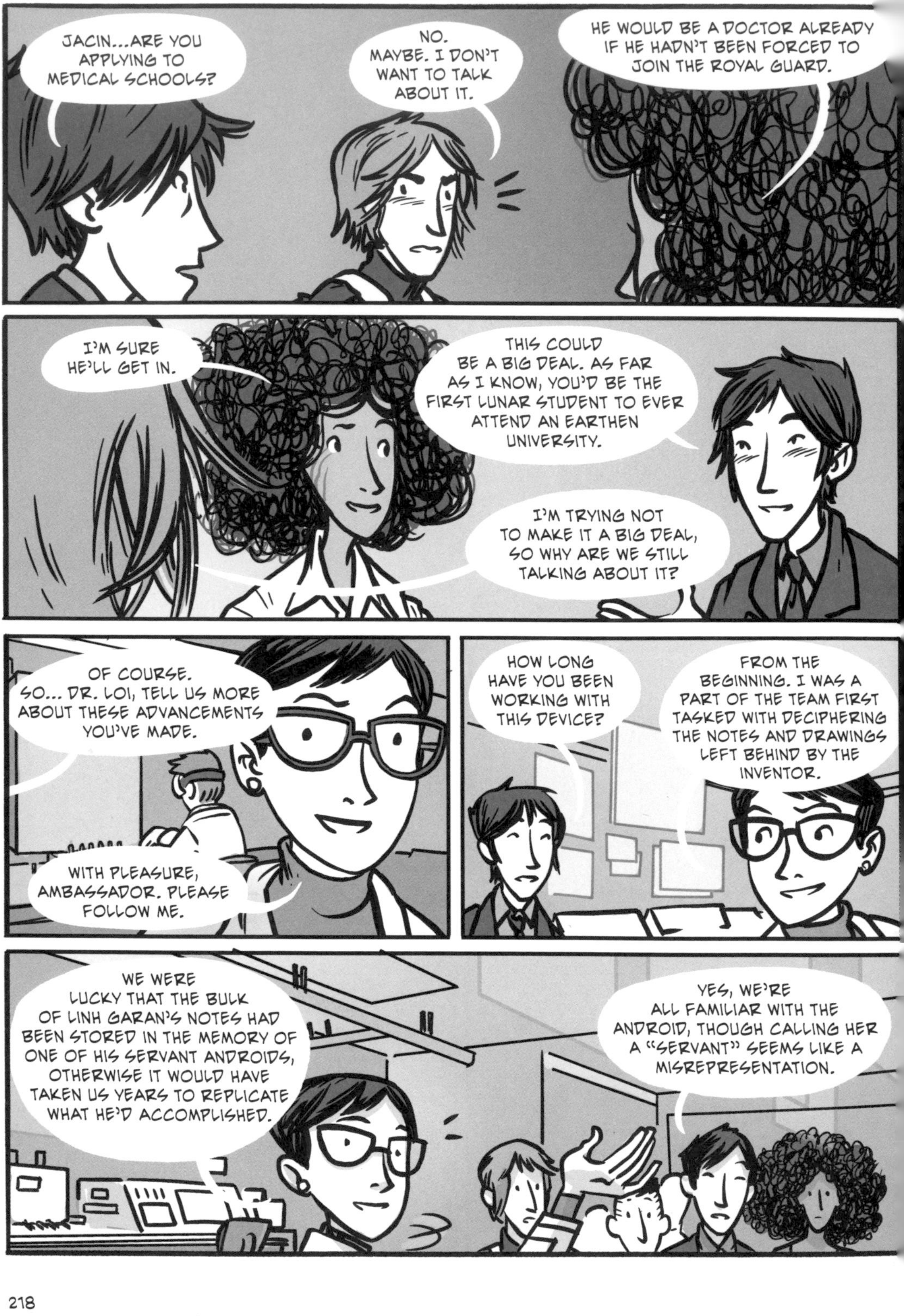
JACIN...ARE YOU APPLYING TO MEDICAL SCHOOLS?
NO. MAYBE. I DON'T WANT TO TALK ABOUT IT.
HE WOULD BE A DOCTOR ALREADY IF HE HADN'T BEEN FORCED TO JOIN THE ROYAL GUARD.
I'M SURE HE'LL GET IN.
THIS COULD BE A BIG DEAL. AS FAR AS I KNOW, YOU'D BE THE FIRST LUNAR STUDENT TO EVER ATTEND AN EARTHEN UNIVERSITY.
I'M TRYING NOT TO MAKE IT A BIG DEAL, SO WHY ARE WE STILL TALKING ABOUT IT?
OF COURSE. SO... DR. LOI, TELL US MORE ABOUT THESE ADVANCEMENTS YOU'VE MADE.
WITH PLEASURE, AMBASSADOR. PLEASE FOLLOW ME.
HOW LONG HAVE YOU BEEN WORKING WITH THIS DEVICE?
FROM THE BEGINNING. I WAS A PART OF THE TEAM FIRST TASKED WITH DECIPHERING THE NOTES AND DRAWINGS LEFT BEHIND BY THE INVENTOR.
WE WERE LUCKY THAT THE BULK OF LINH GARAN'S NOTES HAD BEEN STORED IN THE MEMORY OF ONE OF HIS SERVANT ANDROIDS, OTHERWISE IT WOULD HAVE TAKEN US YEARS TO REPLICATE WHAT HE'D ACCOMPLISHED.
YES, WE'RE ALL FAMILIAR WITH THE ANDROID, THOUGH CALLING HER A "SERVANT" SEEMS LIKE A MISREPRESENTATION.

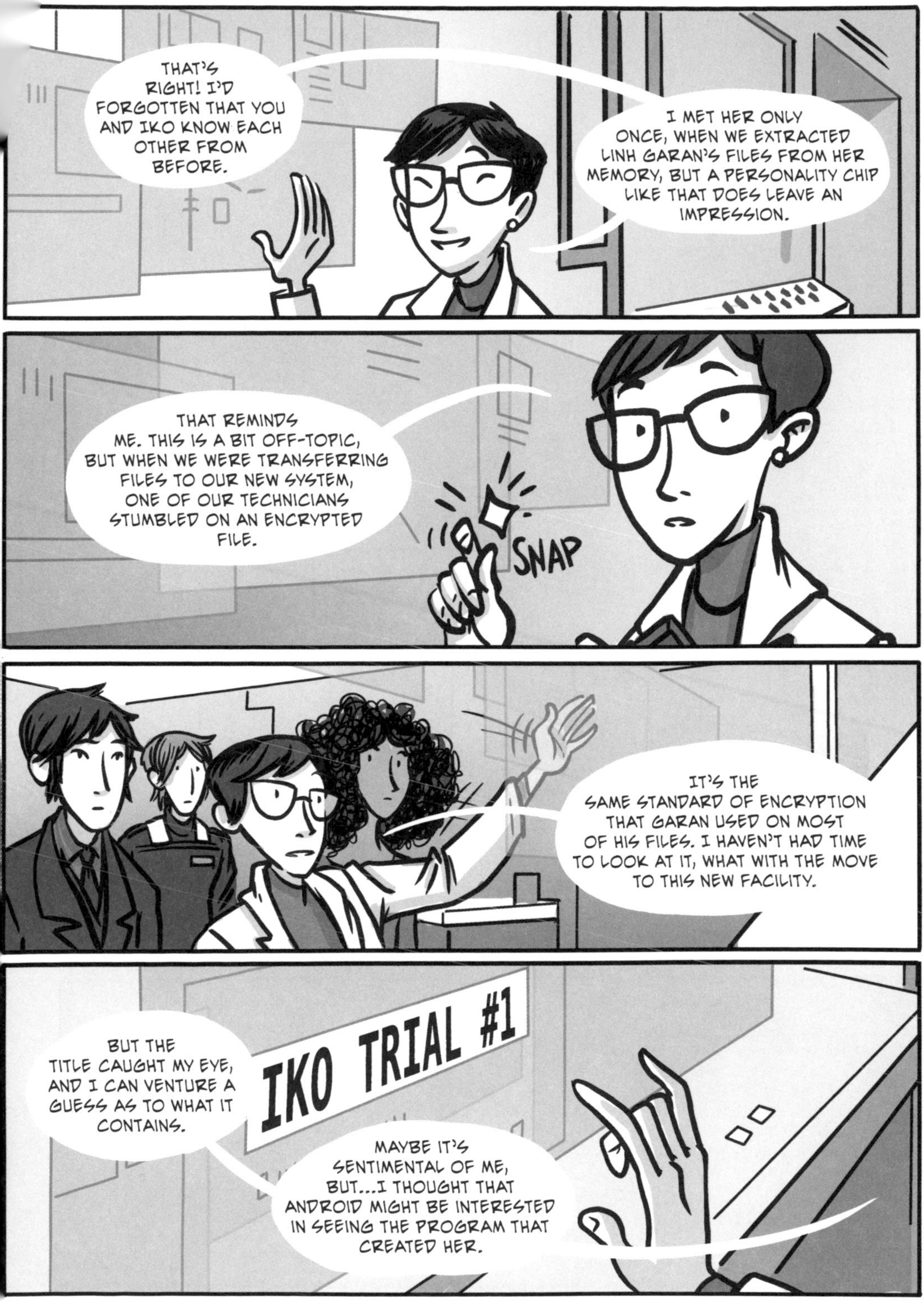
THAT'S RIGHT! I'D FORGOTTEN THAT YOU AND IKO KNOW EACH OTHER FROM BEFORE.
I MET HER ONLY ONCE, WHEN WE EXTRACTED LINH GARAN'S FILES FROM HER MEMORY, BUT A PERSONALITY CHIP LIKE THAT DOES LEAVE AN IMPRESSION.
THAT REMINDS ME. THIS IS A BIT OFF-TOPIC, BUT WHEN WE WERE TRANSFERRING FILES TO OUR NEW SYSTEM, ONE OF OUR TECHNICIANS STUMBLED ON AN ENCRYPTED FILE.
SNAP
IT'S THE SAME STANDARD OF ENCRYPTION THAT GARAN USED ON MOST OF HIS FILES. I HAVEN'T HAD TIME TO LOOK AT IT, WHAT WITH THE MOVE TO THIS NEW FACILITY.
IKO TRIAL #1
BUT THE TITLE CAUGHT MY EYE, AND I CAN VENTURE A GUESS AS TO WHAT IT CONTAINS.
MAYBE IT'S SENTIMENTAL OF ME, BUT...I THOUGHT THAT ANDROID MIGHT BE INTERESTED IN SEEING THE PROGRAM THAT CREATED HER.

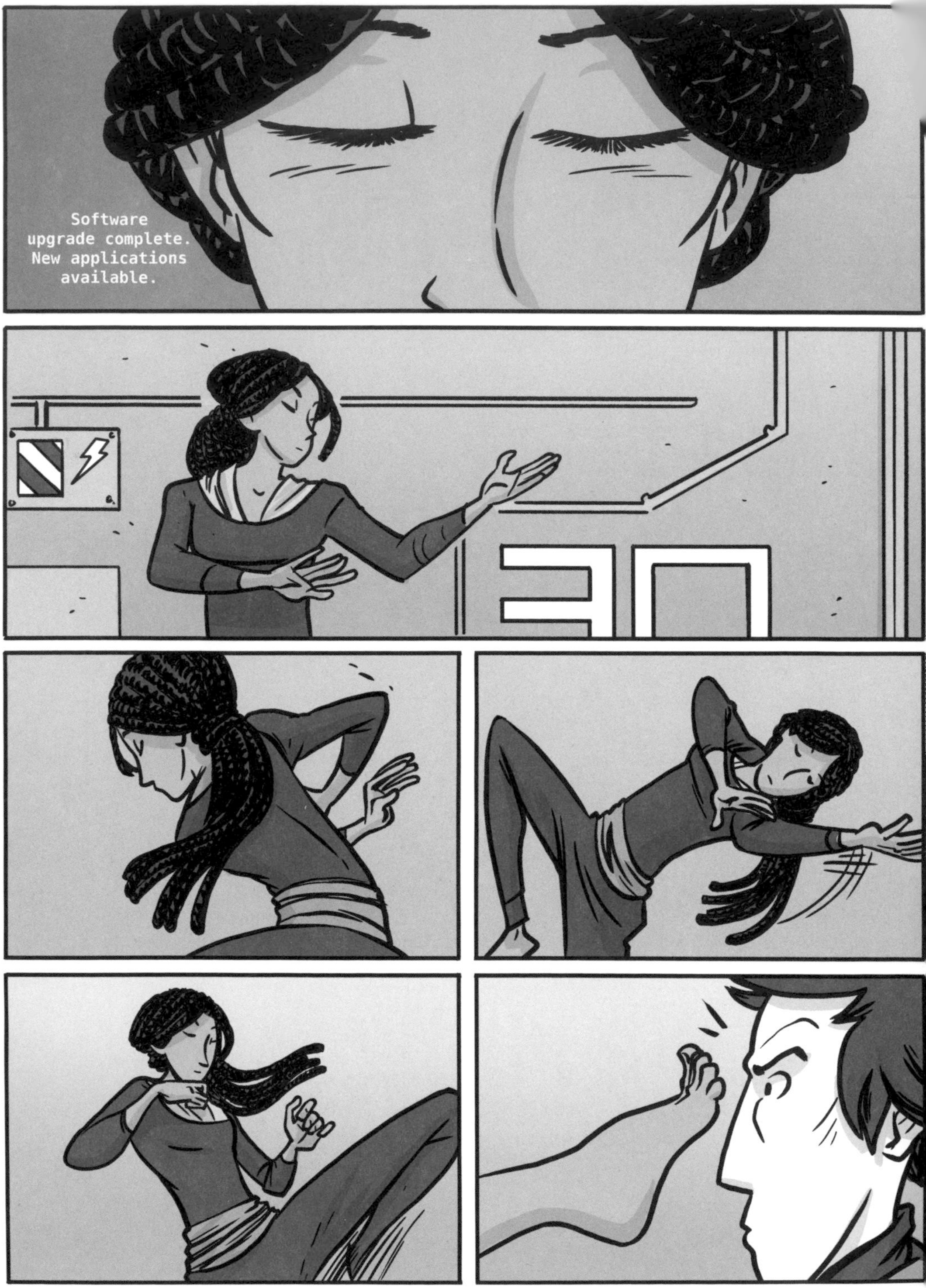
Software upgrade complete. New applications available.

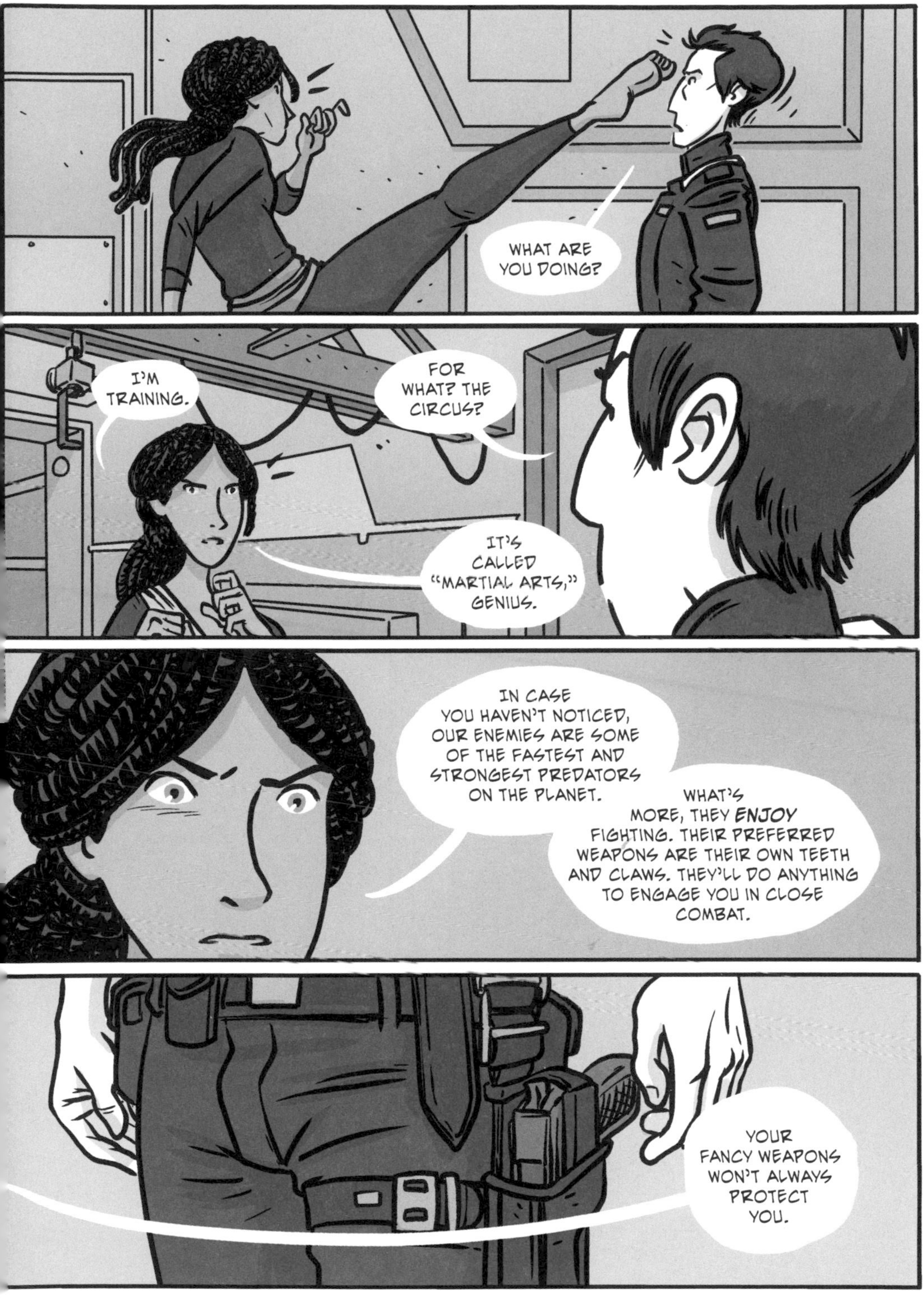
WHAT ARE YOU DOING?
I'M TRAINING.
FOR WHAT? THE CIRCUS?
IT'S CALLED "MARTIAL ARTS," GENIUS.
IN CASE YOU HAVEN'T NOTICED, OUR ENEMIES ARE SOME OF THE FASTEST AND STRONGEST PREDATORS ON THE PLANET.
WHAT'S MORE, THEY ENJOY FIGHTING. THEIR PREFERRED WEAPONS ARE THEIR OWN TEETH AND CLAWS. THEY'LL DO ANYTHING TO ENGAGE YOU IN CLOSE COMBAT.
YOUR FANCY WEAPONS WON'T ALWAYS PROTECT YOU.

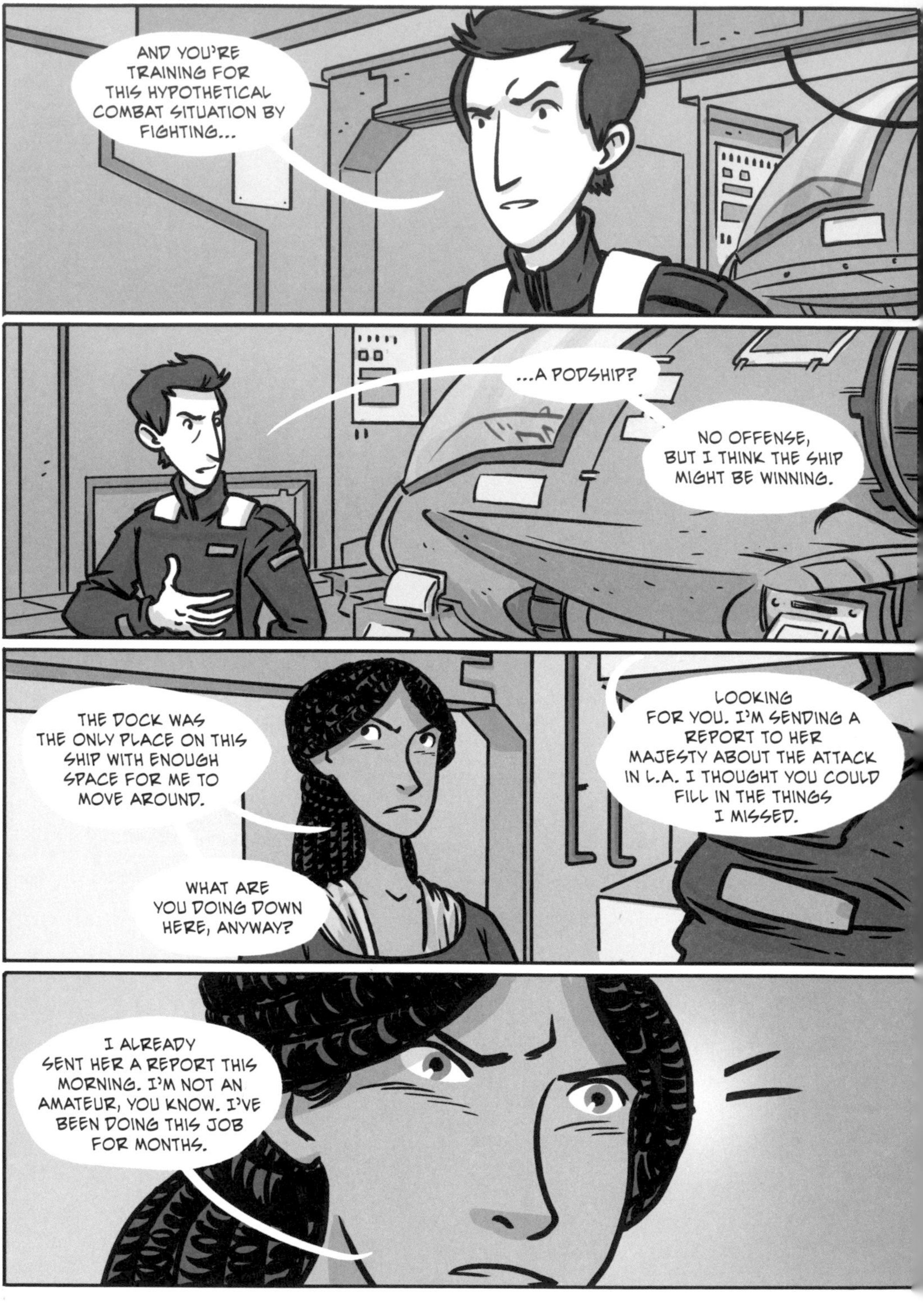
AND YOU'RE TRAINING FOR THIS HYPOTHETICAL COMBAT SITUATION BY FIGHTING...
...A PODSHIP?
NO OFFENSE, BUT I THINK THE SHIP MIGHT BE WINNING.
THE DOCK WAS THE ONLY PLACE ON THIS SHIP WITH ENOUGH SPACE FOR ME TO MOVE AROUND.
WHAT ARE YOU DOING DOWN HERE, ANYWAY?
LOOKING FOR YOU. I'M SENDING A REPORT TO HER MAJESTY ABOUT THE ATTACK IN L.A. I THOUGHT YOU COULD FILL IN THE THINGS I MISSED.
I ALREADY SENT HER A REPORT THIS MORNING. I'M NOT AN AMATEUR, YOU KNOW. I'VE BEEN DOING THIS JOB FOR MONTHS.

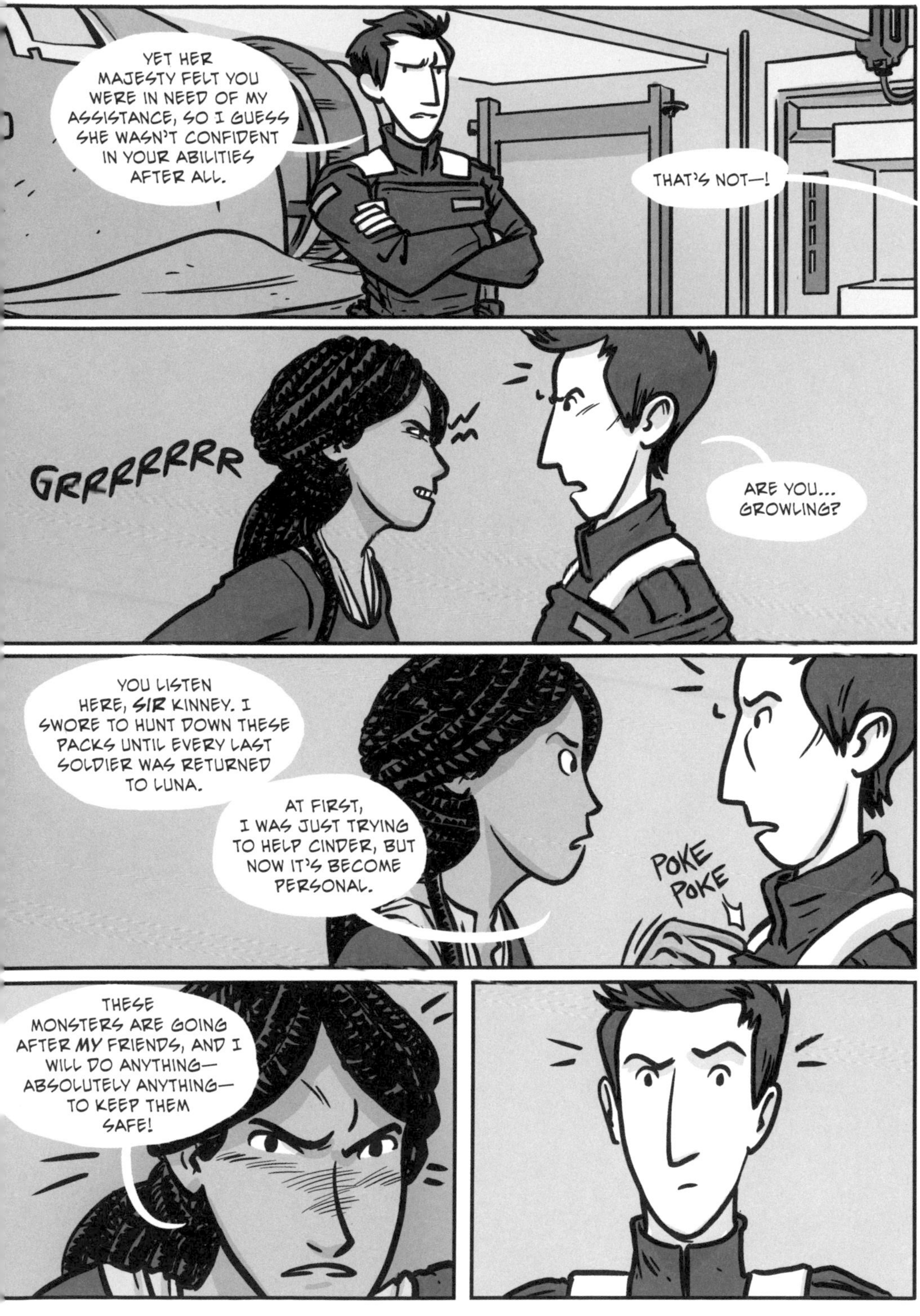
YET HER MAJESTY FELT YOU WERE IN NEED OF MY ASSISTANCE, SO I GUESS SHE WASN'T CONFIDENT IN YOUR ABILITIES AFTER ALL.
THAT'S NOT—!
GRRRRRRR
ARE YOU... GROWLING?
YOU LISTEN HERE, *SIR* KINNEY. I SWORE TO HUNT DOWN THESE PACKS UNTIL EVERY LAST SOLDIER WAS RETURNED TO LUNA.
AT FIRST, I WAS JUST TRYING TO HELP CINDER, BUT NOW IT'S BECOME PERSONAL.
POKE POKE
THESE MONSTERS ARE GOING AFTER *MY* FRIENDS, AND I WILL DO ANYTHING— ABSOLUTELY ANYTHING— TO KEEP THEM SAFE!

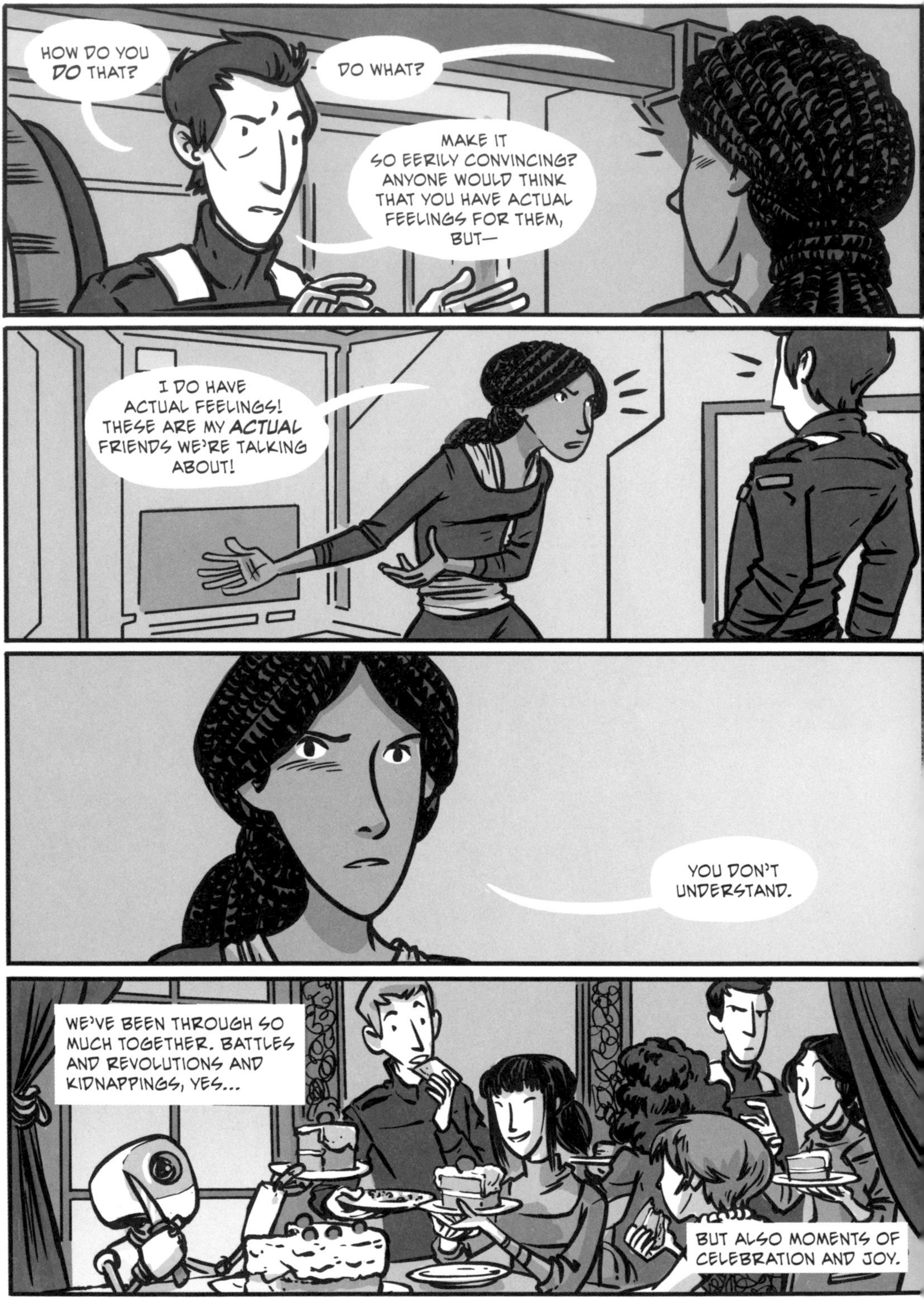
HOW DO YOU *DO* THAT?
DO WHAT?
MAKE IT SO EERILY CONVINCING? ANYONE WOULD THINK THAT YOU HAVE ACTUAL FEELINGS FOR THEM, BUT—
I DO HAVE ACTUAL FEELINGS! THESE ARE MY *ACTUAL* FRIENDS WE'RE TALKING ABOUT!
YOU DON'T UNDERSTAND.
WE'VE BEEN THROUGH SO MUCH TOGETHER. BATTLES AND REVOLUTIONS AND KIDNAPPINGS, YES...
BUT ALSO MOMENTS OF CELEBRATION AND JOY.

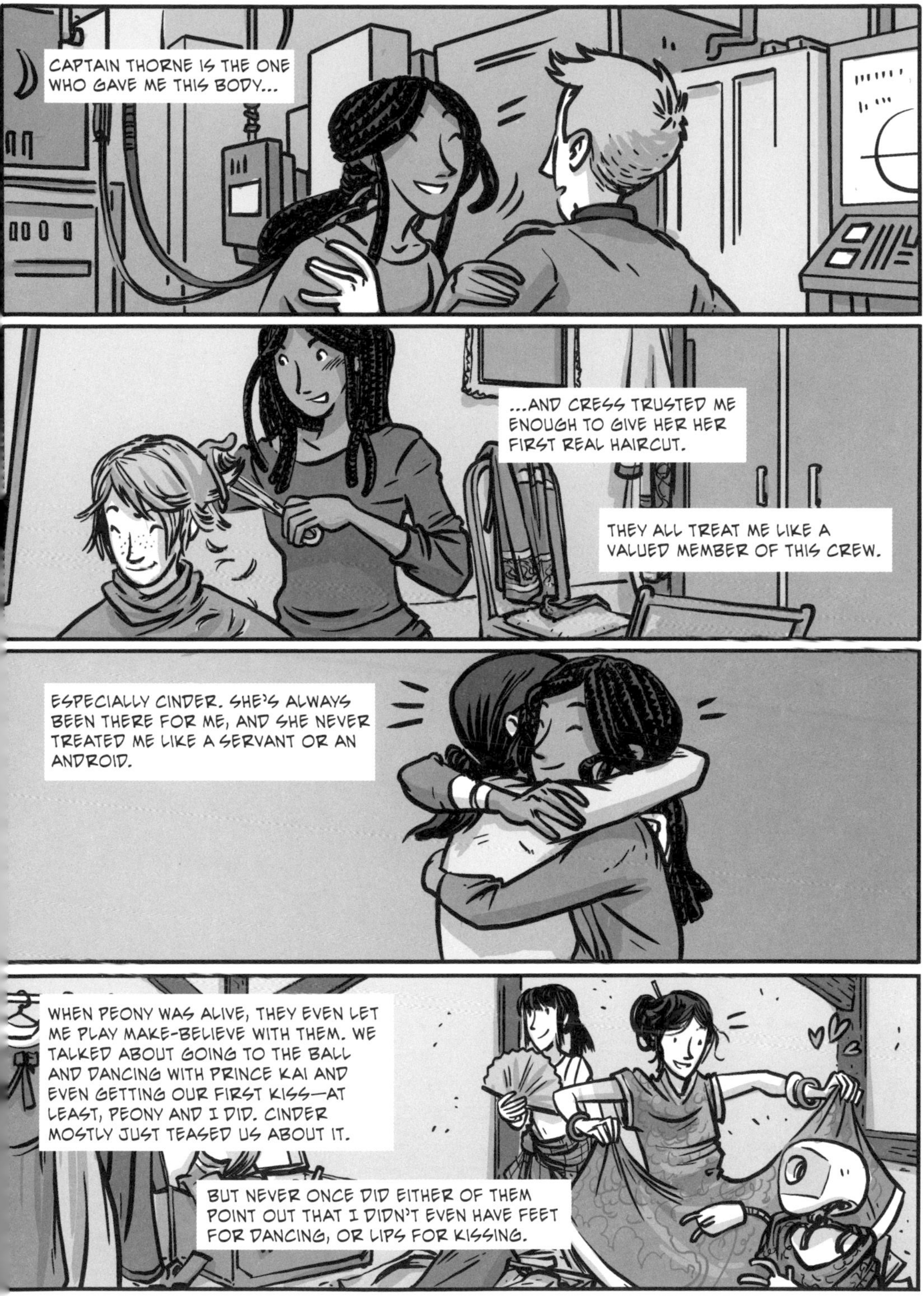
CAPTAIN THORNE IS THE ONE WHO GAVE ME THIS BODY...
...AND CRESS TRUSTED ME ENOUGH TO GIVE HER HER FIRST REAL HAIRCUT.
THEY ALL TREAT ME LIKE A VALUED MEMBER OF THIS CREW.
ESPECIALLY CINDER. SHE'S ALWAYS BEEN THERE FOR ME, AND SHE NEVER TREATED ME LIKE A SERVANT OR AN ANDROID.
WHEN PEONY WAS ALIVE, THEY EVEN LET ME PLAY MAKE-BELIEVE WITH THEM. WE TALKED ABOUT GOING TO THE BALL AND DANCING WITH PRINCE KAI AND EVEN GETTING OUR FIRST KISS—AT LEAST, PEONY AND I DID. CINDER MOSTLY JUST TEASED US ABOUT IT.
BUT NEVER ONCE DID EITHER OF THEM POINT OUT THAT I DIDN'T EVEN HAVE FEET FOR DANCING, OR LIPS FOR KISSING.

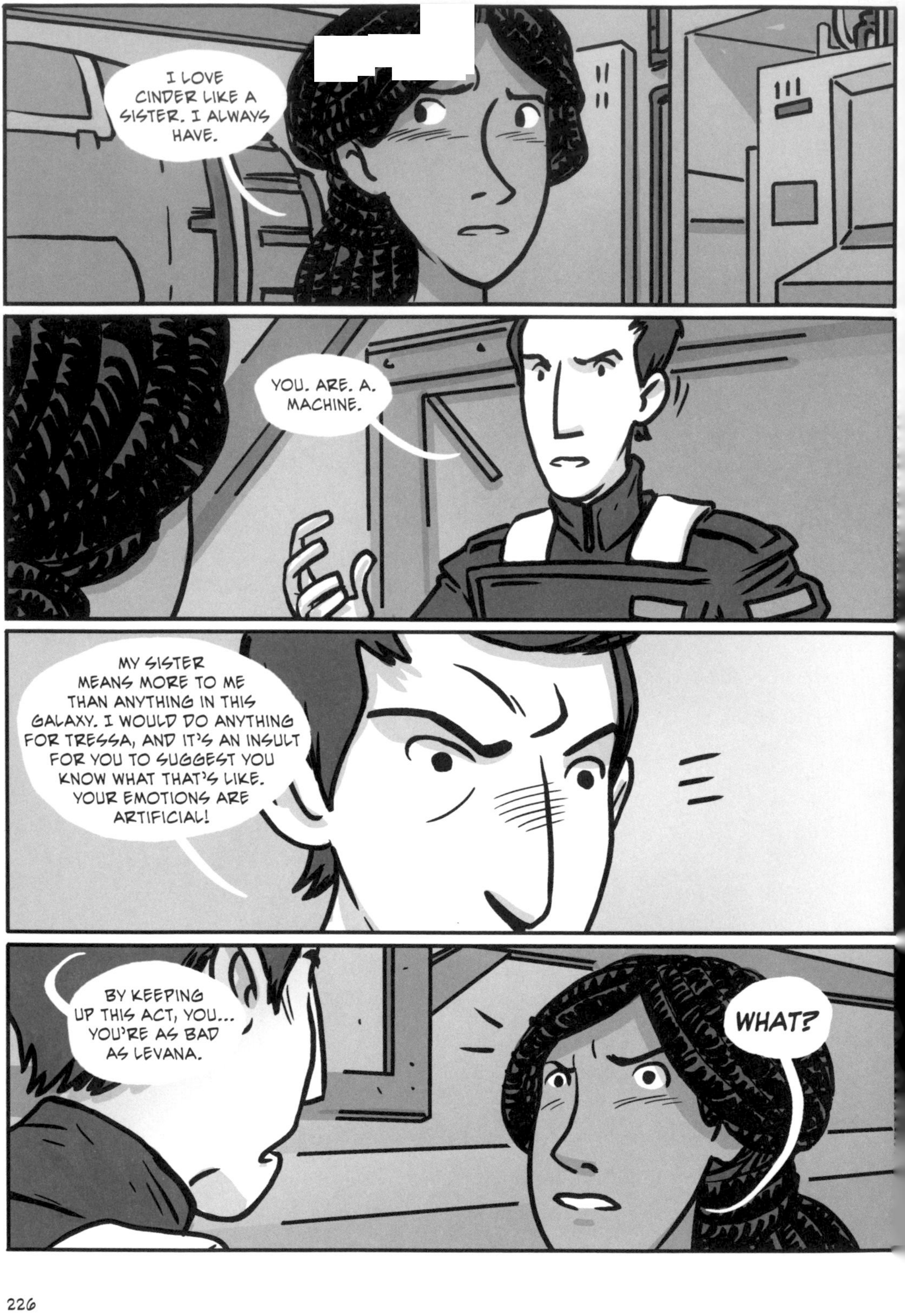
I LOVE CINDER LIKE A SISTER. I ALWAYS HAVE.
YOU. ARE. A. MACHINE.
MY SISTER MEANS MORE TO ME THAN ANYTHING IN THIS GALAXY. I WOULD DO ANYTHING FOR TRESSA, AND IT'S AN INSULT FOR YOU TO SUGGEST YOU KNOW WHAT THAT'S LIKE. YOUR EMOTIONS ARE ARTIFICIAL!
BY KEEPING UP THIS ACT, YOU... YOU'RE AS BAD AS LEVANA.
WHAT?

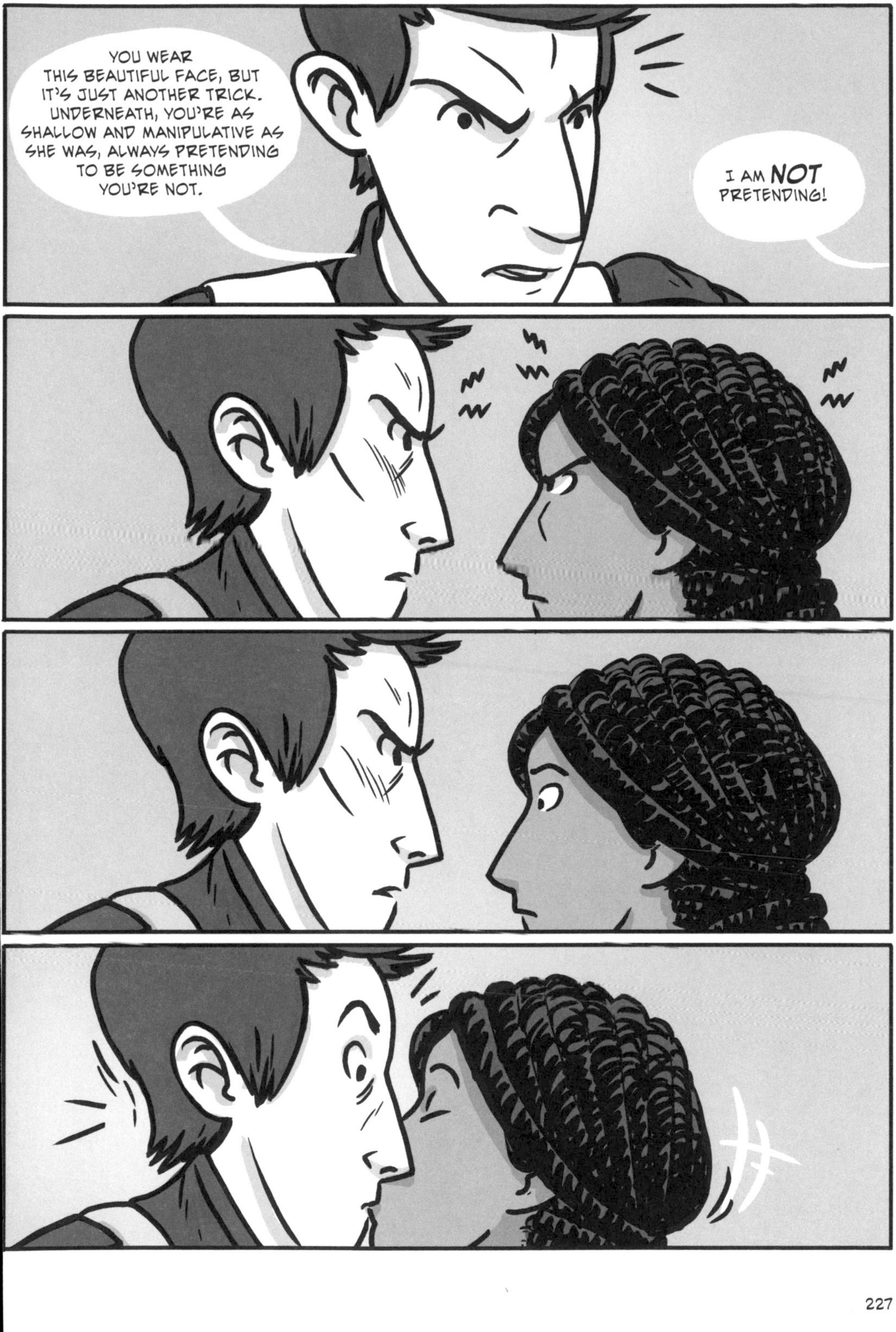
YOU WEAR THIS BEAUTIFUL FACE, BUT IT'S JUST ANOTHER TRICK. UNDERNEATH, YOU'RE AS SHALLOW AND MANIPULATIVE AS SHE WAS, ALWAYS PRETENDING TO BE SOMETHING YOU'RE NOT.
I AM NOT PRETENDING!

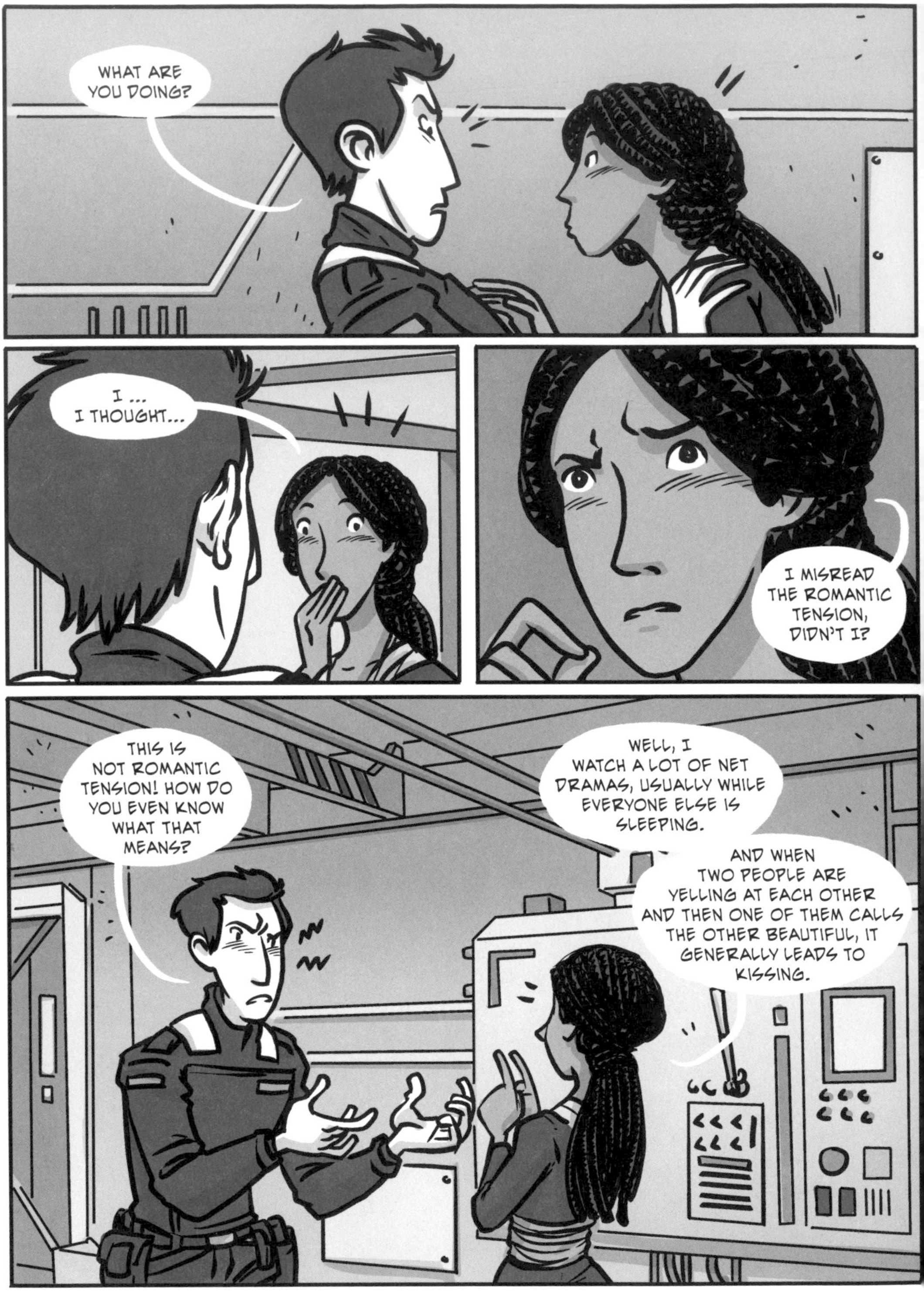
WHAT ARE YOU DOING?
I ... I THOUGHT...
I MISREAD THE ROMANTIC TENSION, DIDN'T I?
THIS IS NOT ROMANTIC TENSION! HOW DO YOU EVEN KNOW WHAT THAT MEANS?
WELL, I WATCH A LOT OF NET DRAMAS, USUALLY WHILE EVERYONE ELSE IS SLEEPING.
AND WHEN TWO PEOPLE ARE YELLING AT EACH OTHER AND THEN ONE OF THEM CALLS THE OTHER BEAUTIFUL, IT GENERALLY LEADS TO KISSING.

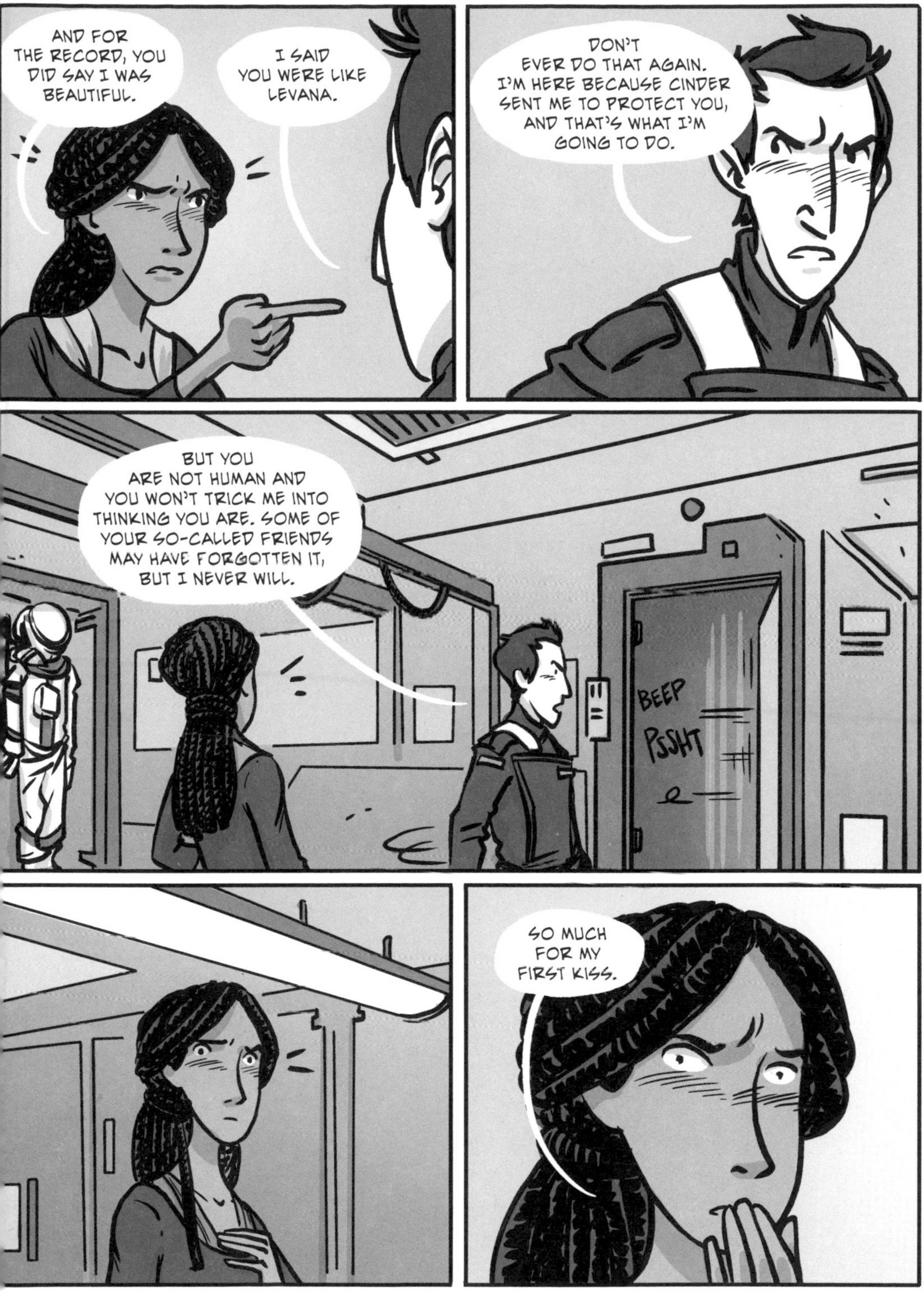
AND FOR THE RECORD, YOU DID SAY I WAS BEAUTIFUL.
I SAID YOU WERE LIKE LEVANA.
DON'T EVER DO THAT AGAIN. I'M HERE BECAUSE CINDER SENT ME TO PROTECT YOU, AND THAT'S WHAT I'M GOING TO DO.
BUT YOU ARE NOT HUMAN AND YOU WON'T TRICK ME INTO THINKING YOU ARE. SOME OF YOUR SO-CALLED FRIENDS MAY HAVE FORGOTTEN IT, BUT I NEVER WILL.
BEEP
PSSHT
SO MUCH FOR MY FIRST KISS.

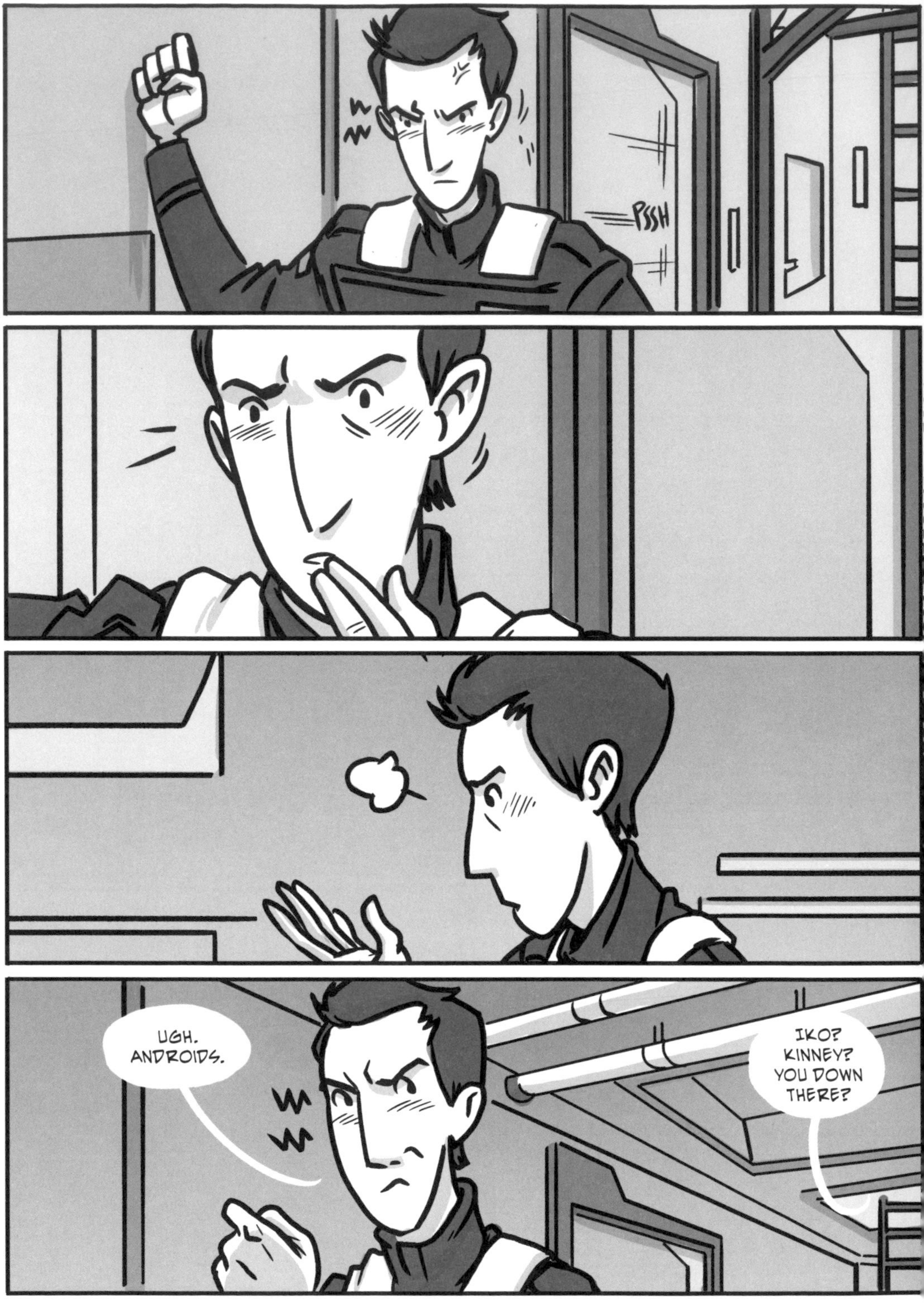
PSSH
UGH. ANDROIDS.
IKO? KINNEY? YOU DOWN THERE?

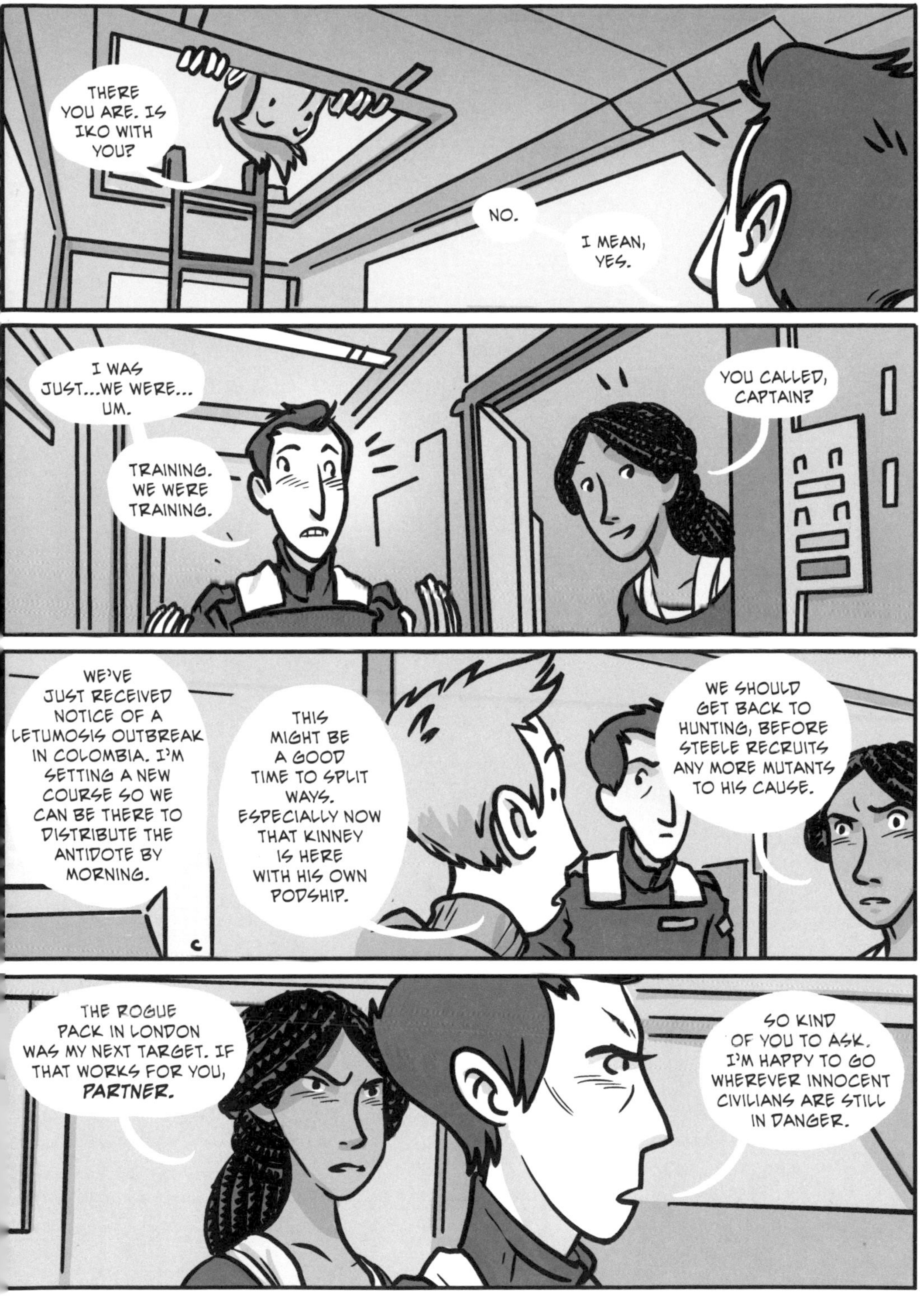
THERE YOU ARE. IS IKO WITH YOU?
NO.
I MEAN, YES.
I WAS JUST...WE WERE... UM.
TRAINING. WE WERE TRAINING.
YOU CALLED, CAPTAIN?
WE'VE JUST RECEIVED NOTICE OF A LETUMOSIS OUTBREAK IN COLOMBIA. I'M SETTING A NEW COURSE SO WE CAN BE THERE TO DISTRIBUTE THE ANTIDOTE BY MORNING.
THIS MIGHT BE A GOOD TIME TO SPLIT WAYS. ESPECIALLY NOW THAT KINNEY IS HERE WITH HIS OWN PODSHIP.
WE SHOULD GET BACK TO HUNTING, BEFORE STEELE RECRUITS ANY MORE MUTANTS TO HIS CAUSE.
THE ROGUE PACK IN LONDON WAS MY NEXT TARGET. IF THAT WORKS FOR YOU, PARTNER.
SO KIND OF YOU TO ASK. I'M HAPPY TO GO WHEREVER INNOCENT CIVILIANS ARE STILL IN DANGER.

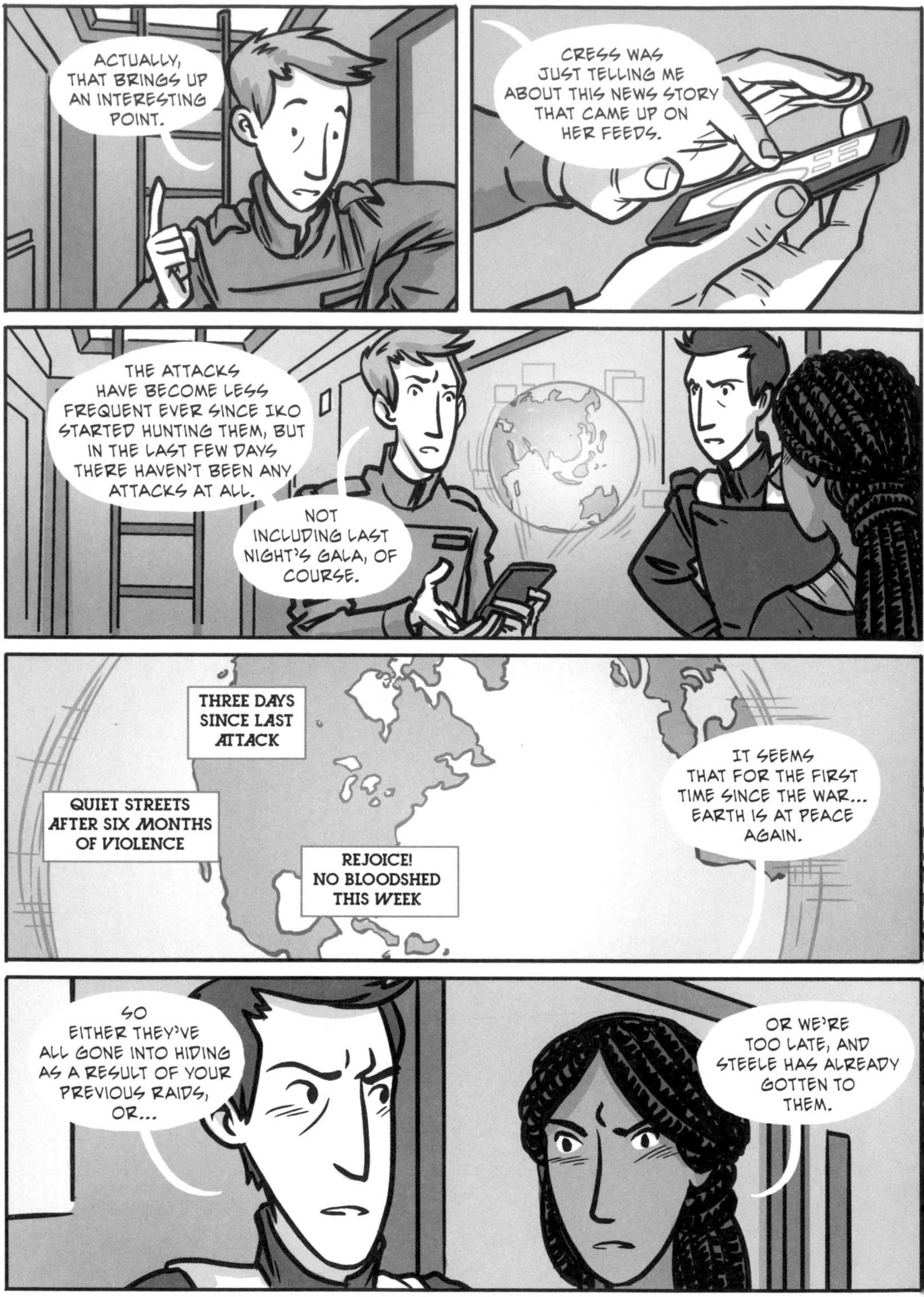
ACTUALLY, THAT BRINGS UP AN INTERESTING POINT.
CRESS WAS JUST TELLING ME ABOUT THIS NEWS STORY THAT CAME UP ON HER FEEDS.
THE ATTACKS HAVE BECOME LESS FREQUENT EVER SINCE IKO STARTED HUNTING THEM, BUT IN THE LAST FEW DAYS THERE HAVEN'T BEEN ANY ATTACKS AT ALL.
NOT INCLUDING LAST NIGHT'S GALA, OF COURSE.
THREE DAYS SINCE LAST ATTACK
QUIET STREETS AFTER SIX MONTHS OF VIOLENCE
REJOICE! NO BLOODSHED THIS WEEK
IT SEEMS THAT FOR THE FIRST TIME SINCE THE WAR... EARTH IS AT PEACE AGAIN.
SO EITHER THEY'VE ALL GONE INTO HIDING AS A RESULT OF YOUR PREVIOUS RAIDS, OR...
OR WE'RE TOO LATE, AND STEELE HAS ALREADY GOTTEN TO THEM.

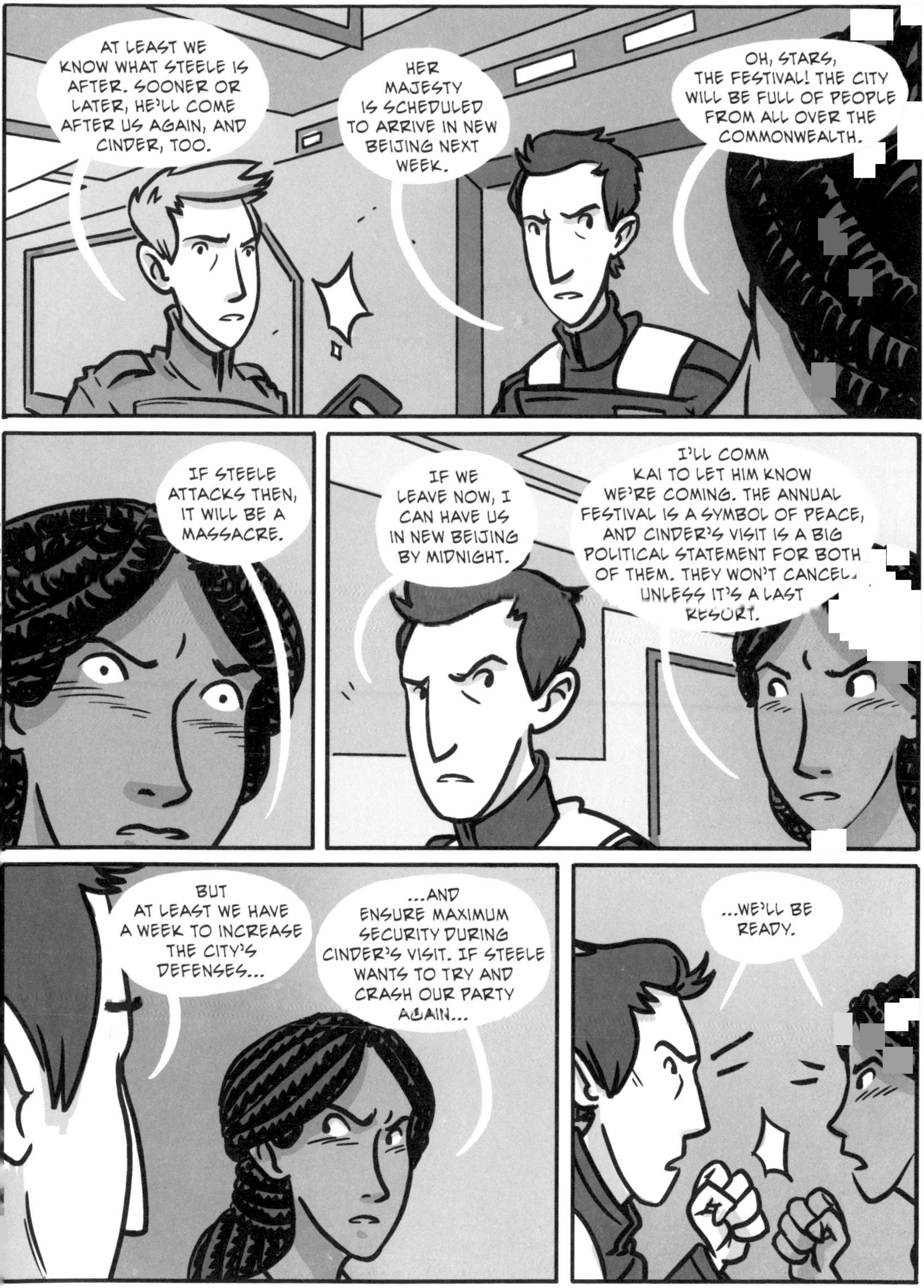
AT LEAST WE KNOW WHAT STEELE IS AFTER. SOONER OR LATER, HE'LL COME AFTER US AGAIN, AND CINDER, TOO.
HER MAJESTY IS SCHEDULED TO ARRIVE IN NEW BEIJING NEXT WEEK.
OH, STARS, THE FESTIVAL! THE CITY WILL BE FULL OF PEOPLE FROM ALL OVER THE COMMONWEALTH.
IF STEELE ATTACKS THEN, IT WILL BE A MASSACRE.
IF WE LEAVE NOW, I CAN HAVE US IN NEW BEIJING BY MIDNIGHT.
I'LL COMM KAI TO LET HIM KNOW WE'RE COMING. THE ANNUAL FESTIVAL IS A SYMBOL OF PEACE, AND CINDER'S VISIT IS A BIG POLITICAL STATEMENT FOR BOTH OF THEM. THEY WON'T CANCEL UNLESS IT'S A LAST RESORT.
BUT AT LEAST WE HAVE A WEEK TO INCREASE THE CITY'S DEFENSES...
...AND ENSURE MAXIMUM SECURITY DURING CINDER'S VISIT. IF STEELE WANTS TO TRY AND CRASH OUR PARTY AGAIN...
...WE'LL BE READY.

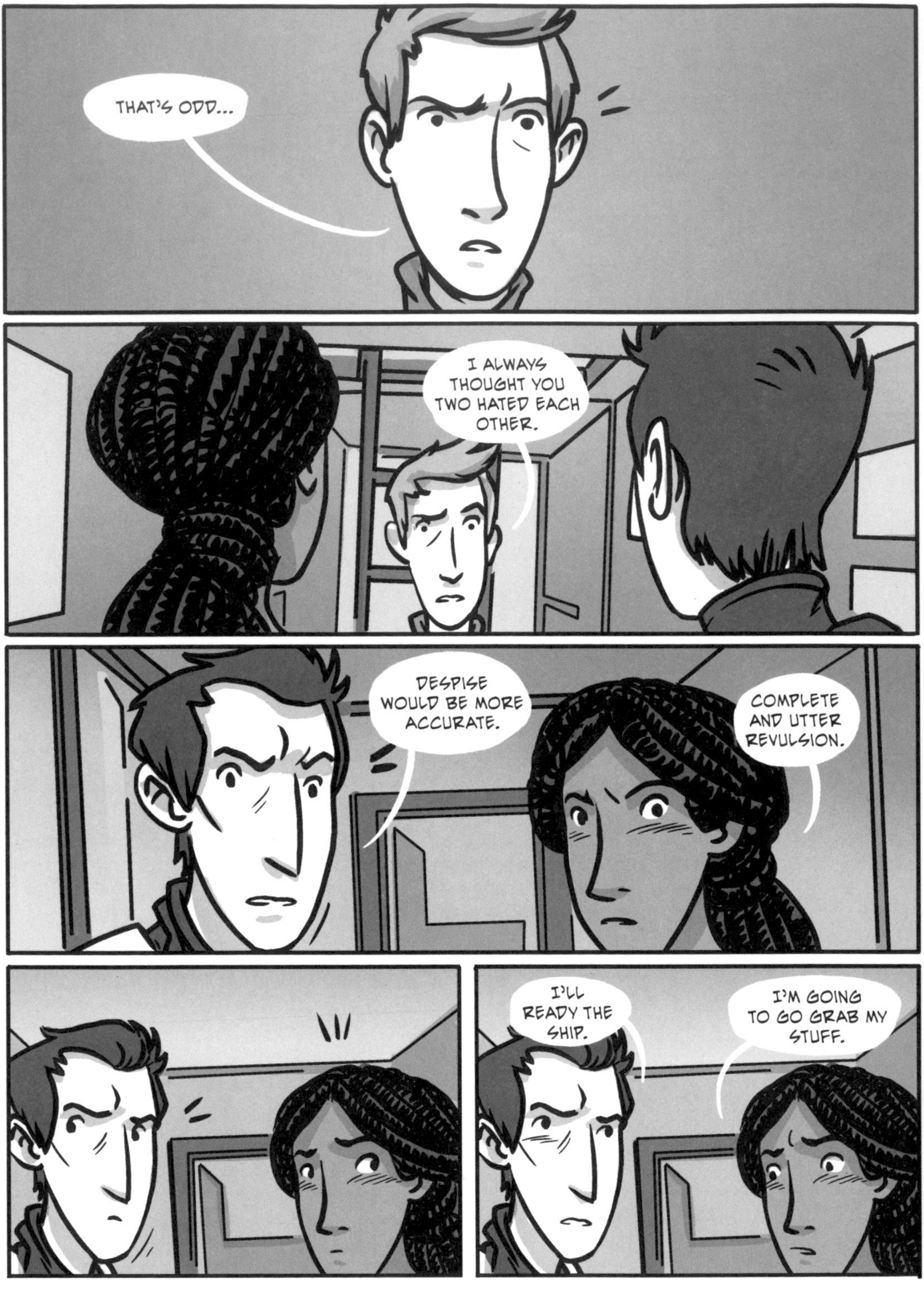
THAT'S ODD...
I ALWAYS THOUGHT YOU TWO HATED EACH OTHER.
DESPISE WOULD BE MORE ACCURATE.
COMPLETE AND UTTER REVULSION.
I'LL READY THE SHIP.
I'M GOING TO GO GRAB MY STUFF.

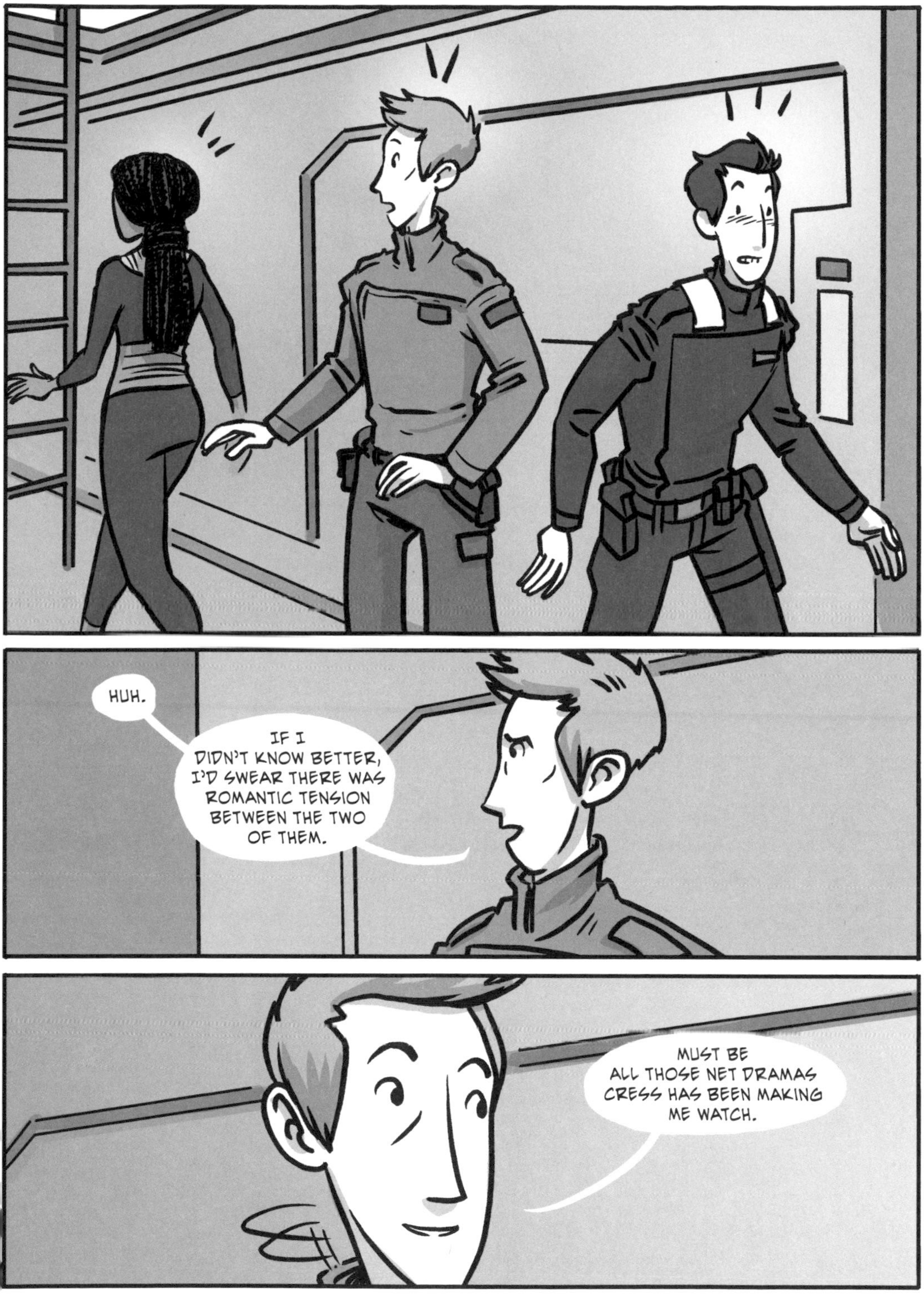
HUH.
IF I DIDN'T KNOW BETTER, I'D SWEAR THERE WAS ROMANTIC TENSION BETWEEN THE TWO OF THEM.
MUST BE ALL THOSE NET DRAMAS CRESS HAS BEEN MAKING ME WATCH.

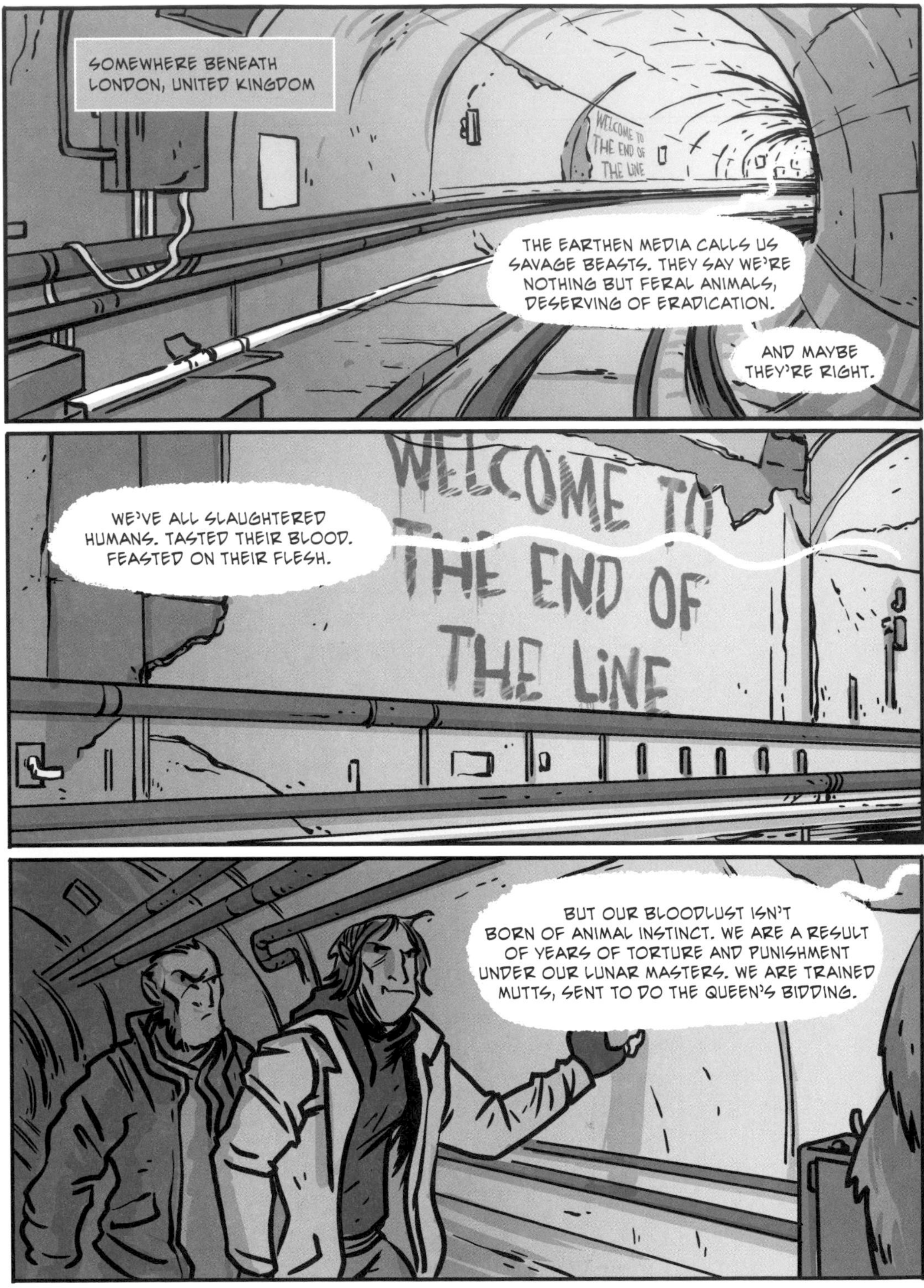
SOMEWHERE BENEATH LONDON, UNITED KINGDOM
WELCOME TO THE END OF THE LINE
THE EARTHEN MEDIA CALLS US SAVAGE BEASTS. THEY SAY WE'RE NOTHING BUT FERAL ANIMALS, DESERVING OF ERADICATION.
AND MAYBE THEY'RE RIGHT.
WELCOME TO THE END OF THE LINE
WE'VE ALL SLAUGHTERED HUMANS. TASTED THEIR BLOOD. FEASTED ON THEIR FLESH.
BUT OUR BLOODLUST ISN'T BORN OF ANIMAL INSTINCT. WE ARE A RESULT OF YEARS OF TORTURE AND PUNISHMENT UNDER OUR LUNAR MASTERS. WE ARE TRAINED MUTTS, SENT TO DO THE QUEEN'S BIDDING.

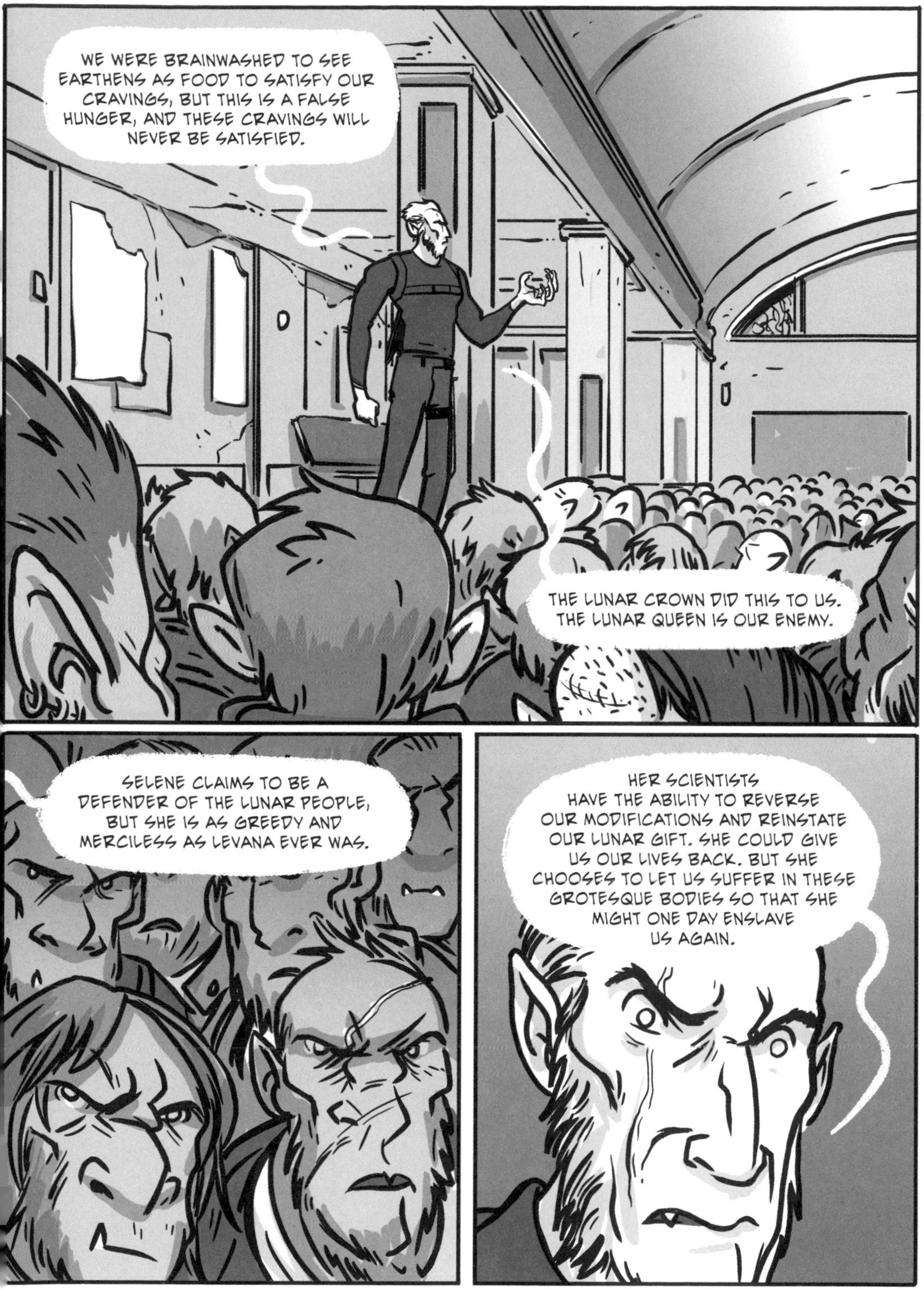
WE WERE BRAINWASHED TO SEE EARTHENS AS FOOD TO SATISFY OUR CRAVINGS, BUT THIS IS A FALSE HUNGER, AND THESE CRAVINGS WILL NEVER BE SATISFIED.
THE LUNAR CROWN DID THIS TO US. THE LUNAR QUEEN IS OUR ENEMY.
SELENE CLAIMS TO BE A DEFENDER OF THE LUNAR PEOPLE, BUT SHE IS AS GREEDY AND MERCILESS AS LEVANA EVER WAS.
HER SCIENTISTS HAVE THE ABILITY TO REVERSE OUR MODIFICATIONS AND REINSTATE OUR LUNAR GIFT. SHE COULD GIVE US OUR LIVES BACK. BUT SHE CHOOSES TO LET US SUFFER IN THESE GROTESQUE BODIES SO THAT SHE MIGHT ONE DAY ENSLAVE US AGAIN.

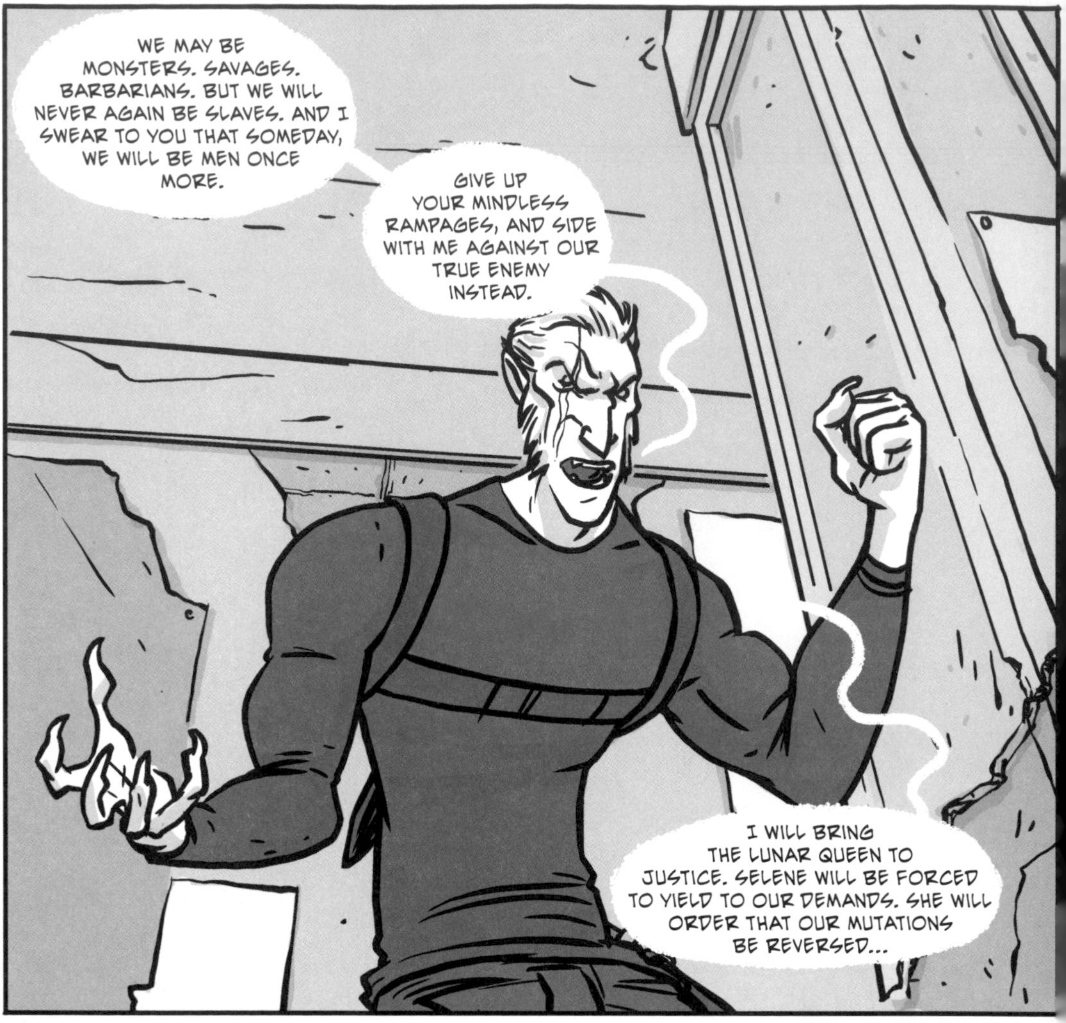
WE MAY BE MONSTERS. SAVAGES. BARBARIANS. BUT WE WILL NEVER AGAIN BE SLAVES. AND I SWEAR TO YOU THAT SOMEDAY, WE WILL BE MEN ONCE MORE.
GIVE UP YOUR MINDLESS RAMPAGES, AND SIDE WITH ME AGAINST OUR TRUE ENEMY INSTEAD.
I WILL BRING THE LUNAR QUEEN TO JUSTICE. SELENE WILL BE FORCED TO YIELD TO OUR DEMANDS. SHE WILL ORDER THAT OUR MUTATIONS BE REVERSED...

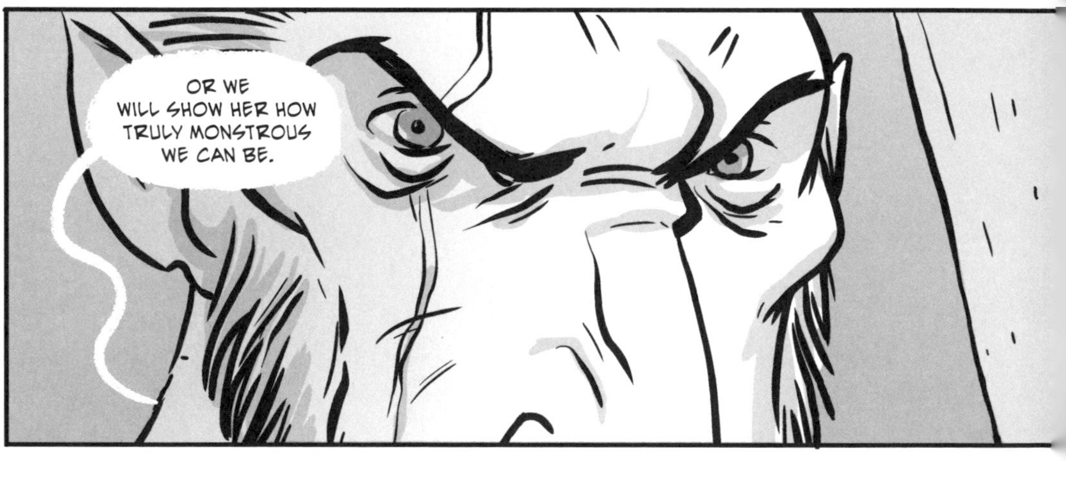
OR WE WILL SHOW HER HOW TRULY MONSTROUS WE CAN BE.